The Accidental Banker

Dan Stringer

Copyright © Dan Stringer 2014
This book is sold subject to the condition that it shall not, by way of trade or otherwise, be lent, resold, hired out, or otherwise circulated without the publisher's prior consent in any form of binding or cover other than that in which it is published and without a similar condition including this condition being imposed on the subsequent publisher.
The moral right of Dan Stringer has been asserted.
ISBN: 1502336324
ISBN-13: 978-1502336323

Dedicated to my Dad.

A man who, if he'd had his way, would've insisted that the whole world wore Wellies.

This is a work of fiction. Names, characters, businesses, organizations, places, events and incidents either are the product of the author's imagination or are used fictitiously. Any resemblance to actual persons, living or dead, events, or locales is entirely coincidental.

CONTENTS

1. The Machete Broccoli Affair... 1
2. Giovanni Erasmo... 22
3. HMS Pedalo... 45
4. The Decapitated Caterpillar... 72
5. Bovine Terrorists... 88
6. Butterflies and Curry... 113
7. Picnics, Sledging and Molestation... 129
8. The Dinner Jacket Virgin... 144
9. Sweet Home Chicago... 165
10. Gym Bunnies... 186
11. Adding Value and Archery... 206
12. JFJFs, CRA(P)s and Go-Karts... 234
13. Squashed Dafs... 253
14. Voodoo Laundry... 273
15. Groin Lending... 297
16. Ocean Therapy... 327
17. Cowboy Boot Crop Circles and a Curious Nipple... 346
18. Summertime Blues... 364
19. Egg-Based Exile... 386
20. Letters, Lakes and Limoncello... 418

Chapter 1

The Machete Broccoli Affair

October, 1995.

Dressed in the sort of budget tyres that would've tested the leniency of even the most broad-minded police officer, four grubby wire wheels mercifully skidded to an unimpressive halt on a vast expanse of drenched, inky black tarmac, the virtually non-existent tread finally managing to coax some much needed grip. Reasonably content that at least a few of the wheels were within the targeted parking space, the driver's trembling hand reached for the gnarled ignition key, with its crumbling ancient fob, paused to ensure there were no witnesses, and switched off the scruffy, 1972 MGB's chronically misfiring engine.

As usual, events were far from over.

The terrified old car and its solitary occupant mentally hugged each other for comfort, bracing themselves against the inevitable, shuddering overrun.

Suddenly, a thunderous judder shook them both to their core, rattling each and every rusty nut and bolt with a seemingly relentless iron grip, reducing the decaying metal body to a quivering wreck of mechanical tears, and leaving the fleshlier casualty once again grateful he'd never had fillings.

Once the violent clatter had eventually subsided, both victims sat quivering for a while, like infants scolded by a sadistic relative when their parents had left the room. As with all storms though, it had finally passed. Now the only noticeable sound came not from tortured metal, but from torrential rain drumming heavily on the barely watertight webesto sunroof, and the ominous ticking and hiss of the aged components, bound as they were for a life of spare parts misery, as cooling water pinged off their edges, and drew thin wisps of steam in the downpour. When he was at last satisfied that the ordeal was over, the driver unclenched his gloved, sweaty hands from the peeling Motolita steering wheel, and breathed a hearty sigh of relief.

He really should get that looked at.

George Butler had turned nineteen that summer. Sadly though, despite spending just over a year now desperately wrestling with the idea, he was still struggling somewhat with the whole notion of becoming an adult. School he concluded was just much more fun.

He shifted uncomfortably, and carefully tried to unpick his trousers from one of the more severe cracks in the decaying leather driver's seat. He wasn't coping at all well this morning, his body's confusing reaction to the unfamiliar challenge that lay ahead overwhelmed him, and he certainly didn't need the pressure of emergency tailoring adding itself to his troubles. Sewing was definitely not his strong suit. Quite what actually was though was still a mystery.

Accompanied by the all too familiar sound of straining stitches, he finally managed to disentangle himself from the seat, and immediately twisted in the cramped cockpit to inspect the damage. No stranger to testing the hardiness of his seams, he soon satisfied himself that he wouldn't need to call upon his Mum's seamstress skills that evening, and, relieved to be free once more, roughly brushed down his matching jacket. Glancing in the misting rear view mirror, he straightened his gaudy tie for the umpteenth time, still somehow completely failing to notice the unfastened edge of his button down collar.

George was very proud of his suit. It had been hastily chosen, thanks to an overly familiar sales assistant with clammy hands, and as such, was poorly sized. Yet something about the polyester, three button navy blue travesty of tailoring, made his heart swell. Although this was its official debut, over the past few weeks he'd repeatedly plucked it from the depths of his wardrobe and taken to parading around his bedroom in it, relishing the feel of the alien garment. This was nothing like a school blazer.

The tie had indeed been a brave choice, but it was the first one that had come to hand, and by that time in proceedings, he urgently needed to escape from the department store. The crisp white polyester shirt he'd snatched in his retreat, at least fitted reasonably well, with only a passing interest in strangling him. The inherent chemical odour however, which no amount of expert motherly hand washing or Old Spice could eliminate, was something he could've happily lived without.

Wiping the rapidly misting windscreen with the cuff of the shirt, he gazed out through the little circle he had created, at the gleaming Audis and BMWs that lined the reserved parking spaces, safely far away from his own antique wreck. He ran his hands down his raw face in despair, dislodging a few small torn balls of tissue, emergency dressings that had earlier been used to stem the flow of blood before it dripped onto something clean. It had been yet another failed attempt at a good close shave.

Try as he might to keep it at bay, the pressure was mounting. What was he doing here, what had he been thinking? He tried to put his thoughts in order once more, but they kept escaping and running off in different directions instead. He was sure they were laughing at him too. After managing to finally grab a few of the slower moving ones by the scruff of the neck, he eventually gathered some of his thoughts together, and concentrated his mind on just *why* he was here instead.

Despite an almost constant, glazed, faraway expression, George had proved to his teachers that his GCSE exam results had not been some horrible marking oversight after all, and he was in fact, actually rather cleverer than he looked. With a handful of impressive A Level grades at his disposal, the world was suddenly his oyster, although his general lack of appetite for shellfish soon proved to be a problem. He should've immediately bid farewell to his comfortable life within the family's respectable semi, a blissful existence, which consisted of three hearty cooked meals a day, all the fresh laundered clothes he could ever wish for, and an endless supply of tea, and he should have either joined the forces, just like his older brother, or embark on a degree of his choosing, far, far away. Unfortunately, neither of these options particularly appealed at the time.

He rather liked his comfortable life, especially the meals and the laundry service, and the thought of being either exiled to some stinking student house, forced exist on takeaways and cheap lager, or squeezed into fatigues and expected to march, filled him with dread. The problem it seemed was that George, despite his ambivalence at the time, was actually one of those rare breed of slightly odd children, who liked school far too much. And he didn't want to leave, ever.

When he'd originally chosen his A Level subjects, three years and a lifetime ago, he'd based his choices on enjoyment, rather than part of a carefully conceived plan for his future, and happily let others form their own opinions about the career path he was intending to follow. But on reflection, Maths had been a horrible mistake.

Art soon proved to be his forte though. In his Sixth Form year, only two grade A's had been awarded. One was achieved by Casper Armstrong, a long-haired hippy who always smelt of hemp and wore bright yellow Doc Martins with green laces. Under the guise of Modern and Experimental Art, for his final piece, he'd spent two days firing paint at a five foot canvas with a catapult, before eventually smearing it with a house brush and a snapped twig. The second grade A went to George, who'd painted a tiger.

Eventually, and extremely reluctantly, he'd concluded that University was potentially the lesser of the two evils. There at least, he shouldn't be shot at too often, and when the time came to apply for places, ahead of his final exams, he'd rather glumly applied to the three nearest Universities he could find, to study Art.

A combination of his impressive mock examination results, remarkably life-like canvases of wildlife, and endless doodles and notes produced in preparation for his work, usually during a Maths class, suitably impressed all three heads of department, and they all awarded him unconditional offers of acceptance. Later at school, as he'd overheard his fellow classmates fret over producing any number of grades to be able to attend their courses, he'd realised that he should've felt very grateful and relieved. But he wasn't.

Something about the ambience of all three Universities unsettled him. As he'd marched through the unfamiliar grounds, desperately searching for the art department so that this charade could be over with, he'd felt totally out of place. Where he'd bundled a collection of his best work together with garden twine, and grappled with the unruly mess as he tried to follow the campus directions, his fellow potential scholars strode purposefully by, nonchalantly swinging oversized leatherette folders, plastered with trendy stickers, not a care in the world. Where he'd worn his school uniform, they'd worn baggy cargo trousers and tie-dyed shirts. Where he'd strived to make a painting look like a photograph, they would've covered a camera with paint. He wasn't going to fit in, and he knew it.

In silence, on the journey home from the furthest flung University on his list, George considered the possibility of gently broaching the subject of taking a gap year. By the time he'd arrived home however, the stress of finding something meaningful to actually fill the gap year with had become almost as unbearable as the thought of leaving school.

As final exams came and went, the long summer holidays stretched ahead like an endless perfect beach, and the wait for the final results began, but enjoying it though was another matter. Before long, mealtimes in the Butler's respectable semi became desperately uncomfortable. Sensing a reluctance to even discuss University, his increasingly concerned parents searched frantically for some reassurance that their youngest son had, however vague it might be, some sort of alternative strategy for his future. Sadly, he did not.

As his eighteenth birthday came and went, and results day loomed ever closer, George begrudgingly accepted that unless he managed to get a job as a janitor, he'd have to leave school behind him soon, and find something else to occupy his time. But there was nothing stopping that something, being another school.

Out of desperation, he'd eventually concluded that a good way for him never to have to face up to leaving school again, was to simply become a Teacher, a primary school Art Teacher to be precise. Naturally he would have to endure four years of University first, but hopefully the other students would be likeminded, and therefore tolerable. His utter hatred of children meanwhile, was just another minor obstacle to be overcome. In any case, in his experience, it seemed to be a prerequisite for the role.

Fortunately the most local University he'd applied to previously also offered a four-year degree in Primary School Education, specialising in Art and Design. More importantly, it was comfortably within driving distance of the family's respectable semi. The treasured lifestyle was safe once more, and he at last had a plan.

After a quick application to change course, and another, slightly less uncomfortable meeting with the heads of department, George managed to secure a place, albeit with conditions this time, and a parental approved future. Harmony was finally restored to mealtimes, and roast potato portions increased accordingly.

However, it soon became apparent that applying to University, even if it was with a genuine intention to actually go this time, wasn't going to be enough. It seemed that he also needed to consider getting some sort of part time job as well, to top up any minimal grant and help towards running a car of his own - assuming he ever passed his driving test. The fourth attempt had not ended well.

After his own half-hearted attempts to find gainful employment fizzled out during the first few days of searching, it was left to his Mum to find her son a paying wage. And after good-naturedly interrogating the checkout girl during her weekly shop, she'd returned home with news that George had an interview the very next day at the local Supermarket.

Part time, third junior assistant to the Hygiene Manager would not have been his first choice, but it was at least something to stop the endless nagging, for now. It had been a very informal interview, and had taken place in a dingy corner of the warehouse that the department used as a base, with the Section Manager, a jolly older man who looked like an Indian Santa Claus. Feeling slightly faint from the overwhelming fumes of the industrial cleaning fluids, George had been asked to identify a few tools of the trade from the racking, and explain how he'd handle a broken wine bottle on aisle seven. Being unfamiliar with domestic sciences, for which his Mum was entirely answerable, he'd needed some prompting at first, but after eventually conceding that evacuating the entire store might well have been an overreaction to spilt wine, he was offered the job nonetheless. Mr Rashid, it seemed, had a soft heart.

Exam results day finally arrived. After ambling to school dejectedly for the last time, he fought his way through a wild throng of his cheering, sobbing or genuinely relieved schoolmates, to see if his own news was worthy enough to send him on his way. They had been. But instead of feeling a great surge of relief, he'd suddenly felt a huge wave of doubt crash into him. Did he really want to be a bloody teacher?

It wasn't long before he had the answer to that question. As feared, he'd found that whilst he was good at Art, he was really rather bad at studying Art, although worryingly enough, he was far, far worse at teaching, almost to the point of being imprisoned.

To begin with, whilst on placement in his first term, and as horrified parents watched from the sidelines, George accidentally hospitalised three five-year-olds during a friendly game of rounders that got dreadfully out of hand. Another time, a pleasant coastal nature walk nearly ended in tragedy when the trainee teacher and the two children in his charge became impossibly lost, and had to be rescued by the Coast Guard from a perilous cliff face. Finally, there was the whole unfortunate business of the electric guitar demonstration he'd given at assembly. An avid novice with an unhealthy relationship with his volume control, he'd succeeded in deafening most of the front row, and had made one poor little girl scream so hard that she'd wet herself. Parents were called and the guitar confiscated until end of class.

Discouraged, George inevitably became very good at other things instead, like finding reasons to be anywhere else but the University. He'd never played truant from school before, largely because he liked it so much, and also for fear of the consequences, but here, nobody seemed to care. Not yet at least.

He befriended another student misfit, Phil, who with his Army boots and shaved head resembled a seasoned bouncer rather than a teacher, and the pair of them often disappeared for whole afternoons, tearing through the countryside to a remote Pub in Phil's heavily modified, black Ford Escort XR3i, listening to the sort of threatening Heavy Metal that would have made the members of Iron Maiden hide under the bed. Naturally, neither of them turned in many assignments.

Unfortunately, after six months of episodic skiving, his lack of progress through the course, along with his absence, was identified. It seemed that there had been a register after all, and he was summoned before the Dean to explain himself. The Dean was an entirely round man with a shiny bald head, bad breath and a greasy complexion, all of which had been very difficult to ignore at the time. He didn't enter personal space, he invaded it. The meeting had been unpleasant and lengthy, and could have been easily shortened if he'd just told the horrified student to bugger off and never come back.

So it was back to square one again. With no immediate fresh ideas about what he actually wanted to do with his life, George decided that, for the moment at least, he'd try and work full time at the Supermarket instead. In order to fill his days, and at least prove to his disappointed parents that he intended to work hard whilst he dreamt up a new plan, he took extra shifts across the various departments. It had been an interesting existence. He could find himself unblocking a customer toilet in the morning, and kneading bread in the afternoon.

As the never-ending, desperate months at the Supermarket eventually turned into a year, even the black leatherette folders, tie-died shirts or machine guns began to seem appealing. Time was running away.

Finally, just when it looked as though he was going to have to gird his loins and join his brother in the forces, a smart advertisement in the local job centre presented a possibility. It wasn't exactly something he'd ever considered, but it certainly seemed respectable enough, and, although no salary was quoted, it was bound to be well paid. It was also reasonably local, and his parents would surely approve. A new plan soon started to formulate.

A few optimistic weeks later, and after completing a heavily embellished, largely fictitious application form, for the purposes of which the last year had been generously summarised as 'Management Training', George found himself facing an imposing, rain drenched, grey corporate building on the edge of the City. It belonged to Cottons Bank PLC, and would hopefully, with any luck at least, contain the doorway to a future he'd been looking for all along.

As usual, his Dad had been right again. He definitely hadn't needed to leave quite so early for his eleven o'clock interview. George had now spent an awkward thirty-eight minutes cocooned in his old rust bucket, with nothing to occupy him but his unruly, rampaging emotions, the endless drum of the rain on his sunroof, and the pleasantly distracting image of a few slender legs emerging from several German saloons. It hadn't been all bad.

Having long ago learnt not to keep the car stereo playing once he'd switched off the engine, the greedy wireless devoured the batteries quicker than he did his Mum's fresh fruitcake, he had no calming music to help him relax either. He glanced at his scratched Timex watch. Still twenty minutes early. Did he want the sweeping, mechanical second hand to speed up time, or stop it altogether?

On one hand, he wanted to get this ordeal over with, so that he could retreat to the comforting safety of his bedroom once more, flick through an ancient Beano on his beloved bed, and wait for dinner. On the other, this was a golden opportunity to escape the Supermarket for good, and perhaps embark on a successful new career. One that would both appease his parents' worries and near-constant nagging, and also provide him with a working day that didn't sometimes start at two in the morning. But was banking really him?

After watching an immaculate Five Series BMW park, and a short, thin gentleman with equally thinning hair, round glasses, and a suit jacket that was far too far big for him get out and wrestle desperately with an unruly umbrella for a few minutes, George decided that it was time to make his own dash into the grey building. He could put it off no longer. All he could do now was hope for the best, and cross every available extremity.

Even in his portly physical condition, the dash to the main entrance seemed achievable without suffering a complete soaking in the rain, which clearly had no plans of letting up until spring time. Confident that once inside he may be offered tea, which he always found to be an incentive, he finally made up his mind. In one wobbly, yet relatively swift movement, he was out of the MG, without pausing to lock it in this company, across the car park, down the steps, and at the reception door, without the prevailing storm causing too much damage to his appearance. Or so he thought.

The severe yet extremely pretty blond receptionist involuntarily almost jumped out of her flawless, pale skin in shock, and sent her neat pen and pencil pot scattering across her desk as the glass door suddenly crashed open and a dripping mess landed unceremoniously onto the grey carpet within. She composed herself, taking a brief moment to look around her domain, ensuring nobody had seen her moment of hysteria, and turned her attention to the soggy new arrival.

She examined George, who was now standing in a small puddle of his own making, looking lost and bewildered, with an expression of polite curiosity and minor disapproval. He couldn't possibly be here for an interview; he didn't look at all like the usual prospects she saw file through her reception. No, judging by the ill-fitting, cheap suit and wayward hair, he was probably a junior photocopier engineer, here to fix something technical and messy. Therefore, he would likely smell horribly of body odour. Hoping that their interaction would be brief, and not involve anything as intimate as civil conversation, she managed to summon a reluctant smile as he dragged his feet heavily across the grey carpet towards her.

"Good morning, umm, how may I help you exactly?"

George had misjudged his dash to the building entirely. He'd failed to consider both the delay that the belly-juddering descent down the unexpectedly long flight of steps would add to the journey, or the sheer force of the violent downpour. It was as though the entire Pacific Ocean was being poured through a giant sieve.

"Err, *oh*, hello! *I'm George!*" He beamed expectantly at the stony face, as though this fact alone should warrant some sort of fanfare, or at least a decent cuddle. "I'm here for an interview, err, today, *I hope!*"

Still regarding him with the sort of disdain she usually reserved for dripping tradesmen who left swimming pools on her desktop, and now utterly convinced that he'd stumbled into the wrong building, she glanced at a schedule of today's interviews and meetings. Surely not, this couldn't be George Butler here to interview for a position of employment with Cottons Bank? He had toothpaste down his awful tie to start with, and what was going on with his hair?

"*Really?*" Try as she might, there was no containing her disbelief. "Do you have you letter of invitation with you please, err, *Mr Butler?*" This would stump him for sure. Clearly there'd been some sort of terrible mistake.

"*Oh!* Hang on a minute!" She watched in horrified amazement as the bedraggled young man started pulling empty packets of chewing gum, a suspicious looking length of toilet roll, and what was clearly a well-travelled emergency Mars Bar out of his suit pocket. Despite this being the suit's maiden voyage, somehow its delighted owner had still managed to stuff its pockets full of endless tat that just might come in handy later. "Ah, *here it is!*"

A crumpled, slightly damp sheet of paper that clearly bore not only Cottons Bank logo, but also an impressive collection of tea cup rings, was placed proudly in front of the receptionist for inspection. Sure enough, there was the evidence to support his fantastic claim.

"*Oh!* I see. Right then. Well, you're a bit early, why don't you take yourself off to the Gentleman's restroom and dry off a bit before your interview?" Completely against her will, and despite being only five or six years older than the dishevelled muddle before her, she was suddenly gripped by a desperate and inexplicable need to mother him, her usual frosty demeanour now melted away. George had one of those faces. "And, you might want to see about straightening that tie, and perhaps try and soak that stain out of it? *Oh*, and button down both sides of your collar." She shook her head in disbelief and grinned hopelessly at him. The poor chap didn't stand a chance. "They're down the corridor over there, third door on the right, good luck now!"

George could be described, by charitable types at least, as something of a work in progress. He wasn't exactly handsome, not yet anyway - more boyish and plump. But nor could he be called plain, and certainly not ugly. Good-looking raw ingredients definitely lurked in there somewhere; the problem was that he didn't know quite where they were, or even what he should do with them if they ever turned up.

He was dark, almost Spanish-looking, thanks to Mediterranean blood on his Mum's side, with longish black hair that, on calm days at least, was swept dramatically back from the temples. The occasional dark comma gratefully escaped the great dollops of gel to fall annoyingly into his eyes. His large, thick eyebrows desperately needed some serious pruning as they resembled a pair rock 'n' roll caterpillars, and clearly had their own ideas about how to conduct themselves in polite company. He had pleasingly dark eyes of indeterminate colour which, along with their furry companions above, spent most of their time looking either happily bemused, or puppy-dog appealing, depending on the circumstances or dietary requirements at the time.

George's skin was now largely blemish free, despite a virulent attack of late onset acne that had plagued him for nearly two years, and which thankfully enough had been in full retreat for the past few months. He had rather smugly cruised through the traditional spotty teenage phase, looking on with glee at his pockmarked contemporaries, as his own skin radiated perfect, spotless health. However, his smugness was to be short lived, as one fateful morning shortly after his seventeenth birthday, he awoke to find that a mass of angry red blotches had invaded his forehead, and had designs on both his chin and cheeks. The war had begun.

There had been long and prolonged battles with casualties on both sides, various chemical weapons had been deployed with devastating effects, troops had been squeezed and bodies ejected, but now at last the campaign seemed to be finally drawing to a close. Fortunately, he'd survived the two-year war with minimal battlefield scaring. But with a few die hard insurgents still hiding out in the trenches, the mirror was still something to be approached with caution.

Physically he was something of a contradiction. Years of devotion to archery had left him quite broad across the shoulders and with relatively thick arms, but an even longer period of devotion to his Mum's cooking had left him a sizable belly, and squeezable cheeks. This, coupled with a complete disregard for any sporting achievements during his school years - thanks to a neat sideline in forged parental notes excusing him from gym class - meant that he had quickly learnt the value of sucking it all in.

In time, with professional grooming and a decent personal shopper, a patient personal trainer and a modest diet that forbid roast potatoes and fruitcake, he might yet prove to be handsome, in the right light at least.

Directions tended to be something George listened to intently, but often failed to absorb. And as he drifted optimistically down the seemingly endless maze of uniform grey corridors, looking hopelessly for the toilets, he considered retracing his steps back to the kindly Receptionist, and asking her if she wouldn't mind drawing him a map.

His thoughts tended to wander like a restless drifter when he was left alone, and so soon he was lost in a sea of inappropriate images about the girl he'd just left at the desk, so lost in fact that he didn't see a short man with an unusual, purposeful gait, come round the next corner, carrying a brimming corporate mug of steaming black coffee.

"*Watch out you bloody idiot..!*" The short, thin man, the same chap that had been wrestling with his umbrella in the car park earlier, shielded his drink with his spare hand and pulled it towards him, away from the advancing polyester belly. But it was too late. A messy, scalding collision was inevitable. "... *Arghhh!*"

"*Oh bugger!* Sorry, I, I didn't see you there!"

The short man bent forward urgently, abandoning his mug, and desperately peeled his sodden, steaming shirt and trousers away from his skin before it raised painful blisters. His reddening attacker meanwhile pulled the dubious length of wrinkled toilet roll from his suit pocket like a magician pulling a ribbon from a sleeve, and started dabbing at his unfortunate victim's groin. He knew it would come in handy sooner or later.

"*What the hell are you doing?* Get off my you fool, *give me that here!*" The short man grabbed the tissue, gave it a brief, doubtful glance, and set to work soaking up the worst of the caffeine. His freshly pressed, white cotton shirt was a complete mess, and the crutch of his suit trousers, tailored in a shade of blended wool that matched the corridors perfectly, bore a suspicious damp patch. "I do hope you're bloody well pleased with yourself. *Now get out of my way!*"

He barged past George before he could answer or even ask timidly for his toilet paper back, and in his confusion and embarrassment, he backed away into yet another grey door. After subconsciously deciding that anywhere else would be better than here, he pushed the long, curious door handle down, without pausing to examine it, and stepped backwards from the scene of one crime, and immediately into another.

Once again, he was outside in the torrential rain.

The first thing he realised as the study metal door clicked shut in front of him, was that it didn't seem to have a handle of any kind on the outside. A stupid bit of design really. The second was that it seemed to be alarmed. Panic suddenly gripped him, and having finally realised his mistake, George desperately glanced around his new surroundings for an alternative exit, his ears ringing from the deafening, howling wail of the tripped intruder alarm.

He was in an almost flooded, square courtyard, bordered on all sides with office windows, a few of which now had curious faces pressed up against the glass. The only other conceivable means of escape seemed to be a slippery metal spiral staircase, which presumably led to some sort of rooftop gantry.

Soaked through now, his heart beating so hard in his chest that he felt quite certain he'd soon faint from all the exertion, George decided that he'd make a break for the stairs, try and work his way back to the MGB, and flee from this dreadful place before any other catastrophes came looking for him. He would join the army instead. A drastic solution perhaps, but needs must.

Just as he was about to make his break for freedom though, the alarm bells were abruptly silenced, leaving his ears still buzzing, and the sturdy metal door that had imprisoned him, was flung open.

"This *isn't* the gentleman's rest room, Mr Butler."

Ten minutes later, and somewhat drier, having pressed as many of his extremities as he could physically manage against the hand dryer he eventually found in the elusive toilets, George sat in reception clutching a blessed mug of comforting tea, and trembled slightly, like a cornered field mouse with a taste for English Breakfast. His hair was massive and tangled, resembling a violated Busby that had been found abandoned in a bush, and he had a slightly singed smell about him. He was also not alone.

Ms Ann Williams, Cottons Bank, Human Resources Manager, here today especially to interview new recruits, had no intention whatsoever of losing one before she'd even had the chance to interrogate him. Not on her watch. She was a tall, middle-aged woman with tight, curly red hair, an enviable figure, and a reassuring tone. It was this tone that was being called into service now.

"...Everyone makes a few mistakes, George, it really doesn't matter. I'm sure no one is going to hold it against you." She rubbed his hunched back supportively, which, thanks either to its earlier soaking, or its owner's relentless perspiration, was warm and moist. She made a mental note to wash her hands afterwards, and smiled warmly into his puppy-dog eyes. "Really, it's okay. Finish up your tea and then come over to room two for your interview." She paused to reflect, glanced up at the Receptionist and added, "Perhaps get Rebecca over there to take you, just to be sure, okay?"

After stretching out his tea break for as long as humanly possible, George finally, unenthusiastically, rose to his feet and trudged over to his rescuer, carefully setting the empty mug down on her desk with both hands, far away from anything that looked even remotely breakable. He wasn't about to risk further embarrassment by cracking a Cottons Bank paperweight.

Rebecca had never known such excitement. To begin with, Mr Varley had burst in red-faced, demanding paper towels and the first aid kit. Then the intruder alarm had gone off, and *then* she had had to talk and interviewee down from the fire escape, just like she was a hostage negotiator. She couldn't wait to tell her friends back at the branches over drinks later.

Still dragging his feet as though they bound to sacks of coal, George trailed behind Rebecca the Receptionist, lost in a fog of humiliation and dejection, unable to even find the enthusiasm to admire the pert bottom which filled the business skirt so pleasingly. Surely he was wasting everyone's time; there was no way he'd get the job now? If only she'd let him escape when he'd had the chance.

Sensing his surrender, and still harbouring confusing maternal feelings, Rebecca the Receptionist stopped in her tracks and turned to face him, just before they reached their destination. She lowered her voice to a whisper. "Now, remember, listen to what Ms Williams said, she's really the decision maker when it comes to new recruits round here, so if she said not to worry, then don't worry, *okay?*" She rubbed his soggy arm despite herself. Poor chap. "I'm sure she'll be able to convince the other interviewer that you meant no harm."

George lifted his bowed head for a moment, baffled. "Err, so there are *two* interviewers then?"

"Oh yes, there always is, one to ask the questions and one to make the notes."

"Oh, *okay*, umm, what's the other one like?"

Rebecca the Receptionist paused for a moment, bit her lip, and furrowed her flawlessly made-up brow. Why did she open this particular can of worms? He was a truly dreadful man. So dreadful that he'd long since had the title of *Mr* replaced with *The Evil* instead. Given this morning's frivolities, his manner was unlikely to have improved any. "*Err, well, he's only here on a short secondment, umm, he's okayish sometimes, I suppose*, but then again, you *did* make him throw a cup of coffee down his front earlier, so, err... *Ah*, I'm sure you'll be fine! *Good luck now!*"

The sensation of sudden, unexpected raw fear is a truly strange phenomenon. It can affect people in a variety of different ways, although generally, it has the initial effect of rendering the afflicted with a temporary illusion common with that of an out of body experience. Whether it is a first bad fall, the result of an overzealous maiden sprint on a brand new Christmas pedal cycle at the age of six, or the news that you have only months left to live at the age of thirty, thoughts tend to be, for the first few seconds at least, largely the same. This isn't happening to me.

At the age of five, George was patiently and tenderly introduced to the notion of school. Whilst he was safe in his bedroom, cocooned in a shroud of his favourite teddy bears, Mr and Mrs Butler calmly explained to him, in a soothing even tone, that very soon he was to go to primary school, just like his older brother Michael, and that he would learn exciting, fascinating things, and make lots of new friends.

However, regardless of the attachment he'd eventually feel towards school, George initially smelled a rat, and hatched a plan to escape to the Amazonian rainforest instead. Once there he'd hopefully find a suitably pleasant tribe and live forever in harmony with nature. School and the new friends, could just bugger off.

Disappointed when his attempts to build an ocean going vessel from his Mum's garden bamboo and wool from her knitting basket failed dismally, he'd finally accepted his fate, and as the dreaded day loomed closer, tried to imagine what the first day of school would hold. The events of that day stayed with him for the rest of his life.

The first day of primary school is the same for everyone. Mums and Dads are encouraged to hang around just long enough for their offspring's fingernails to be prized from their clothing, whilst other children are either performing Oscar worthy fits of hysteria or, in the cases of those destined for a life of crime, stealing the toys from the box in the corner.

To begin with, this was how it had been for George, and he too had hung onto his parents' hands, like the survivor of a shipwreck to a piece of floating wreckage. Yet it was only when the last of the parents had finally been ushered from the classroom that the true horror of that day began to unfold.

Mrs Connelly, year one Primary School Teacher and part time Malevolent Demon, was huge. So huge and vast, in fact, that she seemed to create her own gravity, the plate of chocolate biscuits on her desk seemly drawn to her purse, unforgiving lips by an unseen entity. Nobody ever saw the hands move. The moment the door had clicked shut on last of the relieved parents, the bright false smile she'd been wearing on her dry leathery skin, turned to a picture of pure hatred as she surveyed her young, largely quivering flock, with malicious contempt.

She was quite a sight for the terrified class to behold. A shock of white hair reached for the ceiling from her head, like the hands of cowboys being menaced by a tribe of scalp hunting Red Indians. She had a perfectly round, jowly face, and sunken into it were tiny green eyes, falsely magnified by incredibly thick rectangular glasses, that had long since permanently dented her hooked witches nose. Despite her general Third Reich demeanour, she wore a large apron over her plain clothes, which was elaborately decorated with blue and yellow fluffy bunny rabbits. Clearly there was nothing fluffy about this woman.

During the prolonged silence, she continued to glare at the class. None of the children, all of whom had suddenly become aware of a strange clinical smell, were quite sure what she was waiting for, and all were equally terrified, petrified out of their wits, unable to move. All accept one, there's always one.

None of the class were quite sure whatever became of little Gavin Blake, the crew-cut wearing five-year-old who only moments earlier had been asking his Dad when he could have his first tattoo to go with his stud earring. His crime was letting off an impressive (considering his size) and well-pitched fart, his punishment, swift and savage.

Before the gas had turned even his most immediate classmate green, and in spite of her size, Mrs Connelly was on her feet, and had covered the twenty or so feet between them, plucking Gavin from his yellow plastic chair, and sending it flying across the room, before he'd even had the chance to look pleased with his efforts. As the chair clattered to a standstill, Mrs Connelly, the flailing Gavin now securely clamped under one of her bingo wings, strode back to her desk, hitched out her own chair with a chubby foot, and lowered her not insignificant bottom onto the flattened, rose patterned seat cushion.

She then roughly spread Gavin over her well-padded knee. He seemed almost like a ragdoll in her firm grasp. She roughly pulled down his grey school trousers and bright Spiderman underpants and had begun pounding his bottom expertly and viciously with an open, flat hand. Considering the surface area of her enormous palm, and the Cumberland sausage quality of her fingers, the force per square inch applied to the tiny, rapidly reddening, five-year-old behind must have been excruciating

Many years later, George had found himself happily watching a BBC One wildlife documentary, searching for artistic inspiration, and learning all about the problems elephants cause farmers in Africa. He was alarmed to learn that one particularly savage way of dealing with the issue of fence destruction caused by elephants - and one that nearly made him to switch channels at the time - was for the farmers to shoot one of the herd, skin it, and then drape the remains over the fences as a warning. Mrs Connelly clearly held with this method, and none of the children ever farted in her class room again.

In time, George learnt to file the horrifying events of that day first day at school neatly under the category of 'the most scared I have ever been', a section previously reserved entirely for any number of his older brother's practical jokes, and had quietly got on with his life, content the worst was now over. And until now, it had been.

Standing in front of the bland grey door, George shivered at the thought of the fuming, coffee stained, and doubtlessly vengeful, small man that lay in wait on the other side. Perhaps he could still make a run for it? He felt certain that with the element of surprise on his side, and with gallons of excess adrenaline to speed his chubby legs, he should be able to out run Rebecca the Receptionist, and hopefully make it back to his rusty sanctuary before she realised quite what had happened. But would the MG start first time? It was unlikely at best.

Once again his train of thought was interrupted before he could coax his extremities into action, as the door suddenly opened and Ms Williams, making to stride purposefully out of it to see how the tea break was going, almost collided with her interviewee.

"*Oh!* Gosh George, you nearly had me then too, just as well I left *my* cup behind, *eh?*" She turned to wink at her as yet, still unrevealed colleague. "Do come in, and meet Ray, err, *I mean*, *Mr* Varley properly, and we'll get started."

Taking a few steps that were almost as shaky as his first, George followed Ms William's shock of curly red hair into the grey room, expecting at any moment for a stapler to be launched at him in retribution. But the pelting never came, and instead, like a mouse dropped into a snake pit accepting its slithery doom, he turned slowly to face his foe. He conjured a desperate smile as The Evil Ray Varley rose from his chair and extended a reluctant, thin hand in greeting.

The handshake was unaccompanied by any words, and oddly enough, varied in pressure, almost as if the small man was pumping himself up for a climatic, crushing squeeze. He snarled back into the young eyes, unblinking, before finally conceding a brief verbal acknowledgement. *"Mr* Varley."

They were all seated. Now that George was properly able to examine his stained nemesis, he realised that, physically at least, there was nothing to fear from this man. The Evil Ray Varley was desperately thin, emaciated almost. His suit jacket, which was at least two sizes too big, enveloped his tiny frame, leaving his skeletal shoulders looking like a child's coat hanger that had been swamped with a father's heavy, winter coat. But there was something sinister about him nonetheless, something unnerving in those grey eyes that chilled the blood, and made the mouth run dry.

"Err, once again Ray, *umm,* sorry! I mean Mr *Varley,* I'm really sorry about the coffee, err, and your suit…" He trailed off, hoping this was enough to put things right. It wasn't.

"It seems that you've been rather accident prone this morning, Mr Butler, do try and get through this interview without further mishap, *hmmm?"* He finally broke off his piecing gaze, and instead meticulously studied a file on the desk in front of him.

Ms Williams, who secretly didn't have much time for her soiled colleague, sensed that this was her chance to wrestle control of proceedings once again, and quickly seized her moment. *"Right then George,* it's been a busy morning, so let's wrap this up before lunch, shall we?" One of the three bellies in the room suddenly growled at the mere mention of food. "Err, *okay then.* As you know, today we are going to ask you just four competency based questions to help us understand your capabilities, and, based on your answers, decide if you are a suitable candidate for employment within Cottons Bank. Now, hopefully you had time to read through the candidate pack we sent out a few weeks ago, which gave you a list of potential questions and sample, structured answers?"

George beamed back and nodded as innocently as he could. The pack had indeed arrived safely, and had been glanced through at least once, before being discarded in favour of this month's *Top Gear* magazine. But he'd read the introduction almost thoroughly, and if he was only going to be asked four questions, how hard could it be?

"Excellent! So, just to be sure, you'll remember that within your answers to these questions, it's *very* important that you expand on the *reasons* behind your actions, just like the examples in the pack, and that you need to include any details that you think are relevant. Remember also to structure your just answers as the pack detailed, and try and demonstrate that you have the required skills and behaviours expected of a potential employee of Cottons Bank, *okay?*"

He continued to nod and grin involuntarily. His earlier trembling had once again resumed, beads of sweat were starting to form at his temples. Why didn't you read the bloody pack, George? Was it too late to make a run for it?

"*Okay!*" He had no choice now but to wing it and hope for the best. After all, he'd told his share of tall stories before, elaborated on his excuses for being late to work at the Supermarket, or accidentally forgetting the occasional French lesson in favour of extra Art tuition. And there was always that unfortunate business with the chickens he'd managed to talk his way out of. He'd be fine; he just had to keep his wits about him.

The Evil Ray Varley chose that moment to clear his throat, he sat up a bit straighter, checked to make sure his jacket was covering the newly acquired stains, and glanced across at his colleague. "I think *I* would like to ask the questions during this interview, Ms Williams." The tone of his thin voice left little room for negotiation.

"Oh, *really*, Mr Varley?"

"Yes, *really*, Ms Williams. Now then." He turned and eyed George as though he were a troublesome fly in a summer afternoon lounge, which he'd finally managed to corner with a rolled up newspaper. "*Shall we begin Mr Butler?*"

"*Okay!*"

The short, bitter man had already selected his weapon of choice. A question that was usually left until last, when the interviewee had been given a chance to settle into the format of the competency based interview process, and get into their stride, a question that carried with it the most weight, and that the score of which should determine the candidate's suitability to work with the general public.

The Evil Ray Varley checked his notes, grinned malevolently, and fixed his beady eyes on his victim. "Can you give me an example of when *you* have given outstanding customer service that has likely resulted in the customer remembering *you* for that unique act, and perhaps even told others about?" The words hung in the air for a few moments, leaving just the steady tick of the quartz wall clock to fill the void. Think George, *think!*

His mouth was as dry as the Gobi Desert, his mind as blank as all the canvases he'd ever sat in front of. But this time though, a nice painting of an owl wasn't going to save him. Think George, *think!*

Then finally, at last, a spark of a memory, something that might just work, "Oh, *well*, there was this one time at the Supermarket Ray, *err*, I mean *Mr* Varley…"

A few months ago, George was lucky enough to be transferred to the Produce aisle. It had made a welcome change to the Supermarket's Hygiene department, where lately, his uncanny knack of being able to unblock toilets in record time had given him the sort of notoriety nobody craved. He rather liked the work, the fresh smells, and, although his new colleagues had sniggered behind his back when they told him that all new members of the team had to manage the florist section, he made no secret of the fact he quite liked making the bouquets too.

What he didn't like however, was the rather sporadic working hours. The first time he'd seen his name down for the two a.m. shift, he'd naturally assumed it was some sort of hideous mistake, and turned up at two in the afternoon instead. The only time he'd ever seen two in the morning had been when he'd stumbled home once from a rare pub lock in.

The Section Manager, an aggressive chap with an unbelievably short fuse, had seen to it that George never made the same mistake again though, by giving him every early shift for the next month. Leaving home without a full English breakfast under his belt once a week was one thing. Every day was another matter entirely.

The Manager, and the equally hostile Supervisor, a younger model plagued with delusions of grandeur, also both had rather interesting ideas about how long a nine-hour shift should actually last. And it was certainly never less than eleven hours. And it was whilst George was desperately trying to find the stamina to survive yet another epic nine-hour slog, one that was now fast approaching the twelve-hour mark, that it had happened.

In a fog of acute tiredness, he was lugging a heavy plastic tray overflowing with miniature, treelike clumps of lush broccoli into its slot on the section, when he was suddenly aware of two blurry images on the edge of his fading periphery vision. Oddly enough, the images seemed to grow shoots, and the part of his exhausted mind that was still just about keeping its head off the pillow, told him that these were in fact arms, and the images were people, very old, almost aristocratic people.

They each selected a specimen from the tray and, from what he could see through his deeply sleep-deprived eyes, began minutely examining them with scorn and contempt, pursing their wrinkled old lips and shaking their heads at each other, as though they'd just found a dead lizard lurking within the crop. If they'd been rooting through the bananas earlier, they'd have actually found one.

"Look at the stalk on that thing, Elizabeth? *It simply won't do!*" The slightly larger of the two blurs, perhaps a Gentleman well into his eighties, was dressed from head to toe in tweed, a theme that possibly extended to his underwear, and he held up the offending vegetable for the smaller blur to examine.

"*I know!* It's ghastly, *simply ghastly*! My God, it's all stalk, Piers! I mean *really*!"

During his shift, George had only enjoyed the very briefest of breaks, the full ten minutes of which he'd spent fast asleep, face down in a plate of fried eggs. He had now entered a seriously hallucinogenic stage of fatigue, not helped at all by the drinking the night, or day - it wasn't clear by now - before.

"*Well*, what do you say about it, *Boy*?" Cocooned in his shell, numb to anything but the immediate task in hand, George didn't realise that the question was directed at him, and had continued to fill the aisle, daydreaming about his beloved single bed and roast dinners.

"*Well* I never. *Such rudeness!*" The old blur paused, clearly expecting a response of some sort from the spotty, chubby youth in the tatty apron. "Are you deaf, *Boy*?"

"Hmmm…?" Finally, a brain cell woke up, stretched, yawned expansively, and switched on the lights. But it was too late. The old blur was now in full swing.

"When *we* go to the farmers market, and we comment on the stalks, the young man there chops them off for us, without delay! *What do you say about that?*" A blank, honest face stared back at him through bloodshot eyes, genuinely at a loss. "*Well?*"

The dim light finally woke up another brain cell, who'd been fast asleep in the next room, and before long a few of them were sitting around the breakfast table drinking coffee, trying to agree on the most appropriate response to send their host. Eventually they settled on stalling for a bit whilst the caffeine soaked in. "Err, I am sorry, what were you, err, *saying?*" George was very close to just giving in, and curling up asleep on the floor, cold and hard as it was, he just wanted this unpleasant noise to go away. And some toast perhaps, and a cup of tea.

"So, clearly deaf *and* dumb, *eh?*" The blurred tweed apparition waggled the clump of broccoli threateningly at him. "I mean *really?*" Without warning, he lowered the weaponized vegetable and jabbed George in the chest with a bony finger. "*Really?*"

Intense tiredness makes even pubic hair hurt, and it was the sudden shock of Mr Blur's sharp finger against his aching chest bone that abruptly jolted the young Supermarket employee spectacularly back to life.

"*Stalks?*" He blurted the world, as though it had been trapped in his mouth all along.

"Yes, you stupid Boy, *stalks!*"

"Right then, *wait right there!*" And he marched off the section with a slightly wobbly gait, disappearing briefly through a curtain of transparent rubber into the staff preparation area.

When George Butler returned to the shop floor a few moments later, he was brandishing the ugly eighteen-inch machete that the Produce team used to prepare fruit baskets, like a Viking proudly wielding his freshly sharpened battle axe. There was a frenzied, determined look in his eyes, made even more unsettling by the stains left on his apron from an earlier fatal encounter with a punnet of strawberries.

The Blurs' elderly, pompous faces quickly drained of all colour, and they'd suddenly yearned for the Farmers Market.

The menacing Supermarket employee quickly snatched the innocent green stem from the trembling bony hand and performed an expert if somewhat unnecessarily violent slice, which buried the gleaming blade two inches into the plastic tray he'd used as a chopping block. The Blurs then hastily left the Produce aisle with a perfect head of broccoli and slightly soiled tweed underwear.

Back in his in interview, George decided to give The Evil Ray Varley this as an example of when he'd given truly outstanding customer service. After all, he felt certain that the elderly shoppers would remember him, and in all likelihood, tell anyone that would listen.

Chapter 2

Giovanni Erasmo

November, Monday morning.

Barry Phillips hated his life. He despised his irritating wife and a good deal of his unpleasant family, especially his parasitical offspring. But most of all, he hated his job. He'd once been a relatively successful advertising salesman, but following an unfortunate misunderstanding with the CEO of a large ladies underwear company, he'd been shunned by the industry and cast aside, like yesterday's half-eaten doughnut.

Now he had to be satisfied with the meagre living he made as a Car Park attendant, which despite being a step up the ladder from Traffic Warden, still meant that the world in general wanted him to die horribly. It was indeed a grim existence.

In an effort to stave off the inevitable suicide attempt, he'd recently taken to seeking enjoyment when, and where, he could. His patch included a large T-shaped car park that was situated in a relatively rough part of the city, nearest the decaying shipyards and docks, and which backed onto a certain grand old branch of Cottons Bank, a very greasy Café, and a suspicious-looking newsagent. Of all the Car Parks he patrolled, for two special reasons, this was his favourite.

Cottons employees were always forgetting when their parking was up, and would coyly offer him little cash bribes to look the other way. But perhaps most importantly, it was also a desirable place to park the van and have breakfast, as it allowed him an unrivalled, ogling view of some of the shapely Bank girls that worked within the imposing grey building.

Moist with anticipation, Barry sat huddled in his unloved white Ford Escort van, munching on a greasy Bacon roll, a steaming polystyrene cup of black coffee rested precariously on the dashboard until it was cool enough to drink. It was still raining hard. Any minute now they would start to arrive, each and every one trying to look glamorous and business-like whilst tottering around on high heels, and fighting with unruly umbrellas and handbags. He was bound to see a flash of something unintentional today.

Suddenly, there an unfamiliar racing, throaty engine, a badly blowing exhaust, and surprisingly enough, the unmistakable warble of Neil Diamond. He curiously peered through the misting windscreen just as a battered white MGB flew around the corner of the soaking car park, hit the ever present patch of diesel, which the Council really should've attended to by now, and looked on in amazement as it veered wildly off course.

Inside the cockpit, the driver's gloved hands fought madly to correct the car's trajectory, his apparent inexperience eventually causing the fishtailing old car to suddenly lurch in the opposing direction, clearly now out of all control. After a further elaborate pirouette, which would have scored well on ice, the MG eventually spun to a squealing halt, facing entirely the wrong direction, and shuddered horribly for an age as the engine, and Neil Diamond's classic track, *'America'*, died.

Barry took another thoughtful bite of his bacon roll, and wiped the dribbling molten butter from his stubbly chin with the sleeve of his High Vis jacket. *"Prat,"* he uttered to himself, and reached for his polystyrene cup.

Within the cockpit of the traumatised classic, the trembling driver tried to compose himself again. It had been a very bad morning so far, seemingly fraught with almost every kind of danger imaginable, and it had even been necessary to break out the musical 'Big Gun' in the hope of settling his troubled mind. He had no idea quite why Neil Diamond was capable of sending him into a state of nodding calm, but this was always the case when the *'Jazz Singer'* was eventually plucked from the glove compartment, where is lived nervously between Bon Jovi's *'Slippery when Wet'* and Guns 'n' Roses' *'Appetite for Destruction'*, to be gratefully inserted into the ancient car stereo.

His musical tastes could be described as eclectic at best.

Unbeknown to George, he had been the infant victim of subliminal brainwashing by his well-meaning Mum, who in an effort to get her six-month-old off to sleep, had soothed him into a peaceful slumber with a bit of Neil, and had continued to do so until he went to primary school, and for several months thereafter. Exactly the same effect could be achieved with both Dionne Warrick and Johnny Mathis, but he had limited space in his cramped glove compartment, and there was always the danger, no matter how remote to might be, that a girl might see them and get the wrong idea. So far at least, none had.

However he'd been initiated was inconsequential though, he now belonged to that loyal and dedicated group who believed that in life, people basically broke down into two distinct groups: those that liked Neil Diamond's original version of 'Red Red Wine', and those who preferred UB40's.

Having recovered his composure from his unexpected motoring acrobatics, George eventually managed to get the MG's reluctant engine to fire up again, and he gingerly parked a few spaces away from a grubby white van, the miserable occupant of which seemed to be frowning at him.

He switched off the engine, braced himself yet again for the inevitable overrun, something he'd finally asked his Dad to look at, and when the shuddering had eventually subsided, like the final throes of a dying octopus, he breathed a sigh of relief and took a quiet moment to reflect.

Despite in every sense, having something of a perilous start to his interview four weeks earlier, he'd miraculously enough managed to rescue the situation. Although normally immune to any form of communication that wasn't painfully, and very patiently spelt out to him in large friendly letters, he'd somehow managed to sense that his response to the initial competency based interview question, might've struck the wrong cord with his interviewers, judging by the look of abject horror that crossed their faces, and in a rare moment of insight, quickly rallied his thoughts and answered the remaining three questions rather well. Never in his life had he been so inventive or economic with the truth.

These responses, along with his perceived willingness to press on following a challenging start to his day, had impressed Ms Williams sufficiently to see him pass the interview process, despite her colleagues bitterly strong feelings to the contrary. Other than the whole machete broccoli affair, she'd found him quite sweet and willing, and that went a long way in her book. He would just need to be kept away from sharp objects, full mugs of coffee and fire exits, clearly.

And so now, on yet another clichéd, miserable rainy day, George found himself in yet another soaking car park looking out through another small, mist cleared circle at the Armada Branch of Cottons Bank PLC. His heart was in his mouth. Suddenly it was the first day of school all over again. His only hope was that there wasn't a Mrs Connelly waiting inside.

Although he accepted that he should've probably given the subject some serious thought before now, during his journey into the grey, threatening city that morning it had suddenly dawned on him that he wasn't entirely sure that he actually wanted to work for a bank after all.

But what was the alternative? He'd already wrestled endlessly with the same two options, entirely overlooking any other alternatives that the world had to offer: the military, with all the unappealing screaming and physical fitness, or University again, to study something else instead. But what, or for that matter, to do what in the end? Perhaps the Bank wasn't such a bad alternative after all.

The time had come for George to acknowledge an uncomfortable truth. Beyond sitting in his bedroom painting wildlife, the occasional spirited blast in his beloved old wreck, an hour or so of archery, and the odd alcohol-fuelled night out with his best friend in the hope of finding a likeminded girl to fondle, he simply had no idea quite what he wanted to do with his life. It seemed his academic qualifications were no match for a complete lack of drive or ambition.

He was nothing like his older brother Michael in this respect. He'd always known what he'd wanted to do. For him playing soldiers as a child was never playing at all, it was practice. His younger brother was just grateful that he'd never gotten his hands on any live ammunition or a tank for that matter.

But at least for now, he'd managed to convince a respectable, impressive employer, and one that crucially his parents seemed to approve of, to give him a new chance, albeit a chance that he didn't really know that he wanted. It was time to reflect on the positives. He was going to get to wear a suit to work each day, and that made him feel rather grown-up and important to begin with. The starting salary, although nothing at all like he'd had in mind, was just about manageable, and compared to his employment at the Supermarket, the hours were positively brief. There would also be fewer vegetables to carry, and far fewer toilets to clean.

He glanced at his faithful, scratched Timex. It was eight-thirty, too early to think about going in yet. Heeding his Dad's warnings about the perils of rush hour traffic, George had left in good time, and, having now been inducted into that strange world of the 'Rush Hour Traveller' had come to several startling conclusions of his own.

To begin with, there seemed to be very little in the way of rushing. The cars simply slugged along the dual carriageway that led from the countryside, the direction that he'd come from, and into the grey metropolis, like spilt tins of cold baked beans. There had also been a curious, and largely pointless, game of spirited lane swapping, the goal he assumed, being able to both guess correctly which lane would be capable of the quickest progress, and then succeeding in aggressively forcing yourself into it, as all around horns and four letter words reached a deafening crescendo. It was like being unwillingly involved in an updated version of a slow motion chariot race, although without quite as much violence, and perhaps fewer spears.

George, meanwhile, was just relived to still be to motoring forward, regardless of his pace. He was slowly and painfully coming to the realisation that the old MG just wasn't built for heavy traffic, and certainly not jostling, motorised carnage. Twice he'd needed to pull over, just to allow the car to cool, a challenge in itself but nothing compared to the hell of re-joining the bumper-to-bumper stream of cars. The temperature gauge having now finally proved that not only did it work after all, but was also enthusiastically capable of reaching new, uncharted heights.

Then there was the matter of the rapidly melting clutch. Previously it had been a well behaved and sturdy device, whereas now, it seemed intent on producing a most pungent and foul aroma. This blended unpleasantly with the car's permanent odour of mould to create what could only be described as the Devil's air freshener.

Petrol was also an issue. The MG cost just twenty pounds to fill to the brim, and whilst George had been happily tearing to his best friend's house and indulging in the odd rabbit-worrying drive across the countryside, the fuel consumption hadn't really registered with him. Now, though, he sat uncomfortably, watching the fuel gauge industriously follow a completely different path to that of the temperature gauge, the twin SU carburettors guzzling the precious liquid like an eighteen-year-old out on his first night on the town, and leaving him to scour the roadside frantically for signs of a petrol station.

Finally there was the cost of parking. Shortly after his dramatic pirouette, he'd stood before the greedy little yellow ticket machine, watching in horror as his limited number of pound coins disappeared into its cavernous belly, all the while fretting that he would run out long before it reached the expensive five o'clock position. As depressing and as heart-breaking as it was for him to admit, the MGB's days were indeed numbered, and this was a very depressing note on which to begin his career with Cottons Bank. Growing up and becoming a man definitely seemed to suck so far.

He cast a misty, affectionate eye over the cockpit of his treasured vehicle, and ran his hand along the top of the dashboard, clearing some of the thickening layer of dust. The rear view mirror was held in place with masking tape, the Smiths dials were moist with condensation, and the lingering smell of mould, the source of which still eluded him, was definitely getting worse, but he loved it completely, regardless. In a moment normally reserved for lovers, he still vividly recalled that magical sunny Saturday afternoon when they'd first met, well over twelve months and a hundred years ago. It had been just after the Grand Prix qualifying had finished, a huge lunch had settled, the dishes were away, and perhaps most importantly, a dozing Mr Butler senior had eventually been coaxed into giving him a lift to inspect it.

He'd been delirious with excitement and anticipation at the thought of owning his own car, and had spent most of his waking hours trying to decide quite what he should choose. The rest of his schoolmates had opted for nippy hatchbacks or small sensible saloons with insurance friendly engines, But George yearned for something altogether different, something exotic, and something classic.

In the end though, he settled for a semi restored MOT failure, with blue tits nesting in the wings and newspaper soaking up the leaks in the foot wells. Even though his Dad, an unrivalled Mechanical Engineer, suggested quite genuinely that the car would spend more time with its bonnet up than it would with its wheels turning, his youngest son bought it anyway. He never did listen.

George was besotted, and in that moment he suddenly understood that sacred, mythical bond between man and machine. He simply had to own this car, and he quickly parted with a handful of hard-earned, grubby notes. Later that same day though, when the MGB was bleeding oil all over his parents' driveway and refusing to start, he had to admit to himself that he was struggling to still feel the love.

Back in the car park, he snapped himself out of his daydream. Maybe it wasn't all bad? He did now have a genuine excuse to purchase that most coveted of all petrol heads digest, the best-selling toilet companion for the truly dedicated motoring fan, *Autotrader*. He'd whiled away many a happy hour pouring over the first class postage stamp sized photographs of cars, whilst his feet went numb, his bottom took on the imprint of the toilet seat, and he seriously increased his chances of developing piles. Happy times indeed.

He decided to pick up the most recent copy at lunchtime and save it until nature called, as it inevitably did, around eight in the evening, following yet another well-received, enormous, home-cooked meal. Tonight was Cottage Pie night, and upon remembering this, George's belly growled and rumbled expectantly, despite the four fried eggs, three thick pork sausages and two doorstep-sized slices of hot buttered white toast he'd already taken onboard earlier that morning. Mrs Butler it seemed didn't hold with muesli.

With the most important issues of the day resolved, or at least acknowledged, and a hearty meal to look forward to later, he begrudgingly accepted that the inevitable couldn't be put off any longer. It was now time to get out of the MG, the value of which he had nearly doubled by sticking a fresh parking ticket to the window, step out into the rain, enter this ominous grey fortress, and begin his new career with Cottons Bank PLC.

Ten minutes later, George was still stood alone in the pouring rain, desperately trying to remember quite what it was that Ms Williams had said he should do upon arrival at Armada branch, in order to simply get in. Was it something to do with having identification? He couldn't remember at all, and the cold water was now pouring down the collar as his waterproof jacket, soaking the hair around his neck.

Conscious that very soon he'd be reduced to no more than a mass of wet curls again, he looked for anything that resembled a doorbell. After failing to find one, and having spotted an employee crossing the banking hall within, he banged heavily on the thick glass door in desperation. It was either this, or he'd have to give up and go home for tea and fruitcake instead. It was a close run thing.

Having banged much harder and more enthusiastically than he'd intended, the metal frame of the door rattled horribly against the unyielding doorframe, causing the startled employee to spin around to see what had caused the din. She could only be politely described as massively buxom, with cropped spiky hair that had been dyed a remarkable, and daring, shade of rouge, moist, bright red lips, and a generous application of black mascara. She wore a white smart shirt with the collar turned up, and a red handkerchief with white spots was loosely tied around her ample neck. Her bottom half was covered with a gaudy, long skirt finished off with a large black belt, clamped shut and held in place by a straining, shiny metal buckle.

As she approached the door, George marvelled at the exotic collection of gold rings and chains of varying length that plunged bravely, head first into the endless cleavage, and the abundant earrings that weighed down her lobes. The overall impression was that of a gender confused pirate. One who had grown up with gypsies, probably lived in a wooden caravan, and owned an old Shire horse called Dobbin.

"Ello my Luver, are you *alreet* there?" The strong indigenous accent easily penetrated the bullet-proof glass. "We don't open 'til nine Luver, *see*?"

She pointed to a sign.

Suddenly, George felt a slight sense of relief. She was great, and not at all what he'd expected of Bank employee. Clearly in her early fifties, she was the sort of women who would be a surrogate Mum to all those in need. And right now, he was in need. Things were looking up. She looked as though she might even have a spare slice of fruitcake at her disposal.

"Err, hello. *I am George Butler.* Umm, *I start work here today.*" Suddenly remembering just what it was Ms Williams had said, he plucked his crumpled, soggy driving license out of his jacket pocket and held it up against the wet glass to prove his identify. But the employee took no notice of the squelchy green slip of paper, and instead Gipsy Rose Leigh, as he'd now mentally christened her, fussed over opening the heavy door to get him in out of the rain. He obviously posed no threat to security.

"*Oh my*, let us get 'e in out of that rain Luver, don't want you to go catchin' a cold on 'e first day!" As various bolts and chains were pulled, and the heavy door eventually prized open, George was hit by the strongest, most potent ladies fragrance he'd ever encountered.

Literally reeling from the unexpected chemical attack, he was unable to resist Gipsy Rose Leigh's overzealous greeting, the unexpected wet kiss on the cheek coming as quite a surprise. Concerned that he would now be meeting the rest of the staff with a huge red lipstick mark on his face, he shrewdly wiped the offending area with his hand, whilst she busied herself with sealing the door once more. No doubt about it now, she was defiantly a surrogate Mum.

"I'm Di, Luver, now come on in and us'll find 'e a brew and a chair for that lovely little bum, *eh*?"

He glanced urgently around to see if he'd been accidentally exposed, as Di used a small plastic, electronic key to open the pass door, before leading them into the cashiers run. Most of the positions were filled with staff, all women in various shapes and sizes, busy preparing their individual tills, and George was quietly, unexpectedly, thrilled when he first caught sight of the great wads of cold hard cash, lurking within the drawers. Almost as one, the cashiers turned to look at the new arrival as the pass door closed ominously behind them. The tinkering of coin abruptly ceased, and the flutter of notes, silenced.

"'*ere*, this is George. Fresh meat, *eh girls*?" The unsettling stillness was broken by a warlike cheer, led by an enthusiastic Di, and left him feeling like an unexpected trainee striper at a book club meeting. Thankfully though, despite the bundles of cash at their disposal, none of the grinning women stuffed anything into his novelty boxer shorts as he was paraded past, although if they had, it would have helped with the cost of parking no end.

Each of the ladies greeted him warmly, rubbing his arm or patting his leg, with everyone having an equally peculiar interpretation of business dress, and even more peculiar appreciation of fine perfume. As he passed each of them, nodding nervous hellos, a fresh wall of overwhelming scent battered his senses. Old Spice stood no chance in this company.

"Right then Bird, let's find Linda for you, *she'll know what's best*!" Having survived his long walk past the fragrant menopausal masses, the new recruit was led into an open plan back office. "'ere she is! Linda? Linda? *LINDAHH!*" For her own reasons, Linda seemed to be hastily retreating down a long grey corridor when she was found, but with the piercing voice hunting her down, there'd been no escape.

Trapped, she stopped in her tracks, and seemed to lower her head slightly and compose herself.

"Yes Di?" She was in her mid-thirties, tall, athletic, clinically serious, and dressed as an office professional should be, in a trim charcoal-grey suit with a knee length matching skirt, a crisp light blue shirt discreetly unbuttoned just low enough to display a small gold cross, but nothing else. Her ash blond hair was scraped back severely into a neat bun, and secured in place by a shocking arsenal of pins. A greater contrast to Di would've been hard to imagine.

"This 'ere's George, Linda. *You know*, new boy startin' today?" Linda glanced at the damp young man standing next to Di, sharp pale green eyes flickering over him with mechanical precision. What to make of this new arrival? He appeared harmless enough, a bit messy perhaps and he would definitely need a haircut. There was a vague veneer of confusion about him though, like he wasn't quite sure where he was, or how he even got there, probably another useless lamb to the slaughter then, great.

"Ah yes, *George*, welcome." She shook his hand so briefly that he wasn't entirely sure that it actually happened. "My name, as you might have guessed by Di's gentle introduction, is Linda, Linda Beech. I'm the Branch Manager." Not for a second did the green eyes blink or release their grip on him. "I am sorry, but first thing does tend to be a bit busy around here. Let's get Di to settle you into the staff room and I'll be along shortly. The *others* are already there, waiting…" She hung on to her last word for longer than necessary, smiled a brief, professional smile that looked as though it didn't get out much, and hurried off wondering how on earth this lost little soul ever found his way to the branch without a guide. It was going to be a long day.

Linda already terrified George. She was exactly what he'd been expecting of a Bank Manager, all creases, numbers and professionalism. Was it too late to run away, and what was this *others* business all about?

Before he had chance to form a fresh plan of escape, Di tugged at his sleeve. "This way Luver. Soon 'ave 'e a nice cup of char!" She led the way along a grey corridor that snaked past a maze of back offices. He soon lost his bearings completely, although their actual whereabouts was always unclear, and any hopes of fleeing this drab building were dashed for the moment. Reflecting that he should've tied a length of wool to the door on the way in, he followed his chatty host reluctantly instead, deeper and deeper into the unknown, grey cavern.

After a seemingly endless journey, during which Di asked every conceivable question of her young charge, without ever once pausing for an answer, they eventually arrived at the end of the corridor. To the right there was a door that would lead to a flight of stairs and the next level, and to the left a smaller corridor that was home to three large square units, constantly chattering, whirring, and beeping away to each other.

"*What are those things Di?*"

"Them's cashpoints Luver, well the back of 'um anyway."

"Really, they're so *noisy*, I had no idea!" George was amazed. The part of the machine that the public got to plead with was tiny compared to the huge unit that sat on the other side of the wall. They were almost like overexcited, mechanical icebergs.

Bravely, they began their epic assent, with Di leading the way up the never-ending flights of stairs, her epic bottom swaying magnificently with each heavy step. Accustomed to the hike, and in spite of her padding, she managed to keep her tongue permanently engaged without needing to pause for breath, unlike her companion, and soon turned her good natured interrogation turned into a running commentary instead. On the landing of each floor they paused briefly, a blessed relief for an exhausted George, and as they peered through office door windows, Di gave a brief, but impressively detailed, knowledgeable description of the staff within.

"An' 'ere's where the Business lot sit. Funny buggers, the lot of 'em. One was caught doin' some proper naughty stuff with one of the girls in 'is gardin. Got in the paper in everythin'! *Proper* dirty bugger 'e is!" She grinned from ear to ear as the memory of those interesting few days in the office came flooding back. There was still a copy of the newspaper in here till drawer, perhaps she'd show him later.

Still they climbed ever upwards, through a labyrinth of uniform satin grey.

"*Isn't there a lift?*" George was mindful that his shirt had stuck fast to his back with sweat, despite the weather outside, and he was also quite sure that at least one lung had collapsed.

"No Bay, tis broke'. Some monkey business happened inside, I reckon'." She gave him another of her knowing looks, and the first of what was to be many generous winks.

On reaching yet another floor, Di urgently beckoned the sodden new recruit to another window. "*Look*, Customer Banking Advisors – CBAs, Luver - Financial advisors and Mortgage Advisors. That's what you want to be one day, *one of 'em*, good jobs those." Inexplicably, George was drawn to the window, as though he was at the Zoo, hoping to catch a glimpse of something rare and antisocial. It was a vast open office, home to just six bodies, each sitting studiously at colossal mahogany desks, scattered with all the toys the successful professional office worker could ever demand. They looked as though they'd been there since long before he'd had his own full English breakfast. A dark, powerful-looking man looked up from his work and nodded pleasantly, catching them off guard.

Abruptly, Di shot back and pinned herself to the wall, as though she'd been caught peeping over a neighbour's fence. "I could see 'e doin' one of those jobs, sittin' 'n there like that, smart lad like 'e," She whispered seriously, looking him up and down again with approving eyes.

"*Really?* Well err, what do they *do* then?" George, still in full view, waved back at the man. He would have made a terrible spy.

"They *doos* all the interviewing stuff, lends customers the money, invests it, sorts out mortgages and stuff like 'at, proper professional lot them. Bloody good jobs that. C'mon, *let's bugger off.*"

At last they finally reached the peak, the staff room presumably located in the heavens to deter employees from going there when they really shouldn't.

"'ere we go then Georgie! *Safe 'n sound at last.*" He hadn't been called *Georgie* since he'd been in short trousers and found it quite endearing, despite the images in conjured and the longing it left him with. Whatever else happened today, however many stern Lindas he encountered, he sensed that he had found a unique ally in this strange new world of Banking. Now, just like on that first day of school, he didn't want to let go of her podgy hand, metaphorically speaking at least.

They waddled together across a short landing, before Di pushed open the staff room door with practiced ease and headed straight for the kettle. "'ave a seat Georgie. Wanna a brew then Luver? These are our other new bods startin' today. *Err,* Wesley an' err Belinda wan't it, Bird?" She waved a chubby, bejewelled hand in the direction of the *others*.

"*Yes please,* strong and milky with two sugars." Aware that this was a blend few people could master, he smiled at Di and nervously turned to meet his new colleagues. During the climb, his senses had been so occupied with spurring on his legs and keeping his respiratory system functioning properly, that he hadn't given much thought to the *others* waiting in the staff room. What sort of person normally decided that banking was just the thing for them? Would they be like him, would he fit in? He wasn't holding his breath.

Belinda looked to be expensively dressed in an immaculate black business suit, with sharp tailoring and a reasonably short skirt, which she repeatedly tried to stretch down her slender thighs - an activity that had increased considerably since George had arrived. In his limited experience of women, and in particular Sixth Form girls, he could never understand why they wore skirts so short if all they are going to do is spend all day trying to make them grow.

Belinda was also the sort of girl that should never, ever be addressed as *'Bird'*. She was probably in her early twenties, slim without being thin, and her wavy black hair was styled in a very charming fifties cut. She was pretty with striking blue eyes, but like Linda downstairs, unnervingly rigid. She wore expertly applied makeup, which only added to her air of confidence and professionalism. She was also the sort of girl that George, despite his best efforts, could never, ever imagine being naked.

She stood up, straightened her skirt once more and held out a stiff hand, unburdened by any rings, for the new arrival to shake. "Belinda Jones, pleased to meet you." Her voice was quite a contrast to Di's, well-spoken and clipped, yet free of obligatory pretentiousness.

George had had very little practical experience shaking girls' hands, and what little he did have had almost entirely been gained in the past few weeks. The earlier encounter with Linda didn't really count, if indeed it had happened at all, and the time before that, when he'd met Ms Williams, he'd been so consumed with embarrassment that he'd blanked the entire incident from his mind. What was it his Dad had said that time, firm but not crushing?

"Err, *I'm George*. How are you?" He beamed hopefully at Belinda, hoping to find another ally, and took firm hold.

"*Ow!*" She snatched back her injured paw and glared and him as though he'd attacked her in a darkened alleyway.

"*Bugger!* Err, sorry Linda, I umm..."

"It's *Belinda*, actually." She shot him a withering look that made him wish he could hide behind the grey wallpaper. Sensing that there was nothing he could do or say to improve matters, he turned instead to the second new recruit, hoping not to cause any further bodily harm.

"Wesley Ferrers." Seated a few respectable feet from the wounded

Belinda, a tall man had gotten up to introduce himself, bravely extending his own hand.

"*'ere you go Luver,*" Di was proudly brandishing a steaming mug of tea, like an overjoyed new Grandparent. "*'ave fun, I'll no doubt see 'e later on.*" She rubbed his arm encouragingly, winked one last time at him, and left to begin the steep descent to the ground floor. Although he was completely smitten with Di, and very sad to see her go, he was grateful that she'd chosen not to kiss him again. He took a long sip of her tea, perfect.

Wesley meanwhile, remained perfectly straight, his hand still extended throughout, as though frozen in time. After an age, and after his new colleague had taken several long slurps, he finally cleared his throat.

"*Oh bugger!* Sorry Mate. *I'm George!*" Without thinking too much about it this time, he gripped the long bony hand and pumped it enthusiastically. "I've made a bit of a new friend there. *Great isn't she?*" His bright eyes, having already forgotten the earlier assault on Belinda, gleamed happily.

"Personally, I find it quite unbelievable that Cottons Bank would even consider someone like that suitable for employment. Still, I suppose they must have need of someone who can communicate with the natives." Wesley removed his hand from George's grasp, glanced at it with mild disgust, and made no attempt at all to hide a cleansing wipe with a perfectly ironed silk handkerchief.

Unbeknown to either of them, Wesley Ferrers had actually grown up near the same rural town as George, although a combination of living in a large rambling manor house that his family had owned since the early 1800s, and an education at a reputable private school located on the edge of the countryside, ensured that the two young men's paths had never crossed until now. It had probably been for the best.

Wesley had the sort of historically interbred, upper class face that only a mother could love. He seemed to be permanently looking down his colossal nose at the world, as though the world had been something that the family gardener had just stepped in. Glued to the front of his enormous aristocratic face, it was far from his worst feature, but was still worth mocking for its size all the same. This was not a face destined to grace even the cover of *Horse and Hound* magazine.

He had a huge moon shaped head with equally impressive ears, insipid skin, and tiny unforgiving grey eyes that peered through delicate half rimmed glasses, which balanced precariously on the bridge of his huge snout. His ginger hair was short and fine, slicked into a side parting and unaccompanied by anything as vulgar as sideburns. Although he was the same age as George, Wesley had an old soul, one it seemed to be winning over both his features and dress sense too.

Dressed in the traditional garb of the conformist Banker or Accountant of old, and considering the way he spoke and the contempt he obviously held for the locals, it was quite astonishing that Wesley had made it to Armada Branch alive. A razor-sharp black, three-piece pinstripe suit gracefully hid a scrawny frame that had clearly never benefitted from a wholesome meaty pasty or steak and ale pie. Under the suit he wore a crisp, white, full cut collar shirt, with double cuffs exposed a carefully measured three quarters of an inch below the jacket, complete with enamel links encased in gold. With a private school tie held firm with an ornate pin, and expensive black brogues that were polished to an impressive mirrored shine, Wesley was the quintessential English businessman.

Despite harbouring less than charitable thoughts towards his new colleague, after his obnoxious comments about his treasured Gipsy Rose Leigh, George was mesmerized. He'd never seen double cuffs with cufflinks in the flesh before. They were magnificent.

He was starting to feel seriously out-classed and underdressed. It wasn't that he didn't have some funds available to improve his meagre business wardrobe, it was simply that until very recently at least, he'd mostly been a jeans and T-shirt type of chap, and very happy all the same. Weeks ago, when he'd arrived home from his fraught shopping trip, and proudly presented his new suit, small collection of shirts and a solitary Technicolor tie to his parents. The ensemble of gaudy colours and dubious materials was met with kindly offers of extra cash to perhaps get something a bit nicer. Stubbornly, he'd been determined to stand by his choices. Something he now bitterly regretted.

Sitting in silence, stealing quick glances for comparisons sake, excruciating blisters forming on every square inch of his toes, another consequence of his thrifty purchases, he was starting to understand what his parents had meant. He might very well need a makeover after all.

He sipped his tea, taking comfort in the reassuring flavour, and glanced at his Timex. Would that need updating too? It had once been a perfectly respectable, simple little watch from the Indiglo range, unique in having a button that, once depressed, bathed the white face with a reassuring blue green hue. It looked great under a duvet.

Now though, it was battered and scratched, deeply scared from countless falls from his mountain bike and camping excursion calamities, a constant and faithful friend that had been plunged into icy waters during unsuccessful fishing trips, and subjected to the scorching Mediterranean sun on a holiday to Greece. The plain, black leather strap had long since been torn and replaced with a drab olive green, standard issue NATO strap, which his older brother Michael, had borrowed from Army stores. It didn't really sit at all well with business dress. He continued to sip his tea, reflecting gloomily on the morning so far. Growing up really did suck.

The long awkward silence continued. Belinda casually examined her perfectly manicured nails, whilst Wesley sat perfectly still, pale blue hands resting on his knees. George meanwhile was slumped forward, cupping his tea like an anxious relative in a hospital waiting room. He knew better than to attempt a nonchalant pose.

The grim silence was finally broken by the rhythmic tap of rapidly approaching high heels. Two sets in all likelihood, although the second seemed flatter, as though made by a pair of unseasonal flip flops. The steps reached a crescendo and the door to the staff room suddenly burst open and in strode a purposeful Linda, carrying three personnel files, eager to dispel any thoughts that she'd forgotten all about the new recruits in the heavens. The second pair of feet meanwhile, lingered in the shadows of the doorway, unseen.

Clearly as fit as she looked, Linda spoke brightly and without hindrance, her breathing no different than if she'd just rolled out of her crypt. "Good morning again, I'm sorry to keep you all waiting. I do hope you all have had to chance to get to know each other?" The three of them considered the brief pleasantries they'd exchanged, along with the one count of physical assault, as the best they could manage for now, and murmured various acknowledgments.

"*Jolly good.* Right then, welcome to Cottons Bank. We have a lot to get through today and Summer here will be helping you with most of the computer based activities, seeing to it that you get settled in." She held out a hand to her side, clearly intending to introduce her colleague. Her colleague though, seemed to have vanished. Linda sighed and turned back to the doorway. This was going to be hard work.

"Summer, do come in here, *please?*" Out of the shadow of the doorway, a small, reluctant figure inched into the room, like a timid, startled wren gently being coaxed into taking a peck of seed from an unfamiliar bird table.

In that instant, George's heart fell out bed. After fumbling about on the floor for a while, it sat bolt upright, ran upstairs, and gathered together as many of his fellow senses as it could find. They congregated behind the eyes, and stared curiously out at the vision. What was this, and why was it making them come over all unnecessary?

She was very petit, in her mid to late twenties, and no more than five feet tall. Her mass of thick, brunette hair was enviably long and wavy, yet it appeared to have been recently pounced upon by something savage and mean hearted, with tousled wayward clumps sticking out at odd angles. It desperately needed a good trim, buckets of conditioner, and a bit of love.

She was probably pretty, in a plain sort of way, but seemed to try and hide behind her bedraggled locks, just in case anyone noticed and made a fuss. From what little she'd revealed of her tiny almond shaped face, she didn't seem to wear any makeup, but she did have the bright red rosy cheeks which can only be achieved by having regular hard scrubs with coal tar soap, and a good rough flannel. George recognised the signs, tasted the bubbles, and empathised.

It was difficult to draw any firm conclusions about what Summer was actually wearing. Not unlike the older cashiers at the base of the mountain, she too had an unusual appreciation of business dress. But rather than flaunt what was actually a very nicely cut, slim fitted trouser suit, which a sales assistant had practically forced on her, she instead chose to camouflage the flattering tailoring, and therefore herself, with a collection of patterned, ethnic scarves that would have made a Bedouin green with envy. It was almost as if, under no circumstances whatsoever, did she want anyone suspect that she had a pleasing figure underneath. They also served to hide a near permanent neck flush.

Not unlike Di, Summer also had little restraint when it came to personalised jewellery, although she tended to favour tribal motifs and designs to add to her concealment. It was virtually impossible to establish quite where her tiny wrists ended and her hands began, so burdened were her lower arms with wooden bracelets and seashell bangles. Her slightest movement produced a cacophony of rattles and knocks as the adornments collided, like conkers in a playground, the simple act of reluctantly edging towards the new recruits, creating sounds to rival even the din of George's prehistoric MGB, firing up on a cold winter's morning.

Summer was just a shy, closet hippy. Someone who was merely trying to hide in the Banking industry until either Bob Marley was returned to us, or a wizard turned her into a dolphin. And she was wearing flip flops.

Linda and Summer exchanged whispered, urgent words in the middle of the staff room, muffled in part by the great mound of hair, as the two parties stood nose to nose. With the shorter looking pleadingly up and the more senior, the battle eventually came to an almost violent conclusion as the files were thrust into a tiny pair of quivering hands. It was obvious to everyone but a spellbound George, that somebody was being pressed into doing something way, way outside of their comfort zone that morning. Bless her.

"*Ahem*, right then, sorry about that." Clearly flustered, the cool exterior briefly melted, Linda returned to her flock, a reddening Summer in tow, like a child being dragged to the dentist. "As I was saying, *Summer here* will be helping you get settled in and getting you started on our computer systems, which is *after all*," she turned and shot the tiny girl a perishing stare, "*Her* area of expertise!" The icy cool returned as quickly as winter to the Rockies, and Linda, now feeling her normal indomitable self once more, was looking to wrap things up quickly, remove herself from this utter waste of her time, and get on with more pressing tasks.

"Now, Mr Burton, the Senior Manager of the Armada Group, will arrive shortly after lunch. He will of course be keen to meet you all, and he normally likes to have an informal chat, nothing to worry about, we have, *ahem*, already recruited you all." For some reason, she raised a perfectly plucked eyebrow in George's direction, before turning back to Summer and pulling her towards the doorway by her arm as though she was a ragdoll, spitting her words through hushed, merciless red lips. "*Don't bugger this up*, do you hear me? Get some name badges ordered, go through the packs, and show them the usual rubbish on the PCs, *including* the shock and awe tactics, then let them have some lunch. Do you *think* you can handle that?" Without waiting for a reply, Linda turned back to the confused new entrants, recovered a jovial tone, bid them farewell for now, and retreated to the comfort of some large numbers.

Once again, silence gripped the room. Summer stood near the door at an odd angle, as though she couldn't quite make up her mind whether or not to just run away, make a cup of strong tea at the kitchenette, or jump out of the sixth story window. All of these options were preferable to the task she now had thrust upon her.

"Err, umm, *okay*..." Mumbling, almost to herself, still facing away from the group, the narrow shoulders trembled slightly. "Err, well, *let me see now*. I'm Summer, and err, *well*, as Linda said, I'll be helping you today, with, err, *stuff*." The whispered voice was both tender and soft, with just a hint of an Irish lilt.

Finally she plucked up the courage to slowly turn, and face what she obviously considered to be as fearsome as a fire-breathing, eight headed dragon. Her mind suddenly went blank, struck down with stage fright, her mouth unable to find the next words, until at last, that great British understudy came to her rescue. *"Wouldanyonelikeacupoftea?!"* At least one member of her audience was entirely supportive of the idea.

Normally a properly taught, enthusiastic trainer, one with the boundless energy of a children's television presenter, would be drafted in from Area Office or HR to chaperone the new recruits, and guide them through their first few days. But unfortunately for Summer, Phillip Miles had called in sick that day. A delicate soul at best, he'd probably split a finger nail, and the short straw had been not so much been pulled as thrust into her hand.

Her days were normally blissfully mundane, which was just the way she liked them, and had largely remained so ever since she stumbled into Cottons Bank nearly six years ago. After a year of cashiering, which did nothing to improve some of her social anxiety issues, and following a rare moment of self-promotion, she was accidentally elevated to the position of Group IT Consultant.

New-fangled software had only just been installed in the branches, and with the real IT Consultant already on the motorway to his next job, most of the staff were stumped, especially when a few of the shiny new units failed to reboot. Summer's brother was a complete computer nerd, and it had been impossible for her to enjoy a family dinner without picking up the odd useful tip. After hesitantly suggesting that perhaps the offending units could simply switched off, and then turned back on again, she was immediately branded an expert as the screens flickered into life, and swiftly plucked for obscurity.

The role wasn't particularly demanding, and she seldom needed to write to her brother for technical advice, but it did keep her away from the general public, which she rather enjoyed. When nothing needed fixing or installing, the Senior Manager, who always had something of a soft spot for her, tended to keep her busy as a sort of unofficial secretary, which did nothing for her relationship with his actual secretary. All things considered though, she'd much rather focus on her arts and crafts instead, alone and at home.

The only problem with her role was, when something more traditional was pressing, such as emergency cashiering or staff training, all of sudden it just wasn't that important anymore. Cashiering was almost bearable, she'd long since learnt to control her blushes just long enough to move a customer along without turning into a complete tomato, unless they had an excessive amount of coin of course, but training was another matter entirely. Ever since she'd had her first panic attack, aged just five, playing an angel in the school play, public speaking had been a huge problem for Summer. She even struggled to talk to herself in the bathroom mirror. Somehow though, she was going to have to try and get through this, perhaps build rapport with these new recruits even. The hairy one seemed friendly enough.

After Wesley had pathologically inspected the collection of mugs, eventually selecting the least soiled one he could find, they were all seated in a rough circle of chairs with a steaming brew, a small coffee table stacked with files between them. Summer pulled a bright green notepad from the folds of one of her scarves, and began almost frantically leafing through it, desperately searching for the hastily scribbled training notes she'd taken only moments before from an impatient Linda.

"Ah, err, *no...*" Flushed, she continued her anxious search, before eventually realising her mistake, and, after much more rummaging, producing a crumpled scrap of headed paper from her hip pocket instead, an unintentional brief flash of perfectly fitted trouser, across an unexpectedly firm bottom, not going unnoticed. "*Found it!*" With her notes finally located, at least she now had the semblance of a plan, and possibly even a structure to the morning. "Right, err, okay." She rotated the page, turned it over, and then back again. "Ah, yes, *that's right!* Do you all have your New Entrant packs with you..?"

Almost in unison, Wesley and Belinda pulled perfect leather briefcases from under their seats, unclipped the brass locks, taking infinite care to shield their combinations, as though they contained the darkest secrets of a Superpower, and finally produced two thick packs which looked sharper now than when they'd left the printers.

Completely at a loss, and without even a supermarket bag to aimlessly fumble through, George patted his pockets frantically, sifting through the endless collection of usual tat, hoping that the heavy, ring bound wodge of embossed paper had miraculously fallen in when he wasn't looking. But it hadn't. He knew exactly where it was, or at least the remains of it.

That morning, as he'd battled his way into the grey city, the weather had reached truly biblical proportions, and just for fun, the hole in the driver's side foot well of the MGB decided to enlarge itself. As a great torrent of spray flooded into the cockpit, soaking his polyester suit trousers, George had naturally reached for the first thing that had come to hand to plug the leak, stomping it violently into place with his plastic loafers. Given the embossed covering, the pack had served rather well, only disintegrating entirely towards the very end of his journey.

Summer looked sympathetically at the hairy one. Against all odds of finding what he wanted, he was continuing to fumble through his tissues and discarded chocolate wrappers. She was suddenly overwhelmed by an unusual sense of empathy. Here was a kindred spirit perhaps, and he urgently needed help. She quickly checked her notes.

"Umm, its George isn't it?" The blush deepened dramatically.

Still engrossed in the investigation of his debris, he looked up, surprised to hear his name. He paused. She had the most magnificent eyes. Both haunted and haunting. Uncharitable, jealous types, with narrow, unforgiving eyes of their own, would've branded them far too big for the tiny face. But they weren't. They were just perfect, to him at least, and the most captivating shade of indigo blue he'd ever seen. His heart had another moment. Perhaps he needed to get his Mum to take him to the Doctors for a check-up this weekend, he'd been under a lot of strain lately?

"Err, *George*, its George, isn't it?" Summer anxiously checked her notes again. She had scribbled them in an awful hurry.

"Oh, yes, *yes*, definitely George. Always has been, expect it always will be!" The words falling out of him before his brain had chance to edit, his own blushes now rising from the collar of his polyester shirt, like a spreading red ink stain across a white tablecloth.

"Err, *okay*, umm, well look, if you've forgotten it, *that's okay*, I can get you another...?" 'Forgotten' certainly seemed to be a much more acceptable fate and the trainee nodded enthusiastically. Technically he hadn't lied to her. Part of the pack was indeed still with the car, impaled on a sharp section of rust underneath the pedals perhaps, but it was there nonetheless, and therefore technically, forgotten.

Summer picked up his staff file and made a note in the corner of the first page, pausing mid scribe as something in hobbies and interest caught her eye. "*Oh!* It, it says here that you like to paint, *is that right?*" They both blushed deeply, as though a team of tomato pickers had arrived with great woven baskets of freshly plucked fruit, and had then begun tossing them vigorously in their direction.

"Walls or skirting boards?" Wesley's aristocratic, hateful voice cut through the tender moment of near discovered similarities, shattering the harmony in the room. Summer immediately retreated back behind her curtain of thick hair for safety, leaving George longing for the wonderfully captivating eyes, which only seconds before, had him utterly enchanted. There was no doubt about it, Wesley would have to die.

Sadly, the rest of the morning passed without any opportunity for George to answer Summer's intriguing question, or even understand quite why this small detail about his life had intrigued her so, especially when there was archery to consider. No one seemed to value Robin Hood anymore.

A fresh New Entrant pack was produced, meaning at least there would be something to plug the gap on the journey home, and a few mundane hours past whilst the four of them took turns reading out loud from the endless corporate pages. It was just like class again, only with longer words and more emphasis on customer service.

Unenthusiastically, and in spite of her near terminal flushes, Summer took the lead on a section headed up as the 'New World'. Whispering and stuttering her way through a lecture on how Cottons soon intended to embark on a 'New Journey', possibly in conjunction with another well-known Bank, and one that would both enhance the customer experience, and increase the Banks share of the marketplace. She didn't sound at all convinced.

There was a brief interlude for tea and coffee, but any hopes George had of quietly, nervously picking up the threads of their earlier conversation over a cup of reassuring tea, were dashed as Summer began ordering name badges. Wesley once again adding to his death sentence, by becoming particularly aggravated when it was suggested, quietly and respectfully, that his badge could simply read *Wes*, but only if he preferred of course. Apparently he did not.

Devoid of any mid-morning snack, his hands feeling positively lost without even so much as a biscuit to dunk in his tea, George was giddy with hunger by the time the reluctant Trainer announced at noon, that the mornings training session would move downstairs briefly, so that they could all be logged into the Banks IT system.

Feeling like a lost mountaineer found struggling at ridiculous altitudes, being guided to the safety of base camp by a team of passing Sherpas, he stumbled down the endless flights of steps at the rear of the group, hallucinating wildly, visions of roast potatoes and Cornish pasties floating before his eyes. How on earth did the others do it? It had been four hours since breakfast!

Eventually they settled into another circle of chairs, this time around a solitary computer station within easy earshot of Linda's desk. See kept a careful, watchful eye on the group, especially Summer. She could never understand what it was about this pathetic, nervous little mouse that made the Senior Manager so fond of her. Under no circumstances was she jealous though.

When all three recruits were logged in, a simple task that was delayed somewhat by someone being unable to think of, and then retain, a suitable password, Summer showed them some basic applications which could be used to look up customer accounts, and, after checking through a gap in her hair to see if Linda was still watching, unwillingly pressed on with the 'Shock and Awe' tactics. She didn't agree with this at all, and she hated Linda for making her do it.

Proper Bank Trainers, Trainers that are actually trained in how to provide training, referred to moments like this as making the session 'come alive'. The morning had indeed bordered on deathly at times, but that didn't make this any more acceptable to Summer. She sighed, and grudgingly reappeared from behind her protective mane, she'd need a volunteer. A pair of dark, welcoming puppy-dog eyes gazed longingly at her. *"George!"*

"Hmm?" His mind had been elsewhere for some time now. Not an unusual state of affairs by any means, especially when he was suffering from fatigue induced by near starvation. But this time it wasn't just the hunger that was ruining his concentration. He'd almost completely succumbed to his growing infatuation with his new Teacher as well. It was GCSE art all over again.

"*Err*, would *you* like to have a go then?" Given where his thoughts had just been, this was entirely the wrong thing to say to a trainee banker with amorous intent.

"*Yes please!*" The reply was a little too eager. Grappling with a variety of complicated emotions, not least the all too familiar sense that yet again, he'd been caught out daydreaming when he should've been listening to instruction, he gingerly changed seats, and was handed a well-used scrap of paper containing a sort code and account number. Why hadn't he noticed those perfect full lips before now?

The warmth from the seat padding was both heavenly and distracting. Only moments before the pert little bottom, an essential part of the object of his desire, had sat right here. He gazed blankly at the screen and clumsily grappled with the mouse. Belinda and Wesley, both bored beyond imagination, were now either side of him, their interest briefly restored as it became apparent that the scruffy wretch clearly didn't have a clue. Mutually they willed him to fail, purely for entrainments sake.

George had very limited experience with computers. He'd much rather paint, or wander the woods with his bow, burying his arrows into fallen lumps of tree. On the very rare occasions he'd used the Butler family's BBC computer, he'd play *Elite*, a dated, but nonetheless complicated space ship game, and waste a few rainy afternoons waiting for artistic inspiration, cruising around the galaxy looking for something to shoot at. Invariably, he'd get lost, run out of rocket fuel, and reach for his paint brushes instead.

A growling stomach broke the silence. Clearly he wasn't going to type in the numbers. Taking pity on him once more, Summer leaned over his left side, and, unthinking, rested her small, soft hand over his as it gripped the mouse, rambling aimlessly about the corporate pad, and guided it gently to where it needed to be. The moment had been completely natural. Her many homemade rings pressed lightly into his skin, their cheeks only inches apart. Entirely involuntarily, they gazed for a second into each other's eyes, briefly lost in inappropriate thoughts. George was glad he was sitting down.

"*Ahem*, right then, err, *George*, err, *oh dear*, umm, please type in these numbers, err, for practice and all that..." With Linda still watching on intently, he typed in the two sets of digits, rather heavy-handedly and with one chubby finger. First the sort code, then the account number.

Another pause and another, very different moment of awkward silence soon followed. The three recruits, even the sombre Wesley, leaned in closer and looked in astonishment at the name that appeared on the computer screen. It couldn't be, surely not, *could it?*

George didn't follow football at all, or any sport for that matter, except for two very special weeks in June, and then only the ladies' matches. But unless he'd been captured and held hostage, kept in the deepest darkest cell in some remote, savage corner of the world, even he would've had to have heard of the Italian striker, Giovanni Erasmo.

A flamboyant twenty-something who was as famous for his exploits off the pitch as well as on, Giovanni was a football legend. He was renowned for his poetical sparing with the press, his string of glamorous girlfriends, expensive supercars and exotic holidays. Recently he'd even signed a lucrative three-year deal to play for a prominent UK team, and had moved into a swanky London pad, intent on enlightening hordes of young English ladies. Giovanni was a true celebrity and outstanding sporting figure who was hard to overlook.

Quite understandably then, it came as an enormous shock to the three new recruits of Cottons Bank, when they found themselves looking at Giovanni Erasmo's bank balance, Shock and Awe indeed.

Chapter 3

HMS Pedalo

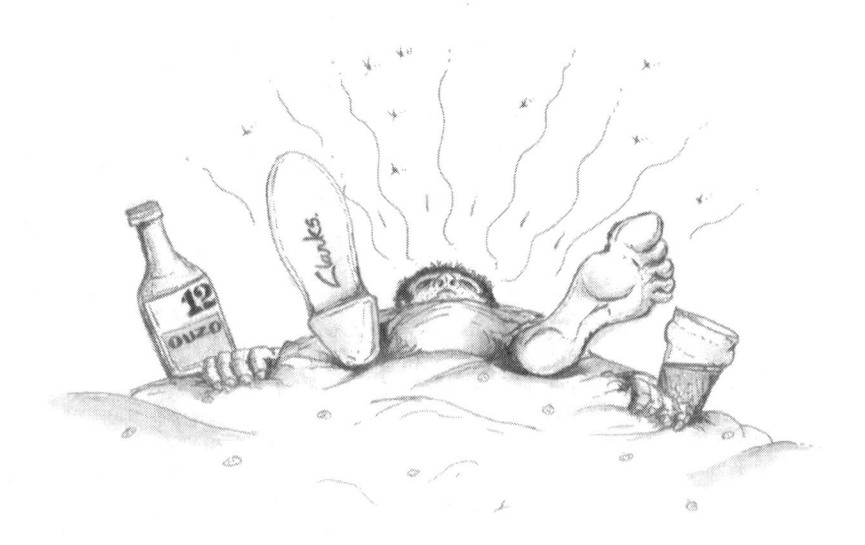

Lunchtime, the same day.

Mr Laurence Burton, Senior Manager of Cottons Bank Armada Group, gingerly lowered his not inconsiderable bulk into a heavily padded leather office chair, let out a slight groan of relief, and gazed wistfully out of his second floor window at the sprawling, grey city. How he longed for the crystal blue skies of the summer months.

The patchwork quilt of angular grey boxes, interwoven with a few precious architectural relics that the German bombs somehow missed, and which often caused people at the preservation society to become very excited indeed, were all being bathed in a torrential, seemingly endless downpour. One thing was certain, the journey home this evening was going to be a truly miserable affair.

Mr Burton sighed as he considered the inevitable dash to his company Jag. His days of enjoying peak physical condition were now a distant memory, and he considered any form of exercise an unnecessary encumbrance to be avoided at all cost. Except for golf of course, golf was wholly acceptable.

For far too long now, he'd been the victim of extended lunches with similarly disposed friends and colleagues. Lunches that typically consisted of plump lamb cutlets, parsnips roasted in butter and honey, steaks cooked so briefly that a good vet might well have been able to bring the animal back to life, rich sauces steeped in heavy wine, and numerous gooey, calorific desserts that had seen his once fine athletic figure slowly take on the appearance of a large, overripe red pear. Yet in spite of this, he still managed to command a great deal of respect and admiration from those around him. His skilled and loyal tailor somehow managed to hide his shame under the finest double breasted suits, and at just over six feet tall, and having recently celebrated his sixty-first birthday, Mr Burton was still an imposing, impressive character.

In the distant past, he would have been described as a traditionally handsome man. The sort of upstanding Chap that wouldn't have looked out of place in 1944 sat in a deckchair next to a fastidiously maintained Spitfire, casually leafing through the dull bits of the Times before thankfully getting to the cricket, twirling his handlebar moustache, and waiting for the order to scramble.

The moustache was still in place, although the handlebars had long since been sheared off, but the hair had now retreated spectacularly, and whilst still mostly jet black, it was now swirled into an elaborate style that ensured Mr Burton managed to cover as much of his head as possible with the limited remaining growth. Unfortunately though, days of dreadfully high winds and rain, such as this one, often played havoc with his appearance, as the long wispy strands that circumnavigated the top of his head broke free, and danced wildly around his ears like skinny cavorting lap dancers.

He stiffly reached down to the well-worn brown leather briefcase at his feet, a constant companion since his parents bought it for him for his first day at the office, clicked it open and took out a single slim card file. On the cover it simply read, Mr L Burton: *Proposed Early Retirement Package.*

Unbeknown to any of his staff, for several anxious months he'd been in talks with Area Office and HR, desperately trying to negotiate his escape whilst trying to appear not at all desperate. It had been a fine line to tread. His wife of forty-one years had been the instigator of this plan. She'd found them an idyllic little cottage in a small village, which boasted all the traditional features of green, pub, church and idiot, and was now quite insistent that her husband retired, before the pressure of his waistline finally evolved into something altogether more terminal.

He calmly closed his eyes and once again tried to imagine the new life that hopefully lay in wait. The tranquil little village nestled in the valley of the rambling green countryside, like a marble dropped into warm putty, the pub that was bound to have abundant *Ye Olde* real ales, and the nearby golf club, where he and his wife had already put their names down for membership. Fingers crossed.

It was definitely high time to put all the stress and pressure behind him, and retire, albeit four years earlier than originally planned, and become the Comb-over Golfer he was always destined to be. Fingers doubly crossed then.

Opening the file, he leafed unseeing through its contents, the words and figures long since committed to memory. Everything seemed in order. The numbers stacked up and were sufficiently generous. Clearly his years of unwavering devotion to Cottons hadn't gone unnoticed after all, but it was his continued devotion to his staff that was being challenged now, in his mind at least. Was he just a coward after all?

Lately, Mr Burton had taken to feeling like a respected General, secretly planning to leave his devoted troops on the eve of battle. The sense of guilt he felt for abandoning them now, when he knew what was almost certainly coming over the hill, was unbearable, almost as unbearable as his near permanent heart burn.

News of Cottons anticipated merger with another high street bank was as secret as a family man's torrid affair on the cul-de-sac where he lived. The only question being, was it with the glamorous new widow in number twenty-one, or the fiery gold digger with the enormous breasts and cheap curtains in number seven? Breasts always tended to win in these situations, and this particularly ample pair, belonged to the NSIB.

The Northern Savings Investment Bank had a solid reputation as a helpful and approachable bank of the people. Compared to Cottons rather stuffy, old school image, the NSIB was considered rather modern and forward thinking by comparison, an image they keenly exploited.

A cunning recent advertising campaign, promoted their ability to grant loans within ten minutes, thanks to their innovative Customer Product Opportunity system, CPO. At the press of a button, the perceived monthly loan budget for a customer could be calculated, based on the turnover through the account, and moments later the money lent. Credit cards and overdrafts were also agreed in the same way, and money was practically lending itself. With the share price soaring, it was time to expand.

The NSIB had a small presence in the south, but were renowned for their large corner of the market in the north of England, this coupled with the ground-breaking framework of CPO, made them utterly desirable and perfect for merger. Cottons, long since consumed with lust, now wanted to abandon the family semi, and leap amorously into bed with them.

Like many cunning mistresses though, the NSIB had plans of its own that went far beyond a quick frolic on the kitchen table. Top Management knew that in order to grow, they needed to expand into the South, and it would be far simpler to attach themselves to a rich old man who already had an impressive property portfolio, rather than try and build one themselves from scratch. Later, when the rings were firmly on the fingers, they could go about discussing redecoration, during some pillow talk, naturally.

It was this potentially destructive redecoration that Mr Burton feared the most. The NSIB had always been the favourite merger candidate, and he knew all too well, not least from a fellow member at his Gentleman's Club, what this would mean for Cottons staff and customers alike.

Behind the modern welcoming façade, the NSIB was run with all the determined aggression of a Bond villain, bent on total world domination. CPO had been developed to speed up sales, not provide excellent customer service, as the colourful propaganda suggested, for they had long ago learnt that financial sales meant massive financial growth.

There's was a perfect, carefully honed machine, managed and supervised at every level by ruthless taskmasters, each motivated and driven by huge targets, bonuses and greed. The Branches were seen as the engine rooms, a place to generate the power and momentum necessary to speed the growing vessel faster still through the icy waters. If anyone failed, they were simply tossed over the side, and fed to the sharks.

It was a marvel of deception and advertising that their customers not only knew nothing of what went on behind the scenes, but also actively praised and supported them. If they'd had even an inclining of how preconceived every interaction with their bank was, how each facet of their private lives had been carefully examined to see if it could be exploited, and twisted into a sales opportunity, they'd have kept all their money under the bed.

By contrast, Cottons, whilst no stranger to the world of financial sales, tended to deal with its customers in a reactive, rather than proactive manner. Targets were considered rather brash and unnecessary, the thinking being that if a customer of Cottons Bank wanted a financial product, they could simply ask for it.

Cottons provided the best and most thorough advisors in the Banking industry to look after such requests, and didn't see any merit in targeting and pressurising these professionals to produce a greater numbers of sales than they already did.

Bonuses and targets didn't motivate Mr Burton at all. Although he'd had to berate the odd member of staff in his time, this was usually for losing the keys to a safe, or perhaps getting rather out of hand at the annual Christmas Ball, and certainly not for failing to hit a sales quota. He just didn't have the required skills, nor did he intend to acquire them at this late stage.

To him banking had always been a noble trade, a good steady career with a defined path for those who wanted to progress, and for those that didn't, then a secure and stable job until they retired with a respectable pension. He'd been a loyal, dedicated employee of Cottons Bank all his working life, starting at the very bottom of the ladder, making the tea and empting the waste paper bins, before slowly and steadily working his way up to his current, senior position, a position of which he was very proud.

But with his trusty foresight ringing alarm bells, he had to agree with his wife. It was high time to get out. Very soon, it was going to be a very different world indeed. The wind of change was blowing through the corridors of Cottons Bank Head Office, like a fearsome tropical hurricane, whipping everything in its path into frenzy.

Top Management, clearly impressed with the profits the NSIB model gleaned, had long ago taken down its pants and handed over the keys to the Bentley. Although the ink on the register still needed to dry, and several concerned relatives would have to be told, a marriage of sorts had already occurred, removal vans booked, and plans to throw out all the old furniture and let the new mistress loose with the decorator, set firmly in motion. Worryingly though, it seemed that no one had any intention to stop to ask the staff what they thought of the new drapes, or the even customers for that matter.

Definitely time to leave then. Mr Burton put the file to one side and refocused his thoughts on the rest of the day instead. For him, it was now just simply a waiting game. He casually picked up the three brown card files that had been placed in his in tray, spread them like oversized playing cards, and peered curiously at them. They contained all the relevant information about the three new recruits, three fresh-faced youngsters that had begun their careers with Cottons Bank on this miserable grey day. Mr Burton had already sneaked a quick look at them without their knowledge on the way to his office, and was now keen to put some meat on the bones of what he had briefly seen.

Firstly there was the girl. Belinda Jones, aged twenty-two, recently graduated from University with a first in Business Studies. Hobbies included eventing horses, ballet and modern dance, and she was due to marry a Pilot shortly. At first glance, he summed her up as an astute young businesswoman who was headed for the top, and would probably be prepared to walk over the bodies of all those who stood in her path. She should do well after the merger then.

Then there was Wesley Ferrers who, despite appearances to the contrary, was quite unbelievably aged just twenty. Mr Burton knew his father from his Gentlemen's club, a stuffy old bugger with a fondness of Cuban cigars, and his son looked to be cut from the same expensive cloth. Mr Ferrers senior was keen that Wesley gained some experience with the common folk before inserting him in the family's export business, and Mr Burton had been approached to facilitate employment, and the necessary strings had been reluctantly pulled.

Finally there was George Butler. What could be made of this character? According to the file he was nineteen and lived with his parents in a little rural town outside of the city. He was the youngest of two brothers and enjoyed hobbies that included archery and painting; he was also teaching himself the guitar. Probably a Hippy then, considered Mr Burton, and one who'd played far too much Robin Hood growing up, at that.

The notes from his interview seemed somewhat muddled, with the two interviewers coming to entirely different conclusions about the poor chap. The man Varley seemed to sum him up as a clumsy, accident-prone slacker, someone with no intention on committing to anything, as evidenced by his all too brief university tenure. Ms Williams meanwhile seemed quite struck with George's resilience, although she didn't expand on her reasons why, but reading between the lines, she clearly found him quite charming.

George was definitely the wildcard of the group then, and as such would probably prove to be the most entertaining. Mr Burton had a soft spot for the underdog, having never been to university himself, he felt that qualifications and family connections were, in his experience at least, no match for natural resourcefulness and willingness to analyses, adapt and overcome.

One thing was certain though, this intake would be entering an entirely different Bank than they'd imagined, or indeed, had applied to all those weeks ago. Despite the outcome of the merger with NSIB, still being classed as unofficial, Head Office was keen that any new recruits should be schooled in a new, innovative manner. Additional sales workshops had been hastily designed, with the NSIB model in mind, and the new entrants were to be the guinea pigs, trained intensively to spot sales opportunities and exploit them. The rest of the staff would naturally have to follow suit at some point, but for now it was deemed easier to mould fresh meat, rather that chew away at the old tough mutton, some of which could well be rotten, and need disposing of in any case.

It would soon be time for the customary meet and greet, he rather looked forward to these brief exchanges. After years of interacting with people, he'd subconsciously become something of an expert in the human condition, and was able to quickly appraise an individual and evaluate their strengths and weaknesses, discover their deceptions and glean the truth from their eyes. It was something that had made him a formidable card player.

There was a nervous, barely audible tapping at his door. Obviously this was not his trusted Secretary. She nearly took the damn thing off its hinges every time she wished to enter. Mr Burton smiled to himself, soft spots didn't get much softer than the one he held for this member of staff. He'd been far too busy over the years to find time to have a family, if he'd had though, he would've liked a daughter like her.

"Do come in, Summer." His voice was warm and reassuring, like the sound of a quality aged scotch being poured into a heavy led crystal glass. The door opened a fraction and a small reddening face, almost entirely concealed by a thick wall of hair, peered through the narrow opening.

"Um, err, *Hallo Mr Burton*! Umm, sorry to disturb you, err, I've sent the new recruits off for a spot of lunch, they'll be back in half an hour, do you, err, *want to see them*, um, *afterwards?*"

"Yes Summer that would be fine. Let's start with the girl, then Wesley. We'll leave Mr Butler to last. I imagine you'll be able to keep him amused while he's waiting?" A deepening rouge hue suddenly consumed the whole of Summer's face, neck, ears and probably even her toes. Judging by her reaction to this innocent question, Mr Burton considered that amusing Mr George Butler was indeed something that Summer was rather partial to. How she'd contain her nerves and prevent herself from exploding though, was another matter entirely.

"*Oh*, err, well, umm..." Mr Burton allowed her to stutter and blush just long enough for his own amusement to be satisfied, before finally deciding to dismiss the poor little creature.

"Will that be all, Summer?"

"Yes!"

"Marvellous, enjoy your lunch." And with that the door was gently closed and Mr Burton, complete with a wicked, mischievous little grin, was alone once more.

Sometimes, on trying days when the in tray looked especially mountainous, or perhaps when his favourite lunchtime restaurant ran out of veal, he often took comfort in the fact that despite his advancing years, thickening waistline, thinning hair and stuffy senior position, he was still a Little Bugger at heart.

George sheltered from the bucketing rain under the awning of the jewellers, and surveyed the vast array of dazzling watches, displayed behind the thick glass. The various faces, dials and brilliantly polished straps gleamed magnificently under the electric lights, their brilliance offering a welcome contrast to the grey clouds and the unyielding monsoon.

It had been a busy, exhausting morning. Having grudgingly accepted his Timex's fate, he'd decided to reward himself for surviving this far, with a new wristwatch. The last of his weekly pay from the Supermarket lingered tantalisingly in his bank account, not the shiny new Cottons Bank Staff Account, which Summer had just opened, but the old Post Office account that he'd had since birth, and a new timepiece seemed like a fitting use for the balance.

He'd been slowly working his way along the window display for a while now, like a lost snail in need of the time, beginning his detailed examination with the hypnotic beauty of the *unlikely to ever be able to afford unless I sell a kidney* range. Eventually, he'd entered the tantalising *maybe one day if I don't get married and have kids* section, before finally arriving at *quite flashy, a bit practical but does the job and you can afford it.*

After much deliberation, and having gingerly negotiated his way around a sheltering tramp, he'd settled on a chunky Seiko diver's watch, the designers of which had obviously drawn inspiration from both Rolex and Omega, but had somehow managed to offer it for sale at a very reasonable eighty-five pounds. Crucially, it had an automatic movement, his Dad was therefore bound to approve. The watch had a simple dark blue face, with pale green rectangular hour markers and a big triangle at twelve o'clock. There was a day and date function, heavy luminous hands that pointed with all the purpose of an enraged Bouncer, and a rotating bezel that was two thirds blue and one red. The robust solid metal strap and case looked heavy compared to his relatively lightweight Timex, and it was considerably larger, but nevertheless, he liked it immensely and was utterly taken with the sporty, adventurous image it conjured.

George had enjoyed love affairs with all three of the watches he'd owned so far. From his first vintage Mickey Mouse timepiece with the eyes that ticked, seemingly possessed, the enormous Transformers digital number, which at least one Teacher thought was a bomb, to his current understated white mechanical Timex, he'd been equally obsessed and infatuated with them all.

Now though it was time to buy something a bit more special, something that would sit well against his finest polyester, and would be more in keeping with his new job, something bold, masculine and shiny. With his mind now set on the diver's model, he was already making up tales of high drama, when diving off the coast of Egypt, just in case anyone commented upon it. In reality though, it was unlikely to be asked to endure anything much more perilous than a warm bubble bath.

However, in spite of his rapt infatuation, nothing would prevent George from performing his usual, fastidious shopping ritual. A time-honoured ceremony that typically involved at least three visits to examine the goods in person, several days of agonising consideration, hours spent leafing through a glossy brochure, if one were available (usually whilst sitting on the toilet), and finally a spell of prolonged guilty soul searching, during which time he'd question over and over again if he really, *really* needed the item at all. Considering the item under the microscope this time was a watch, the whole timely process was going to be quite ironic indeed.

The other two purchases he'd made that lunchtime had, thankfully, been somewhat swifter affairs. The most recent copy of *Autotrader* was safely nestled in a plastic bag under his arm, and the large steak pasty was now lingering heavily over his belt, where it kept his breakfast company.

He couldn't bring himself to spend his lunch break in the company of his fellow new recruits, and when the rest room also started filling up with colourful staff, all of whom seemed intent on unearthing every single conceivable detail about the three new bodies that had bravely entered their world, it had been time to escape. Wesley had managed quite successfully to hide behind the barrier he created, with his droll, unapproachable exterior, whilst Belinda seemed inexplicably, quite happy to talk to the excited gaggle of girls about wedding plans, which had previously remained undisclosed, leaving George to shoulder the remaining attention. Things soon became awkward.

He wasn't good at dealing with large groups of people, he was quite chatty and fun in threes and fours, especially if the others weren't particularly chatty or fun, but any more than that and he began to become, for reasons he'd never quite fathomed, an uncomfortable sweaty mess. At the first suggestion of anxiety, he'd quickly made his excuses and had gone shopping in the rain, seeking the comforting familiarity of both the damp and cold instead. If Summer had braved the staff room things might have been very different, but she'd hastily retreated to another part of the building in a rush of blushing shame, as soon training had finished for the morning, and sadly before he'd had a chance to try and pick up their early conversation. Damn Wesley to hell.

Racing between the shop awnings, trying desperately to limit the effect the relentless downpour would have on his hair, George quickly made his way back to the Bank. His mind was swimming with images and thoughts of Summer. Who was this incredible, magical girl? Why didn't the others seem to notice how fantastic she was, and why the hell did she want to know if he painted? Was she interested in him, would he be able to get her number without making a complete fool of himself? It seemed unlikely.

His lifelong, and therefore by default best and largely only friend, Barney Browne claimed to have rather more confidence and experience with the opposite sex. Despite not ever actually supporting this claim with anything even remotely resembling a real live girlfriend, he'd tried many times to enroll his suspicious friend into 'Barney's Advanced School of Seduction'. But Barney's exuberant methods didn't sit at all well with his rather reserved disciple.

He was two weeks younger than George, and a good inch taller, which to boys of a certain age is a vital detail. He had a thick bush of extremely curly red hair, which if left unclipped for any length of time, would eventually come to resemble a ginger afro, and his face, torso and limbs were splattered with an unbelievable number of freckles. Deep orange freckles.

He was lean and athletic from years of running away from school bullies, and also moonlighting as the school's long distance champion. Yet despite what could only be described as a challenging appearance, Barney positively oozed self-assurance and considered himself something of a Celtic Casanova.

Without fail, each Friday and Saturday night he would typically select an unwary, random girl that had had the misfortune of apparently '*giving him the eye*', and descend upon her with gusto. Fuelled by nothing more than Newcastle Brown ale, lashings of testosterone and pork scratchings, he'd launch into a torrent of cheesy pick-up lines and cringe-worthy innuendo, utterly convinced that he would eventually win her over with his own unique brand of wit and charm.

This was not a method that George felt confident would produce anything like the desired effect with Summer, after all its practice seemed to yield limited to non-existent success for Barney, and he was supposedly an expert in the field. No, if he were to have any chance at all, he would just have to rely on his usual practice of waiting, keeping his head down and avoiding eye contact at all costs, occasionally looking pleading and desperate, and above all else, hope that the girl in question asked *him* out instead. Unsurprisingly, he'd been single for a while now.

Back at the Bank, a soggy George was let into the cashiers run by a flustered Di. She fussed and cooed over him, like a heavily made up pigeon tending to her young, scolding him for going out in such bad weather in the first place. "*...'ll get the flu Georgie!*" she'd cautioned earnestly, whilst pinching his cold damp cheek.

Glancing at his battered Timex, he suddenly realised that he was running a bit late for the afternoon's activities, and quickly freed himself from Di's good natured preening, just as she licked an elaborate hanky, making to rub a mark off his chin, and darted past the other cashiers to begin the mountainous ascent to the staff room.

Fit and Agile had never been good friends of his, and by the time he eventually crashed through the door to the staff room an age later, he was a breathless, soaked mess both from the rain inwards, and the sweat outwards. Having already prepared his excuses, he was both surprised and briefly relieved to find that the room was completely empty. Running a sweaty, podgy hand through his soaking, matted black hair, he leant on the door frame and considered his options. For one important reason, he no longer wanted to escape.

"Oh! *There you are*!" Startled, George quickly spun around, briefly creating an arc of spray as his dripping hair caught up with his head. The draining effort of running up the endless flights of grey stairs had caused his heart to thump heavily in his ears, and he hadn't heard Summer jangle up the last flight behind him in hot pursuit.

"*Bugger!* Oh, err... *I err*, (deep breaths) err (a few deeper breaths and a hacking cough), sorry I'm late Summer. You see, I err..." He trailed off, unable to recall any of the elaborate excuses he'd prepared earlier on his accent, and instead leant against the door frame again, trying to regain some of his inadequate composure. Hopefully fat and exhausted did it for her.

Summer meanwhile, fidgeted nervously with an errant thread that had broken free of her favourite scarf. With the relief that one of her flock hadn't already decided to resign now behind her, she was suddenly confronted by the same confusing barrage emotions that had ambushed her earlier that day, and she could feel the deep red flush already beginning to creep up her slender neck. Thank God for ladies scarves.

"Err, oh, it's umm, *no problem at all really*! I was just err, well, worried about you. Oh! But not in that way I mean, err, *you know*, just that you might've err, well umm, have gotten run over or something! But, err, that's what I meant, not, well, you know, *not anything else...*" She trailed off, the blush having now crept up her neck and enveloped her face, like confused strawberry jam running *up* the sides of its jar. Once again she was acutely aware that the damning redness had won. She hung her head forlornly in defeat, and gestured back down the stairs with a bangled hand. "The others are on the next floor down." She sighed wearily. "Err, waiting to meet Mr Burton, umm, don't worry though, you're going in last, make yourself a cuppa and come down when you're feeling a bit more like it..." With every ounce of self-control she could muster, she managed a pretty, shy little smile through her curtain of hair, before finally giving into her insistent feet, and darting back down the stairs.

George's heart meanwhile swelled to bursting point, and then went for a little lie down to recover. Could this be a sign? Was she interested too? As she left him searching for a clean mug, the Tomato Picker's arrived again for an afternoon shift of pelting Mr Butler. Blushes it seemed were something they had in common. Well, it was a start.

Ten minutes later and significantly drier, having once again worn out a hand dryer in the Gents, George was sat in Mr Burton's waiting room, with gigantic hair and the comforting, familiar smell of his Mum's drying laundry. He was not alone. Wesley was lost in his copy of the New Entrant pack, studiously digesting it contents and busy making notes in a leather-bound pocket book. Summer, who he was delighted to see again, was sat awkwardly in a tall chair at a short desk, aimlessly shifting paper from one pile to another.

Finally, there was a fierce-looking, thin woman of sorts. Somewhere in her late fifties, she possessed every conceivable type of sharp feature possible, and right now, her insufferably steely eyes were slicing through the newest victim that had dared venture into her lair. Her name was Ms Peters, and she was Mr Burton's private, bloodcurdlingly menacing secretary.

Following Wesley's lead, George produced his own pack while he waited to meet Mr Burton, and leafed through it with the same level of interest he would a magazine in the doctor's waiting room. His attention, a fickle part of his mental capacity at the best of times, was now firmly engaged elsewhere. Was she really swinging her legs on that tall chair?

Earlier in the toilet, he'd hastily devised a thin, almost anorexic plan of attack. He would try and bravely engage the object of his desire in a brief moment of knowing eye contact, hoping to refuel their earlier moment and get things off the ground once more. He'd never attempted a knowing look before, if only he had time to call Barney for advice.

Lifting his head from his lackadaisical studies, he gazed longingly in Summer's direction. A second passed, then another, still nothing. Look up girl, please look up! Ms Peters suddenly cleared her throat noisily, and caught George's eye roughly by the scruff the neck, shaking her head malevolently in warning. It was as if she knew his every amorous thought. Thanks almost certainly to a deep and unchallenged knowledge of the Black Arts, she probably did.

They all continued to wait together in silence. The only discernible sound was that of Summer's piles of paper being shuffled back and forth, Wesley's industrious scribblings, and the ticking of the ever present, corporate quartz clock above Ms Peters' sharp head.

With his plan aborted for fear of being lashed, or worse, George tried to lose himself in his pack instead. Not unlike the building he was incarcerated in, it was very, very dull and grey, full of basic banking history and various do's and don'ts colleagues should be aware of. Some of which they'd already seriously breached a few hours ago, when then looked at a certain footballers account. Words and figures definitely seemed to differ here.

He glanced at his Timex, pausing briefly to wind it up, and check it against the wall clock. Belinda had now been in with Mr Burton for over twenty-five minutes. What on earth could they be talking about all this time, or more importantly, what the hell was he going to talk to him about? What would he want to know about him, what was there to say for that matter, would he expect him to be able to talk expertly about the banking industry? He was going to be very disappointed if he did.

The door to Mr Burton's office suddenly swung open and Belinda confidently strolled out into the reception area as though she'd just been promoted. Summer looked up from her piles and checked her own, rather curious looking timepiece. "*Ooo*, that was rather quick, *err*, right okay, umm, if you would like to go back to the ground floor and find Linda, she'll introduce you to our Head Cashier and, err, you can spend the rest of the day learning the ropes with her, umm, *is that okay?*" Through her bedraggled tresses, Summer beamed hopefully at Belinda, desperately willing her not to ask anything taxing. Meaningful answers were in short supply.

Belinda regarded her temporary Instructor with something approaching mild disinterest, and unnecessarily straightened her pristine jacket. "Right then, I'll make my way downstairs, as you say. Thank you." And with that she was gone, stiffly and without a kindly word or nod of acknowledgment for either Wesley or George. She and Linda were likely to become firm friends.

Ms Peters' intercom buzzed excitedly and she leapt at it ferociously, like a panther leaping at its prey. "Yes, *Mr Burton?*" Given her tone and demeanour, *'Mien Heir'* would have seemed more appropriate.

"Send in Wesley, please Ms Peters?" The voice over the intercom sounded calm, warm and level. This brief snippet of perhaps what was to come brought some reassurance to George, who was imagining Mr Burton as an older, even more wretched version of the dreadful Wesley.

"Oh and Ms Peters, could you kindly retrieve the Risk Audit report from archive please? Thank you." The intercom clicked off and Ms Peters rose from her chair, fired a last threatening *don't you even think about it* glare in George's direction and, after showing Wesley the door to Mr Burton's office, reluctantly marched out, her footsteps leaving a sharp, crisp note in the air.

Renewed hope quickly flooded into George. This was his chance! With Wesley and Belinda gone, and Ms Peters now hanging about in some dusty archive, presumably by her talons, he unexpectedly had Summer all to himself, but for how long? He had no choice but to act quickly and rally his wobbly courage if he were to have any chance of success with this magnificent girl. The quartz wall clock ticked on.

Now was not the time to stare at his feet and look desperate. If only he could call Barney for help. He searched his mind desperately for suitable words with which to open the conversation, discarding a few questionable ones that floated by, memories of pork scratching infused hopelessness from too many failed nights in the Pub with his ginger friend. Should he start with the unanswered art question, what if she was just being nice, trying to put him at ease after forgetting his pack, it might kill things dead? Perhaps it was best to start elsewhere, and come back to that one?

Finally, channelling his inner Englishman, he had it. "Err, it's *still* raining outside you know? Err, I, I think it might, err, you know, err, *carry on*..." It was not an opening gambit destined to rival Casanova's finer moments, but it did seem to have the desired effect.

Summer glanced up from her piles of paperwork, looking somewhat puzzled, as though she thought she'd been alone in the room. "Oh, *hello*! Umm, I think so, err, *yes it might indeed*..." The mere act of briefly communicating with the hairy new entrant soon turned her bright red again, but she was comforted to see that he too had taken on a certain pinkish hue.

"Umm, do you like the rain then...?" *Why the hell did you ask that stupid question?* He was now pushing the limits of his patter to the very edge of his ability, and failing badly in the process. *Or was he?*

"Umm, *well*, funnily enough, yes *I do*, actually..." Summer put down her pen and gazed across the room at George with renewed interest. Her head cocked to one side, her face, although still impossibly bright red, open with curiosity. Almost as if he'd just asked her the most significant and important question, anybody had ever asked her in her entire life.

"Umm, you see, *it's the light*, err, and the light that comes after the rain..." She tugged at her scarf, allowing some badly needed air to get at her neck, blushing no longer a concern for the moment. He was just as red as she was, and it was getting seriously hot in the waiting room. "...I, umm, like to paint that sort of thing, err, clouds and landscapes, a, a bit depressing I suppose to some people but, well, *I like it*." All of a sudden, Summer's normal colour started to return to her small, delicate face. The deep hue draining away like an emptied bath, revealing a scattering of bashful schoolgirl freckles. Quite, extraordinarily, talking to George about this subject had somehow managed to put her at ease. "That's why I, err, asked about your painting, *you see?*"

"Oh, *right!*" On the other side of the room, her would-be suitor's progress had not gone unnoticed. With transformed confidence, utterly convinced that he could chat up women after all, he frantically tried to find a way of manipulating his progress into getting her telephone number, before the evil Ms Peters returned from her crypt. Time was of the essence. The quartz wall clock ticked on.

"Umm, I know what you mean, *I think*," he said as smoothly and as hastily and as he could, "My A Level art work was partly about clouds, well, clouds *and* light, and, umm, well, *Elephants*." Thank God for art! He always knew all those years spent splattered in paint, and frowning at some blank canvas would one day prove fruitful. Although, now he came to think of it, when did he last actually pick up a brush? No matter, he was winning.

Summer beamed enthusiastically at him, completely cured of any trace of a blush. Here was someone who at last, might finally just get her after all. Had they found that most cherished and sort after trait between potential partners, common ground?

Suddenly there was the sound of distant, determined high heels on a tiled floor. The moment would soon be lost to them both. They gazed briefly at each other, knowing their time was nearly up. One of them was going to need to summon great courage now, courage and speed.

"NUMBER! *Give me your number!*" Realising that he sounded rather more like robber with a digit fixation than a charming young man with reasonably good-natured intentions, George quickly rallied. "*Sorry, sorry, sorry!* Err, I mean, *please* can I have your phone number, we could talk about, err, umm, *art*, and err, *stuff*, perhaps?" He looked pleadingly, puppy-dog eyes set to stun.

Summer, who'd momentarily been taken aback by his blunt demands, recovered her composure, quickly chose to overlook the incident and, mindful of the approaching footsteps, hurriedly scribbled down her phone number on a scrap of paper, torn from her mountainous pile, darted across the room and stuffed it into his moist palm. He did seem to have kind eyes after all.

She scurried back to her desk, just managing to sit down as the door to reception was flung open and Ms Peters marched in, her face full of accusation and condemnation, all firmly aimed squarely at the new recruit, proving beyond all doubt, that she hadn't heard any of their conversation. Summer and George shared a brief glance, and an even a briefer smile, a mutual mild blush, further down the colour chart than normal, soon returned, and they bent to their individual tasks, safe in the knowledge that they'd escaped the wrath of the Kraken for now.

George's heart was overwhelmed. The sweat poured down his back like a waterfall in February. He'd done it! He'd actually asked for a girl's number and, unbelievably enough, managed to get it, all alone without any prompting or alcohol. This was truly a rare, marvellous moment in his little world, and he couldn't wait to tell Barney.

Meanwhile, Summer was also starting to seriously wonder if she'd require medical assistance before the day was out. She hadn't felt this alive since she'd been photographing a particularly savage storm, high up in the hills, when her beloved car, a very old bright yellow Mini Cooper called Daisy, which was decorated with large hand painted flowers, was suddenly hit by a lightning bolt. Miraculously the Mini seemed to have escaped the ordeal with only minor cosmetic damage, and a strange lingering side effect which meant that the car stereo would now only play Radio Two, and the best of Bob Marley, a tape cassette that had subsequently become entombed within it. Neither of which she considered to be a bad thing at all.

Once again, Wesley demonstrated his uncanny ability to shatter the most harmonious of moments with his unpleasant presence and his customary clearing of his throat. "*Ahem*, Mr Burton will see you now, *Butler*." He said the name as though the letters left a bad taste in his mouth, and glanced down his long nose at the rather dishevelled, exhausted looking mess in the seat beside him. What a peasant, he reflected.

"I see you have taken Ms Peters' job now, *eh Wes?*" George couldn't help himself. He was feeling flush with success, and relished the opportunity to have a good natured dig at both Wesley and the fierce Ms Peters. Before he had chance to be molested by the fury and outrage in the room, he quickly made for Mr Burton's door, leaving all his belongings behind in case they slowed his escape, or caught fire when the dragon spat flames at him. Somehow though, he suspected that at least one little person in that room would be having a quiet giggle to herself.

George was still looking warily over his shoulder, making quite sure he wasn't being followed, as he half crashed his way through the heavy oak door, and into the next room. Fortunately, this one wasn't alarmed.

"Ah Mr Butler, do come in and have a seat old Chap." Momentarily disorientated, he quickly grappled for his bearings, trying to absorb yet another, completely new environment, and one that was clearly Mr Burton's very private sanctuary.

The office was dressed with expensive mahogany furniture, a deep pile rouge carpet and the walls covered in a traditional English wallpaper of burgundy and cream stripes. It was all very dated, but immaculately kept, and made a very welcome change to corporate grey of the rest of the branch. It was like stepping into another world entirely, any minute now George expected an immaculate waiter to appear and take his drinks order, and maybe offer him a cigar from a highly polished expensive wooden box. It was just a shame he didn't smoke really.

Mr Burton himself appeared to be, as his voice suggested, very pleasant and approachable. With his mind swimming in a cloudy pool of emotions, George cautiously shook hands with the older man, suddenly embarrassed as he realised his own palm was wetter than an old sponge which had been lost in a well, and Mr Burton's was firm and dry.

Having been gestured too, several times, he eventually eased himself into the leather guest seat, wiggling his bottom slightly until he was settled, a sense of relief gently washing over him. This meeting seemed at least to be quite relaxed and informal, nothing at all like he'd expected. Perhaps he would risk a cigar, and maybe a brandy.

"So then old Chap, first day with Cotton's *eh*? What do you make of it so far?" Mr Burton leaned back in his padded leather chair and examined the dishevelled, rumpled young man on the other side of the desk with interest. Paying particularly attention to the lump of pasty welded to the gaudy tie, and the shock of wayward, matted hair. Perhaps this was a new fashion trend that had escaped his attention?

"Err, well, it's been a *very* interesting day so far, Sir." Clearly not lying. "And I can't *wait* to see what tomorrow brings!" He allowed himself a mischievous grin as he returned Mr Burton's affable, curious gaze. For some reason, he was beginning to feel like he was visiting a favourite Grandparent.

"Well, I am glad you've brought that up, you see tomorrow, you're going to be packed off to Nelson's Branch. It's a bit of a rough and ready sort of area on the outskirts of town, but it's a small branch and the team there will be able to train you well, and quickly too I expect. The Manageress is a top girl of mine - Miss Hayley Lane - she'll look after you and make sure you learn the ropes. Most of the rest of the team have various strengths, *ahem*, and you would do well to draw upon their experiences, in the main that is. It will be a good for you, *old chap*."

George continued to smile, although his eyes had now glazed over with renewed trepidation. Not *another* new place to find, and more new people to get to know? And then there was Summer, he really needed to stay close to her, she might well change her mind else. Perhaps Ms Peters had heard their conversation after all, and signalled her superior so that he could exile the toe rag before things got out of hand? Or maybe it was Wesley? He really would have to die.

"Err, what's happening to the others then Sir, if you don't mind me asking?" He had the sinking feeling that he may have been given the short straw, without even having had chance to draw it.

"Oh well Wesley has been recruited to become a Business Manager in time, so he'll be staying here, as will Belinda who will learn the ropes for a few weeks and then become Linda Beech's assistant. Don't worry, you'll have just the same amount of opportunity to develop as the others, if not more so. I've based these decisions largely on your experiences, and your interview of course." George cringed at the mere mention of that dreadful, unforgettable day, and sensing apprehension Mr Burton added, "I am sending you, George, because I think you will cope out there." He leaned across the broad desk, as though the two men were suddenly involved in some sort of secret conspiracy. "You know, *I am not sure that the others would.*"

As expected, this had the desired effect. The younger man straightened immediately in his chair and brushed down his suit jacket, dislodging the errant chunk of pasty. This was looking promising, he'd already been singled out as the toughest, the bravest, the least likely to get mugged. Given the competition, this was nothing to become too jubilant about though.

His work done, Mr Burton settled contentedly back into his padded chair with a moderate groan.

"Now that that's settled, let's get to know George Butler a bit better shall we? I've read your CV and I am glad to see you've got some interesting hobbies outside of work, adds colour to a chap's character in my opinion. But tell me something unusual that has happened in your life, George, something that might not have happened to someone else, something unique." Mr Burton scrutinized the nervous young face for signs of reluctance or unwillingness, traits he often observed in these situations, but was surprised to find none. He seemed to be mentally ticking events off.

"Well, *err*, I can't really think of anything that seems, *well*, right to talk about *now*, Sir..." He trailed off, still sourcing material, understandably wary of telling stories, following his previous account of the Machete Broccoli Affair.

Mr Burton's day had, thus far, yielded little more than a dull meeting with a local politician, and a less than adequate lunch in a dreary restaurant, not of his choosing. The disappointing limp salad leaves, cremated potatoes, and pair of parched, stringy pork chops that had threatened to dislodge a gold filling, failing to inspire. He wouldn't be going back.

Any hopes that his day would be brightened by asking the other new recruits the same question, had soon been dashed too, and earlier he'd positively lost the will to live during Wesley's dull response. Wearing a glassy look of mock interest throughout, nodding occasionally in what he hopped were appropriate places, Mr Burton had sat back waiting for the sweet release of death, as Wesley rambled on endlessly in a droll monotone about his stamp collection, and his recent negotiations to secure a particularly rare edition. Clearly the lad didn't get out much.

Belinda had faired a little better, with her tales of horses and eventing. But the equine world held limited interest for him, and he urgently longed to hear something altogether more remarkable, and much more entertaining. Something that could brighten this grey, awful day and stifle the tediousness of the past few hours, something to make the afternoon go a little bit quicker and make his evening meal seem tantalisingly closer. Perhaps something just a little bit wicked was required?

He leaned forward, hoping the gesture would once again yield the same reassuring result. "I'll tell you what George." Mr Burton placed his elbows on his mahogany desk, cupped his hands and looking encouragingly at his guest, as though they were mutual conspirators in a wartime plot. "*Why not tell me something funny..?*"

George raised an unkempt, furry eyebrow, thought for a few seconds, seemed to eventually make up his mind, and grinned mischievously back at the kindly face opposite. "Ah, well in *that* case Sir..."

It had all been Barney's idea, and therefore bound to be fraught with trouble from the outset. George had initially been a bit reluctant to go abroad on holiday with his best friend, but Barney could be a strong persuader when he put his mind to it, and after overcoming a few parental concerns from both households, the boys were eventually agreed on embarking on a week long holiday to Greece. It seemed however that each boy, having both celebrated their eighteenth birthday in the months prior to the planned holiday, had very different ideas about what a holiday to Greece should actually involve.

George had images of picturesque, sun-bleached, whitewashed buildings, with sky blue shutters, olive trees, an endless turquoise ocean sprinkled with tiny fishing boats and, most importantly, olive-skinned, dusky young maidens clothed in linen gipsy tops and floaty white cotton skirts, which became transparent in the sunlight. He had been quite insistent on this last point.

Barney's vision meanwhile couldn't have been more different. Although he too had also concluded that there should be girls, lots and lots of willing, scantily dressed, and very drunk girls. The white washed buildings and gipsy tops he could take or leave.

For reasons George would later come to regret, he left the travel arrangements entirely in Barney's hands, merely handing over a hard earned cheque when required. He then simply packed, bought what he hoped was an adequate supply of drachma and suntan lotion, promised his Mum that he would be very, very careful and that he would call each day without fail, before finally meeting his best friend outside the Supermarket, where they both worked, in order to catch the coach to the airport.

Several hours later, following take off, safely in the company of a few beers, Barney eventually came clean.

It seemed that he'd actually booked the boys on a Club 18–30 holiday to Kavos, Corfu. George had heard about these vodka-fuelled romps, but had never imagined ever embarking on one himself, certainly not with his Mum's blessings, and now at thirty thousand feet, with a can of San Miguel warming in his hand, it looked increasingly unlikely that his romantic idea of Greece was going to become a reality.

The journey from the airport to their hotel was a pot holed juddering, living hell, seemingly without end, but was positively a magic carpet ride compared to their arrival in Kavos town. At a little after ten in the evening, the surly, heavy set Greek coach driver, with an obligatory thick black moustache, grunted their arrival and the boys, along with three other fellow passengers, tried their very best to disembark.

The main street was bursting with wild, drunken revellers, all of whom descended on the coach, like flies around a rotting carcass, as the driver fought to pull the luggage from the storage containers hidden in the bowels of the battered vehicle. The group gingerly left the safety of the air conditioned vehicle, and were immediately hit by a wall of oppressive sticky heat, thumping bass drums from the open fronted bars, the smell of greasy burgers, cheap alcohol, and, most surprisingly considering the hour, suntan lotion. They had arrived.

"WAY-HAY! Newbies!" The closest drunk, who smelt worrying of beer, vomit and kebabs, threw a sun burnt arm around George's neck as he tried to grab his trampled luggage. *"Awright Dude?"*

"Err, no, not really…" He slung his dusty bag over his shoulder and shouted desperately at the coach driver, straining to be heard over the deafening, threatening dance music. *"Where are we supposed to go now?!"*

Suddenly a plump girl with pneumatic breasts, barely contained within a tight, gaudy interpretation of a uniform, elbowed her way through the crowd of drunken partygoers, many of whom enthusiastically hugged and patted her on the back and she battled on.

"Hey, *HEY!* Are you two George Butler and Barney Browne?" Barney, who'd momentarily disappeared into the throng, only to reappear holding two cans of warm lager, grinned warmly at the Club 18-30 Rep. He had a gift for these things.

"Sure are my Lovely, *where're you taking us then?*" The world-weary Rep had heard it all a thousand times before, and from far more handsome men. She shrugged off yet another plastered guest that had draped himself around her shoulders and begun licking her ear, fished around in her bag, and eventually produced two envelopes and a huge, pitted brass key.

"You guys are in 36 D, though that alley and up the stairs to the right, *you're behind this club.*" She pointed at the open fronted neon bathed building, the foundations of which seemed to be literally leaping up and down with deafening music and gyrating, sweaty bodies.

"Great Darlin', *I've always loved 36 D's!*" Barney was wide-eyed and beaming, even his freckles looked ecstatic.

"Excuse me Miss. Seriously, *we're here?* How will we sleep with all this noise?" George looked pleadingly at the Rep as Barney tried to disappear into the crowd in embarrassment.

"*You won't.* Sleep on the beach during the day, and party all night instead. Welcome to Kavos, *Mr Butler.*"

36 D, a second floor apartment within a purpose built block of similarly designed buildings, was unlikely to ever win any awards for its décor or ambiance. The wooden door, which looked as though a light breeze would knock it off its crumbling, rusty hinges, led into a small hallway with cracked terracotta tiled flooring and flaking white walls, stained with the bloody remains of a thousand squashed mosquitoes. Part of the hallway also doubled as a poorly equipped and filthy kitchenette, and to the left there was a bathroom that even the most minuscule of Dwarfs, and one who suffered from a severe case of agoraphobia at that, would have probably found positively cramped.

The hallway/kitchen area led into the main living/bedroom, which consisted of a couple of battered wooden wardrobes, two rickety single beds, and a door to a balcony that, come morning, would reveal an unrivalled view of the nightclubs wheelie bins. The Butler Family's respectable semi, it was not.

"*I want to go home Barney!*" George threw his bag down on the remarkably springy single bed, watched in amazement for a moment as the recoil caused it to bounce onto the floor, and turned to glare at his alleged best friend.

"Now, now come on, *come on*, be reasonable, did you see all the girls out there? They were all hammered, Dude!" Barney looked pleadingly at his roommate, desperately hoping that he would soon share his vision of the sweaty, alcoholic possibilities that lay in wait on the streets below. He was prepared for a reasonable wait this time.

"But, but, *Barney*, you said we were going to Greece on holiday, *not Clubbers' Hell!*"

"Mate, there's girls, music, well noise mostly, but *definitely* girls, cheap booze and sunshine! Did you see that guy's sun burn? You'll be black in a day or two." This was undeniable. George did colour quickly, unlike Barney whose skin could only be politely described as Celtic at best.

"But, but, what about the countryside? You said we would see the countryside, and get inside the real Greece." Clearly, he was not going to be easily swayed.

"No George, what I actually said was you might get *inside* a real Greek!" Barney grinned wickedly, as he'd done so many times before, when he'd been economical with the truth, and had nothing more to do than put his faith in his winning ginger smile.

"*You bloody Git!*" George's face momentarily cracked into an almost imperceptible smile, but Barney knew it was there and that once again, finally, he'd won the battle of wills. Party on.

"Yeah Dude, *but you love me*. Now come on, get changed and let's hit the town, before all the good ones are taken."

George awoke the next day, suddenly and painfully. Apparently, for reasons he didn't yet fully understand, angry gorillas had set about his head with hammers and cricket bats, sometime in the early hours, and had been joined in their melee by a large woodland creature, such as a brown bear perhaps, who'd also chosen to relieve itself inside his slumbering, gapping mouth. Tea. He desperately needed tea.

Through bloodshot half opened eyes, he tried to get his bearings. Wherever he was, this definitely *wasn't* the apartment that he and Barney had hurriedly unpacked in the evening before. He raised his left arm to look at his Timex, brushing something warm and fleshy as he did so. New concerns flooded into his badly hung-over, dehydrated brain. *Who*, or for that matter, *what*, was this?

He gingerly lifted the sweat-stained, white cotton sheet, and was both astounded and relived at what he found. There was a pair of small, suntanned feet and slender calves. Judging by the size and the collection of toe rings and ankle bracelets, they seemed to belong to a girl. He breathed a hearty sigh of relief.

Screwing up his eyes, he tried to recall the events of the previous evening. No, nothing to be gleaned there at all, beyond leaving their shoddy apartment and having that first drink in their neighbouring nightclub. Perhaps he would remember more as the day unfolded? Slowly swinging his aching body out of the squashy wallowing bed, he looked down at his chest and bulbous belly. He was peppered with angry red bites and, now that he was slowly coming to his senses, he realised that his arms and torso also throbbed in stinging, vicious agony. Mosquitoes, Bastards!

For reasons which would never be fully explained, George also found that he was still wearing his jeans, but no boxer shorts, a solitary sock and one boot, but not on the same foot. Despite a stealthy exploration of the cramped apartment, he failed to locate the remaining items of clothing and had to cope with what he had for now. Out of habit, he sucked in his belly.

Eventually, after a few glasses of tepid water from the tap, that his stomach would later come to regret, he decided it was best to leave before the feet woke up. Hobbling towards the front door, he reached for the handle, but strangely enough, there was no handle to be found. He looked around as silently as he could without success, in case it had simply just wandered off, before kneeling down and peering through the hole in the door where the handle and lever should have been. Nothing but circle of mocking, blazing sunshine glared back at him. *"Oh bloody hell!"*

He tiptoed past the snoring feet to the full length shuttered doors and, knowing that he would instantly regret it, flung them wide open. The humidity, the intense dazzling midday sunshine, and the clinging oppressive heat beat him back into the small room, like a novice boxer battered onto the ropes by the reigning champ. Slowly recovering from the assault, he blindly fought his way onto the roasting balcony in an effort to both gain his bearings, and also discover an alternative exit from the feet's apartment. Once outside, things failed to improve.

The apartment was on the first floor, adjacent to what he assumed was Kavos's dusty main street. Immediately opposite, tantalisingly within his grasp, was one of the few things George had originally hoped to see in Greece when they'd arrived just eighteen hours ago. A solitary, slightly depressed looking olive tree.

A plan started to formulate in his parched, alcohol saturated brain. Could he climb his way out?

Without pausing to consider the finer details of this plan, he quickly swung his legs over the balcony and took firm hold of the nearest branch. Glancing down, he noticed that just below the balcony there was a robust-looking bush, which seemed capable of breaking his fall, should the worst should happen.

With the exaggerated care of the extremely drunk, or the extremely hung over, ignoring the tiny voice of reason inside his head, he swung out into thin air and dangled from a startled, creaking olive branch, fifteen feet or so above the bush below. Inevitably, the ageing branch soon snapped.

George finally arrived back at their apartment just after two in the afternoon, following what could only be described as a difficult and unpleasant journey. Unsurprisingly, he found that his travelling companion was to offer him little in the way of consolation or sympathy. The sight of his half naked best friend, twigs and olives tangled in his filthy hair, hundreds of angry looking mosquito bites and scratches from his fall, making him resemble a human dot to dot puzzle, had been altogether too much to bear, and he soon fell about the floor in a fit of hysterics.

By way of an apology, Barney had suggested that he paid for an hour-long pedalo trip around the bay of Kavos town, so that George could see some of the natural Greek surroundings that he craved, and pick up a bit of a tan in the process. There might even be some white washed buildings to see if he was lucky.

It had taken Barney nearly an hour to tend to the many wounds. After he'd coated them all with a heavy smear of Germolene, and patched him up with a whole packet of fabric plasters, the wounded holidaymaker had taken nearly as long again to apply sun tan lotion to the few remaining bits of him that would be exposed to the sun. During the less than delicate medical procedure, the patient had cured his hangover by getting drunk again on a bottle of cheap local ouzo, which tasted a lot better the more he drank, and dulled the pain quicker than any morphine.

Despite an endless interrogation, Barney couldn't get any juicy details about the previous night's escapades from his increasingly inebriated roommate, not least because, despite his best efforts to recall even a fleeting moment of nudity, he simply couldn't remember.

Barney understood entirely though. He too had awoken in bizarre circumstances, somewhere on the outskirts of town in a small stable, in the company of a dusky young maiden with perfect olive skin and who, when she eventually put her clothes back on again, was wearing a linen gipsy top and a white cotton skirt that he had to admit, had a somewhat floaty quality to it.

The pedalo trip had been a marvellous idea. George, whose intense pain had long since been numbed with buckets of ouzo, was starting to relax, and found that Kavos looked almost idyllic from the red plastic vessel that gentle bobbed up and down on the waves, three hundred meters or so from the beach. The boys had packed a small picnic consisting of a couple of greasy kebabs, and yet more cheap medicinal ouzo, and after they had paid the grouchy Greek pedalo owner for one hour, they'd set off for a gentle paddle across the turquoise sea.

"See Dude, I told you this would be fun didn't I? Just look at the mountains over there, and look at that coastline - do you see the mountains and coastline George? George? *GEORGE!*"

"Hmm...?" By now, the pedalo's less than able First Mate was stoned on a heady combination of antihistamine, paracetamol, Germolene and ouzo, and really couldn't care less about the bloody coastline or the mountains, especially as they couldn't be bothered to stay still. All he knew was that the stinging agony from the mosquito bites, the many cuts, and the swollen bruised pain from his bottom, which had absorbed much of his earlier impact, seemed to have thankfully vanished without trace. Comfortably numb indeed.

"Oh well, *sod you then*, I'm going to crash out..." And with that Barney leant back in the red plastic chair and let the sun try and do its worst against his factor fifty sun block.

For the second time that day, George awoke abruptly, although less painfully this time, despite a fitful dream of being chased down Kavos's main street by a large pair of sun tanned feet, a toe ring, and an enraged olive tree who wanted its branch back. He strained his sore back against the hot red plastic chair and sat up, licking his parched lips.

Gripped by sudden, unexpected terror, he frantically looked around. As far as he could see in all directions, there was nothing but a vast ocean, a choppy and rather deep looking ocean. Snatching his cheap, scratched aviator sunglasses from their makeshift picnic basket, he tried to get a better grasp on the situation. Finally, after scouring the hazy, distant horizon for an eternity, he caught sight of what he sincerely hoped was Kavos beach. They were going to need a bigger boat.

"*Oh bugger!*" George looked down at the overcooked lobster, which was fast asleep in the red plastic chair next to him. "*WAKE UP BARNEY!*" Without thinking, gripped with panic, he slapped Barney's sunburnt arm.

"*JESUS CHRIST!*" Barney leapt out of the red hot plastic chair like a startled mongoose and, after desperately trying to regain his balance for a few precarious seconds, eventually toppled head first into the rolling ocean.

"Barney, *give me your hand.*" George reached desperately over the front of the lurching pedalo, grabbed hold of what he hopped was an arm and, with all his might, finally heaved him back onboard.

Barney shivered despite the blistering, relentless heat and looked incredulously across at his shipmate. "What, what, what the *hell's* wrong with you? You nearly drowned me, *and that bloody hurt.*"

"Barney, look around, can you see the coastline?"

Barney, a little short sighted at the best of times, could not. "*Oh shit!*"

"Yes, *oh shit* exactly, it's over there, a good few miles away, and we're stuck on a bloody red plastic pedalo!" George gestured urgently and manically towards first the mainland, and then their now wallowing, inappropriate vessel, just to make sure that he made his point.

"Well, could we, you know, like, *pedal to another island instead?*"

"What, do you mean, like, *Africa?*"

"Oh, Dude, this is not good, not good at all. *What are we going to do George?*"

"Pedal, Barney. *We have to pedal!*"

For the next four hours in the blazing, unyielding Mediterranean sunshine, two boys from rural England, with nothing but a warm kebab and boiling ouzo to fuel them, pedalled as though their lives depended on it. Considering their dilemma, it really did.

Much, much later, in the failing light of day, as evening started to grip the town and the drum and bass music began to throb once more, a surly Greek pedalo owner in a small launch finally caught up with a pair of exhausted customers. Half a mile from Kavos beach, he was not in good spirits.

"Eh, you, you say one hour! *One hour!* You been gone seven, you 'ava to pay more, you hear? *You 'ava to me pay more!*" The boys were well beyond exhaustion now, and close to tears of relief, having finally nearly made it safely back to the shore alive. It was all George could do to waive an accepting hand at the Greek, who threw them a line, before gruffly instructing them to secure it to the front of HMS *Pedalo*.

It is unlikely that a pedalo was originally designed to travel at fifteen knots over choppy water. If this had been intended, then some sort of safety device for disengaging the drive train would have probably been conceived. Regrettably though, this was not the case, and as such the violently spinning, plastic pedals whirled manically beneath the passengers' feet, like a speeding, blood-red combine harvester, and the boys desperately hugged their knees up around their ears in an effort to protect their toes.

Unfortunately for Barney, he lost his grip, and two little piggies in the process.

For several weeks after his meet and greet with a certain new recruit, Mr Burton found himself, quite inexplicably, chuckling away in the most inappropriate of circumstances. The memory of that unexpected afternoon in the company of the dishevelled youth with the huge hair seemed to linger, much to the annoyance of his Bridge club.

Chapter 4

The Decapitated Caterpillar

The Next Day.

There was no doubt about it, George definitely had frostbite. One of the more sadistic leaving rituals practiced at the Supermarket, involved cocooning the unsuspecting escapee in polythene pallet wrap, and then throwing them in the vast minus twenty, frozen aisle chiller for a few minutes, usually on their last day.

To begin with, he'd put up something of a spirited fight, finding speed in his legs that no PE teacher ever managed to coax. But when the heavy set chaps from night crew joined in the hunt, he was soon cornered near the fish counter, wrestled to the ground despite his wildly flailing appendages, roughly wrapped in the oversized roll of Clingfilm, and exported to the vast corridors of chillers, like a freshly caught salmon. The whole process had been completely undignified.

George had seen this happen before of course, to others who'd been lucky enough escape the Supermarket. He'd never got involved in the actual pursuit, that all looked far to energetic, but he'd laughed along when the victim, a fresh layer of ice coating their eyebrows, was unwrapped, patted on the back and handed a bottle of spirits and a leaving card. As he'd lain shivering on the icy floor though, next to a frozen wall of stacked pizzas, he started to suspect that he'd been forgotten about, and thanks to an emergency code nine, *all available staff to the checkouts to help with packing*, he had been. That had been a week ago, and he was now utterly convinced that two of his fingertips were starting to turn black.

For the first time in weeks the rain clouds had finally parted, and the dull winter's sky had given way to a welcome, crisp clear blue. But even this couldn't soften the foreboding air that hung on every street corner here. Bandit land was indeed grim.

It had been a pleasant enough drive through the countryside, and as Nelson Branch was located on the fringes of the great city, the journey had been much quicker and less fraught than the previous day. Not once was he hooted at, and for the moment at least, it seemed that the MGB might have a brief stay of execution, the proverbial axe pausing mid swing. Sadly now though, the old car seemed to face a new, even more perilous threat.

George was still absentmindedly picking at his imaginary frostbite, when a skinny, tattooed and shaven headed man of indeterminate age, banged his hand on the long bonnet of the MG, nearly scratching the paintwork with his vast collection of sovereign rings.

"'*ere*, nice wheels, Mate. *Watcha want fer it?*"

The owner wound down the window slowly, fearing kidnap, and hampered as ever by his broken winder. He examined the cretin at his wing mirror with guarded caution. "Err, thanks, but it's not for sale at the moment, *sorry*."

The man lingered for an uncomfortable moment. He spent an age lighting a thin cigarette that he produced from his filthy jeans, whilst his horribly narrow, bloodshot eyes darted about the interior of the car, pausing for a while to record the make and model of the stereo. "'*ere*, that's no prob Mate, I'll just nick it later. *See ya!*" The awful menace chuckled like the villain he undoubtedly was, and slouched off lazily along the run down street, that was lined on both sides with foreboding, terraced houses. He threw open a galvanized metal gate and mooched past a battered Ford Capri that was resting on bricks in the garden. Eventually, after taking another long squinting look in George's direction, he disappeared into his grim liar, slamming the door so hard, that the huge satellite dish, and last year's Christmas decorations, still hanging limply from the guttering, wobbled precariously. Perhaps it was best to move the car?

The evening before, on his journey home, George had conducted a quick recon of the area, in order to get his bearings and find somewhere to park, keeping his windows firmly wound up, and the doors securely locked at all times. He'd never had an occasion to venture into Bandit Land before, although if he'd ever had, he felt quite sure now that he'd have made up an excuse instead.

It wasn't that the place was poor by any means, a finer collection of satellite dishes would've been hard to find outside of a Radio Observatory, and those brave enough to venture inside one of the ominous looking concrete boxes, would have found vast hordes of state of the art home entertainment equipment, including televisions the size of snooker tables. It was just a very, very rough area.

After a few laps of the curiously designed road that snaked through, and eventually around, a small collection of run down shops and amenities, including the branch of Cottons, he spotted a well-padded lady, somewhere in her late forties, and clearly built for comfort *not* speed, waving in his direction from the curb side. It seemed unlikely that this was some sort of elaborate carjack, but as he slowed and pulled alongside her, he kept the door locked, just in case.

"Ten to nine is more than early enough to start work here *my Lovely*, we don't open until half past!" The high pitched voice had the merest hint of indigenous accent.

"*I'm sorry?*" He smiled back at her nervously, waiting to see if she pulled a shotgun from her suspiciously massive handbag.

"You *must* be George Butler. You are, aren't you, *hmmm?*" She held her head to one side inquisitively, grinning warmly from ear to ear, like the primary school teacher he'd always wanted. She was about five foot two, and shaped like a conference pear. She had quite short, very curly brown hair, and wore just the barest hint of makeup which complimented amazing, sparkling blue eyes that should have belonged to a film star half her age.

It was only the slightest suggestion of wrinkles around the eyes and mouth, her dress sense, and her habit of clutching the enormous bag as though it contained the crown jewels that betrayed her actual age. The perfume was also somewhat mumsy of course.

"*Yes, yes I am.* How did you know?" George was relieved to be spared at least some of the dreaded first day introductions. Here was someone else, clearly put on the earth simply to look after other people. He seemed to have developed a knack of collecting them lately.

"*Oh*, well, Di is a good friend of mine, she described you perfectly." He briefly expected a cursory glance, but although like Di this lady was yet another surrogate Mum to all those in need, she was a *traditional* Mum, whereas Di would have probably dragged him off to her bed by his ankles if he took her fancy, and if she had taken to the gin.

"I'm Rose Saunders, although most people call me *Auntie Rose* for some reason." George quickly reached through the window, made some mental adjustments to his grip, and shook her surprisingly strong hand, nearly slipping off thanks to a thick layer of moisturiser.

"Pleased to meet you Rose, *err,* where can I park my car where it'll be safe, some little Sod a few streets down said he was going to nick it?"

"Was that over there, on South Street?" She waved a hand vaguely in the direction from which he'd fled a few moments ago.

"Yeah, it was a horrible looking place."

"*Nobody* parks over there, I'll jump in and show you where's safe!" In a flash Rose was in the car, hugging her bag close to her, peering through its handles as she navigated animatedly to a safe spot, pausing occasionally to dab parts of the dusty dashboard with an anti-bacterial wipe.

"Will it be okay here then, err, *Auntie Rose?*" The area did seem to have a less, ghetto like ambience.

"*Oh yes*, it'll be fine here my lovely, now come on, *needs must when the Devil drives!*" She led him to the edge of the road that stood between them and the branch and, in a brief and bizarre moment that he would struggle to ever forget, grabbed hold of his hand as though he was five years old and, after cautiously looking both ways, dragged the fourteen stone nineteen-year-old across the street to safety.

"Right then, *here we are!*" Rose let go of his hand, glanced around, and rang the doorbell twice.

George was somewhat at a loss. He looked down at his hand and then over to Rose, who was bobbing up and down to see if anyone was in the branch. What the Hell had just happened?

"Ah, *here she is.*"

A very, very tall, almost Amazonian woman in her early thirties emerged from the dimly lit back office, beyond the modest banking hall, and strode towards the door like a catwalk model that had needed no training, her face coy, heartbreakingly so.

"Morning Rose. Hey, I see you have picked up a handsome stranger. *Good girl.*" The voice was wonderful, quite deep for a girl, but calm and a little rural. Opening the metal framed door, she stood aside so that they could enter the branch, and as George passed her, grinning madly, he was aware of a subtle musky perfume, a world away from the choking chemicals worn by the cashier's at Armada branch. Not once did his eyes run or throat constrict.

"Oh yes, this is George, bless him, he's a bit worried about his car being stolen by the lot over on South Street." Rose took hold of his hand again, and rubbed it reassuringly. He was definitely going to be mothered to death today.

"*Leave him alone Rose.* Hello George, I'm Hayley, the Branch Manager, don't worry about your car, it'll be fine over the road, I promise. Now come on in and we'll get you settled." Hayley shook his hand, now that it had eventually been freed from Rose, in a way that, even given his limited experiences, seemed ever so slightly provocative. In that instant, He fell in love for the second time in as many days. Perhaps banking was for him after all?

Hayley was unlike any other woman he'd ever met before. She was undeniably attractive, but in a relaxed, easy going way that only served to add to her mesmerizing charm. Like Belinda the day before, she too favoured short-skirted business suits, but unlike Belinda, she didn't see the need for constant preening or adjustment. Unabashed, she simply got on with the business of moving around the office. If her skirt rode up a little bit, then so what? She had great legs that went on forever, and didn't seem to care who noticed.

She was a good few inches taller than George's claimed, five foot eleven and one quarter, and the killer heels weren't helping. Slim and athletic but not skinny, she had reasonably pale skin with a few dotted, adorable schoolgirl freckles, similar to Summer's, and big, brown, wide-apart eyes that were accentuated by carelessly applied black mascara. Her thick black hair was slightly curly and cut into a hastily brushed bob, which casually rested just below her delicate, but purposeful jaw. Hayley's mouth was wide and permanently coy, the lips were full and plump, her lipstick the colour of London Buses. In an entirely different way than the day before, George was mesmerised.

Chatting casually, she led the way through the small banking hall and into the back office, via the usual pass door that for the time being was wedged open. Within the banking hall there was another door, again propped open for now, and that seemed to open into to a small interview room. The immediate back office, which customers would see through the security glass, consisted of Hayley's desk behind the three cashier's positions, and two other desks pushed up against the walls. To the left there was a short corridor that led into another room, which was slightly bigger than the first and that eventually led to a doorway at the rear, and a flight of stairs. A section of the front wall, adjacent to the corridor, expanded to create an L shape, the toe of which contained the now familiar clatter from a cashpoint. At right angles to the cashpoint, sunken into the wall, was the sealed solid metal door of the branch's safe. As with the main branch, all the walls were painted a uniform, pale corporate grey, the floors carpeted in dark grey. Somehow though, this little branch seemed so much brighter.

"Cup of tea, George?" Hayley smiled charmingly, suddenly casting him adrift in a sea of attraction.

"*Ooh yes*, that would be great, *thanks*." This was a Boss to love.

"*Well done*. The rest room and kettle are upstairs, Rose will point you in the right direction. I like mine weak with milk and one sugar, please!" She retreated back towards her desk, hips swaying, leaving a preoccupied George alone with a disapproving Rose.

"Now come along, the tea won't make itself! And *by the way young man*, she's too old for you, *and* she's engaged to a huge rugby player!" Whilst half-heartedly scolding her new charge, she pushed the besotted youth up the stairs and out of harm's way. She'd seen a great deal of men, old, young, blind, and gay become bewitched by Hayley. He wouldn't be the last.

The short flight of rickety stairs led to a small dusty, wooden floored hallway that desperately needed a fresh coat of paint. It contained three doors, all of which were slightly ajar. To the immediate right there was the rest room, a simple and slightly unloved space that enjoyed sunlight via a barred window, with an uninterrupted view of the rows and rows of identical terraced houses.

There was a stained old brown kitchen worktop, dull metal sink and drainer, battered yellowing plastic kettle and a shiny black microwave, obviously a recent introduction. An old classroom table dominated the centre of the room, and was surrounded by a variety of chairs of various shapes and states of repair. A pile of well-worn magazines, topped with a fresh copy of *Women's Own*, a few used coffee mugs and a half eaten pasty littered the table top. The whole room smelt of cheap coffee and sweaty pastry. His mum would've had a fit.

"*Oh*, that little Devil, she never clears up after herself!" Fussing, Rose gathered up the mess and straightened the pile of magazines. "I don't work Mondays, the whole place seems goes to wrack and ruin in just one day because of Anita!" She pulled on a pair of bright yellow marigold rubber gloves, snapping them surgically against her skin, and still wearing her coat and with her vast handbag looped over her forearm, began scrubbing the decks industriously. Out of fear and habit, George picked up a tea towel.

"Who's Anita then?"

"Oh, you'll meet her soon enough. And the Bear, although he's a good enough sort, bless him." Rose would soon prove to be one of those unique individuals who seemed compelled in life to hand out more blessings than the Pope.

"*The Bear?*"

"Yes, *The Bear.*" She looked up, as though it was the most normal thing in the world to say.

"What is that, some sort of *nickname?*"

Having run a huge bowl of hot water that frothed with endless excited bubbles, she grabbed a recently bleached, anaemic-looking cloth, and started vigorously on the dishes. "Well I suppose so. I've never known him as anything else but The Bear. You'll soon see what I mean." She blew an errant clump of fleeing bubbles from her nose and attacked a stained mug with renewed vigour. "Why don't you have a look at the stationary cupboard while I put the kettle on and finish up here? The toilet is through the end door if you need them. Don't make a mess, *or splash anything around.*"

Bemused, and a just a little bit insulted, unsure of whether or not he should defend his well-practiced aim, the new recruit left Rose to make the tea and had a look around the rest of the first floor. He pushed open the scruffy door opposite and entered the cavernous stationary cupboard. It seemed to occupy most of the first floor, and was anything but a cupboard. Unlike the staff room, this space was immaculate, the shelves were all neatly stacked and labelled, piles of larger items were placed on the stripped floor boards, and were carefully, precisely arranged so as not to cause any sort of hazard. It had Rose written all over it. She'd get on well with Mrs Butler.

"This is *my* little project, George. We supply stationary to all the branches in Armada Group from this room. *Quite a feat really.*" Rose, still drying a tea cup, appeared at his elbow, swelling with pride.

"*BLACK WITH THREE AUNTIE ROSE!*" A voice like thunder in a bucket, and heavy artillery in a tunnel, came bounding up the stairs from the ground floor, shaking the very walls of the stationary cupboard.

"What are you forgetting, Bear, *hmm?*" Sounding like a Sunday school teacher ticking off an unseen, misbehaving pupil, Rose cocked her head to one side, waiting patiently.

"ERR, *PLEASE?*" Again the roaring voice and this time, as if for dramatic effect, a pile of plastic wrapped forms fell off the shelves onto the floor, and was instantly pounced on.

"Well done *my Lovely,* be down in a jiffy!" She beamed at George knowingly. "*That's The Bear.*"

George sat opposite The Bear in one of the seats behind Hayley's desk and flexed his fingers. He hoped that the feeling would one day, eventually return, and that he would still be able to play the guitar. Moments before, he'd offered a huge steaming mug of very black, sweet coffee to the hairy man mountain and nervously extended his own hand in greeting. Any concerns he'd had about hurting this employee with his overly firm shake were soon forgotten. The Bear was quite simply, a Bear.

Lesley *The Bear* Rhymes stood at six foot six inches tall, and due to an almost all consuming covering of thick, coarse black hair, was of indeterminate age. The hair on his enormous square head, which seemed to have been cut roughly into shape by a blind aunt guided by a cracked pudding bowl, hung low over his short thick, deeply lined forehead and merged with his massive unkempt eyebrows. At approximately the ears, this mass of hair joined forces with his beard, an impenetrable, closely packed legion of hairs that covered his vast square face, save four small lagoons of bright red and brighter blue that were his cheeks and his penetrating eyes respectively. His nose looked like a large pink, dimpled golf ball.

Built like a tank that had fallen into a pit of concrete, he had a belly like a beer barrel, which considering his insatiable appetite for real ale, was understandable. His feet and hands seemed to be twice the size of that of the average man, and he wore a battered brown suit that stretched to bursting at the seams around his shoulders and arms, like a well-worn sock containing a wild boar.

The lapels bore the stains of meals long since devoured, and pints that had somehow managed to miss a cave of a mouth that was full of yellow teeth, which resembled rows of derelict buildings. A cheap white polyester shirt also struggled to contain the bulk of his wide neck, and was held in place by a wide gaudy tie that appeared to be decorated by hundreds of images of Bugs Bunny's head. His Skull and Cross Bones one was in the wash that day.

The Bear loved Rugby, real ale, Led Zeppelin and his Mum. He was the local representative of the Bank Union, CBU, and nobody ever, ever called him Lesley, not even his Mum. It was said, in hushed, fearful voices, that in order for someone to call The Bear, Lesley, they had to first become tired of life. How he'd ever ended up in a bank, was anyone's guess.

Although utterly fascinated by this colossal man, George, still rubbing the life back into his crushed fingers, had to battle against an uncontrollable urge to call him, for a laugh, no matter how brief and painful it may be, *Yogi*. Boo-Boo would have just been insulting.

It was nearly ten past nine when the shrill doorbell ripped through the branch. The small group had been enjoying their beverages, and getting to know the newest member of the team, whilst Rose made ready the tills. A look of resentment briefly flashed across Hayley's serene face, as she grudgingly got to her feet to let in Nelson's branch most demanding member of staff. From where he was sat, George couldn't really see new arrival yet, but he could see that there was clearly an exchange of whispered, aggravated words in the relative privacy of the still closed banking hall. Whispered aggravation seemed to be commonplace within the Bank.

Anita Wright was twenty-nine, yet thanks to hard living, looked forty. She was a uniquely evil and bitter entity. As a child, she wasn't content to simply pull the wings off flies; she'd round up its family too, trap them on a length of double sided sticky tape and make them watch. Antagonistic beyond words, just five minutes in her company, especially when she was in one of her many turbulent moods, would have been enough to send Gandhi into a fit of bloody rage.

Short, at five foot one, she had a slight, almost boyish figure, not helped by a reluctant bosom, which looked like two medium-sized fried eggs. Her close cropped hair was probably originally black or dark brown in another life, but a particularly savage application of bleach had turned all but the rapidly lengthening roots, a truly unnatural shade of yellow, with unintentional green highlights.

She walked, or rather strutted, like a small, vicious dinosaur, one that would've preyed on the weak and the young. Slightly hunched over and heavy footed despite her obvious lightness, each step attacked the floor as though it had wronged her in a previous life. Her perfume of choice was tobacco and strong coffee, and she lived on a diet of junk food and sex-starved sailors who had the misfortune of making port at one of her usual grubby haunts, and whose better judgment and taste was still lost at sea.

Badly offset black eyes, something that can be a charming and alluring quality in others, only served to add to a dreadful picture of slyness and cruelty, each time she glared horribly out of the corner of her distorted eye. She wore a heavy coating of cheap black mascara, and her nails looked as though they had just been plucked from the carcass of a dead wildebeest. Dressed all in black, clutching a severe black handbag stuffed with cigarettes as though it was a sabre, Anita strutted into the back office and glared menacingly at George, clearly planning to flay him alive. There was to be no mutual attraction here.

"You're sat in *my* seat." She spat the words at him bitterly through nicotine stained teeth. Because of her badly offset eyes though, he couldn't quite determine which seat she was talking about, his or The Bears.

Something told him it probably wasn't The Bear's.

"Oh, err, *I'm sorry!*" He scrambled to his feet, offering a recovered hand in welcome and apology.

"*Whatever*, where's *my* coffee?" She threw herself into the swivel chair, ignoring the offered hand, and slouched like drunk in the earlier hours, her short skinny legs wide apart, her arms swinging carelessly over the arms. "Well? Get to it *New Boy!*" She leered horribly at him with black, hateful eyes. Nobody had ever looked at him that way before. His blood froze, he shuddered involuntarily. Suddenly he missed the Produce Aisle terribly.

"You can make it yourself Anita. George is busy." Hayley, returning to her desk, quickly and thankfully, pulled the baby antelope from the gaping jaws of the crocodile, just as the teeth were starting to bite. She'd seen this before. Another second, she'd have lost him in a death roll.

With bloodshed avoided for the time being, it was soon it was time to open the branch, and the staff took up their positions, ready for the onslaught. Rose seemed to be head cashier, as well as chief stationary clerk, and obviously took great pride in her immaculate till. The Bear was a sort of everyman, cashier, enquiries clerk, and doorman. Anita opened accounts, tended to the back office work, such as loading direct debits and ordering cards, and practiced her scowl. She was getting rather good.

As well as holding the loose team together and directing them as best she could, Hayley acted as a Customer Banking Advisor and Team Leader, a role that was considered to be a step up from the average CBA position, and was seen as a starting point to becoming a Senior Manager in one of the larger branches.

Feeling like a spare part, unsure quite what to do with his hands, George fidgeted absentmindedly with his small change as Rose the others served the diverse, colourful customers that piled in once the door had been opened. Rose and The Bear both made easy conversation, catching up on gossip like they knew each customer personally. Those that had misjudged their place in the queue though, and ended up at the harridan's till, were merely glared at, their paying in books crushed under a heavy handed stamp.

George was delighted when Hayley led him into the room that contained the humming cashpoint, placing her hand warmly on his arm; she smiled reassuringly into his wide eyes. How he wished he had more muscular arms.

"Take no notice of Anita," she rubbed softly. "She's just that way to everyone. The rest of us will look after you." As he lost himself briefly in her big brown eyes, nodding hypnotically, it suddenly dawned in him that somehow he had become the baby of the group. It was a role he was both comfortable, and familiar with.

"Okay, this morning I would like you to sit with Rose and learn about cashiering, once you start to pick things up, you can have a go yourself, perhaps after lunch. Does that sound okay?" She slowly secured a strand of loose curly hair behind her delicate, perfect ear. Hayley could have asked him to run naked through a field of brambles and he would still have nodded amiably. He would have preferred not to, but he would have, nonetheless.

A while later, George hovered nervously on the tall swivel chair next to Rose, having already fallen off twice. They were trickier than they looked. He was taking no chances, and had wedged himself between the wall and Rose's heavy bulk cash drawer, which she kept slightly ajar for easy access. She tapped his leg irritably, but good naturedly, each time she needed some coin from it, and scolded him as though he was her own errant offspring. He was starting to feel at home.

It had been an interesting morning. Safe behind the bullet proof glass, the young man from the countryside marvelled at the diverse collection of fascinating, urban characters that filed through the banking hall. Never in his life had he seen so much variety, or so many tattoos.

Firstly there was the man who'd seemed to have been tattooed and pierced in places that George didn't even have. Despite the chill, he wore a sleeveless leather jacket and a tight white vest, just in case anyone wanted to see the mythological battles between the dragons, brawny warriors, and the odd busty maiden tattooed up and down his enormous arms. The knuckles were heavily inked with the obligatory 'Love and Hate', and, along with numerous other metal objects, he had three massive gold spikes inserted through the bridge of his nose. This was a man who clearly knew no pain. If all his piercings were melted down, an entire cutlery set could have been fashioned from the remains.

Then there was the obese mother, clearly no stranger to a Big Mac, and her three young children, all of whom were lashed into a filthy, food stained triple buggy that she'd forced through the front door with the same determined vigour she'd probably used giving birth. Infant arms and legs flayed around wildly, the ensuing horrendous screams of torment so full of anguish and pain that George expected a Constable to burst in at any moment.

The mother, who couldn't have been much over twenty, screamed back at them whilst inserting grubby dummies and offering bribes of cheap, E number saturated sweets and soggy crisps. She wore a bright pink shell suit tracksuit that was unzipped to expose a saggy, stretch-marked and rather frightening cleavage, where dozens of cheap gold chains and pendants dangled helplessly, seemingly screaming for help. Just like a horrific train wreck, he didn't want to look, but somehow just had to. He soon wished he hadn't.

There was an extremely old man, who was clearly mad and should never have been let out alone. A middle-aged woman dressed like a very young prostitute, but who was in fact a very old prostitute, an extremely well-spoken businessman who was obviously lost and very afraid. A batty member of the Women's Institute who paid in enough coin to sink a battleship, a Chinese man whom nobody could understand, a Welshman whom nobody could understand, three giggling Sixth Form schoolgirls who were obviously skiving (George rather liked them), a very tall woman with stubble and an impressive hairy chest, a variety of drunks in assorted states of inebriation and of various sex, a lost puppy, a man who might well have been a zombie, a plastic hairdresser, and, perhaps most surprisingly, a Nun.

And through all of these encounters, no matter how bizarre or unsettling, Rose carried on undaunted. Each customer was treated to a cheery smile and warm greeting, each leaving happily, having had their lives enriched just a little by sunny Auntie Rose. Even those who were turned down for an encashment due to a lack of funds seemed to take it rather well. The woman was a marvel.

Remarkably enough, with all the excitement of the Circus, George's stomach hadn't noticed the time, but when it came for The Bear's turn to replace Rose on the till, his thoughts soon turned to food. And as he watched The Bear lower his mammoth, hairy bulk onto his swivel chair, waiting for the inevitable cracking noise, Rose disappeared upstairs to make the tea and dig one of her Weight Watchers soups out of the cupboard. Like plenty of woman of a certain age and dress size, she was always on a diet, but never actually managed to change either shape or volume, thanks largely to chocolate biscuits, and evening vats of red wine.

George meanwhile, slightly disappointed that The Bear had failed to break anything, quickly recovered his lunchbox from the boot of the MGB, which he was grateful to find both unmolested and where he left it. Having once managed to cross the road successfully, without Auntie Rose's guiding hand, he only narrowly avoided being mowed down by a speeding scooter on the return trip. He desperately hoped she hadn't been watching.

With the all too familiar aroma of bleach and lemon disinfectant making him giddy, he sat opposite Rose in the freshly sanitised staff room, clicked open his blue plastic lunchbox, glancing at the carefully packed contents for a moment in delight, before tucking in.

"*Oh my Gosh!* How much food do you eat, young man?" Wide-eyed, a spoon of almost transparent, thin chicken soup halfway to her mouth, Rose was transfixed.

"I know, *bad isn't it?* Apparently the large lunchbox is *missing*. I blame Dad. Still, I can always get a pasty later, for the journey home." Mrs Butler didn't hold with light lunches. She had always seen to it that the family was packed off each day with enough food to sustain them until they arrived safely back home for the evening meal. A non-family member, supplied with such a feast, could've become lost in the wilderness for a fortnight and still have not gone hungry.

To begin with, there were three enormous white bread baps, filled to bursting with salad leaves, tomatoes, spring onions - always regretted later, cucumber, thick slices of ham, huge slices of strong cheddar cheese, and lashings of butter and salad cream. Wedged next to them for support was the inevitable giant slab of juicy, homemade fruit cake, three homemade buns with icing, a banana that would've embarrassed an elephant, a colossal Golden Delicious apple, two Twix bars, a Wagon Wheel, a small packet of peanuts, a large packet of cheese and onion crisps, and a massive, succulent orange that looked as though it could only be safely eaten naked, and in the shower. At school, everyone wanted to swap lunches with George.

"Well *that* explains the belly then! Oh, yeah, and what's this I've heard about you and that hippy Summer?" It had been a slow on the till, and Anita had been allowed to come to lunch early, after much moaning about needing a fag. George had a large, grateful mouth full of bap, and even if he wasn't terrified of this wretch, would've been unable to retort anyhow. Which was just as well, as it gave someone else a much needed opportunity.

"That is *quite* enough of all that, *young Lady!*" Rose's usual sing-song, Walton's Mountain tone had momentarily been replaced by one that would have caused a drill sergeant to go weak at the knees. The effect was devastating that for a brief moment, inexplicably, George stopped chewing and turned to Anita, who, clearly on the ropes, was stunned and humiliated by the heroic Auntie Rose. The woman really was a marvel.

"I won't hear any more of this, *do you hear me?* Leave him alone! There's nothing wrong with having a belly, and what he and Summer are up to is their own business." She paused for a moment, thoughtfully turning to George who, embarrassed and mid-chew, resembled a hamster dipped in jam. Her face thankfully, once again a picture of serenity. "*Unless* of course, you want to tell me?" He rallied, eventually managing to swallow the huge bite of bread, salad, cheese and ham. He'd been dreading this. But who could've told her though?

"*Err*, well, there's not much to say really." He looked pleadingly at her. Thinking he didn't want to talk in front of Anita, Rose's voice lashed out once more.

"Don't you want one of those awful cigarette things Anita, it would give you a chance to think about what you've done and said, *hmm?*" She raised a quizzical eyebrow. There was no arguing with the eyebrow.

"*Whatever!*" Anita strutted off in her defeat, each petulant step resonating off the stairwell as she retreated. Once again the forces of Evil had been defeated by Good.

Rose turned back to him, before he could take another silencing bite of his lunch, and put on her very best motherly face. "*So*, what do you want to tell Auntie Rose then…?" She would've made a surprisingly unique but utterly devastating interrogator.

When George arrived safely at the Butler's respectable semi, the evening before, his parents had naturally been very keen to hear all about his first day at the Bank, not least to put their minds at rest, and find out if he intended to go back again the next day. Over the evening meal, and after being satisfied that he seemed at least to have a degree of interest in his new job, questioning relaxed a little, and Mrs Butler asked if he'd met any new friends. When he turned bright crimson, she immediately knew that he'd met a girl. This was good news. It would definitely mean he'd go back again tomorrow.

Safe in the knowledge that he didn't have to get up in the early hours to begin a shift at the Supermarket, he'd set off at eight for a spirited drive, culminating in a cup of tea at Barney's family home. As always, Barney had been less reserved with his opinions about George's budding romance. He had no desire to lose his only drinking partner to some slick, sophisticated banker from the city, not unless she had a friend of course, and he'd be invited to join them all for a spirited night on the tiles. That would be acceptable.

These hopes were soon dashed though, as George tried his very best to describe Summer to him. From what he'd said, she certainly didn't sound at all sophisticated, or more importantly, like she'd have a collection of willing, stylish friends. It had all been very troubling for the Celtic Casanova, and he'd made no secret of his disappointment.

As he drove home later that evening, only one thing troubled George. How long *should* he leave it until he called her?

"*Well*, what happened, tell me then, did she give you her number?" Rose cocked her head so abruptly to one side it looked as though it might well snap off. She knew she was overcooking her reassurance now, but, needs *must when the Devil drives.*

"Umm, well, *you know,* we've err, just, err talked a bit and, err, she, err, she did give me her number, yeah." As if to prove it, George produced a rumpled scrap of paper, complete with hastily scribbled numbers, from his pocket. "Look, here it is, *see?*" The interrogation was getting intense.

"*Well,* have you called her yet?"

"Err, well, no, not yet, it was only yesterday, I didn't want to seem, *err,* you know, desperate or anything." He wasn't quite sure what was happening. Was Rose was secretly Summer's Godmother? She did look like the Godmother type.

"Well why on earth would you think that? You must call her tonight, she'll think you've changed your mind else, *the poor Love.*"

He hadn't considered this at all. Summer was the girl and therefore by default, completely in control of the situation as far as he was concerned. Suddenly, his mind flooded with doubt. What if Rose was right? What if she'd been offended that he'd not taken the time to call her last night? What if she met another man today who also painted, and what if he was slimmer and had a nicer suit? Either eventuality was entirely possible. Would she think he was playing childish games? She did *seem* to be a bit older than him, after all. And why was Auntie Rose so interested? And *how* did Anita know about all this? When would he be allowed to finish his lunch? He was starving hungry now, and his bap looked mouth-wateringly good today. What was that funny green thing? Was it some new variety of salad his Mum was trying, or was that a caterpillar in his Bap? There *was* a caterpillar in his Bap.

"*There's a caterpillar in my Bap Auntie Rose!*"

The conversation changed direction somewhat, when he discovered that there was actually *half* a caterpillar in his Bap, the tail half, by the looks of it.

"No George, you want die from eating a caterpillar! They're full of protein, just like chicken." The Bear, now extremely bored of the Caterpillar story, was seriously considering eating George just so that he could enjoy some peace, on what was turning into a very quiet Tuesday afternoon. Anita was busy opening an account for a burly sailor, and as such would be gone for hours, Hayley had popped into Armada branch for a quick meeting, and Rose was busy, happily dispatching stationary to far flung corners of the Empire. That left The Bear training George how to cashier. After just ten minutes, he'd quickly grown tired of the job.

The Bear desperately lacked the basic qualities required of the conventional teacher. Qualities including patience, tolerance and understanding were lost on him, and had instead long ago been replaced with annoyance, irritation and exasperation. His Student was by no means dim, but after the first few minutes of his training, it did seem likely that the elderly customer he was serving was going to expire in the banking hall before he received his change. The Bear had quickly taken over, completing the simple transaction before one of them had died, and he'd had to fill in a form. He hated forms with a passion.

That had been over forty minutes ago, and still nobody had dared to venture into the branch for George to practice on. After covering the basics of cashiering, there was nothing much else for the pair of them to do but chat, much to The Bears increasing annoyance.

"So, seriously, you *can* eat bugs? I mean bugs, *proper bugs*? And beetles? *What about beetles*? Have you eaten a beetle? I mean, not because you're, like, *a real bear* or anything like that…"

Once he was sure that the torrent of questions had eventually finished, The Bear slowly turned to George who was swivelling absentmindedly on the cashier's stool next to his own.

"Which of those questions would you like me to answer first?" The Bear had to admit that there was something strange and rather endearing about this crazy little soul. Despite himself, he was slowly warming to him. Something would have to be done about this.

"Sorry, I do go on sometimes, don't I?"

"That's a waste of a word." With a knowing grin, The Bear continued his silent examination of the street outside, his elbows propped on the counter top, his fingers lost in his bearded chin as fallen trees in long grass. At last, finally, there was peace and quiet.

George fought the never-ending internal battle to stay quiet, as bravely as he could. He'd never been good at it. Silence sounded just too loud to him, and far too awkward. Simmering slightly from the effort, like the lid of a boiling pan of beans, he eventually lost his courageous fight.

"*Hey*, err, so what types of music do you like, *Yogi Bear?*"

And he'd had such a promising future in banking…

Chapter 5

Bovine Terrorists

Later That Same Evening.

In certain homes, there is a silent battle waged each evening, every single day. It is a battle of wits and of courage, a test of nerve, resilience, and of stamina. It is a battle that can only ever have one victor, for the spoils of this particular battle can never be shared. It is the 'Battle of who will help Mum with the Dinner Dishes?' War was indeed, hell.

Since George's older brother had left home, the battle within the Butler household had only two sides. During the campaigns of the late eighties and early nineties, the brothers could pretend to be helping each other out with their homework, and therefore mentally gang up on their Dad for the sake of their education. Occasionally though, if Michael wanted his motorbike fixed, he would quickly swap sides, and pick up a dishcloth for the sake of his freedom.

These days, it was just fought between George and his Dad. Mrs Butler would retreat to the kitchen after the meal and obligatory cup of tea had settled, and noisily begin the washing up, waiting patiently to see who would eventually come to her rescue. Mr Butler senior would then usually begin minutely examining a fascinating article he'd found in the *Daily Express*, despite having owned the paper since early that morning, and having already read it twice that day. This left George channel hoping, praying that Barney would call, as was their secret mutual arrangement. No call meant that Barney had lost his war, and he was on his own. There would be no reinforcements to strengthen his front line that evening.

As the crashing of dishes became every more desperate, and the available space on the drainer steadily diminished, the silent battle intensified, especially as both sides considered the possibility of the runners up prize. Whoever got up to help with the dishes, miraculously enough seemed to get the largest slab of fruit cake for dessert too. It was a very complicated business.

This evening though George was prepared to sacrifice the fruit cake entirely. He had another objective in mind, something that, crazy as it might seem, could well yield greater pleasures than even fruit cake.

The layout of the family home was typical of most modern houses. The front door opened into a modest hallway, which immediately led to a flight of stairs, and a first floor that contained three bedrooms of decreasing size, an airing cupboard and a family bathroom. Downstairs, to the left of the hallway and through a glass-panelled door, there was the lounge, an archway into the dining room, and eventually the engine room of the house, the kitchen.

Crucially the telephone, which was *not* cordless, was located in the modest hallway. This meant that in order to enjoy a private conversation with his parents in the house, George had to either wait until they were busy in the kitchen, or until his Dad had taken Eddie, the excitable family Jack Russell, for his evening walk, and his Mum had retired to the bath with a large glass of red wine and the latest Danielle Steele. In the case of the latter, he would simply trail the telephone into the lounge, secure the hallway door, and guarantee his privacy for at least twenty-seven minutes, the average time it took to walk and empty Eddie.

This would normally be his preference, as the dishes, based on a comprehensive study, generally took only seventeen minutes to tidy away. And there was always the danger that Mrs Butler might emerge from the kitchen ahead of time to offer a small slice of fruit cake, and see who he was talking too.

All these factors had to be carefully considered if his telephone call to Summer was to be a success. The last thing he wanted was to be interrupted with inquisitive slices of cake, or an overexcited, newly relieved Jack Russell.

The conversation needed to be kept brief and to the point. No messing around, simply where and when should they meet. He accepted that this was probably not the most romantic method in the world, but *needs must when the Devil drives*. Where had he gotten that from?

With a monumental sigh, and over exaggerated flourish of his newspaper, Mr Butler senior at last hauled himself out of his comfortable arm chair. Having finally conceded defeat, he was content with the runners up prize that evening. He'd seen it removed from the oven, all moist and fruity, an hour or so before, some things are worth giving up for.

No sooner had his Dad disappeared into a haze of bubbling steam, was his youngest son silently on his feet, and into the hallway, safely securing the door behind him like a tubby Ninja. He carefully removed the precious scrap of paper from his jeans, and paused for a moment, listening intently for the sound of fluffy slippers on deep pile carpets. Satisfied that he'd not been followed, he lifted the beige, plastic receiver and began to press the buttons as softly as he dared.

After an eternity, finally there came the ringing tone. He sat on the second step of the stairs, all his senses sharpened as he waited for her to pick up. Nervously, he peered through one of the doors slightly opaque glass panels for signs of movement, his heart pounding. Still the ringing tone, perhaps she was out with another man?

"Err, *hallo?*" Summer's timid little voice sounded genuinely surprised, as if it was the first time the odd shaped object in the corner of her cottage had made a noise.

"Oh, err, hello, *I'm George.*" This was an introduction he really needed to work on. "Bugger, I mean, *it's* George. *Err*, how are you?" Sweating, he pressed his nose up against the glass. Was that movement?

"*Oh*, err, I'm fine thanks, err, *how are you?*" This could take forever. He was going to have to speed things up a bit if he was to get anywhere before either the dog or dessert arrived.

"*Fine!* So, err, what do you think? *Umm*, do you still want to get together sometime, err, *soon?*" As each word tumbled from his mouth, he winced as though he was being punched. If only he'd planned the conversation as meticulously as he'd planned securing the telephone line. Notes, he should have prepared some notes.

Suddenly things got much worse. Through the glass, the unmistakable blurred image of Eddie bounded towards the hallway door, a squeaking yellow plastic bone in his jaws, all flapping ears and wagging tail. He scratched industriously at the door, barking loudly through a mouthful of plastic bone, which added its own ear splitting shrill to his chorus. Damn the furry little sod! This sometimes happened pre-walk, he would become so overwhelmed with excitement that he'd want to play in the garden, and get a few practice cocks of his leg under his belt first. George had been so focused on his primary objective that he'd somehow overlooked this potential hazard.

"*George,* please let Eddie out will you, he needs to pee?" Mrs Butler's voice penetrated the glass door from the kitchen. Instinctively, he quickly clasped the telephone tight to his chest to drown out the noise.

"In a minute Mum, *I'm just on the phone!*" The Phone! He'd briefly forgotten about Summer.

"Err, sorry about that! Umm, *so when are you free?*" Silence. Had she hung up?

"If he wets himself, *you* can clean it up George!"

He shuddered, and once again muffled the telephone. "Mother, *I AM ON THE BLOODY PHONE!*" He pressed the telephone to his ear. Thankfully he could hear breathing. She was still there, there was still a chance.

"Err, *what was that?*" Cleary bewildered by the call, Summer finally broke her silence.

"Oh, err, nothing, so, how about this weekend then?" Eddie was now bordering on hysterics, and leapt up and down rhythmically against the glass, the yellow bone still clamped firmly in his jaws. It was all very distracting.

"Umm, well, yes that would be nice, *err,* would you like to come over for, *err,* supper perhaps on, *err,* Saturday evening?"

Before he could enthusiastically accept, the hallway door was flung open and Eddie bounded in.

"George, will you *please* let Eddie out for a pee, you can come back to the phone in a minute." Mrs Butler paused, raising a quizzical, mischievous eyebrow. "*Who is it anyway?*" She grinned playfully at her reddening son. It certainly wasn't Barney, that's for sure.

"Err, *no one!*" Pressing the telephone tightly against his chest again, probably leaving a dent in his podgy skin, he desperately fended off Eddie with his free hand. Just when success was in his grasp, it was suddenly all going horribly wrong again.

"*Hmmm,* well, just let Eddie out when you're done, *okay?*" And with a good-natured ruffle of his hair - something he really hated - she returned to the washing up bowl, thankfully taking Eddie and his yellow plastic bone with her. Breathing a grateful sigh of relief, he composed himself as best he could, and returned to the call.

"Err, hello, *are you still there?*"

"Oh, I thought you'd been cut off!"

"*Really?* Oh, probably just a bad line I expect. So, err, where *do you live then…?*"

Wednesday.

George pulled up outside Armada Branch at eight forty-five in the morning, smiled smugly, and reached confidently for the ignition key. After weeks of waiting in intensive care, a surgeon had finally been called, and the once terminal case of overrun, miraculously cured. Good old Dad.

Safe in the knowledge he could claim expenses, he fed the parking meter without a care and turned his face skywards. The sun was still shining, and showed no sign of being replaced with the seasonal cloud or rain. With any luck, the good weather might hold out for the weekend. Life was looking good. Following his success the previous evening, he was brimming with freshly caught confidence, and had even developed something of a fledgling swagger.

He greeted Di at the door like a returning guest to a television game show, relished the obligatory smacker on the cheek, even hugging her in reply, and sauntered passed the other cashiers exchanging pleasantries as old friends. The perfume still watered his eyes though. Briefly released from Bandit Land for good behaviour, he was here for some more training, and when he eventually climbed the stairs to the staff training room on the fourth floor, he found that once again, he was the last to arrive.

Belinda and Wesley sat opposite each other, virtually staring each other down. Wesley seemed to be dressed exactly the same, and Belinda wore the same suit, but this time had teamed it with a very clingy, black roll neck sweater, which emphasised her impressive figure more so than before. Despite this fresh perspective though, George still couldn't imagine her naked. Neither of them so much as nodded a welcome.

Along with the standoffish new recruits, there were three other new faces in the room. Two very different men, both somewhere in their mid-thirties, and a well preserved middle-aged woman with an impressive tan. The man who was seated was very striking, both in his appearance and build. Having removed his expensive looking, black chalk stripe suit jacket, *not pin*, he'd hung it on the back of the free chair next to him, so as not to get it creased, and was sitting in his shirt sleeves, one ankle casually resting on the knee of the other. This was how to successfully execute a nonchalant pose.

He was broad across the shoulders, yet narrow in the waist, in silhouette he would have resembled a large, perfectly dressed carrot. When he stood up, he'd be just over six feet tall, clearly no stranger to a dumbbell, he was muscular and athletic, without looking like a sandwich bag stuffed full of conkers, as some bodybuilder's tended too. His hair was black, flecked with grey, and cropped short in the current fashion. He wore a closely trimmed neat goatee, which looked as though it had been painted on by a very talented artist. The eyes were a piercing, slightly wild, bright blue and his eyebrows, easily as thick and impressive as George's, had been subtly pruned into an impressive, but no less masculine, arch. He looked like a film star from a stylish action movie, and had teeth like an American model.

Like Wesley, he too wore a crisp white cotton shirt, with a wide, full cut collar and double cuffs, but whereas the new recruit's looked stuffy and old fashioned, his was snappy, and of the moment. The cufflinks were Mont Blanc, the heavy knitted, grey silk tie, Aquascutum. The shirt, suit and shoes were all Hugo Boss, and the unusual, huge watch, with the thick black leather strap, a limited edition Officine Panerai. He was elegant, cool and sanguine, qualities that were sadly lacking in the new arrival.

He rose easily to his feet and shook the offered, mesmerised sweaty palm firmly. For the first time in his life, George was properly awestruck by a real human being, rather than character in a film or TV show. Although lately, he'd resented the process of growing up more than ever before, he suddenly decided that if he really had to grow up, he wanted to grow up to be this man. Even his aftershave was confident and welcoming. It seemed saunter up and warmly put its arm around his shoulder, offering him a drink in passing, and made easy conversation about his plastic shoes.

"Hey, I'm Dean, Dean Swift. Good to meet you. It's George isn't it? I saw you the other day when you were with Di." The voice was deep and level, with just a hint of South London about the accent.

"Yes, err, that's right, *I'm George.*" He really needed to stop saying that.

Dean smiled back into the dark, gleaming eyes, released the dripping hand from his own dry, strong grasp, nodded pleasantly and sat down. The new boy was just as he'd expected him to be. Bless him.

The middle-aged lady got to her feet, took hold of George's still outstretched palm, and shook it cordially. She was efficient-looking, in her grey knee length business suit, but still retained a good degree of approachability and warmth. She was also one of those married women who wore at least four highly impressive rings on their ring finger, just to get the point across.

"Good morning, I'm Stephanie King, we've heard all about *you* from Di and Rose. It's good to finally meet you, oh, and the others *of course*, who we already know…" There was just enough of a hint of insincerity about the last part of her sentence, to cause him to wonder if Belinda and Wesley were struggling to make new friends in the big city. Quite what Di and Rose had said about him though, would have to remain a mystery for now.

The second man stood expectantly next to the flip chart, looking frustrated and eager to get a word in edgeways. Crossing the short distance between them, he shook George lightly and delicately by the hand, as though he was afraid of physical contact. He was very thin and sinewy, like a long distance runner with an eating disorder. His hair was short like Dean's, although it was an almost a white blond, with streaks of what looked like orange. Presumably to take advantage of the November sun, he wore cream suit trousers and a pale blue, short sleeved shirt that exposed his wiry arms, a striped tie of white and darker blue and an elaborate, if slightly effeminate, gold watch. Unlike Dean though, this chap reeked of potent aftershave. One whiff made the new arrival sneeze.

"*Oh,* bless you! *I'm* Phillip Miles, I'm your trainer today! Do have a seat." George had very little experience with homosexuals. One of his classmates had once claimed to be gay, but he seemed to change his mind entirely, once the girls started developing breasts. Phillip Miles though, was in another league altogether. He was as camp as a Dusty Springfield tribute act.

"Right then, as you all now seem to know each other *I* won't bother with the usual round of introductions." He was obviously vexed that part of his agenda had been stolen from him. "Okay boys and girls, we're all here today to learn about Cottons' new approach to Credit Card sales. Dean and Stephanie, who as you know, are our Customer Banking Advisors," Phillip gave Dean a quick, approving glance, "Have kindly come along to offer their input and tell us what *they* are looking for, although *that* is all likely to change with the new process." He looked slightly smug, as though he knew something important that his audience didn't.

Dean bristled and stroked his goatee thoughtfully. He had pathological hatred of training sessions. It wasn't that he felt that he knew it all, by any means, nor did he think that it terms of new products or procedures, they didn't have their place. What he hated, was the Trainers. Long ago, he'd concluded that they must have been specially bred in an undisclosed, clinical unit for the sanctimonious.

Stephanie meanwhile wore a permanent, frozen expression of affability. She tended to take these sessions in her good natured stride, and instead secretly pondered on today's share price and whether or not the small apartment in Spain she had her eye on, was still available.

"*Right then!*" Phillip clapped his hands together and 'telegraphed' the audience, moving his gaze from one person to the other, so as to include everyone in the room. Naturally, he'd learnt this on a training course. "I want to start off today with a little game just to get everyone talking and relaxed, *"Is that okay, humm,* everyone - *everyone?"* Eventually, much to his relief, there were a few reluctant mummers of acknowledgment from the group. It was like pulling teeth with this lot.

Dean rolled his substantial shoulders, partly to free an ache from the gym, but mostly to intimidate the feeble Trainer. Soon he planned to start flexing his pectoral muscles under his tightly fitted shirt. That was bound to mess with the little cretins mind.

"Okay, well, *err,* where was I? *Oh yes,* now then, we're going to have a funny story competition! I'm going to tell you one, and then the group has to pick one of you lot to tell me one, okay? Then we'll vote who has told the best one, and whoever wins gets a box of *chocolates.*" Phillip seemed very pleased with this idea. He'd been up half the night trying to decide which story he should use to relax his audience. Given the crowd, it needed to be good.

"George." Dean uttered the name without looking up from his pad, on which he was absentmindedly sketching a picture of a skinny man in short sleeves being beaten to death by a burly boxer. It was rather good.

"Err, I'm sorry Dean, what *was that?*" Phillip was caught off guard.

"We'll choose George." He turned his piercing blue eyes to the bewildered new recruit. "Is that okay with you, my Man? I gather the Old Man found your last story funny enough."

Dean often shared the occasional lunch with his Senior Manager. He enjoyed a good, close working relationship with Mr Burton, despite referring to him as the 'Old Man'. Yesterday, in-between mouthfuls of excellent smoked salmon, Mr Burton had tried his very best to retell some of the new entrants Kavos escapades. It had turned into a very long lunch.

George wasn't quite sure what to do, or what to think for that matter. When he'd joined the Bank, he hadn't expected this at all. They seemed to want to hear more stories than a wide awake toddler at bedtime. But it was oddly comforting, almost reminding him of school on Monday mornings, with 'show and tell', or 'what I did this weekend'. At least this audience was smaller, and they didn't seem to be armed with miniature catapults made from HB pencils and elastic bands. Nothing hurt more at that age, than a high velocity, rolled and chewed strip of paper connecting with a pudgy cheek.

"Err, *really?* Blushing, he raised his eyebrows inquisitively at the rest of the group, but was met with silence and the odd blank shake of a head.

"If you don't mind? *Trainers* think it's a good way to relax a group, gets us to unwind a bit, before they start on the real reason we're all here. I'd rather not bother, but if we have too, I think we'd all rather hear one of yours." Dean paused, reflecting on something else the Old Man had said to him. "Make it a good long one though, anything to keep Phillip here quiet for a bit!"

"Umm, *okay then!*" George was confused. Who was in charge here, it certainly didn't seem as though the Trainer was? It was probably best to do as he was asked. With the challenge now falling to him, once again, he started scratching around in the corners of his memory for inspiration. He was likely to be a while.

Phillip meanwhile, wasn't enjoying this session at all. He'd already lost control of the group and he hadn't even taken out his marker pens yet. Stumbling over his words, he tried to pick up his thread again, before the big man ran off with it for good. "Right then, err, *I'll* go first..."

When Phillip at last finished his 'funny story', a dire account of a train journey he and his 'special friend' had enjoyed a few months ago, involving an inappropriately positioned and therefore hilarious lettuce, there followed what could only be best described as a prolonged and uncomfortable, tumbleweed moment.

"Err, *is it my go then...?*"

During the school summer holidays of 1991, and after endless weeks of relentless pleading, Barney and George were finally granted permission by their respective parents to embark on a weeklong camping trip. Both boys were approaching fifteen, and with this in mind, they were allowed to camp up to, but no further than, ten miles away from home. Just in case.

Over the past year, they'd become keen survivalists, immersing themselves in the after school Army Cadet Force, and secretly watching a terrible pirate copy of *First Blood* more times than was healthy for young men of an impressionable age. Pets in either household were no longer safe to roam the garden, as both boys became adept at setting traps with nothing more than a stolen length of knitting wool and a branch snapped from the rose bushes. Neither of them had the physique for a black singlet though.

Barney had obtained some kit from his Dad, a retired former Royal Engineer who now owned his own Taxi business, and George had been given a box of surplus supplies by his brother Michael, now serving in the Army, and briefly home on leave from Northern Ireland. Much to their disappointment, he didn't bring his gun.

The boys had carefully examined the box ahead of their proposed mission. It was stocked with everything they could wish for. Assorted ration packs, webbing, field dressings, lightweight trousers and combat jackets, none of which fitted, standard issue cooking equipment, and two pairs of freshly liberated army boots. The toes needed stuffing with cotton wool and newspaper to make them fit, but the thought was there nonetheless.

George borrowed Mr Butler senior's hunting knife, and Barney had managed to secure his Dad's treasured, standard issue SLR bayonet, and a relic from his days in the services. They were at last ready to embark on their trek into the unknown.

Finally, on the forth Saturday of the school summer holidays, Barney's Dad dropped the boys off, along with enough provisions and kit to supply a small battalion for a month, on the edge of the countryside. They had a map of the area, a compass and strict instructions as to which grid reference they were to rally too. Once the Taxi was safely out of sight however, in the spirit of excitement and adventure, the boys set off in entirely the opposite direction.

As they hiked across the increasingly remote countryside, like Fisher Price Rambos, their new boots rubbed excruciatingly with each step as the padding shifted, and the overburdened rucksacks reduced their feeble legs to jelly. Each face was a picture of grim determination, as though they were embarking on a secret mission behind enemy lines to capture a corrupt General. A mission so fraught with danger that was it way beyond the capabilities of the regular forces, that's why they'd been called, Barney and George, highly trained mercenaries who knew no fear. Virgin teenage imagination was a wonderful thing. It didn't however, account for a sense of direction.

"*Barney,* where the bloody hell are we?" George was feeling the strain somewhat more than his companion, thanks to his excess body fat, and now that the novelty had worn off, he longed for his comfy bed and a reassuring cup of tea. He leaned against a lonely tree, the tin cups and cooking pans that were securely lashed to his webbing, clanking like cowbells, and drained his water bottle.

The adventure had seemed like a good idea from the safety of the garden shed. Now though, at a little past two in the afternoon, and having already missed lunch, he was hungry, extremely weary, and utterly convinced he was bleeding to death from all his blisters. He needed a Cornish pasty and a cuddle, and not necessarily in that order.

Barney, who was about twenty yards ahead, stopped and consulted the map which dangled around his scrawny, freckled neck in a protective sleeve. The prolonged silence, coupled with the way he seemed to keep rotating the map, occasionally glancing at the surroundings in search of inspiration, only served to add to his teammates anxiety. Overhead, the clouds began to thicken.

"Err, well, we're somewhere between here," he pointed to random expanse of green, "And here, I think…" The second location was three inches from the first, about fifteen miles according to the scale.

"*What went wrong Barney?* I thought you had this all worked out?" George tried desperately to keep the panic out of his voice. Hungry was bad enough, lost and hungry was intolerable.

"Alright, *don't yell at me*. What happened was, it was all going fine and then, err, well there was a thick crease in the map which had torn, it was right where I wanted us to go and I sort of, err, well, lost my bearings for a while. But, *this is nice isn't it?* Look, there's a forest down there." He pointed enthusiastically towards the bottom of the other side of the hill, which actually now seemed to form one side of a wide valley. There was indeed a dense, slightly foreboding mass of thick green trees. "Let's go that way, there's probably a river at the bottom. It might make a good campsite." Grateful that as least they'd now being marching down hill, following an arduous two hour climb, George sighed, shrugged his aching shoulders and led the way, knowing that somewhere buried in his pack there was a tin of Heinz Baked Beans with his name on it.

What the boys failed to notice during their descent however, was the old, almost derelict farm house nestled in the very distance. It looked suspiciously as though it would be home to someone peculiar who probably kept pigs and had a fondness for the banjo.

When they eventually reached the floor of the valley, and having had fought their way through the thick, virtually impenetrable, eerie woodland, the boys stumbled into a lush green field roughly the size of two football pitches. It was completely surrounded by trees and a wide, fast flowing river with a small island in the middle, ran along the furthest edge. On the other side of the river, the valley wall rose steeply and was again, heavily wooded, and slightly sinister.

"Perfect spot!" Barney dropped his heavy rucksack into the long grass, "Protected from the weather on all sides, remote and with its own water supply and fish counter." Just like his Dad, he was a keen angler and had brought with him a collapsible rod and tackle, just in case the baked beans and Marmite ran out.

"Let's have a look at that island. We could camp there. *Cool eh?*" He waded excitedly through the grass towards the river bank, before suddenly tripping on something unseen and falling headfirst into the grass, momentarily disappearing from view. "*Oh hell!* I've landed in something horrible!" He got up slowly, holding his right forearm away from his body, like it was diseased and belonged to someone else. No one else would have wanted that many freckles though.

"What is it?" George examined the circular, hard brown object that had ambushed his teammate. It appeared to have concealed in the long grass, its crust now broken, the insides looked like a pie that had long since passed its best.

"Dude, it's a cowpat!" Both boys grinned at each other. In each tiny brain a light bulb had been simultaneously switched on, so much for growing up in the countryside.

"Oh, of course, didn't expect to see one of those all the way out here, random lost cow I guess?" Barney, still holding his arm before him, gingerly led the way to the river bank and dunked the offending, camouflaged arm into the crystal clear water. Despite the season, it still held the some of the chill of winter, and hopefully plenty of fish.

The river, which seemed to be no more than a few feet deep, was scattered with large rocks and boulders that formed stepping stones to the island. Thunderous white water tore between each of them, like miniature, enraged albino stallions, and the rocks were coated in lethal pea green, wet algae. Walking across them in combat boots was going to be hazardous, and would likely to lead to a good soaking, so the boys retreated to the safety of the river bank, stripped of their boots and thick socks, rolled up their lightweights as far as they could, and waded bravely into the water.

"*JESUS CHRIST!*" They pressed on tentatively through the icy water, the pressure of the fast moving water building on their exposed legs, carefully feeling the slippery pebble strewn river bed for firm footings with rapidly numbing toes.

At last, safely on the island, their ears filled with the roar of rushing water, they sat on a small patch of reluctant grass that grew on top of the two large rocks, and which formed the islands main land mass, trying to rub the feeling back into their extremities. The island was home to two short, but determined old trees, but not much else. Most of the head of the island had been battered into a smooth 'V' by the relentless, speeding river, but on the right hand side it planed away into a long, moss covered slab of flat rock, which the water poured off as small waterfall into a wide, very deep, slow moving pool. On the far side of this pool the river bank rose out of the clear water's edge and large oak trees hung over its depths.

"I'm not sure we could camp here Barney, it's really small and it'll be too noisy to sleep." George continued massaging his feet. He wasn't quite sure what was worse, blisters or frostbite.

"Yeah I know." Barney's eyes were alive with delight. "But I'm *definitely* fishing in that pool!"

They soon set up an impressive campsite twenty yards from the riverbank. After some initial fumbling and a few arguments, the tent and a makeshift lean-to that housed their kit was eventually secured, and a roaring fire, safely contained with rocks from the river bed, crackled comfortingly, whilst they cooked an eclectic and somewhat diverse meal, unlikely to win anyone a Michelin Star. On the menu was a large freshly caught trout, baked beans, burnt bread, which definitely *could not* be described as toast, lashings of Marmite, corned beef, custard cream biscuits, and coffee so strong and sweet, you could stand a spoon up in it. It was going to be an interesting, windy night in the tent.

"Ah, this is the life George, eh?" Sitting in the long grass, Barney leant back on a propped elbow and took another mouthful of fish. Now that he was fed and watered, George too was starting to relax and enjoy himself. A low summer mist was starting to descend on the valley, and the clear blue sky, having eventually beaten away the clouds, was getting ready for bed. With the ever present, hypnotic rush from the river, the occasional call of a nesting bird on the still evening air, and the sizzle of firewood, as a long forgotten pocket of moisture met with the flames, it was indeed an easy place to unwind and reflect.

By firelight, they played poker late into the night, and by the time they eventually retired to the thin nylon tent, Barney owed George just over four hundred and eight thousand pounds. He had been reluctant to take an IOU.

Still fully clothed and cocooned in their sleeping bags, they pressed against opposing walls, so as to be as far away from each other as was humanly possible in a six by four tent, and to avoid any involuntary tactile embarrassment. Exhausted, they soon fell into deep, untroubled sleep.

"*George, wake up!*" Barney whispered as loudly as he dared into the slumbering ear, eventually resorting to a few spiteful, well aimed pinches to rouse him.

"Ow! What the hell's your problem Barney, *get off me you perve!*"

"Shhh!" Even in the dim light, he could see that the fear in the ginger face was very real. "*There are people outside the tent.*"

"*What?* Are you sure?" George unzipped part of his sleeping bag and glanced at his Timex. The faithful indigo light revealing that it was just passed three in the morning. This time though, the usually comforting glow did nothing to quell his nightmares. He reached for a torch instead.

"*No*, no don't turn that on, they'll know we're in here."

"I *think* they'll already have guessed that Barney."

"What should we do?" Suddenly, there was a sharp whipping noise against the side of the tent, and the flutter of material. It sounded as though the lean-to had collapsed. Someone had obviously cut the guidelines. Then, slow heavy footsteps started circling the camp. They seemed to drag ominously through the long grass, as though a heavy axe was being trailed behind them. The cold hand of fear took a savage hold on the occupants of the tent.

"Where's your knife?"

"Under the lean-to, *err...*" George, his heart beating so hard he felt sure it would explode, carefully rummaged around in the tent for an alternative weapon. *"This'll have to do!"* He was holding a wooden spoon, which was coated in cold baked beans. With his dad's bayonet also outside, Barney had to make do with a military issue tin opener. They were hardly a formidable sight.

Suddenly, as they gazed pitifully at their armoury, something gradually pressed itself slowly against George's side of the tent. It crept towards them forming a small mountain of nylon around it. To the terrified junior soldiers within, it looked like a large, unyielding fist. And it was coming to get them.

No longer concerned with mutual proximity, they clung to each other, as the fist loomed ever closer. Trembling, Barney turned to George, his face ashen, utterly gripped in abject terror.

"Grab the torch, we go on three, okay?" His reluctant, petrified teammate nodded. It was a rapid nod, the nod of the totally unconvinced. He brandished his trembling wooded spoon regardless. So this is how it would end? Bugger!

"One. Two. *THREE! ARGHHHH!*"

Their bravery could not be faulted. Spurred on by great bucketfuls of once stagnant adrenaline, they stormed from the tent flaps in a wild, almost feral display of aggression. Screaming at the top of their lungs, violently thrashing their curious assortment of weapons like medieval broadswords at their unseen enemy and tormentor.

Surrounding them, dazed and confused by the torchlight and all the screaming, was a field full of ambivalent, grazing cows. Friesians apparently, according to Barney, who seemed to know about these things.

The cows had clearly chewed through the guidelines, and the fist had actually just been nothing more than an inquisitive snout. Although the threat of gruesome bloody murder, at the hands of a gang of interbred, marauding Hillbillies, seemed to have passed for now, the boys were still faced with something of a problem. If they stayed where they were, there was a good chance that the cows would simply eat the tent, and accidentally trample the novice Commandos in their sleep. Fortunately though, Barney had yet another plan.

"Right, let's put all the kit into the tent, collapse it, roll it up and carry it between us to the island with the kit inside. We'll have to sleep in just our sleeping bags, but it's warm enough. Tomorrow we'll find a new campsite, with no cows, *what do reckon Dude?*" George shrugged his shoulders. The overdose of adrenaline had now been flushed from his system, and had left him with nothing but painful fatigue, and a desperate need for a few bacon butties.

With an audience of curious, munching Bovine Terrorists, the boys recovered their belongings from the wrecked lean-to by torchlight, and roughly threw it all into the tent. After much swearing, and nearly losing a few fingers, they managed to eventually uproot the tent pegs and, with lightweights rolled up firmly past their knees once again, slowly made their way in the darkness to the river bank, the makeshift bag slung between them.

To begin with, things went reasonably well. Despite the stabbing icy needles from the fast river, they made good progress right up until Barney, who was naturally leading the way, stepped into an unseen, underwater hole. He twisted violently, lost his footing, along with the torch, and whilst still clinging onto the tent for fear of being washed away downstream, collapsed spectacularly into the freezing, rushing waters.

"*Hold on Barney!* HOLD ON!" George wrestled desperately with the bucking tent, whilst his soaked teammate fought bitterly to regain his footing on the slippery pebbles. Still desperately hanging on to the tent that joined them together, his freckled feet clawed at the river bed, dislodging rocks and stones, but failing to find any grip.

In his struggle, the muscles in his arms and back screaming from the effort, George also slipped off the stepping stones. He accidentally stood on a large, loose green pebble and, unable to balance himself with his arms fully engaged elsewhere, fell to his knees. He winced as the freezing river first enveloped his waist, and then grabbed hold of his privates in a less than ladylike manner. The torrent enveloped, and then took hold of the tent, tripling its weight. Overwhelmed, his fledgling strength spent, George tumbled face first into an unpleasant combination of wet nylon, and seemingly arctic waters.

The tent was quickly washed away, far out of the reach of the boys flaying hands, and disappeared into the dark shadows of the wide river, never to be seen again. Free of the uncontrollable, impossibly heavy tent, they grabbed hold of each other and battled on through the rushing black river to safety. Finally, after stumbling countless times on the greasy rocks, they eventually managed to make it safely to the island. Bruised and soaked, they sat in the darkness, and trembled uncontrollably. Fearing hyperthermia, they reluctantly huddled together for warmth on the thin grassy patch, and tried desperately to avoid each other's gaze.

Through chattering teeth, Barney was first to break the uncomfortable, awkward silence.

"*Well*, that could've gone better…"

For once, as he motored carefully through the endless backstreets, George paid little attention to either the MG's blowing exhaust, or the heart-breaking blues music from the stereo. It was just past one o'clock in the afternoon, he was heading back towards Nelson's Branch with a large box of Dairy Milk chocolates on his cracked leather passenger seat and a wicked, mischievous grin on his face. Phillip Miles probably wouldn't talk to him ever again.

As the old car growled onwards, past the heavily defended corner shops and the suspicious looking Gentlemen's Clubs, he reflected on the training course and wondered, like a hung-over school teacher who'd been dragged out on the town by his sixth form dance students, if he'd done or said anything he'd later come to regret. He usually had.

To begin with there was the competition, which he'd won almost by unanimous vote. Belinda's support had been unexpected, and it was only Wesley, teacher's pet that he was, who let the side down. Poor Phillip had seemed genuinely distressed to hand over the violet box of chocolates. Perhaps he had them earmarked as a gift?

George meanwhile, already planned to give them to his Mum as a gift, claiming he'd bought them with his first few days' wages. He knew that this simple gesture would easily ensure extra roast potatoes on Sunday, and, much to his Dad's irritation, the biggest slice of fresh fruit cake for at least a week thereafter. Even without giving in to the dishes.

The role playing session that had followed Story Time, had been somewhat enlightening. He hadn't even heard of role play before, let alone be expected to participate in one. It seemed to be little more than play acting, and this wasn't an area of strength for him. During his formative years at a small rural primary school, the vindictive spinster who'd taught year two, quickly realised this and, after taking a dislike to young Mr Butler, following an explosive conclusion to her cookery class, cast him as the lead in every school play, until he finally escaped to the local comprehensive. Even now, he still bore the mental scares left behind by the bright red stockings and endless lines.

Nevertheless, flushed with success after winning the chocolates, and still bubbling with confidence about his date with Summer, he decided to put these nightmares behind him, and give it his best shot. Leading up to the role play, Phillip had been enjoying centre stage for a while, discussing amongst other things, 'Word Patterns', which George thought sounded like something his Mum would have knitted. Belinda meanwhile, keen to win back some ground from the hairy one, and having taken to Word Patterns like a tramp to meth, was desperate to demonstrate her grasp of the concept to the others. The scene was set for an epic showdown.

Phillip arranged a couple of chairs in front of the flipchart, where various enthusiastic Word Patterns were scribbled in his barely intelligible, flowery script, and encouraged them to assume the role of the Bank Clerk and Customer alike, with George being bullied into adopting the role of the Customer. After a quick glance at the flipchart, and the virtually incoherent, hieroglyphic text, Belinda turned her steely gaze on her victim, and prepared to do her worst.

"Mr Butler, I see that you don't appear to have a *Companion Card* to accompany your Debit Card. I will ask one of our Advisors to see you immediately, and arrange one." Belinda was a revelation. She'd already learnt to exploit the whole 'Open', rather than 'Closed', questioning technique which Phillip had touched on earlier. This was a cunning method of communicating with others that didn't allow either a yes or no answer. Barney would have had a field day practicing this on the girls.

George just wanted the role play to be over as soon as possible, and with the minimum amount of effort or embarrassment on his part. "Oh, okay then, *thanks.*" He made to get up from his chair. The show was over.

"Now, *do* come on, George, put up something of a fight, a bit of resistance perhaps?" Phillip was getting frustrated again. He couldn't work with these people. His agent would have to hear of this.

The reluctant thespian desperately sought some deliverance in the polystyrene ceiling tiles. This wasn't what he'd signed up for. "Err, *well*, I'm not really bothered, thanks!" Now the show was over, surely? Unwittingly though, he'd given the star performer yet another golden opportunity to win her Oscar.

"Well, *I think* you should be, Mr Butler. A credit card is a useful, worthwhile item. Do you ever go on holiday, for example? Surely one should always take a credit card on holiday just in case?" She raised a perfectly plucked eyebrow challengingly. Belinda could do this all day long.

"Well, *yes, yes, I have* been on holiday." His mind suddenly filled with exotic, suntanned flashbacks. Toe rings, a drifting pedalo, cheap ouzo and the horny Club 18-30 rep. She never did write to him.

"And *would you* have found a credit card useful when you were enjoying this holiday, hmm?" Belinda was satisfied with the quality of her questioning. She felt she'd clearly demonstrated her superiority over the hairy joker in the cheap suit. Surely she'd left him without meaningful retort.

"Err, well, only if Barney and I could have used it as a paddle."

After arriving back at Nelson's, and enthusiastically updating Auntie Rose on the Summer situation, as well as his morning's exploits, he was overjoyed to be dispatched to the squalid restroom, to share a late lunch with the fabulous smelling Hayley, who always preferred to eat later in the day, in order keep her energy levels up for the gym.

Hayley casually questioned him about the training session, and in a light-hearted, conversational manner, tried to establish if any of the content had penetrated the thick mass of black hair, and been absorbed into his brain. Judging by his answers, it seemed unlikely.

"…And, and, you should have seen the look on his face when I won, it was just sooo funny! And then Belinda, *who I know can't stand me*, was trying to be all, like, well you know, *professional,* and all that, and she nearly exploded when I said what I did! *It was such a laugh!*" He paused briefly for reflection. "That bloke Dean burst into laughter as well. I quite liked him, seemed like a proper bloke, not like the trainer who was a bit, well you know, *Gay…*" He trailed off, eventually taking another stretching mouthful of a huge homemade Bap. Today was corned beef. Great thick slabs of the stuff, lashings of real butter and strong wholegrain mustard that made his eyes run. How he loved his lunchbox.

Hayley thought for a moment, her smile more coy than usual. Finally she came to a decision that amused her. This should be fun. "You know, George, *Dean is Gay too.*"

He froze mid munch. "*Whampht?!*" Trying desperately hard not to shower his gorgeous branch manager with the contents of his Bap, he tried to contemplate what he'd just heard. Surely this was a mistake, he'd misheard her, obviously?

"Yes, *Dean* is Gay too, although he doesn't really talk about it, and I've never seen him with anyone. He's a lovely bloke and, as you said, a proper man. Women *love him* - body of a Roman God, *and* money coming out of his ears. Shame really, I'd leave my chap for him any day…" She winked conspiratorially as her trainee cashier continued to struggle bravely with his Bap. This was all far too much to absorb on a virtually empty stomach.

"No way! *Really…?*"

That afternoon he was let loose on the Till again, the public having been notified in advance. The Bear was close by in case of emergency or adverse queuing, Anita was busy uploading Direct Debits and scowling, Auntie Rose was meticulously ordering the next epic load of stationary, from a vast depot somewhere in the Midlands, and Hayley was hiding in the interview room, laughing and joking with Dean on the telephone.

George was rather proud of himself. Aside from having a date with Summer to look forward to, and of course winning the chocolates, after almost two days of practice he seemed to have finally mastered the complexities of the cashiers stool. Like a novice surfer, finally standing up for the first time in open water, he found that he could now sit on, adjust and swivel his chair without having to frantically reach for stabilizing handholds, each time he felt himself losing his balance. Boasting a thorough and detailed understanding the Banks cashiering system, was nothing compared to this achievement. Not that he had any such an understanding yet.

He sat at the till surveying the empty banking hall, swinging the chair gently from right to left, with an almost unperceivable swish of his hips. Suddenly the glazed, metal-framed door swung violently open and a thuggish looking, tattooed native slouched in. A copy of *The Sun* wedged under his arm, a thin white plastic bag, clearly containing four cans of Special Brew, dangled lazily from his thick, sovereign ringed fingers. He was trouble personified.

"*Cash this?*" He threw a rumpled, heavily stained benefits Giro under the cashier's window, roughly dumping the beer and the newspaper on the counter top. Undeterred, George decided to try his luck.

"Err, I wonder, *would you like a credit card Sir?*" He grinned hopefully back at the brute.

"'ere, *what did you say?*" The man frowned so severely that it looked as though his eyebrow studs might abruptly pop out. His knuckles, which scraped the grey carpet, clenched.

"Err, *a credit card*, perhaps you would like one?"

"Why the *hell* would I want one of those bloody things?" In the back office, The Bear suddenly picked up his furry ears, and dragged himself out of hibernation. One of his unofficial roles was to act as a sort of Banking Peace Keeper. He was rather good at it.

"Well, you know, for holidays and stuff, like, err, your car breaking down or, err well, you know, err, perhaps, umm, *an unexpected pregnancy?*" This probably wasn't a word pattern that Phillip Miles would ever have condoned. Or for that matter, written on his flipchart.

Friday Afternoon.

With things going rather well over the past few days, George was starting to think that banking might just suit him after all. Having decided to treat the training course like any other form of education, he'd simply accepted what was said, acknowledged its content, agreed with its key messages, and then proceeded to do exactly what he liked instead. He soon decided that the best approach to this credit card business was to simply adopt the same method that Barney used to approach girls. Ask as many as you can in any given period, and hope you don't get slapped. He acknowledged that this was going to be somewhat more challenging, as he didn't have the time to get the customers drunk first. The bullet proof glass should provide some protection from the slaps though.

Much to The Bear's surprise, and slight disappointment, the tattooed thug with the Giro hadn't tried to rip the cashier's window off, and had instead sat patiently reading his copy of *The Sun*, waiting for Hayley to sell him a credit card. Something that the new cashier had said clearly struck a chord with him. And George hadn't stopped there.

There was a pleasant old lady who he convinced should treat herself to a nice little cruise, and who, as he neatly put it at the time, should whack it all on a credit card. A bleach blond bimbo who made up her own mind what she would spend the money on, despite a few nervous suggestions. The serial slot machine gambler, delighted that he'd found resources to keep him playing for another month or two, a beautiful girl who, oddly enough, *was* going to Kavos on holiday next year, and a sad, middle-aged man in a raincoat, who'd seemed keen once he'd established that he could draw cash from it.

Hayley was staggered by her new cashier's efforts. The rest of her team had always done their bit, referring the odd confused customer, but in the past this wasn't something Cottons had pushed that hard. There was an expectation that they should try their best in between the daily chores, but that was all. Customer service and tea breaks came first. From what she'd heard from Dean though, who'd heard it from Mr Burton himself, things were likely to change on that front, very soon. It was time perhaps, to leave.

"...And, and, well, you could treat yourself to a new, err trolley or, err *clothes?*" George was stretching both his new found abilities and the constraints of Credit Scoring with this particular customer. The bedraggled Tramp in the old, moth-eaten coat and tattered woolly hat, who'd left his entire world outside in a Co-OP trolley, looked at the cashier in utter confusion. Usually the staff just tried to get him out of the banking hall as quickly as possible, before he leaked something horrible on the battleship-grey carpet. This was a rather pleasant change.

"I think old Reggie just wants to cash his Giro and be on his way, *don't you Reggie?*" The Bear suddenly appeared at the till. It was getting late. Hayley still hadn't loaded the Cashpoint for the weekend yet, and old Reggie probably wasn't an ideal candidate for a card. Real Ale and a hearty steak pie would soon be calling. Something needed to be done. The Tramp nodded his head without comment, collected his weekly state allowance, and shuffled out of the bank, back to his mobile world with the wobbly wheels, and a lonely hot meal in a greasy café.

"George, stop with the Credit Cards now, *okay?*" The Bear loomed over him. His heart was momentarily filled with sadness for old Reggie. Miraculously enough, he'd a few morsels of lunchbox remaining, perhaps he'd like them?

"But, well, he *might* have been able to have one, you know - you hear all the time about Tramps that just choose to live that way, you know, *err*, the ones who are secret millionaires, that sort of thing?" He looked appealinglly up at the large hairy face.

"Don't be making those cow eyes at me, it won't work, *I'm not Auntie Rose*. And Reggie is a proper tramp, he's got the qualifications and everything, so leave it there, serve the bloody customers and let Hayley load the sodding cashpoint so we can all go home for the weekend, *OKAY?*"

It was time to turn off the conveyor belt until Monday, which was a shame really, because he was finding it all rather fun, especially when Wesley had unwillingly called that morning. It had been unexpected to say the least, and George sincerely thought Anita was playing some sort of complicated, evil mind game when she announced that his sworn enemy was on the phone asking to speak to him.

Extraordinarily nosy, and unable to take any call without an interrogation, she'd naturally demanded to know the reason for his call. Very reluctantly, he'd confessed he been asked by Linda to quiz his fellow recruit on his success with referrals, or as he actually put it, ask him to share his 'Best Practice'. It had been a truly wonderful moment.

Compared to the Supermarket, where praise and success eluded him like a seasoned criminal on the run, in just a few days the Bank had positively lavished him with congratulations. Even Mr Burton had gotten his fearsome secretary to call, a moment that had briefly sent a wave of terror crashing through the tiny branch, to extend his thanks and offer a ten pound *HMV* voucher in recognition. Chocolates, music and a girl, things were definitely looking up.

Nelsons branch of Cottons Bank PLC, unlike its larger contemporaries, closed at four thirty in the afternoon, giving the staff a precious half hour to batten down the hatches, shred anything suspicious, and finish off any loose ends. Thanks to George's relentless pursuit of credit card referrals though, Hayley hadn't had much time for anything else besides interviewing a diverse collection of somewhat curious, if not slightly dazed and confused customers. When she eventually emerged from the tiny grey office, looking a little less composed than usual, drained by the afternoon's endless interviewing, she gathered the small team together behind the tills, taking her own slightly more luxurious seat with a relieved sigh. Sod the gym tonight. She needed a large glass of wine.

"Well, that was *quite* a day! George, I think it is safe to say that sending you on that training course wasn't a waste of time! Well done, great job!" She leaned forward slightly, so that he was within easy reach and, much to his delight, rubbed his arm lightly. He was growing rather fond of her arm rubs. He even intended to try a few press-ups this weekend, in order to firm up a bit, in preparation for next week.

Hayley glanced at the office clock. She chose not to wear a watch. It was nearly quarter to five. Should she get a bottle from the off licence before the ghouls started roaming the streets?

"I need a volunteer to stay behind, and help me with the cashpoint, *any takers?*" The Bear, who longed for the rugby club and his pint of cloudy, real ale, suddenly found something interesting to stare at on the ceiling, as did Anita, who needed to squeeze into something cheap and revealing, hit the town and find yet another a desperate sailor. Auntie Rose was just about to offer her help when she was interrupted. This was new.

"*I'll do it Hayley!*" George's services being offered less so out of duty, and more so out of teenage lust. He was after all, technically still single, and obviously wildly ambitious.

An empty Bank, free of any customers, and most of its staff, was an eerie place to be in the dark winter months. Auntie Rose had turned off most of the lights, when she and the others had left just after five, and now, with only a solitary bulb in the cashpoint room for illumination, unfamiliar shadows were cast in every corner. It was all rather unsettling, and not at all romantic.

On the table in the middle of the darkened room, was a dimly lit, three foot square cube of crudely wrapped plastic bundles. Each of these bundles was about a foot long, and contained either ten or twenty pound notes, and each of these was divided into thousand pound wads. George Butler was stunned into an unusual, rare silence. This was real money.

Despite the chill outside, Anita's insistence that the heating thermostat be firmly screwed off the wall at all times (It was hot where she came from, cautioned The Bear), combined with the exertion of lifting the cash from the safe, meant that Hayley had long since discarded her suit jacket and high heels. She now toiled in bare feet, her short skirt, and a fitted, slightly transparent white poplin shirt. A closer, detailed inspection soon confirmed that the material very nearly revealed every embroidered feature of her padded bra. Or rather it did if you were prepared to look hard enough, and the light was just right.

As she fused over the open back of the cashpoint, slightly bent as she wrestled with the cash containers, she seemed to sense that her assistants mind was elsewhere, on many levels.

"If you're thinking of asking me to grab the cash and run away with you George, I'm afraid I've got plans this weekend, and so, *do you*, I gather?" Hayley glanced at her new recruit over her shoulder, grinning playfully. "But there's always next weekend though!" She walked over to the desk, where he'd been lurking, utterly mesmerised, and grabbed a thick wad of plastic wrapped twenties roughly, in way that made his blush deepen. He glanced at his trusty Timex in an effort to distract his thoughts. It was now half past five. His stomach would be craving some attention soon.

He'd thought that, alone in the back office, he would enjoy her company and good natured flirtations, but instead had soon felt completely out of his depth in her presence. She was breath-taking, and she talked like sexy girls do in the movies. His inability to find anything even remotely funny or meaningful in reply to her banter proved to do nothing for his confidence. Suddenly his evening meal with Summer looked daunting. He needed some reassurance.

"*Umm*, so, do you know her very well then?"

"Who?" She was bending over again. Despite the light revealing even more than a bra strap this time, he averted his eyes for the sake of his sanity. Focus George, focus.

"*Summer.*"

"Oh, well, no not really. She tends to keep herself very much to herself, and she never comes out on any of the bank functions. Sweet girl though, perhaps a bit shy for you maybe?"

"*Really?* But, well, umm, don't you think that, err, *I'm* shy too…?"

Hayley loaded the last of the cash containers, straightened up, and walked towards him slowly, the ever present smile causing a number of his more unstable emotional chemicals to react spectacularly. Briefly, no matter how unfeasible it might've seemed, he was convinced she was going to kiss him. Instead, disappointingly, she ruffled his mop of hair. "No George, not in the slightest."

With the pile of cash reduced to no more than a collection of torn note bands and ripped plastic, the cashpoints thick metal door was sealed tight. After leaving her new recruit utterly lost in a wilderness of new and interesting questions, Hayley spent an age inputting data into the unit, via a tiny number pad that was concealed behind a smaller hatch. Finally, it looked as though the whole process, emotional and mechanical, was coming to an end. George was none the wiser on either count.

"I'll show you how all this works soon, when we've got more time and it isn't a Friday evening, it's fairly simple really, it just takes ages to tell it how much money it's holding. Right, *we're done!*" She slammed down the hatch, locked it and picked up her jacket from the chair where she'd discarded it earlier, slipping into it, and ending the show that had earlier driven the audience wild.

She sauntered back to her desk, hips swaying slightly. Picking up her red leather handbag, Hayley fished around in it for the car keys to her pristine, VW Golf GTI, and turned back to George who was now standing a few feet away from the cashpoint. He still had the same look on his face. Poor love. "Can you get the lights please? The switch is round the corner by the cashpoint - make sure you get the right one."

Besotted, confused and casually amorous, despite the odds, he lazily backed up a few feet, not wishing to take his eyes off the staggering silhouette before him. Without looking at what he was doing, he reached around the corner of the room and felt along the wall for the light switch. Groping fingers, tired from the till and playing with his loose change, eventually found what he thought he was looking for. It felt bigger and much chunkier than a normal light switch, and his extended digits struggled at first to flick the reluctant, heavy switch off.

After a lengthy, drunken debate with Barney, George had eventually concluded that his favourite meal was, without question, a Sunday roast. *His* Mum's Sunday roast to be precise, although everyone's Mum makes the best Sunday roasts. It was a fact of life.

George's only caveat though, apart from the obvious issue of the never ending dishes, only became apparent once it had gone. Once Mrs Butler has removed the last of the piping hot roasting tins, once the meal was served and the thick silky gravy ladled into its boat, and once the oven was finally switched off. The relentless drone from a Sunday roast oven, endlessly going about its important business, is one that you don't realise you need relief from until it has finally been silenced, leaving nothing more than the gentle lilt of BBC Radio Two, a steaming plate of fabulousness, and a kitchen full of dirty dishes. Peace at last.

As it soon became apparent, it is more or less the same with Cashpoint machines. Like Sunday Roast ovens, they too emit a monotonous drone, which although doesn't drive you to distraction in quite the same way, it is still rather an unexpected and pleasant relief once they are eventually switched off.

The only problem, however, was that they should never actually be switched off.

Chapter 6

Butterflies and Curry

Saturday Afternoon.

To a soundtrack of grinding metal and a slipping clutch, George Butler performed an entirely unnecessary, and poorly executed racing gear change from third to second, and flung the reluctant old car around the hairpin, budget tyres screaming pitifully for mercy, as they once again fought desperately for grip. When at last the ordeal was over, and a long straight thankfully stretched out ahead of them, the MG still traumatised and quivering like a scolded toddler, rumbled on, leaving its brutal driver to revel in the pleasing, bubbling growl that came from the newly fitted, stainless steel exhaust. It was going to be a good drive.

The exhaust, which had once represented a large chunk of his meagre savings, had been laying on the garage floor for three weeks, waiting to be fixed to the MG. Sadly, a combination of poor weather, and his new found reluctance to get out of bed early on a Saturday morning, soon saw it gather dust. Dust, which once it was attached, quickly caught fire.

His Dad however, had an agenda of his own. And in an unusual move for a normally reserved character, he'd barged into George's Pit just after ten to make his feeling on the subject bitterly clear. It had been one of those rare father and son moments that neither of them cherished. A few hours and a few minor flesh wounds later, the MG was sounding remarkably healthier. The twin SU carburettors had been balanced, the fluids topped up, and after a rather invasive deep clean, both inside and out, the classic car was at last looking classic, instead of just old and decrepit.

In order to take advantage of both the unseasonal pleasant weather, and his newly revitalised transport, George had taken the longer, much more picturesque route over the countryside to Summer's cottage. It was what his Dad would have called 'The Pretty Way'. It normally meant he was lost.

As he turned off onto the B road, which if he'd read the map correctly, would hopefully lead to Summer's little hamlet, he finally opened the lid on the jar of adrenaline that had been sloshing about since he'd woken up that morning. Free at last, it mingled affectionately with the warm glow of joy and happiness, which was already bubbling away inside of him. He was excited and eager in equal measures, yet perhaps most importantly, he wasn't scared anymore.

His first week of employment at Cottons had very nearly passed without any major accidents. But as the drone of the Nelson's branch cashpoint faded and eventually died, so had his hopes that he'd actually managed something of a good start. Hayley was a revelation though. Whereas in the Supermarket, he'd have been virtually strapped to the shelving after hours, and flogged to death for even a minor blunder, through slightly gritted teeth, she'd repeatedly told him not to worry, and that everyone makes mistakes. It was a collection of words he was becoming familiar with since his interview.

The cashpoint reboot process took nearly three hours. But after telephone calls were made to both cancel a romantic dinner date, and to ask that a huge plate of Shepherd's pie was left in the oven for later, Hayley ordered a twelve inch pizza from the takeaway and sent the guilty party out for a bottle of red. In the dim light of the back office, munching on roughly cut slices and sipping wine from cracked corporate mugs, it was practically a date, in George's mind at least.

By the time they eventually left the branch, just after nine, a small but vital change had occurred. Once the guilt had passed, or at least subsided, and the mug of alcohol had dissolved some of the early naivety he'd felt in his Manager's presence, he'd begun to chat freely to her, almost without blushing. It was one thing for Hayley to think he wasn't shy, but actually having the skills to be outgoing, especially in the presence of attractive older women, was something else entirely. Nevertheless, those few hours did wonders for his confidence, ahead of his date.

His parents had been naturally curious, as far as they knew their son had only ever had one girlfriend before. Following a good-humoured, if somewhat inquisitive interrogation, he eventually told them everything, once again proving that he would have made a terrible spy.

Things were definitely looking up for the Butlers. Not only had their son finally found suitable, gainful employment, he was also going to date a fellow Banker, and an older one at that. She even had her own house. Mr Butler senior mentally began measuring up his son's bedroom. Would he at last have the hobby den which he'd craved for so long? His interest in the forthcoming date suddenly intensified, he needed to play his part in making sure it went well. The car! He'd fix it up, and make him clean the old MG. As far as he could remember, girls always like a shiny motor.

After much squabbling, Mrs Butler had finally been able to convince George to let her tend to his wayward eyebrows, something that she'd longed to do since they had sprouted some years previously. Once the hairy caterpillars had been skilfully pruned, everyone, even their reluctant owner, was astounded at the difference it made to his appearance. Ever so slowly, like the very same caterpillars gradually morphing into butterflies, a change was taking place.

But his Mum's involvement didn't stop there. Whilst she had him metaphorically pinned down, she trimmed away his split ends, and tidied the hair around his neck with a few deft, terrifyingly close slices of her razor-sharp scissors. It had all been very distressing.

Somewhat lighter, and breezier around the ears, George retreated to the reassuring surroundings of his bedroom, to select a suitable outfit for his date. He'd read somewhere, that at some point in his late teens or early twenties, a man will start to adopt a style of dress that they usually maintain until either they get old, or get married. He was still waiting for his style to stumble into him, when he found what was to become his most treasured item of clothing, a black waist length leather jacket.

Some months ago, long before his interview, he and Barney had bravely ventured into the city with some hard earned cash. With both boys desperate to improve their chance with the ladies, they'd set out to find a pair of achingly cool leather jackets, in the hope that they would ultimately bring girls flocking to their doors, knickerless and awestruck. At this point they were willing to try anything.

Following a relatively successful sortie, jackets were bought and George at least soon embraced a staple outfit of jeans, T-shirt and leather jacket, regardless of either the weather or occasion. But whist this had been perfectly acceptable in the local pubs, although he was getting a little tired of all the Elvis jibes, his Mum suggested that in order to look the part for a date, it would be necessary for him to temporarily ditch this casual image.

During his epic exploration of the outer reaches of his vast wardrobe, he'd been delighted to find magazines and vintage comics, he'd long since given up hope of ever recovering, always suspecting that they'd been the victim of yet another spring time purge. *Beanos* and *Dandys*, along with a once prized copy of *The Guitarist*, were found unmolested and in a near perfect condition, as was a treasured bag of marbles and, miraculously enough, and ancient Kit-Kat that had somehow escaped consumption.

As he sat on the edge of his bed, munching on his slightly stale find, George considered the outfit he'd unearthed on his adventures. Some particularly spirited foraging, culminating in a tug of war with an unseen entity, had eventually yielded a pair of crumpled chinos, and a half decent white cotton shirt he couldn't recall every owning. Suspecting that it was probably one of Michael's, he gave both the items a careful sniff. Satisfied that they still had the unmistakable, endlessly fresh smell that was a Mrs Butler signature, he set about the task of ironing them flat. Two hours later, he was still at it.

Finally, wearing his Clarks desert boots, a constant companion, until they eventually fell apart and were replaced with an identical pair, leather jacket and a hearty splash of birthday Old Spice, he was ready. As his parents stood hopefully on the doorstep, waving off the gleaming MG, they crossed their fingers, and hoped it wouldn't break down before their youngest son had a chance to make a good impression. It was a proud moment.

The B-road was completely empty. Flanked on either side by beautiful, winter countryside, and with clear blue skies over head, it was almost perfect. Only the addition of a warm summer breeze, rather than the cold November chill, could have improved the moment. Although a committed child of the tropics, in all but the worst rainstorm, George insisted on driving around with his window firmly wound down. And now, with the MG's inefficient heaters battling bravely against the elements, he shivered in the crisp draft.

Keeping one eye on the road ahead, he reached down to the tiny glove compartment and fished around for another tape cassette to replace Bon Jovi. After the initial excitement of the journey, and having enjoyed his rejuvenated toy, something more in tune with the moment was required, something that would settle him down a bit, dilute the adrenaline to a safer level once again. After narrowly missing a bewildered sheep, whist he was up to his elbow in tape cassettes, he finally found what he was looking for. Ever since he'd had taken to listening to late night radio, somewhere in his early teens, he'd been tormented by a song that seemed to be played almost every night, but frustratingly that the velvet voiced DJ failed to either announce or identify to the listeners. The torment was unbearable.

Even at his tender age, he found the song desperately haunting. It seemed to be about regret and reflection about summers past, girls long since lost. For some unknown reason, this angst appealed to him. It conjured images of out of season seaside attractions, always such depressing places once the tourist have finally gone home, and a picture of a beautiful girl driving alone along a deserted road beside a flat, calm ocean. The sun beats down on the gleaming body of her silver Porsche, a 356 speedster, *not* a 911. Her brunette hair streams out behind her, ray bans shielding pretty blue eyes and a white cotton shirt, which occasionally yields to the wind, revealing a modest, pert sun tanned cleavage. But then, he was just fourteen, and positively pickled in testosterone.

It was only years later that he finally discovered the identity of both the song and the artist. Don Henley's *'The Boys of Summer'*. Now, along with the other tracks that accompanied it on the Best Of album, it was one of George's favourites. As such its case was battered, its sleeve creased, and more than once had it needed to be rewound with a pencil.

He settled into the cracked leather seat, turned his collar against the gust from the window, and smiled to himself as the words of the song, and the unmistakable riff, blended perfectly with the throaty growl from the new exhaust. This was the life. At last totally relaxed, his mind got up, dusted the crumbs of his jumper, and decided to go for a gentle wander. Soon he was in the grip of deep reflection. His thoughts drifting off both towards the evening ahead with Summer, and also back in time, to his modest past, and the very few girls that he'd known so far.

George's introduction to nookie had been an entirely unexpected, yet very welcome, affair. During the school summer holidays that would eventually see him turn sixteen, he found that after just a few weeks, he was both bored and in need of extra pocket money.

After some debate, and quickly dismissing the possibility of conventional employment, he and Barney decided that a possible way of generating extra cash would be to offer their services locally as odd job men. Mr Butler senior, despite suggesting that 'odd boys' might be more appropriate, was coaxed into printing off forty or so leaflets from his works computer, all of which were then popped through the most local doors they could find. They were prepared to work, but not necessarily to travel.

Encouragingly, the telephone enquires came thick and fast, and very soon both boys were busy painting fences, mowing lawns and attempting to repair things they had neither the qualifications, or abilities to tackle.

One such enquiry came from Gabriella Smith. She called, enquiring if George would be able to tidy her garden, perhaps take a look at a sticking window, and maybe paint the garage door. It seemed like a good few days' work, and as she only lived at the bottom of the estate, he'd be able to come home for beans on toast at lunchtime too. Opportunities this good were hard to find.

It was a baking hot summer's day when he knocked on the door of Gabriella's two bed semi. Armed to the teeth with tools borrowed from the potting shed, a can of WD40 from his Dad's toolbox and small snack box to keep him going for the morning, he wasn't at all prepared for what happened next.

Gabriella answered the door wearing only the briefest of red polka dot bikinis, and a handkerchief for a sarong. This was nothing like he'd expected from someone called Mrs Smith.

"*'ello* Jorge, do come in *eh?*" Until quite recently, Gabriella Smith had been Gabriella Venturi, but after meeting a dashing Englishman, who worked aboard a cruise ship that was visiting her native Positano, she'd quickly fallen in love and become married, the rather fabulous and exotic name of Venturi being replaced with Smith. The Italian temperament and demeanour though, were not as easily lost.

She was without question, the very definition of a sultry Italian temptress. Twenty eight years old, and a little over five feet tall, she was a slim size six, but an eight at Christmas, yet curvy in all the right places. Her long, slightly wavy black hair reached the middle of her small back, and was layered at the jaw line, falling about her shoulders in a carelessly seductive fashion.

Standing in her hallway wearing old, unflattering, cut-off denims that proudly exposed his newly hairy legs, and a dirty white *Garfield* T-shirt, her odd job boy was stunned into an unusual silence, and left longing for his camera. Barney would never believe him.

With her hands on her hips, in the traditional Italian manner, and with an occasional gesticulation of her right, she then began to list the jobs she wanted doing, and enquired about the cost of his services, all of which suddenly became free of charge. She seemed quite oblivious to her state of undress, and the effect it would have on the scruffy hormonal youth. It was a very long list, and the garden was badly overgrown. George eventually recovered the power of speech, just long enough to offer her a daily rate, which she agreed was very reasonable, and he quickly set to work.

As she watched him toil in the late July sunshine from the comfort of her sun lounger though, sipping a Peroni and twirling a strand of hair between her delicate fingers, a strange feeling began to warm in her tiny brown belly. Her husband, William, was a true gentleman, and it had been this attribute, along with the seemingly glamorous life he led aboard the cruise ship, that had originally drawn her to him. But his work took him away to sea for long periods of time, and soon after they had settled in England, near his family, she'd started to miss her beloved Italy. Recently she'd found herself looking at their wedding photographs, wondering what she ever saw in the pale faced man standing next to her in the first place. She had to constantly remind herself of all his positive qualities, and the fun that they'd once enjoyed together.

Now though, on this sweltering, almost Mediterranean day, there was a new distraction. And it was busy trimming her gladioli.

George had taken on quite a deep tan, thanks to the surprisingly hot English summer, and coupled with his longish black hair and heavy eyebrows, he looked somewhat Italian himself. Gabriella soon discovered that if she squinted a bit, and was charitable about the belly, he was virtually identical to Pablo, her very first love back in Positano. William had been at sea for months now, leaving Gabriella bored, extremely homesick and completely unfulfilled. Suddenly Pablo looked very attractive.

"Eh, Jorge, could you avva looka my bedroom window, *itsa stickin'?*"

And so began the most amazingly explicit, eye-opening weeks of George Butler's life.

His parents never really quite got to the bottom of why Mrs Smith needed their son's services for almost the whole summer. When they asked him casually over dinner one evening, he'd simply told them both, quite sincerely and innocently, that Mrs Smith had a badly overgrown bush which she was unable to tend herself, as she was largely bedridden. George never lied to his parents.

Before long, he was a new man. He wasn't scared of the dark anymore, he found he could talk to girls for almost a whole two minutes without blushing, and he'd even lost a few pounds. Most importantly, everything below the waist seemed to work just fine.

Aside from the obvious, Gabriella also taught him another two important lessons that summer. How to dance and how to cook, although he secretly suspected that some of the dance moves he'd perfected may just have been a little too risky for a family wedding, and he was quite certain that clothes should generally be worn.

Perhaps more practically, he was taught how to cook two important staple Italian meals: Lasagna and Ragu - traditional Ragu mind, of the Sophia Loren variety, and he soon learnt that prepared jars of the stuff were frowned upon in this household.

Sadly, he learnt another, far less palatable lesson that summer when the unexpected love affair suddenly ended. Gabriella's dull husband William had returned home from sea, and all the gardening, cookery and dance lessons had abruptly ceased. Naturally he sulked, in the same way he did when he was denied extra pudding, but this time there was to be no third helpings.

When it became apparent that the door to Little Italy had well and truly been closed for the time being, and having grown rather fond of his new hobby, he decided to set out and seek a replacement for his Italian Goddess.

Despite being ruined for girls his own age by his ravishing Italian tutor, he eventually met Amy, a fellow A Level art student who had an unusual passion for saving the orang-utans of Borneo. She shared their strawberry-blond colouring, and was averagely pretty, had an average sort of figure and average, amiable personality. They enjoyed an unspectacular relationship of sorts for a while, which meant neither of them was lonely on a Saturday night. But compared to his summer long, unbelievably passionate affair with the spectacular Gabriella, the whole thing was like a much anticipated, but hugely disappointing sequel to a favourite film.

Hoping to find some passion in his life again, he separated from Orangutan Amy, an almost mutual decision at the time, and took his chances in the pubs again with Barney instead. The months that followed were barren and frustrating, and until he arrived in Kavos, what seemed like a lifetime later, a vital part of his anatomy was living on nothing more than bread and water.

From what little he could remember of events, once in Kavos, he vaguely recalled two nights of drunken nookie. Firstly there was the girl with the feet, but no door handle, and secondly a wild evening with their Club 18-30 rep, which had come as quite a surprise to all those involved, not least her boyfriend, who found them the next morning.

A few miles away, safely cocooned in her tiny cottage, Summer was also reflecting on her own life, and desperately fretting over the complex Indian meal she was preparing.

Chaffinch Cottage was an extremely old grade two listed, former miners dwelling, which she'd been renting the for the past five years. Refusing to move any closer to the city, she rather liked the relative solitude of the tiny hamlet it was nestled in. People tended to keep themselves to themselves, and nothing untoward ever happened. Perfect.

The cottage had a freshly painted, bright red door, and whitewashed walls both inside and out. It was in the middle of a terrace of five and had a small garden in the front, and a slightly more generous one at the back, allowing Summer to grow a diverse herb garden and vegetable patch, with varying success.

Not unlike its inhabitant, the home was scrubbed industriously twice daily, with traditional, time-honoured products, and a good degree of elbow grease, yet still somehow managed to remain slightly dishevelled. The stripped wood floorboards were polished to a slightly lethal, but none the less impressive, glossy shine and the collection diverse, slightly disconcerting ethnic ornaments were buffed and in perfect order. At the last count, forty-eight tea light holders of various designs were scattered about the lounge, and when they were all ablaze, the tiny inglenook fireplace was hardly needed for warmth, even on the coldest, loneliest night.

For the moment though, both Order and Reason had packed their bags and had left Chaffinch Cottage for quieter shores. Every surface of the tiny kitchen was littered with some sort ingredient, flour, tins of tomatoes and coconut milk, various Indian spices and powders including garam masala, gloves, turmeric, and chili. A huge damp bush of coriander, freshly plucked from her herb garden, and quickly rinsed to remove any unwanted visitors, which might add yet more flavor or the occasional crunchy bite, rested next to her well-worn copy of *Indian Food for Beginners*. Summer's cookery skills never managed to graduate beyond the beginner's stage.

Looking even more tousled than usual, her disobedient hair under attack from random sprigs of coriander and a dusting of flour, she read the page again and tried to establish quite where she'd gone wrong. Was it somewhere around the first paragraph perhaps?

The brown mess that had welded itself to the heavy, bright orange Le Creuset pan, and that also covered most of the stove, the kitchen tiles, a small section off the ceiling and Summer herself, looked nothing like the picture in the book that the charming Indian lady was holding. It might well be time to order a takeaway.

The naan bread had been a much easier affair, and apart from the many types of seeds that the recipe dictated, it wasn't too dissimilar to making regular bread, which she was rather good at. Her lunchtime experiment had gone rather well, even the oven didn't smoke, and she now felt capable of making nice, fresh naan bread without causing an explosion or a small fire, when her guest arrived later.

But this small success didn't detract from her sneaking suspicion that she should've simply bought a readymade curry mix, and poured it over the chicken instead of ambitiously attempting to cook one from scratch. Wine, wine would help. She opened the fridge door that was covered in postcards from far flung corners of the globe, photographs of her family, and the odd enthusiastic painting from a five-year-old nephew, and pulled out a chilled bottle of chardonnay. It was too early to start drinking really, but Summer needed to find some balance and calm her nerves. Wine was always a good leveller.

Summer Roberts was twenty-six, and well aware that her life, so far at least, had contained very little in the way of romance or passion. She'd only ever known one man in that way, and it had been a very, very long time since she'd known him. David had been her sort of boyfriend during their A Levels, and as they'd both ended up studying Art at the same university, the role was continued tentatively through those three years as well.

Apart from very occasional, almost dutiful moments of physicality, which became every more scarce as the years passed, they were largely indifferent to each other, like brothers and sisters who don't get on. As their university degree came to an end, so did their relationship. There were no explosive hysterics though. No long drawn out deep and meaningful conversations about wanting different things, and no arguing over who bought what. They simply packed up and drifted off to different corners of the country, and never saw or spoke to each other ever again.

Since then she'd been on just two dates. Neither of them made it to a second, and neither of the frustrated suitors was ever allowed to offer even so much as a peck on the cheek goodnight. They just didn't feel quite right. As such, Summer's lady garden had been left unattended for a very, very long time.

In her mind, she wasn't conventionally pretty, nor was she a dedicated follower of fashion. She'd adopted a style of her very own that was loosely ethnic and heavily inspired by a treasured family holiday to India when she'd been at an impressionable age. She had long since learnt not to care what other people thought, or at least, to try and not care.

Ironically enough though, Summer actually *was* the sort of girl, that if she'd ever been spotted by a modelling agency, would've found herself working for Calvin Klein before her ankle bracelets could've rattled in protest. Work would be required of course, and plenty of conditioner, but the basic bone structure and slight figure were perfect. Her natural, almost ethereal quality would have been bewitching on the catwalks of Milan. All she'd need to do was simply learn how to pout.

She calmly sipped her Chardonnay, and gazed wistfully at her fridge door. Amongst the images, there was a recent photograph of her wayward older brother, James. After his A Levels, he'd soon decided that conventional life just wasn't for him, and instead embarked on a mind expanding, soul searching gap year. That had ten years ago, and now, at twenty-eight, he was still wandering the earth in search of everything, from the meaning of life, to the perfect cappuccino. Everything, thankfully, still eluded him.

Did she quietly envy his wild abandon, should she have tagged along when he originally set out for Australia all those years ago? What sort of person would she be now if she'd found the courage to follow that path? It didn't pay to dwell on these questions for too long.

Her younger sister April was twenty-four and happily married to Kris, an Austrian classical musician. She was the perfect stay at home mother to three unbelievably adorable girls. The photograph of them that had been taken last Christmas in Austria was all snow, love and thick woolly jumpers. Bless them.

Finally there was the monthly postcard from her parents. Having spent most of their lives pursuing sensible careers, in order to pay the bills and feed their three children, a few years ago, sensing that their work was done, they'd finally retired, and retreated to an idyllic French village in Provence. At last they were able to pursue a long held dream of resuming their own artistic studies, a family trait that both their daughters had inherited. Summer didn't need to pluck the postcard from its Blu-Tack prison, to be reminded of their constant invitation to join them in the peace and serenity of Provence, to help them run the artists retreat they had now established there.

What was it that kept her here? It certainly wasn't her job, she only considered that a modestly lucrative distraction that kept her from being creative full time. Perhaps it was just a desire to paddle her own canoe for a while, even though lately, she had to admit that she'd considered turning south on occasion.

And what of this new arrival, this unexpected visitor that had suddenly arrived on the scene, what did all this mean, and why on earth had she invited him over for supper? There was undeniably an attraction there. Like the pony she'd learnt to ride on, he had a kind eye, and was handsome enough, in a suitably scrubbed, yet desperately unkempt way. But it wasn't this that had drawn him to her. Nor was it just the revelation that he too had claimed some artistic interests, although this was intriguing. Maybe it was simply that, just like her, George didn't seem to belong in the Bank.

Summer shook herself out of her daydream. It was nearly four and the kitchen diner was not at all ready to receive polite guests. Checking the brown mess for the hundredth time, she finally made the brave decision to disguise any flavour and colouring issues with a generous handful of chilies, the whole bush of damp coriander, a few table spoons of turmeric, and the remains of the coconut milk. It would be fine. All men liked hot curry, surely?

George glanced at his sparkly new Seiko, leapt momentarily from his seat as his prolonged gaze, and subsequent drift, drew a loud blast from the oncoming Ford, and guessed that he was now at least half an hour away from Summer's cottage. He was rather proud of his new watch. The sales clerk might well have lost the will to live, as his customer fretted over the adjustment of the strap, but it was worth it in the end. The problem now however, was that just reading the time had become rather distracting.

After enjoying the reflective melancholy of Don Henley, and in the spirit of what was hopefully to be a romantic evening, he'd switched to Sade's greatest hits, something that Gabriella had introduced him to a few summers ago, and now the voice of the sultry singer was conjuring pleasant, explicit memories. His pulse quickened, dare he hope for more of the same tonight?

The old car was running like a dream. As the early evening darkness of winter started to grip the landscape, he turned on both the headlights and the soft internal map reader, the cockpit was gently bathed in reassuring, orange glow. An unnecessary gesture perhaps, but one that never failed to add to the ambience of night time driving. He really loved his car.

As he negotiated a tight right hand bend, which had caught him unawares, the two wine bottles he'd bought before setting out, clinked together against the passenger door. Yet again he questioned his choices and wondered if he should've ignored Barney's advice, and perhaps bought Summer some flowers as well. The preparation that had gone into this date so far had been exhausting.

It had been a mistake to buy the wine from the Supermarket. It had been a bigger mistake though to actively seek his best friend's opinion. Since transferring to the liquor aisle the week before, Barney had begun to consider himself something of an expert sommelier, despite being a Newcastle Brown ale man himself, and having a deeply ingrained hatred of the stuff.

He'd provided a service way beyond that which would normally be expected of a Supermarket employee, and that had made a couple of passing grannies blush, including an interesting hypothesis regarding the number of bottles he should take. His theory was simple. If you take one bottle, you're obviously expecting to drive home. Take two though, and it shows confidence, like you anticipate staying. Compared to some of his theories, it was rather sound.

George eventually escaped clutching a modest bottle of French Merlot, and a crisp Australian Chardonnay, after accepting a good deal more of the advice than he intended. Thinking about the wine naturally made him think of the meal, and of food, his stomach growled, he was starving hungry. His Mum had cruelly denied him his usual Saturday burger - she didn't think he should arrive full, or smelling of onions, so he'd had to make do with an anorexic-looking cucumber sandwich instead. It didn't pack quite the same punch.

What might be bubbling away on her stove for supper though, maybe Summer was a veggie? He hoped not. Suddenly, George thought that his rather throwaway reply to her question of what he liked to eat might've been a little cavalier, especially considering his somewhat traditional palette. It'll be fine, just as long as it wasn't anything too hot and spicy. That sort of food always played havoc with his digestion.

As if by some miracle of housework, Summer had managed to tidy the kitchen, bury the evidence of her numerous culinary disasters, and make herself look somewhat respectable in less than an hour. Standing barefoot in her small bedroom, she looked at her reflection in the full length mirror that stood in the corner. This was not a favourite pastime. She'd discarded some of her bangles and beads, and flushed from her furious cooking and housework, despite a cool shower, had decided to brave a floaty dress for a change. It was simple, yellow, and knee-length, with a modest neckline that hopefully wouldn't give anyone the wrong idea. Not that she was entirely sure what the right idea was.

On hearing an unfamiliar, throaty exhaust, she rushed across the short hallway, past the bathroom and into the spare bedroom to see if it was him. Nervously twitching the curtains, as she knew her neighbours would be, she peered out of the old sash window. In the failing light, an old white sports car had parked very badly behind her mini cooper. And the occupant seemed to be talking to himself.

George looked at his reflection in the rear view mirror, his new eyebrows still coming as quite a surprise. "Okay, *be cool*, you've been here before, *you can do this*, just don't say or do anything stupid." The reflection nodded calmly in response. This was a good sign. With a last hearty intake of breath, he moved to open the door. It was stuck fast.

Still continuing her surveillance of the old white sports car, safely hidden behind the tie-dyed curtains, Summer wondered if she had enough time to quickly select a pashmina from her vast collection. She felt much more exposed than she'd intended, and had nothing to hide behind when the inevitable blush rushed up her neck. It didn't seem as though her guest was in any hurry to get out of his car yet. In fact, it looked as though the MG was now starting to rock from side to side. How strange.

"OPEN UP YOU BASTARD!" George fought hopelessly and increasingly violently against the door handle, which resolutely refused to budge. This had happened once before. He'd needed to climb out of the webesto sunroof in order escape that time, there was no way he could squeeze through the small windows, neither wound down far enough anymore. The passenger door also wouldn't open from the inside, and having failed to heed his Dad's words of caution, he'd erred on the side of thrift, and bought a cheap, second hand door assembly for the driver's side only. Bugger!

Meanwhile, up in the spare room, Summer had returned from her bedroom, having found the blanket sized pashmina she was looking for, just in time to see her guest dangling head first through the large canvas sunroof of his car, his legs sprawled for balance across the MG's roof. He was certainly far more energetic than he looked. Perhaps he was a bit of a monkey at heart?

Sweating like a chubby girl in a cake shop despite the chill, George's fingers groped for the plastic bag that contained the wine, which still rested on the passenger seat. Why on earth he hadn't wound down the window and placed them carefully on the pavement before he climbed out of the sunroof was a mystery.

Whatever else happened this evening, Summer was content that the show at least, had been rather good. Her dinner guest, having now managed to grab whatever it was he wanted from inside his car, was gingerly sliding down the sloping hatchback on his bottom, tightly grasping a plastic bag to his chest with one hand. Goodness knows what her neighbours would be thinking?

He was nearly there. His desert boots were only a couple feet from the tarmac and the wine was thankfully still secure. All he needed to do after touchdown was roughly replace the webesto sunroof, pop a few poppers, and he could put the whole ordeal behind him, and get on with the date. Thank God no one had been around to see him make a fool of himself.

Summer poured herself a very large glass of white wine and pulled up an old wooden stool to the deep window sill in order to enjoy the circus below more comfortably. Sadly though, it now seemed like the act was drawing to a close. He was nearly safe. All he needed to do was…

They might have been favoured by Special Forces units the world over, but clearly these elite soldiers never had to clamber out of a classic car, and down a polished rear window. With only a foot or so left to go, George's Clarks desert boots lost their grip, and with the momentum of his whole weight to carry him, unable to regain his footing, he crashed bum first onto the sharp, chrome bumper. With a worrying, prolonged rip, he then slowly slid onto the road.

Summer's tiny hand shot to her mouth, she quickly darted out of the room and scurried down the rough wooden stairs to the front door. Forgetting herself and feeling somewhat guilty for not coming to his aid sooner, she rushed barefoot to the bottom of the front garden, flung open the small, white washed gate and rushed to her guest's side.

"*Are you okay George?*" He was still sat on the tarmac, looking more dazed and confused than usual, his back resting against the bumper and number plate.

"Oh, *hello!* Err, I am not sure really, I'm a bit scared to get up, I, I think, *something ripped…*" Bewildered and sore, he was beyond embarrassment, but had decided not to linger on the reasons behind his hostess's quick appearance. She was probably just passing a window.

"Well was it you or, err, your clothes that ripped?" Summer was blushing, again.

"Me, *I hope!*" He was thinking of his leather jacket, anything else was expendable, more or less.

'*Err*, shall we get you up then?"

"Umm, okay. Oh, is the wine alright?" He was still clinging onto the plastic bag, as though his life depended on it. Summer prized it from his grasp and opened the bag, her eyes lit up.

"Ooo, *I like Chardonnay*, I'd just about run out watching…" She trailed off, best not mention that bit.

"*Oh good.*" With both of his hands now free, he tentatively hoisted himself to his feet using the sloping body of the MG, and his hostess's delicate, offered arm for support. He stood perfectly still for a moment and waited for something either to drop off, or fall around his ankles. It was an anxious few seconds.

"Umm, everything seems to have stayed in place then?" Still blushing, she beamed encouragingly at George. It was freezing outside, but neither of them had every felt warmer. "Shall we go inside?"

Much, much later that evening, after supper, and long after her guest had polished off a whole bottle of bright pink Pepto-Bismol, they both discovered something rather intimate and personal about each other. Summer had two small butterfly tattoos on the small of her back, and George had a massive hole in the seat of his chinos. Not that it really mattered by then.

Chapter 7

Picnics, Sledging and Molestation

Mid December.

The winter countryside was as cold and as white as a forgotten Tupperware box, long since abandoned to the icy depths of a freezer, never to be seen again. Thankfully, the roads had been kept clear by an army of snow ploughs, and despite the best efforts of the mischievous, plump clouds that still bobbed about the sky; the traffic was just about able to keep moving.

The more accessible, hillier parts of the countryside were littered with enthusiastic families, all seemingly intent on being hospitalised. Mums, Dads and assorted children of various shapes and sizes, were all wrapped up against the elements. Layers of soft woolly jumpers and an interesting assortment of bobble hats and scarves keeping them snug and warm. Before long though, the slope was bound to be littered with bodies.

Some of the upper class families, those that usually wintered in the Alps, wore brightly coloured ski jackets with florescent brand names blazoned across their backs, and tended to hurtle down the slopes on designer plastic sledges. The more financially challenged however, with nothing more than either a thick black bin bag or Granny's tea tray between them and the snow, still usually won the perilous race to the bottom.

George Butler's old English white MGB almost blended into the scenery as he gingerly drove deeper into the remote frozen wastes. Next to him, bundled up in all the winter clothing she possessed, an oversized black Russian hat occasionally covering her eyes, sat his new girlfriend. It was another proud moment.

Pushing back the skinned remains of the long dead black bear for the hundredth time, she glanced out at the endless, icy landscape and stuffed her tiny hands deeper into the corners of her pockets, hoping to find a trapped pocket of warm air. Quite how she let him talk him into this one was a mystery.

"Are you sure this is a good idea? *It's getting worse.*" Her words drew clouds of icy breath in the cramped cockpit, briefly obscuring her new boyfriend. *Boyfriend.* It was a term she was slowly coming to terms with. She preferred Monkey though. He looked a bit like a monkey.

"It'll be fine Summertime, trust me. Mum and Dad always used to do this with me and Mike!" There was to be no reasoning with him, it was something that she'd quickly learnt about George. As she'd pleaded with him earlier to spend the day by the fire instead, he'd just grinned roguishly, and disappeared outside to chip away at the frozen windscreen with his new Cottons Bank debit card. Once he'd made his mind up, there was little that could be done to sway it.

She nervously peered over her shoulder at the battle scared, two-seater wooden sledge that was tied down with bungee cords in the back. Mr Butler senior had built it years ago, during a quiet spell at the University, the fact that it had survived this many winters at the hands of his lunatic sons, was a testament to his skill as an engineer.

Next to the sledge was a huge picnic basket, practically bursting at its wicker seams. Since first meeting Summer a few weeks ago, Mrs Butler had decided she needed filling out a bit, and had quickly set to work with the carbohydrates. There'd be lots of sandwiches and fruitcake to get through today, providing they survived the sledging of course. A picnic in winter, of all the things to suggest…

A few Fridays ago, against his better judgment, The Bear suggested that George should try a proper man's pint. And come lunchtime, the two of them jumped into his filthy green Vauxhall Cavalier and, whilst being deafened by Led Zeppelin's *'Whole Lotta Love'*, drove at a surprisingly sedate pace to *The Pig and Hammer*, the most derelict and threatening pub the new recruit had ever seen.

As The Bear pushed open the door to the dimly lit pub, every shady customer that lurked within turned to look at the new arrivals. Judging by the collection of unfocussed, bloodshot eyes that tried desperately hard to focus, some of the patrons clearly started their day by pouring vodka on their cornflakes.

Despite his youth, the stranger was wearing a suit, and for some of the clientele of *The Pig and Hammer* this spelled potential trouble. Was he with the law?

"He's with me, Boys." The Bear made for the bar and stood next to a threatening lump that was almost as impressively built as he was. Sat on a barstool that seemed to be stained with blood, he hunched over the grimy bar nursing a tall measure of what looked like petrol.

"That's my seat, *Mate*." The Bear loomed over the man, who slowly turned his unshaved, scared face to see who had interrupted his solitude. Despite his size the seated man quickly got to his feet, grabbed his drink and disappeared into the shadows without a word of protest.

Nervous, uncomfortable, and scared for his life, George followed The Bear, mindful that his feet were sticking to the floor, and sat next to him on a free stool. "*Err*, does this stool belong to anyone Bear?"

"It wouldn't matter if it did." There was something extremely comforting and confident about his answer. Regardless of the glares from tattooed, inebriated undesirables, desperate sorts that looked as if they would have happily deep fried the youth and eaten him with soggy chips given the chance, his fears started to scatter. Clearly nobody messed with this patron.

"Two pints of Ol' Goat, please Geoff." The Bear turned and nodded. "This'll put hairs on yer chest!" Having only a patchy growth so far, he offered no protest.

Half an hour later, George was not feeling quite himself. Ol' Goat was a curious looking liquid, roughly the same colour as stale tea, and had what he sincerely hoped was sediment floating about in it. The Bear consumed his first pint, which looked like a shot glass in his huge paw, in a matter of minutes and, urging his drinking partner to do the same, ordered another round.

The second pint, which had an almost viscous quality and was the colour of Bovril, was called Dragons Bladder; it didn't instil the uninitiated with much confidence. Nevertheless he bravely pressed on, despite the fact that he could no longer feel his toes, and was becoming increasingly worried about driving home that evening.

The Bear was clearly agitated, and had been all week. He obviously wanted to get out of the branch and talk about something that was troubling him, and given his lack of options, he'd dragged the new recruit along for company. Times were hard.

"So, do you like working in the Bank then, Butler?" He wiped some froth from his beard and turned his piercing eyes towards his drinking partner. "What do you make of this new business, you know, the targets and all that?"

"*Err*, well, I don't know really. I kinda like it. Cashiering is a bit complicated, and I'm sorry I keep buggering up balancing at the end of the day, but I don't mind asking the customers to see Hayley, I quite like that bit."

"Yeah, but is that 'cause you fancy her?"

"Err, *probably*."

"Hmm…"

Like an unwelcome guest secretly slipping into a party to steal drinks when nobody was looking, over the past few weeks the Bank had been slowly introducing sales targets to the branches. At first no one really noticed. It was only when Linda, acting as Mr Burton's number two, began calling each day to see how the credit cards or loans were going, that staff started noticing that some of champagne was missing.

To begin with, it had all been rather uncomfortable, and it had raised fresh suspicions about the still undisclosed and unconfirmed merger. Were Cottons having something of a practice run, was this a sign of things to come? The older members of staff, those who had been content to simply make polite conversation with the customers that filed past their tills, found the individual targets the most challenging.

"*Well I think it's crap!* I don't see why we should push stuff on the poor sods, if they wanted a bloody credit card they'd bloody well ask! When you worked in the Supermarket, did you chase people around with bunches of carrots askin' them if they wanted to take a bite? *Of course not!*" Nobody knew just how old The Bear was, or how long he'd worked for Cottons, but he certainly didn't hold with the introduction of targets. Where you have targets, you naturally have people that get into trouble for not hitting them, and as a Union Representative, he expected to be very busy, very soon. "Keep making referrals Mate, that's all I'll say, don't worry about the other stuff. Give it a few months they won't give a damn, so long as you can sell crap, mark my words…"

An uncomfortable silence hung in the air for a while, keeping the stench of dirt and stale alcohol company. George didn't really know what to say. The Bear was obviously disgruntled about being given a few referral targets to hit, and the last thing he wanted to do was aggravate him further, although he had proved to be rather good at this lately. Personally he rather enjoyed having a few targets, especially after the cashier's league table followed them a few weeks later. It had been the first time since leaving school that he'd seen his name at the top of something. Naturally, he'd taken a copy home to show his Mum.

Bored, and having had his say, no matter how brief, The Bear decided to change subject, and see if he could find some amusement before their hour was up. "So, how's it going with Summer then?"

"Oh, well, you know, *really good…*" He stared into his grubby pint glass and longed for his lunchbox.

"Oh come on, details boy, give *me some juicy details.*" He slammed his hand down on the bar suddenly, terrifying the patrons and rattling the empty glasses. Was he going to kick off, should someone save the youth? Probably best to not get involved.

George had never been much of a bragger. Apart from one notable Italian exception, there hadn't ever been that much to brag about and he certainly didn't want to start now. During the past six weeks, he'd soon realised that two unseen members of staff seemed to linger in every branch. They didn't help with the cashiering though, or ever make the tea, but they did listen and talk. Gossip and Rumour didn't miss a thing.

There was only one sure way of changing the subject. He braced himself. Last time this had yielded a dead arm. "I don't want to talk about it, *Yogi!*" In a flash of movement, unheard of in men his size, The Bear grabbed him roughly by the lapel of his cheap suit, and dragged him halfway across the bar as though he was a made of polystyrene.

"*Don't Call Me Yogi you little Git!*" He pulled him closer to his reddening face, even his golf ball nose trembled with anger. He lowered his voice. "If you use a nickname like that in a Pub like this, before long they'll be calling you Boo Boo, and askin' us if we have picnics together. Then I'll have no choice but to bloody well *kill them all!*" None of these words sat cheerfully together.

George's face suddenly lit up, the fear of being mauled to death draining away. "*Picnic!*" It was as though he had just won a line at scrabble.

"*What?*" Still clinging onto the polyester lapel, the huge man frowned quizzically.

"That what I should do! I should take Summer on a *picnic!*"

A while later, safely outside *The Pig and Hammer*, somewhat dazed both by the contrasting brightness after the relative gloom of the Pub, and the questionable ale that sloshed about in his bladder, someone decided it was time to clear the air. "Err, sorry Bear, I just, well, you know, it's just that, well, *err…*"

He trailed off and hung his head, apparently feeling slightly sorry for himself. This tactic had proved useful before, with Auntie Rose at least.

"I know, I know, you don't want the whole Bank to know about Summer's tattoos, *right?*"

"*How the hell do you know about them?*" In a heartbeat, his mind flooded with doubt and insecurity. The unexpected delight of their fledgling romance shattered. How on earth would he know that? Oh no, she couldn't have, could she? She seemed so sweet and innocent. Had she slept with The Bear? The colour drained from his face.

"Calm down Mate. *Calm down*, I didn't know at all, it was just a lucky guess!" He paused, wicked, fresh mischief desperately wanting to molest the relief he could see crystallising in the young face. "So what are they of? Are we talking skulls and snakes here, or just butterflies?" George exploded.

"Are you sure this blanket is waterproof, Monkey? I don't like it when my bum gets wet." Still shivering despite her layers, Summer held up the rolled tartan blanket and eyed it suspiciously. How she missed the warmth of her cottage.

"Yeah it'll be fine. Mum said we used to use it all the time when we were kids, and the grass was wet." He heaved the massive wicker basket from the boot of the MG, slid out the sledge, and used a few of the bungees to strap it onto one of the seats.

"But, we're not talking wet grass here. It's fierce weather, it's been snowing for a week, so!" Whenever she became agitated, a little leprechaun wandered absentmindedly into her voice, sat down, and started sipping a pint of Guinness. It was utterly endearing.

"Summertime, *it'll be fine!*" No stranger to a nickname himself, George's response to being christened Monkey had been obvious, but effective. Her tendency to noticeably drift towards Ireland was too infrequent to be inspirational, and after briefly flirting with 'Bangles', and suffering a surprisingly solid, unexpected kick in the shins, he soon settled on Summertime instead. She loved it. And despite all her efforts to the contrary, she suspected that she also loved her Monkey too.

Like any fledgling relationship, there's had started with an intoxicating, almost psychedelic blend of hopes and fears. The hope being that everything would stay this great forever. That neither party would suddenly confess to belonging to some sort of cult, or have an odd collection of something undesirable, such as ears. Everything would continue to blossom and grow; there would be no dark clouds, no rainy days, just endless sunshine and a light breeze to keep things fresh. The fear meanwhile, simply being that everything would change, and everything would be snatched away.

Albeit subconsciously, Summer had spent most of her life avoiding moments just like this, quirky adventures or days out, tales you'd bore the grandchildren with. For her, fear outweighed any hopes. But for some unfathomable reason, she was drawn to this chubby, hairy bundle of bewilderment, like a kitten to a ball of wool. Despite the odd protest, she wanted to share in his wide eyed enthusiasm. For too long she'd been trainee spinster.

Christmas was just around the corner too, the perfect season for any budding new relationship. Since her parents had moved to Provence, Summer had always taken some leave from work and spent Christmas and New Year with them, only returning back to the UK once the pudding and sherry ran dry.

Naturally, George had only ever spent Christmas at home, and with Michael on leave, this year looked set to be extra special. Even thinking about the roast potatoes made his stomach growl in anticipation. Summer had been keen for her new boyfriend to join her in France, but when this idea was met with stiff, unyielding resistance, and sensing a cold wind drifting in to their lives from the south, rightly or wrongly she'd accepted the invitation to join the Butlers. It was time to meet the parents.

Meeting the Butlers was an interesting affair. As they arrived at the respectable semi, Mr Butler senior was toiling away in his garage, on the Velocette motor bike he had owned since he was a teenager. Wearing heavily soiled, navy blue overalls, covered in oil, surrounded by dismantled engine parts, empty tea mugs and a well-thumbed owner's manual, he was swearing colourfully as the happy couple entered his workshop. Someone had moved a sprocket.

Mrs Butler fared slightly better. She wasn't swearing, but regardless of the season, she was tending to her immaculate garden, with half a bottle of Shiraz for company. Barbara Streisand was blaring out of the Hi-Fi, and with the patio doors flung wide open, the garden was like a winter music festival in full flow. Knelt on a plastic bag, and with her head buried in the last of the Begonias, she was immune to the cold. Clearly, she was having another one of her flushes.

"George, its *sooo* cold! Why don't we just go for a Pub lunch instead? My treat." Summer was fighting her way through the knee deep snow, a few steps behind him, waving her arms around for extra momentum and balance. The Monkey, meanwhile, was pressing on regardless, breathing in great gulps of frosty air, still towing the sledge and the wicker picnic basket, the thick blanket slung around his neck for extra warmth.

"Summertime, don't worry, it'll be great when we get there, *honest*." They were slowly making their way up a steep slope, even without the burden of deep snow to contend with, it would've been a strenuous, demanding walk at the best of times. Now though, in these conditions, it was bordering on impossible. The promised view had better be spectacular.

"Oh, *okay*. Just please slow down, *my legs aren't as long as yours*." Given her height, it was becoming a frequent complaint.

After an uncomfortable, almost ruinously expensive meal in a fancy restaurant, pub lunches had soon became something they were both familiar and relaxed with. Keen to keep the ball rolling, before she changed her mind or came to her senses, and conscious that he couldn't really return the offer of cooking for her, George bravely suggested a romantic meal at a restaurant, a week after their first date. Or, as he suavely put it at the time, 'at a little place I know well'. The problem was that he didn't actually know any little places. Well or otherwise.

He spent a frantic Friday evening leafing through the Yellow Pages for a suitable local venue, eventually settling on a charming little Italian restaurant that was hidden down a cobbled backstreet near his home. He nervously called and booked a table for eight whilst the charming Italian lady on the other end of the telephone line stirred up colourful memories for him.

They only opened for business in the evenings, and, hoping to get a better understanding of their menu, or perhaps more importantly, their prices, he'd completed a brief reconnaissance of the premises that afternoon. Rather alarmingly, the menu that hung in a gilt-edged frame behind the window was written entirely in Italian, and didn't quote any prices.

With Mrs Butler able to create traditional culinary delights that no restaurant could match, and Gabriella reluctant to be seen in public with her teenage lover, the only meal he'd ever had out before was a disappointing burger and chips with Orang-utan Amy at his local Pub, with Barney making faces behind her back.

Having had his suspicions that Summer was a few years older than him confirmed during a slightly awkward confessional as they wildly peeled off each other's clothes, George felt he needed to try and act a little bit more mature in her company. It was a tall order, and one that filled him with dread. A fancy meal at a decent restaurant seemed like a good place to start.

Sadly though, the evening did not go as planned. Both parties were strained by the circumstances, and with communication stilted, they each started to fear that the previous week's relaxed conversation, and eventual wild, physical abandon had been a unique experience not to be repeated. As they sat awkwardly in the minuscule restaurant, music of the region playing softly in the background, the other diners laughed, shared whispered secrets, and generally seemed to be having a much nicer time than they were. The pressure was immeasurable.

Summer had been quite surprised by the invitation. She had the impression that like her, George wasn't really that fussed about this sort of charade. Perhaps her brutal curry had given him cause to change his mind? The new little black dress she'd bought especially for the evening, also made her feel far too exposed. Having stripped off most of her bangles and beads for the occasion, and spending hours wrestling her hair into something approaching acceptable, she didn't recognise the quivering person in her mirror at all, when the door bell had rung at seven.

Unfortunately, the menu at the table did contain prices, very large prices, as did the wine list. A quick, hastily rounded up review soon confirmed George's worst fears. A three course meal and a modest bottle of house wine were going to put him seriously overdrawn. Maybe he could get away with a child's portion and a burger on the way home?

As if by mutual agreement, they both ordered a small plate of spaghetti bolognaise, some garlic bread, and half a bottle of house red wine. Dessert and coffee were politely declined. According to his mental arithmetic, even this modest feast would leave him scratching around for petrol money until pay day.

After tearfully settling the astronomical bill, and leaving an unintentionally insulting tip, they quickly escaped. Still unsure of each other, or what this evening actually meant for their fledgling relationship, they took a refreshing walk in the moonlight through the park. After the subtle lighting and uncomfortably claustrophobic atmosphere of the tiny restaurant, the crisp winter's night air was a soothing relief. Soon, they found themselves on the old iron bridge that crossed the river, staring hopefully into each other's eyes. One of them needed to break the silence.

A week later, they were snuggled in thick woolly jumpers and jeans, sat next to a roaring fire, tucking into a steaming plate of steak and ale pie, shiny green peas, and chips the size of chocolate bars, a pint and a half of Fosters battling for space on their tiny round table. They'd agreed that if they went out to eat, they'd be pub grub people, and very happy all the same.

"Now will you look at that view?" Exhausted, Summer clambered over what she'd been absolutely promised, was definitely the last ridge, and, swaying slightly in the strengthening wind, gazed out over the countryside and beyond. It was indeed, quite a view.

"Right, we'll sledge down the other side and have a picnic at the bottom, *okay*?" An anxious debate quickly developed.

With the Italian Restaurant affair safely behind them, the new couple soon settled into a comfortable and somewhat predictable routine. Whilst there was absolutely no talk whatsoever of anyone new moving into Chaffinch Cottage, from Friday evening through to Monday morning, it seemed that somebody actually already had.

George's toothbrush was now enjoying long holidays away from the Butlers' respectable semi. Although the destination was generally a lot colder, and smelt of joss sticks, at least the toothbrush holder wasn't as crowded, and it had been some time since it had suffered a cleansing dunk in Dettol.

Much to Barney's disdain, the couple spent most of the weekends together at the cottage, only surfacing for supplies, and to visit his parents for a Sunday roast. They cooked together, listened to an eclectic selection of music from both their collections, some of which was clearly uncomfortable in the other's company, and watched old movies on Summer's little black and white television. She'd even been persuaded to show him some of her artwork, none of which, strangely enough, hung on her walls. She considered such a display egotistical and showy.

The paintings were of a quality and depth way beyond that of George's talents or understanding. Typically, the images were metaphors for how she'd felt at certain times in her life, menacing skies and lonely silhouetted trees, struggling to hold onto life in a desolate threatening land. Despite being incredibly realistic, and impossibly detailed, he'd struggled to find the right words to praise the heartfelt, faintly unsettling pieces. In the end, he told her that her clouds were very good indeed. She took it well, and was far more expansive with her own, very generous critique of his collection of wildlife art.

"Could you pass me one of the egg mayonnaise ones please, Monkey? I can't imagine they've gone off in the heat." She tugged at the Russian hat, pulling it down further over her bright red ears, and huddled closer to him for warmth. Thank God she'd talked him out of hurtling down that terrifying mountain. They would have perished for sure. He pulled out two thick, overflowing sandwiches, inspected them carefully, handed her the smallest one, and with gloved fingers, they nibbled their frozen lunch.

"It is a very pretty spot George." Like an unbalanced washing machine on a spin cycle, her whole body shuddered. Yet, there she was, against her better judgment, sat with *her* boyfriend, building a memory, experiencing what must surely be a previously unheard of means of developing frostbite. Memorable times indeed.

A few weeks later a new dilemma wandered into their perfect life and began stomping its feet about, making its presence felt. Each year, the employees of Cottons Bank are treated to an extravagant Christmas Ball, where excess, decadence and debauchery are commonplace, as the staff let their collective hair down, and enjoy one whole night of hedonistic overindulgence. Summer had never been before.

In the weeks leading up to the Ball, the business of actual banking takes a back seat as preparations get underway. The ladies try and discover what each other are planning to wear, in a bid to both try and outdo each other, and also, perhaps more importantly, to make sure that they don't all wear the same dress. Crazed lunch time sorties of the boutiques were commonplace.

For the men it was a much simpler business. Those of them that had already invested in a dinner jacket, merely had it dry cleaned in preparation, and perhaps updated the bowtie and cummerbund, depending on the damage it had sustained the year before. The poor bowtie tended to suffer the most at these functions. The rest of them, those who leaned towards the eventual false economy of hiring an outfit, simply headed off to the tailors to see if they'd grown any thicker over the past year. Invariable, they had.

Summer was adamant, she wouldn't go. For her the Ball had always been a melting pot for all her fears and anxieties. Everything from searching for a suitable gown, to worrying about who she'd end up sat next to, caused her to feel faint from uncontrollable apprehension. Even the thought of all those faces gathered together in one loud sparkly room, all those people looking at her, meticulously dissecting her outfit and lack of makeup, and giggling to themselves afterwards, filled her with dread. She had no evidence that this would be the case of course, she'd never been, and nor would she. It just wasn't worth the risk.

George however, had other ideas. Whilst he'd never been much of a party animal, the opportunity to dress up like James Bond wasn't to be passed on lightly, and as soon as Mr Burton's fierce secretary started collecting names for the event, he'd started work on his girlfriend.

He endlessly pleaded with her to go. Puppy-dog eyes were deployed hourly, cheap bouquets of wilting, reduced flowers from the Supermarket presented daily, and three loving mix tapes produced, and all were double sided. He even gave her one of his prized, ten inch square elephant paintings. His determination could not be faulted.

In the end though, it was Di that convinced her to go. Twenty or more new computer terminals had curiously arrived at Armada branch, and although she wasn't instructed to replace anything yet, Summer had been asked to set them up next to the old ones. It was all very strange, and fresh suspicions regarding the merger began to circulate amongst the staff.

It was whilst she was unpacking one of the units, and set about unravelling the spaghetti strands of wiring, which spilled out of the plastic wrappings that Di descended on her.

On reflection, after the good-natured lecture Summer liked to think that the colourful Number One cashier simply had the young couples best interests at heart. That she genuinely believed that if they went to the Ball together, all dressed up, and glowing with happiness, especially at this time of year, it would be a fantastically romantic evening. And she'd also believed her when she'd said that the rumours of these parties resembling some sort of Roman orgy were exaggerated, completely untrue. Of course Di had their best interests at heart. It couldn't possibly be anything to do with the whispers that she wanted to dirty dance with her Monkey. Could it?

And so, with Summer going to the Ball after all, the hunt for a suitable dress was on. Things did not go well. She found the ladies boutique's strange and uncomfortable places. No sooner had she gingerly pushed open the door, was she pounced on by over familiar, tactile women, who immediately began groping her extremities and fondling her waistline. Or at least, so it seemed.

Her petit size six frame was bullied and squeezed into revealing, hideous, sequined monsters, and her modest cleavage - something she'd always been rather keen to conceal - was forced into a frightening-looking padded bra. It was miracle of engineering though. Not only did it support her in places she didn't know she had, but it also seemed to make her assets double in size, and pop out of the top of everything she tried on. Never before had she felt so violated or exposed.

Exhausted, and ever so slightly traumatised by the experience, she eventually gave up on the idea, and decided that with just over a week to go, she'd make one herself instead. A tie-dyed hessian sack would do if necessary, with maybe just a few beads for decoration.

Whilst his girlfriend was recovering from her ordeal, George, despite being a bit nervous himself was rather looking forward to hiring a dinner jacket, although he was somewhat concerned that, following an unexpected sequence of events, Dean was going with him. Concerned, and to a degree at least, relieved.

Dean had been visiting Nelson's branch to finish of a loan for a longstanding customer. After the paperwork was drawn up and the delighted borrower sent on his way, he and Hayley seemed to spend the rest of the morning flirting outrageously with each other. It had all been a bit confusing for the newest member of staff. Was this how Gays normally acted?

Inevitably, the subject of the Christmas Ball soon came up, and Dean teased Hayley about how much flesh she managed to expose last year, the mere thought of this setting one pulse racing. Before long the rest of the team, minus Anita of course, was dragged into the conversation, it had been a quiet day on the till.

It seemed that The Bear, despite all evidence to the contrary, had an expansive wardrobe and already owned a Dinner Jacket, although for some reason the mention of this made Auntie Rose and Hayley snigger. Nevertheless, he intended to dust this off, and stuff his pockets with emergency cans of real ale.

In passing, Hayley asked if George needed to hire an outfit, and as soon as it transpired that he did, Dean swung into action. This presented something of a problem. On many, many levels, George was totally in awe of Dean. He was effortlessly smart and stylish, muscular and athletic. Everything he was not. Whilst in some respects he reminded him of his older brother Michael, his well-groomed appearance and build had been born out of the military, whereas Dean's was born out of fashion. He was the perfect guide into this new, unfamiliar world of tailoring. Doubtless he'd make sure everything looked at it should, dispel his concerns, and metaphorically at least, hold his hand. Strictly metaphorically though - he was Gay after all. But what if he made a move on him?

Not once did it occur to George that a six foot two, gorgeous Roman God with amazing dress sense and a winning personality might not find a hairy nineteen-year-old with the belligerent remains of teenage acne still dotted about his face attractive in the first place. He'd have probably been relieved, rather than insulted.

After being reassured that if they were late back, he'd still be allowed to tuck into his lunch, the miss matched pair set off to see Dean's' Tailor in his immaculate 1986, graphite black BMW M3. George was dumbfounded. Having a ridiculous, and largely useless encyclopaedic knowledge of certain cars, including this one, he'd gabbled away without pausing for breath about the merits of the older M3, compared to the newer model, for almost half the journey. Dean, who already knew all there was to know about his treasured vehicle, nodded politely, as if all these details were coming as a pleasant surprise. They weren't, but it was good to hear them again.

Still reeling from the experience of being in such a coveted machine, and having relaxed into both the unfamiliar left hand drive cockpit, and the company of a man who he was unsure of, he continued to ramble on. He was completely unaware that, like an experienced skipper taking charge of a boat before it crashed horribly on an unseen reef, Dean was expertly steering the conversation as he wished.

W. B. Bowden & Son's Traditional Menswear and Tailors, didn't look at all content with its location. It had a distinctive, old world charm which set it apart from the ramshackle grey houses, and heavily fortified off licenses that lined the streets on either side. If it had been a lesser shop, such as an electrical store or stationers, it would have trembled nervously, expecting to be attacked by its neighbours at any moment. But not this shop, this one had pedigree, and the sort of stiff upper lip that had won the battle at Rorke's Drift. If anyone dared to break in, bayonets would be fixed.

An old ship's brass bell signalled their arrival, as the thick wooden door was pushed open, and at once the two men were transported into another world. The walls were either panelled in rich mahogany or covered in thick, flock wallpaper, all lined with rails from which hung rows of immaculate suits in every size. The carpet was deep and dark, a dwarf would have been lost up to his knees, and the air heavy with both the smell of freshly ironed shirts from an unseen room at the back, and the complimentary essence of Geo. F. Trumper Limes aftershave.

Dean was greeted as an old friend by a slight man in his sixties with thinning hair. He wore an immaculate three piece, navy blue suit, a white tape measure draped causally around his skinny neck. A more polished individual couldn't have been conceivable.

His colleague was introduced and his needs explained, and whilst Dean examined the vast collection of bowties on a nearby counter, the old man took of his suit jacket, carefully hung it up on a wooden hanger, and approached his new client, who completely subconsciously, slowly backed away from him. This was quite normal the first time.

Once he'd cornered him with deft skill from years of dedicated practice, the Tailor quickly measured George's various appendages and girths', making the appropriate allowances as the belly was sucked in, and the chest thrust out. Once again, this was nothing unusual.

Feeling something of the unfamiliar proximity, and uncomfortable probing that Summer must have endured, George stood frozen during the ordeal. It was only the mental image of seeing himself, resplendent in full regalia, with possibly even a cap gun from his old toy box tucked under his armpit for added effect that kept him from fleeing.

When the Tailor unexpectedly went down on one knee in front of him though, his heart rate quickened, and fresh alarm bells started to ring. What on earth was he doing? Before he had chance to ask, the Tailor ran a length of his measuring tape up the inside of George's thigh and, very briefly, yet quite firmly, placed his thumb in a very private spot that even Summer hadn't touched yet.

Later that evening, safely huddled in Chaffinch Cottage, the warm glow of an open fire at his feet, and one of Summer's thick, reassuring homemade throws wrapped tightly around his trembling body, he still couldn't quite shake off the nightmare of that afternoon.

Unsettled by his strange mood, and naturally fearing the worse, she gently pressed him for the reason for his melancholy. Hours went by, and still nothing. Eventually, whist sipping his eighth cup of sugary tea, he relented.

"Summertime. *That Tailor molested me!*"

Chapter 8

The Dinner Jacket Virgin

The day before Christmas Eve.

Wearing an elegantly tailored, double-breasted dinner jacket, a wine-red cumber band with a matching bowtie, a heavy white silk dress shirt, and with the remains of his hair coiffured expertly into place, Mr Burton stood before the full length mirror in his wife's dressing room, critically examining his reflection. Unbeknown to his staff, it was to be his last Christmas Ball, and likely the last time he did this.

He picked up the heavy, led crystal tumbler and took the edge off the ice cubes. Swirling the expensive single malt gently around in the glass, until he was satisfied that some of the fire had been taken out of the scotch. He downed the measure in one swallow, immediately refilling the tumbler with a generous three fingers from the matching decanter. It was certainly going to be an interesting evening.

Soon the car would be here to pick him up. Despite his best efforts, his endless pontificating, and harassing his wife to the point of divorce, he still didn't have a clue how to tell his staff the news. He swallowed the second glass whole and, as he felt the warm glow of the alcohol slowly run through his body, once again reflected on his predicament. Perhaps he should call in sick, but who would he call?

After weeks of anxiously waiting for news, his early retirement package had finally been approved by Area Office just two days ago. From 1 February 1996, he would be officially be retired. His relief was only matched by his nagging feeling of desertion.

Nevertheless, soon it would be somebody else's problem. He just needed to convince his conscience first. January would be spent enjoying gardening leave, or more accurately Southern Spain. The impressive five bedroom town house had been put on the market, and an offer made on the quant cottage in the tranquil village. Everything was finally going to plan. Despite his months of worry that his dream of early retirement would be snatched away from him, especially as talks of the merger with NSIB intensified, the impending changes had actually worked in his favour. After months of negotiations, and having finally gained the approval of the Governments Monopolies Commission, the Cottons Bank PLC, NSIB merger was set to be finalised in January. From that moment on, all hell would probably break loose.

There would be redundancies and redeployment of course, particularly among middle management and Area office staff, where there would be a good deal of duplication, and there would also be a consolidation of the Groups. Mr Burton had simply been an early victim of this consolidation. Not that he considered himself much of a casualty.

A new computer mainframe was to be installed, based on the highly sort after NSIB system. Innovative, modern advertising would replace Cottons old, rather traditional marketing, and the staff would be retrained and pre-programmed to sell, ruthlessly and efficiently. He worried about some of them. From what he'd seen of the new business model, no quarter would be given to underperformers, at any level.

Still, the new-fangled propaganda he'd seen in development at a recent visit to Head Office looked as though it should provide some amusement. At some frightening cost, the Bank had employed the services of a progressive, inspiring Think Tank. Their objective was simple. Develop a campaign to be used for internal purposes only, which would inspire the staff to adopt and absorb a new sales culture, and motivate them to become successful, driven members of their teams. The Think Tank worked hard, yet their solution was baffling. Needless to say, the heads of both the merging Banks approved their ideas wholeheartedly.

Legendary celebrities from the world of sport would be employed to appear in a collection of short, yet rousing internal videos. Dressed in tracksuits, with colourful images of them winning medals playing behind, they'd talk energetically about what it meant to be the best in their chosen field. The hours of work it took, the dedication, the sacrifice, and finally the sense of achievement. Naturally, a suitably rousing soundtrack would accompany their words. With the viewer hooked, various high ranking Suits would then slowly begin to fade into view, eventually replacing the athlete in question. They'd then talk about how this mindset, this unrelenting desire to be the best, should be applied to all that we do at Cottons NSIB. Stalin would've approved.

To Mr Burton, it was all utterly ridiculous. Cottons was supposed to be a Bank after all. He worried about how some of the timid souls would cope. A lot of them didn't look the sort to put on tracksuits. It was definitely time to leave.

There was still one task required of him before he jumped ship, though. It had almost been a term of his release, and he wasn't relishing it at all. Head Office had decided that news of the merger should be communicated to the staff by their Senior Manager, in unison, and at the Bank's annual Christmas Ball, which by tradition, took place on the same night throughout the country.

The news would also be confirmed in writing, but it was the hoped that this way, as many of their people as possible would receive the same message simultaneously, thus minimising leakage ahead of the planned Press Release on Christmas Eve.

Mr Burton didn't agree with this at all. The Christmas Ball, as well as being somewhat sordid and colourful at times, was a celebration, and supposed to be fun. This wasn't the appropriate moment to announce what was likely to be both life-changing and worrying news. It was Christmas after all. It also selfishly presented him with a bit of a dilemma. Which news should he announce first, his or the Bank's?

On that first day, during his first meeting with his Senior Manager, George Butler had been both shocked and disappointed to be told that he would be leaving Armada branch, and heading out into Bandit Land. When he'd been told by Hayley that he was going back in a week's time, he was shocked and disappointed all over again. He was a difficult lad to please.

His unrelenting shotgun approach towards generating sales referrals for his beloved Hayley had accidentally put him in the spotlight, and with change imminent, and keen front line sales staff in demand, his successes were quickly identified, and his ticket back to the big city placed in his reluctant, moist hand.

George struggled to see quite what all the fuss was about. He rather enjoyed talking to his customers, it made the day fly past and mealtimes seem closer. Most of the customers he served on the till seemed quite happy to talk to him too, especially if it was raining outside. And he soon found that getting them to then talk to Hayley about some sort of financial product, was merely just another little bridge to cross, a much less perilous bridge than end of day balancing, for example. It was easy really, but if it meant he could stay in Nelsons, he'd happily stop.

Nelsons branch had become a second home to him, or third, if Summer's cottage was taken into consideration, and the staff like a surrogate family. Anita was still pure evil of course, but then, every family has a black sheep that nobody wants to visit. There's just happened to be far blacker than everyone else's. The Bear was like a well-meaning, slightly terrifying distant uncle that was occasionally a bad influence. Auntie Rose was the maiden aunt, who fussed over the family and made cakes three times a week, and finally Hayley was like the exotic older cousin that, even though he knew it was very, very wrong, he still harboured unrequited, explicit feelings towards.

Although moving to Armada would obviously mean that he would be closer to Summer, and they might even be able to enjoy the odd lunchtime fondle on the fourth floor, he couldn't for a moment imagine that the branch would hold the same place in his heart. For a start, who would make the cakes? Perhaps Di, she looked as though she enjoyed a good sponge.

Nevertheless, from the second week in January, he was going to become a trainee Customer Services Advisor in the main branch. A step up the ladder already, and at least his Mum and Dad had been pleased. It was sold to him as a great opportunity, yet Hayley seemed genuinely sad to tell him the news, but equally proud that his efforts had been noticed. At least with him gone, she'd get some more time to herself again, when the referrals inevitably dried up.

His basic cashiering skills still needed a good deal of work, but fortunately this new move meant that they shouldn't be called upon too often. If they were, Di would have to step in and take over from Auntie Rose, patiently overseeing his dire attempts to balance his till each day. He still missed the occasional thick wad of twenties, and sometimes a whole drawer of coin managed to escape his attention. But as The Bear had said, if you can sell or refer, they won't care, just keep doing it. And it seemed that he was right.

The unavoidable reunion with his fellow new recruits had troubled him at first, they didn't exactly bond, and now it seemed they would all be competing under the same roof. However, George had been interested to learn from Hayley that Wesley had since resigned his position and had retreated back to the family manor. People, it seemed, were not his strong suit.

Belinda had now married her pilot, and the happy couple had recently returned from a fabulous honeymoon in the Maldives, which, thanks to his terrible grasp of geography, George had wrongly assumed was in the Caribbean. She'd also managed to carve out a permanent role as Linda Beech's personal assistant; they did seem to have been separated at birth, and the pair of officious businesswomen had gained the joint nickname of *Lindabelinda*, which had to be said quickly for maximum effect, and preferably when neither was in earshot.

The move was technically a promotion, but thanks to a torrent of other, unnecessarily complicated words and phrases contained within his letter of confirmation, such as *Opportunity Mapping*, and *Selective Secondment*, it seemed that there was to be no pay rise. It was a shame really, as the fate of the MGB had rather relied on one.

The journey to Nelson's had been just about affordable within the old cars restrictive twenty-five miles to the gallon, but now that he was likely to be sat in traffic for a large part of his life, he knew that the same old issues would soon rear their ugly, costly and overheated heads. It was time to pick up a copy of *Autotrader* and make for the toilet.

George never thought that his love for his old wreck could have ever deepened. But all the fun that he and Summer had enjoyed tearing around the countryside in it, had somehow made the rusty old collection of odd noises and disturbing smells, an integral part of their relationship. And now it was time to let it go.

As depressing a conclusion as it was, he soon decided that an Mk 2 Ford Fiesta, with a lacklustre 1.1 litre engine and minimal running costs, was probably a sensible choice. He didn't like the thought of sensible at all. At least the whole transition was going to be made a bit more bearable thanks to a visit to Ashton's Vintage and Classic Cars, a garage that specialised in both restoration and resale. The owner had seen that there was profit to be made in restoring the old B to its former glory, and had eventually agreed to buy the car off the tearful, hairy young man. The poor Chap.

George desperately wanted to hang on to the MG until just after the Christmas Ball, so that he could proudly take Summer to the Ball in his soon to be former, pride and joy. Also, with them both dressed in their finest, even if it was hired or homemade, and with the car given a decent wax beforehand, the inevitable photograph a neighbour would be pressed into taking before they set off from Chaffinch Cottage, would look so much better against a classic car, than it would a sedate, mundane hatchback. It would probably be dark by then too. No one would see the rust.

Not unlike her new boyfriend, Summer also had reservations about him coming back to work at Armada branch, although hers had nothing at all to do with them working under the same corporate roof.

Ever since he'd first arrived at Cottons, for one reason or another, George had slowly become a person of interest to a certain select group, which operated largely out of Armada branch. Unofficially at least, this group was collectively known to the rest of the staff, as 'The Pretty People'. There were only a few of them. They were either Customer Banking Advisors, Financial Advisors, younger members of the Business Team, or a few handpicked individuals from the lower ranks, usually Customer Service Advisors. They were all in their twenties or thirties, single, gorgeous, invariably well thought of by Senior Management for some reason, and nearly always involved in some sort of light-hearted scandal.

Each Friday and Saturday night they'd descend on the town together. Always ending the night by relaxing in the VIP lounge of some swanky club, sipping complimentary champagne, whilst whispering meaningless sweet nothings into the ear of whatever willing partner they'd found to keep the bed warm that evening.

The girls were fanatical about every aspect of their appearance. Lip stick was deftly applied and finger nails honed to perfection. They were Gym Bunnies, with perfectly toned figures, limitless wardrobes and expensive German cars. Each morning, no matter how late the previous evening's activities ended, they never failed to arrive at work looking as though they were ready to be part of some sort of classy photo-shoot for a glossy magazine. It was a miracle of mascara, foundation and Pro-Plus.

The men were equally obsessive. They attended the same fashionable gym as the girls, dressed immaculately, and owned the very best of everything. No one was safe, or immune to their mesmerizing charm. And as with most groups, organised or otherwise, there was always someone at the top. Leaders who even the most belligerent members of the group look up to and admire. For The Pretty People it was Dean Swift.

Dean was something of an enigma. He was independently wealthy, though nobody knew why, or how. Beneath the surface, he was actually very complex and largely miss-understood, but he kept that particular card very close to his cliff like chest. Everyone knew he was Gay, but he was never seen with a partner, casual or otherwise. Even his own gang couldn't profess to see him show an interest in anyone during their many nights on the town, male or otherwise. Conceivably, the whole thing could have been a rumour that he just wasn't that bothered about challenging.

He owned a spectacular penthouse apartment in the fashionable Marina part of the city, a BMW M3, a Ducati 916, bright red naturally, several wardrobes of expensive clothing, and a beautiful twenty-seven foot sail boat he'd christened 'Solace'. Dean seemed to have it all. He positively reeked of confidence and charisma, and unlike others in his group, everybody in the Bank loved him. Somehow, no matter who he was talking too, he always managed to find the right words to put everyone at ease. He was the most hugged man in history.

When he'd joined Cottons, aged eighteen, he made a point of getting along with all the right people straight away. He was quickly promoted to the role of a CBA and, after familiarising himself with the role, chose to stay. The job afforded a good degree of self-management and motivation, there was nobody to directly manage and the salary was reasonable. Having little in the way of outgoings, it kept him comfortably in champagne, lobsters and tailored shirts. He quickly formed a circle of likeminded, attractive colleagues, and before long, his group became known as 'The Pretty People'. Members came and went, the lifestyle remained unchanged.

Membership it seemed was by invitation only, Dean's invitation. And yet the recruitment process was bizarre. At first the new member didn't appear to be an obvious candidate, gangly or overweight, bookish or slovenly, totally out of place with the rest of the flawless pack. After a few weeks under Dean's muscular wing though, a spectacular transformation started to occur. The once ugly ducklings or hairy caterpillars seemed to somehow morph into either an irresistible, graceful swan, or magnificent emperor butterfly.

And this was why Summer was worried. She'd overheard a conversation between Dean and one of his lipstick brigade earlier in the week, which she'd wished she hadn't. Soon after he arrived at Armada Branch, her very own hairy caterpillar was going to be invited out for drinks with The Pretty People.

In George's opinion it was a very bad idea for Mrs Butler and Summer to team up to make a ball gown. In the days leading up to the Ball, he'd done his level best to persuade his new girlfriend to take a fresh look at the ones on offer in the shops, even offering to go with her for moral support. An offer he didn't take lightly. But it was no good. He was going to be nagged.

Shortly after he'd proudly introduced Summer to his parents, he had been lectured by Mrs Butler for two solid days about needing to *look after this one*, and *not messing this one around*. As far as he could recall, he'd never given his Mum reason to believe that he would either fail adhere to the first rule, or was ever likely to default to the second, either now or in the past. The chance would have been a fine thing.

As he feared though, working closely together on the pine dining room table, huddled over an old Singer sewing machine, sharing ideas and occasionally checking dimensions, the two seamstresses bonded, and the nagging intensified.

George was far too young to be married off, but with his limpet like attachment to the Butlers' respectable semi showing no signs of releasing its grip, it didn't hurt to get the ball rolling. Family life had noticeably changed since Summer had arrived on the scene. Number Two son now spent far less time festering in his Pit than before, although he still managed to make it home for all his favourite meals, and somehow always cunningly avoided liver stew night, despite the occasionally irregular mealtime itinerary.

He also tended to arrive home with a black bin bag bursting with dirty clothes. Quite naturally, he assumed that they would wash and iron themselves in readiness for the following week, even if it was midday on Sunday. Bless him.

Usually, when the last of their offspring eventually fly from the family nest, parents can experience a wide range of emotions. Feelings of emptiness and a lack of purpose are commonplace, as the home suddenly becomes an empty, barren environment, and husband and wife are suddenly left with nothing to do but to talk to each other. This can lead to all sorts of problems. However, in Mr and Mrs Butler's case, they had been seriously contemplating moving house without telling George.

Summer stood in her living room and gently swished the skirt of her new dress from side to side, critically examining it in the full length mirror she'd brought down from her bedroom. She wanted to see how the dress reacted to her movement and having fallen over her bed for a second time, concluded that there was much more space in the lounge for this sort of messing around, and had relocated accordingly. Happily, she was also now much closer to the fridge, and the chilled bottle of Chardonnay she'd developed an unhealthy relationship with. Still unsatisfied, she might even make a move on his younger brother soon.

Mrs Butler, who Summer now loved almost as much as her own Mum, had done a truly marvellous job. Although she hadn't covered quite as much flesh as she would've preferred, the dress was perfect for the Ball and she looked, and even felt, amazing. It was a unique feeling that she desperately wanted to hold onto for as long as possible. Perhaps staying in would be best?

It was a long, flattering halter neck made from a silky, royal blue material. It fitted Summer's small frame closely, and perfectly. She had no idea her body could look like this in a dress. When she'd first tried it on, and had shown George's Mum, it had all been quite embarrassing to begin with, especially when her husband and youngest son stumbled in from the garage. But then, once they'd opened a bottle of wine, and the men were banished, everything thankfully settled down a bit. And it did look rather good.

With an ever-present, reassuring pashmina from her vast collection wrapped around her shoulders for extra warmth and concealment, Summer felt that this was just about as confident as she was ever going feel wearing a Ball Gown. The neckline didn't allow for any sort of necklace, yet determined to maintain a degree of individuality, she'd selected two bracelets to wear, which her brother had bought her during his travels through the Dominican Republic. They were heavily decorated with the bright blue gem stones that are particular to that region, and were held together with a silver rope.

Despite the freezing weather, on her delicate size four feet she wore a well-loved pair of elaborate leather sandals, fearing that any sort of high heel - not an item of footwear she had much experience or success with - would end in disaster. There would probably be enough opportunity for ridicule this evening without courting unnecessary spectacle.

Content that the dress did indeed swish correctly, and after employing a second mirror to ensure it wasn't too clingy on her bum, she returned the mirror to her bedroom, poured another generous glass, and perched on the edge of her sofa, so as not to crease her new dress. She anxiously sipped her wine. Nervous, excited butterflies darted about inside of her, their wings tickling and tormenting in equal measure. Without even a whisper of music for company, she waited patiently for the familiar rumble of the MGB. Something nagged at her though. There was something vital she was forgetting. Hair! She needed to do something with her hair!

In the end, it had taken the combined efforts of Hayley, Auntie Rose, The Bear and eventually Dean, to convince George that the Tailor had in fact *not* molested him after all, and that it was quite safe to return to *W. B. Bowden & Son's* Traditional Menswear and Tailors to collect his dinner jacket. It had been a long afternoon for all concerned.

When he arrived at the Tailors, shortly after work the Friday before the

Ball, he was still cautious of the old man and his probing thumb, and at first he'd been extremely reluctant to try on the full ensemble before he left his shop. Everything changed though, once he did.

Stood proudly before the old mirror, chest thrust out, a smug grin spreading across his chubby face like wildfire, he was now without question, a certain Gentleman Spy. The Tailor, who in his clients mind, had now suddenly transformed from being a perverted old man, to being his own personal outfitter, had seen this transformation many times before. Dinner Jacket Virgins were all the same.

He roughly adjusted his client's poor attempt at the black cummerbund, and pulled his shirt sleeves down to the correct length, absentmindedly fiddling with the tangled cufflinks as he did so. After nearly thirty patient minutes of dedicated tutorage though, the Tailor eventually gave up trying to teach George how to correctly fasten his bowtie, and with his professional pride hiding in embarrassment behind the curtains, provided him with a black clip on version instead. It smelt heavily of another man's aftershave.

The Tailor had also insisted that he hired what he'd referred to at the time as some decent shoes, to both compliment the outfit, and perhaps make dancing possible without rendering his client lame. Until that moment, George hadn't given any thought to dancing. From what he could remember of his time with Gabriella, he rather liked dancing, nude or otherwise.

Despite the crisp, chilly night air, a scattering of staff and their partners lingered on the marbled steps of the Mayflower Plaza, the largest and most spectacular hotel in the city, sucking in the last drags of their cigarettes before the frostbite crept up their legs. Several dozen cars and taxis had stopped to drop off guests, and as they emerged from the vehicles, each new arrival, especially the ladies, had been subjected to a thorough, critical examination by the group. They appraisals hadn't always been very pleasant.

The throaty roar from the old MG had sparked particular interest. Who was this? The driver, clearly relishing every minute, had driven up to the entrance at quite a pace, blipping the throttle unnecessarily, the exhaust replying by popping and gurgling in confusion. As it skidded to a halt, inches from the first step, narrowly avoiding losing its chrome bumper, the diver threw open his door and, in a flourish of exaggerated movement, leapt out of the car, and run a hand through his mass of black hair. George Butler had arrived.

After momentarily misplacing his manners, and pausing briefly to glance at his audience, he hurried around to the passenger side, and after fiddling with the handle for a while, eventually opened the door.

"Come on Summertime, *we're here!*" He was as excited as a puppy with two tails and a bowl full of roast beef, flushed with anticipation, and, for now at least, not at all daunted by the evening ahead. His partner though, still hiding in the reassuring cockpit, looked as relaxed as a field mouse who'd accidentally wandered into a cattery. Given the audience, it was not far from the case.

After stalling for an eternity, fusing over the contents of her small clutch bad, and checking her appearance in the ancient, almost opaque vanity mirror, a new, unfamiliar pastime which bought her vital seconds, Summer finally emerged. All eyes turned to see if the rumours were true. They were! That little elf, the computer nerd with all the wild hair, had bagged herself a Toy Boy!

It had taken a moment for the smokers to realise this. With her hair swept up in a serviceable but relatively elegant pony tail, and wearing a dress that suggested a surprisingly enviable figure before it was hidden behind a huge, sheet-like pashmina, she didn't look at all like the timid, jangly little girl that scurried about the back offices. Fresh criticism would be required tonight. She did appear to be blushing at least, some things clearly never change.

Even from this distance, Summer could feel the watchers gaze stabbing viciously into her. The eyes looking her up and down, the whispered comments, the inevitable catty giggles, hushed at first, before building into a crescendo that destroyed the victim. She desperately wanted to go home.

George meanwhile was swelling with pride, his chest puffed out, his freshly shaven chin held high. Bless him. She took his offered arm and smiled as confidently as she could, adjusted her pashmina for the hundredth time, and fought hard against the urge to wrap it around her head.

The plan had been to drop her off at the entrance. He'd then park the MGB, out of sight, collect their overnight rucksack from the boot and meet her back at the steps. The old cars shuddering overrun had been periodically recurring, knowing this would seriously ruin their grand entrance, he wasn't taking any chances. Now though, in the close company of the well-dressed, smoking vultures, Summer wasn't at all sure that she liked this plan very much.

"Monkey, I'll, err, umm, *well look*, I'll come with you and we can, err, walk around together. That'll be nice, *won't it?*" She was shivering terribly, though not with the cold.

"Summertime, go inside and get warm, I'll be seconds, honest. If you go to the desk and find out what we need to do about the room, I'll grab the bag. *Please?*" During the impromptu photo shoot at Chaffinch Cottage, as a kindly seventy-nine year old neighbour snapped away in arctic conditions, and throughout their journey into the city, he'd been wearing an unwavering look of staunch smoothness. Listening to Sade's 'Smooth Operator' eight times probably hadn't helped matters. But now, needing to get his own way again, he suddenly switched to his more usual puppy-dog eyes instead. The sharp contrast took Summer quite by surprise.

"Oh, *okay*, but please be as quick as you can?" With a quick peck on her freezing cheek, he was back in his old car, and with a few more, completely unnecessary blips of the throttle, he tore off towards the hotel car park to shut down the engine in private.

"*Changed his mind already has he?*" Startled, Summer spun around to see who had called out. Her heart sank. Anita, dressed in an extremely low cut, glossy black dress that looked as though it had been sprayed onto her thin body, was leering horribly at her, the ash from her cigarette poised to fall at any moment.

"Umm, err, *no*, he's just parking, actually…" She trailed off, the butterflies in her belly suddenly joined by a squadron of wasps. Without waiting for another cutting blow, she quickly made her way up the steps and through the heavy glass door, her leather sandals flapping on the marble, catty giggles ringing in her ears. She really wanted to go home now.

Ten minutes later they were both safely nesting in their hotel room. George had never stayed in a proper hotel before, and was delighted to find both a kettle and a selection of exotic complimentary tea bags. He immediately he set to work making a brew.

The Mayflower Plaza offered Cottons staff a discounted rate for those that wished to stay the night, and enjoy the hotels quality breakfast the next day, which by then, would be Christmas Eve. Cottons had always used the Mayflower for the Christmas Ball, with the main event taking place in the hotel's huge function room. Not that that prevented some staff from finding their way into other, more secluded and private corners as the night unfolded, or even, as was the case one year, into the vast swimming pool, naked.

Following the incident on the steps, Summer was quite content to get into her brushed cotton tartan pyjamas, snuggle up with her Monkey on the king size bed, indulge in some moderately energetic nookie, and then fall asleep watching the small TV. Anything rather than face the crowds downstairs. Convincing George though, would be another matter.

She gazed lovingly at him. He'd made such an effort to look the part this evening. He'd even let his mum trim his hair again, the second time in as many months, and had slicked it into a sort of neat side parting. Quite a lot of the fringe clearly had other ideas though, and was already falling across his eyes, which she found rather charming.

Miraculously enough, the hired Dinner Jacket fitted his challenging physique perfectly, something that could not be said of his own cheap suit. He looked slimmer, toned even. To add an extra touch of sartorial elegance, Mrs Butler had finely pressed a white silk handkerchief, one that had been liberated from the more affluent end of her husband's sock drawer, thankfully cleansed of all deposits, and tucked into George's breast pocket. He looked the business, and he knew it.

Summer was struggling desperately to contain her nerves. There were so many voices inside her little head now, filling her mind with worry and apprehension, some of them she'd never even heard before. Whilst they were safely locked away in their hotel room, she didn't have to confront or try to silence them. It wasn't home, but it was safe, it would do until morning came. But it wouldn't be fair to him, and so the voices grew ever louder.

She was acutely aware that in all the many years she'd worked for Cottons, this was her first ever Christmas Ball, and embarrassing questions were bound to be asked. Then there was the issue of her boyfriend being seven years younger than she was. Whilst this didn't cause them any concern, it would probably be ridiculed by those women on the steps. Also, although she loved her dress completely, and it meant the world to her that George's Mum had made it, she just knew that a homemade dress would be mocked and derided for not having a designer label, or price tag. Finally there was the issue of dancing. Summer couldn't and wouldn't dance. How she wanted to go home.

George's thoughts were somewhere else entirely. In preparation for the Ball, he'd given a lot of consideration to what Hayley had said to him the evening he'd turned off the cashpoint, especially the nicer bits, after things had settled down again, and after they'd opened the wine. She didn't think he was shy, so therefore, he *must* appear confident. If tonight he could muster some *actual* confidence, everything would be fine. So far at least, it seemed to be working, but so far, they'd only seen a handful of other guests, and hadn't had to talk to anyone yet.

Summer always fussed before leaving home. Hours would seem to pass as she checked the gas was off, checked the taps weren't dripping, checked to make sure the windows were firmly shut, and checked that the back door was locked. Once she was in the car, she'd invariably need to go back to check something she'd forgotten to check. It was just the way she was. It was endearing, so long as they weren't running late. But then, they never really had anything to be late for. Tonight though they did, and quite why she needed to perform the same endless ritual in their hotel room, was a mystery.

"Come on Summertime, it won't matter here if the taps dripping, I don't think we'll get charged extra!" George glanced at his Seiko. The bright, chucky watch did look really rather cool against the double cuff of his shirt. Distractions over, he read the time. "Come on, *we'll be late!*"

Eventually, pre-Ball checks completed, they made their way back down to the lobby. It was deserted, save for a few stragglers, and after being pointed in the right direction by the beautifully polished girl at the desk, they made their way towards the hotel bar that served as a reception. As they got closer, the roar of voices grew louder and louder. There must have been hundreds of them. There was laughter now too, great belly laughter, mixed with squeals of excitement. The happy couples pace slowed.

The double doors of the bar were open. Two immaculate waiters stood either side. Silver trays loaded with bubbling champagne flutes, which stood to attention in one gloved hand, the other free to offer one to each new arrival. Behind them, there was a raucous mass of black jackets, white collars, and colourful ball gowns, packed to the edges of the room, almost spilling out of the door like great handfuls of Smarties and Humbug sweets. There didn't seem to be a way in. Perhaps they should go home instead?

George felt uncertain now too, his newfound, thin veneer of confidence beginning to chip at the edges. There were lots of people. Alcohol would probably help. He gratefully took two of the offered flutes, passed one to Summer, downed the second, and as the bubbles went up his nose, waited expectantly for another. The waiter raised a quizzical eyebrow. He'd been strictly told to offer only a single glass to each guest. Nodding at his companion, he eventually plucked another flute from the tray. The poor chap looked like he needed it. Bless him.

Clinging onto each other's hands like an old, partially-sighted couple lost in an unfamiliar Bingo hall, they found a chink in the wall of bodies, and slowly made their way into the bar. Surrounded on all sides by a great wall of noise and faces neither of them could ever recall seeing before, they instinctively headed for the back of the room, where they stood sipping their excellent drinks in silence. Now, they both wanted to go home.

From their vantage point, safe in the gloom, they were able to watch the last guests enter the bar. With a few exceptions, all of them fell into one of two groups. Firstly, like them, there were the 'Nervous Shufflers'. Clutching their complimentary glasses of bubbly, they stuck to the edges, slowly making their way around the room, as though they expected the floor to fall away at any moment. They drank alone, or with their equally reluctant guests.

Secondly there were the 'Confident Strollers'. There were more of these. They headed straight into the centre, as though they had been launched from a harpoon gun, selected a group to join, usually the largest and the loudest, and then made for the centre of that too. Immediately introducing themselves to any strangers, and offering rounds of drinks. Dean Swift, last to arrive, seemed to have invented the second technique.

"*George!* What are you doing hiding at the back, my Man? Get over here and bring that gorgeous creature with you!" Only moments had passed, but since arriving, Dean had taken over the main group, which was peppered with 'The Pretty People', bought everyone drinks, and told a few choice jokes that had reduced those within ear shot to tears.

With Summer dragging her sandals reluctantly across the oak floor, they were quickly plucked from the shadows of obscurity, and brought into the body of the boisterous, excited group. To begin with, it was difficult for the couple to decide if their situation had improved or not. Dean was a gregarious host, and with a click of his fingers, that managed to be both assertive and respectful towards a passing waiter, quickly freshened up their drinks and introduced them to his flock.

George had become familiar with shaking hands now, he'd even learnt how adjust his grip accordingly, to avoid injury, and he shook the firm, dry hands with a degree of moist confidence. But neither he nor Summer were prepared for the girls' offered cheeks. Having spent time in France, Summer fared better, and although she was still awkward and uncomfortable, she shared none of her boyfriend's head bobbing as, fresh from one peck, he was expected to plant another on the opposite side. The collection of aftershaves and perfumes were intoxicating, though, and a fresh waft of which drifted pleasingly past with each introduction. Coal tar soap and Old Spice stood no chance in this company.

The whole experience was completely overwhelming. George had never been invited to join a group before, either at a party, in the pub, or even just in the school playground. He and Barney had always been Social Gypsies, and had spent most of their formative years simply drifting from one spot to another, sometimes quite quickly, especially if Barney had upset a random girl with a huge boyfriend. Here though, for some unknown reason, there was a group of unbelievably beautiful, likely successful people who seemed to want to get to know him better. Involve him in their conversation and, perhaps most importantly, buy him drinks. He most certainly didn't want to leave anymore.

Summer meanwhile, was starting to feel isolated. After the initial greetings were over, she felt as though she'd been forgotten about, which was absolutely fine normally, but didn't seem quite right now that she was part of a couple, especially when her partner seemed to be doing so well. He was still holding tightly onto her hand, but she could feel a definite change of atmosphere. It was as if he was a novice swimmer, treading water in a swimming pool, still clinging onto the side, just until he could finally muster the confidence to let go, and swim off all on his own. Or was she overreacting, were her nerves and anxieties getting the better of her?

She knew wasn't helping herself. To begin with, a few of the flawless, plastic girls had tried to bring her into the conversation by asking her, with genuine interest, about her dress, her shoes, her blusher, and her curious perfume. But when she'd shyly replied in a barely audible whisper that it was homemade, they were old and from India, it was just soap, and it's actually just a real blush, they eventually grew tired of trying to hear her, checked their nails and gave up. She really wanted to go home now. Perhaps put on her PJ's even, and light the fire.

Seemingly unaware of the trembling hand that still clung desperately to his own, George had become increasingly involved in a passionate discussion with Dean about his M3. As the conversation deepened, gesticulation was called upon, and it was during a particularly zealous exchange of words, that he eventually let go of Summer's hand.

The heavy, highly polished brass ships bell that hung behind the bar was ceremoniously rung twice, and the deep booming voice of the Mayflower Plaza's Head Waiter announced that dinner was to be served.

Slowly, the horde of dinner jackets and ostentatious ball gowns started to move towards the entrance of the function room. Or at least, they hoped that was the direction they were all heading for. Almost as one, they shuffled in the same sort of vague direction, still deeply engrossed in their conversations, merely following the person in front. Hopefully the individual at the head of the group knew which way they were going, and wasn't some sort of lemming.

The happy couple had at last reconnected their hands. Having recovered his full attention by accidentally brushing past his gentleman's region, they followed the crowd, eventually arriving at the heavy oak doorway and the entrance to the vast room. Any anxieties, stresses or fears that remained, in that moment at least, were quickly forgotten. The room was quite simply, spectacular.

The twenty tables were all dressed the same. Immaculate, heavy white table cloths were lit with huge golden, ornate candle holders, thick white candles, fully ablaze, dribbled rivers of molten wax down their long stems. Imaginative, decorative displays of entwined holly and poinsettias had been placed in the centre of each table, vast carafes of red wine, frosty coolers of white and large jugs of iced water sat waiting to be greedily consumed.

Each place was set with polished silverware and crystal glasses that gleamed in the candle light. Heavily pressed expensive white napkins were squeezed into shiny gold napkin rings and place markers, made from a 'V' of thick, coarse cartridge paper, were individualized in elaborate calligraphy.

The room itself was adorned with evergreen garlands woven with Clementine, cinnamon sticks, yet more holly and pine cones. Several hugely impressive chandeliers hung overhead, glittering delicately. In the far corner there was an enormous Christmas tree, as beautifully decorated as everything else, the terrified gold fairy that clung to its peak, clearly suffering from vertigo.

At the far end there was a stage, where a band had set up their equipment some hours before, immediately in front of this there was a wooden dance floor, thankfully clear of any obstacles. Nothing caused more carnage than gyrating office staff.

A seating plan, framed as though it was a priceless work of art, was displayed on an easel at the doorway, giving the guests their first chance to see who they'd been dining with. It often caused a backlog. Thankfully the Mayflower Plaza had the foresight to supply additional waiters to help overcome the challenging complexities of the seating arrangements. Provided that the guest hadn't drunk too much yet, and could still remember their name, the process was reduced to simply pointing them in the right direction. Any disappointments they harboured about who they were sat with, was their concern.

The decorations, seating, and general organisation of the entire event were the sole responsibility of Mr Burton's fierce secretary, Ms Peters. In the past this had been something of a sore subject. She was the Queen of all Spinsters and by nature, despised anything that might even slightly resemble a budding office romance, or cause for celebration. Following many years of complaints however, Mr Burton had been forced to intervene and set out a few ground rules. He needed to avoid a seasonal staff uprising, and reduce possibility of Ms Peters being burnt at the stake in a banking hall. Good secretaries were hard to find.

The rules were simple, and fair. Firstly, couples should be allowed to sit together, regardless of whether or not they were married, Gay or just simply cohabiting. Ms Peters' personal feelings on the subject of sex before marriage and homosexuality should be kept out of the equation. This was The Christmas Ball after all and not The Gates of Hell.

Secondly, wherever possible, and in keeping with the spirit of the first rule, friends should also be allowed to sit together and enjoy themselves.

The availability of alcohol on the table should not be limited based on the events of previous Christmas Balls.

Finally, regardless of the budget, each table, and the entire room for that matter, should completely radiate the very spirit of Christmas. Under no circumstances should either resemble a church hall Woman's Institute afternoon tea party, as had unfortunately been the case with the Christmas Ball of 1991. People were still taking about it.

"Here we are Summertime. *Oh look*, we're with the Nelson's lot, *oh*, and Di!"

Still stood in the doorway, conscious of the vast ocean of bodies at their backs, Summer froze. *"Nelsons?"* Clamping her comforting pashmina around her tighter still, she bent slightly to examine the seating plan, fearing the worst. *"Oh*, oh thank goodness, not Anita though, *phew…"*

As they weaved their way through the labyrinth of tables, dodging the occasional, over refreshed early reveller, they lost their bearings for a moment, until a familiar colossal image rose to his feet and bellowed at them to join him. The Bear was clad in an ill-fitting purple dinner jacket, a stained cream dress shirt with enormous ruffles on the stretched chest, and a huge, comical, tartan bowtie. He was surrounded by empty cans of smuggled real ale, and by the look on his face, his stores were running low.

"'ullo you two! *Crikey Summer*, you look like a proper Bird for a change!" He downed his last can, gazed longingly at it for a second, and crushed it into his huge paw. "I might have to go on the gin now!"

"No you *won't* Young Man!" Auntie Rose, dressed like the Queen Mum, suddenly appeared at the table, towing a very thin, submissive-looking man behind her. "You know just what happens when you have gin, and there is no way I am allowing Ronald here to carry you home again this year, *do you understand?"*

Ronald, who must have possessed hidden strength, was introduced to both George and Summer by his wife, who managed the impossible by making Summer's blush deepen further still by saying how wonderful she looked tonight. Ronald was a quiet sort of chap. He nodded constantly, regardless of whether or not he had been asked a question, and wore a look of permanent agreement on his long bearded face. Both were coping mechanisms. He'd endured thirty years of marriage to a wife who never let him get a word in edgeways, and who continually asked multiple questions, without ever pausing for a reply. He got by as best he could.

A deeply wicked explosion of belly laughter signalled the arrival of the resplendent Di. She was accompanied by a barely contained, heaving cleavage and her equally colourful husband, Bill. With his sequined gold cummerbund and bowtie, shock of shoulder length white hair, and deep sun-bed tan, he looked as though he'd be more at home in a Las Vegas casino. They made quite a couple.

George was still standing, his arm casually slung around the slender waist of his still trembling girlfriend. He was feeling confident again now, almost properly confident. He could relax with this group, even practice his socialising skills. If only Summer would loosen up a bit.

"You okay Summertime? Are you still cold?" He pulled her closer, feeling that he was getting to grips with this boyfriend business, but she was stiff, unyielding, like a well-dressed, nervous lamppost. "*What's wrong?*" He still had a lot to learn about women.

"Oh, err nothing, nothing at all, just, *well…*" She trailed off, following his longing gaze. Suddenly she'd lost his eye contact. Hayley had entered the room.

Seemingly oblivious to her audience, and dressed in a stunning, slinky emerald dress, she had every gawping man spilling their drinks down their shirts as she sauntered past. Her hips swayed hypnotically, the slightly tousled, curly hair bounced with each purposeful yet casual step. Steps that revealed a thigh length slit, and a flash of perfectly toned flesh.

"Good evening all." She retrieved her clutch bag from where she'd absentmindedly left it on an early visit to the table, pulled out her London bus lipstick and reapplied generously. "Look at you two! *You look great!*" Application over, she moved around the table hugging everyone, including a desperately intimidated Summer. Not in her wildest dreams, she thought, would she ever be that spectacular. Around the rooms, tongues were still being stuffed back into mouths by jealous wives and girlfriends, and jaws hoisted off the oak floor.

Her fiancé Jeff soon joined the group. Blond and broad, he was almost as striking and as well-built as Dean - almost, but not quite. Hayley introduced him, yet she seemed disappointed to see him arrive, her gaze often wandering around the room, as though she was looking for someone else.

The tables were set for ten guests. As The Bear lacked any sort of partner, or perhaps mate, this left one chair free for discarded jackets and handbags that concealed Jerrycan-sized hip flasks, topped up with emergency supplies vodka and gin. Each year, as the evening progressed, the bar staff became suspicious when guests, although clearly becoming increasingly intoxicated, insisted on ordering only tonic on ice, with perhaps a slice of lemon peel. It was a mystery indeed.

The menu had been circulated weeks ago, and everyone had made their individual choices of starter, main course and dessert. The choice was generous, especially considering that the Mayflower Plaza would be catering for nearly two hundred Cottons Bank staff that night. As an army of waiters began filing in carrying trays of starters, everyone was seated. Protective napkins were stuffed into collars, and knives and forks brandished in anticipation.

After a long period of enforced self-composure, which had seen her fall worryingly silent, Summer managed to recover some of her nerve, and, safe in the company of colourful, yet non-relationship threatening guests, tried to unwind and enjoy herself. She was here now, and the evening wouldn't last forever. She'd soon be in her PJ's, alone with her beloved Monkey.

George was clearly bewitched by Hayley, but then, so was every man in the room, even a few of the girls for that matter, it was forgivable. And although she kept giving his thigh a spirited squeeze when she thought she wasn't looking, Di was no threat either. Pinching his cheek was becoming tiresome though.

After a third patient attempt by Hayley, who was sat on her left, to talk about her unique dress, Summer eventually relented. She took a deep breath, downed a whole glass of white wine, slipped the comforting pashmina off her tiny shoulders in order to reveal more of Mrs Butler's handiwork, and dived in headfirst. Being this exposed was genuinely stressful, as was the eye contact, but she was proud of herself. The wine had hit home.

Elsewhere around the table, conversation was mixed and good natured. With an inexhaustible river of wine being poured into crystal glasses by attentive waiters, who seemed to miraculously appear at the elbow each time a glass was drained, it was impossible not to fall under the festive spell. The background roar of laughter and banter from the other tables filled the air, thankfully drowning out the dreadful Christmas music that was dusted off and inserted into tape cassettes the world over this time of year. With the meal underway, the party was getting into its stride.

The quality of food was unbelievable, and the plates piled high. After each course, most of the exhausted, bursting diners had leftovers, and it had normally been The Bears responsibility to Hoover up the remains. Now though, it seemed he had completion, as George too, having at least politely asked if the diner was finished, devoured excess roast potatoes and unwanted mountains of cauliflower cheese. As good as it was, none of it held a candle to his Mum's.

Expensive crackers were pulled, paper hats adorned, and tasteful jokes exchanged. Shortly after rounds of luxurious gourmet coffee and quality after dinner mints, the belly of every guest left in ruins, all of the chandeliers and wall lights were abruptly dimmed, leaving the faces of the surprised staff illuminated just by the flicker of candlelight. Everyone held their breath.

Up on the stage, a single spot light fell upon unmistakable silhouette of Laurence Burton. Immaculately dressed as always, and still holding a reassuringly large glass of single malt, he stood centre stage, in front of the singer's microphone.

"Don't worry everyone, *I'm not going to sing*!" The warm soothing voice washed over his audience like the gentle waters of the Indian Ocean, those staff that were Christmas Ball veterans relaxed. Finally, the customary End of Year speech, this was usually one of the best bits. The veterans topped up their glasses in anticipation.

Mr Burton was a fine entertainer. His speeches were typically peppered with humorous anecdotes, uplifting stories, and reflections on Cottons Bank's contribution to charitable causes throughout the year. He delivered his carefully chosen words with genuine, heartfelt sincerity, somehow managing to seize the attention and interest of every listener, as though he was having a quiet word over drinks at the bar. In part at least, for this reason he was an esteemed and much loved leader.

"My friends, I have some news…"

Chapter 9

Sweet Home Chicago

Half an hour later.

The lights came up again leaving Nelson's table sat in silence, like concerned relatives gathered outside the hospital room of a dying Aunt, quite unsure what to say or do next. For a moment, every table was exactly the same. Finally, unsettled by the stillness, conversation slowly started to build again, gathered momentum and eventually filled the void left by the startling news.

"That can't be good, *can it*?" Hayley turned to Auntie Rose, who was still dabbing her eyes with a small, delicate handkerchief.

"Ahem, *no*, I don't believe it is." She took a quick, deep sip from her gin and tonic. "I can't imagine we'll see his like again. As for this merger business, *well*, I - I just can't understand quite what they are all thinking of, I mean, *the NSIB*, really? *Whatever next!*" Auntie Rose was only echoing the voice of every other table around the room. Fear and uncertainly had jumped out of nowhere and gripped the mass of drunken staff firmly by the neck. This was not what any of them had expected, especially not this evening. Why make the announcement tonight, and why the NSIB? The two Banks were just so different in terms of both heritage and business model. Which Bank would be the dominant partner, whose characteristics would win through? Things were going to get messy.

As if to break the mood the band, No Rush, chose that moment to start their set, opening with a spirited rendition of the B-52's 'Love Shack'. It could have been much worse of course, they could have played 'There May Be Trouble Ahead'.

Dean wandered over to the table, shook Jeff and the other partners warmly by the hand, and knelt down next to Hayley, the pair of them suddenly lost in a private, whispered conversation spoken into each other's ears. The rest of the staff, oblivious to their partners, spoke in low, concerned voices. All ashen faced, all fearful.

Elsewhere, the alcoholic bubbles from all the guzzled champagne had now reached George's extremities and he was beginning to worry that any movement required of him would end in disaster. Summer was nursing a large glass of complimentary wine and had suddenly turned even paler than usual. She was gazing into the middle distance as though in a trance, completely lost in thought.

"Talk to me, *Summertime*." He nudged her bare elbow with his own, harder than intended, and grinned encouragingly. "*What's wrong?*"

She smiled feebly, shrugged her tiny shoulders and shook her head. "Oh, err, nothing, *nothing…*"

Although not a complete stranger to relationships, George was not overfamiliar with them either, and still had a fundamental and important lesson to learn. When a man asks a woman 'what's wrong' and she says 'nothing', this absolutely does not mean that nothing is wrong. Something is always wrong, and invariably, it's the man's fault. What he needed to do now was ask again, and again, and then, for good measure, again. Eventually, he'd need to apologise too.

"Oh, okay, then… *Err*, look, people are starting to get up and dance, *do you want a boogie?*"

"*Boogie?* George, *really!*" She rarely called him by Christian name these days. He knew enough about girls to know this was a bad sign. "Do you understand what Mr Burton just said?" Her indigo eyes flashed at him. They were bright, but for the first time, not with desire. Was this anger? He should've paused for a moment. Perhaps considered the look on his girlfriend's face and measured his response. But he didn't.

"Yeah, *I guess so*, but what's the big deal, Summertime? Mr B is retiring and, umm, well, some other Bank is joining up with our Bank, *I think?*" He drained another glass that had come to hand, a heavy red that, judging by the thick crust of pink lipstick on its rim, originally belonged to Di. It tasted of gin.

"What it means is the end of Cottons Bank as we've known it! The end of working under that lovely Man, the end of an era! *It's really sad news, George!*"

"*Oh*, err, sorry Summertime…"

There was no escaping it, she was definitely angry. This was uncharted waters for them, Summer just didn't do angry, not yet anyway. He was lost for something meaningful to say, for the first time he felt the age gap between them, perhaps someone older would know the right thing to do? Her gaze fell away from his, with a slight hint of exasperation. With her normal hiding place swept up, and out of the way, she instead hunkered down into the folds of her pashmina and rested her delicate chin in her hand, once again lots in an ocean of thought.

Around the table, the hushed conversations were starting to conclude, partners were reunited and a few headed off for the bar with offers of drinks for the others. George had never been in detention, but from what his older brother had said, this must have been what it felt like. He didn't even dare slump in his seat. This wasn't how he'd imagined their magical evening together going. What should he do now?

"Butler, bar, *NOW!*" It wasn't a question. The Bear plucked George out of his padded seat and pulled him towards the bar, where they'd all gathered a lifetime ago. The Bear parted the sea of dinner jackets and ball gowns like an enraged hairy Moses, as he made a beeline for a beer, towing his confused reluctant follower behind. "Two pints of whatever passes here for ale please, Barman?"

"Err, I'd rather have a Bud, please…?"

"You're having ale!"

Two frothing glasses, which looked positively cultivated compared to the last ones they'd shared in *The Pig and Hammer*, were placed on the bar, and having cleared some room amongst the raucous mass of bodies, busy fighting for drinks of their own, the pair of them sat down on bar stools. The Bear leaned in closer, even his booming roar having to battle hard against the din.

"What you fail to understand, my young friend, is that the last thing any of us wanted to do was join up with the NSIB - or lose old Burton, for that matter. It is the beginning of the end now. Things will change very quickly, this bloody sales business that you enjoy so much, well that'll become all that *they* care about, you mark my words. The likes of us that just aren't cut out for that sort of thing, those of us that have become institutionalized too, the likes of Summer, Rose, Di, Me and loads more besides, well, we're gonna be in for a hard time. Not straight away mind, but soon George, *very soon*, and when you've given years of your life to a company, it'll hurt. *It'll hurt a lot.*" He leant back and took a deep pull from his pint, wiping the foam from his beard and moustache, just a hint of emotion in his usually vacant eyes. "And that's why Summer is *pissed off*."

George reluctantly picked up his pint and examined it against the light. Satisfied that it didn't seem to have lumps floating around in it, like the last one, he braved a sip, cringed and took another to show willing. "But, *err*, how can you know all this Bear? I - I mean, it might not change at all."

"You don't work in Banking for years on end without hearing what all the other buggers are up to Mate. The NSIB is an animal, *a sales animal*, and they make huge, huge profits. You wait, give it two months, probably less, and they'll have us doing the same as them. Sellin', just sellin', they won't really give as shit about anything else." He took another huge mouthful of ale and turned briefly to glare at someone who'd had the misfortune of bumping into his colossal purple back. "Trust me, I've known plenty of people who've worked for these buggers, they're absolute sales bastards through and through!" He finished his pint and leaned in again, "Summer knows she couldn't cope in that world. Really, it's all she can do to cope as we are. Old Burton's looked after her for years, and now that's ending too. Be nice to her. I reckon you're the only thing stopping her from packing up and leaving for France right now."

George placed his elbows on the bar, cupped his hands, and hunched over his cloudy pint. He wasn't quite sure what was expected of him now. Just an hour ago, the world was a wonderful, shiny place, filled with beautiful, happy people who smelt great and waiters who handed out free drinks. He had so looked forward to this evening. Now he just wanted to go home.

The Bear slammed down his empty glass, glared critically at the barman, and rose to his feet. "I'm going for a pee, I'll meet you back at the table, don't be afraid to get me another pint eh?" And with that, the broad purple back parted the drinkers and eventually disappeared into the crowd.

George was good at bars. He'd had a lot of experience of propping them up in the past whilst Barney was off tormenting some random, unsuspecting girl. He wasn't at all bothered to be left alone drinking. At the moment it seemed preferable to being sat with his forlorn girlfriend. It was time to collect his thoughts, to try and think of something nice that he could say to her that would rescue the evening, and hopefully, put nookie and dancing back on the table. Perhaps not in that order though.

The crowd around him had slowly started to expand, and he could feel his own hired dinner jacket brushing against the back of another as he lifted his arm to take a sip. Soon he was completely isolated, encircled by an extravagant, verbose wall of uniform black jackets and an assortment of ladies bare spines, draped in an diverse array of colourful materials. It wasn't quite as pleasant as it sounded.

The wall seemed completely oblivious to the solitary young drinker it had trapped at the bar. As the wall became even more engrossed in heated, gesticulating banter, the din of their conversation coupled with the distant band, now playing Bryan Adams 'Can't Stop This Thing We Started', became overwhelming. The prisoner desperately needed to escape.

"*Hey*, George, are you okay there?" Incredibly, out of the human barricade stepped Natasha, one of The Pretty People Dean had introduced him to earlier. Completely unruffled by what must have been a tough journey, she sidled up next to him and, without any hesitation, looped her arm through his, as though they were dating, giving his forearm an affectionate squeeze with her free hand. Suddenly, the world looked a lot brighter.

"So why are you here on your own?" Still standing, she cocked her head to one side and moved her body closer to him. When they'd met earlier, George had been swimming in a lake of new, unfamiliar emotions and experiences. Her beauty had registered of course, but so had the increasing pressure of Summer's hand on his own. Now though, with some of his feelings also joining him at the bar, he was able to safely appreciate just what a breathtakingly stunning girl she was.

There was a slight hint of Hawaiian about her features and colourings. She was compact, slim and toned, an unashamed fact that her slip of a dress happily advertised. The big brown eyes dazzled, her long, almost jet-black hair was swept up into an elaborate style, and like most of the people that he'd met that evening, she smelt amazing.

Although initially startled by Natasha's unprompted warmness and proximity, having always had a keen eye for the foreign and exotic - an engrained lasting consequence of the whole Gabriella affair - George began to relax in the company of his new, olive-skinned companion. It made a welcome change to worrying about the logistics of delivering The Bears pint, or what he would say to Summer next. It wasn't like he was cheating after all.

"Oh, umm, *hi*! I, I was just waiting for the barman to serve me. *Err*, how are you enjoying the evening, does this merger stuff bother you much, our lot seem really down about the whole thing?"

Without acknowledging his question, Natasha let go of his arm and clicked her fingers in the air. For a brief moment, all warmth and affection left her voice. "Over her please, *we're waiting*!" The barman swivelled as though he has just been shot in the shoulder, and quickly darted over to the commanding voice.

"*I am sorry Miss*, what can I get you both?" He stood with his hands behind his back, awaiting further instruction. There was something about her tone that forced him to obey.

"Good, that's more like it. *Right*, I'll have a glass of Champagne." She turned to her confused companion, pouring tenderness back into both her voice and manner. "*For you, Darling?*"

"*Oh*! Thanks, err, I'll have a Bud please?" George was amazed. He genuinely couldn't recall a girl ever buying him a drink before. In his experience, it had been hard enough the other way around. Things were definitely looking up.

The drinks were served. Natasha coerced another guest into providing her with a barstool, which she demanded was placed close to George, and she sat down next to him, seductively sipping her glass of excited bubbles. Her dress gaped slightly, deliberately, taunting his eager gaze.

With his all senses melting into a puddle on the floor, he tried to distract his eyes by instead glancing at his new, chunky divers' watch. With the electric bar lights glinting off the metal casing it looked fantastic, but it was no match for Natasha's tanned cleavage. But it did prompt him to at least remember the time.

The Bear had been gone for at least ten minutes. Soon he'd be back, looking for his pint and a bag of pork scratchings, he was bound to be hungry again by now. This left him with something of a dilemma. He needed to return to the table to satisfy The Bear's never ending need for real ale and, perhaps more pressingly, re-join Summer. But on the other hand he couldn't just leave Natasha. She'd just bought him a Bud after all, there were rules about these things. And she was a complete vision.

"Now, where were we? *Oh yes*, the merger. No, it doesn't really bother me at all. I'm a CBA and if we follow the NSIB model, that'll probably mean that the Bank will start paying bonuses, so more money for shoes and holidays, which doesn't sound that bad, *does it?*" She winked at him, slowly, and took another sip. There was something about her surefooted confidence that inspired him. Natasha was probably less than an eighth of The Bears overall body mass, but she was clearly taking the events of the evening in her stride, and planning her future around change, whereas The Bear and Co. were busy contemplating their doom.

He pushed the pint of horrible real ale away and happily replaced it with an ice cold bottle of Budweiser. Ignoring the equally iced glass the barman provided, he took a long luxurious swig. As was always the case, his body was revived by the crisp, clear taste. Natasha had removed her arm from his when she sat down on the stool, but she was still very close. She hadn't taken her eyes of him for a second either, even when she sipped her champagne. What did it all mean? As the music and banter continued to build around them, and with a delectable drinking partner at his side, George started to enjoy himself once again. This was the sort of evening he'd imagined. The only slight fly in the anointment now was that he was enjoying it with the wrong girl.

"So then George, are you staying here in the hotel tonight?" A dark, perfectly plucked eyebrow ever so slightly began to arch.

"Err, yes, yeah, I, *err*, I mean, *we*, have a room, umm…"

"*We?*" The eyebrow continued in its quest.

"Umm, *yeah*, err, me and Summer."

"*Summer?*"

"Summer, my girlfriend, you, *err*, met her earlier…"

"Plain-looking girl, blushes a lot?" The eyebrow suddenly dropped and was joined by its evil twin. They frowned inquisitively at him.

"Well, I, I *err*, I don't think, that's to say, I - I, *umm*, I think she's pretty, don't you, *err*…?"

"No, not at all." She glanced at her Gucci watch. "Find me later darling, when you get bored of them again. We can dance together." It was not a question.

"BUTLER! Where's my bloody pint?" The human wall tumbled and suddenly the couple were joined by a large, hairy, purple mass of ale-deprived Bear. He didn't look at all happy at what he'd found at the bar.

"Oh, err, *hello*, sorry, I got distracted by, umm…" He fumbled desperately for her name. The blood that fuelled his memory was urgently pumped back from his loins.

"*Natasha*," she whispered gently into his ear, her breath raising goose bumps all over his body.

"Oh yes, *Natasha*, yes, umm, *of course*, Natasha! So, *err*, a pint of ale then?"

Back at the table, all was not well. Summer had entered into an alcohol fuelled, deep and meaningful conversation with Auntie Rose, and other than briefly stroking his hand when The Bear returned him unceremoniously to her side, she seemed unavailable to him for the immediate future. He considered retracing his steps back to the bar, and an encounter that had been altogether more in keeping with the spirit of the evening.

In the meantime, Di and her husband had been causing something of a stir on the dance floor. It seemed increasingly likely that at any moment causalities would be incurred by the wildly gyrating couple. At least someone was having fun. Dean and Hayley had apparently disappeared, leaving a desperate Jeff stranded with Auntie Rose's husband Ronald. His eyes looked pleadingly into the distance, hoping his emerald beauty would return and rescue him from Ronald's endless lecture about his model trains.

The Bear meanwhile continued to glare at George. He didn't approve of Natasha, or any of The Pretty People for that matter. Only Dean commanded his grudging respect, thanks to a shared love of Rugby. Despite his obvious shortcomings and sledge hammer personality, The Bear was actually quite sensitive to the feelings of others, just as long as the others in question didn't aggravate him or call him Lesley. He'd known Summer for years, largely by reputation, but he knew enough about her to suspect that given the evenings shocking news, she'd be even more vulnerable than normal. If she'd seen her new boyfriend in the presence of a scantily dressed *Hawaii Five-O* extra, it would have certainly have been enough to tip the poor, insecure little waif over the edge.

Elsewhere, the party goers settled into two distinct groups. Those that had a real and immediate problem with the announcement, which as the alcohol continued to flow proved to be in the minority, were either huddled in tight groups hidden in the shadows, or bent in intimate conversation at the table, quietly whispering about their mutual uncertainties and fears.

The rest seemed to have adopted a sort of 'Free Bar on the Titanic' mentality, and were busy making the best of the evening before it was time to leap into the lifeboats. Fuelled by the complimentary food and abundant alcohol, they'd collectively decided to make the best of the situation, and apart from a circular exclusion zone around the madly gyrating Di and Bill, imposed for health and safety reasons, the dance floor was now packed with drunken revellers.

No Rush, in an effort to prevent the two most enthusiastic members of their audience from causing a pileup, had slowed the pace down a bit by performing a sultry rendition of Alannah Miles' 'Black Velvet'. Disaster was averted, but the couples resulting dance moves were somewhat explicit. A few of the staff, already clearly the worse for drink, had slumped in their chairs, mumbling incoherently. Others though, alert and brimming with twelve months' worth of desire and lust, were coyly planning intimate, illicit liaisons. Whispered room numbers were exchanged, and secret rendezvous arranged for the small hours. There would be blushes all round when the

Banks opened again next week.

As he sat watching the others, absentmindedly peeling the label of his bottle of Bud, George wondered if he would ever be allowed to enjoy himself this evening. Summer was still lost in conversation. He was sure at one point she even wiped away a tear, but he didn't have the nerve to step in an offer his carefully pressed, silk hanky. A barrier had gone up between them, a great divide, and nothing he could say seemed able penetrate it. Why was this happening to them tonight? Was it just the merger, or something more? He looked at her small back, wrapped tightly once again in the comforting pashmina; it was turned from him, seemingly disinterested. Where had all the fun from their relationship gone? His thoughts drifted off, back to the earlier chance encounter at the bar. *She'd seemed interested in him.*

Suddenly, and to a degree, thankfully, he was unceremoniously sat on by a very sweaty Di. His wayward thoughts scattered in terror. "*Awright Luver*, why aren't you up *dancin'* Bay?" She flung her hot, damp arm around his neck and wetly kissed his cheek. "Ooo you're such an *'andsome* little Bugger!" For the hundredth time, she pinched him roughly.

"I would Di, but Summer's having a bit of a chat here with Auntie Rose. I don't think I…" He trailed off, conscious that his lap was slowly going numb.

Undeterred, Di leant across the table, crushing her victim further into his seat. "'ere, Summer, *SUMMER!* Kin' I take your 'andsome man 'ere *dancin'*?" Her gin-infused breath and booming voice managing to capture Summer's attention in way that her boyfriend had failed to for the past hour. Startled, she turned, frowning at the odd apparition before her.

"*Oh*, err, yes, by all means…" She lightly rubbed his arm again, briefly smiled at him, and returned to her deep and meaningful with Auntie Rose. His heart sank.

"Right then Georgie. *Best brace yourself, 'andsome!*"

After just two minutes on the dance floor with Di, George seriously doubted he would ever be quite the same again. He desperately tried to avert his eyes as his partner's bouncing heaving, bosom leapt this way and that, threatening to escape from her dress like dislodged, overripe melons at any moment. She repeatedly whirled him, spun him and crushed him to her hot, wet body. During the ordeal, he suffered severe chafing and scratches from the army of sequins that were sewn onto her skin tight dress, as he was forced to cling onto the spinning fifty-year-old for fear of being flung into the crowd by her momentum. Just when he thought his legs would finally buckle under the strain of an unexpected, back breaking *Dirty Dancing* move, the music finally stopped and the air was filled with applause. He'd survived, for now at least.

"*Oh bugger me*! I'm gonna need a stiff G 'n' T after that. I'll leave you to it, '*andsome*." And with another unwelcome, if nonetheless good-natured, smacker on the cheek and a ruffle of his sweat-soaked hair, she staggered off the dance floor bandy legged, like she had just ridden a wild, unbroken stallion through a burning field of corn. Suddenly, he was alone again. It wasn't much of an improvement.

The lead singer of No Rush announced a short break, and the dreaded traditional Christmas music quickly replaced their efforts whilst they refreshed themselves at the bar. Not wanting to return to the table of misery and confusion, George put his hands in his pockets and wandered up to the stage to get a better look at the guitars that rested quietly in their stands.

"How are doing, my Man?" It was Dean, looking as cool and collected as ever. His immaculate, unruffled appearance was a complete contrast to the red eyes and half tucked dress shirts that were starting to dominate the room.

"Oh well, it's been an, err, *interesting* evening so far..." He looked down at his hired dress shoes. The tailor was right. They hadn't caused blisters at all.

Dean, holding a fresh glass of champagne, placed his free hand on the younger man's shoulder and squeezed it reassuringly. "Don't worry George. I would have saved you from Di before she dragged you off to her bedroom. Come on, let's take a seat and have a chat."

They found two free chairs at the table closest to the dance floor. Dean sat down and adopted his usual relaxed position, the ankle of his left leg resting across the knee of his right. He took another sip of his champagne. "So what's going on with you and Summer then? I thought you too were practically living together." It seemed he didn't miss a thing.

George shrugged his shoulders. His bowtie was aggravating, choking him almost. Unconcerned about the Tailor's intricate lecture on etiquette, he unclipped the wretched thing. Mindful of his twenty pounds insurance deposit though, he carefully rolled it up and put it in his pocket.

"The thing is Dean, I err, *well*, all I did was ask her to dance and then she just got all funny about this merger thingy and started to sulk!" Unthinking, and beginning to relax once more, like a patient with a trusted therapist, he unbuttoned his shirt to the third hole. "I mean, I can understand her getting a bit, you know, worried and everything, but we're supposed to be enjoying the bloody party. I spent a fortune on this suit, *and the room!*"

Dean listened intently, nodding slowly. He would do so until he was finished. He was a good listener.

"*Also*, I - I know she didn't really want to come to this party, but, but now *she* is ruining it for *me*. That's not fair, *is it?*" George stopped himself. Was he being disloyal, should he have just said that? Yet now those words had been said, he felt a degree of relief for getting them off his chest. It suddenly dawned on him that he was actually a tiny bit angry with Summer. She'd pushed him away and left him alone with a room of drunken strangers, alone in a heavily decorated strange land he didn't really understand. All he wanted was for them to be like they'd always been, to be like nuts and bolts again.

Content that he was done, Dean took a sip of his champagne to make sure. "There's going to be changes, my Man, lots of them. Summer and a few others know that the little worlds they've built in Cottons, their safe houses, are going to crumble. It won't be a place to hide, or coast along anymore. It's sad, but it's true. When we join up with the NSIB, it's going to be inevitable." Once again, he rested his strong hand on the younger man's shoulder. It was a very reassuring gesture. "The difference between them and us, my Man, is that we know that there's nothing we can do about it tonight. We're the lucky ones. While the music is still playing and there's wine on the table, we should all just have some fun while we still can, don't you agree?"

George nodded. Some of the unwanted, unexpected tension and stress born out of the evening slowly started to ebb away, leaving him yearning for some of the fun Dean talked about.

"You play the guitar, don't you?"

"Err, well a bit, *yes*, sort of I suppose. *How did you know that?*"

"Hmm, Oh, I looked at your file." The response was completely natural, as though he had every right to do so. "And another thing, Natasha has taken quite a shine to you…"

With his self-confidence reeling from an unexpected, although entirely welcome, boost, George made his way back to his table via the bar. He ordered two bottles of Bud and a Southern Comfort chaser to keep them company, and as he waited for the bourbon to be poured over some ice, he reflected on his brief conversation with the breath-taking stranger he'd met earlier. It was slowly beginning to dawn on him that here, in this new grown up world of banking; he might not be quite as invisible to girls as he'd always thought he'd been. It was quite a startling revelation.

He walked back to re-join his group with newfound Gunslinger

Swagger. The two beers clutched by their chilly necks in his left hand, swung casually with each step, the tumbler's ice tinkling slightly in the right. Any thoughts he'd had about transforming into a brooding heartbreaker were suddenly scattered though, when he saw that at last he had a chance to talk to Summer again, alone. His heart lifted and he quickened his pace.

Auntie Rose and Ronald had already taken to their bed, and a clearly exhausted Di was dozing peacefully, her head in Bill's lap. Or at least that's what everyone hoped. Hayley and Jeff were nowhere to be seen, which left just the Bear and Summer, who didn't look entirely comfortable in each other's company. George placed his drinks down next to her and went to top up her empty wine glass from the decanter.

"Oh, no thanks, Monkey. I think I've had enough." She put her small hand over the top of the glass and smiled half-heartedly at him. This couldn't be a good sign, but at least she was calling him Monkey again. Think positive.

"*Really*, you normally love your wine, Summertime." Echoing the use of their nicknames, he sat down next to her, considered his options carefully for a moment, and tentatively placed a hand on her back. Her eyes were red, and she had slightly swollen cheeks. This was definitely not a good sign.

Having already established that asking what was wrong was unlikely to glean any new information, and more than likely land him in trouble again, he decided to adopt a new approach. He moved his hand. Gently put his arm around her quivering shoulders and pulled her in for a good old fashioned hug. She snuggled in willingly, her earlier stiffness now melted away. The move seemed to have had the desired effect. They were finally a couple once again. George was relived on several levels. He wasn't quite sure how he would've explained to his Mum just how he'd managed to ruin things with this lovely girl a day before Christmas. The punishment didn't bear thinking about. This was the season of roast potatoes and fruit cake after all. Being denied a good portion of either, would've been hell.

Judging by one or two stumbles, some ear splitting feedback and a crash of cymbals, the band, clearly over refreshed, were preparing to start up again. Strangely enough though, Dean had joined them on stage. He was probably requesting a song.

"*Err, COULD GEORGE BUTLER PLEASE COME TO THE STAGE?*"

Shit!

George was under no illusions at all about his limited abilities with the guitar. Since the age of eleven, he'd been self-taught, thanks to an unfortunate misunderstanding between himself and Mr Fenhollinder, the Dutch music teacher who ran the weekly after school guitar class. It was the closest he'd ever come to being expelled.

Having expressed an interest in the guitar from a tender age, his parents, keen to nurture a new found potential hobby, bought him a three-quarter size Spanish acoustic from *Argos*, along with *The Children's Guitar Book One*, for his tenth birthday, and duly enrolled him in Mr Fenhollinder's class.

From the outset, he struggled, more so with the class than he did the guitar. Mr Fenhollinder was an altogether odd character, clearly the tallest man in the world, and so skinny that when he turned sideways, he seemed to almost disappear. His long, floppy hair was prematurely grey, and his moth eaten, reluctantly beard looked like a diseased garden lawn. He endlessly drank some sort of foul-smelling, thick black treacle from a huge green thermos flask, and talked aggressively to himself in his native tongue when his students aggravated him, which was most of the time.

George's fellow classmates were a cultural cross section of misfits and oddities of various shapes and sizes. Once in full flow, their combined racket was enough to drive even the strongest willed primary school teacher to the cliff tops to end the suffering, and no matter how long they spent tuning their wretched instruments, somehow they always sounded utterly dreadful.

Nevertheless, after six months of frustrated and somewhat hostile tutorage, Mr Fenhollinder somehow managed to coax most of his class into playing 'Row, Row, Row Your Boat' and his own personal favourite, 'Old Macdonald Had a Farm'. Given their limited attention span, it was nothing short of a miracle. With the annual Christmas Show looming, it was decided that the class would perform at the event, both as a group, and in some cases, individually. On reflection, it had been a bad idea to let the guitarists choose their own piece.

After months of practicing dreary children's songs until his tiny fingers bled, young George decided it was time to learn a new song for his solo. At least then, he hoped the disturbing recurring dreams he was having about Mr MacDonald's farm animals escaping in a rowing boat would cease. Nothing gave him a restless night, like the image of a cow with oars.

Fortunately though, his older brother Michael was on leave from the Army, and having picked up a few basic guitar skills himself whilst posted in Germany, he was more than happy to step in and offer some much needed advice. Bless him.

George always blamed Michael for the stir he'd caused at the School Christmas Show. Once the group had performed a collective, and by now hugely reluctant rendition of 'Old Macdonald had a Farm', with nervous, bright red faces, they each began their individual acts. The opening solo was by Asiff, a tiny Indian boy, barely visible behind his guitar, who strummed out a spirited interpretation of 'London Bridge is Falling Down', to great acclaim. Next, there was a workmanlike execution of 'What Shall We Do with the Drunken Sailor', a surprise choice from the pigtailed and bespectacled Jennifer. Once the applause had died away, and the ten-year-old Diva had eventually been led off the stage, various other well-known children's classics were performed with trembling, sweaty little hands. The solos were going well. There were a few missed notes, and Mr Fenhollinder had to shout out a few cords when one of his flock stumbled, but on the whole, the act met with the approval parents and staff. Dutch blood pressure remained virtually constant.

George was last to perform. Strangely enough, he ambled out on stage like a Cowboy wearing school uniform, freshly polished, his cheeks rosy red. Mrs Butler had trimmed his pudding basin hair the day before, and, taking no chances, had sealed it in place with a hearty blast of Silvikrin hairspray. His trousers were pressed, his tie still straight.

Unlike the rest of his class, his guitar was slung around his shoulders on a black leather strap covered in skulls and cross bones, a good luck gift from Michael. As their youngest son wandered into the spotlight, Mr and Mrs Butler held each other's hands tightly in excited anticipation. Unlike his athletic brother, George lacked anything even remotely resembling sporting ability. Sports Days had been painful to watch, and waiting in the rain for the exhausted runner in last place at Cross Country, frightfully dull. This then, was their first real chance to cheer him on in public. Michael, still home on leave, had also come along to pledge his support to his youngest brother. The whole thing was almost too much for the eternally overemotional Mrs Butler to bear. There would be tears and fruitcake before supper.

After a brief round of pre-performance applause, the hall fell silent. George cracked his fingers, and began.

Shortly after the show, barely containing himself and quivering slightly, Mr Fenhollinder had a quiet word with The Butlers. In his opinion, Black Sabbath's 'Paranoid' was perhaps not the ideal song choice for a Primary School Christmas Show, and nobody had expected their son to sing along either. Michael left home the next day for the safety of his military base.

In the years that followed, George was left to teach himself. He soon out grew the old acoustic and longed for something altogether noisier. After the embarrassment he'd caused his parents though, he didn't think it wise to ask for a basic electric guitar for Christmas, and decided to save up for one instead.

Five and a half years later, he finally had enough to buy the Encore Stratocaster replica that endlessly taunted him from behind the bay window of Tremolo's Guitar and Piano Shop. It was pearl white or cream if you were being cruel, and had a rosewood fret board and maple neck. He'd visited the shop hundreds of times to try it out, secretly feeling as though he owned the instrument already. Mr Clegg, the owner, was relieved when his most regular, if least profitable customer eventually rushed in one afternoon and began counting out a creased, slightly soiled collection of five pound notes. Any longer, and the guitar would have been virtually second hand.

Impressed that he'd been able to save up the required funds to purchase the guitar, his parents bought him a basic amplifier for his birthday and two pairs of ear plugs for themselves. A week later, and strangely enough without any prompting, they also bought him an electric guitar tuner too.

Although a passable strummer on his old, questionably tuned Argos acoustic, he soon found that his new electric beast was something else entirely, strung entirely in steel, playing it felt like an act of self-mutilation, and the medicine cabinet's supply of plasters soon ran dry.

Having neither the patience nor aptitude to learn proper music, he relied on guitar tablature instead, and soon the simple diagrams became second nature to him as he wrestled painfully with famous flashy riffs, and roof rattling power cords. Despite near constant agony, and regular breaks to tend to a fresh laceration, George slowly started to pick up a few basic electric guitar licks, but he desperately wanted to master something flamboyant, something he could show off. Something people would recognise.

After months of tireless practice, rivers of blood, and breaking countless strings, it finally happened. He'd been perched on the edge of his single bed for hours, his fingers bleeding down his fret board, his eyes screwed up in frustration, agonizing pain and exasperated anger. Then, out of the tangled mess of miss hit notes and poorly bent strings, there was a note, a collection of notes even, which sounded familiar.

He was suddenly hit by an overwhelming sense of both relief and joy. Had he finally stumbled upon the sound that he was desperately searching for? He composed himself, downed a stone cold mug of forgotten tea, clicked and flexed his fingers, and tried again. At last, there it was! The unmistakable opening riff to Derek and the Dominos' 'Layla', his own unrequited love of his guitar had finally been repaid.

For George, the sense of relief and happiness that he'd mastered something new was second only to his first sweaty passionate experiences with Gabriella. From that moment he was hooked, and dedicated all of his free time, and a great deal of homework allocated time besides, to his guitar.

At least twice, Mr Butler had been compelled to confiscate the instrument.

Undaunted, he continued his practice. Before long, and providing his parents were out of the house, he found that if he set the trembling fifty-watt amplifier's overdrive to a neighbourhood threatening level, he could also manage a passable rendition of Dire Straits' 'Money for Nothing'. Only the best bit though, the start.

And this soon proved to be his undoing. Once he'd learnt the flashy riffs, or the solo halfway through, he lost total interest and moved on, failing entirely to learn the remaining rhythm section, obsessed instead with the next searing riff in his new book. Before long, if he was ever asked what he could play, he would usually have to confess to only being able to play the opening of this, or the solo of that.

This was disheartening. After the unbearable pain he'd suffered to learn the bloody instrument, to not be able to lay claim to a single song, was utterly frustrating. Reluctantly at first, still addicted to the high that the solos gave him, he decided to set about learning something from start to finish. Something he could play along to, if the original recording was inserted into his tape cassette. But what should he learn?

During his endless tormented studies, he'd stumbled across a basic blues guitar riff which could be adapted to any key. Initially he'd abandoned it in favour of Layla, but after carefully listening to an assortment of tracks on his treasured Best of Blues cassette, George realised that many of the lead guitar licks followed the same basic pattern. If only he could simply master this pattern, and perhaps add a few Chuck Berry flashy bends and slides, he'd be able to play along with anything bluesy.

A few weeks later, Mr and Mrs Butler returned to the family's respectable semi, after the weekly shop, to find the blues blaring out of their stereo system. Expecting to have to scold their youngest son for playing his music too loud again, and conscious of their neighbours, they barged through the back door. The front door was only ever used for guests.

For a moment, they were frozen in stunned silence. Their son was stood in the centre of the lounge on their prized Chinese rug. His eyes were screwed up tightly, his face twisted into an expression that alarmingly resembled constipation, his fingers darting almost expertly amongst the strings with the occasional painful bend or slide. Clearly oblivious to his parents' presence, he was playing along, quite expertly, to Buddy Guy's version of *Sweet Home Chicago*. Involuntarily, in spite of the inevitable complaints, they swelled with pride.

When the song finally died, he opened his eyes again. Yet instead of retreating to his room in embarrassment, as he'd done when he'd been caught doing the same thing with a tennis racket years before, George smugly put his hands on his hips. "Mum, Dad, *DID YOU HEAR THAT!*"

As Mr Butler pointed out at the time, actually the whole street had heard that.

"'ere you go Mate, take it easy with her, she's my pride 'n' joy!" George nodded nervously as the heavily tattooed lead guitarist slung the black Gibson Les Paul over his trembling shoulders. He was now holding a guitar that was worth roughly twice as much as his MGB. Should he make a dash for it? It would solve lots of problems all at once.

With one type of abject terror temporarily distracting him from another, he gingerly adjusted the strap, which the guitarist had set for somewhere around his ankles. The stage lights dazzled him, but despite the spots in his eyes, he could still see a drunken mass of curious, intrigued staff. Their expectant eyes all waiting to see what was going to happen next.

Dressed entirely in black with curly blond hair, and clearly harbouring a fetish for eyeliner, the singer bounded across the stage to meet the newest member of his band. *"Dude*, top man for getting up here, *let's do this Man!"* He bounced up and down excitably, his eyes wide and crazy, the massive black cross around his neck leaping violently about. He was quite terrifying up close. *"What do you wanna play then, Dude?"*

Utterly petrified, and uncertain of just how he let Dean talk him into this mess, George nervously whispered into the singer's ear. *"Err*, well, umm, I can only really play bits and pieces really. *Umm*, I can play one song, err sort of at least, I - I, well, *I play along with it on the stereo!"* Any embarrassment this confession might have sparked was also busy trembling in a corner of his head.

"Dude, we all do that! What's the track, Man?" The singer grabbed hold of both of George's shoulders. Was he planning to shake the information out of him?

"Err, well, it's a Blues track..."

"Cool Man which one?"

"Err, well its, umm, 'Sweet Home Chicago'..." The Singer went mad with joy, slapped him twice on the cheek and bounded back to his microphone. Clearly he was on drugs.

"Ladies and Gentlemen, we are proud to play for you, with the help of one of your own, *SWEET HOME CHICAGOOOOOO!"* Although most of the audience had probably never heard of the song, they all exploded in a riot of applause, cheers and badly pitched whistles. This was encouraging at

least. Now, he just had to hope he wouldn't bugger it up.

Leaving the microphone wobbling slightly, like a violated Weeble, he bounced back over to his guitarist. "*What key Man?*"

"Err, *sorry?*" Fear suddenly chased a large amount of the alcohol out of his bloodstream. His heart thumped harder still.

"What key do you want the band to play it in, Dude?"

"Umm, well, err, *I don't know!*" This wasn't a bit like Eric Clapton.

Sensing a fellow musician's terror, no matter how unbelievably incompetent he was, the bass player, a very round man in a badly fitting, sweat-stained denim shirt wandered over.

"Dude, where do you normally play the song on your fret board?" He nodded encouragingly. It had been a long night. He was the designated driver, and he just wanted to go home and dive into a bucket of fried chicken.

"*Oh, I see!*" A light bulb was finally lit in a very dim room, "Err, *here.*" He pointed to his favourite, much loved twelfth fret.

"Right, thank God for that. *KEY OF E BOYS!*"

When the very last note was eventually wrung from the terrified Les Paul, and the great wave of belting blues finally came to an enthusiastic, string-bending climax, the audience of staff, thanks to either being extremely drunk, or unbelievably charitable, went mad with applause. The lead singer, who'd been brilliantly encouraging throughout George's traumatic yet uplifting experience, bounded over to embrace his guest guitarist, ask him his name, and introduce him to his new army of devoted fans.

"Ladies and Gentlemen, I give you, *The Butler!*" He yelled through his microphone and the ecstatic crowd immediately started chanting "BUTLER, BUTLER, BUTLER". It was a uniquely overwhelming, and truly emotional moment in his life. But now, as through his whole performance, George desperately searched the room to see if Summer had been watching him play. She wasn't.

The next morning he awoke on his back to find that he'd slept fully clothed on the king size hotel bed. His head throbbed terribly, and his throat and mouth were parched. This was a familiar unpleasantness, and something he'd learnt to deal with, yet it was nothing compared to the vicious pain that emanated from the fingertips of his left hand.

He sat up slowly, and looked at the dried blood that had stained the cuff of his hired shirt. His Mum would have her work cut out before he returned it to the Tailor. Desperately searching his hung-over, dehydrated memory for clues, he glanced at his watch. It was ten o'clock in the morning, it was Christmas Eve, and he was alone.

Through the alcoholic fog, events started slowly coming back to him. He remembered playing with the band, literally until his fingers bled, and he remembered everyone being really rather excited about it. He grinned at the memory in spite of the pain. He remembered all the drinks that people had bought him afterwards too, the endless and somewhat strong drinks, all of which seemed to be served in very large glasses.

Suddenly, a good measure of adrenaline flooded into his weary body. He'd remembered dancing with Natasha. Quite closely and seductively, now he came to think of it. New, urgent questions started to form in his freshly troubled mind, all of which boiled down to the same thing. Had Summer seen him dancing with Natasha? And perhaps more importantly, where was Summer?

A knock on the door startled him. He instinctively leapt to his feet, his head pounding as the blood sloshed against the sides. Had she just locked herself out, gone for breakfast maybe, and didn't want to wake him? His heart swelled, everything was going to be okay after all.

He flung open the door, unconcerned with his appearance. Stood waiting patiently in the hallway, was an immaculate member of the reception staff. He was holding a square box that had been carefully wrapped in Christmas paper, and he examined the dishevelled guest with an expression of quiet, but polite, repulsion.

"Mr Butler, *Sir*, this was left for you yesterday evening." He held out the package for the confused young man. "Just to remind you, *Sir*, check out for all Cottons Bank Staff is at twelve noon, *sharp*. Good day to you."

His heart sunk again. Tea was urgently required before anything else happened. He vaguely recalled there being a kettle and some tea bags in the room, and set about tending to his unbearable thirst.

Nursing a passable brew, George sat on the edge of the bed and examined the package. It was clearly a gift. Solid to the touch, roughly twelve inches long, six wide and two deep. Taped to the front of the Christmas paper there was a white envelope. He detached it carefully and opened it. Glancing at the unmistakeable writing, he immediately knew who it was from.

He closed the card without reading it, and took long sips from his steaming cup. If only he could remember what had happened. Up until he'd played with the band, events were reasonably clear in his mind. Beyond that moment though, things started to become somewhat hazier. All evidence so far though, tended to suggest that very bad things had occurred. It was time to read the card, time to face the music.

My Monkey,

I am so sorry. I know I'll have upset you by leaving on Christmas Eve, but I felt that I must get away and clear my head. I also feel that you might need to spread your wings and fly for a while. You are so very young and tying you down at this stage in your life to someone who just wants to settle, is the wrong thing to do right now. I don't want to lose you though, and I certainly don't want anyone else in my life.

Last night, Mr Burton kindly agreed to let me take a few weeks holiday, to get my head together. I'm not sure that the Bank is really the place I belong anymore, and the merger will only make things much, much worse for me. That's why I was so upset. It really is the end of an era for me. I need to leave to find myself again, perhaps find something that I really want to do.

So for now at least, I am going to join my family in Provence for Christmas, and try to find some solace and make some decisions about my future.

I do know that I desperately want to have you in my life, regardless of whatever happens, and as long as that's still okay with you, I urge you to stay close to me George, if only by letter?

Most importantly, please promise me one thing, promise me that you will pick up these brushes and paint again?

Always yours, with all my love,

Summertime. X X

Confused and lost, George held the card away from him, as though it was a stained, dirty shirt that belonged to someone else, not unlike the one that he was wearing. Eventually, after reading it again and again, he let it fall to the floor. He drained the remnants of his cooling tea for comfort, and finally picked up the present from where he'd left it on the bed sheets. Very slowly, he opened the gift.

When the last fragments of torn robin and holly bush wrapping paper had been removed, and he'd pulled the unruly, clingy Sellotape from around his fingers, he was able to finally see exactly what she'd meant. It was glossy hardwood paint box, full of thick tubes of Daler Rowney acrylic paints, and a neat, impressive collection of quality horsehair brushes. He'd always wanted one. How did she know?

A great surge of guilt tore through him like a hot bullet. He should have done more to comfort her last night. He should have asked Auntie Rose what he needed to say to make it better. He should have taken her to their room instead of showing off on stage. He should have. He should have.

He fell back on the bed and clasped the box tightly to his chest. She'd buggered off, she'd properly buggered off. His mum was going to kill him.

Chapter 10

Gym Bunnies

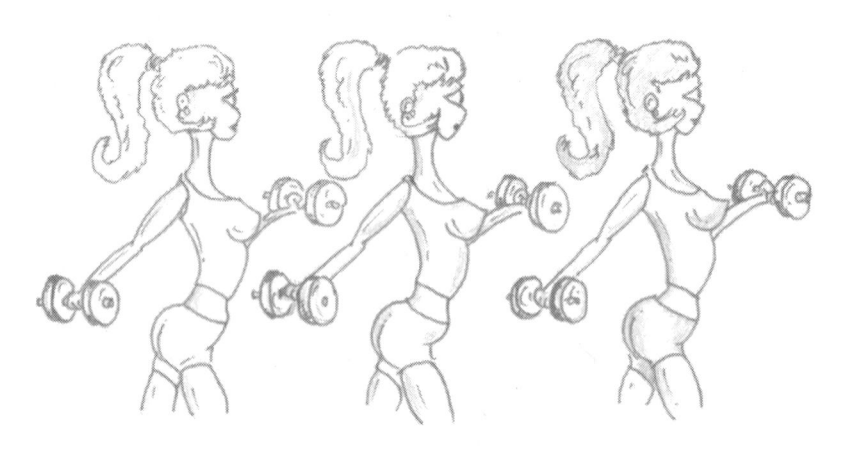

Monday evening, early February, 1996.

Inadequate, it was the only word to describe how he felt right now, and he didn't expect things to get very much better once he'd summoned the courage to step inside the impressive looking gym, which loomed ominously ahead of him, either. Yet it was a welcome change to some of the other emotions George had become familiar with over the past six weeks.

Nevertheless, there was just no way his 1.1 litre, powder blue Ford Fiesta Mk.2, with its plastic wheel trims and grey velour seats, stood a chance in this company. The immaculately kept, metallic black BMW M3 seemed to almost smirk at the quivering shopping trolley, which had just pulled up alongside its flared, muscular arches. Bless it.

So far, 1996 had thrown the Fiesta's reluctant new owner into a world of misery, loss and confusion. Although he'd encountered these sensations before, they seemed far more grown up and severe this time around. The sense of agonising loss he'd felt in his formative years, when he'd misplaced a cherished Lego man for example, paled into insignificance when compared to his separation from his girlfriend, on the whole at least. He did after all eventually find the little yellow chap behind his moneybox.

The year had gotten off to a very bad start when Summer announced, via an inventive combination of international telephone calls, postcards and mix tapes, that she had definitely decided to leave the Bank, and now planned to move to France to help her parents run their artists retreat. Leaving the Bank was one thing, but leaving the country was another matter entirely. Naturally, despite the contents of her Christmas Eve letter, George assumed that this meant she'd also be leaving him too, his experience in these matters being somewhat limited. The whole affair resulted in a particularly miserable festive period on both sides of the Channel. Summer fretted over her decision to leave, and George moped about and fumbled for answers to his Mum's increasingly threatening interrogations. Soon enough, she concluded that he had obviously buggered things up. His slices of fruitcake visibly thinned.

The rationing went largely unnoticed though. His brain had been far too busy dealing with a never-ending stream of questions to tell his stomach that it was being short changed at supper. What did it all mean, had he been dumped at Christmas, quite the worst time of all to be dumped, was he a single man again? Whilst this was a relationship status that he was all too familiar with, it was not one that he particularly craved.

The torrent of emotional phone calls, wistful postcards and poignant notes hadn't helped answer any of his questions either. They only served to prompt new ones instead. From the moment he'd read that first letter, dazed and alone in his hotel room on Christmas Eve, he'd been truly baffled. The tone of all her subsequent letters, postcards and the numerous heartfelt calls, suggested that she was simply waiting for him, and would be continuing to do so for some considerable time. Quite what she was waiting for him to do though was a mystery, but she did seem to be giving him a free reign to do as he pleased. Or rather, as she'd kept on putting it, time to 'Spread his Wings'. But what on earth did all this mean?

In the past, George had never had much of a private life, or opportunity to do much wing spreading for that matter. Unlike his older brother, he'd never had reason to request an audience with his Dad for what was bound to be awkward, father and son time. Now though, with his head spinning with questions to which he urgently needed answers, he felt that if ever there was a time to draw upon the experiences and wisdom of Mr Butler Senior, this was it. With Michael away, there should at least be a free slot too.

Timing was essential, especially if he was to avoid any unwanted input from his Mum, who still seemed to harbour some quite strong views on the subject. Given that his Dad's movements were fairly easy to anticipate, George soon identified that Saturday afternoon would be the best time to strike. The ritual lunchtime beef burgers would've had sufficient time to settle, and the vintage Velocette motorbike that lay in neat scattered piles on the garage floor, would begin to beckon. The next weekend, he'd set his plan in motion.

He'd gingerly entered the garage, taking extra care not to stand on any of the precious mechanical parts that littered the concrete floor, and slowly approached the oil stained apparition in overalls. His Dad was holding a crank case in one hand, and a very well-thumbed owner's manual in the other. He didn't look very happy.

Mr Butler was without question one of the most talented and brilliant mechanical engineers ever to grace the halls of the University, where he'd worked for over thirty years. His unwavering ability to overcome complex and challenging engineering conundrums confounded his contemporaries, and awe struck the students alike. In his spare time, usually from around ten in the morning to three in the afternoon, he'd invent household gadgets for fun. He'd constructed a washing line powered by a two stroke motorbike engine, an automatic can opener that could have easily doubled as an angle grinder and a skateboard for Michael, skilfully moulded from *borrowed* carbon fibre. Not only did it go like the wind, it was also invisible to radar. He was great with his hands, though not so ingenious with his relationship advice.

In the end, George found that although his Dad's exasperated response to his relentless questioning was somewhat curt, it did seem to somehow put things into perspective, and shed new light on recent events. "It means you've got a first reserve. *Now bugger off.*"

To make matters worse, during all of his emotional upheaval, George's treasured MGB was at last sold to the owner of Ashton's Vintage and Classic Cars. He'd handed over the keys to his pride and joy, like the reluctant owner of a misbehaved Rottweiler, giving his lead to the vet with the court order. As he clutched a dirty envelope, stuffed with soiled twenties, his heart had sank as the man in the grubby overalls jumped into the driver's seat, where he'd spent so many happy hours at the wheel, and unceremoniously tore off to the back of the yard to find it a place among the other wrecks that rotted there. Out of sight, but by no means out of mind. Never to be seen by its tearful former owner, ever again.

The following day he unenthusiastically handed over five hundred pounds to a very old lady who was selling her perfectly respectable 1.1 litre Ford Fiesta, as she could no longer summon the strength to depress the clutch. It smelt faintly of lavender.

Despite the persistent, oddly disturbing aroma of old lady, the Fiesta at least proved to be an economically sound choice, especially given his imminent move to Armada Branch. Compared to the voracious thirst of the MG, the fiesta was practically teetotal, and he was now able to cover great distances without having to plan his route between petrol stations. The Fiesta also had no inclination towards overheating, melting, randomly cutting out, stoutly refusing to start or, most importantly, leaking fluids, in or out. And, whilst the old lady fragrance was unwelcome, it was an improvement on the MG's occasional 'Au d' Devils Armpit'. But these benefits were of little consolation. The Ford lacked the one thing the old wreck had had in abundance, that almost intangible quality that made him look fondly over his shoulder every time he parked it. The Fiesta lacked soul.

Having been incessantly nagged by his Mum about not wasting Summer's lovely gift, or for that matter, his talent, in the past weeks George had also picked up his new brushes and paint set, and spent hours planted at his easel. A fresh blank canvas stared hopefully back at him as he searched for inspiration. He'd read somewhere once that when someone paints during a time of emotional turmoil, the painting they create somehow absorbs these emotions and feelings, and becomes a record of that chapter in their life. He considered this notion very carefully, and eventually set about painting a lonely baboon in a tree. It was very lifelike.

To begin with, George dreaded the welcome desk at Armada branch, as he had his first day at secondary school. He was comfortable at Nelsons. He knew where the toilets were and he knew how to avoid the resident bully, he'd even managed to become teachers pet. Now though, in this largely new and unfamiliar world, he was in a state of near permanent anxiety, fuelled in part by his emotional vulnerability. He dreaded the moment he'd be faced with a challenging query that would pitch him several miles outside of his minuscule comfort zone.

Any opportunity to relinquish his position to make the hourly tea run was seized upon enthusiastically as a means of escape. He'd drag out the task for as long as he could, squeeze the life from the tea bags and polish the cracked mugs to a brilliant shine. If his return to the welcome desk could be further delayed by popping out to the shops to buy more semi skimmed milk or PG Tips, more so the better.

He was now part of a team of four staff. They all manned the desk and rotated their lunch breaks to ensure that it was adequately covered at all times. Sadly though, this meant that at least twice a week, he found he was either having brunch, or late afternoon tea, rather than lunch. It played havoc with his digestion. Not unlike a Giant Panda, he needed to eat for at least fourteen hours a day in order to avoid digestive crisis, and he soon became adept at hiding digestives and fruit cake in his suit pockets.

The Team Leader, Adriana, was a hot-blooded, raven-haired woman in her early thirties. She was of Spanish origin, single and extremely passionate about customer service. She favoured impossibly tight, pencil skirts which forced her to walk from the knee down, and extremely close cut white cotton blouses, buttoned adequately enough to conceal the structure of her desperately overworked bra, but very little else.

Adriana was prone to mad fits of gesticulating rage, expressed in her native tongue, and usually as the result of some avoidable, minor incompetence. But these moments tended to pass quickly. Almost as soon as the blood had risen to her slender neck, the fury was replaced with tactile cooing and soothing reassurances. It was all very confusing. As it had been left to Adriana to teach George the complexities of the welcome desk, his first few days had done nothing to improve either his understanding of the female creature, or his grasp of the Spanish language. Both were still something of a mystery to him.

Acting as number two was Doug, a married father of three in his late forties. He had impressive middle-aged spread and even more impressive bushy moustache. With thick black, curly hair flecked with grey and big brown eyes, he looked just like an overweight, aging Tom Selleck. Doug had a wicked sense of humour, read the Sun newspaper at every opportunity and took his coffee black, except on Thursdays.

Finally there was Kelly. She was gorgeous, twenty-five, tall, slender and very, very blond. She was warm, generous and, most importantly, shared George's obsession with tea.

In his first few weeks though, and despite his best efforts to the contrary, it wasn't long before the newest member of the team was mugged once again by Blunder and Muddle, the two unseen members of staff who seemed inclined to pounce on him from behind the coin trolley when least expected.

Firstly there was an unfortunate incident involving an urgent money transmission. Frozen in terror, with no tea run to save him, George had nervously taken the instruction from the head partner of the Cities most prestigious law firm, Gilders LLP. He was an impossibly rigid man, all pinstripes and spectacles. His firm had been a respected, long standing Business customer of over eighty years, and he knew it all too well. He was acting on behalf of an equally prominent client, and therefore was understandably concerned a few hours later, when seven hundred and thirty-two thousand pounds left their client account and disappeared into thin air.

After a fraught afternoon spent checking the records, during which time George considered making a run for it, the monies were thankfully located. It transpired the fault, quite naturally, rested with the new recruit. Having failed to check his work thoroughly enough before processing, he'd inadvertently delighted a random fisherman in the Ukraine, rather than an elderly spinster from the UK.

Having narrowly survived this fiasco, the following week, obviously not content to sit quietly at the desk and serve customers, he caused another spectacular cashpoint incident. Adriana had done her very best to explain the complexities of the machines to her new charge. He desperately scribbled notes in his *Red and Black* jotter whilst his passionate Spanish tutor pointed out the essentials, the basics and the absolutely vital. He broke his pencil three times and he blushed eight.

"This *leetle* button 'ere, donna press it *eh*, causa massif problemo for me, *ana for you*, hey?" Adriana pinched his ample, pudgy cheek affectionately; it was unfortunately becoming her habit, having borrowed it from Di, and returned to the now familiar prone position that enables the cashpoint operator to load the money containers, and affords the cashpoint novice a spectacular, uninterrupted view of the operators bum. It was indeed a spectacular bum, and George made a quick sketch of it alongside his notes.

She observed him three times before handing over responsibility, eventually satisfied that he could load the machines and enter all the data correctly, without inadvertently causing a massive system failure. He was understandably tense, and checked his notes constantly, the nub of his pencil tucked behind his ear, but at least he hadn't broken anything, yet, or accidentally switched them off.

A few days later he stood apprehensively before the machines, sleeves rolled up, tie loosened, and a buckling trolley full of money wrapped in plastic at his side. The operator's manual and his jotter were on the floor, wedged open with a stapler and a spare coin weight. A very large mug of reassuring tea cooled on top of one unit, and a gentle dose of nervous Delhi belly troubled his paunch. He could do this, he'd done it before. It would be fine, concentrate. Don't bugger it up.

A few hours later he was back at the welcome desk, flushed with success and relieved that he'd been able to successfully complete his task without having to scream for help. He happily soaked up the warm praise from Adriana, and nods of encouragement from Kelly and Doug. Mission accomplished, he couldn't wait to tell his Mum.

George was still brimming with pride and satisfaction when a very small, old lady in thick glasses, towing a tartan, wheeled shopping basket behind her, slowly made her way towards his desk, a look of utter distress carved into her crumbling features. In an effort to appear caring, he leaned over his desk and looked down at the quivering little soul, beaming encouragingly as others had done to him. Not unlike his Fiesta, she also smelt faintly of lavender. "Good afternoon, how can I help you today?"

"Oh, umm, sorry to be a bother young man, but, but I think there's been an awful mistake!" Her barely audible voice trembled with distress.

"Oh really, what's the problem?" He cocked his head to one side, he'd seen Kelly do this hundreds of times to convey genuine empathy and it seemed to work a treat. Customer service was a doddle.

"Oh, well, it's the cashpoint you see, young man. I don't believe he's thinking straight!"

Clearly she was barking mad. The poor old love thought the cashpoint had a person living inside it. He had seen this sort of behaviour before of course, at Nelson's Branch, when he used to yell *"I'M CLOSED"* at the drunks through the open back as Hayley was loading. It had been great fun, especially for The Bear when the plastered and the legless stumbled into the banking hall declaring with terrified, bloodshot eyes that the cashpoint was *alive*. Happy times indeed.

Nevertheless, he continued with his good natured assessment of the old ladies predicament, after all, she didn't seem to have had any sherry yet today.

"I'm sorry, but I don't understand madam, what do you mean, *he's* not thinking straight?"

"Well, umm, I only asked him for ten pounds and he's given me twenty, *look!*" Still trembling, she held up the cashpoint receipt, which clearly read ten pounds, and the cash itself. It was definitely not a ten pound note. Suddenly his heart started pounding heavily, his body filled with adrenaline. A familiar warning alarm went off in his head. Danger George Butler, DANGER!

He sent his chair clattering across the grey carpet, left his behind his bewildered customer, and in one impressive flurry of movement, especially given his level of fitness, dashed towards the glass front door of the branch. There was a rapidly growing queue of ecstatic customers forming at the cashpoints.

"*Oh Bugger!*" George's eyes were wide with fear, like a dozing traveller suddenly discovering he was waiting in the wrong departure lounge. He ran back past the old lady, nearly sending her spinning as she stood patiently, still clutching her receipt and the offending twenty pound note, grabbed his cashpoint keys and sped off towards the back office as fast as his confused legs would carry him.

Kelly, who'd been absentmindedly loading direct debits, half an ear on the conversation, looked up, startled by all the excitement. "George, *calm down*, what on earth's wrong?"

Halfway to the pass door he paused briefly, a blessed relief to his badly over stretched cardiovascular system, his face ashen. "I – I - *I've put bloody twenties in with the tens!*"

After a second day of pouring a king's ransom of pound coins into the gluttonous ticket machine, George decided that it was time to cautiously approach Adriana, and ask her where she and the rest of the staff parked their cars. If things carried on as they were, he would have to take a second job in the evenings just to cover the cost of parking.

Several minutes of enthusiastic, gesticulating Spanish directions followed. An impressively detailed, yet hastily scribbled map, which might well have revealed the hidden location of lost Aztec gold, was produced and the new recruit left none the wiser. Once Adriana had safely gone to lunch, he asked Kelly instead.

It seemed that most of the City's work force parked on a stretch of waste ground, a ten minute walk from the main streets. The site had originally been a thriving Business Park, but had fallen into disrepair and was now predominantly demolished or crumbling, leaving the streets and abandoned forecourts free for parking. Unbeknown to George though, an entirely new enterprise had risen up out of the ruins.

The Fiesta had slowly crept along the rows of cars, its tiny engine barely ticking over as its driver struggled to find a free spot. He'd decided to move the car during his lunchtime, to get a better understanding of the area without being distracted by the usual early morning panic. Staying in his warm single bed for just a few more luxurious minutes each day was starting to become a problem. The waste ground was packed. An assortment of cars, vans and motorbikes of various shapes, sizes and condition were parked either on the kerbside in close single file, or scattered haphazardly across the abandoned areas of tarmac. Clearly the key to securing a space here was to get in early. No more lying in bed, then.

George was about to abandon his search and return to the ruinous car park when he spotted a small slot that might just be able to accommodate his tiny hatchback. He quickly pulled up alongside the space to measure, once satisfied that the car would indeed fit; he pulled forward and prepared to perform that most dreaded of driving lesson manoeuvres. Which mirror should he look in again?

Just as he looked over his left shoulder to begin reversing, he spotted a colourful girl in an extremely short skirt, running towards him along the broken pavement. How strange. Already startled by the sudden appearance of the running girl, he nearly jumped out of his skin as a bright red, Ford Escort XR3i raced past him. Its windows wound down, the three young, male occupants all yelled something that sounded like encouragement, the horn honking wildly. How very strange.

Bemused by the events, he shook his head and turned to continue his tricky manoeuvre, only to be unexpectedly joined by the running girl. Without any invitation, she'd flung open the passenger door and thrown her unbelievably skinny frame into the seat next to him. She positively dripped with poorly applied makeup, and reeked of cheap perfume. As well as the skirt, which was more like a belt, she wore a cropped bleached denim jacket, fishnet stockings and a see-through mesh vest, which caused her to shiver in the seasonal chill.

"*'ere*, git going then, *before any Pigs sees us*!" Her voice was high and indigenous. When she opened her mouth to speak, the stale stench of a smoker's breath briefly overwhelmed both the cheap perfume, and even the Fiesta's ever present smell of lavender.

"*Who the hell are you?*"

"I kin be anyone 'e wants 'us to be, Luver, but git going, the clock's runnin'!"

"*What?*"

"Aww, you shy Luver? *First time eh?*" She nudged his arm and winked knowingly at him.

"*What the hell do you want with me?*" George was terrified. Whilst this awful woman of indeterminate age and questionable dress sense, didn't seem to be robbing him, he sensed a definite an air of criminality about her.

"Business, Luv. Now come on, *clock's ticking*!" She seemed to be very keen to get moving, although quite where to was unclear. Perhaps she thought he was running some sort of unlicensed taxi service, hence the urgency? That would explain it.

"What sort of *business?*" His voice trembled. Nothing like this ever happened in the countryside, not often anyway.

The Hag sighed and rolled her heavily massacred eyes. She grabbed her bewildered customer firmly by the jaw with a bony, bejewelled hand. "*Monkey Business, Luver*!"

Later, back at the branch, having downed three cups of very sweet, strong tea and four bourbon biscuits in the reassuring company of a chuckling Doug and a caring Kelly, George physically shuddered as he relived the horrendous ordeal. He couldn't get the smell of cheap perfume off his clothes from where the Lady of Horizontal Refreshment, as Doug had described her, eventually gave up waiting, and pounced on her horrified customer mid park.

When all the warning bells had finally gone off in his head, he'd taken his life in his hands and, fearing an armed, hidden Pimp, physically thrown the Lady of Horizontal Refreshment out of the Fiesta and onto the street, before she leaked something awful onto his grey velour seats. His Mum might sit on that seat. He then tore off as fast as the meagre 1.1 litre four cylinder engine would carry him. Sweating with a combination of cold fear and a sudden rush of adrenaline, he headed back to the car park in a cloud of burning rubber, cheap perfume and lavender.

When the police stopped him a few streets later, he naturally feared the worse. In a rare moment of good fortune however, they'd simply wanted to caution the red faced youth about his erratic driving. They'd apparently seen nothing of the earlier exploits. George was so relieved he very nearly hugged the officer. The thought that kept racing through his mind, was how he'd have explained all this to his parents, had the police caught him in the act. Innocent or otherwise, it's not the sort of subject to bring up over a family dinner.

The welcome desk was at right angles to the cashiers run, meaning that both groups had a good view of each other. This had caused some embarrassment for George. Di had been overjoyed to see her little dance partner again, insisting on waving incessantly and blowing him kisses through the bullet proof glass. Nevertheless, despite a narrowly avoided scandal, a few forgivable operational losses, disappointing news for a Ukrainian fisherman, and Di's unrelenting rapture, he eventually started to settle into his new working environment.

Once his confidence had picked itself up off the floor and dusted itself off again, he'd also started to set a pace with his sales referrals too. The clientele at Armada were generally more sophisticated than some of the dregs that lurked in Nelsons banking hall, and he soon found his feet, quickly sending a steady flow of willing, unwary customers in the general direction of either a credit card or a home insurance policy.

Armada Branch was used as a convenient walkthrough by the general public. The doors at the back led onto the massive car park, which he'd skidded into a few months ago, and the front opened onto one of the city's main streets. Although there was always plenty of fill in work to keep the team out of mischief during the quieter spells, George understood very little of it, and Adriana, exhausted from the first few days of tuition, had decided to ease off the training for a while. This allowed him to just sit quietly at the desk. Although Adriana always kept a keen Spanish ear open for any possible signs of trouble, or an innocent misdirection of funds, he was able to fill his quieter moments simply people watching. It was a welcome distraction, and it helped him keep his mind off Summer.

Before long he started to recognise a few of the regulars. He acknowledged them accordingly with either smiles or nods, depending on the perceived character or, in the case of the plethora of young ladies who passed smartly by, the shortness of the skirt. But despite the catwalk of beauty that occasionally paraded past, he couldn't shake his thoughts.

He kept expecting Summer to walk through the pass door and smile shyly at him, to bravely pat his bottom in passing when no one was looking, or to leave a freshly made cup of tea on his desk with a loving Post It note stuck to the side. This is how he'd imagined things to be if they'd ever worked together. But now, he'd never know.

Some of the staff, those that had gotten to know him better, and especially those that had seen him play the guitar at the Ball, had begun to ask questions about their relationship too, questions to which he didn't have any answers. Before long he started to avoid the staff room altogether, not least for its mountainous accent, and spent his lunchtimes shivering in the cold winter's air on a park bench instead, battling the with hungry, persistent pigeons.

He missed Summer desperately. Although their relationship had been nothing short of brief, they'd connected on so many levels. Despite a few differing character traits, they'd fitted together like the proverbial peas in a pod. He missed so many things about her, trivial little things, that didn't seem to matter at the time. Like the way that she insisted on warming her beloved, bright red teapot twice. Why on earth did she do that?

He missed sleeping next to her too, and the way she seemed to enter a primeval state of hibernation in the early hours of the morning. Many was the time he'd bravely left the comfort and warmth of her old cast iron bed, to tend to a desperate, lifesaving need for water, only to return to find that she was entirely cocooned, hidden from the world in the folds of her duvet, the only visible clue of her presence, the exposed nub of a tiny nose.

He missed the way the way that despite her wayward hair's prolonged, bitter campaign against anything even remotely resembling neatness or style, she religiously insisted on brushing errant strands from her forehead, once she felt safe, and the need to hide behind it had passed.

George missed the all little things that made up his memory of her. Summer's many foibles and idiosyncrasies. The things that would've been lost just as easily on a stranger passing her in the street, as they had been by a colleagues who had worked with her for years. Most of all though, he just missed his Summertime.

He endlessly reflected on the ill-fated Christmas Ball which had seemed to have been their undoing. Had he done anything wrong? Was it his fault for getting up to play guitar? Had she seen him talking to Natasha? He had to admit though, playing with the band in front of all those people, and socialising with Natasha and the rest of The Pretty People, had been a real buzz. It was completely different to any other sort of party he'd experienced before. To his shame, he desperately wanted to be invited to it again. But was that wrong, and did that count as spreading his wings?

With his head occupied with thoughts of Summer, and his body doing its level best to land him in either prison, or at least the local newspaper, George had been almost immune to the general atmosphere of thinly veiled trepidation that lingered within the Branch. In the absence of Mr Burton, who strangely enough never returned following his Christmas announcement, Linda Beech had taken up the role of acting Senior Manageress. In her typical brusque fashion, she had insisted that the staff put their individual concerns and questions about the merger to the back of their minds for now, and concentrate on the day job instead. But it wasn't as simple as all that.

Apart from the hasty rebranding, and the never-ending torrent of colourful advertising, promising great things to come, nothing very much had actually changed yet. Cottons NSIB had arrived, but that seemed to be it for now. The wait became agonising for the apprehensive, fearful masses. Only one item of official communication had been sent from Head Office to alleviate any fears. It was a short video, strictly for internal use only, presented by a rather modern looking chap in his early thirties. He was polished and suited, but wore no tie, perhaps in an effort to appear more relaxed and open, and he talked about the massive amounts of planning that was taking place at Head Office, and the great new Bank that was going to be created as a result. It all sounded very suspicious.

Echoing Linda's words, which must have meant she'd been told to say them, he also talked about the need to keep the wheels turning whilst the finer points of the plans were agreed, to keep momentum, to maintain 'Business as Usual'. It was very suspicious indeed. Did 'Business as Usual' actually mean 'hold steady until we decide how many of you are going to get the chop?' The plot thickened.

Meanwhile, throughout all his unexpected brushes with the law, cashpoint debacles, unwelcome proximity to Ladies of Horizontal Refreshments, and accidentally misplaced sums of money, George had been comforted by Dean's steady, reassuring presence. With his homophobic anxieties buried for the moment, under a mountain of more pressing drama and crisis, he'd started to look at him as something of a banking older brother, someone to look up to with admiration and respect, someone who was considerably bigger than he was.

During that first traumatic week at Armada, Dean had been there at the end of the day to offer soothing words of encouragement to the eternally dishevelled younger man. Clearly, he needed a bit of guidance, support, or even at times, possibly legal representation. Of course, this was simply all part of his well-conceived plan.

Dean had a tried and tested approach to recruiting new Pretty People. It tended to work particularly well if the subject in hand had the required potential, but was not currently enjoying peak prettiness. After allowing his new recruit a week or two to acclimatise to his surroundings, he decided that it was now time to put Phase One into motion. It was time to rebuild George Butler. He relished a challenge.

A master of structure and method, a trait he used to great success in his day job, Dean had a mental checklist of assignments that needed to be completed if the subject was to be accepted by the rest of The Pretty People. He was well aware that this approach was both arrogant and narcissistic, that it had an air of elitism and superiority about it, but he simply didn't care. To him, transforming a bedraggled, uncoordinated mess into a sharp suited vision of physical perfection was a welcome diversion, an escape from the trivialities of life. Where some people built model aircraft as a hobby, Dean Swift built People, Pretty People.

There was always one feature that was virtually impossible to build though. No matter how promising the raw materials seemed physically, the complete absence of this one quality meant that the subject would invariably be no more than just a pretty shell. Nice to look at and hang off your arm, but not someone you would wish to become trapped in an elevator with for too long. As such, they never made the cut. That one important feature was character.

Thankfully, George didn't lack character. Along with excess puppy fat, it was something he had enormous reserves of. Although at times it needed to be tempered somewhat and perhaps taught when to shut up, at least he could never ever be described as being dull. Dean very much liked this quality. He liked the way that he seemed to have a scattergun attitude to life, and the way that he often had no idea at all what he was saying, but simply kept talking anyway, just to see what would come out next. The young man seemed to be stuck permanently on transmit.

Physically though, he knew he had his work cut out this time. The puppy fat was in danger of soon becoming a fully grown St. Bernard, and he desperately needed a haircut, a new wardrobe, aftershave that didn't belong to a fifty-year-old engineer, and a decent pair of shoes that wouldn't raise static electricity every time he crossed a carpet. The divers watch was okay though, but that was about it.

The first order of business was to encourage him to join the gym. Once he'd lured him into that spectacular world of Lycra clad Gym Bunnies and protein shakes, he'd soon be able to go to work moulding the wobbly jelly into cold, hard steel.

There would be endless, gruelling workouts and regular, healthy meals that didn't include mountainous portions of roast potatoes or homemade pies at every sitting. Dean needed to set his new disciple off on the first leg of his physical journey. He called this initial stage, the Fruit to Veg process, the part of the procedure where the subject transformed from a pear shaped blob into a carrot shaped roman god. It required a huge amount of effort on the subject's part. There would be a strict diet to follow, and they'd need to summon a tolerance of pain and anguish to rival that of a prisoner of war, held captive, and without hope, in a Japanese concentration camp. But it would be worth it in the end.

"Have you ever worked out, my Man?" It had been a quiet afternoon in the banking hall. Fresh from a brief meeting with yet another of George's many referrals, Dean had sauntered nonchalantly over to the welcome desk for a chat.

"Err, no, not really," he reflected for a moment, briefly lost in thought. "*Well*, Barney and I used to spend a lot of time running away from the bullies when we were younger, *does that count?*"

Diamond Fitness - Building Better Bodies. The words were scrawled across the vast glass frontage of the gym in four foot high bright red letters, like a neat doodle in lipstick left on a bathroom mirror. George stood before the three storey building and gawped helplessly at its magnificence. It was an impressive piece of architecture. The chunky, almost industrial framework was proudly exposed, safely concealed behind the acres of double glazing and painted red to match the sign outside. On each level he could just about make out the rows of perfect, sweaty bodies, pounding away on something mechanical and challenging. Yet again, he began to feel inadequate.

He looked down at his own PE kit. Hand-me-down grey jogging bottoms, which had been totalling abused by Michael, an old Def Leppard T-shirt with tour dates on the back, and a pair of lightly used school trainers that he just about managed to still squeeze his feet into. Given that he expected to die this evening, it didn't seem to make sense to buy anything new to wear. Clutching his empty squash bottle for comfort, he took a deep sigh and advanced towards his doom.

The company had clearly put a lot of thought into creating a positive, dynamic environment. The staff looked impossibly healthy, if slightly orange in some lights, and once inside, he was quickly descended upon by a buff chap who seemed to be wearing eyeliner. As instructed, he nervously asked for Dean to be called and waited at the reception desk, leafing through a very glossy brochure, trying to breathe in and push his chest out, all at the same time. The effort was slowly killing him.

Located in the swanky Marina part of the city, near Dean's apartment, Diamond Fitness offered a range of classes, including tai chi, yoga and Pilates, none of which George had ever heard of before. This fitness centre was clearly so much more than a just simple gym. He read on intently, desperately hoping his chaperone would materialise before he was coaxed into signing up for something painful and expensive. By the time he'd finished the brochure, he'd learnt that there was a number of health and beauty treatments he could enjoy, an Olympic sized pool to drown in, a Jacuzzi, sauna and steam room, and a comfortable club lounge, bar and restaurant. There was also a Gymnasium.

Immaculate as always, dressed in a black, zipped up Nike tracksuit and impossibly white Puma trainers, Dean briskly ran down the flight of open paddle stairs from the floor above. "My Man, you turned up, *well done*! Turning up the first time is the hardest bit, *right Mac?*" He turned sharply to the receptionist, catching him admiring his rear.

"Hmm, *Oh*! Yeah, sure thing Dean, top marks for sure!" Dean raised a critical, perfectly formed eyebrow at him, and took firm hold of his victim's arm.

"Come on George, I'll show you around."

Mac composed himself, and snapped out of his day dream. "Err, Dean, *well*, what about his induction, he needs to have an induction, *it's the rules*!"

"No, he doesn't, he's got me."

The Club was vast. As well as the reception, downstairs housed the huge pool and the saunas, various treatment rooms and changing areas, leaving the second floor free for the gym, and third floor for the open plan club lounge, bar and restaurant. George had changed at work before venturing out. He'd secretly dreaded this part. Even though his concerns about Dean's sexuality had abated somewhat of late, changing rooms were still filled him with terror. They had done ever since primary school. Whilst he accepted that there was probably little chance that he would fall victim to a towel whip in here, there was still the issue of male nudity. Quite the worst form of nudity. Fortunately, and somewhat surprisingly though, the changing rooms were unisex, with rows of individual teak changing cubicles, lockers, and low benches scattered around the white tiled floor. Things were indeed looking up.

With the downstairs tour complete, the two men, who looked really quite odd together, walked back through the reception area, ignoring Mac's renewed pleas, and up the stairs to the next floor. All of a sudden, George began to enter a new, alien world.

A strange combination of noises washed down the stairs and into his ears. There was heavy, drum and bass dance music, not the sort of rubbish he'd heard at the school disco or in a few of the shady pubs around town though. This was quality, well produced stuff. It blended, almost in time with a constant whirring noise, and a second thumping beat which kept time with the music. The closer they came to the top of the stairs, the louder the racket got. When at last the source of the commotion was revealed, he couldn't help but stand in stunned silence, staring in wide eyed amazement at the abundance of physical exertion.

There were two rows of eight running machines. All of which were pointed towards a bank of suspended televisions, hung from robust metal frames, and they were all being mercilessly pummelled to death by a diverse collection of training shoes. Apart from two extremely lean men, both of which looked as though they weighed no more than a bag of sugar, each machine was occupied by a vision of female perfection.

They all wore a similar, hypnotic uniform. Skin tight, black pedal pushers, and an equally skin tight, although colourful, sports bras, leaving their slender, lower backs exposed to admiring glances, and a welcome cooling breeze from the frosty air conditioning. Aside from the rows of mesmerizing, pert little bottoms, each of which resembled two very firm cherry tomatoes that had been squeezed into a small Lycra sack, the thing that struck George was the way that their ponytails swished from side to side. They were completely synchronized. It was quite a feat of timing and co-ordination.

Beyond the mass of energetic Gym Bunnies, there were rowing machines, exercise bikes and a few bizarre looking contraptions that looked as though their primary function in life was to tear people limb from limb. They were cross trainers. Dean led the way past the cardiovascular suite of pain and toil, acknowledging one or two sweaty faces as he did so, down a small flight of stairs and into a vast weights section. At this point, his new disciple started to panic.

The power bar from the club restaurant's self-service vending machine tasted vaguely of dried raspberries dropped in glue and sawdust. It did nothing to suppress George's longing for a greasy pasty. As he chewed his way through its cardboard texture, like an industrious beaver gnawing through an old log, he reflected on his brief tour of the house of pain, and started to question his reasons for being here, again.

As well as Dean's curious invitation to join him, surprisingly enough, his Mum had also been quite adamant that he'd started to put on weight. She'd never said anything like this before; she usually just heaped on the roast spuds and told him to tuck in, it was all rather confusing. The problem was though, that unlike his Dad, who spent a good deal of his day manhandling metal and machinery, or his brother, who endured daily runs over a military assault course in full kit, her youngest son didn't do anything to burn off the beautifully cooked calories. Not since Summer had left him, anyhow.

Dean had taken his time explaining in graphic, torturous detail exactly what each of the terrifyingly complicated training apparatus did, and which parts of his body would scream out in agonising pain for days on end, once they'd been used. It seemed to beg an obvious question. Why the hell would you use them then? He pointed out the groups of machines they would use in close succession, when concentrating on training a particular muscle group, and also the free weights, great racks of dumbbells, ranging from the embarrassingly light, to the monumentally heavy.

Conscious that he was eking out his power bar for as long as possible, hoping to delay the inevitable agony, George eventually finished the last mouthful of woodchip and raspberries, washing it down with a generous gulp of water from his brand new training bottle. The empty squash bottle apparently wouldn't do.

Mac was delighted when they returned to reception, to at least fill in the membership forms and the Direct Debit mandate. It gave him the opportunity to use his favourite item of reception equipment, The Laminator. George was given a special key ring, which doubled as a locker key, a voucher for two free protein shakes, and a newly pressed membership card. Against all the odds, for the first time in his life, he'd finally committed to physical exercise. Or at least to paying for it, regularly turning up might soon prove to be another matter.

Pre-workout, sat comfortably in the club lounge, Dean explained the training methods and routines he tended to adopt. He broke his training down into four distinct sessions, legs, back and biceps, chest and triceps and finally shoulders. After each weights session, which typically lasted for forty to fifty minutes, he'd work his abdominal muscles until he could no longer stand the pain, and then finally complete his work out with thirty minutes of cardio.

Monday was chest and triceps, Tuesday shoulders, Wednesday was a rest day, thank God, Thursday legs, and then finally back and biceps on Friday.

Depending on how the evening's frivolities went the night before, he'd also visit the gym again on either Saturday or Sunday morning, to work his abs and run for at least an hour. Dean was clearly mad.

As if all this wasn't enough for his horrified student to absorb, he then went on to discuss diet and nutrition in excruciating detail. Very soon, it became glaringly apparent that George's diet was going to need considerable alteration. Roast spuds and fruitcake needed to be a thing of the past. He very nearly cried.

Since he'd started working at Armada Branch, George found that time in the mornings had become even more precious and scarce than before, especially if he lay in. Before long though, he'd made some cunning alterations to his usual breakfast routine to compensate. He reluctantly shunned his home cooked full English, and instead substituted it with a hearty bowl of Cornflakes and two slices of thick white toast, which positively dripped with butter and marmalade. Once he'd driven to the derelict business park, and was safely outside of the Whore Zone, and was just inside the Safe Zone, he'd then pick up a freshly made bacon and egg bap from his new best friend Stavros, a larger than life Greek with a stained apron who ran the popular mobile Greasy Spoon on the very edge of the Whore Zone. His clients were nothing if not diverse.

Hopefully, this would sustain him until his allocated lunch break. Depending on how short his straw had been that day though, he'd normally need to smuggle a couple of chocolate bars and lump of fruit cake back to the welcome desk, to keep him going through either the long afternoon, or the longer morning. Wily stealth was the key here. Adriana, who seemed to live entirely on couscous and grapes, did not hold with eating in front of customers, and had once reduced him to a pleading, grovelling mess when she'd confiscated a Double Decker she caught him nibbling at his desk. Of late, he'd gotten much sneakier, and started concealing them in Bank Statement paper.

After the gargantuan lunchbox had been consumed, he'd then start planning his homeward bound snack. This would either be another calorie packed, deep fried offering from Stavros, a huge pork pie from the corner shop, or an extra-large steak pasty from the bakery. All of these proprietors greeted him with open arms.

Once the perilous journey through the Whore Zone had been successfully negotiated, and he'd made it safely back to the Butler's respectable semi, he would usually be greeted with a steaming mug of sweet tea, a plate topped with three bourbon biscuits, two custard creams, a few homemade buns and, if he was lucky, a pre-dinner slice of freshly made, moist fruit cake.

The Butler evening meals were varied, vast, hugely nutritious and able to feed most of Africa. It seemed to have escaped Mrs Butler's attention though, that her eldest son, a strapping, fit young man, now belonged to the army and had left home, and she continued to cook in the same volumes as she'd always done before.

The meals were usually of traditional English grub. Cottage pie, Shepherd's pie, roast beef, roast chicken, roast pork, the odd spaghetti bolognaise for international flavour, and invariably, as a result of all those left over roast potatoes and vegetables, at least once a week, bubble and squeak, served with extra thick Cumberland sausages and stiff, lumpy gravy. It was a welcome feast, but one that always made for a windy night.

Finally, whether it was late in the evening, after staggering in with several pints and a few bags of pork scratchings under his belt, or earlier, after the TV had dried up and thoughts of Summer came flooding back to him, George would round off the day's nourishment with a doorstep sized sandwich, full of butter and marmite, and a final, cleansing mug of steaming tea. The next day, he always woke up hungry.

Dean considered the Butler Diet for a moment. He sat back in the comfortable club chair and rested the ankle of his left leg on the knee of his right, absentmindedly fiddling with his trainer's shoelaces. How best to put it then?

"George?"

"Err, *yes Dean?*"

"Just out of interest, how many times a day do you need to go to the toilet?"

"Oh, at least four. *Sometimes five though!*" There was a touch of pride in the younger man's reply.

Dean smirked, reached across and placed a strong hand on his disciple's hunched shoulder. "Why does this not surprise me...?"

Later that evening, having completed a gruelling, seemingly endless chest and triceps workout, countless agonising sit ups, and an eight-minute gentle jog that had made him see stars, George eased his way back home in abject agony. His triceps, a part of his body he was vaguely aware of, but not exactly on first name terms with, screamed in torment as he desperately tried to steer the Fiesta. To take the pressure off his arms, he'd tried leaning forward in his seat, but this only caused a burning sensation in his overworked stomach muscles, which caused him to feel queasy and he had to relent. He was surely going to die.

His chest felt as though molten lava had been poured under his skin, and every time he reached for another gear, he felt certain that some vital part of his anatomy was going to drop off, and end up in the foot well. He hurt in places that he didn't even know he had, and in degrees of discomfort he didn't think were possible, let alone survivable.

But all of this unfeasible discomfort, all the worry that he'd permanently damaged himself beyond medical repair, all the embarrassment he'd caused himself when his legs went wobbly and he accidentally sat on a resting Gym Bunny, was nothing compared to the one inescapable, unavoidable horror that hounded and tormented him on his long, slow journey home.

Tomorrow evening, Dean expected him to do it all again.

Chapter 11

Adding Value and Archery

Mid February.

My Monkey,

HAPPY VALENTINES DAY! Life here in France is just so nice. I am just helping some early season visitors get settled into the art studio, and then I'm off to the market. They sell bangles!

I miss you so much, and I think of our time together constantly. When I feel low, I draw and I paint and I remember all the fun we had in those few weeks. I'm glad you're having fun with Dean, although it does all sound very painful to me! Still, as you say, at least soon you will be able to see your toes again!

Write soon, have you used your new paints yet?

All my love,

Summertime. x x x x

George read the handmade Valentine's Day card once more, before pinning it to his bedroom wall, where it joined the diverse collection of other postcards and letters that Summer had sent him so far that year. Frowning slightly, he reflected on its content again, attempting to unravel some sort of hidden clue or message within the few lines. There were more kisses on this one than the others, what did that mean? *Valentine's Day*, what was he missing here…?

It was eight-thirty in the evening. Having gratefully survived yet another of Dean's gruelling workouts, he'd taken a reviving, long hot shower at home. He still didn't trust the ones at the gym, despite the privacy afforded by the cubicles, and now stood naked in front of his wardrobe mirror, just a fluffy pink towel wrapped around his waist to cover his modesty. He was rather proud that he could now actually wrap a regular towel around his rapidly reducing waistline. Regardless of the colour, it wasn't a bath sheet. This was progress.

Thanks to un-relenting, life threatening sessions at the gym, willpower he wasn't aware he even had, and some miracle of nutritional science, over the past two weeks, he'd actually already started to shift the flab, and in not unnoticeable volumes, judging by some of the compliments he'd received from a few of his kinder colleagues. He was starving though, all the time.

He even had the beginnings of a proper, manly chest. Not the flabby, slightly worrying man-boobs he'd hidden under his heavy metal T-shirts for years, but firm, square pectorals. Apparently they'd been there all along. They just needed a bit of encouragement, and careful excavation from the ruins.

Whilst the physical exertion in the gym was torturous at best, the horrendously strict diet was nothing short of utter torment for the carbohydrate loving, full fat, double cheese and chocolate sprinkled George Butler. Even worse though, was the constant temptation thrown in his path by his increasingly concerned Mum, the evening offerings of tea and doorstop sized slices of fruitcake becoming harder each day to refuse. At times, he wasn't sure how much longer he'd hold out. God, he was so hungry.

But for some reason though, he did continue to hold out. His new meals were at least regular, even more regular than his previous grazing habits, but where he used to munch on fruitcake, huge white baps, and crisps at every opportunity, he now ate from a carefully planned, high protein, low carbohydrate diet every two to three hours. Some of it had to be adapted though. Cottage cheese tasted far too sour, and had awfully painful side effects at the other end, and he was never keen on yogurts, low fat or otherwise. As for avocados, well they looked like alien eggs.

At least the protein element proved to be less of a burden. George had always enjoyed something of a passionate love affair with chicken, although he still maintained it tasted much better roasted in butter and its own juices than it did skinned and grilled to death. Eggs, too, had been a staple part of the Butler diet since birth, and now, whilst they were poached, they did at least look like they'd been fried. Protein shakes were another matter entirely. Regardless of alleged flavour, they all tasted like feet. Yet still, he soldiered on.

But what was driving him? Perhaps it was a desperate need to fill the void left in his life when Summer emigrated? For a few miserable weeks after she'd gone, George tried to fall back into his old routines and habits, but reading old magazines on his bed for the hundredth time, or trawling through the same old, familiar pubs with Barney, absentmindedly keeping his eyes open for a potential replacement, soon became tedious. So perhaps it was something else?

During the first two evenings training together, possibly in an effort not to intimidate his new disciple, Dean had kept his tracksuit top on, its zip firmly sealed all the way to the top. On day three, soaked with sweat, he took it off and stripped down to his ribbed vest.

George had seen muscles before of course, a few of the other members of the gym were rather buff, and his own brother was stocky and thick set, but this was something else entirely. Michael had the coveted vein running down both biceps, a sure sign to boys of a certain age that someone was strong, and as hard as nails, but Dean's veins seemed to have a mind of their own. Like wide, bulging pipes, they crisscrossed and zigzagged over his shoulders and chest, as well as his arms, each one having countless, equally engorged offshoots steaming from the main body. His tanned skin was taught, way beyond toned, and underneath it, his spectacular, swollen muscles rose and fell like the Rockies.

Not since his new follower had sneaked into his older brother's room to watch *Predator* had he seen such a thing. He felt, as before in the car park, totally inadequate. The difference now though was that he wanted to do something about it, even if it meant being in agony most of the time and hungry - desperately, achingly hungry. Training was causing him no end of trouble with his Mum as well, not least for invading her kitchen.

"*I never born you like that George!*" Mrs Butler barged into his *Pit* with armfuls of perfectly ironed laundry, and a face like she'd been chewing a wasp. "It's not right, young man, your brother's fit and strong, but he's still got a bit of a podge, *and I don't like all these lines,* you look as though someone's been drawing on you with a biro!" Mrs Butler set the laundry down on his bed and prodded her youngest son in the shoulder, which really rather hurt, pointing out the beginnings of some veins that were slowly being un-earthed from under the layers of fat. He was really rather proud of them.

"Oh but Mum, *it's how we're supposed to be*, Dean says that..." He was abruptly cut off, yet again.

"I don't care what this *Dean* says. I would like to meet this man and give him a piece of my mind, corrupting my son with his modern haircuts and funny diets. He obviously doesn't have to share a toilet with you!" She picked up an item of his laundry as though it was one of his Dad's oil-stained hankies. "And what's with all this fancy new underwear with men's names written on the elastic, what's wrong with the ones *I* bought you for Christmas? *I bet Summer would have liked them*!" The torrent died away as she eventually left his Pit and headed for her immaculately organised airing cupboard, still muttering to herself about her sons Strange New Friend, and his new-fangled underwear. It plainly belonged to someone called Calvin.

She did have a point though. His new Tightie-whities were taking some getting used to, and he still twitched nervously when he reflected on how much they cost. Still, overall he was snug, well contained and significantly less likely to be laughed at in the gym changing rooms if he was spotted. Perish the thought.

His new haircut had been a traumatic experience, but had at least come with an unexpected treat. Dean had eventually given up persuading him to have a decent trim at a proper salon, and kidnapped him instead. He imprisoned him in leather back seat of his BMW, and drove him to his stylist, whilst George pleaded bitterly to be set free. Briefly, he even cried.

Once he'd been bundled unceremoniously into the heavily padded bright red chair, the work bench of the frighteningly busty young blond, who seemed to wear nothing more than underwear and pink lipstick, the thick black mop was attacked with all the ferocity of a band of marauding tree surgeons.

Up until now, his Mum had always cut his hair, and he'd always found that distressing enough. His experience at the hands of the buxom stylist though, had proved to be an unexpected affair. It was an experience of both pleasure and pain. For every ear threatening slice of the scissors, scrape of the clippers and lump of cherished hair that fell about his feet, there was a consolatory, if brief moment of utter bliss, as the busty blond brushed her enormous assets against either his cheek, or as was the case on more than one occasion, actually into his ear. It had been a brutal, deeply disturbing ordeal, but one that left him feeling strangely aroused.

He eventually left the salon twenty-two pounds poorer, and several pounds lighter. The chilly February winds had whipped at his newly exposed neck and ears, and made him hunker down into the collar of his leather jacket as he climbed into the passenger seat of the M3. He'd had mixed feelings when the busty blond proudly showed him the back of his head. He certainly looked smaller, and it was a much more contemporary style, but as the blond surgically applied a final blob of wax to the finger length hair, one thought kept nagging at him. Mum won't like this at all.

That had been a week ago now, yet it already showed signs of recovering some of its original bulk. On balance, despite the stylist's unexpected foreplay, he'd much rather it was long again. A bit of length came in handy when the occasional spot took up residence on his forehead. Tearing himself away from his reflection, he looked down at the neat pile of clothes on his bed, and tried to decide once again, quite what he should take with him on his unexpected journey.

The past few weeks had proved to be nothing short of interesting for the staff of the newly formed Cottons NSIB. After a relatively tight lipped period of nothingness, change had arrived with all the devastating force of an unexpected tsunami. Many of the staff were still mopping out the kitchen. Wave after wave of crashing turmoil and transformation smashed into the workforce, with all the care and thoughtfulness of a wrecking ball at a listed building.

First on the agenda was the Staff Contracts of Work. Within Cottons there were three very different, historic contracts. The first dated back to the dawn of time, and only applied to a handful of older staff, like Di and presumably The Bear. It had a desirable final salary pension scheme, working hours that excluded weekends and unpaid overtime, and sick pay arrangements that actually made coming back to work following an illness, financially unsound.

The second, slightly less attractive contract, had a money purchased pension scheme, a clause to allow paid overtime, at Manager's discretion, and six months full, six months half sick pay. Dean, Hayley and most of the staff who'd been employed for at least ten years, served under this arrangement.

Finally there was the most recently introduced contract, the one that George and his fellow new recruits signed upon joining Cottons. This contract was very much the poor relation in comparison. Working hours were defined as simply forty per week, quite when these hours started or finished was very much decided by the needs of the business at that time, and unpaid overtime was all but expected. The pension scheme was so meagre that death seemed like a realistic alternative to retirement, and the measly sick pay arrangements meant that unless a member of staff was turning up for work with anything short of a limb hanging off, they should really make the effort to come in.

This was the contact that the newly formed Cottons NSIB Senior Management Team wanted all of the staff to sign, regardless of their current arrangements. There was a keen desire to release them from all the privileges and perks of the existing ones, and perhaps more importantly, get every single member of staff under the same working arrangement.

Ironically enough, the former NSIB staff found the new contract rather generous in comparison to the medieval version they'd signed. There was no mention of floggings, beheadings or having to ask your Manager permission to get married. Although this was likely to present a few commitment phobic staff a whole new set of problems.

Whilst the Bank made it quite clear that it wouldn't force the staff to sign the new contracts, they did intend to virtually starve them out of their old ones. Pay rises would be refused until they had relented, and if a member of staff wanted to apply for a new role within the Bank, they'd be expected to relinquish their old contact and sign the new one, even before they would be considered for an interview. That should soon get the Buggers to sign.

Naturally, the Unions challenged this radical line and demanded an explanation, but the response had been long, complicated and laced with management jargon that no one understood. Ultimately though, it seemed it was the customers fault. The new Bank apparently wanted to put the customer first, and to have branches open at the times customers wanted them to be open. With all the staff on the same contact, it would be far easier it achieve this goal. It was for the customers, of course, not the Bank. It was nothing at all to do with saving money and increasing profit. A new word emerged from Head Office, 'Customer-Centric'. It soon seemed to be a justification for almost everything that was happening, putting the customer first. But had anyone actually stopped to ask a customer what they wanted?

It seemed unlikely, especially when Sales Targets were inevitably introduced at the staff training meetings. They weren't directly referred to as sales though. Instead they were labelled as Fulfilling Customer Requirements. This confused the Cottons heritage staff no ends. Surely if a customer had a requirement, they'd simply come in and ask someone to fulfil it?

Each member of branch staff, from the cashiers to the Senior Managers, was expected to play their part in delivering stretching sales targets, or rather, help to Fulfil Customer Requirements, whether they wanted them to be fulfilled or not. Every financial product imaginable was to be aggressively offered for sale. From credit cards to unit trusts, pensions to personal loan insurance, simple savings accounts to investment funds, there wasn't a product that Cottons NSIB didn't want to promote and sell to its customers. They were even rumoured to be flirting with the idea of selling gas and electric too.

It was no longer simply a nice thing for a cashier to smile sweetly, and convince a customer to apply for a credit card with one of the CBA's. It was a necessary evil, an expectation in order to avoid being managed out of the Bank for sustained underperformance.

For some though, the changes weren't all bad. As well as benefitting from a much more lenient contract, the NSIB heritage staff also found the targets positively merciful, in comparison to the herculean goals they'd been set in the past. If anything, the changes presented opportunity to progress and earn more money.

And Opportunity, or rather 'Opportunity Mapping', had become something of a buzz word of late, that and the other new favourite, 'Adding Value'. In some expensive office, nestled in a comfortable corner of Head Office, someone was being paid a ridiculous amount of money to come up with this crap. 'Opportunity Mapping' was about putting the right people in the right roles, for maximum effect. 'Adding Value' was something the Bank wanted the each member of staff to think very seriously about. What they could they do for the company to add value?

Short films, intended to be both inspirational and encouraging, were produced by the Bank for everyone to watch and absorb at the team meetings. Each focused on the 'New World', and featured deliriously happy, alleged members of staff going about their daily duties. Serving or interviewing, depending on their role, equally elated customers who seemed overjoyed to be sold whatever it was the member of staff was selling. The more cynical members of Cottons suggested this was nothing more than subliminal messaging. The Bear suggested it was propaganda. He was given a cautionary file note.

Yet for every Branch Manager that resented the changes, there seemed to be two who, strangely enough, believed the hype, accepted the party line, and were eager to start their the new role as a fearsome whip crackers and bean counters. They likely had large mortgages, greedy ex-wives, or both.

George was usually in too much pain from the gym, or suffering from sustained, unrelenting bouts of calorie withdrawal to really have an opinion either way, and tended to keep out of the regular, heated lunchtime debates. He kept his pigeons company on the bench outside instead, although curiously of late, his new-fangled lunch seemed to hold little interest for them. For this reason, when news of a series of residential 'Team Building Events' leaked into the branches, it didn't really register with him either. Not until he was randomly selected to attend one.

"Mum, *MUM*! Where's me boots?" He was really concerned about this trip. Apart from his holiday, a few sleepovers, evenings at Summer's, and various eventful camping trips, it was the first time he'd been properly away from home since his weekend residential course with primary school. And he'd hated that with a passion, especially the showers. "Oh, don't worry, found them!"

Details of the Event were vague. Each carefully chosen, *random* candidate had been given a list of clothing to take and a time and location to catch the coach, which would transport them to an undisclosed location. Every part of this worried George. Clothes generally troubled him; school mufti days had been a living hell. He was fine messing about in jeans and T-shirts in familiar company, but as soon as he was thrown into an unfamiliar group or situation, he usually began fretting endlessly about everything from his shoes, to his underwear. Now at least, he felt considerably more confident about his underwear.

Then there was the issue with the coach. Each candidate was expected to meet at the city's main bus station at five-thirty on Tuesday morning, in order to arrive at the venue by nine. Even with his poor mental arithmetic, this meant at least three and a half hours on the road, three and a half long hours of trying hard not to fall prey to his old adversary, travel sickness. In desperation, he'd gotten out his scientific calculator to check his workings.

He'd been suffered from this horrendous ailment for years, often looking at his fellow passengers on the school bus in envy, as they read the latest copy of The Beano or munched happily on a leftover lunchtime sandwich without a care in the world. It was so bad for him, that when he and Barney stepped on the plane for their trip to Greece, he'd quite sincerely asked a bemused air stewardess if he could sit up front with the pilot. He felt a bit better if he could see where they were going.

The candidates were asked to pack a smart outfit for an evening function, old clothes that didn't matter if it they got muddy or ruined, and casual attire for the classroom exercises, but strictly no jeans. This caused him no end of difficulties. Apart from his suit bottoms, the only other pair of trousers he owned that could be reasonably described as smart were his newly repaired chinos, other than that, his wardrobe was home to a collection of jeans in various different shades and states of repair. They ranged from his newest and smartest, which despite his protests, his Mum had ironed creases into, to his Rock Star pair, with strategically torn holes in the knees. They constantly faced denim death row.

With no time to shop for new ones, he begrudgingly added his suit trousers to the pile and hoped nobody would notice. With a couple of cotton shirts, his faithful leather jacket, two pairs of his extortionately expensive new Tightie-whities, socks, belt, smart, plastic shoes, desert boots, a few plain t-shits and an old rugby sweater, he was almost ready. What could he use for rough wear bottoms? He scratched his head and pulled at his unfamiliar, cropped hair. "Mum, *MUM*! Where're Mike's spare combats?"

The coach journey had been an unrelenting misery, but had been made almost bearable by an unexpected travelling companion. Even at this unsociable hour, Natasha somehow managed to not only to be immaculately presented, and as fresh as a daisy, but also smelt just like heaven, and during the trip, she did her upmost to keep things that way. She kept George talking, which was never much of effort, rubbed his knee affectionately when he turned white, and when the sun eventually came up, started pointing out various objects of interest. All of which seemed to be on the horizon.

They were the only two members of staff to be *randomly* selected from the Armada group to attend the Team Building Event, and during the endless journey, the coach stopped to let yet more bleary eyed candidates on board from other Groups. They were always in twos, and as suspected by a few of the more cynical passengers, they'd all been carefully selected.

Only a small number of staff, those who were either demonstrating the desired competencies and behaviours at the moment, or showing promise that they could be moulded and influenced in the future, had been chosen. Depending on the feedback they received from the course instructors, those staff not already in a sales role could well be fast tracked into one upon their return.

Natasha was extremely driven. Just a few months after joining Cottons three years ago, she'd quickly been promoted to CBA, and in the years that followed, had made a name for herself as an ambitious member of staff who desperately wanted to succeed, no matter what. Many of the girls also envied her impressive collection of shoes. Unlike Dean, the undisputed king of all CBA's, she wasn't too opinionated, and seemed the most likely of all CBA's in the Group to adopt the New World ethos without objection. Whilst she might not truly believe all the propaganda, she'd certainly pay it more than mere lip-service if it meant earning more money for clothes, cars and holidays. Some people were easy to predict.

George, meanwhile, had been a curious choice. Yet despite his many faults and numerous shortcomings, he did seem to grasp the whole referrals concept. Quite why was a mystery. What was his goal? Perhaps his success was merely down to an inability to identify the exact moment that he started to aggravate the customer, something that caused others to stop, but that he seemed to blindly push on through, until they eventually relented. He was certainly tenacious, if nothing else. With the right amount of training, brainwashing and encouragement, he might even be a reasonable CBA. And soon, the Bank was going to need a lot of CBAs.

'Back Woods Field and Adventure Centre' emerged from the early morning mist like a foreboding, remote hotel from a slow burning, deeply disturbing horror movie. The old grey buildings, once part of a large rambling farmhouse, had been converted into an impressive residential venue. It played host to corporate team building events, school trips, and getaways for small independent groups of people, who liked to test themselves at the weekends, rather than just put their feet up with the papers.

The scattered barns, outbuildings and farmhouse provided accommodation, a dining area, classrooms, a gymnasium, swimming pool, and even a small lecture theatre and bar. The surrounding farm land, which included a menacing forest, contained challenging assault courses, off road tracks for motor bikes, playing fields and an enormous orienteering course spread over a huge area of mixed terrain. Some of the guests were bound to get lost over the next two days.

The fifty weary passengers got off the coach and were immediately met by two very different men, both in their early fifties. The first was very well dressed in a suit and tie. He introduced himself as Raymond Barnes, had a slight build, greying hair and the sort of nondescript face normally associated with a serial killer. By comparison the second man was built like tank, had a thick black moustache and, despite the February chill, wore a tight military singlet, lightweight combat trousers, gleaming black boots and a red beret. He was simply called Drill Sergeant Nash, and had probably been so since primary school.

There was a short introduction. It seemed that the Serial Killer ran all the classroom exercises, lectures and so forth, and the Trained Killer was in charge of any activity that involved getting wet, muddy or covered in blood. Starting to feel somewhat unsettled, the group collected their belongings from the belly of the coach, and wistfully watched it disappear into the mist as it drove away.

It was just past nine o'clock, and breakfast seemed like a long time ago to the majority of the group. The Serial Killer rambled on in his unhurried voice about fire exits, meal times and the recreational activities available in the evening, before finally handing out a map of the facilities and a brief guide. After settling into their rooms, they were to gather in the main hall at ten, where they'd be given coffee and croissants, briefed on the planned activities and split into groups.

George took his room key and hoped that nobody heard his stomach growl. He was even hungrier than normal, if that were at all possible. His four poached egg whites and dry, half slice of wholemeal toast had ceased to offer any comfort hours ago. Despite his protests, his Mum had packed him off with three freshly cooked bacon baps for the road, clearly oblivious to his travel sickness. But a combination of his loyalty to both Dean and his diet, and the remorseless waves of nausea that battered him, meant that he'd sold them to the fat chap in the next row instead. Although this was something that would've been unheard of in the past, it did yield a tidy profit to spend in the bar later.

Now though, giddy with hunger and fatigue, the mere mention of a croissant chased away any allegiances he held, and for the moment, his stomach was as excited as a kitten with a stolen ball of wool. It was only an innocent bit of butter and pastry after all, Dean wouldn't need to know.

"What's your room number, George?" Despite her size, Natasha, his only ally in this unfamiliar, slightly unsettling environment, parted the sea of milling staff like a bull through the streets of Spain. She sidled up next to him. Close enough to brush elbows, but not so close that they'd appear to be an actual couple. She might still get a better offer.

"Err, fourteen, what about you?" His eyes looked pleadingly at her, desperately willing the number fifteen to come out of her beautiful mouth.

"Fifty-one, over in that other building, by the looks of it." She held the map up for him to see, having already gained a full, detailed understanding of her surroundings, including the location of the small bar. "You're here, in this building, not *too* far away from me, Darling…" She winked so briefly at him that he wasn't even sure that it had happened. Smiling coyly, she sauntered off with the rest of the women, all of whom seemed to be incarcerated in a separate block from the men. No doubt there'd be plenty of careful, midnight manoeuvres later this evening then.

George's ground floor room was small and spotless. It contained a tiny en-suite with a shower, a modest wardrobe for belongings, a desk with an unforgiving wooden chair, and an extremely hard double bed. There were no bedside tables, just a modest shelf on one side. No television, no radio and nothing even remotely resembling a mini bar. The Ritz, this was not. There was however, a sizeable window taking up much of the far wall. It opened wide and afforded far reaching views. Or rather would have done, if it weren't for the ominous mist that still clung to the surrounding countryside, like a blanket of wet cobwebs. He was so hungry.

A large red warning sign hung on the wall. It cautioned guests against drinking alcohol anywhere on the premises, except for in the bar, or eating food anywhere but in the dining room. Rooms could be inspected at any moment, if any evidence of alcohol or snacks was found; the individual and their company could be fined anything up to five hundred pounds. That could make for a very expensive pint of beer, or packet of crisps. He considered his Tupperware box full of vile protein powder, should he flush it down the loo just in case? Food, he was so hungry.

Trembling slightly from famine, he packed away his few items of clothing and looked around his bleak quarters. Regretting not bringing the latest issue of Guitarist Magazine for company, he thought instead about finishing his letter to Summer, or even starting it for that matter. It was going to be a very long two days though, especially without any means of making a cup of tea. He was still allowed tea on his strict new diet, although skimmed milk took some getting used to, as did the lack of sugar.

He sat heavily on the sparse bed, a wave of weariness washing over him, forcing his eyelids to close. He hadn't felt this tired since working the night shift at the Supermarket. Glancing at his Seiko, he slowly, gratefully lay back on the rock hard bed, and looked up at the beamed ceiling. It was quarter past nine and he'd been up since half past four. Surely there'd be no harm in having just few minutes rest before the meeting at ten?

George barged into the main hall at eighteen minutes past ten, and immediately, each croissant munching face turned to curiously examine the blushing new arrival. His short hair was flattened on one side, a sure sign that he'd dozed off, and his trouser fly was plainly gaping open for all to see. The new underwear *had* been an essential part of his wardrobe after all.

Drill Sergeant Nash took him outside, and yelled at him for five minutes without pausing for breath, before leading him back into the hall to let the Serial Killer publicly mock him for his time keeping, appearance and narrowly avoided moment of partial nudity. Presumably as punishment, he was denied either a reviving mug of coffee or freshly warmed croissant. Sitting alone at the back of the hall, he listened as the Serial Killer explained the day's activities to his audience. Above everything else, he wished he could just go home and hide behind his bedroom wallpaper. He was so very hungry, tired and humiliated.

Later that evening, back in the relative safety and discomfort of his barren room, George sat at his desk with his head cradled in his arms, and tried his very best not to cry. It had been a truly awful, unrelenting day of misery, made much worse by the fact that everyone else seemed to be having a really good time.

Unfortunately, he'd been placed with a group of former NSIB staff. Since the merger, word around the camp fire had been that some of the diehard members of this Bank rather resented being thrown into a pot with their new southern cousins. It had never occurred to the staff of Cottons that this might be the case. Whereas many shared Auntie Rose opinion that the largely northern based Bank was beneath them, no one had stopped to ponder quite what *its* staff might think about Cottons. Sissies from the South, just about covered it. Unfortunately for George, most of the diehards seemed to be in his team.

Armed with morning's tardiness, as well as an arsenal of new nicknames the embittered members of NSIB had invented to throw at their contemporaries, the day had been spent happily ridiculing their youngest member. No stranger to the odd playground or Supermarket dig, he did his best to cope, but having only worked for the Bank for a few months, some of the insults were lost on him. It was like being insulted by an unpleasant, foreign mob. By the end of the day though, he felt utterly alone, especially as Natasha had wandered off with another group. He hadn't seen her since the coffee and croissant affair. She was probably a Team Leader by now. She'd have no doubt sent one of them out for illegal pizza and wine, and perhaps organised a party in her room.

As his own day unfolded, he'd been constantly sidelined and derided by his older team mates. He'd hoped that his new, modern haircut would make mockery a thing of the past for him. None of them had called him Elvis at least. Everything else had been launched at him, but not Elvis. He almost missed it.

There'd been three separate activities, all concluding at five, giving the candidates a couple hours to themselves to freshen up, socialise and bond, before the formal sit down evening meal at seven. George meanwhile, simply hid in his room, reflecting moodily with a rumbling belly. He was so hungry. A packed lunch had been provided, but he'd been pushed, or *maybe* he did trip, and most of it ended up in the mud. Ironically though, if his teammates had actually allowed him to offer an opinion, he could've added some valuable input to the tasks at hand.

To begin with, before they changed into rough wear, each team took part in a classroom exercise. Based on Pictionary and Charades, the aim to encourage candidates to identify exactly what a person was trying to communicate, either by miming or with drawings. Whilst George was terrible at charades, apart from donkeys, he could draw anything on demand, and in record time. Or at least he would have, if he'd been allowed. Instead he sat at the back with a rumbling stomach.

Next, after they'd changed into their rough clothes, they were issued with a packed lunch and sent off on an orienteering exercise. The aim it seemed was to find a hidden object, which rather disappointingly proved to be nothing more exciting than a small, brass bell. Not that George's group actually found it. They'd become quite lost instead, and were late back for the final task. If they'd listened to the one member of the group who'd actually grown up in the countryside though, the one who after he and his best friend had become lost yet again on camping trip, had been taught how to read a map properly, they'd have probably won.

The final task of the day, an activity designed to encourage communication, logical thinking and observation skills, was blindfolded tent building. George and Barney had camped so often, and in such inhospitable weather that both boys could not only erect a tent blindfolded, but also whilst a force ten gale was making it rain sideways. This time though, demoralised beyond words, he just watched from the back and said nothing. He was so sad and hungry.

The small, beige plastic phone that sat on the desk next to him rang excitedly, snapping him out of his thoughts. It rang again, almost more urgently than before, irritated that it hadn't been picked up the first time. He gazed at it quizzically. Who'd be ringing him here? Suspecting a cruel, practical joke from his teammates, George gingerly picked up the receiver.

"George, *George*? Talk to me Darling." His heart soared. There was no mistaking Natasha's husky voice. "I think it's time we broke out of here and had some fun, *don't you*?"

The next morning, he awoke with a dry mouth, a piecing headache and what could only be described as an unexpected attack of cramp in his right hip. As the fog slowly cleared, further mental examination of his body also revealed a mild burning sensation in his neck and back, a split lip, something that looked suspiciously like bite marks on his chest, and more alarmingly, very little feeling at all in his most personal, and private area.

He looked around the meagre room and sat up. There was something different about his surroundings. He scratched his cropped hair, pulling at it absentmindedly while he waited for his brain to engage. What was different about the place? Suddenly he had it. The window was on the wrong side of the room! Somebody had moved his window in the night, a cruel practical joke perhaps?

The door to the en suite abruptly opened and Natasha, very, very naked and slightly moist, sauntered into the bedroom, still drying her long black hair and grinning mischievously at him. She was completely at ease with her spectacular nudity. Why wouldn't she be?

"Good morning Darling. How's the hip?"

During the course of the following morning, after he'd been yelled at some more for missing the formal meal, breakfast, and being sporadically unshaven, the evening's events slowly came back to him. To begin with, there was the half hourly news round. Initially, these stories included little more than just flashbacks of unlawful drinks in Natasha's room, with George pointing out the alcohol warning sign, and the possible issue of being fined. The news reports did become more interesting as the morning unfolded though, and by the time his team was engrossed in a bridge building activity around eleven, he finally remembered climbing out of Natasha's bedroom window and dashing for the tree line behind her, like a convict on the run.

The midday news brought him up to date with events at the small village pub they'd stumbled into. The massive T-bone steak and the half dozen poached eggs he'd consumed, and the six bottles of Budweiser he'd washed it all down with. Dean would have been proud of him though, he didn't eat his chips or his onion rings. He used to love onion rings.

It was during the final leg of yet another orienteering exercise that he finally remembered, in all its hip crunching, chest biting, and back scratching intensity, the rest of his evening with the incredible Natasha. For the first time in two days, or at least the first time whilst sober and clothed, George smiled to himself and felt briefly happy. Then he thought of Summer, and his feelings stopped dead, blushed, and rapidly changed direction. Should he be feeling guilty now? Did this count as spreading his wings? They certainly ached a bit.

The final hateful task, before the coach returned and thankfully took them away again, had been kept a closely guarded secret. All that was said by either of the trainers was that the assignment was designed to prove that, even when faced with a new and unfamiliar skill, an individual could prove themselves to be successful, if they listened to instruction, and tried hard enough to win. At least there would be a prize.

Whatever it proved to be, it was unlikely to hold any interest for George though, and when Natasha pulled him into a rhododendron bush, as the group made their way to the main playing field, he didn't care in the slightest if the stolen, passionate kiss led to another unpleasant yelling episode. It would be more than worth it, guilty feelings notwithstanding.

When he finally stumbled onto the playing field twenty minutes later, sprigs of bush in his short hair, a fresh love bite beginning blossoming on his neck, for the second time in as many minutes his spirits leapt. In his estimation, the archery targets were set at roughly thirty yards, an easy shot for him. The collection of bows and arrows at the shooting line looked like novice equipment compared to his kit, but serviceable none the less. This was more like it.

Finally excited, and hoping to at last prove his worth to his horrible colleagues, regardless of what his bullying group tried to pull, he bounded over to join them. They were already kitted out with arm guards and bows, and he looked around desperately for his own equipment to join in. Suddenly though, Drill Sergeant Nash grabbed him unceremoniously by the arm, and dragged him away from the line.

"Right you horrible slovenly little shit, *you listen to me*! You've right royally got well and truly up my nose, sunshine! If this was the Army, I'd have you flogged, *FLOGGED*, do you hear?" He gripped George's arm harder and harder, pulling him to within inches from his nose. "If you think I'm letting you near one of *my* bows, you've got another thing coming, boy, now bugger off over there and stay out of my sight!" He shoved him brutally backwards to make his point. He needn't have bothered. Predictably, his group who'd been watching the exchange, laughed and pointed as, crestfallen, he sloped off to sit on the cold, grassy bank.

"*George*! What the hell do you think you're doing?" Having survived a telling off for being late by cunningly feigning ladies problems, Natasha wandered over and sat down next to her despondent lover, her face a picture of genuine, exasperated concern.

"Sitting this one out I guess. I don't care, really, it's okay, I just want to get out of here, *don't you*?" Forgetting all of Dean's insightful lectures about posture, and holding your head up high at all times, he let his shoulder slump and the remains of his belly sag. But not for long. The brutally expert, well-aimed blow to his thigh nearly caused him to weep in pain.

"*You listen to me, Butler*! Get off your sorry ass now, grab that bloody bow off that lanky shit over there and *fire the fucking thing*!" Utterly stunned and astounded, George gawped at her, his mouth hanging open in shock. He'd never heard anyone this small and pretty use bad language before. She wasn't finished either.

"You've got muscles now! You could knock any of those bastards out if you wanted to. Maybe not the Drill instructor, he's obviously a psycho, but those little shitheads who've been giving you crap, you could punch the living daylights out of those assholes! Now go and give 'em shit, or there's *no way* I'm letting you play with me again!"

Abruptly, she jumped up, clipped him round the back of the head, kissed him lightly on the ear, a confusing combination at best, and strutted off back to her own group, leaving him to stare openly at the pert little bottom, barely concealed behind the smallest pair of white shorts imaginable. Bugger, what just happened?

He eventually broke out of his bubble of astonishment and, for only the second time ever in his life, girded his loins. It felt terrifyingly good. Thrusting out his chest and throwing back his shoulders, he offered up a silent, agnostic prayer, and marched determinably back towards the firing line. Pushing past the group of people who'd derided him, patronized him, and generally made him feel utterly useless for nearly two days, he eventually confronted Phillip, the obnoxious, statuesque git who'd become the unofficial head of the 'Let's Make George Butler's life Hell' Club. They were considering printing membership cards.

"What do you want, *Butler*?" Phillip, like some frighteningly tall people, had sauntered through life naturally thinking he was better, generally more evolved than the rest of mankind. He looked down his perfectly developed nose at the dishevelled wretch. It seemed to have gained some interesting new injuries. "*Well*?"

"Give me the sodding bow Phillip, or I'll batter your lanky ass purple, *you git*!"

His heart in his mouth, George grabbed the bow and arrows out of the suddenly shaky, confused hands and, whilst trying to control a body which was shuddering like an unbalanced washing machine on a spin cycle, approached the firing line.

"Err, *young man*! We'd much rather you had some *proper* instruction before using that!" The Serial Killer stood with hands on hips, his head held to one side, eyebrows raised the very picture of aggravated authority. He desperately hoped the Trained Killer would appear from nowhere, as was his custom, and shoot the errant candidate before something awful happened.

Ignoring him completely, his adrenaline still trying to fathom out quite how long it had been asleep for, and where the hell it was, George expertly slotted an arrow into place, and drew back the fibre glass bow. In impressively quick succession, he fired all six arrows, each landing dead centre in the thirty-yard target, one no more than a pinkie fingers width from the other. Robin Hood would have been proud. He could have at least split one down the middle though, for dramatic effect, if nothing else.

"I've already *had* proper instruction." He glanced angrily over his shoulder at the dumbfounded group, and the gawping Serial Killer, just a touch of pride spreading across his white face. *"From my Dad."*

Pity, thought Natasha, he'd sounded really rather cool up until then.

Weapons-grade nagging was to blame for George's foray into the world Archery. Whilst her eldest son enjoyed hobbies and interests that included football, cricket and rugby, pursuits that naturally developed fitness and, more importantly, ensured he was subjected to massive doses of good old fashioned fresh air, Mrs Butler's youngest just painted pictures of wildlife, indoors. This troubled her, and it was high time something was done about it.

To begin with, having dismissed the whole Ozone Layer issue as simply nonsense, she'd insisted that he set up his easel in her spectacular garden, rather than his bedroom, to at least get some colour in his pale cheeks. George however was not convinced. Having removed yet another paint-encrusted blue bottle from his canvas, he soon retreated back to the safety of his bedroom whilst his Mum's head was buried in her azaleas. Then things really got interesting.

Steps would have to be taken. He needed a hobby that would drag him out of his Pit and back into the sunshine.

Mr Butler was not a particularly sporting man. He'd no interest in either rugby or football, but he did rather like cricket, and he and Michael often enjoyed a light hearted game on the flatter parts of the surrounding countryside. George had joined them once, but it had proven to be a complete disaster. To begin with, he absolutely could not catch a ball, even when it was thrown gently, and directly, straight into his hands. He swung the bat like a tennis racket, despite endless instruction, and often wandered off when he spotted something shiny in the undergrowth, even if he was in bat.

Fearing that the nagging would never cease if he didn't find some way to engage his son in a meaningful outdoor pursuit, his Dad decided to try a more obscure sport instead, one that had held his own interest through his early twenties; Fencing. A spirited and somewhat unnecessary remise, soon put pay to this idea though, especially when his wife saw the hole in her son's new jumper. She wanted him to be healthy, not skewered.

Undeterred, Mr Butler changed tack completely, and chose something that by its very nature required not only the great outdoors, but also great dollops of fresh air, and more importantly, wind, lots and lots of wind. They were going to build and fly a massive kite.

Thankfully, George became engrossed in the project. It appealed to him on many levels, and didn't involve too much physical exertion, or anything even remotely resembling a bat or a ball. After digesting several books on the subject in preparation, father and son set about building a monstrous, triangular ten foot beast. Following a week of arguing over what it should resemble, it took another week to paint a fearsome bright red, raging dragon across its vast wingspan. Once it was finished, it terrified the family Jack Russell.

For the line, Mr Butler bought some tough fishing line, capable of reeling in a shark and, leaving it on the reel on which it was supplied, simply threaded a sturdy piece of dowel through the centre. Handles were made from rubberised tape, and it was secured to the three corners of the kite. Finally, it was ready to fly. All they needed now was a suitably windy day.

Eventually, one extremely blustery Sunday morning, the Dragon Kite was finally granted its maiden flight. High up on the rolling countryside that surrounded the rural town where the Butler family lived, the magnificent beast, the product of several weeks' worth of dedicated father son time, at last soared gloriously into the clear blue summer sky. The reel spun wildly on the smoking length of dowel, and, gripped tightly in young, terrified hands, the Kite raced ever skywards.

By the time they eventually realised that the end of the fishing line was not actually attached to the reel it was supplied on, it was far, far too late to do anything about it. Still buffeted by the howling gale, they stood in stunned silence, watching all their hard work disappear higher and higher into the stratosphere. They decided it was best not to tell Mum. It crashed, it broke and it was beyond repair. End of story.

Several miles away from the launch site, nestled in a green and pleasant valley, lay a quaint pocket-sized village, home to a pub, a green, a tiny church, a scattering of picturesque cottages and very little else. It was on this village, or more accurately, onto the church yard, that the bright red fluttering, screaming Dragon Kite eventually descended. Tearing out of the heavens like a Demon just as the elderly congregation left Sunday morning service.

The aged mass of worshippers screamed in terror, and scattered like startled geriatric mice as the Dragon Kite, which by now had built up quite an impressive landing speed, bore down on them. The Vicar, a spritely seventy-eight year old, held up his hands as 'The Beast' grew ever closer, belting out scripture to defend his flock against the terror from above.

When the Dragon Kite eventually came crashing to the ground, tearing itself on an elaborate headstone nearest the pathway, the spectacle sent most of the remaining parishioners into the graveyard. It was left to Doris

Arkwright, a ninety-two year old former Royal Naval nurse, to hobble slowly forward on her Zimmer frame, and beat the fluttering red Devil to death with a discarded walking stick. End of story.

Just when it looked as though all was lost, and that George was destined to spend his life indoors with a whitish pallor and thickening waistline, he made an unexpected discovery in the loft of the Butlers' respectable semi, which would change his life forever. Having run out of white acrylic paint, and with his parents safely out of the house, he'd bravely entered the loft, fearing the ever present danger of randomly un-boarded roof beams and of course, spiders. It was his intention to raid his father's long since abandoned paint box, an item which was last seen heading loft-wards following the relentless and unforgiving Great Spring Clean of 1988.

With just a single, naked thirty-watt bulb dangling from the roof beams to guide him, throwing shadows into every nook and cranny of the loft, he took infinite care with his footing. All the while wondering just how big the spiders got up here, and if there was any chance he might find his long lost Star Wars figures. He didn't.

He spent two hours trying not to fall through, and gingerly prodding boxes with his reclaimed lightsabre. A welcome find that had been propped up in a corner, miraculously still worked and as an added bonus, now helped him see where he was going, albeit with a slightly malevolent red glow. He'd always favoured the Dark Side.

Suddenly, in the crimson half-light, he found a curious wooden box, with elaborate artwork painted on the front. Behind the box, lent against a supporting roof strut, was a long narrow brown bag made from leather. In a sea of uniform and meticulously labelled cardboard boxes, these new finds stood out like a sore thumb. Clearly Mum didn't know about them.

George balanced the lightsabre on a box marked 'Michael's Primary School Books', checked his footing, and knelt carefully in front of his new discovery in order to get a better look. The wooden box was sturdy and robust, just over three feet long, ten inches wide and six deep. Two solid looking brass latches held the lid firmly shut. He'd found it! He heard about it before, but never actually seen it. It was Dad's revered, much talked about and, if you happened to be French and knew your history, politically incorrect Archery box.

Archery used to be a treasured hobby of Mr Butler senior. He'd only reluctantly given it up when the children came along and the nagging to spend time with them intensified. But to begin with, in an effort to add a touch of humour to the stuffy old club he belonged to, he'd constructed a bomb-proof arrow and accessory box from timber reclaimed from a discarded University lab bench. Then he set about personalising his creation, for fun.

On the lid, he'd painted a detailed, period piece from one of his many historical text books. It depicted the famous 1415 battle at Agincourt, complete with a realistic scroll that bore the St. Crispin's Day speech from Henry V. Things got much, much more entertaining on the sides of the box though. In uncanny, almost unbelievably realistic detail, he'd painted imitation flag stickers, such as those found on old, well-travelled leather suitcase, intended to identify the places the owner had visited. But instead of Paris, New York or London, these flags read Crecy, Hastings, Poitiers, Agincourt, Bosworth and Orleans. All places a self-respecting longbow archer of yesteryear with an ingrained hatred of the French and a quiver full of arrows would have happily battled.

The leather bag gathering dust next to the roof strut, contained his longbow. A fearsome piece of equipment, painstakingly constructed out of an unfortunate yew tree that grew in the garden of his then bachelor pad. Once the yew had been left to dry and season, for almost as long as it had taken it to grow, he'd then set about building the six foot longbow with nothing more than a well-worn library book on the subject, and a carefully selected assortment of hand tools.

It was this very bow that young George Butler carefully pulled from its sheath. In the half-light of the attic, a look akin to that of a young King Arthur, gingerly plucking Excalibur from its stone, crept across his pudgy face. Somewhere deep inside of him, his inner Robin Hood suddenly woke up.

After finding his slightly dusty, youngest son in the hallway, clutching his longbow and wearing a wicked grin, Mr Butler senior wasted no time at all enrolling them both in the local Archery club. Finally, providing he didn't get shot, he'd found a hobby for him.

The Club had been established for over forty years. It was run with military precision by a close knit committee of retired and rather dull, former Officers. For the past thirty-eight years, the Club had been lucky enough to base itself within the vast grounds of the local private school for boys, an imposing institution that could itself trace its history back to the dawn of time. There had never been any complaints or any accidents.

They leased a modest store room to house the targets and equipment, and had use of the main playing field for practice, once the pupils had gone home, naturally. The field was enclosed on all sides by a dense border of oak trees, and the main school building grandly overlooked the far end of the seven hundred yard, square area of perfectly manicured grass.

Not long after joining the Club, Mr Butler senior soon resumed his old favourite position at the one hundred yard target. Trusty longbow in hand, with its impressive sixty-pound draw weight, he steadily and consistently buried his ash arrows deep into the centre of the straw target, at a rate that would have driven fear into the heart of any passing Frenchman.

To begin with though, George couldn't share in his Dad's enjoyment. All he could do was look on in envy as he struggled with an impossibly underpowered, unexciting beginner's bow. To make matter worse, his tutor, a condescending, thin man somewhere in his forties, had a fondness of cough sweets, despite any evidence that he actually ever suffered from a cough, and the constant sickly honey aroma made his pupil nauseous.

In order to maintain his son's interest, or perhaps more importantly, protect his enjoyment of his now fully revived hobby, Mr Butler senior decided that after a few weeks of suffering basic tutorage, his son should be treated to a decent bow of his own. Sadly, this wasn't to be the simple purchase he'd hoped for, with both archers having very different opinions about what a decent bow should look like. It was going to get messy.

Mr Butler senior thought that his son should have a modest re-curve bow, with a twenty-five pound draw weight, until his strength developed and maturity finally kicked in. Meanwhile, George's thoughts on the subject had been thoroughly corrupted a few weeks earlier, by the film *Rambo: First Blood Part Two*. Once safely hidden from view behind the end of Michael's single bed, and apart from occasionally having to hide behind a pillow during the gory bits, he became fascinated by the hero's black bow, with its curious wheels and cables. His mind was made up. He simply had to have one.

'Adams Archery Supplies' had played host to a many squabbling families before, and Joe Adam was no novice when it came to refereeing such conflicts. Often the child in question wanted a bow that was simply too big, or too powerful for them to be able to draw, and he would gently and calmly meditate between Ungrateful Brat and Aggravated Parent until a compromise, often a more lucrative one at that, could be found.

Therefore, when the Butler family descended on his modest commercial unit, something told him that the plump lad with wide eyes and a mass of black hair, was going to be trouble, and he prepared himself accordingly for the onslaught. When the family left a few hours later, he was so relieved that he'd closed for the rest of the afternoon, and went to the pub to regain his composure and steady his nerves. However he considered it, there was definitely no way on earth that that kid should've been let loose with a Barnett Safari compound bow. No way at all.

In the weeks following the events at 'Adams Archery Supplies', and after George had written a sincere, heartfelt letter of apology to Mr Adams for accidentally shooting an arrow into his cash register, enthusiasm for the hobby had once again been restored, and perhaps more essentially, aim improved.

With his new if slightly menacing black compound bow, and a gleaming set of aluminium Easton arrows, he'd soon found that not only could he consistently hit the target he was aiming at, but also that his patronising tutor now seemed inclined to leave him alone. The rest of the Club looked down their noses at the contraption though. Traditionalists generally took a dim view of the compound bow. Obviously they just needed to watch Rambo.

Before long, its destructive force started ruining the straw targets at close range, and George was swiftly banished to the one hundred yard position, to join his Dad and Tony Sheldon, the only other member of the club who could actually see a target at this range. Tony was an unusual companion for Mr Butler senior. Being something of a loner himself, despite his wife and two sons, he tended to collect friends at the same rate that most people collect tropical diseases. Tony was thirty-two, but could just have easily been either forty-eight or twenty-seven. He wore a pair of battered National Health spectacles, which were held together with a heavily stained fabric plaster, and had very closely cropped, thinning hair that in certain lights looked orange. He had permanent stubble, a smattering of timid freckles, was extremely tall and wiry and smoked very thin roll ups incessantly, which he kept in a small black tin that he'd etched a rough skull and crossbones into.

Every Tuesday and Thursday evening, and for four hours on Sunday morning, before the epic family roast dinner, the three archers battered the solitary one hundred yard target with a combination of arrows, let fly from an old, handmade longbow, a relatively inexpensive one piece re-curve, and a lethal compound bow nobody approved of. It was only when Simon Peck arrived one balmy Thursday evening that they began to question where it was all going to end.

Simon worked for Ford. As he arrived in a brand new, extremely loud, bright yellow Ford Escort Cosworth R.S, it was clearly something he wasn't bothered about keeping to himself. He was a bachelor in the grandest sense of the tradition, having managed to avoid marriage and, as far as he knew at least, children all through his fifty-one years. He was impossible not to warm to. With a Friar Tuck haircut, bulbous midriff that constantly caused his expensive shirts to escape from his belt, and thick hairy, apelike forearms, he wasn't blessed with good looks, but was utterly charming, had boundless energy and an unrivalled zest for life. Women loved him.

Like most bachelors who have secured decent jobs, he was also obsessed with his Toys, and having recently discovered archery, his new Toy was a jaw-dropping compound bow that made George's effort look as though it had come free with a box of breakfast cereal.

By the close of Thursday's shooting, having politely asked to join the archers at the one hundred yard target, the four of them were friends. By the following Sunday, they were as thick as thieves, and by the end of the next week, they had a plan. They were going to introduce a new arm to the stuffy old Club, Field Archery. It was going to get messy again, and very probably muddy too.

Field Archery was as close to hunting with a bow and arrow as any of them were likely to get, without having to actually murder anything cute and furry. Once they'd found a suitable remote, rural venue, they intended to make life sized animal targets and set up across rivers and deep into wild forests. According to the rule book Simon had bought, they needed to set three shooting stations from which the archer must then attempt to hit the targets, without any idea of the actual range. There were various other complicated rules and regulations, regarding scoring and so forth, but the newly formed band of field archers soon chose to ignore all of these, in favour of simply having a good time playing bows and arrows in the woods. Boys never really do grow up.

Naturally, and in keeping with tradition, George somehow managed to find both Peril and Danger lurking behind every tree and outcrop of rock, each time he set foot on the newly adopted field archery course. Firstly, despite his girth, he was the smallest of the group and as such the logical choice to fill the role of Chief Arrow Spotter. This unenviable task, simply involved cowering behind something large and protective, close to the chosen target, whilst the others took turns to pelt the straw animal with arrows, fired with an unpredictable degree of accuracy. It wasn't much fun. He soon found that the trick to being an effective spotter was to try and not close his eyes and cower each time and arrow was fired at him. This was all well and good in theory, but impossible in practice. Basic self-preservation really made quite a strong argument against sticking his head out from behind the relative safety of an oak tree to spot arrows that are travelling at twenty-five metres per second in his general direction. Bugger that.

Towards the end of the course there was a particularly challenging long shot over the narrow river that cut through the land. The three shooting stations had been cunningly arranged for maximum Robin Hood effect, with the archer having to shoot between several trees and across two bends in the river, before finally attempting to bring down the large wildebeest that had inexplicably trekked all the way from the Serengeti Plain, to rural England.

The island itself was not much bigger than the wildebeest, and offered little in the way of cover for the petrified spotter. The only real option was for him to stand in the shallows and wedge himself behind a pathetic-looking beech tree, which grew out of the far side of the river bed. Then it was simply a case of breathing in, covering his vitals with his shaking hands, and hoping his fellow archers aim was considerably better than his own.

On at least on occasion though, Simon's aim had been off. That evening, Mr Butler senior had no choice but to sneak out to his garage, whilst his wife was safely immersed in her chin deep bubble bath with a large glass of merlot, a questionable scented candle and the latest Danielle Steele novel for company. He needed to repair the carbon fibre, arrow sized hole in son's Wellington boot before she discovered it, and put an end to all their fun. It wasn't like he'd lost a toe or anything.

After a few weeks of sinking his costly carbon fibre arrows into make-believe bears, zebras and lions, Simon was obsessed with their new found sport and, following a particularly expensive evening meal with the glamorous head of stationary at the Ford plant where he worked, turned up at the next shoot with novelty gifts for his fellow archers. It seemed that after a rather eventful second date, he'd eventually managed to persuade the head of stationary to make a selection of tiny stickers for each member of the unofficial, and as far as the proper club was concerned, un-authorised, Company of Field Archers.

The sticker was no bigger than a thumbnail, and depicted a brilliant cartoon of a Robin Hood style archer drawing back a bow and aiming an oversized arrow. The image was printed on clear, sticky back plastic and had just black outline, except for the feather in the hat. These came in four different colours, one for each member to wrap around their individual arrows just ahead of the flights. It would identify them as Rebels to the rest of the main club. They'd giggled like schoolboys as they peeled off the backing and stuck them onto their arrows. For some unknown reason though, George's was pink.

As the evenings began to draw in towards the end of the summer, the poor light meant field archery was strictly limited to just Sunday mornings, and the ragtag foursome had to reluctantly make do with target archery for the rest of the week. It was nothing short of mundane compared to their adventures in the woods. Somehow, firing a steady, consistent volley of arrows at a target of known distance just didn't hold the same level of excitement as shooting off a hard earned length of aluminium, carbon, or ash, whilst never being quite sure if you were ever going to see it again.

Therefore, it wasn't long before the four hooligans at the one hundred yard target found some other means of enjoying themselves. Late one misty

Thursday evening, Mr Butler senior presented his suggestion to the others.

Flight archery was inevitably, most people's first introduction to the sport. The simple act of pulling back a bent bamboo cane with a nylon string, and launching a smaller length at forty-five degrees into the air whilst the garden peas fell over, was basically flight archery. For the rebellious Company of Field Archers however, it simply boiled down to seeing just how far they could shoot their arrows. Or, more importantly, who had the best bow.

Simon and George immediately set about adjusting the limbs of their compound bows to the maximum draw weight. This quietly worried George. The last thing he wanted was to be embarrassed by being unable to pull the thing back. Victory would be worth the risk though.

Once the rest of the geriatric archers had hobbled off the field, and their fleet of impossibly beige Volvos had slowly driven away, the four extremist, giggling like naughty school boys, lined up with their backs to the trees, a good six hundred and fifty yards of clear playing field ahead of them. It was time. They drew lots, made from discarded flights, to decide the order of shooting. Mr Butler senior was to go first, Tony second, and then George. Finally Simon would shoot for the heavens with his terrifying bow. Worryingly though, since he'd set the thing to missile launch mode, it seemed to be quivering slightly in its stand.

Holding his longbow at the correct angle, as instructed in his newly acquired archery digest, Mr Butler senior held onto the ash arrow just long enough to allow a roosting crow pass out of his line of sight, and released. There was the usual powerful, stately twang of the longbows string, and the arrow soared magnificently into the air. It arced perfectly, before coming back to earth three hundred yards away with an audible thud into the sun baked grass.

Tony was next. And despite his bows modest forty-pound draw weight, he still managed to outdistance the older man's more powerful, vintage weapon. There was a brief, slightly awkward moment of silence between them. Just as George readied himself for the effort of pulling back his own, much heavier than usual bow string, he was interrupted by an awful collection of noises from Simons bow stand. Having been stretched to a limit that it was franking not prepared to work at for long, the string snapped spectacularly. They all ducked.

Panic over, everyone waited whilst Simon dug around in the boot of the Cosworth for a spare string. When his frantic search failed to yield anything more useful than a suspicious pair of ladies stockings, he returned crestfallen, only eventually being brought out of his childlike sulk by Tony kindly offering his own bow. Forgetting the shooting order entirely, he pulled and fired the borrowed bow before George could protest. Finally managing to regain some of his usual gusto in the fading light, he convinced himself that he had outdistanced the other two archers. Naturally, this sparked intense, heated debate, and the three of them quickly set off to retrieve their arrows at a brisk trot, still muttering away, leaving a fully armed and un-tested junior at the firing line.

Certain that he'd easily beat the conventional bows, and with a few moments of solitude in which he could attempt to draw his bow, without any pressure from the others, George girded his loins for the first time. He slotted an arrow, complete with a new sticker of a pink feathered archer, onto the rest, and pulled the bow string back with all his might.

It wasn't his most graceful draw by any means, and he was convinced he'd torn something vital in his groin, but nonetheless, despite the extra thirty percent increase in power, he'd finally managed to get the arrow back under his bum fluffed chin. Trembling from the effort, he quickly angled the bow upwards. Conscience that the others would be nearing their arrows by now, and wincing from the effort of holding onto a string, which felt as though it was tearing through his finger guard, he held his breath and fired.

A week later the Archery Club held its annual AGM in the local town hall. The Company of Field Archers secretly suspected that some of the members actually enjoyed the AGM far more than they enjoyed shooting arrows. All four of them sat at the back, glaring and shivering. The local town hall, like all town halls, was freezing cold all year round.

It was a seemingly endless, sober affair, with various dull points of discussion raised by the incessantly smarmy Mr Chairman, but if a member wanted to ensure the survival of something they held dear, it was best to attend. The unofficial and un-associated Company of Field Archers clearly had the most to protect, fearing banishment at every turn from their contemporaries.

As the meeting drew to close, many, many frozen hours later, Mr Chairman raised an issue under AOB. This was unusual behaviour for this most serious-minded individual. Normally he didn't hold with the frivolous nature of AOB. Everyone, even the dead, sat up with renewed interest.

With unnecessary drama, he quickly produced a battered aluminium arrow shaft from under his wooden desk, and held it up for all to see. It had lost all of its flights, and was so scratched and damage that it looked as though it had been sanded down. Mr Chairman then asked that the offending arrow be passed around the room, to see if any of the members could identify, or claim its sorry remains. As he did so, he took great pleasure in regaling the group with the story of how it came to be in his possession.

It seemed that he knew the Headmaster of the Private School where the Archery Club practiced rather well, with both men being members of a prestigious Gentleman's Club. Reading between the lines of endless waffle and self-praising twaddle, apparently a few days ago, quite out of the blue, Mr Chairman had been invited, or rather, requested, to attend a meeting with the Headmaster, most urgently, in his private office.

Mr Chairman arrived promptly, of course, and was shown to the Headmasters office by his extremely flushed secretary. As usual, hands were shaken and pleasantries about the weather and family members exchanged. But it was only when the Headmaster slowly stood aside, allowing Mr Chairman, an unrivalled view of his pristine, regency mahogany desk and the beautiful, period stain glassed window that overlooked the playing fields, that he fully appreciated just why he had been summoned.

By now the remains of the arrow hand reached the Company of Field Archers. They all looked at the arrow, looked at each other, and then finally, three pairs of eyes looked accusingly at George. To anyone else the arrow was unidentifiable. It had been stripped of all characteristics and features by its violent, seven hundred and fifty yard journey through the cooling autumn air, through the period stain glass window, and eventually by burying itself into, and eventually three inches through, a once pristine regency mahogany desk.

To a certain brave band of loyal, and for the moment at least, more importantly, *silent*, members of the Company of Field Archers though, all the evidence they needed was there before their very eyes. The damning proof was no more than a barely visible fleck of coloured plastic. It was a seemingly innocent speck that could easily have been anything at all, but was actually the remains of a small pink feather.

The coach journey home had been almost unbearable George. Waves of travel sickness battered him endlessly against the rocks, and darkness prevented Natasha from pointing out anything of interest on the horizon to distract him. But he did have a spectacular gold trophy of an archer to keep his mind off things, and his travelling companion found something far more interesting than his knee to rub, to reassure him on their long journey home.

Chapter 12

JFJFs, CRA(P)s and Go-Karts

Late March.

Rebecca the Receptionist was puzzled. For the umpteenth time, she glanced down at the meetings schedule, which rested on her neat, impossibly organised desk, and then back at the relaxed, smart young man that sat nonchalantly in reception. It just couldn't be him again, could it?

Battling desperately against the never-ending urge to fidget, George, meanwhile, remained as still as he could, and waited nervously for his interview. This didn't come at all naturally to him. The ankle of his left leg rested on the knee of his right, his hands on his thighs, unmoving. Under Dean's patient guidance, he'd been practicing this pose for weeks. Until he'd eventually mastered it, he'd fallen off the chair, twice.

When he'd arrived a few minutes earlier, and reported to the desk, he'd been rather disappointed that the severe, yet extremely pretty blond receptionist didn't seem to remember him. Disappointed, and to a degree at least, relieved. Yet it seemed unlikely she'd fail to recall the devastation he'd caused last time, so why didn't she acknowledge him now?

Having quickly checked through her pristine files, Rebecca eventually found the date she was looking for, a day forever imprinted on her memory. People were still talking about it. She pulled out the meetings schedule, which was neatly stapled to a bundle of staff and visitor information, and leafed through until she found the one she was looking for. Dear God, it was him! Identical address and identical date of birth, the name hadn't simply been a coincidence. This was the very same George Butler who'd caused havoc in this very building just five months ago.

Rebecca looked at him again, confused, but now equally curious. She recalled harbouring a strange desire to mother him before. Now though, her desires were far from motherly. He'd lost a good deal of weight to begin with, and the black pin stripe suit, which fitted his frame perfectly, revealed something of an athletically muscular physique, which he definitely didn't have before. The thick mop of unruly hair had been cropped short, and looked modern and neat. It suited him, he looked older, but not in a bad way. Perhaps he was single? Involuntarily, she smiled at him, disappointed that he wasn't looking in her direction. He seemed to be gazing out the window. Now he was gazing at a chair, now the new vending machine.

'Periodic Lighthouse Glances' was how Dean described it to him, a method to prevent his student from permanently staring into space, a robust system to hopefully keep his famous glazed expression at bay. He needed to look at something, appear to take an interest in it, and then look at something else, a few degrees to either the right or left. Repeat the process and avoid being robotic, keep it fluid and natural. It seemed to work, so far. It was time to look at the receptionist again.

Rebecca blushed. He'd caught her looking longingly at him. At least he'd returned the smile this time though. She smiled back at him, grinning like a schoolgirl. Perhaps he'd been on some sort of television makeover show? They'd certainly done a marvellous job.

The past few weeks had been something of a blur. George had returned from the Team Building Event proudly clutching two new trophies. One made of gold, and another that was altogether more entertaining, pert and warm. Shortly after though, events took a turn for the unexpected. To begin with, despite his lateness, slovenliness and general lack of interest in almost all of the tasks undertaken during the Event, the brief report compiled by Drill Sergeant Nash, led the Bank to believe that he'd be an ideal candidate for the newly revised CBA role.

The report read as follows: *Always late, frequently disinterested and slovenly in appearance, does not engage at all with his Teammates, seems to have his own agenda, and only became interested in competing once a prize had been identified. Which regrettably I must report, he won.* To the Human Resources Manager though, whose job it was to interpret the reports and Map the candidate's path accordingly, this translated into: *Will probably work hard for cash prizes*. Fortunately, this was exactly what the Bank was looking for.

Top Managers had given a great deal of thought to designing the new CBA role. Production had even interfered with a few rounds of golf. But it was time well spent. Those colleagues that held this position would likely generate the main source of revenue for the Bank, and they needed to be well trained, and well-motivated to ensure that the sales came flooding in as hoped. The current Cottons heritage CBA role, and the equivalent position within the NSIB, simply entitled, Seller, was fastidiously reviewed by costly outsourced industry experts. Positive characteristics of each were identified, analysed and debated for days on end, before eventually being discard, and replaced with something far more complicated and profitable. After much more expensive discussion, the new role was eventually christened Customer Relationship Advisor or CRA for short. And because they were fun to make, and the expenses were generous, a whole collection of rousing internal films were produced to explain the new, exciting role to the plebs. Corporate popcorn was not provided.

Training courses were organised and thick workbooks dispatched to the existing CBA's and Sellers alike. This caused some dissatisfaction amongst the older guard of both heritages though. They found the whole process of being trained to do the same job they'd been doing for years on end, completely unnecessary, with one or two rebels suggesting that the new CRA title was only missing a solitary P to fully encapsulate its true meaning. Cautionary file notes were issued accordingly.

However, the frightening reality was that the new role was actually going to be significantly different from either of the historic jobs it replaced, especially for the Cottons Bank refugees. To begin with, there was the matter of 'Relationships'. Those that blindly accepted the internal propaganda, likely accepted the important message that the new Bank wanted to get to know its customers better, and sought to build lasting Relationships with each and every one.

The Bank wanted to be the only conceivable point of contact for all their financial needs. Apparently, it firmly believed that only by properly interviewing its customers, by collating detailed facts about every facet of their lives, would the Bank be able to provide a truly exceptional, Customer-centric experience. For the cynical members of Cottons heritage staff however, this was where it all started to sound suspiciously false.

Whilst the NSIB Sellers had been happily churning out financial sales for years, without even knowing if their customers were still breathing or not, Cottons staff had actually been developing Relationships with its customers all along. The only difference was, they didn't call them Relationships, nor did they have an agenda. Now though, they feared that if Cottons truly planned to adopt its new roommate's philosophies, and attitudes towards retail banking, then the only reason it would want a CRA to get closer to a customer, was so that they could sell them something. Lots of somethings for that matter. Unfortunately, for all of it customers, the cynics were right.

The new job description was cunningly written. Interwoven with unnecessarily long, complicated words, which most employees would need to look up, it detailed every aspect of the revised role. An entire page was dedicated to the 'Individual Financial Interview Form' or IFIF for short. A new-fangled, highly intrusive tool, designed to capture every aspect of their customer's lives, and to help the CRA identify sales opportunities. *Clearly* this device was nothing if not Customer-centric.

There were great paragraphs, which concentrated on the behaviours and responsibilities that the Bank now expected the CRAs to demonstrate. Complicated charts detailed an even more complicated target and bonus system, and a diagram, that looked suspiciously like an ancient drawing of a Egyptian pictogram, explained that, along with the Mortgage Arrangers, Financial Advisors, Customer Advisors and even the Cashiers, CRAs would now be expected to work as part of a 'Pentagon of Protection'. It was all very disturbing.

However, when the endlessly complex waffle was strained from the epic document, all the new CRA's were actually left with was a huge shopping list of financial products and services to sell their customers, and the hope a getting a decent monthly bonus in return.

It was no use, he couldn't take it anymore. After glancing around to make sure no one was looking, George broke his pose, which in any case was starting to give him cramp, pulled the collection of interview notes from inside his new suit pocket, and looked over them for the hundredth time. He was much better prepared than before. According to the pack he'd been sent, and forced to digest, his interviewers had eight possible competencies based questions to choose from. And so he had eight carefully constructed answers to give them. There was a lot of fiction on those few creased pages. As Dean had explained though, it wasn't the best candidate that got the job. It was the candidate that had the best answers, and his memorised answers were a marvel of diligently rehearsed excellence. Complete bullshit, but excellence nonetheless.

He put the thick wad of paper back in his pocket. Dean had been quite right. All this stuffing did ruin the line of his flashy new suit. Hoping that no one was watching, he battered the bulging side as flat as he could with his bent arm, like a hysterical chicken flapping a broken wing. That did the trick, sort of. Falling back into his old habits, he brushed down his jacket and fiddled with the buttons. Panic was starting to seep in again. As instructed by his mentor, he tried to shift focus, to think about something else. What did he say again? Have confidence in your new armour, this outfit will convey nothing but self-assurance and style to your interviewers. George started worrying about the dent the expensive, slim fit suit had put in his meagre bank account instead, he needed to get this job in order to top it up again. Panic returned, joined swiftly by hunger. It was half past ten, and he was overdue a feeding. Somehow munching a cold chicken breast whilst he waited didn't seem quite appropriate.

Although it caused him an equal amount of anxiety, he knew what would do the trick. Discarding his thin veneer of nonchalance, he rummaged about in his expertly stitched hip pocket, eventually freeing the letter he'd been struggling to write to Summer. Delicately opening up the sheet, which had been carefully folded for ease of concealment and transportation, he reviewed two weeks' worth of sincere, heartfelt work.

Dear Summer,

How are you?

It wasn't going terribly well so far.

"George, err, *George Butler*, the Interviewers will see you now, be sure not to get lost this time, *okay*?" Did Rebecca the Receptionist just wink at him, was that another smile she gave him as he got up to face a second grilling? Surely not.

Two days later, George was coolly propping up a well-polished, swanky bar with Dean and the rest of The Pretty People. Up until now, he'd politely declined the numerous offers to join the tribe for evening drinks in their favourite watering hole, *The Significant Other*. The glamour of it all seemed far too intimidating. Meeting at the gym was one thing, but socialising on the town was something else entirely. However, today he'd cause for celebration. So much so, that they weren't even training this evening. Instead, they'd hit the town straight from work.

"...I still *can't* believe that they bought all those stories! *I mean*, I know we rehearsed them and all that, but they didn't guess it was all made up!" He was on his third bright green cocktail, and positively bubbled over with excitement and adrenaline. It was a dangerous combination.

Just a few hours ago, Linda, ably assisted by a slightly resentful looking

Belinda, relieved him from the welcome desk and took him quietly into one of the interview rooms. Naturally he feared the worse, he'd been here before. But luckily enough, this time it seemed he hadn't caused any cash losses, or accidently telegraphically sent funds to the Moon. Much to his amazement, he'd actually been successful in applying for one of the new CRA roles. George was so relieved that he nearly cried, and he couldn't wait to tell his Mum.

Linda also told him that he'd be based in the exciting new, city centre Profile Branch, once it had been fitted out, and that more details about this, along with a revised contract, would follow shortly. By now though, he'd glazed over, his mind already elsewhere, busy spending and fantasizing. Business cards, he was going to have his own business cards! Each time he'd seen Dean, or any of the others, hand one of these coveted, individualised statements of personal importance to their customers, he'd thought it looked achingly cool. *'Take my card'*, it just sounded so unbelievably smooth. He would need to practice at home, in front of the mirror, naturally.

When Linda asked if he had any questions about his promotion, he also proved the analysts in the Human Resources Mapping Centre entirely correct. All he wanted to know was when his new salary would start, and how much it was going to be. He definitely had the right stuff.

"Well done, my Man. I told you, *bullshit always wins*. I don't think it's going to be quite the job it once was, but at least it gets you a reasonable salary increase. I better take you shopping again soon, *eh?*" Dean squeezed his young protégée's shoulder affectionately, and absentmindedly picked a piece of lint off the otherwise immaculate, black pin stripe which he'd picked out for him prior to his interview. "Do you just roll in fluff when I'm not looking?" He briefly faked a frown, winked at him, and returned to his vodka and slim line tonic.

Dean had been nothing if not dismissive about the endless schooling he'd provided to ensure the younger man's interview was a success, the incessant role playing in coffee shops at lunchtime, the endless rehearsals in the gym changing rooms, and the hours of practicing his answers until he knew them off by heart. He'd also taught him how to walk properly, without dragging his feet, how to sit up straight, and how to hold a seemingly relaxed pose, which would convey just the right balance of confidence and respect. It had been a challenging few weeks for both men, but in the end, just like everything else, it had been worth it.

Before emptying his bank account and heading out earlier, George wasted no time calling the Butlers' respectable semi, to give his parents the good news, and to tell them not to wait up, as he was hitting the town to celebrate with a few new friends. He'd felt very cool saying this. In characteristic fashion though, his Mum had brought him back down to earth, by reminding him to have a decent evening meal, to avoid deep fried fatty food, as they gave him heartburn, and not to use anybody else's tooth brush. Bless her.

"Another Frog in a Blender then, George?" So it was definitely back to George again, *not* Darling. What did it all mean? He was very confused by this particular relationship, more so than he'd ever been by his one with the spectacular Gabriella, his only other real comparison. Although he'd been disappointed to learn that their evening of passion on the Team Building Event didn't actually mean they were now enjoying a relationship in the traditional sense, he'd been grateful when Natasha invited him around to her small, but perfectly formed apartment to indulge in more of the same three weeks later. Since then though, disappointingly enough, it had all gone rather quiet again.

Even though he'd been very young at the time, not to mention utterly terrified, after their first sweaty entanglement - once he'd gotten his breath back - Gabriella had been very open about what she was looking for from him. The boundaries of their time together, as she'd put it at the time. He couldn't have cared less of course, as long as she continued to take her clothes off, but with Natasha, things were entirely different. She expected him to work it all out for himself. So far at least, he hadn't, and he certainly wasn't going to ask for his Dad's advice on this one. He might tell his Mum.

"Oh, *thanks Tash*, I think I'll have a Bud this time, please." Bravely, he decided to try his luck once last time. Smiling warmly, he tentatively put his hand on her slender hip. Almost shocked, she abruptly turned to him, raised a perfect, quizzical eyebrow, and gently removed it before anyone noticed. She bought him his beer, handed it to him without further comment, and moved to the far end of the group, turning her slender back on him, perhaps for the last time. It was all very confusing. "Oh, err, *thanks...*"

Another morning, another strange, unfamiliar place, and yet another raging hangover for Cottons NSIB's newest Customer Relationship Advisor. Having laid flat and still just long enough to realise that he wasn't going to get away with the inevitable, he sat up in the vast, king-size bed and tried to compose himself. His liver wasn't happy. It protested bitterly about the evening's activities, threatening to pack its bags and leave him for good if he didn't get a cup of tea inside him soon.

Dean's apartment was, quite simply, stunning. Or at least the spare room was. Knowing his host reasonably well though, it seemed likely that the rest of his home would be equally sleek and impossibly white. Once again, George remembered very little about his evening, and even less about stumbling in, but he was certain that arrangements had been made for him to stay with his Guru. But did he let his Mum know? Crikey, he hoped he had.

He appeared to be completely naked. This troubled him, he never slept completely naked. Someone might walk in when something was hanging out of the duvet for one thing. Slowly at first, some of his senses were starting to stretch themselves, shake off the evening's frivolities and begin thinking about making a strong pot of coffee. The spare room had its own en-suite, which he thought was very posh, and further examination proved that the door was slightly ajar, and that the shower was running.

Gingerly, he swung out of bed, wrapped the duvet around him and over his ruffled hair, and looking like a giant conical pillow on feet, shuffled curiously over to the en-suite. Nudging the door open, he frowned slightly, and waddled in. Behind the frosted glass there was a very shapely, soapy girl. She was a severe, yet extremely pretty blond, and from what he could gather, naturally so. There was something oddly familiar about her too.

As silently as possible, the duvet cone padded slowly in reverse until it was back in the spare room. It quickly located the bedroom door, and then trundled off towards the smell of fresh coffee and grilled bacon. In this household, it was likely to be extra low fat, extra lean bacon, but bacon was bacon. As Auntie Rose would have said, *Needs must when the Devil drives*!

Wearing nothing but white cotton PJ bottoms, busy making breakfast in the vast, open plan kitchen diner, Dean was stood with his back turned when the duvet monster waddled in from the connecting corridor. He turned, and raised an inquisitive eyebrow. Was he about to be abducted by a quilted alien?

"My Man, why are you wearing your bed?" He handed George a cup of thick black coffee in an oversized white mug, and forgiving him dietary sins for now, pushed the equally white sugar bowl across the counter towards him.

"There's a *strange girl* in my bedroom, Dean!" A hand darted out from the duvet and grabbed the mug, and several lumps of energising sugar.

"What do you mean a *strange girl*? It's the same one you came back with, *isn't it*? Rebecca, that receptionist from Area Office? Or did you go out again and get a spare one? *That's impressive if you did my Man*!" He turned over the bacon that sizzled away in the stainless steel tower oven. "Am I going to need to put some more bacon on then..?"

The following Sunday morning George slouched on his single bed, listening with half an ear to Dire Straits' 'Brothers in Arms'. With his electric guitar resting on his knee for comfort, he tried again to process the information he'd just been given by his tearful Mum. It seemed that after almost two years of messing around in the relative safety of Germany, Michael's unit was being posted to Iraq, to help with the humanitarian effort.

His Dad was quite philosophical about the situation. He explained to his inconsolable wife, that being in the Armed forces surely meant that from time to time, Michael might be expected to be in some sort of danger. But she wouldn't have any of it. Undeterred he tried to draw comparisons, suggesting that it would be like expecting George to work for a Bank without ever seeing a customer. Although the Top Managers fell quite neatly into this bracket, his youngest son didn't think mentioning it would help matters. Mrs Butler retorted through her sobs by saying that George's customers weren't likely to shoot at him. Clearly she'd never been to Nelsons branch.

Apparently the redeployment had been on the cards for some time, although the last time Michael had been home on leave from Germany, he'd been so busy, excitably showing off his new Audi Quattro, that somehow it slipped his mind. Still cradling the Stratocaster, George looked around his bedroom and smiled to himself, reflecting on all the good natured torment, light-hearted beatings and high spirited persecutions his older brother had subjected him to over the years. Bless him.

Michael was very different from his younger brother. He'd achieved little at school besides setting the still unbroken record for the most detentions, without having actually ever managing to be expelled, though it wasn't for lack of trying. His saving grace had always been his sporting achievements, being far too valuable a member of the football, rugby and cricket teams to be banished. He was also utterly charming, somehow always managing to hold hands with the prettiest of all the pigtailed girls. And despite being a complete sod, entirely worthy of a 'Dennis the Menace Prize for Outstanding Achievements in the field of Mischief and Tomfoolery', everyone loved him.

Regardless of any evidence to the contrary, he worshipped his younger brother too, and was totally in awe of his academic abilities and artistic skill. He just simply chose to express his adoration by tormenting the life out him. George lay back on his single bed, his guitar now resting on his stomach, and remembered the many times in the evening that Michael would sneak silently into his room, on his hands and knees, like the solider he'd eventually become, just as he was sipping his last steaming mug of tea of the day, and reading the latest Beano. Crouching as close to the bed as he could, breathing so shallowly that he began to feel dizzy, he'd wait patiently for the optimum moment to strike. From experience, he knew this was just as he heard his younger brother take a sip of tea, and turn the page of his comic. Then, like a coiled jungle cat, unexpectedly doused in boiling water, he'd spring up and yell *"ARGHHHHH!"* The effect this had on his startled brother was nothing short of spectacular. He did the same thing the night before he left for basic training. Bless him.

The track finished, and George rolled off the bed, hit the repeat button and rested his guitar gently against his chest of drawers. In an effort to distract his thoughts, he glanced over the wall of postcards and letters that Summer had sent him. Suddenly he felt very ashamed of the brief, solitary note he'd posted at the beginning of February, and of the cheap, belated Valentine's Day card he'd finally remembered to buy. None of this came naturally. What was wrong with him? When they'd been together, they'd talk for hours, but somehow, trying to replicate the same thing on paper was as hard as nailing jelly to the wall.

He pulled his carefully folded work in progress from his jeans once more, unravelled it and slowly lay the creased piece of paper down on his desk. Ever since the passionate night with Natasha on the Team Building Event, and the unexpected episode with Rebecca the Receptionist which, frustratingly enough, he still couldn't remember, he'd been feeling unbearably guilty, although still not entirely sure if he actually needed to be. Somehow though, it just didn't seem right to ask.

Summer's letters contained such rich detail about every facet of her life in France, that anything he wrote short of *War and Peace* would look positively half-hearted in comparison. Whilst his recent social events were nothing if not newsworthy, the overall content didn't seem quite appropriate, regardless of any license he'd been given to spread his wings. Scratching his cropped hair with the end of a biro, he sought for inspiration amongst the *Airfix* models that still hung from his bedroom ceiling on lengths of thin cotton. What could he fill this damnably blank sheet of white paper with? Suddenly, thankfully he had an idea.

Dear Summer,

How are you? Did I ever tell you about my brother Michael? If you think I'm mad, listen to this…

For as long as anyone could remember, each year, the residents of the modest cul-de-sac where the Butlers lived competed in a friendly yet highly competitive go-kart race on the steep surrounding hillside. Because this race was organised without a committee or formal meeting, or without a Chairman to oversee proceedings, it meant each competing family had a really great time preparing, and didn't spend the rest of the year avoiding their neighbours. Although that's not to say things didn't get ruthless at times.

Like Salmon suddenly waking one morning with an unexplained urge to swim up river, somewhere around the third weekend of the school summer holidays, each family's garage transformed into a miniature Formula One workshop. Parents and excited children of all ages banded together to either re-build last year's kart, or if they had a particularly bad season, return to the drawing board to start all over again.

From dusk till dawn, the noise of hammers, saws, and - if budgets allowed - power tools filled the air as they toiled away on their machines. There was an unspoken rule that spying was strictly prohibited, yet this didn't stop the odd family from dispatching their most innocent, wide eyed child to a neighbour's garage, under the pretence of borrowing some sheers. Health and Safety was nothing if not relaxed. When they returned, they'd usually be given thick crayons, and encouraged to draw whatever they'd seen on the back of a spare roll of wallpaper. The hoax often failed to yield any industrial secrets, but often ended up on the fridge.

The Butlers were always seen to have an unfair advantage over the rest of the residents, given that the head of the family was a mechanical engineer. Nevertheless, his efforts to win were usually thwarted by two sons who seemed incapably of steering straight, and somehow always managed to crash into at least three competitors.

The actual race was a simple affair. Twenty or so go-karts would line up at that top of the steepest hill, just after the farmer had cut the long grass and then race to the bottom, three hundred yards below. The trick was to stop your go-kart before you reached the narrow stretch of overgrown woodland that ran along the valley floor, and which concealed a slow moving, deep river where most of the cul-de-sac's children fished and swam in the summer months. A finishing line, made from ribbon and bamboo, was stretched out twenty yards ahead of the wood, where the only impartial local, Mr McGregor from number sixteen, eighty-one and unlikely to compete again following a spectacular crash three years ago, stood bravely with a flag made from a pillow case and garden broom, to wave the karts through. This year, he desperately hoped he wouldn't be hit again.

Although the actual race took a fraction of the time it took to construct the go-karts, setting up the collapsible tables and laying out the feast of sandwiches and cakes took hours, with everything having be hauled up the grassy hill by hand. Deckchairs were scattered, and red faced grandparents were finally allowed to collapse, with a well-earned cup of tea and slice of moist fruitcake. Elsewhere team mates discussed race tactics, ate thick corned beef sandwiches for energy and stamina, and made final, minute adjustments to their karts.

The go-karts themselves varied massively in design. Some were no more than wooden boxes with pram wheels, basic steering and brakes that required terrified children to simply stamp their feet down hard on the tyres. Over the years though, some karts had become much more evolved and sophisticated. There was only one un-written rule. The framework and body should be made from timber, and not, as Mr Butler senior had attempted one year, from anything as exotic as carbon fibre. Bloody spoil sports.

Despite being restricted by this rule, the Butlers kart was impressive nonetheless. Each year, when it was ceremoniously lowered on ropes and pulleys from the specially designed storage unit installed amongst the rafters of the garage, it drew a huge grin from each member of the family. It was essentially a miniature, two-seater replica of the Lotus Formula One car. Painted black with gold John Player Special decals, just like the original on which it was based, the neighbours watched in envy as it rolled out onto the street.

As it had been designed to take two passengers side by side, it was quite square, but other than that it was a completely faithful imitation. The main chassis was constructed from marine grade teak, and the bodywork from special, impact absorbent plywood that had been *borrowed* from the University. The axles, steering and braking systems had been painstakingly designed and engineered by Mr Butler senior, for maximum efficiency and strength, and would've easily coped with a jaunt around Brands Hatch, if he'd ever fitted the kart with an engine, as he'd often threatened too. Unfortunately his wife wouldn't let him.

Inside, it had two, handmade Recaro style seats, with frames of oak, and comfortable, thick padding made by Mum, although she did have to be gently guided away from her original choice of material. It had been terribly flowery.

Yet despite its technical brilliance, with the Butler brothers at the wheel, the go-kart had enjoyed a chequered racing history. Even with their exasperated Dad bellowing race orders from the starting line, the boys had only ever managed to win once. Three years ago, and then only after Mr McGregor had managed to roll his own kart and take out most of the field. An ambulance had to be called that year. It wasn't pretty.

This year though things were going to be different. It was the last time that Michael would probably be able to compete. He was bound for Army basic training in a few weeks' time, and it was likely that the rest of the neighbourhood would object to a trained killer lining up alongside their seven-year-olds in the future. However, he was determined to go out in style. The night before the race, he'd diligently applied grease to every moving part, checked the steering and brakes, and had even sat up with the go-kart for over an hour, softly talking to it, offering words of encouragement and inspiration. George meanwhile stayed inside, painting a rather realistic elephant for his Mum.

The next morning it was a beautiful, crystal blue summer's day, the sort of day that only really exists in childhood memories. Everyone got up early to begin the hike up the steep grassy hill, dragging behind them an assortment of go-karts and picnic hampers. For the first few hours, the starting grid was a buzz of excitement, as each team finally got to see exactly what the competition had been up too. Those children that were too young to race, or that had crashed badly the year before, and were still mentally scared by the ordeal, played happily in the grass, while Mums and Grannies shared gossip and biscuits in the glorious mid-morning sunshine.

The Butler-Lotus team had managed to secure a good position at the centre of the start line. Michael was intense and focused. He'd barely spoken to his younger brother through the visor of his motorbike helmet, as the grid prepared for the start. Their Dad stood behind the go-kart with his strong hands resting on the sturdy rear wing, ready for the single, authorised initial shove to get them going. After that it was simply a case of gravity and aerodynamics.

As they waited for the start, two things troubled young George. Firstly, there was the look in Michael's eyes. Secondly, his oversized motorbike helmet, despite the socks and woolly hats his Dad had stuffed it with, still spun around on his small head every time he moved, impairing his view. However, considering that he and his psychotic older brother were about to hurtle down an extremely steep hill, in a wooden Formula One car, blindness might not actually be such a bad thing.

Tensions mounted. All eyes watched the unofficial, race official raise the starting pillow case. Silence gripped every team and spectator. Time stood still. At last, finally, the makeshift flag dramatically fell. *'GO!'*

The Butler-Lotus team won the race that year, in spectacular fashion. But victory came at a terrible price. After a hearty push from their Dad, the boys tore off down the grassy slope at incredible speed. George struggled to see quite where they were heading, and Michael grappled with the bucking steering wheel which, thanks to a welcome late growth spurt, rested precariously between his knees. The Butler-Lotus soon left the rest of the field far behind as it bore down on the finishing line, and a terrified Mr McGregor. The low front spoiler whipped at random sprigs of uncut grass, and as the kart tore into a still shaded area of hillside, where the sun was yet to reach, it drew an impressive rooster tail of dew from its wide rear tyres.

Unfortunately though, it was this layer of moist dew that was to be the teams undoing. Despite the kart's impressive brakes, it didn't have an anti-lock braking system. That was planned for next year. In the past, the twenty-yard run off had been more than ample to slow it down, but this year, having built up massive speed by avoiding any crashes, there was just no way that the Butler-Lotus was going to stop in time with soaking wet brakes.

After Michael nearly broke his ankle, desperately pressing the pedal into the floor, their predicament quickly dawned on him. Realising that they weren't slowing down, in a split second he decided not to bother, and aimed the kart towards a gap in the woodland instead. As they narrowly avoided a wide-eyed Mr McGregor, they flew over the finish line in first place. With victory theirs, Michael let go of the wheel, grabbed hold of his younger brother and screamed *"YEAAAAAAAY"* at the top of his lungs, as they disappeared from sight into the trees.

The Butler-Lotus crashed violently through the narrow stretch of overgrown bushes. Countless branches snapped as they whipped against the immaculate paintwork, yet still it hurtled faster still towards the riverbank, the famous outcrop of moss encrusted rock, and towards the four foot drop into the deep, slow moving pool, where children dive-bombed during the school summer holidays.

Over the coming years, some families moved away, children became adults and eventually the annual Go-kart race faded from memory, only ever recalled when a veteran racer was asked about a curious scar. One or two original households remained though, not least the Butlers, and every summer, especially after a new family had settled into one of the respectable semis, there would be a gentle knock on the front door. A member of the Butler household would politely answer, and not be at all surprised to be faced with a dripping wet curious child, wanting to know why there was an upside down, wooden replica of a Lotus Formula One racing car, resting at the bottom of the deep pool in the river.

A few hours later, with a hearty chicken roast dinner under his belt, albeit with a solitary, sinful, crispy potato for digestive company, George was feeling much better. Michael had called just after Sunday lunch, and all his talk of 'Safe Zones' and 'Advisory Roles' had managed to dilute some of the initial Butler panic. In the relative calm that followed, he'd also managed to finish his letter to Summer, all nine, double sided pages of it. His hand was killing him. Flushed with success, he'd even managed some illustrations, small pencil sketches of a cute dormouse, and another of an oversized snail. They were curious choices perhaps, but endearing nonetheless.

Completely out of the blue, Barney had called too, wondering if his best friend was still alive, and if he was, did he fancy a beer. It had been a long time since the two young men had been out together. Although their friendship had been kept alive with slightly stiff, succinct telephone calls of late, alcohol might just provide the necessary catalyst for an evening of good old fashioned boyish fun.

George quickly changed into a few of his new clothes, fussed impatiently with his cropped hair, having it all cut off hadn't reduced his styling time in the slightest, and left the Butler's respectable semi with thirty-five pounds in crisp new fivers in his wallet, and an optimistic grin plastered across his face. He'd forgotten how much he'd missed this. The moments before a night on the town with the Celtic Casanova, the anticipation, the hope he used to harbour that perhaps tonight he'd meet a girl that wouldn't need too much encouragement. It would be a stark contrast to his evening with Dean and The Pretty People of course, far less civilised, and much more likely to conclude with a diet forbidden kebab. But right now, it sounded just perfect.

"Crikey Butler, you been ill or something, *where's your belly gone?* And what's happened to your hair? You look like *George Michael*, Dude!" His optimistic grin soon fell to the grubby wooden floor of their local pub, as the other patrons turned to see the pop star that had wandered into *The Bull and Goat*.

"Hello Barney, it's good to see you too, *you git!*" He slapped him warmly on the back, secretly hoping some of his new found strength would lightly wind him, and nodded at Keith, The Bulls long suffering head barman. "Vodka and slim line tonic, please Keithy, what do you want Barney?"

Nursing the dregs of his bottle of Newcastle Brown Ale, his ginger companion frowned severely. "Bloody hell Mate, *vodka and tonic*. When exactly did you start drinking like a girl?"

"Calories, my friend, calories - far fewer calories in this, trust me! Newcastle Brown for you then?"

Barney shook his head in disbelief. "Well some of us are loyal to old friends!"

"That's a bit harsh, Mate!" George sipped his tipple, and set it down on the bar.

"*I meant the beer.* Now, tell me what you've up to in the big city, other than having your head scalped and your belly sucked out."

Three hours later, having consumed a great deal more alcohol than had been intended, the pair of drinkers were happily rounding off their evening of catching up by debating the last six jukebox songs they'd subject *The Bull and Goat*'s regulars too. So far, they'd discussed a range of colourful topics, dear to each of the young men's hearts. As the evening unfolded, they'd philosophised on the really big issues of the day, such as the true origins of the beer mat, quite what colour a Smurf would turn if it were strangled, and why girls should never, ever drink pints.

In other news, it seemed that Barney was in love, a startling revelation to accept, even when sober. Yet it seemed to be true, and he and his new girlfriend Amanda were planning a holiday to Spain. The photographs produced from the darker recesses of Barney's long-suffering, dubiously sticky wallet, proved Amanda to be small and reasonably attractive. The first shot wasn't particularly flattering. Clearly caught unawares, and wearing huge, pre-self-aware round glasses, she looked like a startled pygmy owl.

The second was much better. Like her new boyfriend, she was also pebble dashed with freckles, had beautiful wavy red hair, and the sort of skin that screamed for factor fifty sun block, each time the sun was exposed from behind a spring time cloud. Perhaps most importantly though, it seemed that she'd only recently move to the area with her parents, which explained why she'd agreed to go out with Barney in the first place. His reputation hadn't spread quite as far as he'd once feared.

Apart from Amanda, little else had changed in Barney's life. With a willing girl at last in tow, he seemed to have calmed down a bit. He still worked on the liquor aisle of the local Supermarket, still thought he was something of a wine connoisseur, and still borrowed his Dad's car to get to work. But he no longer made up stories of wild philandering. He didn't really need too anymore.

Meanwhile, George talked about his amazing night with Natasha, or at least as much of it as he could remember, his important new job that started in a few weeks' time, and about how he'd been delighted to find Rebecca the Receptionist in Dean's en-suite. Although he left out the bit about her nervously munching bacon toasties, whilst making polite, awkward conversation with a young man wrapped in a duvet. He talked about his brother for a while, but changed the subject when he found himself beginning to feel sad again, and instead listed the things he wanted to buy with his new salary.

"Another watch? You've got a bloody watch, *you've got two watches*! What the hell do you want another one for?" Barney didn't hold with his friend's fascination with shiny things. He'd clearly been a magpie in previous life. "You're mad, Dude, *mad*!"

"Oh but this one's, err, hang on, I'll get it, oh yeah. *It'll go deeper*!"

"Deeper where?"

"In the bloody sea!"

"You don't dive, though!"

George considered this for a moment. "*I might*, one day…"

Barney banged his hand down on the bar, laughing drunkenly. "Seriously though, *seriously*, you're really thinking of getting a flat of your own?"

"Yep."

"But *why*? What about your Mum's cooking, and ironing - *you can't iron*!"

This was true. Yet although he'd never given any thought to leaving home before, ever since he'd first seen the swanky, compact, modern apartments advertised in the cities local paper, George had started to form a plan. Due for completion the middle of next month, they were located on the very outskirts of the city, the perfect spot for a young bachelor with a very particular set of requirements.

The apartments - *not flats*, as he kept impatiently reminding Barney - were close enough to the Bank to make travelling less of an ordeal, but far enough away to avoid city life when he wanted too. More importantly though, they quite literally bordered the countryside, with a clear run over the rambling hills, he'd be back at the family table, starring at a freshly roasted chicken in twenty-eight minutes flat. Even in the Fiesta. Whilst he was visiting, it also made sense to also pick up his fresh laundry and ironing at the same time. Clearly, he'd thought of everything.

Having his own pad also meant he didn't have to rely on anyone else to put him up when he went out on the town. After that first, entertaining night, this was something he hoped would soon become a frequent occurrence. Furthermore, providing he wrote his address down and gave it to the taxi driver on his way home, there would also be less chance of him waking up in the morning, with no idea whatsoever of where he was either. Also, it was apparently an investment or something like that.

"An' investment, *investment*? Dude, it was only a year ago you thought a leather jacket was a good investment. You've changed Mate, *bugger*!" Barney slid off his barstool and, much to the dismay of his fellow drinkers, loaded *The Bull and Goat*'s jukebox for the eighth time. George set up another round of drinks and smiled drunkenly to himself as Bob Marley snuck up behind him and started to caress his ears with all the warmth of the Caribbean Sea.

"Summer used to love a bit of Bob, Barns, did I ever tell you that? Barns - loved him she did. I miss her Barns. I do, *I really do!*" He took another heavy pull from his now large, vodka and slim line tonic, wincing slightly. Large quantities of alcohol and very little carbohydrate were proving to be a hazardous combination.

"Why 'ave you started callin' me *Barns* all of sudden? You've never called me Barns before." Barney reached for his tenth bottle of Newcastle Brown Ale, missed completely, eventually connected on his third attempt, and glugged it back noisily, slamming it down hard on the battered wooden bar when he'd had his fill. "KEITHY? Give us some pork scratchings Mate?"

"Perhaps I should go an' see her when I get a decent car. She'd like that. *D'reckon she'd like that Barns?* I reckon she would. How the hell do you drive to France anyway, there's, well, *a sea* in the way, isn't there?"

"*Well*, this new watch you want should be okay then." Barney swivelled unsteadily on his barstool to face his old friend, nearly losing his balance. He waved his hands around erratically, desperate to find something solid to steady him. Eventually, blindly he managed to find a firm anchor. It was George's shoulder. A look of drunken shock quickly washed over his freckles. Unthinking, he began roughly squeezing, enthusiastically. "Crikey, *you've got muscles Dude!*"

"Get off me Barns, *you great Queer*, they're for the girls, *not my ginger Mate!*" He battered away the freckled hands and returned to his drink, which was slowly numbing his tongue as well as his senses.

"I'm sorry, *I'm sorry*, my bad. But listen to me, listen. 's really important, *you need to listen to me George.*" Barney leaned in closer, overwhelming him with the familiar, repulsive stench of real ale and pork scratchings, his face a picture of orange, drunken conspiracy.

"What, *what is it?*"

"*Shush!* Listen, you need to know this Dude, '*simportant!*" The smell was horrendous, but he leaned in regardless. His sloshed heart beating hard in anticipation of the coming revelation, what exactly was he going to tell him, was it bad? Was it about Summer? It was possible he was becoming paranoid.

"What Barney, *tell me!*"

Suddenly, Barney leant back dramatically. Wobbled for a bit, somehow managed to compose his balance, and eventually sat up, straightening himself, his hands tightly gripping the edge of the bar. "Your new haircut really does *suck*, Dude!"

After battling with the lock for a few moments, George eventually stumbled into the Butlers' respectable semi at eleven fifty-two. He tried in vain to calm down an ecstatic Eddie, so as not to wake his parents, and quietly made a bedtime protein shake by the light of the fridge freezer. In his drunken state however, he inadvertently used whole milk rather than skimmed. It didn't mix particularly well with all the vodka and slim line tonic. He tip-toed up to his bedroom, finally flicked on his bedside lamp after a few failed attempts, and pulled his letter to Summer out of the buff envelope he'd stuffed it into for safekeeping, before hiding it on his bookcase between *Watership Down* and *Casino Royale*.

Despite his dire state of inebriation, on the long, meandering trek home, it had suddenly dawned on him that his letter, for all its colourful, entertaining content, was missing a vital bit of information. Something he felt sure she'd want to know. He picked up his chewed biro and concentrated intently. Squinting in the half-light, he aimed roughly at a spot just below his signature and all the kisses, and went for it.

P.S. I've got a new job! X x x x x x x

There were probably too many kisses now, but what the hell.

Chapter 13

Squashed Dafs

Mid April.

Danny Garson ducked under the frame of the pass door and surveyed his new banking hall with a critical eye. The Profile Branch still had a thin protective layer of plastic covering most of its surfaces, and a thick layer of dust covering everything else. He ran a chunky finger across the top of the welcome desk, examined the mound of grime that dared to collect on its wide tip, and made a mental note to yell at someone until it was cleaned properly. The Bank would need a thorough scrub before being officially unveiled next Friday, but other than that, he was reasonably content with his kingdom.

And he was a difficult man to please at the best of times. After fighting his way up the NSIB's ruthless career ladder the hard way, Danny eventually became a Branch Manager three years ago. Not through hard work, dedication or determination, but by simply being one of life's born leaders. Completely bald, with striking blue eyes the size of chicken eggs, he stood at six foot six inches tall, his hands were twice as large of most, and his shoes had to be specially made in order to contain feet the size of farmhouse bloomers.

Like all NSIB staff, he wore the compulsory uniform. A cheap ill-fitting grey suit, a white polyester shirt and a plain navy blue tie, the now defunct NSIB logo emblazoned across its width. Ties though had always been a problem for Danny. His torso was considerably longer than normal, meaning that the knot he was able to fasten with the remaining length of material, was usually no bigger than a mid-sized marble. It looked especially odd around his twenty-one inch neck. When he'd joined NSIB, the HR department had to specially order oversized suits and shirts from their man in China, in order to accommodate their giant member of staff. But with ties for some reason, he was on his own, and frequently chose not to wear one from late April through to September. It wasn't as if anyone would be brave enough to reprimand him.

Physically, there was something rather peculiar about the thirty-six year old. With his permanent pot belly, thick, long forearms, impressive stature yet relatively narrow shoulders; he uncannily resembled a shaved orang-utan with a fetish for stilts. Not unlike the great ape, Danny was also capable of both destructive force and playful humour in equal measures, and commanded utter respect and admiration from all those around him, eventually.

He'd been something of an NSIB Nomad for years, and given his rather unique set of skills, he naturally fell into a trouble-shooter role, often dispatched to an unruly underperforming branch with bothersome staff and weak leadership. Just a few weeks under Danny's rather intimidating, iron rule was usually all it took to return the offending Bank to order again. Sales would come flooding in once more, the staff uprisings having been firmly quashed. Sometimes, he even managed to achieve this without bloodshed, or public floggings in the banking hall.

In the past six months though, much had changed. Remarkably enough, he'd quickly fallen in love with, and married a stunning cashier he'd met whilst battering an unrelenting, unruly enquires clerk.

Hannah was one of life's Angels, a true beauty both inside and out. She simply wanted to make everyone around her, happy. For reasons she'd never share, she immediately fell under Danny's spell, despite the bloody clerk at his feet, or the blossoming bruises on his walnut knuckles. The couple had enjoyed a lavish wedding in Antigua a few months ago, and both still had a healthy summer glow, although Danny's did rather highlight a few battle scars on his forehead, from one head-butt too many in his formative years. They added character.

All they wanted now was settle down somewhere nice and create a clan of their own. Hannah had had an amazingly soothing effect on her new husband, and apart from a lecherous waiter in Antigua, who he'd thrown unceremoniously off a restaurant balcony into the pool, he hadn't strangled anyone for months. Not even the staff. The Profile Branch Manager position was a perfect opportunity, and Hannah could easily slot into a role at one of the Groups satellite branches. Given his impressive track record, and with some of his more violent characteristics toned down a bit, the role was his for the taking, and the newly formed Cottons NSIB Area Office had been equally delighted to appoint Hannah as Number One Cashier at Armada Branch, aggravating Di no end in the process.

The newlyweds had their eyes on a flashy townhouse in the city, and a new BMW convertible to park on the drive. Life was indeed looking rather good for the happy couple. Or rather it had been until the Profile Branch's Manager discovered the identity of one of his new Customer Relationship Advisors.

Billy Reed was from the North of England and had an unhealthy appetite for bingo, female cashiers and killer chip butties. Having made a name for himself as a successful Seller early in his career, he'd quickly applied his natural gift of the gab to climbing the career ladder, charming all those who dared interview him, eventually gaining a branch of his own. Unfortunately, almost as quickly as he'd achieved this status, he lost it again thanks to a badly timed, ill-judged Sexual Harassment case that threatened to ruin him. Only his ability to sell and dodge bullets saved him from dismissal. Sales were without question, far more important to the NSIB than a pinched cashier's bottom.

Billy was enormously fat. Long ago his thick neck had given up its thankless battle for independence, and was finally swallowed up by his upper body, leaving his squat head sat perilously on top of his round body, like a poached egg served on a beach ball. Over the years, he'd developed numerous, time saving meals that enabled him to absorb the maximum amount of calories with the minimum amount of effort. He was considering writing a book on the subject. His favourite amongst them was without question, the lunchtime chip butty.

He'd buy a whole, uncut loaf of white bread and two large portions of thick greasy chips, coated in vinegar and liberal dustings of salt. Once safely back in the staff room, he'd then set about sawing off the end of the loaf, hollowing it out, and stuffing the hot chips inside the cavity, along with lashings of tomato ketchup and yet more salt. Having greedily consumed this massive feast, wiping the worst of the slops from his slimy chin with the wrappings, he'd then use the discarded innards from the loaf, to mop up the odd chip that had managed to escape. It wasn't a pretty sight.

Astonishingly enough though, despite truly horrific eating habits and household management that would have forced even the most hardened sewer rat to pack up and leave his squalid home, women loved him. They virtually queued up to climb aboard his bulbous body. All twenty-two stretch-marked, cellulite ridden stone of it. It must have been his aftershave.

Danny first worked with Billy at one of the NISB's Northern Strongholds, two years ago whilst on troubleshooting duties. Although they very rarely socialised at the time, they'd enjoyed a successful working relationship, borne out of mutual desire to earn good bonuses. And so when Danny relocated to London, Billy, having always been something of a drifter, simply tagged along. The Seller needed to be kept on a tight leash to prevent scandal and libel action, but their pairing worked well, right up until they went their separate ways and Billy got his own branch, and an uncontrollable desire to pinch something squidgy that he shouldn't.

"*Ay-up Danny*, grand looking branch, in't it, *eh?*" Billy lumbered up behind his manager, having satisfied himself that both the canteen and toilets were adequate for his needs, and stood next to him, craning his chubby head upwards, grinning encouragingly.

"Yeah, I guess so *Chief*, it'll do." Curiously, it was Danny's habit to call everyone 'Chief', everyone except his wife. He wiped the grime from his finger tip and turned to Billy. It was time to have a stern word. "Right you *chubby shit*, now you listen to me! Let's get this straight, don't go causing me any bloody grief okay? No ass pinching, thigh stroking, rubbing shoulders or *accidentally* brushing against anyone's boobs. *Clear, Chief?*" He loomed over the much shorter man, and subjected him to his most severely piecing glare. The steely blue eyes gleaming like diamond arrowheads. Sadly, it failed to have its usual devastating effect.

Billy stared back defiantly. He wasn't going to be beaten down just yet. "*Eh*, now come on, don't come over all *Yul Brynner* with me! Remember Duck, *I know* where all the bodies are buried."

Danny placed a shovel-sized hand on the wobbly shoulder, squeezing firmly enough to make his point, but not so hard as to break his collar bone. Not yet anyway.

"Yes, *Chief*, and I know who helped me bury 'em..."

It was beginning to dawn on Phillip Miles that he might not be cut out to be a Bank Trainer anymore. Since the merger, the training courses had been relentless. The preparation he needed to put into each one took up more and more of his precious evenings, playing merry hell with his salsa practice. Yet perhaps more importantly, he just didn't believe in any of the new stuff. He actually found it all rather unsettling. The new sales courses and training materials were ruthless at best, and some of the ideas and best practices that fell out of Head Office seemed frankly unethical.

Sadly, as well as the inspired, merciless sales techniques, another of NSIB's crude management terms had also slipped through the net. When an uncomfortable or contentious message needed to be delivered, Trainers were simply told it was a JYBDI - '*Just You Bloody Do it*!' This was Cottons NISB's new Staff Objection Handling Tool. Phillip didn't feel that he was up to using it sincerely enough for it to have any real impact with his audience. Nor did he wish too, for that matter.

Unfortunately enough, today's JYBDI was the innovative, Head Office approved, new sales process, 'DAFS', and he had to deliver it to a small group of largely militant CRAs. It was going to be a difficult morning.

In the few quiet, peaceful moments he had left before the onslaught, he flicked open the Trainers pack and reviewed the content one last time. He cringed again. There was no escaping the fact; DAFS was a truly appalling sales process. He'd always been able to cope with the courses before, objection handing, and open, rather than closed questioning techniques, were positively tender in comparison to this. The whole concept was just morally wrong. How on earth was he going to present the course convincingly enough? He flicked through the rest of the pack, hoping that maybe he'd missed something. Perhaps it was just an elaborate joke?

DAFS was an acronym. Banks had always loved a good acronym. Phillip took comfort that this grandest of traditions at least, was still alive and well.

D was for Disturb. The competent CRA needed to ask the customer a series of unsettling questions from an approved list, each one designed to unnerve and fluster with increasing degrees of intensity. An example of such a question was; *have you thought just how bad your life could become Mr Customer if you couldn't make your loan payments after being hit by a bus, but you survived your injuries?* Phillip couldn't believe his eyes when he'd first read that one, but that was positively understated compared to; *if you were lying on your deathbed, Mr Customer, wouldn't you feel better knowing that you wouldn't be leaving any debt for your widow to sort out?*

A was for Anguish. Here, a CRA was encouraged to make the pain and suffering of their customer's poor life choices really come alive. They needed to stress the suffering and torment that lay in wait for them if they didn't heed their expert advice. Examples included the cheerful: *how would you feel Mr Customer if your wife left you because you lost your job and couldn't make payments on your loan, causing you to become bankrupt?* And the unbelievable: *what would you have to do to survive Mr Customer, what would you have to sell, your home, your pets, yourself?*

Strangely enough, F was for Feeling. At this point in the interrogation, it was hoped that the proficient CRA would begin funnelling all this raw emotion and distress into a cauldron of pure misery, and begin stirring vigorously. Just ahead of the final death blow to the jugular though, they'd needed to ensure that their message was deeply embedded: *I imagine if all this happened to you Mr Customer, you would feel just awful; bankrupt, divorced and left with nothing in your life to bring you any joy. How do you think you would feel Mr Customer, what does that look like to you?*

Finally, S was for Seize. By now, providing the CRA had done their job properly, the customer should have been reduced to a quivering, tearful wreck. Totally consumed with fear, dreading just how awful their lonely, sherry soaked miserable existence was going to be if they didn't do exactly whatever it was the CRA told them to do. It was at this precise moment that the CRA needed 'Seize the Sale': *So Mr Customer, if I could offer you a solution to this problem and save you from all this misery and heartache, would that make you happy?*

Phillip closed the pack, and then his eyes. What on earth was happening to the Bank?

Unsurprisingly, the meeting did not go well. At the first mention of DAFS, Dean erupted into a furious torrent of disgust. He ridiculed the process for blatantly attempting to brainwash not only the customers but also the staff too. Summarising, he labelled the method *'an unforgivable means of manipulating innocent customers who just wanted advice'* and called the word patterns *'Banking Mind Tricks'*. He also found it ironic that such an unpleasant sales technique had been named after a flower. A flower that was associated with a time of year which celebrates nailing a man to a tree for suggesting people should be nice to each other.

Phillip, who remained silent and red faced throughout, didn't disagree with him in the slightest. Especially the last bit, which he made note of.

Dean was infuriated. He'd been successful in the role for years by simply listening to his customers and gently suggesting solutions and ideas that might help improve their situation. The thought of effectively manipulating people into feeling that they had to buy a product to prevent them from becoming destitute, had been the final straw. He'd woken up that morning in the same, carefully constructed, positive mood he did every day. When, as he stepped out of his shower, he'd remembered about the course, he decided to try and find some positives, something he could share with his young protégée over coffee, later. He certainly didn't imagine for a moment, that he'd storm out of the meeting room in a fit of barely controlled rage, nearly taking the door off its hinges in the process.

When the dust eventually settled, just four pairs of eyes looked up at Phillip with a mixture of mild disinterest, hunger, sympathy and bewilderment. Stephanie King shared her colleague's emotions and empathised accordingly. She just didn't have his energy. Instead she sat quietly making plans to cash in her healthy portfolio of Bank shares. It was definitely time to retire to Spain. Thankfully, the flat was still available.

Selfishly, Natasha wondered just how long it would be before Dean resigned, leaving her a larger slice of the Armada branch pie to play with. The first thing she'd done after the new CRA bonus structure was unveiled, was to calculate exactly how much she needed to sell in order to upgrade her car. Perhaps a red one this time, with black leather interior, and of course, some new shoes.

An NSIB veteran, Billy had seen this countless time before. He sat patiently, his chubby hands folded neatly on his enormous belly, hoping that the big man would stop shouting soon. It was nearly time for a chicken pie. He also wondered about having a go at the olive skinned girl to his left, he was quite sure she'd winked at him earlier.

George meanwhile, wasn't entirely sure what had just happened. He was vaguely aware that Dean had got annoyed about something and stormed out, but he'd been so consumed with a sketch he was doodling on his notepad, a rather realistic barn owl sitting on an upturned rusty bucket, that it had been lost on him. No doubt Dean would explain it all to him later.

Lately, he'd been an invaluable guide through the new world of customer interviews. Having only recently graduated from a Post Office Juniors account himself, George had been understandably concerned about offering sound financial advice. But with trademark patience, once the dumbbells had been put away for the evening, his mentor had filled in a few of the blanks and offered some words of wisdom. The only trouble was from what little he'd understood from the official CRA training, much of Dean's advice stood in stark contrast to the Banks.

It would probably all become clear eventually. As nothing seemed to be happening for moment, he gazed over at Natasha instead, his mind drifting off again. During the past few weeks, she'd continued to barely acknowledge his existence, either on the three nights out he'd enjoyed with The Pretty People, or on the rare occasions their paths had crossed in the Bank. But this morning, on their way up the stairs, she'd patted his bum and coyly winked at him in passing. It was all a mystery. Much of his life had been lately. But at least growing up didn't seem to suck quite as much these days.

The nights out on the town had been enlightening and entertaining in equal measure. The neon bathed bars and nightclubs that The Pretty People frequented, were unlike any he'd ever imagined, let alone experienced. During each of those endless, almost surreal evenings, he felt as though he was living someone else's life. Someone better looking, with a healthier bank account and a superior wardrobe. He was on a journey from innocence to experience, and the ride was just spectacular.

On all three nights, he'd been delighted to meet new, extremely friendly, beautiful girls. In complete contrast to his desperately hopeful years of trawling the rural bars with Barney, these girls positively welcomed his advances. Spurred on by his mentor, armed with colourful, meaningful patter, his insecurities extinguished with just the right amount of vodka, he'd approach them with, if not unwavering confidence, then at least something approaching self-belief.

Yet the following day, once the alcohol had worn off and his ears stopped ringing from the drum and bass, he was left feeling confused and slightly disheartened again, as his temporary lover, whose name he struggled to recall, virtually shook his hand and disappeared, never to be seen or heard from again.

It was during these cold, almost business-like moments of parting, stood in the doorway of Dean's apartment, wearing a duvet and an expression of post-nookie bewilderment, that George missed Summer the most. Where were the cuddles, the plans for the day ahead, the endless cups of rehydrating tea and the playful tickling? One thing soon became abundantly clear. These sorts of girls didn't do tickling.

In an effort to derail these thoughts, he examined Billy. It took a while, there was plenty to examine. Having discovered that they'd be working together at the Profile Branch, he was relieved to find that he rather liked Billy. He liked his jolly manner and his unusual accent, which up until now he'd only ever heard on the television or radio. Most of all though he liked that he was no longer the fat kid. His continued dedication to both the gym and his diet, meant that his days of sucking it all in were numbered. But even if his trousers *had* still been leaving their judgemental teeth marks in his waistline, next to Billy, he'd have still looked positively emaciated.

After recovering his some of his limited composure, Phillip handed out a few copies of the new IFIFs, grateful that Dean at least never got to see one, and set about packing away his flipchart pens into his small leather satchel. He'd had quite enough. Wishing his audience the very best of luck, he left the meeting room to find a quiet corner to sit in. After eleven years of loyal service to a now forgotten, once grand institution, it was time to write his letter of resignation. The exodus had begun.

"Right *Chiefs*, I'll make this as simple as I can." Danny Garson paced up and down in front of his nine new members of staff, like an officer inspecting his troops. His huge hands held behind his back, occasionally he'd pause to ensure he had their full attention. "All eyes are going to be on me when we open these doors later, and my eyes are going be on you lot. Any one of you let me down, and I'll personally see to it that you are transferred to some ass-end pigsty of a branch in the middle of a warzone. Do I make myself clear, *Chiefs*?" All nine heads nodded obediently. He grinned, rows of pearly white, tombstone teeth glinting under the electric lights. It unsettled a few of his staff rather more than his words had.

"And if he's not watching you, remember, *I will be*!" The thin smoker's voice came from a nightmarish vision in a wheelchair at Danny's kneecap. The words, which hung in the air like a toxic fog, contained nothing but pure bitterness and loathing. Mary Faulkner, the Profile Branch's able Number Two, was, despite her frail body and tiny frame, pathologically terrifyingly. Former NSIB, she'd no interest in customers, apart from those that bravely dared to complain. Nor did she have a desire to make any sales herself, but she did devour paperwork, staff issues and administrative tasks like a ravenous, wheeled wolverine.

Danny hated paperwork. Or anything that even remotely resembled a distraction from selling for that matter, and although he'd always thought Mary was verging on edge of psychotic, he'd grudgingly agreed that she was ideally suited to the job, despite her oddities.

Mary insisted on having her wheelchair in the branch at all times, yet she very rarely used it. Most of the time it just sat gathering dust in the back office, occasionally cunningly deployed to help deal with a complaint, a sort of visual pacifier, as she wheeled herself towards an irate customer. Otherwise, she seemed quite able to stalk slowly around the office, poking her nose into every facet of branch life, meddling in business that didn't really concern her. Working with Mary was like living on a perilous knife edge. Those chosen few who fell into her good books, found her support unconditional, but for the majority, those poor souls who fell down the other side of that sharp blade, the day job was a living hell.

Smoking and strong coffee seemed to be her only sustenance. Nobody could ever recall her actually ever eating lunch, and she only ever went outside during daylight hours to spark up yet another death stick. She claimed to be married, despite any evidence of an actual husband, and the only joy she seemed to have in her bitter little world, were three small lap dogs. One brave member of staff once dared to suggest that one of these might actually be her husband. The body was never found.

At nine AM precisely, the cities Lord Mayor, a pretentious chap who would have happily attended the opening of a crisp packet if it meant getting his picture in the local newspaper, ceremoniously cut the bright red ribbon and Cottons NSIB's new Profile Branch was officially declared open for business. The press did a fine job of capturing the challenging image of the gigantic Branch Manager shaking hands with the dwarf like Mayor, and a suitable newsworthy piece about the new Banks virtues and qualities, rigorously scripted by Area Office, was passed to the journalists to help them save time. Carefully selected photogenic, compliant customers were invited to attend the grand opening, mostly from the Cottons heritage, and each member of staff, even Mary, wore a compulsory welcoming smile on their faces. So far, things seemed to be going to plan, with each carefully selected member of the team, specially chosen by Area Office for a specific reason, performing admirably.

At the heart of the new branch were the cashiers. Often the first member of staff a customer encounters, they have an amazingly positive effect on sales. Under the new regime, each cashier had a daily referral target to pass over at least five customers to a CRA or similar. Booked appointments also counted towards their targets, but immediate referrals were usually more desirable. Stack them high, sell them cheap.

Danny's cashiers were chosen for either being ruthless or professional. They were all former NSIB staff, some of which he'd worked with before. To begin with there was Rich. In his mid-thirties, lean and clean cut, he was a career cashier. Once he'd achieved his Number One status, he showed no further interest in promotion, instead being content to run whatever little team he was given with a mixture of good natured efficiency and pride. He quickly built excellent rapport and had a staggering memory. Once he'd served a customer, not only could he recall their full name on sight the next time he saw them, but also their children's names, which football team they supported, what their pets were called and which of their relatives were feeling under the weather. He couldn't, though, ever remember his name badge.

Rich had three cashiers to manage, Ryan, Sally and Beth. Ryan was nineteen, permanently glowed with health and was unbelievably enthusiastic about anything he was asked to do. He was a good looking, in an American sort of way, and had been lucky enough to win a competition the NSIB had run shortly before the merger. The prize was to appear in what would be their last television advertisement. He was something of a familiar friendly face therefore, and Area Office wasted no time capitalising on his brief moment of fame.

Sally was in her late twenties, a devastatingly exotic beauty of mixed blood, with walnut skin and thick hair, as black as the inside of an olive. She'd joined the NSIB from school, and thanks to an impressive, machine gun referral rate, she'd earned good cashier bonuses over the years, meaning that like Rich, she'd no desire to move on.

Finally there was Beth, an extraordinary odd character who was difficult to age thanks to the thick layer of make-up she coated onto her challenging features each morning. She was in fact fifty-three and had been married and divorced five times. She had slightly hazardous looking, spiky hair dyed several shades of beige, and her body was slight and hunched from a lifetime spent bending over a till. Despite her shocking appearance though, Beth was a gluttonous sales animal, mercilessly dedicated to the pursuit of bonuses and praise. Often she'd abandon her till position to chase a fleeing customer down the street, still spouting the merits of a credit card or home insurance policy whilst in hot pursuit. In the NSIB, this was the stuff legends were made of.

To add some much needed Cottons flavour to the branch, Kelly had been freed from Armada and prompted to head Customer Advisor, leaving Ash, a former NSIB head enquires clerk, somewhat disgruntled. A few hours in Kelly's charming presence however, soon melted away any animosity between them, and Ash, who at thirty-one had never even so much as held a girls hand before, fell in love.

He lived with his Mum, collected rare *Batman* comics and spent most of his evenings playing complicated computer games. He'd only joined the NSIB when he ran out of schools and universities to attend, and soon found that his ability to fix computers when they inevitably blew up put him in good stead with his new employer. Having effectively hidden from the world for most of his life, he also found talking to customers an exciting novelty too, and more out of fascination than instruction, demonstrated genuine interest in all those he came into contact with.

Kenny was the branches long suffering Financial Planning Advisor. Like all good FPAs, he was frequently broke, usually in the throes of a divorce, and constantly staring into a pit of bankruptcy and depression. However, in order to prevent himself from being completely tipped over the edge by the many obstacles life threw at him, he retaliated instead with scotch and soda, loose lonely women, and jazz. He was quite a character. As any breeder of championship fighting pit-bull knows though, the leaner and hungrier the dog, the more likely it would be to rip the throat out of the opposition, and with Kenny the same applied to financial sales. Naturally, he was chosen for the branch.

Finally, there was George Butler. To begin with, Danny decided he'd save time, and took an instant dislike to the flashy little sod, with his modern cropped haircut and ostentatious three piece pinstripe suit. But then, that was before he'd sat in on his first customer interview.

"So, definitely an Audi then, and *not* a BMW?" Mr and Mrs Randall were not at all prepared for this. They'd expected to pop into the nice new branch, politely ask for a loan to buy a new car for the family, and then leave as soon as possible. But it wasn't meant to be. The rather unusual young man they'd ended up seeing, seemed eager to become their new best friend instead.

George was stalling for time. His mind had gone blank and he was desperately trying to remember what came after Rapport Building, before any other random thoughts sensed an opportunity to wander into his head. The hateful role-plays he'd endured during the week long CRA training course had obviously covered this. A whole day had been allocated to interview structure, but now he was faced with real, live customers, he just couldn't remember anything beyond Rapport Building. He'd rather liked this bit, having a good old chat came naturally to him. If only he could remember the next step though.

The training course had been packed with vital learning and ample opportunity to practice interviewing before being thrown into the field. In was so intense that George had little time for his usual doodles or sketches. Even more elaborate and disturbing word patterns, designed to complement the merciless DAFS process, had been introduced, along with yet another example of innovative sales practice, The Diamond Suite of Protection. The brainchild of one of the Banks more colourful, flamboyant product designers, the idea was for the CRA to first draw a diamond shape on the customers IFIF. At least for George, this was a chance to sketch. Then, at each corner of the diamond, they'd highlight the four products the customer should buy in order to fully protect them against everything from the common cold, to the bubonic plague.

Products including Personal Payment Insurance, for loans and credit cards, Critical Illness Insurance, Accident Protection, and finally the Hospital Bed Plan. A novel cash payout scheme for every night the customer spent in hospital, although which crucially, did *not* include the first night's stay.

For George, it was all starting to get just a bit too complicated. He understood it all; he just didn't enjoy the subject very much. It was GCSE Chemistry all over again. It didn't help matters that Dean had becoming increasingly negative too, and reluctant to keep up his afterschool classes.

Seemingly unaware of his recent outburst, Area Office had foolishly tried to pressure him into applying for the new Senior CRA role, something that had seen his rage reach new, vein splitting levels, and had ended badly for all concerned. In certain corners, bets were being placed as to how long it would be before he resigned.

Natasha, meanwhile, had been delighted to accept the new appointment instead. Along with a significant increase in pay, it meant that she'd have a unique portfolio of the most profitable and prestigious customers, those most likely to buy from the Bank and earn her good bonus. Naturally, she wasted no time in tottering off to the BMW dealership. Suddenly, everything seemed to be changing very fast.

"...*Err*, well yes, *I think so*. I just thought the Audi would be, you know, a bit more grown up! So, err, can we have the loan then, George..?" Joe Randall looked pleadingly at his interviewer. He'd trodden a long, rocky road on his journey to convincing his wife that they really should upgrade the family Ford Sierra, and any possibility that even a glimmer of doubt could be thrown into the path of his fickle wife, needed to be quashed immediately.

George rifled through his mountain of scribbled notes, pressed a few buttons on his keyboard, for no other reason than to appear efficient and desperately tried to avoid his manager's steely gaze. In order to be inconspicuous, Danny had positioned his enormous bulk in a corner behind the Randalls, but directly in his CRA's line of sight. It was proving to be rather unsettling.

"Err, well yes, *I guess so*, we just need to, *umm...*" George scratched the back of his cropped head with his biro. What the hell was he forgetting? He hadn't warmed to the Trainer on the CRA course. Phillip was positively butch in comparison, and he was starting to think that his reluctance to listen to the thin, high pitched voice may have done him a disservice. Out of desperation, he flicked through the crumpled IFIF. On the back page there was a customer friendly version of the Banks approved interview structure. He'd forgotten all about that. "Ah! Oh yes! *I need to process the application!*"

Danny rolled his eyes, muttered something inaudible, and made yet another note on his observation jotter. It had been a very, very long interview. This cretin was supposed to be the next best thing, yet he'd lost count of the times he'd fought the urge to jump in and take over, before Audi stopped making cars altogether. He loathed sitting in on other people's appointments at the best of times, but this was purgatory. His feedback was going to need to be censored. Resting his huge chin in the palm of his right hand, he let his body sag further into the chair. It squeaked in protest. Soon, he's going to start talking about loan protection. Please God, before the Pubs close.

Fortunately, the third hour of the Randalls' epic interview had been marginally better. George managed to identify that they had two young girls, a mortgaged house, and a small cat called Molly, who was scared of mice. His meandering approach to unearthing these facts were far from Bank approved, but had been somewhat entertaining for his observer. In fact, it had been quite fascinating to watch.

Now that he'd finally remembered some of the structure he was supposed to follow, there was no stopping him. Although his questions were definitely not listed on any of the standardised, official Bank word patterns that Danny could recall ever seeing, they did seem to work. He talked to the couple as though they were propping up the bar in his local, he'd even loosened his tie, and after a while, they'd relaxed and just went with it. In the end, they told him things they hadn't even told each other.

By the time George actually started talking about financial products again, his IFIF looked to be covered in the deranged scribblings of a mad man. However, amongst the barely legible notes, scrawled figures that had been totted up long hand, a small sketch of a frog, and a drawing of a house with a number on its roof, it was all there. Against all odds, he'd managed to collect together a complete picture of the Randalls' life, everything from their credit card balances to their favourite TV show. It really should have been framed.

All he needed to do now was convert some of this hard earned personal information into, not only the loan they'd come in for, but also the range of other financial products they could easily be sold. His next few words were vital for his survival. Danny held his breath and trembled as he tried desperately not to step in. The temptation was overwhelming.

"Err, *do you know what?* I reckon we can probably help you out with some of this other stuff, *umm*, shall we get brew though, *I'm gasping...?*" George looked up pleadingly. His exasperated Manager rolled his eyes for the hundredth time, tore a sheet off his jotter and stood over the Randalls. He was the most terrifying waiter in the world, ever.

"Right then *Chiefs*, so, tea or coffee?"

"*Oh*, you must be George! Danny's told me all about you." Hannah Garson was the most beautiful girl ever to look down on him since secondary school. Although it had become clear of late that he'd stopped getting any taller, he was reasonably content with his five foot eleven and one quarter inches. But now, in the land of the giants, he felt like a hobbit.

Hannah was at least six foot, three, without heels. Yet when she stood next to Danny, in the absence of any shorter comparison at least, the pair looked quite normal. It was only the crick in their guests straining neck that reminded him, that he was amongst people who had obviously been grown in fertilizer.

She was breathtakingly stunning. A statuesque woman somewhere in her early thirties, Hannah had thick brown, wavy hair that was layered and fell about her shoulders. Her features were soft and pleasing, and her figure curvy, but athletic. The wide apart, welcoming blue eyes were hypnotic. And for some reason, Danny called her, 'Bird'.

"*You must stay for supper.* You looked half starved! Danny, please get the poor chap a beer or something?" Since he'd first met his Manager, it had never occurred to George's that anyone would be able to ask him to do anything, let alone survive and gain a favourable response. Clearly at home though, things were very different from work, and a few moments later he found himself sipping an excellent, ice cold pint of Stella. This was more like it.

"*Bird*, Butler here's on some sort of funny diet, he won't want to eat with us, *will you Butler?*" He loomed over his employee, frowning intensely. Hoping his meaning would sink in quicker than everything else seemed too.

"Oh, no, no, *it's okay.* Wednesday's a rest day, and Dean says I can eat what I like once a week, now I've lost a bit more weight..."

"Really Butler, *are you sure?*" The frown deepened.

"Oh, yeah, yeah, *its fine, thanks*! So, what're we having then?"

A while later the three of them sat around an enormous dining room table. The chairs were so tall that George's feet only just brushed the waxed, oak floor. Hannah served a vast meal of thick spaghetti bolognaise with huge wedges of homemade garlic bread on the side. It positively dripped with molten butter and roughly chopped chunks of garlic; even the most fervent vampire would have been kept at bay until the weekend. Before long, having resigned himself to spending the evening with the employee, Danny steered the conversation in the desired direction before his wife started asking him about his love life. After all, earlier he had practically kidnapped their impromptu dinner guest. And the ransom was his art.

One hundred and ninety two minutes after Mr and Mrs Randall originally sat down with George to begin their marathon loan interview, they finally left the premises, blinking in the sunlight like miners freed from an unexpected cave in. At last they had their loan and they were free. Yet it was odd. Apart from the suits and the ties, and perhaps the occasional question about something vaguely financial, neither of them felt like they'd just spent several hours in a bank.

It had all been rather surreal. For some reason they couldn't quite put their finger on, they'd told the disorganised young man everything about themselves. Even things they'd never intended to tell their family. Like a shambolic Ring Master who kept losing his clowns, he'd spent ages suggesting solutions to some of their financial woes, even bringing on a new clown of his very own. The bedraggled financial consultant reeked of scotch, but talked energetically about the pitfalls of under insurance, suggesting viable, affordable solutions. The terrifyingly huge waiter had talked to them about mortgages too, and once the alcoholic fog had left the room, the giant stood up, conducted the most succinct interview ever, and concluded by telling them that they could indeed afford to move house. This had been fantastic news.

Finally their old friend had picked up the threads of his interview. In his usual confused manner, which they'd learnt to warm too, he mopped up all their external debt, as well as the balance required for the car, into one new loan. They'd also signed up for Cottons NSIB home insurance, Credit Cards and PPI. And as they walked home that afternoon, satisfied but bewildered, the Randall's reflected that it had definitely been a bizarre experience. Not unpleasant, by any means, but bizarre. They'd definitely go back when they needed some more cash.

Danny chose to debrief Mr Butler in the relative sanctity of his private office. He'd seen quite enough of George's modest den for one day. Having counted the all perforated holes in one of the ceiling tiles twice to pass the time, and then mentally calculated how many there were in the whole ceiling, he never wanted to step foot in that particular interview room ever again.

"Right *Chief*, well, we're all a bit older now, that's for sure!" He grinned mischievously despite himself. "I have to say though, I reckon if we sold kitchen sinks, you'd have flogged 'em one eventually!" George sat expectantly on the edge of his seat. This sounded like praise, he chose to beam nervously. He could still be wrong.

"Seriously *Chief*, if we can shorten your interviews down by a few hours, I reckon we could make a decent *seller* out of you yet. Just don't do what Billy does, and put your thumb over the loan insurance premium before the punters realise what they're signing for, *okay Chief?*" Grinning expansively, he downed the cold remains of his black coffee, slammed his hands down hard on the table top and rose to his massive feet, glancing casually at his Rolex Submariner. It looked like a child's novelty watch against his thick wrist. "Crikey, *it's half six*! Bird's gonna kill me! Right Butler, OUT, NOW!"

Shocked by the sudden, unexpected change of tone, George leapt out of his chair in fright, accidentally bumping into the desk, sending a framed picture hurtling into the air. "*Easy Chief!*" Carefully picking up the photo, like he was rescuing a drowning butterfly from an oil slick, Danny gently turned it over to see if the glass had shattered. It hadn't. He wouldn't have blood on his hands just yet.

Bright red with fear and embarrassment, George cursed his clumsiness. "I, *err*, I'm really sorry Danny, *is it okay?*" He crept forward gingerly, craning his neck to see what damage he'd done. Fortunately everything seemed to have survived its brief moment of aerobatics, and was delicately placed back on the desk. "Sorry Danny, *what is it anyway?*" He never knew when it was best just to leave.

The picture frame held a treasured wedding photograph of a couple on a tropical beach. Danny's head was badly sun burnt, but he was resplendent none the less in a cream linen suit, and his beautiful bronzed wife at his side, wore a flowing white dress with a classic neckline, Caribbean coral flowers in her wavy hair. In the background, silhouetted against a setting sun and fluffy, pink clouds, there was a wooden jetty and a pier, which supported a colonial style building.

"*That's beautiful, Danny!*"

"*That*, Mr Butler, is MY WIFE!" He screwed up his fists. What was it Hannah had said about counting to ten before hitting people?

"*Oh, I see*! Yes she is very beautiful too, *of course*, but I meant the pier and the sunset. It's a great picture, would make a lovely painting." There was a moment of appreciative silence and confusion.

"What do you know about painting, *Chief?*"

After the enormous meal had settled and been washed down with several pints of strong coffee, Hannah set about retrieving their wedding albums from the enormous bookshelf in the study. Counting Crows', 'August and Everything After' whispered softly from the impressive Bose stereo, and Danny collapsed onto one of the vast sofas, doing best not to belch. It didn't last long.

Not unlike their earlier customers, almost against his will he'd started warming to his new CRA. To begin with, amongst other things, his typical

Cottons habit of wearing his own flash suit had rather clouded his opinion. But now, with several bottles of red wine and a fine meal under his belt, he was almost bearable company. The fact that he also claimed to be capable of creating a painting of the Garson's tropical wedding venue, didn't hurt the fledging relationship any either.

"Here we go George, *this is the best one!*" Hannah wedged herself snugly between her artistic dinner guest and the armrest. Opening the vast album to the first page, he was delighted to be greeted by a full length picture of Hannah, barely clothed in the skimpiest of white bikinis. There was also a pleasing turquoise ocean in the background, some palm trees and other stuff. But that didn't really matter. He had to agree with Hannah, this was definitely the best one.

Hannah was fascinated by artists. As George carefully selected the photographs he'd need in order to paint a suitably impressive picture, she didn't hesitate, pulling those chosen out from behind the protective plastic and placing them in an envelope without question. Obviously this young painter knew what he was doing. When she'd left the room to get some more wine though, Danny grabbed the envelope and began editing. Carefully removing all traces of his wife tanned cleavage, even if the backdrop had been vital to George's work.

The evening grew late and conversation meandered somewhat before finally arriving at fitness and sport. Danny wasn't at all relaxed with this topic. When the couple had first met, it seemed he'd been quite the sportsman. A keen tennis player and proficient at squash, he'd also been the sort of competent windsurfer that was capable of circumnavigating the globe, with nothing more than slightly wet ankles to show for his travels. But a combination of sudden, unexpected contentment, a lifetime ban from the tennis club, following an unfortunate incident involving a ball hopper, and a general thickening of his waistline, had seen most physical activity grind to a lumbering halt.

Hannah said that although she was extremely proud that her husband had managed to give up smoking, she really wanted him lose a few pounds before their holiday to Spain. In a rare moment of self-preservation, George chose not to mention his Manager's hourly fag breaks, and instead listened intently. It was a novel experience for him.

The gym it seemed was out of the question. There were far too many people to aggravate Danny, but maybe something like squash would be a good idea, after all, he already had all the kit, and wasn't there a squash court at that Diamond Fitness gym? Hannah talked about her gigantic husband as though he was an oversized, misbehaving primary school pupil. Busy pulling the wings off blue bottles in the next room, whilst the grownups decided what was best for him.

The black squash ball hurtled past George's head, like something lethal on its way to sink a Spanish Galleon. Once again, he uncoiled his shoulders and relaxed for a moment, safe in the knowledge that at least this violent projectile hadn't connected with any bare flesh. Quite how he'd ended up in a white concrete box with a psychopath this evening, was beyond him. Things seemed to have been going reasonably well lately, but now it looked as though he was going to die, horribly.

"I think that's *game*, Chief?" Danny twirled his racket absentmindedly in his huge right hand, recovered the hot rubber ball with an expert flick, and started bouncing it hard against the wooden floor to maintain its heat and spring. It was very upsetting. Any hopes George had of enjoying a gentle knock about this evening, had been dashed by his opponent's opening, deadly thwack. He'd never even held a squash racket before, and now, with huge red, perfectly circular welts forming on his exposed shoulders and arms, it seemed unlikely he ever would again.

"My serve then, ready?" With another ear-splitting whack, his opponent launched the ball at the wall with brutal raw power, leaving George no choice but to hide behind his left forearm, cower into his corner, and weakly hold up his own trembling racket in anticipation of the thunderous impact.

"*JESUS CHRIST!*" His squash racket clattered to the floor, and he limped around the court clutching his left leg, trying desperately hard not to cry in front of both his Branch Manager, and the ever increasing crowd their one sided, David and Goliath match had drawn in the viewing gallery above. In this case though, David looked to be properly buggered.

"Sorry *Chief*, I thought you had that one?" Danny recovered the melting ball and proceeded to bounce it rapidly once more, as his opponent massaged his newest wound.

George was an exhausted, battered wreck. Having already covered several painful miles of squash court in his hopeless attempt to return serve, he gleamed with stinging sweat, and was peppered with bright red, swollen bruises, brail for the seriously blind. Although he was clearly fitter than his adversary, after forty-two minutes of continuous play, Danny was hardly breaking a sweat. He'd barely moved from the T during his absent minded demolition of the younger man's game.

"Ready then *Chief*, last point I reckon?" The bouncing ceased abruptly, and George prepared himself for the final death blow. Suddenly he regretted all the things he'd ever done wrong in his life. Perhaps one of the spectators would tell his Mum that he had at least died game. Here it was then, the end.

But the inevitable whack and thud never came. Slowly at first, in case it turned out to be a cruel trick, he lowered his badly damaged, protective forearm. Through squinting eyes, one of which was slowly closing, having developed an impressive shiner, he looked over at his challenger. Curiously, rather than preparing to end the suffering, he instead seemed to be examining his own racket. He looked totally bewildered, as though someone had just handed him an aroused garden gnome.

"*Crikey*! Err, Chief, I may owe you an apology Mate…" Danny turned. His usual wicked, half grin joined by an almost reluctant pang of guilt. "… I've been using my tennis racket, *Chief*?"

Chapter 14

Voodoo Laundry

Late May.

Dressed in brand new Pirelli tyres, that wouldn't ever fail to grip like limpets wearing crampons, even in the harshest weather, four polished fourteen inch alloy wheels crunched across the gravel of Shady Glade Cattery's car park, before stopping, sharply. The immaculate, bright red 1988 Toyota MR2's perfectly tuned, mid-mounted, double overhead cam engine, was then silenced, without drama.

Leaving his gleaming pride and joy in first gear, revelling in the mechanical clunk as he slotted the bespoke gearshift into position in the carefully milled aluminium gate, the delighted driver run an affectionate eye over the low slung cockpit. Words couldn't to describe just how good he felt to be back in a sports car again, especially one that didn't leak or smell horrible, and one that always started first time, every time.

Apart from the Ferrari style gear lever and gate that his Dad had made, the car was completely original and unspoilt. It had just one fastidious previous owner, prior to being sold to the delighted young man with the handful of used twenties, having clearly been loved and cherished all its life. The original sales receipt was tucked inside the religiously stamped service booklet, and despite being eight years old, it still smelt new.

In stark contrast to his heart wrenching separation from his beloved MGB, the quickly agreed part exchange of the fiesta, had been a positively liberating experience for George. Even with four lemon air fresheners hanging from the rear view mirror, come the end, it still smelt faintly of lavender. Most importantly though, it did nothing for the carefully constructed image he'd been busy creating for himself of late. And these days, image was everything.

After a great deal of time spent on the throne with a copy of *Autotrader*, and having terrified several used car salesmen with his spirited test drives, George eventually settled on the Toyota. With its mid-mounted engine, sport bucket seats, and low slung driving position, it just looked so exotic, and much more expensive than it really was. But mostly, he just loved the pop-up lights. Never before had he let so many of his fellow drivers out of the side roads. He'd even started to leave home earlier, just to account for the extra time it took. But it was worth it. Each time those square units popped up, he grinned uncontrollably, and his heart swelled.

The Fiesta had yielded him very little in part exchange, meaning that the balance had to be met by a three year staff loan instead, which Billy had happily arranged for him. It had been a strange feeling, sitting on the other side of the desk for a change, and the whole processes of borrowing money for the first time, felt altogether alien. He'd worried about telling his parents too, they didn't hold with borrowing money. But this was the world he lived in now. With his new salary, he could afford the repayments, and as a man about town, he desperately needed a car that didn't smell of old lady. But perhaps most importantly, he wanted something flash to mark his new position. And a bright red sports car seemed like a good place to start.

It had been a busy and expensive few weeks for George. Firstly, despite numerous last minute reservations, he'd finally moved out of the Butler's respectable semi and set up a little home of his own in the modern, ground floor one bedroom apartment he'd fallen in love with several weeks earlier. The apartment was modest in comparison to the family home, which although not flash, was a good size and extremely cosy, thanks to Mrs Butler's obsession with Good Housekeeping magazine, and her disturbing love affair with soft scatter cushions.

In contrast the apartment - not *flat*, as he kept reminding anyone who would listen - was contemporary and somewhat cold. With an oak effect laminate floor running throughout, except for in the bedroom where there was a serviceable, if rather thin, beige carpet, and plain white washed walls, it was quite bland too. The apartment was really not much more than rectangular box, measuring just twenty-two feet by sixteen, which sat quite happily amongst the five similar shaped boxes that made up the block. The whole development, which also contained houses, was located on the very outskirts of the city, bordering undisturbed woodland that marked the very start of the countryside.

Once safely inside the small communal lobby, via the secure intercom system, a private front door led into a small but perfectly serviceable hallway, which was of an uneven shape thanks to a small corner store, and an almost octagonal shower room. It wasn't big enough to accommodate a bath, but with its gleaming chrome work, brilliant white suite and matching tiles, the new owner's eye had been rather drawn away from this shortcoming.

Two more doors led to a double bedroom straight ahead, and left into the open plan kitchen/diner/living room, which ran the entire length of one side of the apartment, narrowing slightly for the kitchen. Patio doors at the far end led onto a small private courtyard. The bedroom had a window that overlooked the courtyard and the kitchen had a novel porthole, looking onto communal gardens. With the full width patio doors, the apartment was relatively bright at least, apart from the hallway which, starved of all natural light, especially if the doors were pulled closed, was as dark as the inside of an oil drum, having to make do with recessed, sparkly halogen bulbs for illumination. But they did look rather cool.

The kitchen had a range inexpensive, but robust oak effect cabinets, and a black marble effect roll top surface extended to form an island to sit around, and which overlooked the lounge. Everything else that could be, was made from shiny stainless steel. Being something of a magpie, George liked his new kitchen best of all.

The actual legal conveyance had been an interesting affair. His chosen solicitor, Mr Obayomi, a Nigerian former marine lawyer who'd escaped to the UK to set up his own firm of solicitors, of which he was the only partner, the secretary, and the tea boy, had a unique and somewhat precarious grasp of the English language, let alone its legal systems. His most recent client was still uncertain as to whether or not he actually legally owned his new home. Nevertheless, he was extremely cheap, especially compared to a few of the other firms that the Business Banking Manager at Armada Branch had suggested. But he did unfortunately lack anything that even remotely resembled efficiency, expertise or organisation. Naturally, he got on very well with his newest customer.

Eventually, despite the endless paper trial, the lost, found and then lost again legal documents, and a perilous last minute panic, during which time the Cottons NSIB mortgage department seemed to suspect Mr Obayomi of money laundering, the purchase finally went through. And George was a proud property owner, with a twenty-five year mortgage around his neck.

He'd expected to have sleepless nights, to wake up worrying about his new, colossal responsibilities, about the inevitable bills home ownership was bound to attract. But it never happened. Whether he'd just been anaesthetized by weeks of lending money to the public, or perhaps it was simply some new found confidence, born out of his position in the Bank, was unclear, but spending money was certainly becoming second nature.

During the past few months, the very essence of cash had changed for him, and since he'd become a CRA, his feelings towards debt had changed too. By the time he'd signed the loan agreement for the MR2, he no longer shared his parents' stern views on the subject. He'd been brought up with a simple, cast iron rule that if he wanted something, then he needed to save up for it. Mortgages were the only exception. Working for the Bank had soon changed all that though. These days, if he wanted something, he simply whacked it on his new credit card, and worried about it later.

His parents were becoming increasingly concerned about their youngest son. Although they were surprised that he'd gone through with it, they'd been pleased that he'd bought a property of his own. But they'd hoped that he would be sensible about furnishings and household items, simply buying the bare necessities for now, such as one cup and saucer, and maybe a plate. Make do with a deckchair as a sofa perhaps, and an inflatable bed until he had enough saved to buy a new one. But their son had other, expensive ideas.

The huge furniture stores positively welcomed him with open arms, especially after he expressed an interest in store credit. As the salesmen filled in the colossal application form required to fund the purchase of two black leather sofas, a glass coffee table, a king sized designer bed with matching wardrobes, bedside tables and chest of drawers, George happily sipped a passable brew whilst listening to endless pan pipe music. Not a care in the world.

An impressive stainless steel fridge freezer, which matched his new oven and hob, was also whacked on his credit card, as was every single other conceivable item of household goods imaginable. A huge television, sleek modern crockery, a wildly colourful rug, sharp bedding and a coffee machine that looked capable of a moon landing.

Ironically enough though, apart from the fridge freezer, nothing arrived on time, and his very first evening in the shiny new bachelor pad, was spent eating cold baked beans from the tin, sat on a borrowed sun lounger, wondering why the fridge in his parents' house didn't sound quite as loud as his. In that horrible moment, he missed his Mum, missed his bedroom and had started to think that he'd made a terrible, terrible mistake. Never before had he wanted a slice of freshly made, moist fruitcake so much.

But knowing that he was fully committed, he bravely stuck it out. The last cuckoo had finally dive bombed from the nest, and it had been an emotional business for all involved. His Mum had been emotional because, with Michael having left years ago to join the Army, George was the last of her brood to waddle out the door. His leaving marked the end of an era. Although he wasn't really going to be that far away, and she knew that he'd still be turning up with soiled laundry, and expecting to be fed at all hours of the day, it didn't change the fact that he wasn't going to live at home anymore. No longer would she be able to nag him for not picking up his dirty socks, or for leaving coffee rings on the dining room table. It was all very sad.

Her husband meanwhile had just been emotional because he was finally getting a study.

George had naturally suffered a number of last minute worries about being a homeowner. His Mum was a Domestic Engineer without equal, but even she seemed to spend her entire life keeping the whole household running. There just always seemed to be something that needed cleaning, polishing, scrubbing or cooking. This troubled him. When would he find the time?

He'd also had mixed emotions about his old bedroom. Almost in a heartbeat, he'd go from living quite happily in his little den, with its curling Star Wars posters, *Airfix* models and impressive collection of Beano Books, to a slick, modern environment, which looked like a Tupperware box with a plywood base. It was all so grown up. How would it feel to live there, alone, permanently? He'd rolled up a favourite Jedi poster, just in case.

But there was something else troubling him too, something even more disheartening. As he packed up the things he wanted to take, he carefully unpinned the many cards and letters Summer had sent him, placing them together in a large brown envelope. Should he seal it shut for good, had she already grown tired of waiting for him? It had been over six weeks now since anything new had arrived from her, and despite his superficial aloofness, he ached for something to come with the next post.

To begin with, corresponding with her, whilst the memory of another naked girl floated about in his mind, had seemed decidedly wrong, immoral almost. For a while, he'd even dreaded the arrival of her distinctive, handmade envelopes, with all their painstakingly detailed decorations. They only served to make him feel guilty once again, to remind him that at the other end of this letter, a really rather lovely girl was waiting. But was she?

In addition to his heartfelt, epic letter about Michael, in quick succession, he'd written another, equally emotional note about his plans to get his own place, inviting her to perhaps come and stay. And that with Danny and Hannah's picture well underway, he was also painting again, even taking on a few more commissions as more and more people saw the

Garson Beach Scene when he brought it in to show his Boss. Yet still nothing in return. Not even a postcard from her local village shop, something she'd previously sent him with clockwork regularity.

It was strange, and for the first time, unsettling. What was she up to? The same as him perhaps, but with someone called Pierre, on Jean-Philippe? It didn't bare thinking about, and jealously had flushed bitterly through him. But he wasn't sure if it was right to feel like this anymore, not when he'd been spreading his wings as much as he had been lately. Maybe it was just time to forget all about her? But this thought only made matters worse.

George had taken a rare day off and moved into the apartment on a Wednesday. By the following weekend, most of his new furniture and household goods had arrived, a good deal of which was coated in bubble wrap, which he always found to be a welcome distraction. It was three days before he'd popped every bubble.

Armed to the teeth with every conceivable item of domestic weaponry, Mrs Butler had whipped through his new place like an unstoppable, cleansing whirlwind, giving it the inevitable, inaugural 'Mummy Clean'. Large terracotta flowerpots miraculously appeared in the courtyard, already brimming with healthy looking palms and ferns. A vase of brilliant white roses materialised on the coffee table, seemingly out of thin air. The bathroom cabinet was stocked with Vosene medicated shampoo and Wrights Coal Tar Soap, and the whole place smelled strongly of lemon disinfectant and bleach. It was the very essence of clean, and more importantly for George, the very essence of home.

Like most first time buyers though, during his first few days, all alone in his apartment, he'd been startled and confused by an array of puzzling, unsolved Domestic Mysteries:

Why is it that once you've washed all the dishes, and you're quite sure the washing up bowl is empty, somehow there is always a solitary tea spoon lurking in a corner when you pour away the dirty water?

What happens to socks once they've been loaded into the washing machine? Why is it that although a pair goes in, sometimes only a lonely single sock emerges at the end of the cycle? Was the washing machine secretly some sort of portal to another world for gentlemen's hosiery, and who taught it to dance?

Why was it that, despite the fact that both the larder and the fridge were brand new, the larder somehow seemed to come complete with a suspicious looking tin of beans, which was already a year past its sell by date, and after a few days, the fridge somehow had a resident single can of Fosters Beer welded to the back by a thick layer of Arctic ice?

What troubled him most of all though, what caused him restless nights as he tossed and turned endlessly on his impossibly uncomfortable sheets, was his inability to create fresh laundry like his Mum did. He'd carefully selected exactly the same washing powder and softening fabric conditioner that she religiously stuck too, and even though he'd already blown his budget for white goods on his shiny, stainless steel fridge freezer, had also bought exactly the same model of washing machine as her non-wobbly one. Yet despite his care and diligence, the laundry just didn't smell or feel anything like his Mum's. It just wasn't fair.

Mrs Butler's laundry smelled of fresh clean air and warm summer's days, even in the depths of winter, and had all the soft, snugly qualities of a new born Persian kitten. George's didn't. After yet another failed attempt, during which the washing machine attempted to perfect the samba, he finally came to a startling conclusion. Clearly some sort of 'Voodoo Laundry' was at play. As he had no business trying to understand the strange, magical rituals or customs his Mum obviously practiced, he'd have to make do with cardboard sheets and shirts until Sunday afternoon eventually came around, and he could take a load home instead. Home, that had been an interesting point, where exactly was home now?

George stood naked at his new kitchen counter and checked his ingredients. The scribblings he'd studiously taken many years before, as he'd stood just as naked in Gabriella's kitchen, were faded, but his memory would hopefully fill in any gaps. And what a memory it was. He'd decided long ago that his maiden voyage in his unspoilt kitchen should take him to Italy. Back to those warm explicit evenings with his patient, sultry Italian temptress, and perhaps more importantly, back to the Island of Ragu.

It had taken him quite some time to convince Dean that Ragu would neatly fit into his Auschwitz diet, from which the only respite from boiled chicken breasts and egg whites was a solitary day of indulgence. Considering the staggering amount of weight his young disciple had now lost though, Dean eventually conceded. Allowing the dish under the strict understanding that he didn't serve it with pasta or bread just steamed broccoli, and maybe cabbage. Surely one helping of fresh pasta wouldn't hurt though?

Partly out of tradition, yet mostly to avoid staining, George also chose to draw the blinds and the curtains, put Sade on his new Sony stereo, and strip off to cook his opening dish. His memories of cooking with Gabriella were hazy to say the least, and inter dispersed with far more pleasant images of bare olive skin, and an uncontrollable urge to keep saying 'thank you', but according to his notes he seemed to have successfully gathered everything he needed from the Supermarket. He rather liked his new local Supermarket and one young checkout girl in particular, unnecessarily lapping the isles several times with his bulging trolley, until she was free and he could turn on his newly acquired charm. Quite what she made of his shopping though, with the endless cartons of eggs and dozens of chicken breasts, was another matter.

With everything spread neatly before him, a very large, reassuring glass of Chianti within easy reach, he was at last ready to begin. He vaguely recalled Gabriella lecturing him about the diverse types of Ragu cooked across Italy, and how each region tended to use different types of meat according to tradition. But being tutored by the first girl he'd ever seen properly naked, had an adverse effect on his ability to retain such facts, and now sadly, these historical details were lost to him. His notes however, were not, and he smiled to himself as he recalled scribbling her instructions ridiculously fast in the flickering candlelight of her kitchen, as she fiercely stirred the thick broth with a slender, bronzed arm.

He heaved his shiny new stainless steel pan out of a cupboard and placed it heavily on the largest of the gas rings. It was a vast item of cookware, well over a foot in diameter and just as deep, built from the sort of weapons grade metal that would easily withstand small arms fire and shrapnel damage. Gingerly, he set the gas to full. Stepped back slightly, to avoid singeing his pubic hair, and lit the hissing hob with a flick of the ignition switch. After taking a very deep pull from his goldfish bowl wine glass, he scrutinized his notes one last time, and began. It was a proud moment.

Firstly, he carefully sliced and fried five red onions and two whole bulbs of garlic. His scribblings had been a bit smudged here, probably by Gabriella's sauce, but he considered that you can never really have enough garlic, and pressed on bravely. Through watering eyes, he added a kilo of minced steak and a large glass of red wine, giving him ample reason to refill again, and vigorously stirred until he eventually broke up the meat and couldn't see anymore. His fire alarm, obviously suffering from paranoia, went mad.

After running to the bathroom to wash out his eyes and tend to a minor cut, he seasoned generously with salt and cracked pepper, from his new, faintly intimidating wooden grinder, before slicing and adding ten whole fresh tomatoes, finally pouring in six tins of chopped ones and a whole tube of concentrated puree. It was starting to look real. He took another deep sip of wine, this was exhausting stuff.

Everything seemed to be going quite well, all things considered. The wound to his thumb didn't seem to need stitches, and apart from having to desperately leap out of the way to avoid a scalding splash from a particularly zealous stir, all was relatively calm and composed. The Ragu was simmering nicely. According to the recipe, he needed to start thinking about frying off the rest of the meat now, and adding it to the sauce before throwing in four or five handfuls of fresh basil, a few bay leaves, some dried Italian herbs and brown sugar.

Taking another deep glug of wine to compose himself, he carefully checked his splattered notes before opening his gleaming new fridge, and removing the assorted chunks of meat. In the spirit of Dean's diet, and his constant mantra of *Protein, Protein, Protein*, George had decided to go overboard on the flesh department. As well as the kilo of steak mince, he'd also chosen twenty-four lean chipolata sausages, two whole packs of streaky bacon, and a huge smoked gammon joint. It seemed to have just enough fat on it to give the required flavour. Brandishing his new, frighteningly sharp Sabatier knife, like a psychopathic nudist, he savagely cut it into manageable lumps with glee.

Despite knowing that his mentor would disapprove, He decided to stick to his notes and fry off the meat rather than grill, the juices of which he'd then add to the mix for flavour. Bugger it. Unfortunately though, this had proven to be a rather painful affair. Although his recollections of events were rather clouded, he was quite sure that his nether regions hadn't been scalded quite this badly in Gabriella's kitchen. Not by boiling olive oil at least.

It was whilst he was sealing the last of the gammon in readiness for the pot, long after opening his second bottle of Chianti that his intercom buzzed excitably. Taking care to turn everything down from its blast furnace setting, much to the relief of his hypochondriac fire alarm, George quickly dashed into the hallway to answer it. Hopefully something new and shiny had been delivered whilst he was at work.

"Hello, *hello?*" There was prolonged silence, followed by a slight clearing cough and barely audible breathing over the crackling line.

"Umm, err, Mr Butler, its Penelope, err, *from upstairs*, umm, err, I took a parcel in for you earlier, *would you like it?*" The voice was nervous. Its owner clearly wished it hadn't gotten involved.

He hadn't met Penelope yet. From what little he could glean from the apartments poor soundproofing, it seemed that his neighbour in the floor above went to bed at ten o'clock sharp, judging by all the frantic switching off of the plug sockets, and that she was obsessed with hovering and Dolly Parton.

"Great, thanks, *let me get the door!*"

It was only later, as he added the last of the seared gammon to his huge vat of Ragu, once again accidentally scorching his naked gentleman's region, that the reason for his bashful neighbour's horrified refusal to come in for a quick drink, and subsequent swift exit suddenly dawned on him.

Much, much later, when the last of the Ragu had finally been cleaned off the kitchen floor, ceiling and some of the light fittings, George slouched alone on his cold black leather sofa. His belly full, he was still glugging Chianti, aimlessly flicking through the latest Guitarist Magazine. Aside from wondering if Penelope would ever look him in the eye again, something else was troubling him. His apartment was starting to feel a bit like home now. The familiar waft of garlic mixing pleasantly with the lemon air fresheners his Mum had dotted about the place, a light spring breeze outside the open patio doors, rustled through the potted palms, creating an almost tropical atmosphere. But something important was missing. To begin with he thought his feelings had been ambushed again by the confusion caused by Summer's abrupt silence. But this was different. What on earth was it?

He lazily rolled off the sofa, stretched his aching muscles, and hobbled over to switch on his huge television. An advert for Whiskers Cat Food was drawing to a close. That was it! Suddenly he had it. He needed something furry to cuddle of an evening.

Like most children, George's earliest memories of pet ownership stemmed from his all too brief relationship with Gary, a small, slightly emaciated looking Goldfish that Michael had won for him at the Summer Fair. Sadly, no sooner had Gary the Goldfish been introduced to the Butler family, he was found floating upside down on in his bowl by their youngest son, who, quite naturally, had been inconsolable for weeks on end afterwards.

In a bitter attempt to lift him out of his pit of grief and despair, Mr Butler senior, after carefully seeking his wife's approval, decided that another creature, preferably one with a slightly longer life expectancy, was in order, and father and son headed for the local pet shop to buy a hamster.

Boris the Siberian Hamster was an Escapist and a Revolutionary. He was the leader of a loyal band of furry brothers and sisters who were, for the moment at least, incarcerated against their will at Percy's Pet Palace, in a large glass tank. Since he'd first arrived in this shabby little shop, and had been confined to the vast glassy cage, Boris had been secretly hatching a cunning plan. He intended to escape and flee back to his native Siberia, taking with him as many of his countrymen and women as was possible, and especially before the 'Large Pink Hand of Doom' reached into the cage once again, dragging yet another of their number to some horrible fate. Time was running out, for them all.

His carefully constructed plans had been ruined though, by the arrival of the hairy child and the faintly aggravated adult. The smaller of which had pointed to Boris the Escapist, something that all the imprisoned hamsters knew triggered the arrival of the 'Large Pink Hand of Doom'. Boris was finished, all their hopes of freedom, dashed forever.

He squealed bitterly in protest as the 'Hand' grasped him roughly by the scruff of the neck, causing him to dangle his modesty for all to see. This was no way for a leader to go. As he was pulled ever skywards, small legs flaying wildly, he squeaked heartfelt promises to somehow escape his fate, to return and free his brothers and sisters.

That night, when all the lights had finally been turned off in Percy's Pet Palace, and there wasn't a sound to be heard, save the deranged curses of Sid the parrot, the remaining captive Siberian Hamsters built a statue in memory of their fallen leader, from sunflower seeds, crushed oats and their own faeces. It was very lifelike, considering.

After just a few days of incarceration in George's bedroom, Boris considered that death would indeed be a welcome alternative to a life spent with his new captor. It was only his solemn promise to free his people that kept him from ending it all, from hanging himself from the roof of his cage with a twisted length of newspaper. Somehow he must escape.

His new prison warden was a cruel tormentor. He constantly seemed to be finding new ways to test his furry resolve, to try and break him. Solitary confinement was bad enough, but there was also the endless handling. The warden seemed intent on plucking him from his quarters at all hours, fondling him endlessly, especially his head and ears. The brutality was unbearable. Time and time again, he had sunken his fangs into the fleshy fingers, but this only led to audible torture, the high pitched scream coming from nowhere, making his tiny velvet ears throb in agony. But still he held out, he would not be broken.

'The Sphere of Terror' was an especially cruel means of torture though. A transparent plastic ball that the warden locked him into, before releasing him into some sort of vast grassy wilderness, with nothing to do but scurry about wildly, dazed and confused. Just a few tantalising plastic millimetres from freedom, yet still cruelly detained nonetheless. But still he kept his head.

In order to keep his sanity during captivity, Boris focused his efforts on planning and personal fitness. He would spend as much of his day as the warden would allow, hiding in the bright yellow plastic house that sat in the far corner of his cage, silently hatching a plan. He tried to hide extra supplies of sunflower seeds and nuts amongst the straw bedding, ready for the day of his escape. But they were always found, gutted and cleaned out, forcing him to start over. At night he'd train endlessly in his exercise wheel.

His only means of release, and would build up his upper body strength but performing sets of pull ups from his roof bars. Soon, the fat hairy warden would make a mistake, and he'd have his chance to escape.

Sadly though, Boris the Escapist never did free his people. Instead he drowned horribly during a brave bid for freedom when 'The Sphere of Terror' unexpectedly cracked open after crashing into the rocks around the garden pond. As he'd always planned, sensing an opportunity, he'd seized the moment with both claws, and swiftly clambered out of the plastic wreckage, like a determined, furry ninja. Scurrying over rocks, which were encrusted with some sort of slime, he quickly darted towards what he assumed was an expanse of a smooth green moss.

Later, once George's inconsolable wailings had been reduced to an exhausted, quivering sob, and after all attempts to revive a soggy green Boris had failed, it was concluded by the Butler Board of Enquiry that the hamster's untimely watery death was entirely Michael's fault for not cleaning the algae from the garden pond as promised.

Reflecting on pets long since been buried next to the vegetable patch soon found George slipping into a melancholic mood. It was deteriorating by the minute too. Endless thoughts of Summer, and the inevitable Frenchman she'd obviously shacked up with, had barged into his head, and were running around all naked and sweaty. It was horrible, and the three bottles of questionable red wine probably didn't help matters either.

Suddenly he really needed a hug. Not from some random girl that would never call again, but from a loving, unquestioning pet. His mind was made up; he definitely needed some sort of animal to share his home with. A goldfish was definitely out. What he needed was something independent, but that would still be there for him at times like this. Something that would be content to just curl up and listen, but not ask too many questions, something that purred perhaps. What he needed was a fully grown Tom Cat, but where to find one?

Fred and his two siblings had been the result of a late night, illicit tryst between a one-eyed, street-fighting alley cat of questionable standing, and a prize winning, perfectly groomed Maine Coon with an unquenchable thirst for a bit of rough. The Maine Coon, a truly beautiful example of the breed, with a thick, glossy white coat faintly striped smoky grey, was, despite her not inconsiderable size, called Minnie. A name she detested. She lived in complete luxury though, so she didn't complain, and her wealthy spinster tended to her every need.

By comparison, the battle-scarred alley cat was a muscular stray with no given name. He was a predatory Ginger Tom who lived off the generosity of the neighbourhood butcher, the kindness of several lonely old widows, and the lax security of the local bird sanctuary.

When Minnie fell pregnant, her owner naturally assumed that her prized feline had finally relented to the charms of Reginald, a handsome Maine Coon with similar colourings and markings that a friend from her ladies bridge club often brought around for afternoon tea, hoping that the two of them would eventually make some pretty grey and white kittens of their own. It wasn't to be though. Unbeknown to her owner, Minnie had become increasingly bored of the social scene, and above all, Reginald. He was both pompous and tedious in equal measure, and drove her to despair with his endless preening. What she wanted was a real Man, or rather, a real Cat.

And so when Minnie eventually gave birth a few months later, in the presence of her excited owner and the bridge club acquaintance, all present were somewhat surprised to be presented with what was quite clearly, a litter of three tiger cubs.

Eight weeks later the enormous, illegitimate ginger kittens were advertised for sale in the commoner's local newspaper by the spinster's gardener. They were adorable, and each one was bought by eager parents, destined to be welcome presents for three families of excited young children.

Maine Coons are normally gentle giants, placid cats of above average intelligence, easy to train, loyal, but not overly clingy; they're both playful and loving. Yet whilst his siblings shared much of their mother's inherit traits, despite his physical resemblance to her breed, Fred was just like his feral dad.

He'd been sold to a family of seven, two parents, an incontinent, moaning grandparent, and four wild children. They lived together in a three bedroom terraced house in the middle of a town in the north. Named after a much loved family member who'd recently died in unexpected circumstances, the family doted on their newest furry member. But despite the endless saucers of milk, piles of generous leftovers, and the handsome collar and name tag he'd been bought, he hated them all bitterly. The first time the kitchen door was left open, he was gone. Over the stone wall and far away, leaving nothing but a small orange ball of fur as evidence that he was ever there.

The next four years were interesting ones for Fred. He spent the first two battling alley cats in dirty backstreets for scraps, occasionally letting a friendly human to adjust his collar to allow for his thickening neck, before finally deciding to see what all the green stuff on the distant horizon was all about. By the age of three and a half, he was fully grown and blissfully happy in his new, rural territory. Now a gigantic beast, he lived on a diet of wild rabbit, the occasional lamb, side orders of field mice, and, given his breed's affinity with water, even the occasional surprised salmon.

Well over a foot tall at the shoulder, and almost three feet in length, including his huge bushy, raccoon like tail, his shoulders were square and strong, and his paws were like snowshoes, which proved particularly useful during the winter months. His long flowing coat was dense and thick, and as his broad back and tail had taken on all the Ginger Tom characteristics of his father, with his belly, chest and lower jaw being bright white like his mother's, he looked just like a Siberian Tiger. Unfortunately though, it was his resemblance to a fearsome, roaming Big Cat that eventually ended his reign of terror in the rural province he'd carved out for himself.

It had taken the combined efforts of three bordering farms, a team of terrified locals armed with shotguns and pitchforks, and the local Territorial Army unit to eventually capture the fearsome 'Beast of the North'. When the exhausted group finally cornered their quarry in a lonely barn, following an eighteen hour pursuit over unforgiving countryside, they were somewhat relived and surprised to find a ginger Maine Coon curled up on top of a discarded tractor tyre, preening itself luxuriously, and not, as they'd feared, a wild, savage tiger hell bent on making a bloodthirsty last stand. Foolishly though, no doubt thinking the worst was behind them, the pursuers made the fatal mistake of trying to put Fred in a box.

The Commander of the Territorial Army unit that had been dispatched to hunt down The Beast had been impressed with the tenacity of his prey. Despite permanently losing the use of a thumb during the ordeal, he'd personally seen to it that Fred was re-homed rather than machine gunned to death, which had definitely been a favourite suggestion amongst his badly lacerated, blood-soaked troops at the time.

His sister owned a string of catteries across the country, which not only took in waifs and strays as part of their charitable work, but also offered lodgings to domestic pets too. And so, like an unwanted, troublesome foster child who nobody can cope with, and whom everyone is secretly suspicious that they might wake up to find stood over their sleeping bodies with a carving knife, Fred was moved from cattery to cattery for the next year, as terrified staff drew lots to clean out his pen and take him his dinner.

Sadly though, in spite of their efforts to re-home him, something about the way he looked at potentials owner's children as though they'd make an ideal afternoon snack always saw them take home a timid kitten instead. Shady Glade Cattery was Fred's last chance. He'd outworn his welcome at the others, and had been personally responsible for a total of fifty-eight stitches, two counts of partial paralysis, a circumcision, and, although evidence was lacking to indisputably sentence him, the brutal murder of at least two of his fellow inmates.

After yet another blood-splattered transfer, he was eventually securely locked in solitary confinement and left to groom, licking his scalpel like claws clean of human flesh as though he'd just enjoyed a saucer of milk. It wasn't that he was a particularly evil cat, or that he especially hated humans, it was just that he couldn't bear to be fussed over and fondled by strangers. He was really a wild cat at heart, he needed to warm to someone, and give them a good sniff before he'd allow them to touch him.

However, fortunately for the terrified staff of Shady Glade, his fellow inmates, local wildlife, should he ever break out, and even for Fred himself, George Butler knew this. He'd had experience of wild cats before.

After Boris the Escapist sadly departed in watery circumstances, Mr and Mrs Butler had, quite understandably, been somewhat reluctant to buy their youngest son another pet. His deep love of the animal kingdom, coupled with his inability to moderate his grief, troubled them, and in an effort to divert his attention, bought him a new BMX instead. A week later, he crashed it into a lamppost, bending the frame beyond repair. It was back to the drawing board.

Fate had other plans though, and during that same long hot summer, a stranger came down from the surrounding countryside, climbed over the natural hedge, that formed the lower bounder of the Butler's back garden, and sat, preening itself, carefully surveying its new surroundings.

Daisy, Mr and Mrs Butler's beloved tabby cat, had sadly passed away the year before, peacefully in her sleep, dreaming of cornered mice and electric blankets. Since then, they couldn't bring themselves to buy another. Daisy had been a devoted, easy-going pet, always happy, always loving and never any trouble. The thought of replacing her didn't sit at all well. Although strangely enough, they'd found that a home without a cat didn't seem quite right either. And so when a mid-sized, heavily pregnant, semi-wild moggy came looking for a home, it had the warmest welcome imaginable.

To begin with, none of the Butlers could get within ten feet of their cautious new arrival, and the family had to be content to watch her feed from the kitchen window. To the Butler brothers, it was like having a their very own screening of *Born Free* in the back garden, with George, who was now in his final year of primary school, talking animatedly about recent developments each morning with his teacher.

After a few weeks of sitting perfectly still on his Mum's manicured lawn, his chubby hand extended in welcome and a permanent look of sincere warmth on his face, Skippy, the universally approved name for the newest member of the family, finally allowed him to gently stroke her head. Everything seemed to be going well. George was living out his own little animal adventure, nothing had drowned yet, and there was the distinct possibility that very soon there would be kittens too.

When Skippy disappeared a few days later, refusing to return despite their youngest son's around-the-clock rattling of the munchies box, Mr and Mrs Butler naturally feared the worse, and prepared for another onslaught of mourning. Fortunately though, the bereavement was to be short lived. When a still grief-stricken George came home a week later, he was overwhelmed with delight to be greeted by a somewhat slimmer, slightly exhausted Skippy.

Gallons of full fat milk laced with breakfast cereal and Bovril was served by the excited twelve-year-old, along with great bowlfuls of tuna chunks and freshly cooked chicken, which had been intended for his Dad's sandwiches. Skippy ate it all down as though she'd just walked across Russia, preened for a few moments, before finally rubbing herself affectionately against her host, and disappearing under the potting shed.

For the next three weeks little changed. Skippy would periodically emerge from her den just long enough to stock up and appear grateful, before retreating again to the safety of her nest. George found it all extremely fascinating, and set up a small watching post opposite the shed, cunningly hidden from view by the hydrangeas, all the while making detailed notes of his observations to show his mum later that evening. Michael meanwhile had since discovered girls, and as such, had little interest in anything else. Despite his diligence though, school attendance unfortunately interrupted his twenty-four hour feline surveillance, and the precious moment he'd been waiting for was sadly lost to him.

As part of her weekly, incredibly detailed household cleaning schedule, Mrs Butler would spend Wednesday afternoons cleaning the windows of the family's respectable semi. Unlike the rest of the cul-de-sac, she refused to waste money paying for a window cleaner - he'd be bound not to clean them properly in any case, and instead she risked life and limb perilously hanging out of the flung open first floor windows with a soapy sponge, and nothing but Neil Diamond and a large glass of Merlot for company. The neighbours couldn't watch.

It was whilst she was gripping onto the frame of a bedroom window by her outstretched fingertips, desperately trying to free a stricken fly from an unsightly cobweb that had had the audacity to attach itself to her house (she hated seeing anything suffer, apart from spiders of course, which she regularly beat to death with a pink fluffy slipper), that she caught sight of something small and furry.

By the time her youngest son came home from school, his face its usual pale green from his brief, yet nonetheless traumatic bus journey, she was giddy with excitement. Pulling him quickly into the kitchen, she pressed him up against the window without so much as an explanation, or even his usual afterschool slice of fruitcake. Silently they waited together, barely breathing, so as not to fog the glass, nothing but the distant wind in the fields and 'Sweet Caroline' on the stereo to fill their ears. Time stood still.

After what seemed like an eternity, finally, there was movement amongst the Geraniums and Busy Lizzies around the potting shed. Slowly at first, four tiny faces eventually emerged into the daylight, blinking and wide-eyed in the sunshine like a mole who had forgotten to wind forward his watch. The four kittens couldn't have been much more than four or five weeks old, but had already established some sort of pecking order.

The largest of the group, a black, plump bruiser who'd clearly been hogging most of Skippy's milk, strode forward fearlessly, out of the flower bed and onto the lawn. It was followed cautiously by a slightly smaller, black sibling with a white bib and paws, who briefly paused to attack a snail, and then the remaining two, a tabby with huge black tufts on its ears, and finally an odd little creation that seemed to be a mixture of all three. Judging by a few stumbles, this one hadn't quite come to terms with balance or composure yet. All four kittens looked to be in the best of health, despite being reared under the potting shed. With perfectly round, plump bellies, which looked as though each had swallowed a tennis ball, they waddled about the lawn, pouncing on butterflies and sniffing at everything with a curious nose.

The weeks that followed were amazing for young George. He couldn't wait to get home from school, regardless of the daily travel sickness, and would sit on the lawn for hours, desperately trying to coax one over with lengths of knitting wool. Although their sex was unknown, he named all four of them. The leader became Garfield, a favourite comic book at the time, the smaller black kitten with the white paws, Socks, and the tabby, Tigger. The uncoordinated one, who was obviously a little bit special, was named Wilber.

When they got a bit bigger, Mrs Butler began putting out vast serving platters of full fat milk and cereal mixed with kitten food, to help build them up and soon, like anything that comes into contact with the Butler kitchen, all four furry bodies got considerably plumper. It wasn't long after this that Skippy disappeared. Her work was done. Her litter was in safe hands. Naturally, George was devastated, but still continued to try and tame her four kittens, regardless of his sobs. After all, if Joy and George

Adamson could do this with a lion, he could do it with cats.

Finally, his patience was rewarded. After a few false starts, and a quick dash to the emergency ward to re-attach the end of his little finger, he eventually won the trust of the litter, ironically enough, having fallen asleep in the grass one baking hot summer's afternoon. Awaking slowly to find four round balls of fur curled up around him, sleeping peacefully, twitching occasionally, and dreaming of mice yet to come.

Keeping all four kittens was never going to be practical. He was allowed to keep just one. A heart-breaking decision needed to be made by the young lion tamer, before they destroyed the respectable semi for good. The curtains were already in shreds. He'd built up a strong bond with each kitten, and especially loved the way that Garfield seemed hell bent on head butting the horizon. But his favourite was Wilber. He shared George's tendency towards enthusiastic bewilderment.

Wilber was quite odd. He talked incessantly to himself throughout the day, early evenings, and sometimes even in the small hours of the morning, leaving the Butlers to conclude that he must have some sort of imaginary friend to converse with. Although he sometimes played with the other kittens, he was normally content to just sit by himself, gazing out at nothing in particular, chirping away happily, waiting for the next interesting thing to happen. And so, it was decided that the crazy little bundle of patchwork fur, along with his imaginary friend, who was allowed to stay as long as he didn't make a nuisance of himself, should become the official Butler family cat.

"Oh yes Mr Butler, *yes*, I remember, you called the other day didn't you? Hang on a minute, I'll just get Geri and she can show you the inmates!" Wearing a new, white, spray on T-shirt to show off his equally new muscles, George couldn't quite decide if Fiona, the receptionist in the blue overalls and ponytail, was pretty, or whether or not the overalls did anything for her figure. But he did know that he desperately needed to chat up a new girl, to find a replacement lover somewhere other than in a swanky night club.

Summer still hadn't written to him and there was just no way was he going to call her, despite what his Mum had said. Without question, in his mind at least, she'd definitely shacked up with some garlic infused Frenchman. He'd also decided that he was definitely called Pierre, and that he'd brought her fresh bread every day, and serenades her each night with his piano accordion. The bastard, how dare he!

It was time to move on. But on the other hand, according to his Seiko, Shady Glade had been a good hour from his new apartment. This meant that Fiona probably lived a similar distance away, therefore logistics might prove costly and timely if his planned charm offensive went well. These sorts of factors really needed to be taken into consideration. His train of thought was thankfully side-tracked, as Fiona the receptionist returned with Geri.

Geri was probably some sort of woman, judging by her enormous jutting breasts, but this was where any similarity to the fairer sex ended. Her overall sleeves were rolled up tightly against thick, hairy forearms, her face had a scattering of unsightly moles, each one sprouting random clumps of course black hair. Her Mum probably loved her though.

"I hope Fiona here told you that we 'ain't got no kittens. You look like the sort that would want a kitten', well we 'ain't got none, *see?*"

"Um, no that's fine, I just want a fully grown tom cat really, I've just got a new fla- I mean, *apartment*, and I don't really want to worry about it scratching everything, *I haven't paid for it all yet!*"

Geri considered this for a moment and turned to Fiona, shrugging slightly. "Well, there's always *You Know Who* in Solitary, what do reckon?"

"Really? But Mr Butler's a young man, *he's still got his whole life ahead of him.*"

Following Fiona through the rows of pens towards Solitary, all the while trying to see if the ill-fitting overalls actually contained a pert bum or not, George tried not to look at the pleading, small faces that stared hopefully up from behind the wire meshing. Some of the cats jumped up on the wooden ledges, rubbing themselves against their cage. Others barely moved, and some simply just sat still, mentally willing the stranger to pick them over their fellow inmates. They were all very lovely, but they were all girls, and it was definitely time for some male company.

Unusually, Shady Glade only had three adult male cats to re home. A very, very old tabby, who appeared to have already been stuffed and mounted in a curled up sleeping position, a Siamese who looked a bit sly, as though he might make off with the stereo whilst his owner was asleep, and finally the notorious *You Know Who*.

Solitary was literally just that. It was a large, single pen with its own airlock to prevent escape, a sizable house that had an open door at the front and a cat flap at the rear, leading onto an enclosed lawn. But unlike the other pens, the mesh seemed just a bit thicker, the timber construction a little more sturdy.

After quick tour of the perimeter, Geri concluded that the inmate must be sleeping inside his house, and quickly ducked into a nearby shed, eventually returning with a small medical kit, a power-hose and a large yard broom.

"Right, I'll flush the bugger out and you see if you like the look of him, *okay*?" She tried a few blasts of the hose to make sure it was set to its maximum level, and reached cautiously for the airlock handle.

"Err, well, *hang on*! Why don't I just go in and sit down, I'm sure he'll come out, *won't he*?" George was beginning to become just a bit puzzled by all this overdramatic security. What on earth did they have in here, a lion? The two members of Shady Glade's staff exchanged knowing glances. Fiona shook her head slowly at Geri, who also, having suffered more than her fair share of stitches at the paws of this moggy, nodded slightly in response.

"Well, that might not be such a good idea. This one's a bit, well, *wild*!" Fiona had warmed to the young man. She hated the thought of seeing his pretty little face scarred for life.

"Well, come on now Fi, if Mr B here wants to go in an' have a look see, we should let him. Come on, it's his choice after all. *He did sign the insurance waiver an' everything.*"

George frowned for a moment. "Oh, is that what that was? You didn't say."

A few minutes later he sat on the hard floor of the pen with his legs stretched out in front of him. Now that he had become accustomed to his surroundings, he was slightly unnerved by all the patches of dried blood. Geri and Fiona were just the other side of the internal door. The hose had been trailed into the inner airlock, and was trained on the doorway to the pen's house in Geri's unwavering, iron grip. Fiona meanwhile was as white as a sheet. She held onto the yard broom with tiny trembling hands, knuckles equally white, the medical kit open at her feet, a fresh bandage already unwrapped and ready.

Despite the paranoia, there didn't seem to be any sign of life, or movement within the dark recesses of the house. Succumbing to his usual goldfish like attention span, George started looking for something else to amuse him until the cat, if indeed that's what it was, decided to put in an appearance. At the entrance of the house, there were the remains of what looked like a teddy bear. Its head had long ago been sheared off, and it was missing an arm and a leg, but it definitely had a certain soft toy quality to it. He decided to pick it up and investigate.

"NOOOO! *Don't pick up his teddy bear!*" Geri took aim with the hose in readiness for the furry death that was bound to come. The curious hand shot back from the teddy, as though it had just sat up and pulled a knife on him.

"BLOODY HELL GIRLS! *What's wrong with you two?*" Momentarily shocked, his heart beat hard in his chest, this was all getting a bit much. Distracted and disorientated by the outburst though, he failed to notice that in that spit second, suddenly he wasn't alone anymore.

Fred sat and calmly examined his guest with keen feline interest. This was new. Clearly the creature was too big to be lunch. It wouldn't fit in his bowl for one thing. It also still seemed to be alive, and was smiling nervously. How odd.

George sat perfectly still and said nothing, he barely breathed. Suddenly he understood everything. All the security and all paranoia *had* been justified. As a result of his own foolishness, he was shut in a cage with a small Siberian Tiger. Not that *small* was a word that anyone would associate with this creature. Keep still. *Keep very, very still.*

Fred stood up and frowned at the human. He stretched; content that this didn't seem to be yet another attempt to move him, and continued to scrutinize the new arrival. Moving forward slowly, placing one tea cup sized paw in front of another, he briefly sniffed the human's legs. Denim, he'd shredded this before.

Don't move your leg. Just keep very still.

Fred was impressed. The human had made no effort to engage him in meaningless conversation. There was none of that dreadful 'here puss' some of the others had tried on him, shortly before bleeding. Yet most importantly, he hadn't attempted to touch him yet. Maybe there was hope for this one?

Just keep still George, he'll come to you when he wants to, or maybe he'll just eat me?

Another curious sniff of the denim reminded Fred of what he was missing. Fresh smells, another world beyond his cage. A world that probably still contained terrified wildlife he could kill and eat. Maybe this creature would like it if he killed him something, a field mouse maybe, or perhaps a small deer?

Why's he's frowning at me?

It was time for a closer inspection. With infinite care, first one paw, then another, Fred climbed on the outstretched legs and slowly made his way up the trembling body. His huge bushy tail raised high in the air, twitching slightly, his massive furry ears rotating independently, like machine gun turrets seeking out bandits from above.

Bloody hell, this cat weighs a ton!

He continued to sniff the human periodically, all the while stalking his way up the semi-pliable flesh, pausing to keenly examine a new spot, before eventually coming to the right-angled chest. Fred decided to sit down. His eyes level with the human's.

Oh God, he's sitting on my Willy, and he's looking right at me!

Fred was content with his decision. He was a very clever cat, he'd seen his fellow inmates come and go, and he knew the score. In order to bust out of here, he needed a human pet of his very own to take him. This business of taking chunks out of them had been all well and good, but enough was enough. Frankly, if he had to be escorted out by one of these pink idiots, at least this one seemed vaguely bearable for now. His mind was made up. He would allow himself to be stroked by this human. In order to announce his decision, he would curl up on his lap and do the one thing he'd declared he would never do. He would purr.

Geri and Fiona looked at each other in utter disbelief. They slowly lowered their makeshift weapons, completely stunned by what was happening. This massive cat, this huge beast that'd terrorised each and every member of staff, this violent aggressor that managed to even scare the owner's German Shepherd, was curling up and purring, like a Harley Davidson ticking over. Busy nesting in the lap of the young man, he was even letting him gently stroke his head, without lashing out at the fingers.

"Err, *Mr B*, what's your first name, lover?"

"Umm, George. *Why?*"

"Are you sure, you sure it ain't *Daniel*, love?"

He pondered her question for a moment, and without thinking, briefly stopped stroking the massive cat on his lap. Fred had become rather accustomed to the hypnotic petting, and immediately looked up at his new human with a faintly threatening, disapproving glare. The stroking quickly resumed. "Err no, it's *definitely George.*"

"Oh, well that's okay Mr B. It's just, well *I* thought we had our very own *Daniel in the Lion's Den* for a moment there...!"

The journey home had been traumatic for both occupants of the bright red Toyota MR2. Fred had taken serious umbrage to being rather sneakily trapped in a thick cardboard box by his new human, and had become positively enraged when Geri had quickly sealed the lid. The last thing he saw of her before the lights went out was her ugly, mocking grin. Vengeance would eventually be his.

Given that the car lacked anything even faintly resembling practicality, George had no choice but to place Fred's box on the unmarked black leather passenger seat. Throughout the entire journey, it leapt and bounced about as though it was full of angry, drunken Goblins as its contents fought bitterly to escape.

The MR2 eventually pulled into its allocated parking spot just as a strong ginger paw finally punched its way through the cardboard. Partially free at last, it began clawing desperately at the edges, threatening the leather seat. George quickly jumped out, ran around to the passenger side, and heaved up the violently shaking box with all his might. The solitary paw meanwhile, sensing a change of circumstances, swivelled around looking for something to gorge, like a menacing submarine periscope.

Balancing the box on his trembling knee, George quickly entered the code for the communal entrance, failing twice, before bursting through it and across the hallway, finally reaching and unlocking his own door. He pushed it open with his back and stumbled in, accidentally tipping his new housemate's box over onto the laminate. It bounced twice and eventually skidded to a halt by the bathroom door. He scurried over to the upturned box. It was still bucking violently. At least he was still alive. Peering nervously down through the roughly clawed hole, the movement abruptly ceased. Staring back at him from the darkness within, glowing, golden eyes clearly enraged, the furry occupant looked decidedly pissed off.

"Fred, *are you okay…?*"

A few hours later, having consumed two freshly grilled chicken breasts, three cans of tuna, some scrambled eggs and four large saucers of delicious ice cold milk, Fred decided he would not, for the moment at least, kill his human pet. His new surroundings, which he'd subjected to a thorough and detailed sniffing, seemed reasonable enough. He certainly had a good deal more room to move about in, too. But what really intrigued him was what lay beyond the glass doors. Something small and furry out there was bound to have grown tired of life. He decided to sit by glass and meow loudly and endlessly, until the human got the message.

"*Aww*, come on Fred, if I let you out now, you're just gonna run away on me aren't you?" The howling intensified. "Do you promise you won't run away?" Abruptly, the meowing stopped and the huge Maine Coon looked pleadingly up at him. It was the very picture of feline honesty and devotion. "Oh, *okay then…*"

No sooner had the patio door been slid a mere nine inches open than Fred was gone. He squeezed through the gap that both instinct and his thick, wiry whiskers told him should be just wide enough, shot across the small courtyard, in-between the plant pots, and leapt over the four foot fence, and into the neighbouring garden like a scolded gazelle.

"*Oh shit!* Fred, *FRED*, come back. *I've got salmon!*" George was crestfallen. He'd been an impatient fool. He knew better than this; he should have waited for a few days before letting him out for the first time, and then he should've put butter on his paws.

"Err, hello there, I say?" The elderly voice, which seemed both frail and powerful in equal measure, came from the other side of the fence. George rushed across the patio and peered hopefully into next door. There, sat in a battered, steamer chair, nursing a small frosted glass of something yellow and possibly alcoholic, basking luxuriously in the last rays of afternoon sunshine, was the neighbour he'd yet to meet. And he was busy feeding custard creams to an enormous cat.

"Err, is this *your* Tiger, Sunshine?"

Chapter 15

Groin Lending

June.

George awoke slowly and blissfully in his beloved king sized bed, the morning sunshine streaming in through the angled slats of the white venetian blind, welcoming him into the day. He stretched his arms and legs under the impossibly soft, white duvet which smelt fresh and heavenly, and made a snow angel on his ruffled fitted sheet, relishing in the quality of his laundered bedding with half-conscious delight as it caressed his bare skin. Even though these days he had to make it himself, it was a small price to pay for bedded bliss.

The day before, he'd enjoyed his usual Sunday lunch at the Butlers' respectable semi, by now, he'd become something of an expert at extracting as much from his weekly visit as was humanly possible. And having finally accepted that his own abilities with his washing machine were somewhat limited, fresh bedding was top priority. The damn thing was more consumed with learning to salsa than it was cleaning his clothes, and he'd resigned himself to laundering nothing more exotic than socks and gym gear. His Mum, bless her, did the rest. Providing he arrived by eleven in the morning, not always easy considering his Saturday night exploits, a week's worth of washing could be cleaned and aired in the early summer's breeze, by the time he left again at five. With the weekly car wash and a mini service thrown into the trip, logistically, it worked a treat.

His mouth was parched. That would probably be the booze again. With a last generous flap of his angel wings, he reached over to his bedside table and downed the tumbler of water he'd the foresight to pour the night before, accidentally swallowing a drowning blue bottle in the process. At least he'd kicked off the day's protein intake.

Suddenly, he was aware that the radio alarm clock hadn't yet gone off yet. Where was 'Wake up to Wogan'? Why wasn't Terry easing him gently into the day as he did so every week day at seven-thirty sharp? (George was a Radio Two man and very proud of it. As far as he was concerned, Terry was a God.) Senses slowly recovering, he glanced at his Seiko. It was just after six a.m. That would be why then, but what had woken him so early?

He rolled out of bed and scrunched up his toes in the course bedroom carpet, a newly discovered method of self massage which seemed to get his blood moving a little quicker first thing. With his feet tingling slightly, he at last got up, and strolled out of the bedroom and into the small hallway, completely naked. It seemed that for all his years, without ever knowing it, he'd secretly been a bit of a closet nudist all along. Now that he had his own place, and a body that he wasn't scared to catch a glimpse of in a mirror once in a while, he positively loved to pad about in the buff, even if it did scare the Postman.

The shower was running. That must have been what woke him up. Apparently it had been one of *those* nights again, and therefore it was going to be one of *those* mornings. And on a school night too! It was time to boil the kettle, tea never failed to bring back his memory, and if he was lucky enough, usually before he had to remember the girl's name again. As he waited for the shiny, stainless steel kettle to boil in the kitchen, he wandered back into his bedroom to grab a pair of baggies and open the blind. Sat periously on the narrow windowsill, not at all amused at having been shut out of his home for the night, a small mouse that was either very dead or extremely calm, hanging from his large jaws, was Fred.

"Aww, now come on, you can't bring *that* in, we've got company this morning!" He pushed open the double glazed window and let the tiger in. Normally, he left it wide open all night, allowing him to come and go as he pleased, much to the alarm of every living creature within a five mile radius. But when he was entraining, he'd found it best to banish him for the evening. Nothing ruined a moment of passion like a dead rabbit.

"Now, come on Fred, *give it to me.*" George had become something of an expert in disengaging his fearsome cat from whatever poor, unsuspecting animal he'd murdered the night before. Where legions of cattery workers would've been savaged, he'd found that as long as the blood-soaked mass of dead fur was quickly replaced with milk and tuna, all seemed to be well between the two of them. It was a happy home.

The remains of the mouse were unceremoniously flung out of the bedroom window. Yet another short, private service would have to be conducted later. Knowing the drill, Fred quickly padded into the kitchen, huge fluffy paws beating the laminate flooring with all the rhythm of an excited bongo player, and sat patiently by the fridge, waiting for his breakfast. A steaming pot of tea was brewed, a whole tin of tuna lumped into a metal dog bowl; the recently purchased cat bowl just wasn't up to the job, and ice cold, full fat milk glugged generously into a dinner plate. A saucer full was never enough.

Conscience that the shower was still running, and that his memory was still refusing to get out bed, George dropped to the floor beside Fred, and quickly bashed out twenty slow press-ups. His reasons were twofold. Firstly, Dean told him to, and secondly, it gave his muscles a last minute pump before whoever was in the shower re-emerged, and could possibly be persuaded to engage in some pre-brekkie nookie. Planning was everything. Just as he got up off the floor though, the bathroom door opened and in that brief moment, the whole night came flooding back to him, in glorious Technicolor.

"Oh, you're up, *good!* Make me an espresso Darling. I see you've got a decent machine there." Natasha turned her naked, dripping wet back on him again, paused briefly, and looked over her tanned shoulder. "Actually, you've turned into a half decent machine yourself!"

Twenty minutes later, the three occupants of the apartment sat on shiny new bar stools in polite silence around the kitchen island. Despite her enviable ability to appear polished at all times, Natasha, who looked disapprovingly at her fresh espresso, needed only ten minutes or so to achieve visual perfection. Helped no end by flawless olive skin, which required little make-up, and hair that was simply too afraid to be anything but perfectly styled and chic at all times. She was wearing another new designer power suit, which was cut very close to her small, but purposeful frame, and finished in a striking black pin stripe. The skirt was short and tight, revealing slender, athletic legs, the jacket broadened slightly at the shoulder. With the killer black heels, the whole outfit screamed success.

George felt considerably underdressed. Sat in his brightly coloured baggies, sipping strong tea from one of his new, extremely oversized teacups, and sucking in the remains of his belly so that his virgin abs would appear tighter, he was also trying not to fret about his laminate flooring. So far this morning, his guest had managed to break both of the unbreakable rules the Developers had taken care to detail in the new owners welcome pack. *Don't let the laminate floor get too wet, and don't walk on it in high heels.* He was too scared to mention either.

"So, Darling, that was a great evening wasn't it? Tell me, do you remember *anything* yet?" She eventually relented and downed the suspicious looking puddle of coffee. Shuddered briefly, and quickly took a mint from her bag.

"*Err*, well, I, um, remember the Bear belting that chap who asked him why he had a girl's name, and, um, I sort of remember you arguing, err, *with Dean?*" He took another long sip of tea and flicked back through his most recent memory files, absentmindedly stroking Fred, who sat in his usual post-breakfast spot atop one of the barstools next to him, purring loudly, hoping for seconds.

"Oh yes, well, he needed to be told in *my* opinion. The man needs to either shut up or resign if he doesn't like the way things are going!" She slid gracefully off the stool and straightened her skirt. "I need to get home and change, it was a lovely evening George. *You're getting much better, you know.*"

"Oh! Err, umm, *thanks*!" He was lost, embarrassed and confused. She had that effect on him. In the weeks leading up the Bears sudden resignation, and impromptu Sunday evening bash, Natasha had continued to be distant, almost to the point of rudeness. Now though, things happily seemed to have taken a turn for the explicit again, even if it was at the cost of his new flooring.

Sensing that her young suitor was struggling to process events, she moved closer to him and put both her arms around his neck. A rare gesture once the passion had left her eyes.

"Now, listen to me Darling. Don't go reading too much into this, or letting that overactive imagination of yours get carried away. I look at sex just like *tennis*. It's nice to have a challenging game with a new player from time to time, but equally, sometimes, and particularly on a Sunday, it's nice to have a gentle knock about with someone familiar. And like I said, *your game's improving.*"

She kissed him lightly on both cheeks, fearlessly ruffled Fred's huge, furry head, and turned her back on both of them, leaving the pair looking dumfounded at each other, for entirely different reasons.

"Oh, and Darling, will you please get some decent coffee in for next time? One hundred percent Arabica, *okay*? *Ciao*!"

It had been a busy few weeks for George Butler. Aside from briefly rekindling his affair with Natasha, he'd been tending to his carefully concealed heartache by burying it under a mountain of new conquests. It had now been two months since he'd heard anything from Summer. But of course, he was fine with this. There was nothing wrong with him at all. He absolutely did not miss her notes or letters one bit. Not even for a minute, not ever.

Despite his Mum's very strong views on the subject, there was no way he intended to relent and call her. For the first time in their semi-quasi relationship, he felt that he was in the right for a change. In this, he at least took some comfort. He'd written twice without any response, after all. Rather than mope, he'd decided to continue to seek solace in alternative, equally friendly female company instead, and had hit the town like an atom bomb in a Lego village.

But here things had changed too. All of a sudden, Dean seemed to have grown tired of the whole nightclub scene, and had taken to spending a lot of time with Hayley. Recently, she'd called off her engagement with Jeff, no doubt upset and in need of comfort, the pair of friends seemed to favour quiet little restaurants, or nights at Dean's waterside home, instead of the neon bathed, heaving sweaty cattle markets. You couldn't really blame them. But without any warning, The Pretty People seemed to have suddenly vanished.

A few followers remained. Natasha and three or four others were often seen out together, sipping complimentary champagne in private booths. But for some reason, this new micro-group tended to alienate George, making his most recent conquest all the more puzzling. Fortunately though, he'd found a new group to attack the pubs and clubs with, although their methods were somewhat different from those he'd been used to.

Despite being thrown together like a band of ill-fitting mercenaries, all of whom had been unceremoniously discharged from the military, the Profile Branch Sales Team had quickly bonded, like careless Superglue to inexperienced fingers, and it was largely thanks to their skilful Manager. Internal squabbling was permitted, but only briefly, and then only if only relatively good natured. Blows should not be exchanged.

Although his CRAs technically competed against each other, Danny created a culture where all the other branches were the enemy, it was them that needed to be beaten, not each other. When they'd worked together before, he'd always kept Billy on a tight leash, and almost isolated him from, not only the other Sellers, but also anything even remotely resembling a league table, or figures that gave away his current position. If nothing else, at the end of the month, Billy's larger than expected bonus always came as a pleasant surprise.

Danny's method was simple, keep them all lean and hungry, make sure the Team gets along, and begrudgingly hand out some sort of praise at the end of each month. Then rinse and repeat. Before long, the Profile Branch sellers became as thick as financial thieves.

It probably helped matters that each Friday Danny was always up for a quick, cheeky pint after work, although this innocent drink usually descended into fully fledged, booze fuelled trawl through the cities pubs and clubs. Eventually concluding when either one of the group were cautioned by the Police, or guilt eventually bobbed to the surface, and he retreated home to his wife, a huge greasy kebab in one hand, and a bunch of wilting flowers from a twenty-four hour petrol station in the other. She was a very understanding wife.

During the intervening hours, the rag tag band of Bank employees did their absolute best to end up in either prison or hospital. Usually it was just the four of them, Danny would naturally lead the way, closely followed by Billy who struggled to keep up, Kenny who, being the oldest of the bunch at fifty-one, always looked slightly out of place in his corduroy trousers, and finally George. He was the group's ticket into the smarter clubs, having been granted access many times before in the days of The Pretty People.

Occasionally, if he was feeling brave enough, Ryan would venture out with the hooligans too. Still wearing his NSIB uniform, the harmonized Cottons NSIB version was still thankfully under review, complete with a drab tie, and a look of utter, and unwavering enthusiasm. The gang was quite a sight to behold as they staggered down Main Street.

As the Friday night sessions became a permanent fixture, the group organised themselves accordingly, with the men's toilets in the Profile Branch turning into a tarts boudoir from around four in the afternoon. Jeans and Ben Sherman Pulling Shirts were tugged onto bodies that really needed a cleansing shower, but instead were freshened up with great handfuls of aftershave and potent deodorants, with all the subtlety and finesse of a crop duster.

In was no secret that George had strayed a little from Dean's original Master Plan lately. He still trained regularly enough with his Mentor, and if anything, even harder than before, but the once carefully constructed, neatly polished image that had been created for him, was slowly coming away at the seams. To begin with, he'd let his hair grow back. Apart from a quick, all too necessary trim around the ears by his delighted Mum, so far he'd managed to avoid being kidnapped and scalped again. Although not as long as it had been a few months ago, at least it had some length again, and could at last be whipped back into the Elvis quiff he'd sadly missed.

He'd also taken to blending in with his new drinking partners. Wearing boot cut jeans rather than the modern, sharp tailored ones he'd worn before, only the slim fit designer shirts remained. With their figure hugging tailoring and darts running down the back, they showed off his rapidly developing physique to anyone who happened to notice. There was no way he'd turn his back on them. Unfortunately though, the rest of his new social group mocked him endlessly, asking him if his Mum minded that he borrowed her blouses for the evening. Bless them.

However, despite their good natured taunts, even they'd have to concede that George had turned into something of a successful philanderer of late. And to think, it had all begun with a seemingly innocent splodge of paint.

Aside from Summer, he'd rarely talked to girls about his artwork before, yet over the past few weeks, he'd made a truly startling discovery that soon change all that. Much to his surprise, he'd found that in the lurid wasteland of clubs and pubs, a lot of the smarter looking girls, those that looked faintly bored as their mates danced around their handbags in stratospheric heels, actually welcomed a decent chat over the din. As art was a relatively unexpected topic of conversation in this world, it also succeeded in creating something of an air of mystery about this dark stranger. If only he'd known before, the sixth form could have been so much more enjoyable. The rationale behind his new discovery was, as always, not entirely straight forward.

One Thursday evening after the gym, George finally finished Danny and Hannah's painting. Having stayed up into the small hours applying the finishing touches, he'd woken very late the following morning, just as Terry was attempting to make the eight o'clock pips. He'd quickly darted about his apartment, grabbing clothes for the usual Friday night drinking session, feeding his persistent tiger, and tying to flatten his wayward hair with great handfuls of wet look gel. The finished picture, which he'd been very pleased with, was propped against one of his barstools so that it wouldn't be forgotten, and it was whilst he dashed past the kitchen island, that he caught the corner of it with his boot, sending it skidding across the laminate floor.

Fortunately, the damage was minimal, nothing more than a small scruff across an expanse of beach, which could easily be touched up at lunchtime. He grabbed a few key tubes of acrylic paint, and a couple of horse hair brushes, briefly paused to reflect on just who had bought them, bundled up all his belongings and rushed out of the door to the waiting MR2.

Later that day, he'd drawn quite a crowd in the staff room as he carefully repaired the damage to the painting. Nobody from either banking heritage could recall a time when a member of staff had actually painted during office hours before. Judging by the mess he'd made of the walls and flooring though, it seemed unlikely anyone would ever forget.

Danny was uncharacteristically impressed and immediately took George out for a quick lunchtime pint to celebrate. It was whilst he was downing a well-earned Stella, talking animatedly about his work, that he'd noticed his hands and nails were speckled with yellow ochre paint. He made a mental note to scrub it all off before they hit the town later, and returned to his beer. The large splodge that had somehow managed to land on his left ear went undetected for now.

Much later that evening, the young, very beautiful blond that George had set his sights on was relieved to find that the orange mark on the rather charming young man's ear was in fact acrylic paint, and not, as she'd feared, some sort of horribly contagious skin disease. From there, conversation about art had naturally blossomed, drinks were shared, glances exchanged, and before long, a variant of that very old, well used cliché was dusted off and handed to George by whatever deity deals in these matters. '*So, do you want to come back to my place and look at my etchings?*' Yet remarkably enough, it worked, time and again. Although etchings were exchanged for paintings - he hated to etch.

The apartment's pristine white walls had been altogether too plain for their new owner. Having been convinced by his Mum that Star Wars posters didn't really work, George settled on the next best thing he had at his disposal, his A Level artwork.

In the open plan lounge/diner, he hung two of his Sixth Form pieces. A four foot canvas inspired by David Shepherd's *Wise Old Elephant*, with a moody sky, heavy with an impending storm, and also a brave attempt at copying *Tiger Fire*. Which at nearly five foot long, drew threatening glances from Fred whenever he passed by. Over his bed, he'd chosen to hang an original piece, painted for his final exam.

Wilber the Fearless Hunter had been an attempt to capture the true character of the Butler family's beloved, simple natured cat. The artist had also hoped to make people chuckle. The canvas depicted the extremely content moggy, fast asleep in a flowerbed, completely oblivious to the world. Perched immediately next to him, atop an upended flower pot, was a totally unafraid, relaxed blackbird. It was Wilber to a tee. Girls seemed to like this one the most, and it was merely coincidence that it just happened to be hanging in George's bedroom.

A string of recent commissions also meant that his multi-coloured, paint-splattered easel was permanently set up in the corner of the lounge, right by the patio doors, where the light was best. His long serving wooden stool, a few new claw marks scratched deeply into its battered legs, was positioned underneath it, a paint encrusted palette and a scattering of brushes and tubes carefully balanced on top. Whatever was underway at the time, be it another wretched pet portrait or, heaven forbid, an actual person portrait, was concealed from view by a well-worn, splattered denim shirt, and would remain so until it was finished, adding to the mystery.

It was the easel, which sat apart from the rest of his modern, sleek furniture, which had drawn the girl's attention that first night. By the time the wine was poured, a few candles lit to set the mood, and appropriate music inserted into the CD player, his work was done. It was only going to be a matter of time before he found out if, with this particular blond, words and figures differed.

After more than his fair share of one night stands though, nookie quota more than exceeding expectations, George finally decided to find a semi-permanent replacement for Summer. He missed the sweet romance and snuggles absent from his nocturnal activities, he wanted someone who'd stay for longer than it took for his bed to cool, or for the uncomfortable morning after coffee to be drunk. His search did not go well.

To begin with, there'd been Debbie, a curvy, red-haired secretary who was a couple of years older than him and full of life. Their wildly passionate, nine-day relationship, practically a marriage by comparison, had ended abruptly when, during a particularly spirited moment of passion, a pillow was accidentally kicked onto a flickering tea light and quickly burst into flames, threatening his beloved bed. Strangely enough, the hypochondriac fire alarm did not go off though, and it was only the extra illumination that alerted the two sweaty bodies to their predicament. Debbie had not been at all impressed to be doused with a bucket of cold water, and promptly left the apartment clutching her shoes and underwear, never to be seen again.

Next there was Paula 'Chattybath', a pleasant enough girl who shared George's interest in art, being a Design student at the local University. They'd met on one of Billy's new, and now habitual, Thursday night trawls through the city, enabling the boys to take full advantage of Student Night. It was fresh meat, literally. Their fledgling relationship fell short on three counts though. To begin with, she drove like a complete lunatic, looking at her passenger the whole time they conversed, rather than the road ahead. Presumably, the only reason she avoided fiery death each time she got behind a wheel, was thanks to some sort of subconscious sixth sense, or possibly a third eye hidden somewhere in her right ear.

Secondly, she lived in complete student squalor. George only visited her shared house once, but that had been enough. The bath alone looked as though a filthy mammoth had shaved and soaked itself in it for a month, hence, the nickname.

Marginally worse though, was her terrible circulation. The first night she'd stayed over, he'd quietly slipped out of bed in the early hours to tend to Fred. With a dead wood pigeon hanging from his jaws, he was banging its bloody remains on the window, presumably in protest at being exiled again. Having removed the feathery body from his tiger, once again replacing his quarry with tuna and milk, he returned to his bedroom only to find yet another dead body. The exposed foot that dangled from the bedding was a deathly, pale blue. Paula had clearly passed away in the night. Time stood still. Never in his entire life had he ever been so relieved to hear a girl fart.

Finally, and in complete defiance of Dean's golden rule, he'd also very briefly dated a Gym Bunny. But in fairness, it hadn't been entirely his fault, at least for those who subscribed to his new, interesting theory.

As far as George was concerned, even now, at this advanced stage in his physical development, all forms of cardiovascular exercise were pure evil. He'd grown rather fond of weight training, especially as his body developed, and even more especially when they worked out in front of one of the vast mirrors. He soon found there was nothing like the discovery of a new vein or muscular bump to spur on a weary limb. But when the dumbbells were put away, and the resistance machines wiped free of all his blood sweat and tears, for him that was when the real torture began.

Dean favoured treadmills. He could effortlessly pound away for hours if needs be, miles and miles of rubber belt whirring away under his gleaming white trainers. George, meanwhile, hated the damn things. To begin with, it had been weeks before he could even lightly jog without feeling as though he'd be flung off the end. He'd look on in marvelled bewilderment as the other members ploughed through the pain barrier, seemingly transfixed on either the large, suspended TVs, or lost in their own private Walkman cocoon.

Although his mentor didn't hold with any such distractions, choosing instead to stare fixatedly at a spot in the distance until it was all over, George decided he needed all the help he could get, and bought the loudest personal stereo he could find, re-recording Metallica's *The Black Album* in preparation for his inevitable slog.

The weeks passed painfully, and slowly at first, his fitness improved and his balance and co-ordination steadied. Although it was never going to be love, he learnt to accept cardio for what it was. Thirty minutes to an hour, depending on the day, of seemingly unrelenting misery that would make his muscles easier for girls to admire. It was worth it.

True to form though, once his body started to accept the horror of it all, he started letting his mind wander again, despite the roar of thrashing electric guitars in his ears. Even finding the energy to let his eyes evaluate the shapeliness of the Gym Bunny in the row ahead, or perhaps speculate about any that might be alongside. It was then that his theory started to take shape.

The treadmills were in two rows of eight. Dean tended to favour the front row, and he'd always isolate himself if possible, choosing one that was at least two machines distance from the next member. He'd never explained why, but had told his protégée not to take it personally, and that had been that. George meanwhile was less fussy. He couldn't care less where he sweated, as long as he survived. But he did start to notice something of a pattern emerging amongst the other runners.

Typically, if it were quiet, a member could discreetly choose a treadmill perhaps one or two away from the next runner, similar to choosing seats at the cinema. There was nothing rude about this; members were simply respecting each other's personal space whilst they were able. Early most evenings when it was busiest, this was never the case. However, if it was quiet, and a member was busy padding along in isolation, several machines free on either side, and yet another member chose to run alongside instead, surely that meant something else entirely?

Perhaps this meant they were attracted to this member, perhaps they hoped to share an empathic word during a rest period, or maybe a protein shake in the bar later? This was the essence of George's 'Treadmill Theory'. If there were other machines to choose from, but a girl chose to run next to you, *you were in*. And one very, very quiet evening at Diamond Fitness, Alison chose to run next to him for an hour. He very nearly died trying to keep up.

Ali, as she preferred to be called, wasn't quite a fully committed Gym Bunny though. Her ponytail wasn't quite severe enough; her Lycra outfits just didn't have the same spray-on, limpet like quality as the rest of the herd. She was, however, seriously fit. And as he found to his cost, ran like a racehorse for hours on end. Although utterly determined at the gym, she proved to be a gentle soul at heart. Of all of the girls he'd met, she reminded him the most of his long lost Summer. She was studying to be a primary school teacher, and in her spare time, helped out at a local centre for disabled children, as well as taking time to visit an old people's home at least twice a week, to read to the inmates. It was all very humbling.

With her perfectly toned figure, dark brown, bobbed hairstyle and wide apart, green eyes, she was perfect. And although it all seemed to be a bit quick in his opinion, and would play havoc with his laundry routine, after just a week of dating, George accepted an offer to join her for a family for Sunday lunch.

Disappointingly, up until to now all physical activity had been confined to extremely light petting. But this gave him cause to reflect on one of Billy's more insightful observations. Some girls, especially those whose tattoos are spelt correctly, occasionally take a week to ten days to get into bed. Or, as he tended to put it, the same length of time it takes for a credit card to be processed and arrive. He was an old romantic at heart.

As soon as he arrived at Ali's parents' house though, and the door was thrown open, he knew he was in trouble. A two-foot wooden crucifix, the first of many, hung in the hallway, looming ominously over him. Ali's parents, and as it soon became apparent, Ali herself, were deeply religious God fearing folk, and conversation had quickly turned to interrogation, as their guests own religious views were challenged.

Fearing that he might also end up nailed to a tree if he said, or did anything that might have been misconstrued as even faintly agnostic, he instead regaled the group with a tale from his primary school days. He'd been cast as Jesus in the annual Easter play, and, spurred on by his mischievous older brother, had brought the house down the first night by replying to the six-year-old peasant girl's offer of *'Would you like a date Jesus'*, with a genuinely misunderstood, *'Sure, I'm free next Tuesday!'* He wasn't asked to say Grace.

"I have to say, Sunshine, those cuttings that your Mum gave me are looking great. I think they'll be ready to go into pots soon." George handed the tray of piping hot bolognaise over the four foot fence to his spritely, eighty-seven year old neighbour and nodded with a knowing grin.

"Yeah, you can always rely on my Mum, Arthur. Now mind the plate my friend, *it's hot!*" One of his earliest childhood memories was of being out walking with Mum, and asked to stand guard, like an underage GI somewhere in occupied France, as she liberated a cutting from someone's garden. She'd then patiently explain to her puzzled youngest son that she wasn't stealing, it was simply spreading the beauty of the countryside. That's okay then.

"I don't mean to sound ungrateful, but hope this isn't like that curry you made last week. It played havoc with my knees, all that getting up and down to go to the toilet. *I'm an old man you know.*" Arthur took hold of the tray with hands that, despite his advancing years, were still as steady as a rock, and winked at his new best friend. "Good lad, you look after me well, Sunshine."

George had taken to experimenting with his cooking lately, even bravely trying to tame his old adversary, curry, with some interesting results. But the one thing he did still struggle with was the size of his portions. Being a Butler, it was naturally ingrained deep within him that when he cooked, he needed to feed the world. Or in his case, his new neighbour.

Arthur Hathaway had been retired and widowed for longer than his young neighbour had been alive. He was the last surviving member of his family, having long since buried both parents, who'd survived well into their eighties, even though they'd decided somewhere in their seventies that they really rather hated each other. His younger brother Reggie, despite being a veteran of countless dives during his career in the Royal Navy, had also sadly perished shortly after retirement. He'd been attempting to break the over sixties world free diving record in the Bahamas. To a degree at least, he succeeded.

Reggie had always been an eternal bachelor, the quintessential Peter Pan. All he'd left behind as evidence that he'd ever existed, was an old cardboard box full of medals, an impressive collection of scuba diving masks, and an immaculate Royal Navy issue, Omega Seamaster 300. Arthur often reflected on the day he'd spent picking through the remains of his siblings life. The watch had been recovered and sent back to the UK, along with an outstanding tab from a shady seaside bar, and a crumpled napkin on which some besotted island girl, having fallen prey to the old boy's charms, had excitedly scribbled her number in thick red lipstick.

Arthur chose not to call her and explain, but instead had carefully picked up the watch, wiped the dry crust of sea salt off the threaded canvas strap, washed its case under the cold tap, and put it on. These days it never experienced anything more aquatically perilous than a heavy winter's downpour, but at least it was still loved.

In contrast to his adventurous, well-travelled brother, Arthur had devoted his own life to education, and to his beloved wife Rose. He'd eventually become Headmaster of a small private primary school, and spent the last ten years of his career, dividing his time between teaching English and PE to those who would listen, organising fetes and sports days, and occasionally dabbling in minor accountancy fraud in order to balance the books, and keep the ever decreasing budget on track.

When he finally retired, he'd naturally assumed the he and Rose would fulfil their long held dream of buying a ramshackle old cottage in the country. Sadly however, in the space of just a week, the ink still wet on his final salary cheque, she promptly packed her bags and announced that she was leaving him for a coach driver, eleven years her junior. It was whilst she was crossing the road outside their marital home, carrying two large suitcases bulging with clothes and years of hidden love letters, that she was run over and instantly killed by a double-decker bus. The number fifty-four to be precise, which was just beginning its afternoon school run.

Arthur had been overwhelmed with feelings of loss and betrayal, utterly confused about all the years they'd spent together, with her living a lie. Through his desperate sadness and despair though, and despite all the questions which would never be answered, in a brief moment of mournful reflection, he considered that if God did exist, he not without a sense of irony.

With his world lying in tatters around his fraying carpet slippers, and no family left to console him, Arthur decided it was time to change his stars. He sold up, put his vast collection of books, Johnny Cash LPs and other, less cherished belongings into storage, bought a modest mobile home and spent the next fifteen years on the road, searching for nothing, but looking for everything. He'd decided that a life spent reading obituaries, wondering when his own name would appear, just wasn't for him. He felt certain that he'd be much happier lost in new, beautiful places than he would be alone, in beige familiarity. As he'd put it at the time to his few bewildered friends, he intended to Properly Bugger Off.

To begin with, he toured the English coastline. Once he'd arrived at a spot he was quite sure he'd seen before, content that he'd completed a full lap; he headed for the ferry port and to France. He lazily motored down to Bordeaux, where he lingered for an unhealthy length of time to sample the wine, before eventually crossing the Pyrenees into Spain, and heading for Barcelona. After a few weeks in the sun, trying to avoid the football, he crossed the width of the country to Portugal, up past Porto, picking up several cases of fine Port along the way, before settling in the North for a while. Here he sipped iced cold Vinho Verde of an evening, and planned the next leg of his journey.

Eventually he left Portugal, drove clear across Spain, back over the Pyrenees, across to the South of France and into Monaco, just in time for the Grand Prix. From here it was a short jaunt into Italy where he decided to rest for nearly a year, in the small town of Limone, on the shores of Lake Garda. Enjoying the limoncello and warming his old bones in the sun.

This, he concluded, was definitely his favourite spot so far, it was time to put his bare feet up. For the first time since his sadness, he sat on a small deckchair by his motor home, looking out over the lake, and breathed a heartfelt sigh of relief. At last, he'd found some solace.

Arthur spent years touring Italy. He saw some wonderful sights, and experienced a life he never thought possible beyond the stuffy walls of his old classroom. He met an array of fascinating, colourful people who welcomed him into their lives as a long lost friend. There were even a few sultry lovers along the way, and nights of passion he'd hold dear until his memory failed him. He picked up the language as best he could, and enjoyed a retirement that his dear departed wife would never have approved of, adulterous old bag that she was.

Sadly though, on his seventy-ninth birthday, after far too much celebratory grappa with more dear Italians, he slipped and fell down a flight of steps in Sorrento, breaking both his hips in two places. Undeterred, he drove back to the UK, having only begrudgingly received scant medical attention, and stoned out of his head on painkillers and the remains of the Port. Once home, he finally relented and went to see his doctor, who promptly packed him off to hospital where both his battered hips were eventually replaced, and the last of his limoncello confiscated.

His epic journey had taken quite a toll on his health, and an even bigger toll on his bank balance. But he didn't care a jot. He'd enjoyed every second of his travels, and happily sold his worn out mobile home, gathered together the remains of his savings, and bought a minuscule cottage in the village he'd always intended to retire too, some fifteen years earlier. Once settled, and with his mobility never fully recovering from his fall, Arthur began looking for new, interesting hobbies to keep his mind active, and the Devil at bay.

Much to the delight of the villagers, he started dabbling in the production of alcohol from his tiny kitchen, brewing everything from mild dandelion wine to faintly toxic vodka, which caused at least on case of temporary blindness. He also used it to make his beloved limoncello. Everyone was happy for a while, except the landlord of the local pub, and six months ago, when Arthurs Still spectacularly exploded, destroying his cottage, the local community sifted through the rubble for hours, desperately trying to unearth the buried eighty-six year old.

One carefully considered insurance claim later, and following another brief spell in hospital to mend his broken arm and dislocated shoulder, he found himself on the housing market once more. It was probably time he concluded, to move somewhere on level ground, that was easy to maintain, had no steps, and perhaps most importantly, was in close proximity to an emergency ward.

"*Ah*, you just can't beat a glass of chilled limoncello after a decent meal, can you?" The old man sat back in his steamer chair, warming his craggy, lined features in the last of the evening sun. "Sometimes, you've got to remember to enjoy your blessings." Despite his age, Arthur just didn't look that old. Walnut coloured skin covered a handsome, deeply lined face, his hair style was borrowed from Picasso, and he wore a neatly trimmed white beard, which sat pleasing against the permanently tanned face. He could easily have passed for a sixty-five year old sailor, who still refused to come ashore.

Regardless of the injuries he'd sustained over the years, his body was strong and reasonably capable, his grip was like iron. Unlike every other old person his young neighbour had ever encountered, he tended to favour comfortable, baggy old chinos and brightly coloured linen shirts he'd picked up on his travels, rather than beige cardigans and cords. He only ever fastened the bare minimum of buttons required to prevent his shirt from falling open, instead, proudly allowing his wide brown chest a full view of the world, giving its healthy covering of course curly hair, as white as fresh fallen snow, an opportunity to sway in the breeze. He never wore shoes, and seemed to have nothing but utter contempt for socks.

"You know, I used to really enjoy making my own vodka to put in this stuff. *Oh*, that was before the explosion of course. I have to make do with shop bought stuff now. Do you know it's usually only about thirty-seven percent proof? *Dreadful, dreadful...*" He trailed off again, as was his habit, swilling the large glass of yellow liquid around in the thick tumbler before downing it in one swallow. "Still, at least I can remember how to make the bloody stuff, most people my age can't remember where they live. *Ha!*" He hobbled back inside to refill their glasses, leaving George to lean on their dividing fence. He was completely chilled and relaxed. His new neighbour was great company.

In a very short space of time, they'd adopted each other, as Granddad and Grandson respectively. Sadly, George's own Grandparents had died when he was very young. He'd never known what it was like to have another generation of family to torment. Arthur, meanwhile, had been too busy teaching other people's children to ever get around to breeding any of his own. Now though, all alone in the world, he discovered he rather liked the company, and at least some of the increasingly ambitious meals.

"So, even with my terrible hearing, that last girl you had around seemed to enjoy herself. Is this one staying for a while?" Arthur had a way with words not normally associated with the elderly. It had taken some getting used to.

"Oh, that was *Natasha*. No, apparently she seems to think of me as some sort of tennis partner, or something..." George gratefully took a second, generous glass of limoncello, finishing the first, and balancing it on the top of the fence, whilst Arthur creaked into position on his steamer chair.

"*Oh*, do you play tennis then?"

"*Err*, no, not really…"

As if by magic, without a word of discussion, they'd fallen into a mutually beneficial evening routine, which suited them both down to the ground. George would return home from the gym around seven. He'd release Fred from his most recent kill, feed him socially acceptable cat food, and jump in the shower ready to join Arthur for a quick aperitif over the fence by seven-thirty, just as the sun was going down behind the distant tree line.

In the kitchen, something would be either bubbling away on the younger man's hob, or roasting in the oven ready for supper at eight. This would then either be taken around, so that they could eat together at the large oak table, which dominated the older man's apartment (like many old people forced to downsize, the remains of his furniture overwhelmed his small home), or if either of them had a date, would simply be passed over the fence. The old man didn't seem to date much these days though. George made the meals. Arthur made the booze, perfect.

"Do you know what I think is wrong with you, Sunshine?"

"I'm too damn handsome for my own good?" The young, fresh face grinned back mischievously.

"No, no, *definitely not*. What's wrong with you, my young friend, is that you've already met the right girl, and you let her go. Now you're regretting it, and trying to fill up your life with empty sex instead." He paused briefly to let Fred jump up on his lap, winced until he eventually settled and began purring loudly. "Where was I again? *Oh yes*! Although I imagine this is great fun, from what I remember, it doesn't really make you feel any better. *Am I right?*" The old man leant back in his chair, tickling the tiger absentmindedly. He wore a good natured look of smug satisfaction on his weathered face. As a retired school teacher, he still relished being right occasionally.

"I *really* do wish that I hadn't told you about Summer, Arthur…"

"No, *no you don't Sunshine*, you can't keep anything from me, that's why you confess your sins each week! You just remember what I said the other evening, at the end of the day it gets dark, and all cats are grey in the dark, except that is, for the bugger that can reach the light switch! Now, *what's on the menu tomorrow?*"

"They want us to do what, Duck?" Billy sat perched on the edge of the staff room desk, munching a large bar of Dairy milk chocolate. It was just past nine in the morning, the desk bowed slightly, and he looked faintly puzzled.

"They want us to start predicting what we're going to sell at the start of each day, Chief. Says it right here on the briefing, don't worry about it Billy, I'll just put up the Crap Umbrella like I always do and hope the shit bounces off." Danny took another mouthful of strong coffee from his enormous mug, and read through the head office document once more. "This bit makes me laugh, Chief: *the Bank has made a conscious decision to go ahead with this structure...* What the hell would an unconscious decision have been - *a bloody dream?*"

Billy choked briefly, spat half chewed chocolate down his tie, cursed and ran to the kitchen sink to clean it off, just as George sauntered into the room to make his second cup of tea in five minutes. "Everything alright boys?" He patted Billy on the back as he brought up the last of the chocolate squares.

"*Chief*, you're gonna have to start making up stories each morning, shouldn't be too much of a stretch for you, just carry on doing what you've been doing. You know, just like when you stroll in late."

"Danny I swear to you, *I was mugged by a gang of field mice the other day!*"

After spending an inordinate amount of time arguing like a group of five-year-olds, struggling to agree what they should build with a fresh box of Lego, Cottons NSIB Top Management had at last finished designing the Banks new structure. Everyone was relived. A suitably ruthless, oily Chief Executive Officer was elected by his peers, and from there down, a whole army of unnecessary, hugely overpaid hangers on could be traced down to the Cleaner.

In an effort to give them something to do in-between lunches, Top Management was tasked with rolling out 'Sales Delivery', a massively detailed approach to gathering sales data at Branch and Area level in every location. Vast wall charts were dispatched, along with a good supply of non-permanent marker pens. These charts needed to be placed in a prominent position in the back office, so that the data could be viewed by each member of staff, at any given time. Top Management lived blissfully happily under the assumption that staff wanted to know if the branch was ahead, behind or just on track for any individual target. It was probably best nobody told them otherwise.

There were six main white boards in total. One collected the daily sales data, another was a weekly summery, there was a monthly summery, a chart detailing average footfall, a customer referral board for the cashiers and enquiries staff, and finally, what would inevitably be a seldom used, CRA self-made appointment summary.

Once collated, this information was to be hand written onto miniature versions and faxed off to Area office daily, weekly and monthly as dictated. There, it would finally be written once more, onto another, larger wall chart, in a vast room that contained identical charts for each Branch within the Area. The Area Director would then critically scrutinize the information, compare the Branches output, and bestow his judgment on to one on his many assistants, who'd feedback accordingly on his behalf. It all amounted to a lot of non-permanent ink and hot air, and far less information was recorded the first time a man was put on the moon.

In the Profile Branch, things were going to be very different though. Danny had his own method of accurately tracking exactly what his Branch was doing, and he had no intention of changing it now. Far from complex, it involved nothing more complicated that a battered notebook containing his targets and a stubby, well chewed HB pencil which seemed to be immortal. No one was allowed to look in his little book, which was rumoured to contain a naked photograph of Hannah, and, up until now at least, it was all he ever needed to ensure that he and his team finished first.

In order to appear willing though, and just in case they had any unannounced, surprise visits from the new Area Director, once one was appointed, he'd populated the majority of the charts with impressive, fictional numbers, proving his Branch to be both enormously efficient and incredibly successful. Everything would be just fine, as long as nobody visited twice.

As well as the exhaustive data capture, Top Management also devised a new league table for both the CRA, and Senior CRA population. In the past, Cottons version of this had been no more than a gentle list of names. It allowed those staff who could be bothered, to see what the rest of the country was up too in comparison. And, although there was absolutely no expectation here at all, maybe lift the phone to a particularly successful colleague, if they wanted to ask any advice. It was all very civilised and non-threatening.

The NSIB league table though, from which Top Management had naturally drawn inspiration, was completely different. NSIB Sellers were awarded additional bonuses if they finished in the top ten percent. The league table was a vital tool therefore, to understanding just how close an individual was to achieving an extra payout, and perhaps more importantly, identifying just who was preventing them from earning it. The employment of professional assassins to remove the threat from above was not beyond the realms of possibility. It all simply boiled down the amount of bonus achieved, net of the hit.

When the revised Cottons NSIB league table was eventually published, it contained four weeks' worth of historic data to give the CRA's a starting point. Eyes were naturally drawn to individual positions; however, George, who was pleased to be in the top twenty-five percent, couldn't help notice two other colleagues' rankings. Natasha, who was near the top nationally, and Dean, who was heading south like a bandit fleeing for the border.

All of a sudden, it seemed that to be successful in banking, an effective employee was not, ironically enough, a good banker at all, but instead an efficient, manipulative seller.

"*Bloody word patterns*, load of old crap if you ask me, Duck!" Billy leaned back, wiggling his not unsubstantial bottom until he was settled. The large leather sofa creaking in protest at the unrelenting force from above. "I mean, we always used to have this type of old tosh in the NSIB, but we never paid it any bloody attention, its total, and utter *crap*, in my opinion!"

The word pattern briefing had arrived earlier that day, when Danny, who normally shielded his staff from the majority of the 'Propaganda from the Top', was out on an unofficial, and completely deniable fag break, leaving Billy free to open and digest its contents with disgust.

Cottons NSIB had recently refined and developed their original arsenal of interview questions, clearly seeking to further hone the CRA's interrogation skills, leaving some to wonder if they'd employed a veteran torturer as a consultant. They now included a whole range of new questions for both cashiers and enquiries clerks to deploy as well. Very soon even the Cleaner would be issued with a sales target.

Danny remained reflective though. His CRA was right, they'd been here before, and then it had been paid a polite amount of non-committal lip service by the sales force. Given that the targets, stretching as they were, were still achieved, the revolutionary sales processes of the day had eventually been abandoned, just like every other bright idea to come out of NSIB Head Office. His only real concern this time was that the new Cottons NSIB Top Management seemed to actually mean it every word of it. This could well mean trouble.

"Eh, *Butler*, you know what we should do for a laugh, Duck, we should make up our own bloody word patterns." George was returning from the bar with their drinks. Having gained access to the Nightclub's VIP lounge, the group was enjoying an entirely new level of comfort and luxury, thankfully shielded from the rest of the throbbing masses by a thick layer of soundproof double glazing. The music was funky, but not overwhelming -

Morcheeba according to Billy, and the service, excellent. They didn't really belong here, but they didn't really care.

He passed out the frosty bottles of Bud, and sat down in the luxurious club chair next to Kenny. In the lavish surroundings, he looked even more nervous than usual. "What's that Bill?"

"*Word patterns*, we should make up our own, you know, like just sign here for further information, Love, or, this is great this is, *I tell you what, its saying you can't have the loan, unless you take the Protection, you're too high a risk, okay?*"

"Easy there *Chief*, I am sat right here you know." Danny, crushing his beer bottle in his shovel sized hand, so tightly it caused undetected hair pin factures to form under the label, turned his steely gaze threateningly on his bulbous employee. Count to ten, just count to ten, like Hannah said. One, two...

"Oh alright there *Yul Brynner*, calm down, Duck! That vein in your forehead will pop out one of these days. *I was only joking!*" Billy downed half of his beer, and wiped his rubbery lips with his shirt sleeve. He kept a watchful eye on his Branch Manager, just in case he took a swing at him, as he was prone to on occasion. "*Hey*, I tell you what, let's have some *chat up* word patterns instead then."

George hadn't joined the others in their choice of beer. Instead he sat sipping his usual, relatively weight conscious vodka and slim line tonic. Calories tended to sneak up on him when least expected. He picked up his ears, always eager to expand his skills when it came to ensnaring the ladies. "You mean chat up lines?"

"Aye, like when a girl says to me *I'd eat you for breakfast love*, I always say, *no you won't Duck, I'm far too big and in any case, I'd be in McDonalds by the time you woke up!*" The four drinkers chuckled, the mood relaxing once more.

Miranda, the manageress of the Nightclub's VIP lounge, sauntered towards to the shabby group, no more than a pleasingly shapely silhouette against the low key neon. "Is everything alright here gentlemen? Is there anything else I can get for you, some canapés or a complimentary bottle of champagne perhaps?" She was a tall, very elegant blond, somewhere in her late twenties. Although not classically beautiful, something about the way she carried herself caused men to melt. And just two days earlier, she'd successfully reduced George Butler to a puddle on his interview room floor.

Billy, a graduate with distinction from the 'University of Lecher & Gawp', invented 'Totty Alert', *patent pending*, almost as soon as Cottons NSIB installed the impressive, technically advanced computer system into their branches. One of the many useful functions now available to staff was an internal messaging system. Originally intended to make sales referrals easier, it allowed colleagues to send a message around the branch, which would then appear on every single screen, and could enable a cashier to call for a CRA to see a customer referral. Billy, though, used it to tell George when there was a bit of Totty in the banking hall, and Miranda's presence had been detected the moment her stilettos had stepped over the threshold.

Danny had to flip a coin to decide which of his hormonally unbalanced lenders would provide her with the funding loan she badly needed. She'd racked up a level of debt comparable to that of a third world country. It was really rather impressive. George won, much to Billy's consternation, his pleading calls for best of three, sadly ignored. As his colleague led the sultry goddess into his interview room, he grinned smugly over his shoulder, although he soon came to regret this passing shot.

Ever the sore loser, Billy wrote a torrent of endlessly crude messages, all of which flashed up on the screen in his rival's office. Thankfully, they abruptly stopped when Danny found Billy and locked him in the safe. He was starting to think he was running some sort of mental institution for the sexually deranged. Still, it was better than banking.

Loans processed on the new systems were either accepted, referred, or were declined. A CRA had discretion to override refer codes up to ten thousand pounds, but no ability to overturn declines. Instead they needed to present a strong case to the Manager as to why they felt that the lending, however marginal, was appropriate. Given that the Managers had sales targets to achieve, and that lending and payment protection insurance earned them the most sales credits, unbiased sanctioning was a rare thing. Also, if the Manager in question was single, and the desperate customer attractive enough, a degree of 'Groin Lending' could be blamed for some truly questionable overrides.

Danny wasn't single, but George was, the book having firmly been closed on this topic, and he'd pleaded like a child in a sweetshop for his Manager to override Miranda's declined loan. There was a very long list of adverse information codes to consider, but there was also the matter of the daily sales charts. It was Wednesday. This loan, if agreed with protection, would mean they'd hit the branch's weekly sales target. Anything else they generated would be a bonus, literally. Perhaps more importantly though, she was the Manageress of a VIP lounge at a popular local Nightclub the group often failed to get into. What to do...?

"Gentlemen, we have assorted canapés, the smoked salmon crostini is particularly excellent, try not to let *him* have it all." Miranda looked down her nose at the slovenly, obese member of the group, who kept gawping at her legs and licking his grotesque lips. "And of course your champagne. I'll put another bottle on ice for when you're ready." She poured them each a delicious flute of Taittinger. Placed the remains of the bottle back into the silver bucket, where it crunched amongst the perfect cubes of ice, and sauntered off back towards the bar, gently brushing past the young man who'd solved all her financial woes, as she did so.

"*I've got it!*" George downed his flute in excitement. "*I've got my word pattern!*"

"Go on then Duck, *let's have it.*"

"*Ahem*, I know you want me, but it's probably best we don't get together. *I'd only end up ruining you for normal men!*"

As it turned out, Miranda wasn't ruined for normal men at all. She did, however, spend the rest of the weekend wondering if the large cat that lived with her young lover was going to eat her whilst she slept. Thankfully he didn't; he preferred brunettes.

"*Oh no Fred*, not a bloody budgie! *That's someone's pet!*" The enormous cat sat insolently on the small patio. Clutched tightly in his jaws was the bright yellow remains of a once treasured bird. He dared his human to just try and disentangle him from this victim. For some reason, he was rather taken with its playful colour. "Come on now, give it to me…" The tiger stood up and backed away, swishing his tail threateningly.

Suddenly the budgie lifted its small head and twitched into life, with a look of bewildered panic, it somehow managed to free a sodden wing and fluttered hopelessly, bravely fighting for its life. "Oh hell! *It's alive! Arthur! ARTHUR? We've got a live one!*"

Since arriving in the pleasant little cul-de-sac, Fred had thoroughly explored his new territory, methodically examined its indigenous population, and systematically begun murdering as many of them as possible, carefully bringing home each bloody body to share with his human pet. He felt quite certain he'd appreciate the gesture.

The killing sprees were relentless. Like a popular village churchyard, burial space amongst the potted plants was quickly running out, and very soon George would need to start burying the bodies under the small patio instead. As well as the dead rabbit, which had been unfortunately heaved onto his human's bed mid-nookie, Fred had also succeeded in decimating an entire colony of field mice, a stealthy murder of a couple of surprised grey squirrels, a quick and clean assault on a careless magpie, and the rather drawn out, unpleasant assassination of a large brown toad. That had been a messy one.

Despite his bloody safari though, the tiger had become increasingly frustrated by his failed attempts to bring down a winged mouse that had been circling the patio for nights on end. It tormented and teased him, taking tantalisingly low swoops just out of claw reach. The bat had become a regular evening visitor to the housing estate. Just as the sun set, it would emerge through the failing light, like a tiny, out of control jet fighter, beginning its own hunt, feasting on the small insects that buzzed around the gardens.

Fred had been monitoring its movements for several evenings. He felt certain he could catch the curious furry projectile, if only he could somehow get above it. On the fourth evening, he decided to climb atop the six foot pricey fence panel, which divided his human pet's domain from that of the old man with the biscuits, and waited for the optimum moment to strike. This time there'd be no escape.

Unfortunately, he'd rather underestimated the speed and stealth of his quarry. By the time he was mid leap, the bat had performed a string of impressive manoeuvres, whizzed through the open patio doors, and into the lounge, just as George was returning to the garden with a large glass of merlot. Once the initial shock of their unexpected collision had passed, the pair stood in silence in the doorway, mesmerized as their new house guest did high speed laps around the living room, somehow narrowly avoiding anything breakable.

George was no stranger to bats. When he was much younger, his Dad had often taken him on long evening walks with Eddie, the family Jack Russell, and as they rambled across the countryside, conversation often turned to the natural world, especially as the light faded and a great deal of it suddenly woke up. Being a fearful soul, thanks to watching far too many scary films through the gap in Michael's bedroom door, to begin with, George had been completely terrified of bats.

During their long walks, as father and son strolled up what they would eventually christen 'Bat Alley', Eddie would disappear in and out of the shadows looking for fresh smells, as the nervous ten-year-old scoured the heavens for the winged devils, his head darting about like a spitfire pilot hunting for Jerry. Tired of his youngest son's phobia, and of being nagged by his wife for causing him to have disturbing nightmares, which he then felt compelled to retell in graphic detail over breakfast each morning, his Dad decided it was time the quash his fears for good. He'd show him how to play with the bats instead, that should do the trick.

With infinite patience, he explained that by tossing a very small piece of bark or twig into the air, the passing bat would swoop quickly down towards the object, before their sophisticated internal sonar identified that this was not supper, and they pulled out of the steep dive to begin their hunt for insects once more. Being easily distracted, George soon forgot all references to Dracula, and instead, started tormenting his Dad each evening, until he eventually relented and took him back to 'Bat Alley' to play with his new found friends. Still, it was better than being nagged.

As it turned out, brown rice worked just as well as fallen tree bark, and the apartment's resident bat was soon tricked into flying back out through the patio doors, into the still night air, with Fred still hot in pursuit.

"Do you think he'll be okay Arthur, do you think he'll, well, you know, *make it home*?" George held out the tattered bundle of yellow feathers for his eighty-seven year old neighbour to examine. Fred had eventually been distracted by a large, raw slice of sirloin steak he'd been saving for a hot date that Saturday. Distraction was starting to get expensive.

"Back home Sunshine? what, you mean *to Australia*?" Arthur rested one of his brown, leathery hands on the four foot fence panel, and gently stroked the small quivering head. Just like the evening sunshine, it was clearly fading with every passing second. He looked into the watery eyes of his adoptive Grandson. "I'm afraid he's a goner old Chap." The old man placed a reassuring hand on his shoulder. "Listen to me Sunshine, sometimes with animals, it's much kinder if you can help them into the next room. Now, give me the poor little soul and go and pour us both some of that wine. I'll take care of him…"

Hours later, the memory of the budgies unfortunate passing dulled somewhat by an unhealthy quantity of mid-week wine, limoncello, and a second play of Bob Marley, the two neighbours, still outside enjoying the warm night, were doing their best to avoid the subject altogether.

"I've never really grasped what it is you actually do, Sunshine. Are you some sort of Bank Manager then?" Arthur passed yet another thick tumbler of yellow homebrew to his neighbour, who still propped up the fence, and carefully lowered himself back into his steamer chair, echoing its creaks with his own failing joints.

"Well, no not really, *although* that's what I tell all the girls I do. I guess I just sell bank stuff really, you know, like loans, credit cards, that sort of thing, oh, and insurance, they do like it if we sell insurance." He took a deep pull of limoncello and picked an errant slice of lemon rind from his teeth. It only served to add to the drinks distinctive flavour.

"So you're sort of an insurance salesman then? You seem a bit young for all that nonsense."

"Oh no, no, we've got one of them as well, a guy called Kenny, *but he's always broke*! No, I just have to sell a few bits of insurance, you know, like loan protection, that sort of thing. I don't understand what all the fuss is about really, they sort of tie in sales credits with the things you sell. Insurance earns you a lot of credits and increases your bonus each month, that's *always* a good thing! He drained his glass and balanced it on the top of the fence until his neighbour, falling behind for once, caught up with his drinking.

"Sunshine, why on earth are you doing this for a living? I thought you were some sort of artist."

"Painting doesn't pay as well, though."

"But what makes you happier?"

George paused for a moment. *Happier.* He'd never actually given this any consideration before, and especially not in the past few weeks. He'd been far too busy spending money, and entertaining girls in an effort to forget Summer to give any thought to anything else. Particularly now that, as much as it pained him to say, he was finally a proper adult. He had a mortgage and everything. But the old man did have a point. "Um, well, *painting,* I guess…"

"*Paint then*, you silly sod! Don't waste your life making money for an ungrateful employer, Sunshine. I never followed this path myself, *much to my regret*, but I gather that some of the happiest people in the world are those who chose to paddle their own canoe." Arthur got unsteadily to his feet and collected their tumblers together. "In the meantime though, shall we have another while we plan your future…?"

The following Sunday, George sat on the edge of his old single bed. He'd arrived in good time. Lately, his Mum had taken to threatening domestic industrial action if he didn't get home at a reasonable hour. Unless the washing was on in time to be finished before lunch, it wasn't going on at all. This wasn't really aimed at his timekeeping though. It was a demonstration against his relentless philandering. She'd much rather he'd just call Summer and fix whatever damage he'd done, rather than waste his time with all these loose women. Often, she'd warn her youngest that 'it would drop off' if he wasn't careful, and that his Dad would soon need to scrub him down with Swafega and a wire brush, before she'd let him in the house. Dirty little sod.

In reality though, both Butler brothers could've returned home looking sheepish, eventually admitting that they'd accidentally got mixed up in a bit of harmless genocide, only to be given a stern ticking off, a hearty slice of homemade fruitcake and a steaming mug of tea, providing they promised never to do it again, and if they agreed to write a brief letter of apology to all those concerned.

The bedroom had once been his most favourite place in the world, his own private sanctuary, a place where dreams had been made, forgotten and replaced. Nothing lasts forever though. And as he did his best to absorb the dramatic change in décor that surrounded him, he also tried to process new, upsetting news that, like the smell of breakfast kippers, wasn't going away anytime soon. He couldn't recall being this upset since the first time he'd seen *Watership Down*.

And it didn't help matters that his bedroom clearly wasn't *his* bedroom anymore. No sooner had the last of his belongings been packed up, and either moved to his new apartment or exiled to the loft, than Mr Butler senior had invaded, occupied and claimed the space for himself. When Michael left home to join the Army, and following a brief spell of parental adjustment, his wife had quickly transformed his bedroom into a lavish, soft pink sewing room whilst her husband was distracted by the cricket. This time he wasn't taking any chances.

Only the *Airfix* models remained. Still silently frozen in battle, the lengths of white cotton that suspended them from the Artex ceiling were still unique in being the only part of the house that was ever able to gather dust. Gone was his treasured collection of empty guitar string packets, and the drunkenly peeled labels from endless bottles of Newcastle Brown Ale and Budweiser, precious relics from nights on the town with Barney, carefully pinned to the wall over his white melamine desk. Gone too, was the desk, along with the overloaded bookshelves laden with *Beanos* and the rest of his beloved, battered bedroom furniture too.

In its place were tall, slightly foreboding oak bookcases containing equally tall and foreboding books. A matching spotless desk, the latest copy of Classic Motorcycling Legends resting on its polished surface, a few small framed pictures of treasured motorbikes, and a scattering of components from the ancient grandfather clock his Dad had been restoring for just over eleven years, even though there was no way his wife would ever allow it in the house again. But this was far from the worst of it.

Michael's letter and been brief, hastily scribbled on a 'Bluey' that no doubt rested on a trembling knee. George had never seen nervous looking handwriting before. His older brother's penmanship clearly looked as though he'd sooner be writing a postcard from holiday, a chilled bottle of San Miguel in hand perhaps, the beginnings of a worrying, well-earned itch, somewhere in his boxer shorts, rather than from a bleak military base in an undisclosed, threatening location.

It seemed that Michael had been promoted. But in this case, it wasn't necessarily good news. Something about his new position meant he wouldn't be able to write, or call for a while, and that he might not be able to send his younger brother a birthday card, until he was back from wherever it was he was going. Wherever it was, he didn't, or couldn't, say. It looked like George's older brother, was going to war. But still, this wasn't the end of it.

The pile of unopened letters, unread postcards, and what was clearly a large greeting card, probably a housewarming gesture, were neatly bundled together, and tied with a course, fraying length of string. The most recent of them, judging by the postage date, sat expectantly on top, desperate to be opened and read.

Just a few short hours ago, George had been happily waving off yet another willing, extremely friendly brunette he'd met in Club Land the night before, contentedly taking in the collective breakfast smells that collected each morning in the communal hallway, relishing the thought of having his home to himself once more.

Fred was separated from a dead grey squirrel and fed his usual, and as the kettle boiled again, he'd looked at the number the girl had given him. He was sort of sure she was called Jenny. He'd screwed it up and thrown it into the stainless steel kitchen bin, along with the egg shells, empty tins of tuna, and every other number he'd been given of late. Just like all the others, Jenny, if indeed that was her name, somehow seemed to suffer from the same problem as the rest. She just wasn't Summer.

As he drove the MR2 over the countryside earlier that day, his usual basket of dirty laundry wedged in the narrow bucket seat beside him, his mind went through the same process it did each week. Why couldn't he shake off his attraction to Summer, even now that she had clearly grown tired of waiting for him? Although he had no photographs or pictures to remind him of her, every detail of her tiny face, and shy petite body had been permanently etched into his memory. And he didn't even like etching. But it was always there, just before his eyes, even when someone else's face and naked body was vying for his attention. It was quite distracting at times.

Even though he'd tried to convince himself that a few of the girls he'd enjoyed drinks and horizontal refreshments with, had been more attractive than Summer, they'd been so in a beauty magazine sort of way. Once the layers of make-up had been eroded by sweaty, nocturnal activities, and left all over his expensive white pillow cases, the façade faded for him. Once again he'd long for fresh faced rosy cheeks, and clear bright eyes, free of any camouflage.

It was beginning to dawn on him that Arthur might just well be right. Maybe he was pinning for her after all, merely filling the emptiness with a string of meaningless, if enjoyable at the time, one night stands. Somewhere, in the dark, dusty recesses of his befuddled mind, carefully filed away next to Denial, lurked a painful question.

If Summer was still in touch, would he still be living the life he was, and what would she think of him if she knew of what he was really up to? Had he taken her good natured, liberating invitation to 'Spread his Wings', and stretched it into an albatross?

Carefully, like he was handling a newborn kitten which had fallen from its mothers nest, George delicately freed the first envelope from the bundle. The flowery handwriting, itself a beautiful work of art, was unmistakable. Gently, he ran his trembling thumbnail along its length, eventually freeing the perfectly folded letter from within. His heart beat like a thousand bass drums in a lonely cave. There was no escaping this.

My Monkey,

I'm so, so sorry, you must have been worried sick about me! You've probably seen on the news that we've had some terrible, unseasonal weather here in France, and being a bit out in the sticks, we've been completely cut off!

I've been leaving endless letters and cards for you in the post-box at the end of the track, but Jean-Philippe, our lovely local Postie, hasn't been able to get to us because of all the fallen trees, and I've only just found out! I'm so sorry George, but as you know, when I'm sure you tried to call, all the phone lines have been down too, including the one in the local village!

It's all well and good living in a tranquil Artists Retreat, but when you really want to talk to someone, someone you love, it can be just awful…

As you will see when you eventually get all my letters, I've been thinking about you all the time and how your new job is going, and how you're settling into your new home.

I miss you so very much George, have you missed me too?

All my love,

Your Summertime x x x x .

George slowly rested the letter on his lap. Almost in a trance, he stared out of his onetime bedroom window at the lush, green countryside beyond. His mind was back in the hotel suite they'd booked, but not shared, just a few short months and a whole lifetime ago. That night they'd gone to the Bank Christmas Ball together, as the happiest couple in the world. How things had changed since then.

Mrs Butler very rarely cursed. But when she did, she had a unique, somewhat sing-song, favourite. It managed to combine both mid and low range swearwords in a pleasing expression. Never to be used lightly, it was only uttered in special moments of alarm, crisis or culinary bloodshed.

George had been accidentally exposed to the phrase when he was just four years old, and no amount of Kermit the Frog, or moist fruit cake, would distract him from remembering to use it in the most inappropriate of circumstances, for years to come. The Doctor's Surgery was never safe again.

Somehow, it just seemed to say it all, summing up moments of pain, anger or frustration like no other. For this reason, it wasn't the first time that Sunday morning that those few, choice words had echoed loudly through the Butlers respectable semi.

"Oh Bugger 'n' shit 'n' hell"

Chapter 16

Ocean Therapy

Sunday 14 July.

The bow of *Solace*, Dean's gleaming white, twenty-seven foot yacht, cut through the frothing water just outside the marina like a compliment through a virgin's heart. The wind in his estimation was roughly below twenty knots, so he decided to risk it, and let out the remaining mainsail. Still pointing upwind, he expertly pulled out the Genoa halyard and winched it in tightly, slowly bearing off into a closely hauled angle. Dean loved all this.

Content with the set of his sails, he turned off the modest, nine horsepower engine, a mechanical oddity that somehow never seemed to need refuelling, and set the battery control switch to domestic only, to save power and also to keep the fridge, which was well stocked with frosty Peroni, as cold as a Siberian winter. He darted about the deck, tending to his various lines and winches, wearing nothing but an immaculately pressed pair of khaki skipper shorts, a look of blissful serenity, and his treasured Panerai watch, the leather strap of which he'd swapped for a more serviceable rubber number.

Meanwhile, his new, and judging by his worsening colour, no doubt *temporary* First Mate, was still to clinging on to the frame of the spray hood, like a stubborn red wine stain to a favourite white shirt.

As usual, many thoughts were busy sailing their own meandering course through George's head, not least today though, was a sense of utter disappointment that his body didn't seem to share one of his hearts long held dreams. He'd always thought that sailing would be in his blood. His Granddad on his Mum's side had been a sailor, man and boy, and although he'd never met him, his Grandson was convinced that some of his salty blood had found its way into his own bloodstream. Sadly though, it had not.

Until now, George's only experiences of anything remotely nautical had been his ill-fated pedalo trip in Greece, and fond memories of tormenting the university lecturer his Dad knew who lived down the road from the Butlers respectable semi. He owned a modest yacht that was permanently moored on his driveway awaiting repair, propped up on quivering wooden struts, miles from the ocean. Whilst Mr Butler senior teased his colleague by building a 'Build Your Own Barnacle' kit, his youngest son tried in vain to push it over. It was a wonder the old lecturer was never pleased to see them.

Having given up trying to squeeze his body into a second lifejacket, George hugged the spare one instead, like a child clinging onto a precious teddy bear, his bare toes gripping the edge of the teak decking for extra stability and comfort as the boat leant over further still, crashing endlessly into the lolling waves. Quite why he hadn't considered that he might experience travel sickness on this trip, was a mystery.

The buff Captain Ahab, though, couldn't have been happier. On days like this, when the skies were clear and the wind had woken up in a wicked mood, intent on having some fun, the modest twenty-seven footer could be a bit of a handful in anything approaching a force five. Yet Dean loved her completely. Although his finances, especially given recent events, could easily manage an upgrade, the thought of replacing *Solace* with a larger, heavier boat, didn't appeal. He'd just much rather have the exercise.

"She won't tip over, my Man, no need to worry, trust me. I've been out in far worse than this before!" The Captain, now standing at the helm, strained to look past the leaning mast at the endless ocean ahead, "I mean, it's not even as if the whales have come up alongside yet!"

"*What bloody whales?*"

The lives of both crew members had changed somewhat of late, and today's voyage marked a special moment for both men, although for very different reasons. Dean was celebrating the sale of his waterside home. A place he'd kept so immaculate and pristine, that the very first viewer, a brash American playboy looking for a UK pad, offered him the full asking price without even stepping foot on the balcony. When Dean offered to throw in the Ducati, the drapes and the coffee machine, so long as the purchaser paid his agents fees and solicitor costs, the American agreed readily the moment he clapped eyes on the gleaming red, Italian superbike. The deal was done, it was time to pack up and leave, in every sense of the word.

He'd reached the point where he'd finally had enough. He could no longer stand by and watch the grand old Bank, which he was once proud to be associated with, be stripped of all its morals, or bear witness to the ruthless financial assassination of its customers.

After a torrent of complaints to the Union, Cottons NSIB eventually softened their approach to the brutal sales training courses, and this had briefly given him hope that it had all been a horrible mistake, that order would now be returned. But sadly, it wasn't to be the case. Under the surface nothing had really changed at all. The Bank was just using longer words to disguise their agenda now, flowering things up a bit for effect. Like a thief renaming his crimes as the 'Permanent Reallocation of Goods without the Former Owner's Written Consent', it took a while to unravel the meaning, but the messages were still essentially the same.

The training session which had proved this to be the case, and that had been the final straw for him, claimed to focus on extending and strengthening customer relationships. It was delivered by yet another spineless wretch, who'd clearly never interviewed a customer in his life. He'd drivelled on endlessly about how the CRA role was all about getting on the customers' agenda, about the need to find out what is important to them and understand their needs, develop robust, lasting relationships that can be built on, so that the Bank could serve the customers better throughout their banking life cycle. At least new propaganda sounded more user-friendly, to begin with at least.

His slight, pigeon chest had positively swelled with corporate pride, as he continued by saying that only by understanding our customers and their needs, will the Bank win a greater share of the customer's purse, inevitably becoming a valued financial companion. Increasing its growth within the market by simply listening to what our customers wanted from their bank, and then responding to those needs once they have been identified. Naturally, they might need help with the identification process, a bit of a push here and there. It was basically the same message as before. Find out what makes them tick, exploit this weakness, and flog them everything you possibly can.

For the younger, naïve members of the audience, it all sounded rather positive, and customer friendly. It had left George somewhat confused though. He'd only just returned from yet another intensive advanced sales course, full of yet more 'Banking Mind Tricks'. It focused on 'Advanced Disturbance Techniques'. He'd been surprised not to be issued with thumbscrews and a bag of hot pokers on his way out. Now though, he wondered if maybe he'd gotten the wrong end of the stick again. Perhaps he wouldn't have to learn how to hammer splinters under his customers' fingernails after all. Thankfully, Dean soon put things into perspective for him.

As all the veins in his muscular neck stood out, like wild snakes under a single silk sheet, he got up, drawing surprised glances from the rest of the audience. Was he going to ask to go toilet? His needs were even more pressing though, he'd held his temper with a strong leash for long enough. Slowly releasing his choking, black knitted tie, he looked around the room. So, this is how it all ends.

George had been sat next to his Mentor throughout the meeting. He was probably the only member of the group who knew who this once respected man really was. The former leader of The Pretty People, someone who'd had the ear of the now retired Area Director, someone who many had looked up to as a reliable, honest and successful Manager. Perhaps then, it was only he who noticed the slight tremor in his voice when he eventually spoke.

"Can you please explain to me, exactly *how* we are getting on the customers' agenda when we spend each morning agreeing what we are going to sell the poor sods even before they've come in? Every day we're forced to commit ourselves to selling products to people we haven't even met yet, often on the strength of nothing more than hope or blind luck, only then to have to explain *why* we haven't sold the products we predicted if for some reason, *heaven forbid*, they didn't actually want them in the first place? How exactly is that *getting on a customer's agenda?*" He didn't pause for an answer, it didn't seem as though one would be forthcoming. "Surely if we were truly getting on the customers agenda, we'd go into a meeting with nothing more than a blank sheet of paper, a list of their balances and an open mind, which is exactly how things *used* to be done!"

He wasn't usually given to dramatic gestures. Despite his size and the respect he'd once commanded, he'd always carried himself with an air of cool grace and dignity. But the moral decline of the Bank he'd once held as a dear, treasured employer had been enough to crack through the veneer of calm, something that had slowly been wearing away for weeks on end now.

He'd been dressed in his usual immaculate uniform. The black, chalk stripe suit was perfectly tailored, the crisp white shirt with it thick double cuffs, enviably trim against his body, the knitted black silk tie, reminiscent of one that might be worn to the funeral of a dignified friend. It was quite fitting really. Perhaps this *was* best, maybe this is how it was all supposed to end?

Slowly, deliberately, he pulled off his tie, carefully rolled it up into a neat circle of silk, and passed it absentmindedly to his protégée. He unfastened the first three buttons of his shirt buttons to relieve some of the enraged heat from his body, delighting the mesmerised watching girls, and unhurriedly headed for the door, pausing briefly to turn.

"I understand a new uniform is going to be issued shortly. If things carry on like this, they'll need to issue highwayman masks as well…"

Then, without a backward glance, Dean was gone. He'd properly buggered off.

The yacht was now a good few miles offshore. The prevailing wind, which was considerably higher than had been forecast, meant that the planned voyage to a small marina along the coast was likely to be completed in well under two hours. Relieved that he could still see the shoreline at least, through the endless buckets of salty spray, George was at last starting finding his sea legs, thanks in no small part to great handfuls of travel sickness pills, and three bottles of chilled Peroni. As the potent combination took effect, he started to relax his grip on the spray hood and unclench his toes.

Today was his twentieth birthday, and he'd bid farewell to his teenage years with a lump in his throat. He was still trying to fathom just how it had managed to sneak up on him so quickly. The trip was Dean's present to his young disciple, a parting gift as such, before he dropped him off at the Butlers respectable semi later that afternoon, to enjoy a hearty roast dinner with his family. As it was his birthday, the roast potato embargo had even been relaxed.

Naturally, Dean had been invited to join the Butlers for supper, but for reasons he didn't expand on, he politely declined. He'd met George's parents the week before, and despite any initial reservations they harboured, he'd been welcomed into the clan with open arms. They'd been relieved to find that, contrary to their suspicions, he was engaging and utterly personable, and not at all what they'd expected of the man their youngest son seemed to have become worryingly obsessed with in recent months. They'd been rather sad to see him leave. He had such nice manners.

Should she ever meet him, it had always been Mrs Butler's intention to give Dean a piece of her mind, a threat that would've poured fear into the heart of any Third World Dictator. She didn't approve of the way he seemed to have influenced and dominated her youngest son of late, let alone the awful haircut he'd once forced him to have. And so, when her badly hung-over youngest announced that they were popping out to visit, so that Dean could have a final blast on his Ducati, she'd dusted off her rolling pin, and prepared to clip his elbows.

George's Dad followed the same routine as he'd always done when he sensed trouble or conflict ahead, and retreated to the safety of his garage to continue the restoration of his vintage Velocette. He'd been eking out the project for just over fifteen years now. The oily frame and carefully stripped engine parts, never failed to provide him with a welcome alternative to getting involved in complicated family matters.

Should the project ever near completion whilst one of his sons still lived at home, it had always been his plan to sabotage the bike in some minor way. Nothing major of course, but something that would give him an excuse for yet another, full engine rebuild, or possibly even an extra respray of the gleaming black petrol tank. It was beginning to dawn on him however, that although both of his sons had now left home, the little Buggers kept coming back, bringing with them new and even more complicated troubles. If this carried on he was going to have to seriously consider buying a second restoration project, to keep him occupied, greasy and perhaps most importantly, well out of the way.

One of George's few redeeming features was that he was an excellent pillion rider. Able to read the road ahead just as well as the rider himself, he'd anticipate the lean of the bike through the oncoming bends, and hardly ever burnt his feet on the exhaust. It all began when his Dad first sat him on the petrol tank of his Triumph Tiger Cub. A battered work horse of a motorbike he used to compete in organised Club Trials, before it all became too painful and expensive.

The initially terrified five-year-old would sit astride the warm metal tank in shorts and a Muppets T-shirt, trying not to let his bare legs touch anything hot, gripping the cross bar as tightly as he'd held his Mum's hand that first day at primary school. His Dad would then kick the lumpy trials bike into gear, pop the clutch, and tear off through the woods like a startled fox.

Once he'd opened his eyes, George soon became addicted, and an honorary biker for life. Although he'd no interest in actually learning to ride himself, the simple pleasure of being able to whizz about the roads, taking in the countryside or coastline without having to be bothered with trivial things like braking or traffic, was somehow enough for him.

Dean had been quietly impressed with his pillion. To the point where he'd almost forgotten he was there, and had fully opened up the Red

Devil's throttle on one of the few straights between the city and the rural town. Only remembering to ease off again when the squeezing around his waist intensified. When startled, George was a hugger.

Mr Butler senior was hiding in his garage with door up when the Ducati rumbled into the quiet estate. His original plan to be both aloof and unapproachable soon evaporated when the charming leather clad gentleman hopped off his ticking motorbike and extended a freshly un-gloved hand in welcome. Moments later, the two enthusiastic bikers were examining various engine parts, and discussing the relative merits of the Italian beast. Dean was even led into that most sacred of places, The Butler Garage, where all of a sudden he seemed to transform into a giddy schoolboy in the presence of the partially restored, vintage bike.

The two men were engrossed for so long, that Mrs Butler, desperate to meet this man and set about his elbows, eventually left the kitchen and her rolling pin behind, to see quite what was going on. She opened the back door of the garage just as Dean was being led through it, and in that brief moment of surprise, and as if by magic, he pulled a beautiful bunch of unbroken yellow tulips from his leathers, kissed her very lightly on the hand in greeting, and begin a detailed and knowledgeable appraisal of her spectacular garden. All this before she'd even had chance to open her mouth. It was something of a miracle, and she immediately fell under his spell. The rolling pin remained safely in the kitchen drawer.

By the time the two of them screamed up the road on the Ducati a few hours later, Dean was both a lifetime member of the Butler family, and a few pounds heavier, having been tempted more than once by Mrs Butler's deliciously moist fruitcake. He needed fattening up a bit, in her opinion. Suddenly he understood just how hard the strict diet must have been for his protégé. Bless him.

"You're not looking quite so green anymore, my Man, how're feeling, is the beer helping?"

George was now sitting on the side of the cockpit, trying his best to look both nonchalant and cool, whilst still gripping a nearby hand rail with one hand, a fifth bottle of Italian beer in the other. "*Oh yeah*, not too bad now, just took a bit of getting used to that's all. Do you want a beer?" He handed the Captain a Peroni and looked out at the white horses that littered the endless ocean. Now that his nausea had faded, he could at last appreciate where he was, and just what he was doing for the first time. As the yacht continued on, propelled by nothing but the wind, a strange sense came over him. He couldn't quite put his finger on it, but he'd never felt this alive before, or this free.

"I really like sailing Dean, thanks for this…"

Solace's tiny engine was coaxed into life just as the yacht entered the mouth of the estuary. With the natural wall of the hillsides to shield it from the winds, progress became far less turbulent, especially as Dean lowered the sails. The tiny marina was a favourite haunt of his, as was the neighbouring coastal village that clung to the side of the water's edge, like a stubborn limpet. It was somewhere special to escape too, somewhere seemingly lost in time. The few villagers mostly fished the waters, and had so for generations, only the occasional contemporary, seafood restaurant or bar hinted at progress.

It was approaching midday. The plan was to come ashore, have a few beers in one of scattering of waterside bars or quaint old sailor's taverns, and then find some sea bass to cook aboard *Solace*, whilst George continued to get drunk and feed the seagulls. Dean had radioed ahead when *Solace* was fifty minutes out; requesting a berth at one of the marina's floating pontoons for a few hours. As he came into dock, he was relieved to see that, as mysteriously was always the case, a friendly looking stranger just happened to be waiting to take his in mooring lines.

With the good natured, if somewhat graceless assistance of his increasingly inebriated First Mate, he made good the deck, cleared away the discarded beer bottles which had been rolling around the cockpit during their voyage, irritating him no end, set the engine to idle and tied up the fenders. The docking lines, which had been cleated in readiness, were thrown to the outstretched hands with words of thanks, and when *Solace* was no more than three feet from the pontoon, Dean put the engine into reverse and the stern started slowly back to port, moving the yacht closer to its berth. When she was safely tied up and the helpful stranger thanked with a chilled beer from the ships supplies, the crew prepared themselves to come ashore. So far, it had been the most civilised part of the journey.

Since resigning, Dean had relaxed his image somewhat. His neatly trimmed goatee was now a neatly trimmed full beard, and he'd allowed his usually closely clipped chest wig to grow and sprout an already impressive covering of thick, salt and pepper hair. It was his interpretation of letting himself go. One rule he had no intention of relaxing though, was one of being seen in public wearing shorts. No matter how perfectly pressed they were. Before heading into the village, he disappeared below decks to change into a relaxed pair of Levi jeans, tan loafers, and a close fitting white linen shirt. For the first time in George's experience, he wore it un-tucked, the bohemian.

His First Mate, meanwhile, wearing boot-cut jeans and a ribbed black T-shirt, gingerly hopped onto the gently bobbing pontoon barefoot, his most recent, and in Dean's estimations, highly questionable choice of footwear, clenched tightly in one hand. He sat on the dock struggling to pull them on. It was rather comical, especially for the locals.

"*Cowboy boots*, my Man? I mean, have you listened to *anything* I've taught you?"

"Dean, *just look at 'em*, they're *sooo* cool!"

After yet more beer, and what eventually became a heated debate about the relative merits of the cowboy boot and its inappropriateness, especially in a nautical setting, the two men agreed to disagree, and retreated back to *Solace* with some freshly caught sea bass. It came as a great relief to the collection of gnarled, long retired fisherman who'd been unwillingly drawn into the conversation.

George, having been sternly forbidden to step aboard the gleaming white yacht until he had taken off his ridiculous boots, sat unsteadily on the pontoon again, tugging drunkenly at each toe. Pleading for help, he flailed about like an upended, Cowboy Turtle. The unusual sight drew quite a crowd.

After Dean had whipped up an excellent feast of pan fried sea bass, Greek salad, and boiled new potatoes, which he hoped would absorb a certain amount of the beer his First Mate had consumed, the pair of them sat at the small pop up table in the cockpit and ate the delicious meal in the early afternoon sunshine.

"Why on earth did you bring that guitar, you haven't even taken it out yet?" Dean pointed a fork towards the grey leatherette case that was just visible below decks.

"Well I didn't know I was going to be near death with travel sickness on the way out, *did I?*" George took another mouthful of bass, its fried crispy skin crunching pleasingly with each bite, and reached for his beer. "I reckon I'll be okay for the journey back home though, *any requests?*"

"Hotel California."

"Oh... Err, *any others...?*"

An hour later, *Solace* was back at sea. The wind had dropped, which depending on which member of crew was asked, was either deemed to be a very good, or very bad change in the weather. Dean kept the engine on, in order to motor sail back to his home port, and hopefully get his First Mate to his birthday roast dinner in good time. He'd been talking animatedly about his Mum's exceptional roast potatoes all day.

Cocooned in his own little world of Italian beer and travel sickness pills, George sat at the bow of the yacht, his legs dangling over the side. Safely encircled by the forward pulpit, happily strumming away on his old *Argos* acoustic guitar, no longer concerned with the endless spray from the ocean, or even the inevitable disastrous effect it would have on his hair.

His repertoire included a few newly learned, poorly remembered Counting Crows songs, his old troublesome friend *Paranoid*, and finally a spirited attempt at his Captains earlier request, which they both sang along to, having to pause occasionally for the guitarist to remember which bit came next, or to give him time to reach a particularly stretching cord.

An hour later, his lips tasting like the counter of a fish and chip shop on a busy Friday night, George gingerly made his way back towards the cockpit on all fours, the guitar slung across his back. He sat down heavily, resting the soaking guitar on his lap, and ran his hand threw his damp hair. He grinned as Fred tended too when he'd killed something hopeless and furry. He was positively buzzing with the cleansing, thrilling effect of the crisp sea air.

"*I want boat Dean!*"

The older man, who'd changed back into his skipper shorts to take advantage of the afternoon sun, looked down at the sodden mess at his side. Making a mental note to take him up to his apartment to shower and freshen up, before he delivered him to his parents later that day, he reached for a carefully folded, white towel he'd brought up from the cabin especially, gently tossing it at his dishevelled First Mate.

"Here, take this and dry off, you look a right mess!"

George clumsily caught the towel and, like an excited infant running in from the rain, immediately buried his salty face deeply into the welcoming, soft fabric, inhaling luxuriously. "*Crikey*, this smells just like Mum's! *How the hell did you do that?*"

"It's a gift that comes with age, my Man, a gift that comes with age..."

Solace was now just an hour or so from docking. The wind had all but dropped to a gentle breeze, leaving the crew nothing much to do but gently motor back at a modest four or five knots. It was perhaps only a little faster than either of them could swim. But that wasn't the point.

Dean sat back in the cockpit, his brown legs outstretched in front of him, sipping an icy bottle of water, as condensation ran down the side of the plastic and chilled his fingers. "So then, Summer's coming to visit. *How do you feel about that?*"

This delicate subject hadn't so much as been the elephant in the room during their voyage, as it was the blue whale in the galley. But now that the lobster was well and truly out of the crabbing pot, it was almost a relief to the First Mate. He desperately needed some advice.

On that same eventful Sunday he'd learned of Michael's news, and after he'd carefully read each postcard and heavily illustrated letter at least twice, George had rushed downstairs, closed the hallway door, and with trembling fingers dialled Summer's parents' home in France.

The months that had passed since he'd last spoken to her had been nothing if not colourful, and his experiences had done wonders for his confidence. But as he sat perched on the diligently vacuumed, carpeted stairs, he'd found that he was just as nervous as that first time he'd called her. That epic evening he'd desperately fought his Dad to win the 'Battle of who will help Mum with the Dinner Dishes', the carefully folded scrap of a paper he hidden in his jeans, that held the vital numbers, quickly scribbled down before they were caught by Laurence Burton's fierce secretary. Suddenly he was chubby, ill at ease, and terrible at chatting to girls all over again.

After a brief, slightly embarrassing exchange in his best attempt at failed GCSE French, with a patient lady who George wrongly assumed had been Summer's Mum, there followed a desperately long silence on the other end of the line. Eventually tiny rushing footsteps, that could only have been size four flip flops on flagstones, came tapping ever louder. The receiver was eventually snatched up and a heavenly, familiar voice clearly on the verge of tears, shouted into the receiver, *"GEORGE, George, my Monkey?"*

It had been one of those epic, hazy telephone conversations that seemed to somehow transport both the callers into another place, well beyond the reaches of both space and time. Rather than being yelled at for spending far too much time on the telephone, George was instead brought endless cups of perfect tea by his Mum, and had even managed to unconsciously devour three slices of moist fruit cake during the call. Calories were now far from his chief concern.

Later that same day, as he drove the MR2 lazily over the countryside back to his apartment, he'd listened to one of the mix tapes she'd sent him earlier, of all the music that reminded him of their time together, whilst frantically leafing through his memory of the telephone call. Like the hung over drunk he often was, he tried to recall the finer details of the endless conversation. Had he said anything yet that was likely to land him in trouble? More than anything else, he hoped not. He couldn't bear to have buggered things up again. Surely she would've said if he had, this time?

George was due holiday. The Bank had adopted an old NSIB's rule, and insisted that CRA's took an annual two week break, presumably to allow enough time for the bodies to float to the surface, and for any wrong doing to be identified. It had long been Billy's custom to take every shred of sales evidence on holiday with him, even going as far as paying extra luggage allowance in order to hide the damning evidence in a foreign country. It just wasn't worth the risk.

Although it was far from an ideal time for either of them to take leave, especially as the Artist's Retreat Summer's parents owned was likely to be inundated with hairy, creative types for the next six weeks, they'd mutually, passionately agreed that she should visit him. She'd then bring him his birthday present, to save risking the post, and they'd spend a week enjoying the local tourist haunts and his new apartment. Although a short break in France appealed, Fred couldn't be imprisoned in a cattery for a week. The death toll alone would be catastrophic.

As the week of her planned visit loomed ever closer, George had begun to worry about how he'd handle her inevitable questions. Just how far would she have expected him to take her invitation to spread his wings, had she even really meant it at all? Seeking some reassurance, he'd taken to reading the letter she'd written on the night of the Christmas Ball over and over again. He was desperate to find some comfort in those few words, proof that would convince him he'd done nothing wrong. Proof that in fact, for once in his life, he'd actually done what he'd been told to do. Albeit probably far more times, and with far more people than she'd ever intended.

In an effort to bury any signs of his philandering, he'd also scoured his apartment for evidence, focusing his attention on the back of the leather sofa, and behind his king sized bed. He was looking for spoils of war, hastily discarded ear rings, bangles or any other kind of detachable article, which might cause an embarrassing tumbleweed moment, should Summer stumble upon them.

But he knew his efforts just wouldn't be sufficient. In order to fully fumigate his home, to ensure a complete pre-visit purge, George had no choice but to wheel in his Mum and ask her to unleash a weapons grade, nuclear biological 'Mummy Clean'. It was just the only way to be certain.

"Well, the fact that you're worried about all this must mean something. I mean you obviously care a great deal about this girl." Dean absentmindedly checked his ropes, preparing *Solace* to dock. They still had at least forty minutes of sailing ahead of them, but he seemed excited about something, eager to arrive almost. For the moment at least, whatever it was, he kept it to himself.

"Err, well, kinda, yeah, well, umm, *I guess so...?*" George had eased off the Italian ale in past hour. He was now entering that dangerous period, somewhere between the hangover and drunkenness. It was a precarious time. He had a limited window of opportunity in which to decide whether or not to delay the inevitable, dehydrated head splitting agony, and carry on drinking, or suffer a lesser misery and sober up now. "Is there any more beer left, Dean?" It was probably a sensible choice.

The sun continued to beat down on the ocean, and the lonely boat that slowly motored onwards. It was blisteringly hot, and exposed as they were on deck, the two men were both taking on an impressive tan. Sadly though, given that he was still suspicious of his Captains sexual preferences, in spite of all the time they'd spent together, George's was very much going to be a Famer's Tan. He still refused to take off his T-shirt.

Concerned that if he delivered his charge to Mrs Butler in a drunken state, she might well whip out the rolling pin she'd joked about when they first met, Dean bribed his First Mate into drinking a litre of water before handing him the last chilled Peroni. It was an especially large rolling pin, after all.

"...Anyway, I always thought you didn't like Summer?"

"Whatever gave you that impression?"

"Well, you know, at the Christmas Ball, when you, *err...*" He trailed off, unsure of quite where he was going with his line of thought.

"George, I wasn't the one who let go of her hand, or danced with Tasha and played guitar with the band, was I? All I ever wanted to do was help you shift a few stone and get you out of that terrible suit, you know, *make you look better*! Anything else that's happened along the way has been down to you, my Man. And anyway, you've got to admit, your new body is a vast improvement on the old one, *isn't it?*"

"Err, yes, yes it is, sorry Dean..." Taking hold of a line for balance, he looked down at his bare feet. He could now clearly see them past his once bulbous pot belly. Evidence, if any were required, that his physical appearance at least had indeed been re-engineered for the better.

"I haven't got a problem with Summer at all. She could do with maybe buying a brush, and even using it once in a while, but other than that she seems like a fine girl. If she's the right one for you George, then don't let her get away again, and certainly don't let working for the bloody Bank be a reason not to be together. You'll just end up losing something special in order to make money for an unappreciative employer, *believe me.*" There was new weight behind his words, bitter experience perhaps?

"But I need to work, Dean! I've got all sorts of commitments these days. What would I do if I left?" He was thinking of his most recent credit card statement, and the reminder from the overly friendly Furniture Stores that his payment holiday was coming to an end.

"Sell up, get rid of everything like I've done. Streamline your life, hit the road - or ocean for that matter. Go to France maybe, work with her in this retreat, I'm sure they'd find you something to do."

"But - but what if it all goes horribly wrong, I'd..." He trailed off again. It did sound like a reasonable plan. Sunshine, painting, Summer in a summer dress, nookie in the meadow perhaps. But he wouldn't have the comfort of a healthy bank balance to support him like his Captain had, far from it.

"Life can be full of ifs, buts and maybes, George, sometimes you've just got to take a deep breath and jump in with both feet!"

"That sounds like something Arthur would say..."

"*Arthur?*" Dean raised a quizzical eyebrow.

"Oh, my neighbour, Arthur, you haven't met him yet. I always know when he's going to say something deep and meaningful because he starts off with, '*Sometimes...*'"

Solace coasted on through the calm sea. Onboard, the conversation still lingered around the Bank, and the possibility of a life beyond its corporate walls. But it was time for George to reluctantly broach a difficult subject, something that had been troubling him for a while. He needed to get it off his chest, to be done with it.

"Err, *Dean*... You know when you used to sell products, did you, well, tell the customers *everything*? You know every detail of what they were getting?" He stared at his bare feet again, absentmindedly picking the label of the drained bottle of Peroni, sheepishly trying to avoid the Captains gaze.

"Well, first of all, I never sold anything. I *introduced* customers to products that they might benefit from. And yes of course, I went through *everything* in fine detail, and insisted they went away and thought about it, even if just for a few hours, to make sure they were happy. Why, *what have you been up to?*" For the first time during their trip, the mood altered significantly. The sun's glare was even briefly extinguished by a solitary cloud, which had clearly misplaced his friends. The First mate empathised. There was no going back now, he should press on.

"Oh, umm, well, it's not so much me, *as Billy*, that NSIB bloke I work with. He does all sorts of dodgy stuff, like putting his finger over the loan insurance when he gets people to sign, and telling them they *have* to take a credit card out when they order a debit card, else it won't work properly."

George looked up at the disapproving, handsome face at the wheel. He knew he looked like a primary school infant, caught red handed with a catapult when a window had been smashed. His only defence was to say '*It was him Sir!*' It was pathetic really.

"What about you though, what are *you* doing wrong?" The voice had lost all its playfulness. It was low, almost menacing, and heavy with questions. He wasn't going to let this drop.

"Err, well, *nothing like that*, I promise you! But, well, you know, I don't always bore them to death with every single little thing. You know, like if they want a loan, I just say something like, *I think you should have some insurance*, and if they say *okay then*, I just sign them up!"

Dean checked his heading, paused to reflect briefly on his thoughts, and knelt down, some calmness restored. "Listen to me very, very carefully. Soon the world will wake up and realise just how the Bank has changed. All these little sales habits you and the rest of your cronies are all picking up, no matter how minor they might seem now, will be stamped on, heavily. When this happens, you can guarantee that the Bank, even if it is turning a blind eye to it all now and enjoying the sales while they last, will deny everything, any knowledge of wrongdoing at all. They'll just blame the staff."

"But - but they send us on all these courses and stuff, and some of the people on them talk about the same sort of things Billy gets up too, and *much* worse besides! All they do is just laugh, *even the Trainers!*" He looked pleadingly at Dean, genuinely confused as always. It was supposed to be his birthday.

"I know. I did attend a few didn't I? It doesn't matter, it *will* happen. The Press will get wind of mis-selling and before you know it, there will be secret filming, like they did with the double glazing salesmen on *Watchdog* last year. The walls will tumble down, and fingers will be pointed at the sellers, *not* Top Brass, trust me on this." He stood up again, and rolled his shoulders, conscious that he was picking up a burning tan, "What you're doing is nothing as bad as this chap Billy, *granted*, but at the end of the day, you're *still* not doing things correctly! You need to spend time seeing if the customer is even eligible for a product before you let them take out a policy. Promise me you'll do this from now on?"

"What do you mean *eligible*?"

For a while there was nothing but the sound of the ocean lapping gently against the hull, the brief flap of canvas as a light gust filled the mainsail, or the occasional call from a seagull overhead. The two men sailed on in uncomfortable silence. George had exiled himself to the forward pulpit, almost in self-imposed detention. Eventually Dean, conscious that he probably wouldn't see his First Mate again for several months, perhaps even years, decided it was time to put their day together back on course.

"Do you want your birthday present then?"

The younger man, who'd been gazing sightlessly out to sea, immediately spun around. The word 'present' had always been like concentrated cat nip to him, "But I thought this trip was my present?"

"Part of it, but your main present, providing you want it that is, actually involves you giving *me* some money!" He grinned warmly back along the length of the teak deck. The wind was thankfully strengthening once again, flowing through the hair on his chest, like a warm breeze through an uncut meadow.

Order had now finally returned to the voyage once more, wrongdoings and lectures forgotten, enthusiastic bewilderment, at least on George's part, at last restored. And this comment had indeed caused some him bewilderment; a present for him that would cost him money? Nevertheless, the word present had been used. Regardless of any other additional words that just happened be loitering around that sentence, his bodies default reaction to the word 'present' was to reduce him to a quivering, wildly grinning five-year-old.

"I, err, I don't understand, *what do you mean?*"

"What do I have that you really want? Something that I own?"

George considered Dean's vast collection of enviable, coveted possessions. "Err, well, there are your suits I guess? But I'm still not big enough for them, and Mum would have to take the trouser legs up…" He scratched at his scalp; it had become itchy with the drying sea salt. "Oh, your coffee machine! I rather like that, but I'm not quite as scared of mine as I was, I'm not sure I could cope with another new one?" Staring off again towards the distant horizon, he continued to mentally list the belongings.

"*Bugger*! The BMW, *the M3?*" His eyes suddenly wide, madly so, like a game show contestant who's run of bad luck at last seemed to be coming to an end.

"You got it, *finally*, but I'm not *giving* it to you, I'm letting you buy it off me, at a heavily reduced price. I want it to go to a good home, and I know your Dad will make sure you look after it properly. So, five grand and she's yours. I'm sure you'll have that put back by now, especially with all those bonuses you've been earning lately?"

"Oh yeah, err, *definitely*. Thanks Dean, I promise I'll treat her well.

Crikey, *an M3!*"

George's habit of hitting the town at least three nights a week, and burning through hundreds of pounds each evening had, along with otherwise crippling finance repayments, soon eroded any bonuses he'd earned. His savings account was now as empty as Billy's fridge. He'd taken to relying on his overdraft to sustain him, until his basic pay and sales bonus arrived at the end of each month. The desperate hope always being that the bonus covered any shortfall. Lately, the bonus had a lot of ground to cover. But now, through a haze of alcohol, blazing sunshine and drying sea salt, five grand didn't sound like that much money. Once he'd sold the MR2 and Billy had worked some miracle of re-financing, he'd probably be just fine, probably. It was too good an opportunity to pass on. He'd worry about it later, much later.

"Just transfer it into my account next week sometime, no rush, we'll sort out the paperwork when I drop you off later, and just be careful with her, don't treat her like the other girls you've met recently, she's a rare one, just like Summer, *okay?*"

The end of the voyage loomed like the last day of the school summer's holidays. Apart from a brief moment of discontentment, both members of the crew had enjoyed a fantastic trip. They were sun burned, but not so deeply that they'd complain, one was comfortably semi-detached by alcohol, but not so much as to ruin the meal ahead, and the other felt as though, for the last time perhaps, he'd managed to bestow some badly needed advice before it was too late.

"So, what are you going to do now then, you know for work and that?"

"I've got no idea at all, probably nothing for a while, I'm going to sail over to France to begin with, and then maybe head further south along the coast, see what happens next." *Solace* was closing in on the marina. Dean took in the mainsail and eased back on the chugging engine.

"Aren't you going to buy another flat or something?" Despite staggering through life a little uncertainly at times, George had been brought up surrounded by stability. This new found vagueness in a man, who'd also once seemed to be anchored in bedrock, was unsettling to say the least.

"No, I don't need one, I've got *Solace*, I'll live aboard her, she's plenty big enough, it's not like I'm taking all my suits with me!" He winched in a line and checked his course once more.

"But you'll be, well, sort of *homeless* then?"

"Well, I suppose so, but plenty of people live aboard a boat, and in any case, with the apartment sold, I'll be *loaded* and homeless, which makes all the difference in the world!"

"Won't you be, err, you know, *lonely*?"

"I'm not going to be alone George, I've got a travelling companion coming along. We're meeting up when we dock in a minute. I'll need a lift back from your folks place if I'm leaving you with the M3, *won't I?*"

Panic, and a great lump of apprehensive adrenaline suddenly gate crashed the party. George shuddered. In all the time he'd known Dean, he'd never seen him with a *partner* before. The thought of finally seeing him in the presence of another man and, heaven forbid, perhaps even kissing, terrified him. Should he just leap overboard and swim for it?

"Oh, err, *okay,* well look, *err,* I can always ask Dad to pick me up, umm, *I'll collect the car tomorrow instead?*" The panic was obvious. Dean had been expecting this, he grinned wickedly back at him. This should be fun.

"My Man, don't worry, it's all arranged, and it'll be fine. Besides after we drop you off, I'm stocking up and sailing this evening, I didn't want to worry you about all this earlier, I just wanted you to have a nice day..." He dropped down into the cockpit, reached out and, perhaps for the last time, placed a firm reassuring hand on the younger man's shoulder, smiling warmly into his eyes. "Like I said, don't worry, *you know already who it is.*"

"*I do...?*" He began mentally listing all the eligible men he'd met since he'd joined the Bank. Which of them could have secretly been gay all along, who would be attractive enough to stand beside this Roman God of a man? The Bear was quickly eliminated from his enquiries. "Err, well, *who is he then?*"

"*Her.*"

Solace was now just a hundred yards from her berth. George, who'd been facing his Captain, rather than looking at where they were heading, swivelled around so quickly to see who Dean had pointed at, that he nearly lost his footing and toppled over the guard rail into the sea.

Stood on the dock, surrounded by a scattering of luggage, her thick brown hair dishevelled charmingly by the revived afternoon breeze, was the familiar slim figure who'd once welcomed the new recruit into Nelsons branch. The same strikingly attractive girl who'd skilfully reduced him to a quivering, spotty schoolboy with her mesmerizing charm and London bus lipstick. "...But - but *that's Hayley.* She's not gay is she?" Bewildered by an unexpected turn of events, he'd lost all sense proportion.

"No, she's not, *and neither am I...*" Dean waved at the beautiful girl. She looked to be brimming with excitement. The pile of luggage she'd brought with her was a little concerning though. He threw *Solace's* engine into idle, allowing her to coast slowly towards the dock, towards the wonderful new life that waited for him, towards all the possibilities it might yet hold.

"But - but - *I don't understand,* why, what, *eh*…?"

"George it's really quite simple my Man. It's Hayley. It's *always* been Hayley…"

Chapter 17

Cowboy Boot Crop Circles and a Curious Nipple

Early August.

Exhausted, and unable to find any lingering reserves of strength to call upon, George slammed the pair of thirty-five kilo dumbbells down on the thick rubber matting, either side of the padded bench that supported his sweating body. He lay still for a moment. Waiting for the excited fireflies to vanish, for his chest to stop burning from the effort, for someone, anyone to ask him if he was okay. It would probably take some time,

He slowly sat up, winced, and looked around the gym. Although he'd been horizontal and lifeless for a while, no one seemed to have noticed. His apparent death had gone unnoticed, again. Since he'd begun training on his own, he'd found that Diamond Fitness, despite being quite crowded at times, was one of the loneliest places on earth.

Dean had been a much loved and respected member, and his dishevelled, sweaty sidekick had been accepted accordingly, if only out of reluctant politeness. But now without his presence, George found that, for some reason that eluded him, both the Gym Bunnies and Gym Foxes kept their distance. Even the scattering of orange bodied instructors seemed disinclined to offer him a much needed spot, or even the odd friendly word of encouragement. All of a sudden he just didn't seem to fit in anymore, and he couldn't quite understand why not.

Fortunately he was still being spurred on from afar though. His mentor's weekly postcards from quaint French ports were crammed to the edges with constant reminders of the importance of consistency, diet and the right mental attitude. George had no intention of letting him down, or of letting all his months of starvation and agony go to waste, and ploughed on regardless, countering his solitude with his Walkman and a healthy selection of good old fashioned Hard Rock.

It was the Friday evening before Summer was due to arrive. And rather than hit the town with the usual suspects, he instead rounded off his week of intense fitness and stringent diet, with a last battering session of his chest and triceps, with a side order of lateral raises for good measure. Much to Arthur's disappointment, this week's evening meals hadn't yielded anything much more exotic than steamed fish and broccoli. Perhaps more alarmingly though, where he'd normally make a fresh batch of limoncello twice weekly, he still seemed to have an ample supply left in the fridge from the week before. It was all very concerning.

Fortunately, the purge was drawing to a close, and normal service seemed likely to resume once his neighbours 'Special Guest' arrived. Whilst George was far from being his old tubby self again, the endless nights on the town, coupled with vats of red wine and limoncello, had taken their toll on his physique. Some of the carefully constructed sharp edges and his enviable vascular network, had been either gently rounded off, or partially buried once more under a thin layer of unwelcome fat. He'd realised this of course, but with just a week to go before his guest arrived, it was his Mum who'd inadvertently encouraged her youngest to clean up his act. She'd innocently commented that it was nice to see him getting a bit 'cuddly' again. That had been enough. The very next day he'd hit the gym with a vengeance.

He'd spent much of the following week feeling light headed and exhausted. The pre-work out, bland Power Bar from the local health food shop, provided a vital energy boost, but it wore off the minute he sat down on the carefully positioned towel, he'd lay across the M3's black leather driver's seat for the painful journey home. Yet still he battled on. The last thing he wanted was to become one of those retired Gym Bores, who spend all their time recounting stories of when they *used* to be ripped or *used* to be muscular. He didn't even have any photographs to prove he had been yet.

With his ears stilling ringing with the best of Def Leppard and Aerosmith, his body once again longing for the days of fruitcake and thick white bread, dripping with butter, George gently, and extremely carefully, motored home in his newest and most treasured possession. With the Blaupunkt stereo switched off, he was content to have the window wound down, just the deep burble of the twin exhaust and the gentle breeze of the warm evening air for company.

The BMW M3 was an ugly beauty. A fabulous beast from another age of motoring that didn't care what it looked like, but instead just got on with the job of being the best at what it was. Although a newer, more powerful version of the E30 model was available, Dean's motor was the 1986 original. As old as some of George's favourite T-shirts, it was one of the first batches of road going race cars produced by the German company, to enable it to compete in the World Touring Car Championships of the time.

It resembled the standard BMW saloon in the same way that a heavy weight boxer resembles a Derby winning jokey. With its widened track, flared arches, purposeful rear wing and menacing stance, it was a formidable sight on the roads, especially finished in black. The four cylinder 2.3 litre engine produced 195 bhp, and this, coupled with a relatively lightweight shell and uncompromising driving composure, ensured that in the hands of a skilled and experienced driver, the BMW would positively fly.

George wasn't a particularly skilled driver though, nor was he desperately experienced. And for these reasons perhaps, the malevolent beast scared him silly every single time he turned the key. Sometimes, even turning the key proved to be problematic.

Like all E30 M3s, it was left hand drive. And during his first week of ownership, usually early in the morning, before his third espresso had chance to take full effect, he'd often hop into the passenger seat and wonder who'd stolen his steering wheel. After a brief pause to reflect, and to glance around to ensure nobody was looking, he'd then either clamber over the wide transmission tunnel, especially if it happened to be raining, or quickly leap out and dash around to the driver's side before anyone noticed. Then things got really interesting.

In keeping with its racing pedigree, the M3 had an entirely different gear shift pattern to the other cars its new owner had driven. Reverse was where first should've been, second and third were where third and fourth are usually found, with fourth and fifth off somewhere else entirely, presumably holidaying somewhere pleasant with first.

His Dad had patiently explained to his red faced, extremely late son one Sunday afternoon, that in terms of racing, it all made perfect sense, with changes between gears less likely to involve either first or reverse. And later that afternoon, after a much delayed Sunday roast dinner, a quick nerve shredding blast over the countryside succeed in both proving his point, and reducing to his young passenger to a green, quivering mess.

Unfortunately though, even this lesson didn't prevent him from having daily near misses in traffic, with reverse being dangerously selected instead of first, resulting in panic and screaming horns from behind. He'd also often sit patiently, wondering why the car was making very slow forward progress, and producing an unpleasant burning smell, rather than backing smartly into a parking space as intended. Dean would not have approved.

Thankfully, with a few weeks experience under his belt, locomotion was slowly improving, literally. He'd even briefly flirted with the idea of engaging fifth gear. Sadly, in all the excitement at the thought of owning a car like this, not once did he stop to question whether or not he'd actually be able to safely drive it.

True to his word, after Billy performed some act of Financial Witchcraft, which Danny had been both delighted, if somewhat surprised to have to override, George transferred five thousand pounds to the previous owner's bank account, and the car was officially his. It had been a rather fraught experience. After just a week of advertising the MR2 in the *Autotrader*, he'd quickly become tired of all the test drivers and dreamers. They'd descended on his shiny red sports car in baseball caps and huge training shoes, burning the clutch and his Pirellis. Crippled by two lots of insurance premiums though, he foolishly decided to cut his losses, and sold the Toyota back to the garage he'd bought it from. It was at a heavy loss. Deprecation was a sod.

Financially, George had gotten himself into bit of a mess lately. He was earning good money, thanks in no small part to his regular monthly bonuses, but a lethal combination of a personal loan, a credit card that was busting at the seams, an overdraft which he regularly exceeded, and pressing furniture store credit, spread his income as thin as the last dollop of Marmite in the jar.

To a degree at least, he could still just about keep his head above water by ensuring he exceeded his sales targets, and maintained a good level of bonus. The money he'd been making on the side by taking painting commissions was welcome extra cash, but until recently at least, it had been quickly squandered on rounds of expensive drinks in the heaving City Nightclubs. It rarely stayed in his wallet long enough to feel at home, let alone make any new friends.

Billy had treated his colleague like any other customer, and suggested that a consolidation loan would be best. One that would absorb the relatively expensive borrowings he'd accumulated, and would stretch the original MR2 loan over a longer period, making the extra five thousand George needed for the M3, more affordable, if much more expensive in the long run.

Originally he'd planned to pay the proceeds from the sale of the Toyota off the loan, but the thousand pounds he'd recovered from that particularly expensive motoring episode, just looked far too content sitting in the biscuit tin that passed for his moneybox. Instead it stayed there, slowly eroding a little further with each passing day.

"Evening Arthur, I was thinking of grilling some steaks tonight, what do you think?" After three attempts, he'd eventually parked the BMW in his allocated space, made his way into the apartment, and quickly headed for the patio doors and his small courtyard garden. Arthur was basking in the last of the evening sun as usual, stretched out on his aging steamer chair without a care in the world, and with Fred sprawled contentedly on his lap, twitching slightly, probably dreaming of hunting wildebeest. Both creatures were fast asleep.

"I'll take that as a yes then..?"

Later that evening, after the neighbours had shared a delicious meal together in younger man's garden, sat at the small wooden set of table and chairs he'd recently bought, to allow him and his imminent guest to din al fresco, they carefully reviewed the plan once more.

"So, we're quite clear? When she arrives tomorrow, there's to be absolutely *no* mention of all the other girls that have stayed here. If she asks, I just seem to just spend all my free time either painting or going to the gym, *okay?*" George topped up the old man's wine glass and gathered together the empty dinner plates.

"Sunshine, believe it or not, when I'm introduced to new people, I'm not normally in the habit of opening with, *'by the way, do you know what a dirty little bugger this chap is?'* Give me some credit, and don't be frugal with the wine my boy?" Arthur held up the half-filled glass until his host finally got the message, and topped him up with the full bodied red.

"Well, yeah, I know that, *but*..."

"Don't worry, I'll behave, I promise. Now, am I to wear a smart suit when I meet this girl then, or just pants and a string vest?"

George awoke relatively early the next morning. He was well rested, and suffered only from the barest hint of a hangover from the heavy red, something his body had briefly gotten out of practice with. It was a glorious day. Fred was splayed luxuriously in a sunbeam on the white duvet, yet another small furry victim lying in an advanced state of Riga Mortis next to his relaxed jaws. It was long dead, finally, gratefully, at peace.

Once the remains of the mouse had been buried in a new garden pot, the patio slabs wouldn't lift easily enough, he fed his tiger, showered, and devoured his usual breakfast of double espresso, four poached eggs, and two slices of burnt brown toast, with just a thin scrape of butter for once. With any luck, later, he'd need the energy.

Summer had said that she would make her own way to the apartment, and that she'd probably drive over in her trusty mini, Daisy. Detailed directions were provided, including an impressive hand sketched map. It showed the route she should take from the ferry port, directly to the spare communal parking space alongside the apartment. It even had carefully drawn, tiny little feet that then led to the front door, and an impressive rendition of the intercom, including the button she should press to gain access. Nothing had been left to chance.

Apart from the occasional Bank holiday, this was George's first break since he'd joined the Bank. In the weeks leading up to it, Danny had, figuratively speaking, thrashed the living daylights out of his fledgling CRA. He wanted to squeeze ever last financial sale out of him before finally, reluctantly, allowing him to leave the branch. Seller's holidays had always been a bone of contention for him, not least because he might have to actually see some customers himself. God help them all.

Lately, despite trying his very best to convince himself otherwise, George had found that he'd become increasingly concerned about Summer's impending weeklong visit. As the day of her arrival drew ever nearer, he battled desperately against his old adversaries. Emotions that he thought he'd managed too, if not exactly banish entirely, then at least send away for a long holiday somewhere foreign and remote.

But now they'd returned. Nervous Energy and Adrenaline were back with a vengeance and armfuls of duty free. And this time they'd brought with them a few new friends they'd found loitering in the hotel bar too, Doubt, Guilt and the obese, heavy drinking slob that was Insecurity. They'd comfortably collapsed into an armchair, somewhere within their host's belly, and clearly had no plans to leave whilst the fridge was stacked with beer.

George couldn't quite process all his raw emotion, nor would he allow himself time to dwell on its origin, even when his mind was at its most open to wandering, typically during Bank training sessions or cherished *Autotrader* moments. He was desperately worried that if he thought too much about why his body was reacting so spectacularly to Summer's visit, he might have to start confronting some difficult questions about the way he actually felt about her. And that wouldn't do at all.

Instead, he bundled his unwelcome guests together with the promise of a free bar and a running buffet, shut them away in a tiny room marked 'Deep and Meaningful Issues - avoid', and nailed the door shut. Content that the door should hold for now, and as a welcome means of distraction, he allowed himself to worry about something else entirely. Quite what his guest would think of his first beard?

George and his facial hair had enjoyed a mixed relationship. Like most Butler's, especially his Dad, he'd been born with almost a full moustache, which he'd proudly kept until puberty kicked in and his parents pinned him down and shaved it off. He was starting to resemble a thirteen-year-old Mexican bandit. Confident that the rest of his face would eventually catch up, he'd put this particular element of teenage physical development to the back of his mind, and willed his chest hair to grow instead.

However, unlike the rest of the clan, his facial hair failed to sprout magnificently. It just grew in patchy sporadic clumps, the only consistent growth being his sideboards and moustache, something for which he was eternally grateful. Nevertheless, he was determined that this most recent attempt at true rugged manliness, would be a success, and inspired as always by Dean, he made the brave decision to reach for the beard, shortly after their boat trip together.

Predictably, his moustache and sideburns soon germinated and took root. The rest of his face sadly remained a largely barren wasteland, with nothing more than the occasional lonely prickle to keep the odd battle hardened, teenage spot company. In order to give this unfertilized ground time to catch up, he'd decided to shave off the more densely populated areas, and for the first few weeks, this approach left him with a truly unique appearance.

Undeterred by any references his colleagues made of his resemblance to the Wolf Man, George pressed on, until finally it seemed that, in the right light at least, he at last had something that could more or less pass for a beard, more or less.

As well as carefully cultivating his face wig, he'd also been giving a lot of thought to the outfit he should wear when Summer arrived. It needed to show off his new body, but also look both costly and cool. Clothes had become far more important to him than they'd ever been before, and he wanted her to see that, although he'd taken to living in jeans and T-shirts again, they were expensive, well cut jeans and T-shirts, and this made all the difference. Having tried on most of his rapidly expanding wardrobe, he eventually gave up looking for the right outfit, and took his freshly cleared credit card shopping for a new one instead.

In the end, he settled on a trim, slim fitting white linen shirt, which clung to his chest and arms as though it had been soaked by a passing shower. That should do the trick. He liked it so much he bought in ever available colour, in spite of the groans from his all too briefly liberated plastic. To complete his ensemble, he then picked out yet another pair of expensive, faded boot cut jeans, which his Mum was bound to say looked as though they were at least, second hand. But he wasn't finished just yet.

For some time, George had been flirting with the notion of accessorising. He'd been quietly envious of the 'Ethnic Dangly Thing' that Billy had taken to wearing recently, and had soon become engaged in finding one of his own. He felt sure his guest would approve, and had gingerly ventured into the friendliest looking Surf Shop he could find, in search of suitable pendant of his own.

It had been lunchtime, and wearing his black pin stripe suit and newest, flashiest tie, he felt not unlike a lost monk, who'd accidentally stumbled into a brothel, as he browsed as nonchalantly as he could. The curious staff, all of whom looked as though they spent most of their lives wishing they were dolphins, grinned encouragingly at him, quietly hoping he wasn't there to inspect their tax records.

With the pleasantly addictive, if not alien smell of what he would later discover to be surf wax, making him feel slightly light headed, he was eventually guided towards a Koru pendant by the pretty girl behind the counter. She clearly belonged to some sort of shell worshipping tribe. Her eclectic outfit was skimpy and difficult to define, so skimpy in fact, that he'd been quite sure he'd briefly glimpsed a curious nipple amongst the braided threads. It was a very nice nipple though. Ordinarily, he'd have asked to see more.

The Koru, which she'd reliably and very seriously informed him, was Maori for loop, apparently symbolised new life, growth, strength and peace. Sensing that at least some of these qualities would be welcome additions to his life at the moment, he quickly bought it, along with a length of leather cord to hang it from, and puck of Sex Wax surf wax, to use as an air freshener.

A few days later, his apartment smelt like a Californian beach hut, and after a few false starts, and a disturbing dream about being hung from the gallows, George finally became accustomed to his new 'Ethnic Dangly Thing'. Asides from school and offices ties, the only other thing he'd ever had around his neck before, had been his brothers hands during some exceptionally spirited play fighting. It had seen him turn a particularly interesting shade of blue. Or as Michael had put it at the time, Smurf like.

George stood in his shower room with a brilliant white towel around his waist, and lovingly stroked his fledgling beard. Once again, he went over his plan for the day ahead. It was a good plan, well-rehearsed, as best it could be, and long since committed to memory. Everything would be fine, just as long as his old neighbour didn't let him down. As content as he could be for now, it was time to wrestle control of his hair.

Recently, he'd found that if he allowed his mind to wander, being a nomadic entity this was its natural state in any case, the whole process of sculpting his locks into something vaguely approaching acceptable, seemed to take care of its self on some sort of subconscious level. His recent 'Trim 'n' Edge', as his Dad tended to label it, had been an emotional affair, with neither his Mum, nor her hung-over Son, quite able to agree on what exactly qualified as a reasonable haircut. There were frequent, anxious pleas of *"Not that bit Mum!"* often countered with *"I have done this before, my Son!"* before an ear-splitting scream that had the neighbours twitching their curtains. The whole experience left George with a slightly smaller earlobe on his left side.

Back in his bathroom, suitably trancelike, he swept back his lightly gelled quiff, and quickly gassed it with a liberal blast of Silvikrin Extra Firm Hold Hairspray, before it could flop forward again. If anyone ever asked, it was actually quality Spray Gel he'd bought from Dean's barber, and *not* hairspray.

Summer said that given the Ferry times, she'd probably arrive around lunchtime. This would give George not only the whole morning to apply finishing touches to his home, but also a welcome opportunity to show off his new, if not *entirely* honed cookery skills. He'd toyed with a variety of dishes, before eventually settling on his seldom used, but delicious 'post nightclub, three AM and no takers tonight' feast, Spanish omelette. Although this time, he hoped to break a good deal more eggs in the bowl, rather than on the floor. He planned to serve the omelette with some sort of Greek salad, a recipe for which he had liberated from one of his mums Women's Own magazines when she wasn't looking. They were both foreign sounding after all and therefore bound to impress.

In an effort to persuade himself that he was in a tranquil place emotionally, he stopped pacing nervously around his apartment barefoot and instead considered the remaining jobs that were outstanding. Like the slightly confident host of a Saturday evening dinner party, who started on the Pinot at three in the afternoon, rather than peeling the spuds, George was convinced that he had loads of time to finish tidying up, to change into his carefully selected outfit, and prepare the ingredients for lunch, before she arrived. He didn't. The first item on the list didn't appeal though. The last time he'd attempted it, things had not gone well.

A few weeks ago, following some rapport building that had gotten well out of hand, George had been lectured about the merits of brushing his cat, by a well-meaning customer who owned eight Persian's. Feeling sufficiently guilty that he hadn't considered this before, he'd immediately bought a bright red brush from the local pet shop.

For a number of days though, the brush lived in the kitchen drawer. Fred just didn't look bedraggled enough to risk it. When he wasn't comatose in a sunbeam, he tended to divide his time equally between episodes of casual murder, eating gargantuan meals, and tireless self-grooming. His human, understandably, also had a lingering desire to live.

Nevertheless, the cat lady customer had been insistent, and in the end he decided to try his luck. Later that same day, after a good deal of wailing, hissing and some near misses from rapier like claws, George came to two conclusions. Firstly, the cat lady was mad, and secondly, brushing the back of his pet near the base of his bushy tail, tended to be far less fraught with danger than say, his nether regions.

Fred meanwhile, decided enough was enough. He'd murder his human that night whilst he slept. Really, the indignity of it all! But not just yet though, first he'd allow him to brush his long spine once again, just for good measure. That bit was rather pleasant.

With another life threatening groom over for now, the huge cat bounded out of the open patio doors with his tail indigently held in the air. He'd probably spend the next hour grooming endlessly, carefully putting everything back to where it should be. His owner meanwhile, happy to still be alive, swept up the great handfuls of fur into an orange pile on the lounge floor. Skilled hands could have conceivably knitted another Fred.

George flushed the huge bundle down his toilet, offering up a rare, silent prayer in the hope it wouldn't block, and scattered the few remaining tuffs with his bare foot. The last thing he wanted to do was to have to dig the vacuum cleaner from the cluttered hallway cupboard again. It was a perilous place these days, where an imminent cave in seemed inevitable, He checked his Seiko. It was ten twenty, loads of time.

Crossing the life threatening task off his list, he licked a small flesh wound, and moved onto the next item. There were a few outstanding jobs left that his Mum, following her own purge, had identified, along with some more pressing tasks he'd added himself. Such as showering, changing the bed, and searching the premises once last time for any evidence of philandering. To begin with though, he needed to touch up the paintwork in the kitchen. Something he should have embarked on before showering. It seemed that although his Mum's cleaning equipment was ruthlessly comprehensive; even she wasn't quite prepared for the carnage in her son's kitchen. The many haphazard splatters, fallout from his prized ragu sauce.

Still wearing nothing but his damp towel, George carefully dabbed each of the affected areas with a square brush from his paint set, before finally balancing precariously on one of his barstools, in order to reach a few splashes that had ended up on the ceiling. One thing was certain. If he didn't learn to stir less vigorously, soon his whole kitchen would slowly become somewhat narrower.

With the crime scene successfully concealed, he checked the job off and considered the remaining chores. Changing the bed and, more importantly, checking underneath it again for evidence, seemed like the next logical step.

Annoyingly he hadn't found time to quickly dash home in the week, and have his Mum iron his new shirts. The thought of dashing anywhere in the M3 terrified him, so late the night before, he'd thrown caution to the wind, braved his chaos cupboard, extracted the unused ironing board, still in its protective wrapping, and pressed his linen shirt himself. It proved to be unique and utterly painful experience, one which, although successful to a degree, resulted in him burning his belly twice. It seemed that nudity and ironing were not good bedfellows.

As he sincerely hoped that some of the week ahead would be spent both naked and closely pressed up against another, equally bare sweaty belly, in an effort to quickly repair the damage, he'd generously applied a great dollop of Germolene, and a vast fabric plaster. It already had designs on ripping out great chunks of his happy trail when it was later gingerly removed.

He held the linen shirt up against the morning sunlight which streamed in through his open bedroom window, and critically examined his evening's work. There was no escaping it. Despite suffering second degree burns, and spending forty-eight minutes trying to achieve fabric perfection, he'd still managed to iron tramlines down one of the arms. Bugger it. It was time to move on to the next job.

Since planning Summer's visit, all had been quiet on the nookie front, but he decided to strip the bed of the lightly soiled sheets in any case. Pulling back the king sized mattress, he checked under the slats again for anything shiny or thong-like. The coast was clear, he'd done well. As he grappled with the heavenly smelling fresh laundry though, a worrying thought broke down the door inside his head. Was he being presumptive? What if his guest expected to sleep alone? Doubt and Insecurity, having emptied the fridge and escaped, were looking for some light entertainment to amuse them. But maybe they were right?

Before he could dwell on this for too long though, these thoughts were quickly chased away. Having heard the familiar rustling of sheets, Fred bounded into the bedroom and leapt up, diving paws first into the huge duvet.

Quite what it was about changing the sheets that drove the tiger into a state of rapture was uncertain, but every week without fail, he turned into an overexcited kitten each time the bed was stripped. For those few moments, even if there was an extremely *pressing* need to change the sheets, a fresh set high heels tapping ever nearer outside the apartment perhaps, Fred became so downright cute and loveable, that George couldn't help but join in, and a sort of wild feline game of 'Parachutes' would commence. But there really wasn't time today.

"*Nooo Fred*! Not today, *please*?" With the crisp white duvet now covering his vast body, the tiger chased his tail around and around in increasingly fast circles. He was bound to be making an orange, furry mess of the fitted sheet below. "Come here, *or I'll brush you again*!" He pinned down the edges of the thrashing bulge until it stopped bucking, and then carefully reached underneath until he touched warm fur, and tugged on the strong hind legs. Claws eventually retracted from the mattress, Fred emerged, somewhat bedraggled, from his white cotton cave.

"Aww Fred, *look at you*! You're all messed up again, let me get the brush. Wait there." Without pausing to see if the game would resume, the tiger quickly darted out of the room and into the garden, leaving his human to battle with vacuum cleaner and remove all traces of frenzied moggy.

Finally, everything seemed to be ship shape and in order. The kitchen was spotless, with even his breakfast dishes washed and stowed. His egg poacher very rarely saw the inside of the cupboard. The laminate floors had been swept clean and mopped, and the perimeter checked one last time for evidence. All that remained now was clothes and aftershave. George himself was more or less ready for his guest, if only superficially.

According to his Seiko, he still had ample time to play with, time which he could be well spent choosing appropriate music. With the exception of Def Leppard's *Hysteria*, a solitary CD that had always felt extremely conspicuous, until he'd moved into his own place, George's music collection had consisted of an assortment of battered tape cassettes and scratched vinyl. There were dodgy copies of dubious quality, well used originals that had long since lost their Christmas day shine, and a warped

LP of the best of Shakin' Stevens. It was an eclectic collection at best. Now though, in spite of the groans from his bank account, each week he treated himself to at least two new albums. Slowly replacing his decaying collection with upgraded, if somewhat costly, Compact Discs.

Naturally, Dean's M3 had been fitted with a CD player, although this luxury presented a unique problem. The music he wanted to play in the apartment on a rainy afternoon would inevitably be in the car, even if he'd been quite sure he'd brought it in the night before. It was a mystery indeed.

The CDs that ended up in the car had a hard, miserable life. One filled with neglect and abuse. George was terrified of letting his concentration lapse even for a second when piloting the M3, in case the Beast should tear off in some random direction without warning, leaving them wrapped around a lamppost. So instead, he would change CDs by feel only. Often dropping them into the foot well to be scratched by his boots, or crumpling their inserts as he desperately wrestled blindly with the case.

For much of the past week, he'd been listening to Bob Marley's *Legend*. This album had long since been the soundtrack to his weekends. Once the evening's temporary nocturnal guest eventually tottered out on a Sunday, leaving him with an empty wine rack and a nagging feeling of guilt, he'd reach straight for a bit of Bob for comfort. Suddenly all would be well with the world once more. Each song, regardless of their actual meaning, be it a celebration of love and life, or deeper issues about revolution and struggle, always reminded him of Summer. Even when he was sure she'd given up on him, he still played it.

A quick rummage through the oak CD rack proved that Bob was indeed missing, presumably exiled to the BMW. There was no choice but to make a quick dash out to the car, recover Bob, insert the album into the apartment stereo, and let the Caribbean lilt work its magic. He'd then change into his outfit, and splash on several gallons of aftershave. His plan to do a few pumping press ups would have to be discarded though. Exercise and reggae didn't really work for him.

Outside, the sun was getting into the swing of things, considering that both Arthur and Penelope had seen him far more naked before, albeit completely against their will, he decided that his damp towel was an adequate outfit for the twenty-yard dash, and pulled on his cowboy boots to avoid injuring himself on the scattered gravel. Regardless of Dean's strong feelings, the cowboy boots had proved themselves to be an excellent choice, if ever so slightly insulated for the season. He loved them so much; he'd even forgiven them for instigating an earlier case of minor paranoia.

Unlike his chin, from the age of thirteen, George's legs had always enjoyed a good, healthy covering of thick, dense hair. Being able to show them off in shorts at school to the giggling groups of girls had been the only reason he tolerated PE at all. He was therefore, devastated a few weeks earlier when he'd discovered two small bald patches appearing on each leg, on the inner and outer calf muscle. Initially, considering some of the bizarre injuries he'd already sustained at the gym, he assumed they were the after-effect of some sort of exercise, and welcomed the excuse to shy away from training legs for a week or so.

But the patches got worse, much worse, and before long he'd convinced himself that they seemed to be getting bigger overnight. He'd wracked his brains for the cause of his affliction. What could possibly be the reason for such a strange occurrence? In the end, he reached a startling conclusion. He'd clearly been the victim of an attempted alien abduction.

Arthur had done his very best to listen sincerely to his young neighbour. Clearly consumed with a mixture of blind fear and genuine enthusiasm, he detailed his theory over the garden fence, a large quivering glass of limoncello in his unsteady hand. His thesis was indeed interesting. The bald patches were actually a previously undocumented type of Crop Circle. According to George, it had only been a miscalculation of scale, on the U.F.O's part, that had prevented him from being abducted whilst he slept, and subjected to any manner of probing and experiment.

Eventually, the true source of the bald patches was identified and explained by an exasperated Mr Butler senior. Having been in an even more pragmatic mood than usual, following an unpleasant afternoon wrestling with a greasy gearbox, he suggested that the issue could be swiftly resolved by simply buying longer socks. It wasn't quite as exciting as his youngest son's theory, but it did the trick nonetheless.

Arthur was extremely disappointed though. He'd decided to torment, rather than sympathize with his adopted Grandson, and had invested a good deal of his week painstakingly constructing miniature Flying Saucers from discarded baked been tins, which he'd hammered flat, silver painted Ping-Pong balls, and tin foil. He'd intended to haphazardly crash land his replicas into his neighbour's plant pots whilst he was at work. This, he was quite sure, would drive him completely over the edge. He'd keep them though. They'd be bound to come handy at some point, especially living next door to him.

George retuned from the BMW with one hand full of CDs from the glove compartment, and the other full of serious looking letters he'd retrieved from his startled Postman. The Postie had soon shrugged off the experience and got on with his round. It wasn't the first time he'd seen this particular resident half naked. He felt fairly certain that it wouldn't be the last.

As an afterthought, George quickly wedged open the communal pass door with an unopened copy of the Yellow Pages, in an effort to let out the mid-morning cooking stench that emanated from his elderly neighbours apartment. Given that he'd suggested that the Butler kitchen might be closed for a week, Arthur had obviously defaulted to 'Old People's Food', and had taken to boiling Brussels sprouts, cauliflower and cabbage for his evening meal, a mere eight hours in advance, leaving the whole hallway smelling like an Old Folks Home.

With a warm breeze whipping under his front door, Bob safely installed in the Stereo and 'Is this Love' already working its Rastafarian magic, he looked smugly around his spotlessly clean home one last time. Summer should be left in no doubt that he'd moved up in the world over the past eight months, even if it had been at the cost of his credit rating. But would she really care about all the shiny new stuff he'd bought?

Mrs Butler had sanitized and fumigated both leather sofas, but not before first taking the added precaution of pulling on a pair of fresh, industrial thickness yellow rubber gloves, and now the usual masculine smell of leather mingled awkwardly with the aroma of lemon disinfectant. The glass coffee table was for the first time since new, completely transparent and free of coffee rings or enormous cat prints, and the vibrant rug had been coaxed back into life with a good hard scrub, and a liberal dusting of Shake 'n' Vac.

George's guitars, the Stratocaster and his original cheap acoustic, rested contentedly in two new stands next to the smaller of the sofas, an equally new Marshall Amplifier squatting between them. Unhappily, during his Mum's purge, he'd been forced to dust these, and as he was physically unable to pick up either without having a decent strum, cleaning had been briefly suspended in favour of some impromptu blues. He was soon told off.

It was time for a brew. Something familiar and reassuring to take the edge off, and considering he rather fancied taking his guest out for a gentle drive in the M3 later, it needed to be something non-alcoholic for a change.

George was starting to suspect that he might be bordering on the fringes of alcoholism. Indeed he couldn't remember the last time a day had gone by without at least half a litre of frosty homemade limoncello, and a few very large glasses of full-bodied red passing his lips. He shrugged off the notion though, and boiled the kettle instead. Rolling his slightly stiff shoulders, he reflected on the excuse he often trotted out at times like this. With all the time he spent at the gym, drinking didn't really matter at all, did it?

The damp towel was starting to chaff, making his waistline wrinkly. With a steaming brew for company, and Bob well into 'No Women No Cry', he made for his bedroom and the fresh, carefully considered outfit that lay waiting for him. The towel was banished to the endlessly overflowing wash basket, and he examined the wrinkled skin that circumnavigated his waistline, considering his options. Standing naked in his bedroom, save for the cowboy boots, he carefully hair-dried his moist midriff. The blast of warm air was intoxicating. Soon, feeling reasonably content, his mind got up for a wander again, only for it to be mugged by Doubt and Insecurity as it sauntered down an innocent-looking backstreet.

A few nights ago, in a desperate effort to assemble his thoughts, he'd tried his very best to break the whole Summer affair down into three separate sections of equal confusion and bewilderment. He'd nothing to help guide him on this mental journey, but two bottles of Australian red wine, that had been on offer at the Supermarket, and BB King's 'Best of the Blues'. It proved a lethal combination.

With some reluctance, he eventually admitted that Section One was all about *his* guilt. Although he had the whole Spread Your Wings invitation to fall back on, something he'd often bring to mind when something pleasing and warm lay next to him in expensive underwear, he still couldn't quite escape from the fact that he'd completely covered himself in feathers with this one.

Section Two focused on doubt and uncertainty. Summer was staying for a week, but what if everything went horribly wrong within the first half an hour? What if neither of them could stand the sight of each other anymore, or, if he was being completely honest here, what if she'd gotten fat on garlic bread? It didn't bear thinking of.

Finally there was the painful Section Three, the worse part of all. From his position at least, this Section seemed to completely invalidate Section Two, and yet gave him fresh concerns about her reaction to any revelations that might inadvertently slip out of Section One, when he wasn't looking.

Although some of the girls he'd know of late had been looser than the rusty old exhaust that used to bang about on the underside of his trusty MGB, it never bothered him at all. Not even if he'd seen them again in another nightclub, on another evening, draped around yet another man. It was just part of the game, and he didn't care a jot.

But with Summer things were very different. Although the note she'd left him on Christmas Eve, did indicate that she didn't want anyone else, there was still the small matter of the endless weeks of silence between them. Her great bundle of letters certainly suggested that she was still very keen on him, and they had chased away any fears that she'd permanently moved on, but now they'd been replaced with fresh concerns.

George had begun to fret that during that desperate time, she might have taken an amorous Frenchman as a lover. Some sort of muscular Gaul with forearms like his own thighs, who was more than happy to appease her emotional pain in between servings of fresh Escargot, and for some reason that his twenty-year-old mind couldn't, or perhaps more tellingly, wouldn't, fathom, the thought of this turned his stomach into knots.

Thankfully though, someone else managed to channel his wayward thoughts for him, to lead him gently by the hand to the correct path. Arthur put it best when, over the garden fence, he simply said, "*Sunshine, sometimes you've got to lose something for a while before you realise just how much you really needed it after all. And better still, how great it is when you find it again, and discover that it's not been damaged or molested, it's okay, it's just fine, and just as you left it.*"

His meaning had sadly been lost for a few moments though, and the old man had to patiently explain to George that he was speaking euphemistically, and not talking about misplacing his wallet or car keys. But they got there, in the end.

The warmth of the hairdryer was addictive, and George continued to blast his midriff with hot air, long after the whitish wrinkly skin had returned to its seasonal, medium olive brown. Fred meanwhile, no stranger to the dryer himself having been well and truly fluffed up after being caught in a summer downpour, watched his human suspiciously from the edge of the freshly made bed. His human was acting very strangely this morning.

Bob was just coming to the end of 'Three Little Birds', and it was just as this song faded that George was quite sure that he heard a knock at the door over the roar of the hair dryer. He flicked it off and stood perfectly still, clutching it like a pistol.

There it was again. Given that there was the pass door to negotiate, it had to be someone from within the apartment block. It couldn't be Arthur. He was under strict instructions to sunbath in his steamer chair from midday onwards, to look distinctive and charming at all times, and await further instruction.

That just left Penelope from upstairs. The other residents were very rarely seen, let alone coaxed into conversation. It was strange on her part though. Other than venturing downstairs to complain, extremely timidly about the excessively loud Blues coming from his Stratocaster a few Saturday's ago, in an effort to impress some girl he'd brought home, she seemed inclined to just happily hibernate and Hoover.

There was another knock, this one more urgent than the others. Bob wasn't that loud surely, and the guitars were both safely resting in their stands, what on earth was all this about? He really didn't need hassle from above right now. Perhaps if he ignored her, she'd just bugger off?

Again the persistent knock. It was obviously not a man's aggravated thumping boom, which would have surely rattled the door hinges by now. No, it was clearly a woman's insistent rap. Judging by the tempo, it was being played with a small knuckle. Clearly there was no escape. He'd have to deal with Penelope and whatever her problem was, hopefully the sight of him naked again, except for his cowboy boots, would be enough to drive her off for good.

George marched purposefully towards the front door, irritated beyond belief that his carefully thought out timetable was going to be interrupted by his reclusive neighbour. Damn the woman! He paused briefly to grab a fresh towel from his shower room. No sense in ruining *her* for normal men after all, wrapped it around his cooling waist, and clip clopped across the remaining hallway, eventually flinging open the front door with all the exaggerated force he could muster.

"*Oh*! Err... *My Monkey*, you've grown a moustache!"

Chapter 18

Summertime Blues

Thirty-eight minutes later.

George lay spread eagled and alone on his bed, starring sightlessly at the plastered white ceiling above him. His chest was heaving, despite all the hours he'd put in on the wretched treadmill, and a thin layer of perspiration covered his naked body. The gentle breeze that drifted in through the still wide open bedroom window, drew goose bumps all the way down to the toes of his right foot, the left still safely protected from the elements by a persistent cowboy boot that somehow seemed unwilling to join its fallen comrade on the floor.

No more than an hour must have passed since he'd carefully made the bed and vacuumed off any orangey traces of Fred. But now it lay crumpled and creased under his exhausted body, like a screwed up treasured handkerchief, ready for the wash.

Over the past few months, he'd been lucky enough to enjoy more than his fair share of pleasurable female company. He'd learnt new, invaluable life skills too. Skills that helped expedite the evacuation of a temporary nocturnal visitor, such as making sure he'd always had a good supply of taxi numbers at his disposal. But now, such thoughts couldn't have been further from his mind.

He didn't want this one to ever leave, ever again.

Before the inevitably flush of the toilet signalled the return of his amorous guest, he tried to recall the details of the past forty minutes or so. Not the explicit details, those would be etched into his mind for a lifetime, but the little information he'd gleaned in that brief moment between Summer finishing the word 'Moustache', and when she'd flung her tiny, yet deceptively strong, slender arms around his neck.

Like a perfect morning sunrise appearing from behind a misty window, fresh images finally came flooding back. To begin with, there was her face. A beautiful face he knew so well, but that seemed to have changed ever so slightly. Was she even more beautiful than he remembered? It certainly seemed so. Her eyes, which had once been shy, hidden from the world by a bowed head and a fallen mass of hair, now blazed with joy, positively sparkling with excitement. Her wavy brown hair also seemed to have finally given up its pursuit of being unruly and disobedient, yet somehow still managed to maintain a cool, nonchalant air of uncontrollability. The difference now being, it looked as though it was a statement, not a curse.

She dressed completely differently too. Previously she'd had a somewhat ambivalent approach to clothing, seeing it as a necessary evil that prevented people from starring, and from her getting a chill in the kidneys. But in the months that had passed she'd clearly wandered off in the direction of 'Boho-Chic'. Judging by how naturally, if briefly, she'd worn the outfit that now lay scattered randomly across the bedroom floor, she'd obviously been very happy and at ease with what she'd found there.

She still clearly had her eclectic and unique approach to accessorising though. But where her appendages and neckline had once been weighed down with heavy ethnic bangles, which in capable hands could have conceivably brought down a grazing water buffalo, she now wore delicate charms and handmade necklaces. I was all far more complimentary, far more feminine, and devastatingly attractive.

And then there was her body. Regardless of all the high heels that had tottered in and out of his apartment over the months, leaving a trail of make up on his pillow cases, and using up all his toilet roll in a single sitting, it was always the image of Summer's pale, delicately curved figure that uniquely stayed with him. But like her face, this aspect had also changed. Thanks to the endless sunshine that had bathed Provence, save for the devastating storm, this once perfect English Rose had transformed spectacularly into a glowing Mediterranean Sunflower. She was breathtaking on a whole new level. And knowing her, she wouldn't have a clue.

The bathroom door opened a fraction and the tiny bronzed face peered through the gap, ocean blue eyes ablaze. The sight of the splayed body, which hadn't moved an inch from where she'd left it earlier, made her reddening blushes, deepen. She retreated briefly, and giggled in the safety of the shower room.

"*Monkey*, don't you think you'd perhaps be happier, *err*, under the covers now, and maybe you could kick off the other boot?"

George was aware of a voice somewhere out in there in the void, but it was a moment before he fully returned to consciousness. Like a drowning man who'd happily accepted his fate, and was letting the warm sea gently take him, he had mixed feelings about the kind soul who'd dragged him aboard his boat. Feelings which quickly crystallised into delight however, when reality was eventually restored.

"No, *make me*!"

"*Monkey*! Please, you know how embarrassed I get!" It crossed his mind to challenge her playfully on just *where* her embarrassment had been hiding a few moments ago, but rather than risk ruining any inhibited future nookie, he instead tugged off the boot, which had stuck fast to his calf muscle with drying sweat, and pulled the crumpled duvet over him.

"*Ready*!"

Summer finally emerged from the bathroom, not naked and coy as he'd hoped, but almost entirely cocooned in George's impossibly white, fluffy dressing gown, which only the week before had been subjected to all the unbending might of his Mum's 'hand wash and comfort'. It was just as well.

Two small brown feet, which he noticed were decorated with a scattering of toe rings, poked out from bottom, and she quickly made for the bedroom across the laminate floor, her hands wrapped so tightly around her tiny body, that they became lost somewhere in the deep folds of the gown. She pulled back the duvet and jumped in. Still wearing the dressing gown, she quickly pulled the duvet over them both, and up under her chin before either she saw anything rude, or George did something ruder.

Bob meanwhile, had been playing on throughout the all excitement, and now, ironically enough, had reached 'Waiting in Vain'. It prompted a question.

"*Summertime?*"

"Yes Monkey?" She lowered the duvet slightly, unnerved by the barest suggestion of change in his tone.

"Have you missed me then?"

Relived, she pulled the duvet right up under her nose again, to hide her unabashed honesty and conceal her relief. "Oh, err, well, *only when I was breathing...*"

Whilst the passion had been raging inside the apartment, as the reunited lovers rekindled their relationship and tested the bedsprings, those left outside had a far less pleasant morning. Fred, who as usual had been watching his human's antics with bemused interest from the windowsill, had been caught on the nose by some sort of airborne item of underwear, and had quickly retreated to the relative calm of Arthur's lap.

Arthur meanwhile, who'd been sat patiently waiting in his steamer chair to be introduced to his neighbour's Special Guest, decided at the first hint of a moan from next door, that it was probably best to retreat inside. He sealed the patio door shut, barricaded himself in his bathroom with his wireless and the Saturday papers, and waited the ordeal to be over. This left Fred to wander the estate, looking for something innocent and furry to take the whole experience out on.

"So you definitely think I should shave it *all* off then?" Having dressed in his towel again, George critically examined his hairy chin in the misting bathroom mirror, a sink of steaming water and a fresh razor at the ready. He had mixed feelings about hacking it all off. It had taken him ages to grow.

"Err, *I think so*, it makes you look older, *and it tickles!*" Summer was still in bed, still securely wrapped up in the dressing gown as though it was the depths of winter. Well and truly snuggled.

George wiped a flannel over the mirror and frowned. Like teenagers, desperately hoping to fool the off license owner, he was still at an age where being told he looked older wasn't necessarily a bad thing. Something that he would inevitably change his mind about when he reached his late twenties, when age caught up with him, and he could no longer find the end of a reel of sticky tape. As for tickling, well, it didn't tickle him.

Sensing hesitation, and fearing that she'd spend the week developing a rash, Summer decided it was time to offer a little incentive. "Please shave it off. I'll give you your present..."

"*Okay!*" That did the trick.

Like most men who've grown facial hair though, it wasn't going to be a quick shave. He'd periodically reappear from the bathroom to ask at first whether sideburns and a goatee suited him, then if sideburns and a moustache worked any better, followed by moustache only, before at last emerging clean shaven and cut ribbons. The bathroom looked like a crime scene.

"Where's my present then?"

Ten miles further down the coast from the sprawling grey city was a stretch of perfect shingle beach. It was just over three miles long and bordered by an almost equally long freshwater lake. As well as the beach, a wide bank of grassland and a thick marsh kept the sea from visiting its distant cousin, and a long, almost perfectly straight road divided the two, cutting through the landscape like a rule.

At the closest end, if approaching from the city, a small village clung to the shoreline, its few permanent inhabitants praying each year for a kind winter, desperately hoping the sea would behave. Over the years, commerce had gradually begun to cater purely for the tourist trade. Where once there'd been a thriving, if somewhat bleak fishing industry, operating directly off the beach, there were now a scattering of 'bucket and spades' novelty shops, and the inevitable greasy, fish and chip van.

In contrast to the traditional English seaside fare, parked permanently on an immaculately kept lawn between the sea and the lake, there was a decommissioned Sherman Tank. It served as a reminder and as a memorial to the hundreds of servicemen who needlessly lost their lives on that very beach during a wartime naval exercise that had ended in tragedy. It was an impressive and unflinching monolith. One that had presumably been preserved over the years by countless tins of black Hammerite paint, untarnished as it was by the endless war it now waged against the sea salt.

To the left of the Tank and its patch of lawn, there was a gravely car park. It became unbelievably congested during the summer months, as family saloons crammed full of sweaty children and slobbering dogs, jostled for a spot in which to leave the overheated motor. Regardless of the dust, the overbearing heat and the odd fractious argument that broke out over a space, the car park was within easy walking distance of the shops and a section of beach which they led directly down to. This small fact made the battle well worth winning for the exhausted drivers.

Despite the expanse of largely unpopulated beach that stretched out to the left of the main attractions, no one seemed inclined to explore it. Leaving instead, a throng of sun burnt bodies, spilt ice creams, aggravated over heated dogs, screaming children or belligerent seagulls gathered below the shops. The shingle here would soon become overrun with families of every shape and size, all of whom seemed to fear venturing too far away from either the car or the candy floss. This left the vast stretch of remaining beach free. It belonged to those fit enough to walk any distance on shingle, and those who simply wanted some peaceful ocean therapy of their very own.

"Why didn't we come here before Monkey?" Summer crunched barefoot through the shingle, each step just the right side of a pleasant tickle, her feet naturally exfoliated by the terrain.

"Too damn cold in the winter Summertime, plus you could get washed out to sea if it gets really bad." Having forgotten to borrow the Butler picnic basket, George was carrying two bulging Supermarket carrier bags instead. Both were bursting with burgers and sausages, an assortment of salad, a big pot of coleslaw, a frying pan, plates and forks, and a warming bottle of Chardonnay.

It had been a perfect week, better even than either of them had hoped. But it had gone in the blink of an eye, and this sadly was to be their last day together, before Summer headed home tomorrow morning. Yet they'd planned to make the most of it, before in the inevitable separation, and the inevitable tears. They crunched on, legs and bottoms beginning to feel the strain. But it would be worth it. They'd left the heaving crowds far behind them now, and were heading towards a virtually private beach at the far end.

The weather had been especially generous. Apart from a rainy Wednesday afternoon, which had seen them retreat first to the cinema, and then eventually to bed, the skies had been crystal clear and free of cloud. The Sunday before, Summer had been very carefully driven to the Butlers' respectable semi in the M3, and once there, had been hugged to within an inch of her life, and presented with a feast to rival that of the finest of Roman banquets. The Butlers were clearly very happy to see her again, and they were eventually packed off with bright lipstick marks on each cheek, full bellies and a large tin that contained their very own, moist fruitcake. Clearly, all diets were off for now.

Later on that first Saturday, she'd also eventually been introduced to Arthur. As she stood in George's little courtyard garden though, listening with genuine interest to his charming neighbour, the colour had briefly drained from her tanned cheeks as she glimpsed the wide open bedroom window. He didn't mention it though, which was rather nice of him.

Apart from the odd trip to the Supermarket to stock up on supplies, and refill the wine rack, they'd spent most of the first half of the week in a state of semi hibernation. Not wishing to stray too far from either the sun drenched garden, or the bedroom. It was perfect. Every meal, including breakfast in their PJ's, was taken outdoors, and when the clouds did eventually appear late Wednesday morning, they'd put up the patio umbrella and munched their way through a chicken salad as increasingly heavy rain drops bounced off their brightly coloured shelter.

The trip into the City that followed, eventually finding them in the cinema watching a film neither had any interest in seeing, proved that Summer had become a true country girl. She'd never seemed at ease in town anyway, but now she appeared genuinely uncomfortable. The pace of life, the grim faced crowds and the general lack of consideration for others, as the masses fought their way towards the vast cinema complex, frightened her. She'd clung onto George's arm for reassurance, which naturally in response, he'd flexed to show off his new muscles. Disappointingly, she was still yet to comment on them.

Later that evening, relived to be back at the apartment, the rain continued to batter against the windows, and they'd huddled together under the vast soft duvet like chipmunks caught in a storm, sharing stories, some of which were carefully edited by one party, and devoured steaming mugs of tea, whilst a vast vat of Ragu bubbled away on the hob.

Even Fred was happy. He'd never taken to any of his human's female guests before, except for his Mum of course, who was a master of the ear tickle, but after a just one morning in Summer's company, he'd fallen completely in love. It wasn't anything to do with how she looked, smelt or even that she offered him titbits from the table when his human wasn't looking. It was just the way she patted him on the bum. It was simply bliss.

Summer had been taught by one of the Frenchwomen at her parents Artist Retreat, that the best way to tame the semi feral cats that roamed the countryside was to offer small morsels of food and then tap them quite quickly, and with gradually increasing force, on their lower back just by the base of the tail. The moggy should then collapse in ecstasy and meow with pleasure. Fred was now an addict.

In the midst of all this happiness though, there was just one little wobble, one hiccup that briefly threatened to shatter the harmony. It was on Thursday morning, whilst George was showering, that the telephone had rung. Summer, without thinking, had answered it. It just seemed like the natural thing to do. But when he eventually emerged from his usual ten minute soaking, he found her in the hallway, still holding the receiver, looking a little crestfallen.

"Err, some girl called *Natasha* just called. Was she err, *a girlfriend* or something?"

He'd paused for a moment, stalling, desperately collecting his thoughts. Everything had been going so fantastically, there was no way he wanted it ruined, especially not by Natasha. Finally he had a flash of inspiration. "Oh, err, not at all, *no*, she's umm, just someone I err, played, err, *tennis* with sometimes…"

Summer had looked relived but still confused. "*Tennis*? Oh, I didn't know you played, are you any good?"

"Umm, sometimes, so *she* says. But I've decided to give it up now."

"Really, have you gone off the game then, Monkey?"

Relieved that the whole 'Spread your Wings' conversation he'd feared all week, seemed to have been cunningly avoided, he'd reached for her tiny hands and smiled into the perfect blue eyes, "I suppose so Summer, I just never really got a hang of the rules I guess…"

But he wasn't out of the woods just yet. Later that afternoon, after a hearty pub lunch in the small village where Summer used to live, she'd found something she'd rather not have, something that somehow had managed to evade both the Butler Purge and The Mummy Clean. It was no more than a damning, discarded hair bobble on the bathroom door, but it said as much as if she'd found a spare naked girl hiding in his chaos cupboard. Finally, they had the conversation.

George had perched on the edge of the smaller of the two leather sofas, a spot he found oddly unfamiliar having never sat there before, tried to ignore the new perspective this vantage point threw on his lounge, and instead prepared for the argument that was bound to come. Summer meanwhile had sat equally upright on the adjacent sofa. Her tiny hands cupped, trembling slightly, as she tried to find the right words to express her barrage of emotions. Clearly neither of them wanted to be having this chat. Unable to ever tolerate a period of prolonged silence, George eventually spoke first, and when he did so, it without pause or any discernible need to draw breath.

Like a model schoolboy, who'd fallen off the rails, and wrongly assumed he'd been caught stealing the petty cash, when in fact the Headmaster was rather more interested in finding out who'd been stretching Clingfilm over the toilet seats, he admitted to everything in fine, Technicolor detail. In one great, endless tirade of unfiltered, uncensored information, he'd confessed to the endless parade of girls that had tottered in and out of his apartment, the mornings when he'd been so hung-over and unable to recall events of the night before, that he'd just been grateful to find a girl lying next to him, even if he couldn't remember her name.

He told of the instances of Groin Lending he'd indulged in, including the Nightclub Manageress who'd been more than happy to repay his financial skills in kind, least she become insolvent again, and the lecture he'd had from Dean about being less than open about the financial products he was selling to his customers. Then there was a summary of his brief attempts at relationships, designed to replace her and which ultimately failed dismally, of the odd times when offers of unexpected repeat nookie came out of the blue mid Sunday morning, and he'd needed to quickly change the sheets before the next willing guest arrived.

Yet all through this download, somewhere inside a voice kept screaming at him, begging him to edit his confession before it was too late, to tone down the gory bits and add some much needed pixies and fairies to this Eighteen Certificate tail of philandering and plundering. But still he continued on, perhaps desperate to offload his guilt. It was painful to watch.

Fred had even jumped up and sat next to Summer on the sofa, smugly watching as his human squirmed and rambled on, his ears being tickled absentmindedly. All the while though, she never took her eyes off her young man as he continued animatedly with his story, even when the pit he was digging was well past his ears.

Finally he ran out of steam. He was spent, his epic confession complete. If he'd been Catholic, a whole team of Priest's would have needed to be work in shifts around the clock to process the information.

The silence that had followed had only been broken by the tigers, Harley Davidson purr. Even George didn't feel confident to jump in and fill this empty void. What else did he have left to say? Summer had finally leant forward, and placed her hands on his knees, smiled briefly and got up. This is it, he'd thought, she's going to pack the few clothes she'd hung next to his in the wardrobe, which had made him feel both invaded and grown up all at once, storm out, and head back to France. It's over, again.

He'd braced himself, preparing for the emotional landslide to come. The damning character annihilation, the utter disgust at the life he'd lived, the shame he should feel for the discarded trail of girls he'd left in his wake, the threats to tell his Mum. God no, *not that!* As often he did in times of woe, he'd tried to look beyond the immediate pain. To seek out some glimmer of light at the end of the tunnel, something he'd do perhaps to pick himself off the canvas after the battering he would have to endure. Normally this would be a night out on the town, the promise of a fresh girl to ruin, or maybe a call from Natasha to say that she fancied a quick match. But strangely, none of this had comforted him. Instead it had left him cold, with a desperate yearning to turn back the clock an hour so.

In the end though, Summer didn't storm out. The verbal assault never came either, that just wasn't her style. She did the one thing that she knew needed to be done more than anything else at that moment. Something that might just yet make everything alright, restore order and some degree of serenity to both their relationship and their holiday. She'd put the kettle on.

George had cupped the steaming mug of tea in both hands and took some comfort in the warmth it provided. Fred was moved from the warm spot she'd left when she'd gotten up to make the tea, and Summer had sat down exactly where she'd been before, sipping her tea slowly. And then, in a calm level voice that was controlled and trembling in equal parts, she'd begun to talk.

For a while, George felt the age gap between them. She'd used long, meaningful words about feelings, deep relationships and the importance of trust and respect between partners, which left him wishing he could stop her for a moment, check his spelling and scribble them down in order to ask Arthur to explain them to him later. She'd talked about what she really wanted from him, about accepting his imperfection's as much as all his positive qualities, he'd felt he was on much firmer ground here, and also about what he wanted from his life. Perhaps most importantly, there'd been no mention of spreading any wings this time.

She pressed on though, this time with questions. Did he feel that he was done with that type of life? Did the endless possibilities of a night on the town still hold any interest for him? Was there even any stone left unturned, or would he need to relocate to a new city? This brief, uncharacteristic moment of light sarcasm had caught George rather off guard, and he'd spent a few moments considering house prices further up the coast, before an involuntary, utterly welcome giggle broke the daydream and some of the seriousness that weighed heavy in the lounge, thankfully dispersed.

They'd sat looking at each other for a moment. Unsure as to whether or not they'd should let the giggle grow and mature into a healing, fully formed laugh, or whether it should be suppressed, reprimanded and packed away to its room, in order to allow the grownups to talk.

Fortunately, George Butler was never destined to be a grown up.

The effort of trudging endlessly across the shingle was starting to take its toll. Seldom used stabilising muscles and tendons were straining to keep both of the walkers upright on the constantly shifting terrain. Thighs ached and bottoms winced in spite of daily jogs in the crisp Parisian mornings, or punishing squats in the gym, the far end of the beach stubbornly refusing to get any closer.

"This spot will do, *surely*? Look, there's no one around for miles." Summer stood in mock petulance, her weary hands fallen at her sides, small shoulders slumped in defeat. She had a point though. Despite her usual prudishness, even she'd stripped off her kaftan top a few hundred yards back, suitably content that she was way beyond even the most dedicated of prying eyes, and now risked just her bikini top and linen shorts, much to her partner's approval.

George meanwhile, was already practically naked. It troubled him that all his months of pain and anguish in the gym, still hadn't raised even the barest hint of a compliment from her. In a last ditch effort to coax some praise, he'd slung his muscle vest over his shoulder the minute his feet touched the beach, and now wore just the jeans he'd roughly hacked off before leaving that morning. They were so short, even Daisy Duke would have blushed.

"*Aww*, come on Summertime, look, just a few more steps and we'll be at the end. It's totally private over there - *we can do anything we like…*" He grinned mischievously. However colourful his life had been in the past months, it had failed yet to yield nookie on the beach yet. Now, in the warm peaceful afterglow that followed the near terminal conversation of the day before, he couldn't think of a better way to celebrate. At least it wasn't sandy.

"*George Butler*, really, you're an animal!"

"*Grrr*!"

For all its unpleasantness, the events of Thursday afternoon had been utterly necessary. Summer needed to know what he'd been up to, and George needed to confess. He just didn't know it at the time. Given that she'd also spoken so genuinely about commitment and trust, it reassured him, without having to say a word, that she hadn't strayed into the nearest barn with some random Gaul for a bit of Anglo-French refreshment. It was a massive, if somewhat hypocritical relief.

Summer understood George. Even though they hadn't actually spent that much time together, it felt as though she'd known him for a lifetime. He had that effect. A young man of very, very few soppy words, he didn't do grand gestures of love, or spend hours writing letters that delved into the deepest depths of his heart. But he did do uniquely 'George Butler' things. Like take her for a picnic in the snow, or write her letters about his Brother and the mischief they got up to when they were younger, invite her around to his parents and ask his Mum to make her a dress for a Ball, or serve her lunch outside in the rain. It all added up. Perhaps these things wouldn't mean much to anyone else, but they meant the world to her. She knew now, more than ever, that she wanted to spend the rest of her life with him. It certainly wouldn't be dull.

"*This'll do!*" He bent down and placed the carrier bags carefully on the shingle, so as not to break the Chardonnay, his shorts almost revealing parts of him that Summer had never wished to see, and stretched luxuriously. It had indeed been worth the trek. The road veered off a hundred yards back and disappeared up an unseen hill, bordered by pine trees, and climbed the rising cliffs which curved around the spot George had chosen. The beach here opened up into a vast bay, and at the foot of the cliff there were centuries old boulders that warmed in the lunchtime sun, and kept the chill off the evening lovers that hid there at night. With any luck, they'd be joining them later. At a suitable distance, of course.

According to his salt encrusted Seiko, it was just past one, definitely time for lunch. Calling upon camping skills that had lay dormant for a while, he quickly gathered together a few small rocks, dug out a modest pit in the shingle, and built a wind shelter in which to build his camp fire.

Summer had strongly suggested that they limit their chances of food positioning by adding a disposable barbeque to the shopping list. But as usual, her boyfriend would not be swayed, and now, as he darted about the beach in his ridiculous shorts, expertly gathering wood and kindling, she had to admit, she was somewhat impressed. She was even more impressed a few minutes later when he managed to get the fire going, without losing all of his eyebrows.

The fire cracked and hissed as pockets of moisture and lost slugs, which had sought refuge in the timbers, met with the flames and a grisly end. The sausages and burgers smelt delicious, as they sizzled away on the frying pan, which was suspended between two larger rocks. The Chardonnay was lukewarm, and the tin camping cups were hardly the same as finest crystal, but any wine in the sun is a blessing, and as they stared out over the endless ocean waiting for their lunch to cremate, Summer and George lay snuggled up close together, wrapped in the contentment that only a beach campfire can bring.

They ate messily, without a care, laughing at each other for getting coleslaw in unexpected places, eventually washing down the burnt offerings with the remains of the white wine. Although the August sea temperature was bound to bring on a mild case of hypothermia, he managed to persuade Summer to join him for a quick dip, to freshen up, or perhaps something more.

It was short-lived, though. Partly due to the piercing cold, but mostly because of the huge school of jellyfish that became interested in them. They splashed out of the water as though they'd seen an advancing shark, and tore up the beach to the comfort of their smouldering fire. Stretching out on two of George's finest bath towels, with full bellies and a little wine to carry them on their way, they soon drifted off to sleep in the afternoon sun.

Summer woke up first, although to begin with, she couldn't quite fathom what had woken her. The unmistakable crunch of shingle under foot soon shook away the last misty remains of sleep though, and without thinking she quickly wrapped the towel around her body, covering her bikini, protecting her modesty.

"George, *George!* Someone's coming!" The comatose lump next to her stirred briefly, groaned and sat up. A covering of smaller shingles gradually falling from an outstretched arm and the side of his face. He'd clearly rolled off the edge of the towel during his slumber.

"*Hmm?*" The sun was behind the approaching figure, so it was difficult to make out any details, but it looked like a man, and it also looked like a reasonable group of other people had gathered on the circular beach to their left. A collection of silhouettes were busy running about, playing what looked like cricket. It all seemed quite serene.

As the man came upon their camp though, several things happened at once. The sun briefly hid behind a cloud. All the silhouettes suddenly became clear, three dimensional figures. Summer hid under her towel, and George, having finally rubbed the sleepy dust from his eyes and regained his sight, was greeted by a fat, balding middle-aged man, wearing nothing but socks, sandals and a winning smile. It was all far from serene.

"I promise you Summer, I had *no* idea that end of the beach was reserved for nudists, no wonder we never went up that end when we were kids!" He rolled up his bath towel and put it in the boot of the M3, along with the carefully wrapped plates and the frying pan, holding out his hand for the other one. Summer meanwhile, had no plans whatsoever to give up any item of available clothing. Or indeed, ever be naked again for that matter. She instead kept the protective, fluffy shield wrapped tightly around her body.

"He - *he was just stood there though*, in broad daylight, with, with, that thing just, *err*, dangly there for all to see! *What's wrong with these people?!* I mean, it was just, just hanging there!"

George fished the last of the pebbles from his pockets, knowing he'd still be finding them around the apartment at Christmas, and carefully ushered his girl into the passenger seat. She was still trembling slightly from the ordeal, and just gazed unseeing out of the windscreen. He opened the driver's door and hopped in, having Summer on board made getting in the right side first time much easier. He was still shirtless, still breathing in and tensing, and still hoping for a kindly word. Would it ever come?

The M3's black leather had been baking in the black car all day, and the second his lightly toasted back connected with the roasted seats, he sprung back out of the BMW like Zebedee suffering a sugar rush, dancing around the dusty car park, screaming and swearing at his mechanical torturer. Families scattered, children's ears were covered.

"*Bastard car! I hate it!* All it does is bloody well frighten the hell out of me, try to kill me and now the damn thing's burnt me alive! *Arghhh!*" He was beyond vexed. Summer watched from within the humid cockpit. Still in shock, but now confused too as he stomped back to the boot, pulled out the towel, which showered him in tiny pebbles, listened as he cursed again, before returning in a sulk, to drape it over the offending seat.

"You could always just, *put a shirt on…*" She thought she was being helpfully.

Ignoring the comment, tempted to just ask her once and for all if she thought he looked fit now, he instead fired up the engine, blipped the throttle belligerently, safe in the knowledge that the beast was in neutral, and made to pull out of the car park, to turn right, and head back home for a cold shower, and a tube of Germolene. But he paused instead, and looked at the long three mile stretch of unbending perfect road to his left. Suddenly he had an idea.

"Wanna see what this Baby can do, Summertime?"

"Err, sorry Monkey, *what?*"

"I've never had it out of fourth gear for more than a few minutes! Perhaps it's time to show it who's Boss?" He gripped the steering wheel tighter, still gazing down the long straight.

"I think the car knows its Boss, Monkey."

George turned and raised a quizzical eyebrow, his mind was made up, "I hate that I never open this bloody thing up, and look, you could do with a shock to shake you out of your tree again, *what do you reckon?*"

"I think that I've had quite enough shocks for one day!"

"Aww, Summertime!" The stern racing driver face quickly melted into the more familiar puppy-dog, the bottom lip protruded a fraction for extra leverage. It had the desired effect.

"*Oh go on then*, with any luck you'll run one of them over…"

"*A hundred and twenty-two miles an hour!* I still can't believe it!" George chopped up the last of the ingredients for the ambitious Chinese feast he was preparing, with a huge, freshly bought Sabatier cleaver, as Summer watched, flinching with every absent minded slice. "I mean, it was steady as a rock, if I'd done that in the MR2, it'd have taken off!"

"Yes, yes, quite Monkey, now mind your fingers, that one was very close!"

"A hundred and twenty-two..." He paused for a second, the cleaver half way through another potentially lethal swing. His face suddenly a picture of concern. *"Don't tell Mum will you?"*

Having Arthur over to join them for dinner in the garden was Summer's idea. The old man had been very reluctant at first, suggesting that it was far more appropriate that the young couple spend their last evening of their holiday alone, as long as they promised to close the bedroom window this time.

Blushes aside, she insisted, Summer knew just how important he was to George, and she felt a degree of guilt that her presence had perhaps kept them apart. From that first telephone call, following their prolonged silence, to their idle chit chat on the beach earlier, he'd often spoke fondly of his adoptive Granddad, and now she wanted to get to know him better too. Entertaining also made them both feel like a proper couple too and very grown up.

George was busy in the kitchen dividing his time between tending to a flesh wound, battering the smoke alarm with a dish cloth, and sweeping up yet more small pebbles, when their guest arrived promptly at seven. He was carrying a large bottle of homemade limoncello in one hand, whilst the other felt its way along the wall and surfaces, as though he'd suddenly been struck with blindness. The speed with which he grasped the large glass of red wine offered proved that this was certainly not the case however, but the way he looked so relieved to make it onto one of the barstools in one piece, troubled his Grandson. Something was wrong.

For the first time since he'd known him, Arthur looked like a proper old man, rather than a stout chap who's unintentionally woken up one morning to discover that there was false teeth in a glass beside his bed, and he'd developed a burning desire for a boiled sweet. Once rested and suitably watered though, the old bugger quickly returned, and he soon had his young hosts laughing, enthralled with his anecdotes and observations.

The Chinese meal was something of a success, although Arthur's good natured comparison to it being like greasy string with rocks in it did find George checking that the cashew nuts were in fact nuts, and not yet more shingles from the beach. It could have been much worse though. He'd originally planned to make an experimental dish with squid and baby octopus, but after reducing his kitchen to one of the more disturbing scenes from 'Alien', soon changed his mind.

Presumably expecting some sort of power cut, Summer had packed hundreds of tea lights before she'd left for England, and all week they'd burned brightly in empty jam jars and glass tumblers she'd found about the kitchen. Tonight was no exception, with dozens scattered about the patio, either resting on plant pots, or balancing precariously atop the fence panels, flickering warmly in the cool evening air, as the sun eventually set on the day, and brought with it their precious last night together.

It was a fabulous evening. And once a suitably loosening quantity of wine and limoncello had been consumed, George was eventually coaxed into plugging in his guitar and giving his guests a short performance. His reluctance had been understandable though. The last time he'd played in Summer's company, she'd left him and fled the country. A strong reaction to say the least, one he was desperate to avoid repeating. Undeterred, with the front door firmly locked and secured to prevent any attempt at escape, he carefully synced his backing C.D. to the Marshall amp, tested the volume, adjusted it to prevent deafening his audience, and belted out and instrumental version of Gary Moore's 'Still got the Blues'. It was rather good, and nobody reached for their passport.

Arthur watched in masked amazement. Over the months he'd heard hours of painful practice through the walls. The endless missed notes and bum cords, as his neighbours bleeding fingers desperately wrestled with yet another new song. At times it had been beyond awful, but this sounded great, and naturally he yearned to demonstrate his approval by pretending to through eggs at him when his show was over. Somehow though, the look of complete devotion and pride he saw in Summer's eyes stopped him. He smiled to himself contentedly. If he didn't bugger things up again, George was sorted. And this thought gave the old man a warm, comforting glow deep inside.

The next morning George awoke in an empty bed to the unmistakably homely sound of hot tea being poured into deep mugs. He could get used to this. Summer shuffled into the bedroom wearing a pair of oversized rabbit slippers, which Fred had molested countless times during her stay, and snuggled back under the cosy white duvet next to him. Apart from their proximity, location and relative nudity, the feeling between them now was similar to their first, awkward time alone together outside Laurence Burton's office. Those stolen minutes when his hawk eyed secretary had briefly disappeared, giving them a few precious moments to try and talk to each other. But what should either of them say?

Summer needed to pack and be away by two o'clock at the very latest, in order to catch the evening ferry back to France, and their very late night meant that waking up before midday was never going to be on the cards. Breakfast was shared in mutual silence, with communication reduced to just wistful, meaningful glances, hand holding and long drawn out sighs.

She then packed slowly, reluctantly, as though she was practicing, memorising where everything went in order to do it all again later, blindfolded. Carefully and deliberately, she folded away her few clothes, gently wrapping up the shells they'd collected together on the beach, and later divvied up later over a glass of wine. George meanwhile, sat on the edge of the bed with Fred, still searching for something appropriate to say. Something in keeping with their predicament, something that would make them both feel a bit better about parting company again. But there just didn't seem to be the words.

He glanced at his Seiko. For the first time since he'd bought it on that first rainy day at the Bank, he wished its relentless, self-winding second had would stop sweeping smoothly, and instead grind to a halt, freezing them in time forever. He really didn't want her to go. And not just because his attraction to her now burned like a relentless inferno, making the flames of their first encounter seem like a complimentary hotel matchstick, but also because they seemed to live together so well.

Arthur had said once that, *'In order to really know a girl, sometimes you have to wake up next to her on at least four consecutive mornings, or afternoons for that matter, to see if it will really work.'* It had seemed completely alien to him at the time. But the old man was right, and they did work, really well. She even squeezed the toothpaste from the bottom of the tube.

George made a huge fuss over loading Summer's modest bag into the trunk of her beloved mini. He shifted the small tool box her Dad insisted she carried, although she had no idea what any of the contents actually did, from side to side, trying to get everything to fit. He was stalling for time, and she wasn't about to hurry him along.

But they couldn't wait forever. Finally there was nothing else to do, no further delays that could be invented, no luggage to fuss over, no tyres pressures to check and no engine parts to examine. Nothing, but for her to get in, start up the little 998 cc engine, and leave for France.

In the end, it was Summer who broke the agonising silence.

"Monkey, err, there's been something I've been meaning to say to you all week, but, umm, I never quite found the right words, or the right time for that matter…"

George frowned. What was this, not bad news now, surely? Perhaps she was finally going to tell him how good his body looked? It seemed like an odd time to bring it up, still, better late than never.

"Umm, my parents have offered you a job in France. I've told them all about your artwork, and how good you are with people, they said they'd like you to come over and join in, to help run the place. That is, *I'd* like you to come over, I mean, as well as them, and, err, well, live with me…" She blushed deeper than ever before, quickly hugged the stunned body, which was ready to explode with questions, until her arms ached and she had to let go, kissed him until he finally snapped out of his shock, and returned the gesture passionately, jumped into the mini and turned the starter.

"Promise me you'll think about it? *Promise me, George.*" Tears streamed down her face and dripped off her tiny chin, soaking her gipsy dress as she reached out for his hand through the rolled down window.

George recovered himself just in time to grasp the offered hand tightly, smile genuinely, and slowly let it slip from his grip as she pulled carefully away. "I, *err*, I - I promise, *Summer*, Summer, *I PROMISE I WILL!*" And then she was gone.

He waved off the hand-painted, battered old Mini for what seemed like an eternity, and certainly long after its distinctive, cheeky exhaust note had disappeared behind the surrounding buildings, on the start of its long journey home. The last time he'd done something like this, he'd been waiving off the coach that had taken Michael, along with the rest of his unit, to some undisclosed airbase, and a flight to a remote corner of the world where people shot at each other. Leaving always sucked.

An unusually cool, mid-afternoon breeze whipped through his hair, bringing with it a reminder that autumn planned to visit soon. In that moment, he felt utterly empty and alone, but at least he had the unexpected, surprising offer to keep his mind occupied. It was time to retreat to the safety and comforting familiarity of his apartment, to seek solace in a large glass of something strong and alcoholic. That would probably help.

Once inside, he firmly locked the front door and paused in the hallway. There was her present. Carefully hung, so that it would be illuminated by at least two of the blinding spotlights, it was perhaps the best birthday gift ever, even if it did make him rather envious of her superior talents. Summer's interpretation of Monet's *Champ de tulipes en Hollande* was the brightest, most beautiful thing she'd ever painted. A world away from the bleak, if expertly realised canvases she'd shown him in Bluebell Cottage all those months ago. Just like her, it was a lot, lot happier.

Finally tearing himself away, he wandered into the kitchen and poured the last of Arthur's limoncello into a tall glass. Topping it up with a healthy measure of Smirnoff vodka, and adding a handful of crushed ice cubes, he collapsed on the larger of the two leather sofas. His home suddenly felt so quiet. He was grateful when Fred wandered in through the open patio door, and jumped up on the glass coffee table. Sitting down abruptly, the tiger briefly cleaned his right ear, before proceeding to glare at his human.

He'd developed something of a lasting crush on the apartment's most recent female visitor. Although she'd failed to grasp the ear tickling concept in quite the same way that his human's Mum had, the whole bottom tapping thing was splendid, odd, but splendid nonetheless. Now though, given that every feline instinct at his disposal told him that she'd vanished, he was pissed off again.

Ignoring him, George took a deep pull from his drink, winced slightly as the strong spirits burned everything it touched, and tried to process all that had happened to him over the past few days. His head was overwhelmed with questions. But maybe this was the answer, this opportunity that had come out of the blue to escape the Bank, to try for a new, completely different life that actually suited his few talents? But what would his parents think of such a rash move? He'd already given up on University because he didn't like that, what would they think if he gave up on the Bank too? To them, it seemed to be respectable career, something that they were proud to tell people their son did. It was a proper job, on paper at least. Surely they'd be disappointed in him?

But what if he could make this could work? What if Dean and Arthur had been right all along? George had heard of people taking a career break before, taking up to a year out to pursue a dream, or have children. Perhaps he could work on this angle? But what about his dire financial situation, how could he make that work? Maybe if he promised Danny that he'd get his head down, work like hell for the rest of the year, and stay in of an evening with a video and his elderly neighbour, instead of spending money he didn't have, in clubs he had no reason to visit anymore, he could earn good bonus and maybe pay off some of his debt?

He could paint much more too, perhaps try and get some of the local galleries on board, ask them to sell his paintings rather than just relying on word of mouth for commissions? Then maybe, just maybe, if everything went to plan, at the end of the year he could sell up, clear everything else, apply for a career break and join Summer in France. Once he was sure he liked things over there, he'd then work on his parents. Convince them that he was much better off now, much happier and settled. Surely this alone would go some way to satisfying his Mum? Perhaps his parents would come over for holidays too, maybe even bring Arthur along with them? He'd like that. As the alcohol took effect, it all started to sound very doable, promising even and much more fun than banking.

Even the mere thought of all this, awoke a whole kaleidoscope of butterflies inside of him, their collective gentle wings, tickling a huge smile out of the previously crestfallen young face. That was it! His mind was made up, he was going to France to paint, to do whatever else they wanted him to do at this retreat, and most importantly, to be with Summer. He leapt up and reached for the telephone. He needed to start work on the most important influencer he had at his disposal without delay. It was time to call his Mum.

"Fred, how do you feel about murdering French Bunnies?" The tiger stopped looking angry and seemed to consider this offer instead. He preened briefly, before acknowledging his acceptance by jumping into the warm patch his human had just vacated, curling up and filling the silence with his usual Harley Davidson purr. "Great! Right then, *let's work on Mum*!"

Frustratingly, just as he was about to lift the receiver, the telephone started to ring. He was in no mood for idle conversation. His days of making half-hearted promises to meet a girl whose name he would struggle to recall the next time their paths crossed for a drink were firmly behind him now. He let it buzz impatiently instead, until the caller finally gave up and the lounge fell silent once more.

Before he could snatch it up though, the telephone started ringing excitedly again. Having drained the limoncello, George headed for the fridge, reached for a frosty bottle of Peroni, popped off the bottle top in one an expert, well-practiced flick of the opener, and drained half the bottle in one swig whilst he waited for it to stop, his bare foot tapping irritably.

At last, the caller finally gave up again. Suddenly there was nothing but the sound of the gentle wind through his potted palms in the courtyard garden, and the tigers purr from the sofa. He gazed thoughtfully at his beer, fighting against his sudden urge to jump in the M3 and chase Summer to the ferry port as quickly as his renewed nerve would carry him. Then telephone started up again.

Although the damned thing only had the one tone, this time it seemed even more urgent than before. Who the hell was it? It suddenly dawned on him that it might be his Mum. It might be news of Michael. His tanned cheeks drained of their seasonal colour, he slammed the beer down on the kitchen top and raced across the lounge, clumsily dived over the arm of the leather sofa and snatched up the receiver.

"HELLO, *Mum*, is that you?" It wasn't.

"Easy there, Duck, *this isn't your Mammie*!" Billy's distinctive northern lilt caught him off guard. It was a moment before he could cope with the emotional change of direction.

"Billy, *BILLY*, what the hell do you want?"

"Oh well that's *lovely* that is! He's been hibernating with an old flame for a week, and all of a sudden he's forgotten his old Mate Bill! Far too busy to answer the damn phone, *what a bloody git he is*!" He sounded genuinely hurt, if only for a moment, "Anyway, if you can tear yourself away from the sack for a moment, you're gonna want to turn on the TV, Duck. BBC One, *the bloody Bank's on Watchdog*!"

"...*What?*"

"George, turn on the telly, *BBC One*. I'll call you back when it's finished..." Billy abruptly hung up, leaving his confused colleague listening to a nameless woman telling him that the other person had cleared. Almost robotically, he reached for his television remote and flicked on the wide screen set, selecting BBC One. Sure enough, Billy was right. The show's two honourable Presenters were stood either side of a Cottons NSIB logo. They didn't look at all happy, and talked animatedly about alleged miss-selling at the high street Bank.

"... *And as the secret filming we've taken over the past few months will now show, these employees' of Cottons NSIB, whose faces we've hidden and voices we've changed for legal reasons, are clearly mis-selling personal loan insurance and other financial products...*"

To begin with it was almost comical. As though the whole thing had been staged, some sort of elaborate joke, reverse advertising perhaps. The 'Customer' was a model example of the breed, extremely easy to interview, and as open with her personal financial information as she was to the CRA's suggestions.

The first two examples were shockingly bad. Both CRAs, obviously blissfully unaware that they were being filmed by some sort of spy camera, presumably hidden in the 'Customer's' handbag, managed to make Billy look like a model employee. They quite sincerely claimed that the 'Customer' had to have PPI with their loan. Because of her age and risk rating, she would also have to apply for a Credit card too, also with PPI, to ensure her credit rating improved in the future. At home, Billy was probably making notes.

The second was more inventive. Even going so far as to insist that she also saw a colleague to set up a pension, apparently so that the Bank would feel more secure lending her money in later life. Desperate as he was, even Kenny wouldn't have stood for that.

The final CRA was far chattier and laidback. He'd made the 'Customer' a cup of tea, despite insisting several times that she didn't actually want one, and had rambled on insistently about trivial things that drifted into his mind. He seemed to casually gather together just the barest scrap of her financial information on his Individual Financial Interview Record. At one point he even seemed to be doodling - a monkey, by the looks of it.

He was obviously quite taken with the 'Customer', leaning across the table periodically, and using some questionable interview techniques that seemed designed to identify which Nightclubs she preferred, rather than explaining the finer points of the products he was trying to sell her. He was clearly trying it on.

George chuckled to himself. Poor buggers, getting caught like that! He tickled Fred's ears and retrieved his Peroni from the kitchen, his mind drifting off to warm feelings of Summer, and of the life they would soon share together. Back on the television, the CRA continued to ramble on hopefully...

"...Well, if you do go out on Friday, remember I'll be at Destiny's *from around ten if you fancy that drink? Although I should warn, it's probably best we don't get together, I'd only end up ruining you for normal men..!"*

All of a sudden, the telephone started to ring again. And this time, it didn't stop.

Chapter 19

Egg-Based Exile

Mid November, Saturday afternoon.

Clad in a borrowed, ill-fitting wetsuit that left him feeling slightly claustrophobic, George Butler popped up on his long board from prone position, and tried, for the hundredth time that afternoon, to assume the perfect surfers pose. After hours of practicing paddling and duck diving, he'd just managed to catch a small hiccup of a wave. It had left him coughing and sputtering in the shallows, and he'd been lying down at the time, gripping the edges of the board tightly until his knuckles showed white. Now it was time to try it standing up. He wasn't convinced.

Popping up proved to be an awful lot harder than it looked, even without the added complication of the sea to contend with. The thought of putting the unwieldy slab of fibreglass and foam into a pitching surge of swirling, freezing water, and then somehow trying to master leaping from prone to standing, whist simultaneously shifting his weight from left to right, back to front, or whatever other combination was required to maintain balance at that time, seemed beyond the will of man.

To begin with, George couldn't quite understand what possible joy could be gleaned from this brutal pastime, even when practiced somewhere hot, like Hawaii. Let alone here, on a bleak English beach at the start of what was clearly going to be a harsh winter. Threatening rain clouds continued to gather overhead, as increasingly mountainous waves crashed harder and harder against the shoreline. Nevertheless, the afternoon's aquatic adventures had succeeded in taking his mind off things for a while. And if his mind was focusing its efforts on not drowning, then it couldn't be fretting about its current predicament. And that had been David Weedon's plan all along.

The past few months had been less than pleasant for George. From the very second he'd heard his own damning 'Word Pattern' on *BBC Watchdog*, his world had started to fall apart. All the hopes and dreams that had grown so quickly in his mind, during those few moments after Summer had made her invitation, suddenly fell from his grasp, and smashed into a million pieces on his hard, oak effect laminate flooring. And no amount of his Dad's borrowed Superglue was ever going to put them back together again.

First thing Monday morning, he'd been called into work, despite still being on holiday. Not to his native Profile Branch though, but to Area Office instead, where he was met by two intense, unflinching grey faces he'd never seen before, along with a sheepish looking Danny, and the newly appointed Area Director. Any hopes he'd briefly harboured that perhaps nobody important had watched the show, and that he might even get away with it, soon evaporated as the seriousness of the situation caught up with him.

Having never been in serious trouble before, either in the Bank or at School, he wasn't quite sure what to expect. He had a suspicion that being seen on national television, casually chatting up a Customer, rather than providing sound financial advice, might result in a stern telling off, perhaps by his Manager, or maybe even by the Area Director. But when the two solemn faces introduced themselves as regional Human Resources Officers, the knot in his stomach trebled in size. It seemed his situation was far more desperate than he'd imagined. Suddenly he wanted his Mum and a cup of tea.

The BBC had secretly filmed twenty-seven Cottons NSIB employees across the country. Of which twenty-six could conceivably have been charged with either mis-selling, misleading, or at the very least, failing to provide full product disclosure to the 'Customer'. It wasn't a particularly impressive ratio. The Bank had been given a list of the culprits' names and locations, the challenge presumably being to discipline the suspects, and evidence that the 'Bonus Seeking Predatory Sales Culture', as the report had aptly labelled it, and been both addressed and quashed.

However, the Bank had a number of issues with this proposal. Firstly, they rather liked the 'Bonus Seeking Predatory Sales Culture'. It had grown organically within the organisation, thanks to numerous, carefully constructed and downright ruthless training courses, moral shattering bonus opportunities, and an arsenal of sales words patterns that, if used correctly, could turn even the strongest of minds into a buyer.

The bonuses the sellers were awarded were chicken feed compared to the colossal revenue the Bank earned off the back of the lending interest rates, loan insurance premiums and the greedy margin held back on savings balances, let alone the endless stream of annualising renewal income from home insurance policies. This soaring growth in the market place had seen the share price rocket in recent months, and the potential dividend swell beyond all expectation. Cottons NSIB's Top Management, tended to hold lots of shares.

Secondly, each of the guilty twenty-six members of staff were largely exemplary sellers. And whilst they could be replaced, everyone in Banking was expendable these days; it would take some time, and would probably also have a deeper impact in the short term. The top twenty percent of CRAs in the league tables were a competitive bunch of vampires. Whilst they were endlessly chasing on the tails of the next CRA above them, they naturally sold more and more in an effort to climb the ladder. If twenty-six highly motivated sales predators were taken out of that jungle, then those that had been doing the chasing would start to run a little slower. They'd perhaps hold back a few sales for the next month, as the need for them to box a little cleverer, just to stay ahead, had been marginally reduced.

Finally there was public image to consider. After the recession, earlier in the decade, the country had discovered that it really rather liked the Nineteen Nineties, and was enjoying a period of rapid economic growth. To celebrate, everybody seemed to have decided to borrow excessively and spend well beyond their means.

The *BBC Watchdog* report had caused a stir, and in the days that followed, the report echoed briefly on the tabloid front pages. But there wasn't the catastrophic scandal that Top Management had initially feared, as they'd spat out their Saturday afternoon G&T's when the program was originally aired. The nation instead just seemed to shrug its shoulders, and continue to choose expensive cars, holidays and kitchens they couldn't afford. And it all needed funding somehow.

Nevertheless, if only for appearances sake, a few heads would have to roll. New procedures would need to be introduced that would make mis-selling and half-hearted IFIFs, a thing of the past, to the casual observer at least. Care would need to be taken though, to ensure just the right amount of due diligence remained absent on the Banks part, thus allowing the opportunist CRAs enough scope to still fill the coffers to overflowing, and slip harmlessly through the auditors net, unscathed.

In the meantime, a hastily scribbled, heavily embellished press release, which largely ignored all the evidence, was issued: *Cottons NSIB wishes to reassure its Customers that, in light of the recent BBC1 Watchdog report, Top Management have undertaken a thorough investigation, and have satisfied themselves that the reported examples of miss-selling are in the minority. Unfortunately, the members of staff that were filmed were largely new to the role. It is likely that the undesirable practices we have seen are actually bad habits they have been taught before they came into the Banks employee. Swift action will be taken to discipline, re-train or terminate contracts, where applicable.*

Cottons NSIB wishes to reiterate that they are fully committed to providing a truly exceptional level of customer service.

It would have been much simpler if they'd just said, 'It's their fault, not ours!'

Across the country though, CRA productivity was slowing. Some sellers even insisted that Customers left their hand bags and jackets on the floor, rather than the table top, fearing a hidden spy camera. Steps needed to be taken before the share price was affected by dwindling quarterly performance. The whole BBC affair needed to be put to bed, for good.

It was quickly decided that over the following weeks, the twenty-six would face disciplinary action, and sentenced accordingly. Naturally, the Bank had already decided who would get the chop, who would be reprimanded, stripped of all bonuses, and who would be downgraded until they were satisfied that they had learnt their lesson. Six were carefully chosen to be sacked for gross misconduct, ten reprimanded, and taken out of the bonus scheme for six months, leaving the final ten to be downgraded to a Customer Advisor roll, for a period of no less than six months. Any future bonuses were suspended during probation, and any currently due, cancelled with immediate effect.

The six that were sacked had been fully fledged rouges, cold hearted and ruthless sellers who were difficult to manage at best. Now that they'd been collectively caught with their pants down, it was an opportunity to let them go without a fight. The ten that stayed in role, yet were stripped of bonuses, were top twenty sales staff. Equally merciless individuals perhaps, but better natured and outwardly at least, easier to supervise. They tended to pour honey on their daggers before thrusting it into their Customers' chests. But perhaps most importantly, they were far too lucrative to lose.

The remaining ten were mostly fledgling CRAs. Successful and driven, but they'd been seen doing just enough of the wrong things to warrant disciplinary action. By downgrading them and throwing them back into the workhouse, the Bank hoped that in six months' time they'd be stronger, wiser, and even more desperate to prove themselves. Hopefully, like a first time crook emerging from prison with a few tattoos and a best friend called 'Fingers', they'd also be better prepared to get away with it next time.

The problem for George Butler though, was that he didn't have six months.

The magnitude of what was happening to him, and the potential it had to ruin his life, dropped on George like a falling anvil the moment the HR Officers introduced themselves. His mouth had run dry and his hands trembled uncontrollably. Even the usually self-assured Danny was awkward and uncomfortable. Like all of the twenty-six, he was immediately suspended pending a full enquiry. He'd receive a letter in the post advising him of the date of his hearing, and they suggested that if he was a member of any Union, now would be the time to call them.

As he'd left Area Office, stumbling dazed, almost drunkenly towards the waiting, poorly parked M3; he was on the verge of tears. It was only his desire not to sob uncontrollably on Danny's chest, when he eventually caught up with him that prevented the waiting downpour. The last thing the Officers did before marching him off the premises, was strip him of all his Bank keys. In his horror and confusion, he'd inadvertently handed them the keys to the BMW as well.

Danny felt genuinely terrible for his Seller. He wasn't a bad chap by any means. It was just shear bad luck that he'd won the flip of the coin that day, rather than Billy, and he was filmed, rather than the slovenly sale's Velociraptor in the next office. It was something that without doubt, certainly saved Billy's career. He'd rested an enormous hand on the quivering young shoulder, smiled as reassuringly as he could, and passed him his car keys.

"Apparently they won't take bribes *Chief*, nice try though…"

As George's official holiday came to an end, being suspended proved difficult to explain to those around him. Especially to Arthur, who although was very grateful for lunch, was surprised to still have the weekday company. But his adopted Grandson had no intention of adding this particular confession to his lengthy list. This was far worse than sleeping with married woman, or waking up without any memory of the night before. He planned to keep it to himself, to not tell a soul. Not his neighbour, not Dean or Summer, and especially not his Mum and Dad. The stress of this unfamiliar, high level deception weighed heavy on his mind. A few white lies aside, he just hadn't done dishonesty before. It was beyond horrible.

In some respects, his parents proved the easiest to handle. His Dad was far too engrossed with his latest round of classic motorcycle restoration, to pay any notice to his youngest offspring's haphazard attempts to avoid the subject of work, whilst his Mum was understandably consumed with worry about her eldest son. Information of his unit's exact whereabouts had recently become even scarcer.

Dean tended to communicate simply by crammed, colourful postcards, sent from whatever port he and Hayley had drifted into that week. He'd occasionally call to catch up, but each time he'd devote most of his foreign coins to checking on the condition of *his* M3, and whether or not George had asked his Dad to check the oil recently. He never asked about work, so the subject didn't need to be avoided.

Arthur meanwhile, had long since put two and two together, and decided to keep his thoughts to himself. He'd seen Watchdog and listened intently to the last CRA. Having paid particular attention to his body language, he'd also bought a few tabloids the following day to confirm his worst fears. He knew that George would tell him eventually, he usually did.

The old man felt deeply sorry for him though, not just because of the scandal, but because of what it might mean for him, and how it might change his future. He hadn't confessed as much to his Granddad yet, but Arthur had the sense that his Grandson might've had a plan, a plan to perhaps pick up his own paddle, and row off to some new shores, far away from the Bank, before this all happened. No doubt they'd talk about it, when he was ready. He better make some more limoncello, just in case.

The suspended CRA's main challenge was with Summer. He wasn't at all sure that their rekindled relationship, no matter how brightly it burned with desire and longing, would survive another epic confession. He needed to tread carefully.

"...But Monkey, you said that you *wanted* to come to France?"

He was on the ropes again. George looked down at the pages of notes he'd prepared ahead of the call. The endless scribbles, the highlighted sections designed to prompt his memory, the pages of thinly veiled fiction. God he hated this.

"Summertime, I do, *very much so*! But the thing is I need to save up first." He paused to sip the last of his expensive vodka and tonic, perhaps the last he'd ever taste. "All those nights on the town have cost me a fortune! I just don't have much saved right now…"

It had seemed like a good idea at the time to use elements of his original plan, the one cobbled together on the sofa, shortly before the BBC had ruined his life, to explain why he couldn't leave just yet. But he hadn't counted on actually saying the words to his trusting, besotted girlfriend, or realised how much he'd hate himself as the little white lies dropped from his tongue, like so many winter raindrops.

"You won't really need much money though, Mum and Dad will pay you weekly, like I said, and you'll live in my little barn, *with me*." She was starting to sound tearful again. Not the tears, anything but that.

"I know Summertime, *and that's great*, but I need to sort out my fla- I mean, my *apartment*, too. You know, either rent it out or sell it. And then there's Fred to consider…"

"*Fred?* You know you can bring him along, I said before that…"

"*What I meant was*…" He rooted frantically through his notes, cutting her off. This was a funny bit. Funny bits had saved them before. "…*Oh yes*, I meant that I need to have some cash saved up just in case Fred murders some expensive, prize winning *poulet* or something." It didn't get quite the laugh he was hoping for. "Please Summer, just give me a few months to save up, *please?*"

She knew he'd be making those big puppy-dog eyes again. Even safely hidden in another country and with communication limited to the telephone, for her at least, there was no escaping their power. "Oh, *okay*, but just a few months then, no more! And we need to talk on the phone each day, and write weekly this time, *okay?*" Damn those eyes of his.

"Okay, I promise! Daily and weekly, *which way round was it again?*" After an expensive hour, he'd won, but it was a hollow victory, which no light-heartedness could brighten.

"You're not as funny as you think you are, *Monkey*."

"I know…"

Of course, there was one way he could've eased his financial burden. He could've simply sold the M3. And whilst an overweight security guard eyed him suspiciously, he'd flicked quickly through a copy of Glasses Guide in the local Supermarket, and was soon both ashamed, and quietly relieved to see that the BMW was worth almost twice what he'd paid for it. But this was never going to be an option. He knew that Dean didn't so much as sell him a car, as pass him a baton, after choosing him above all others to run with. If he dropped it now, in this early stage in the race, there would be hell to pay in the changing rooms later.

Sadly, just when things couldn't possibly get any worse, worn out and with little left in the tank to defend him, George came down with that most dreaded of all childhood illnesses, a stinking head cold. Ever since he was an infant, he'd feared that first hint of a snivel. That runny nose which signalled the very start of days on end of fuzzy headed delirium. The inevitable endless green, lumpy harvest, the bunged up ears, clogged sinuses, and ineffective cures that brought on waves of nausea. It was grim stuff indeed.

With the exception of hangovers, which he'd become rather good at self-medicating, this was the first time since leaving home he'd been properly ill. He soon discovered that being alone and ill, was quite the worst sort of loneliness imaginable. But as the days spent waiting for confirmation of his hearing turned into another week, his illness did at least give his parents and concerned neighbour, a plausible excuse for his continued absence from work.

Yet desperate as he was for some maternal comfort, with even great handfuls of his Mum's dreaded *Vick's* vapour rub smeared into his sparsely hairy chest, bearable compared to his congested solitude, he knew that in his weakened state, he might easily let his predicament slip. And the endless lectures that would then follow, about personal finances, taking pride in his work, and about keeping it in his pants, would be far, far worse than spending a few nights wondering if he would suffocate in a sea of bogies.

George shuffled about his apartment for days on end, wearing just his PJ's, and a soup-stained dressing gown, pockets bursting with crusting tissues and sickly throat sweets, reluctant stubble sprouting on his chin, hair like a mess of greasy wool. His dilemma continued to follow his every step like a spectre in the shadows. The unrelenting head cold, coupled perhaps with an increasing need to hide from the world, had him under virtual house arrest. He had nothing to do but succumb to the monotony of day time television, and wait for his summons from the Bank to drop into his mailbox.

Doubt and Insecurity had long since broken down the door of their prison, and were now busy running about the corridors of his mind with some new troublemakers they'd picked up in the bar. Shame and Regret. They'd spray painted the walls with derisory graffiti, and beat the living daylights out of Joy and Happiness each time that they dared to peak around the corner to see what was going on.

The impending disciplinary was the first thing he thought about when he opened his eyes each morning, and the last thing fretted over before he eventually fell into a fitful sleep at night. He was constantly plagued with nightmares of insolvency and visits to the dole office. Where his mind should've been filled with Summer, and how to convince his parents that leaving the Bank would be a great step for him, it had been obsessing over how to avoid leaving the Bank instead, or at least how to avoid being fired from it.

A few days later, when he eventually did emerge from his apartment, clean shaven and blinking in the unfamiliar sunlight, it had been to meet up with the Case Handler the Union had assigned him. It was the first bit of welcome news he'd had in weeks.

George gingerly pushed open the rotten, stained door of *The Pig and Hammer* and, without making eye contact with any of the suspicious patrons that glared at him from the darkened corners, headed straight for the battle scared bar, and the familiar seated figure in a stretched XXXL Rugby top, and faded jeans. Hopefully, this creature would be his savoir.

"I suppose this idiot's you then, *is it Butler?*" The Bear slid a well-thumbed, two-week-old copy of *The Sun* newspaper across the bar, as well as the sticky surface would allow, and turned his massive, hairy face to glare at his new client. "Two pints of Ol' Goat please Geoff, and a couple packets of 'scratchings', he's buyin'…"

Ever since he'd left the Bank months earlier, The Bear had been earning his crust by dividing his time between chores as a Handyman, shifts as Barman at his beloved Rugby Club, and a freelance Union Representative, gun for hire. Usually only summoned for the most desperate and hopeless of cases.

The two of them had sat next to each other like old times on the till at Nelsons branch. The bulky Cottons NSIB file in front of the larger man, already told him everything he needed to know, and he'd watched the BBC show, and read the transcript enough times now to be able to recall every detail without prompting. On the day of the hearing, all The Bear needed his Client to do was to sit still, and try not to say anything that might aggravate the situation further. He wasn't holding his breath.

George's relationship with his mailbox had been an uneasy affair from the outset. Previously, when he'd lived happily at the Butler's respectable semi, post had been something to look forward to with both excitement and anticipation. Whether it was some plastic gift, the long awaited result of weeks of carefully collecting coupons from the side of a cereal packet, or the most recent copy of *Airfix* Magazine, a treasured monthly treat that was methodically freed from its packaging before being digested minutely on the throne, his post was an utter joy to receive.

But the responsibility of a being a homeowner, soon brought with it new, increasingly threatening brown envelopes, and the delight he'd once experienced every time he'd heard the Postman's footsteps, the snap of the letterbox and the bark of the family Jack Russell, was soon replaced with growing dread. Now, the pass door would open, the Postie would work his way along the clattering line of tin mailboxes, and each one would flap metallically or not, like an early morning game of mailed Russian roulette.

Worthless, yet priceless, die cast models, awards from endless cut out and keep campaigns, were swapped for energy bills and water rates, which seemed to question whether or not the occupant had an otter living with him. George soon decided that visiting the mailbox on a daily basis was far too stressful. Even when he'd been waiting for Summer to write, and he instead chose to open it every other day, and not at all at weekends.

With news of his disciplinary likely to arrive any moment though, he couldn't afford to be so careless, and he rooted carefully through the box each morning for anything that looked suspiciously ruinous from the Bank. Leaving the thickening utility bills and bank statements, all of which were easily identified to the trained eye, sealed within their tin prison for another time. There was only so much he could take at once.

In the end, his reluctant diligence proved unnecessary. And a few days after his meeting with The Bear, his Postman knocked on his door and handed him his most ominous looking envelope yet. Cunningly sent by recorded delivery, to ensure there were no excuses for not turning up, the Bank had left nothing to chance, and nowhere to hide.

On the morning of his disciplinary, George had done his very best to create an atmosphere of confidence and calm in his apartment. The Bear had been surprisingly supportive during the ordeal, pointing out on numerous occasions that, whilst his Client had made a bit of fool of himself, by chatting up the 'Customer'; he'd tended to labour this point more often than was necessary, compared to the rest of the suspects, he hadn't actually mis-sold anything. He'd just simply failed to follow procedures, and the 'Judge' was bound to take this into account, hopefully.

George clung onto this barest glimmer of hope like he'd had to his Mum's hand on that very first day of school, and had filled his home with inspiring, uplifting music as he pecked at his poached eggs, and changed his tie for the fifth time. Sadly though, by the time he'd arrived at Area Office, with twelve long minutes to spare, no amount of Journey's 'Don't Stop Believin'' or Queen's 'We Are the Champions', could sustain any dreams he'd held of coming out of this mess unscathed.

Despite being flanked by both Danny and The Bear, enormous, imposing companions that ordinarily would've made him feel smothered with looming protectiveness, he'd felt completely vulnerable as they entered the 'Courtroom'. He was faced by the same two grey, antiseptic Human Resources Officers he'd met before. They'd quickly begun the hearing by reiterating the charges and giving The Bear chance to read an opening statement of defence, which he'd prepared on his Clients behalf, and perhaps most importantly, without his input.

Both Officers took notes throughout, in an almost secretive, devious fashion, and leered damningly at the squirming employee, with every deliberate scratch of their elaborate fountain pens. George meanwhile, trembled constantly. His palms sweated despite regular wipes on his trouser legs, and when he answered the endless questions, his voice was high with fear. It no longer sounded anything like the one he was used to hearing. He kept telling himself that whatever else happened, he mustn't get fired today. Being sacked from a high street Bank would surely look bad on his already anorexic curriculum vitae?

After thirty-eight long minutes, the accusers called for a recess, in order to deliberate and arrive at a decision. Unbeknown to the accused or his Legal Team, this was merely for show, the decision having already been made weeks ago. As they sipped weak tea and nibbled digestive biscuits, arguing over who would drive the Mercedes E class back to Regional Office, George and the others waited patiently outside. Hands on knees, quietly checking watches from time to time, nodding meaningfully at each other. It was a worrying contrast to their usual personalities. Finally, after a sufficiently troubling period of time had passed, the defence was called back to hear the findings of the court.

A guilty verdict was passed, and the sentence was demotion to a Customer Advisor role for a period of no less than six months, with a reduction in wage to suit. This was the position he'd held at Armada branch, before winning the CRA role. During this time, his Line Manager would complete weekly evaluations of his conduct, and report back to HR. He would not be eligible for any bonus, and any bonuses pending would not be paid in this month's salary. In keeping with revised Bank policy, he'd also be expected to work three Saturdays a month. After six months, providing he gave the Bank no further reason to bring about disciplinary action, or had demonstrated any other undesirable behaviour in the workplace, consideration would be given to re-instating him back into the CRA role. If appropriate, and if such a role was available at the time.

As each new piece of information had been launched at him, George had tried to think of the problems they'd cause, and any solutions that might yet be found, before another crashed into his head. To begin with, the weekly reports shouldn't be too much of an ordeal. Danny despised paperwork of any kind. He'd probably get him to write his own, before checking and signing them off for HR. That wouldn't be too bad. But it was whilst his mind was busy tackling the difference in salary, and coping with the horror of shortened weekends, that the final sledgehammer snuck up and drove the last rusty nail into the splintered coffin which now encased him.

In order to prevent 'Customer Confusion', and to ensure there was absolutely no danger that he'd accidentally interview someone he shouldn't have, George would be re-located to another branch, as far away from his home as the current travel policy would allow. Current Bank policy was thirty miles, each way.

Two days later, wringing his hands dryly in anticipation of the entertainment yet to come, The Evil Ray Varley reviewed the staff file before him, with quietly reserved delight. It rested neatly atop his perfect mahogany desk. Infinite care had been taken not to disturb any of the executive office accessories that meticulously lined the polished surface, by the unfortunate cashier who'd nervously brought it up from the post room earlier that morning.

Finally he'd have his revenge on the hairy little cretin that had barged into him all those months ago, whilst he was on his ridiculous secondment with Human Resources. The very same careless idiot who'd ruined his favourite shirt and tie, and scolded him with boiling coffee. Finally, George Butler would be his to command and to torment.

Bay Branch was nestled in a quiet little inlet, just along the coast from the same shingle beach where Summer and George had been exposed to a well-meaning nudist, several months earlier. It was an exceptionally pretty town. The very definition of charming and quaint, it once had an indigenous population that radiated happiness and warmth to visitors and passersby alike.

In recent years though, the town had become something of a middle class tourist destination, and second home owners had invaded like a band of marauding Vikings. Charging into the streets in their Volvos and polar neck jumpers, they bought up the quaint fisherman's cottages and family homes alike, as though there was undiscovered pirate gold lurking in the attic. Before long, they'd priced the locals out of the market, and far out of town.

Now, during the winter months, it became something of a Ghost Town, with the holiday home community retreating to either their city residence, or the ski slopes. It was left to just a scattering of die hard, largely elderly locals to keep the year round businesses afloat, the Post Office open, and the town barely ticking over.

A little further down the coast, along a winding cliff top road, there was an even quainter and even more picturesque harbour. It was much smaller, and here the second home owners had managed to swell house prices further still. There was just a scattering of shops now, and over the years they'd morphed from bakers and fishmongers, into high end designer clothes outfitters and coffee houses. Cottons NSIB had the only branch in this small corner of the world. Although it cut back to just three mornings a week in the off season, it was a welcome and much loved aspect of the community that the true locals treasured.

Too small to be a standalone branch, it was attached to Bay Branch, and was simply known as The Cove, situated at the cobbled water's edge. It was staffed on a rotational basis, without any computers and only manual tills, and it closed at lunchtime. With no heating to speak of, from late October through to early April it was as cold as the Arctic wastes.

George sat quietly in his new Senior Manger's office. He was becoming quite good at sitting quietly these days. Whilst the other man bent silently over a file, he occupied his thoughts by absorbing the vast collection of inspirational, corporate posters that lined the walls behind his desk. He'd seen most of them many times before, *Teamwork, Dedication, Communication, Success*, they were all there, but here each one had been carefully framed in ornate gilt edge. To the artist's eye, they clashed terribly with the dramatic images within. Perhaps he should mention it?

The Evil Ray Varley had a face that somehow managed to look disparaging, judgmental and condemning all at once, and all of the time. At their first meeting, although George had soon realised that physically at least he was no threat, he'd been so consumed with anxiety and stress that he hadn't fully appreciated just what an alarming collection of unsettling features Evil Ray had somehow managed to assemble. To begin with, everything about him seemed to be thin and grey. From his lips to his short, wispy hair, the incredibly narrow face and body, his long hooked nose, and the grey eyes that barely seemed to open wide enough for him to be able to look disapprovingly, at whatever lay before him. All was grey, and all very, very thin.

Like most villains, The Evil Ray Varley also had a Henchman, but in his case, it was a Henchwoman. In stark contrast to Evil Ray's uptight, grey thinness, Susan Wheeler, Bay Branch's second in command, was a blisteringly unpleasant, slovenly harridan. A thickset, knuckle scraping vile excuse for a human being, with all the communication skills of a brain damaged chimp, and charm of a drink addled cockroach.

She had a drooping, hound-dog face, peppered with hairy moles, crusty ears, and an almost full moustache. Her thick, badly neglected brown hair, which she cropped herself with Pinking shears, naked and round shouldered in her filthy kitchen, was, in complete defiance to her aggressive threatening scowl, often pinned back at the sides with childish butterfly hairclips. She was obsessed with her horse, her work and her knitting. Anything else could wither and die an unpleasant death for all she was concerned, and she didn't care who knew it.

She even had her own peculiar catchphrase, which considering that broadly speaking at least, she didn't give a damn, could be considered to be more than just a touch sarcastic. Everyone was met with a grunted, "*Ohlright Mate*," and continued to be called '*Mate*' from then on. Staff, Customers, Area Directors, the lot, even George Butler.

Having misjudged the traffic on his epic journey, George had arrived at Bay Branch a few minutes past nine on that first Monday morning. Every conceivable type of road going vehicle imaginable seemed intent on delaying him. He'd first battled around the outskirts of the City, and then briefly tore up a stretch of motorway, before pulling off a few junctions along, and eventually beginning a perilous, zigzag expedition through a labyrinth of B roads and single tracks that led to the coast.

A few weeks earlier, with Summer in his passenger seat, this same trip had been great fun. Even the odd moment of hard braking and perilous backing up into a passing place had seemed to be a quirky part of their holiday adventure, as they crawled ever closer to the beach. But now, with the M3's digital clock confirming what his trusty Seiko had already yelled at him, each hold-up, each caravan, each belligerent tractor, was just another stress inducing obstruction, another gloating barrier to be screamed at.

As he passed the familiar Tank memorial, which marked the beginning of the three mile straight he'd used to finally overcome his fear of the BMW, and hampered as always by the left hand drive, George had stretched over to the right, and checked the oncoming road was clear before launching the M3 past a line of slower moving estate cars. They were all loaded with children still enjoying the school holidays. Lucky buggers.

He rounded the tight left hand corner at the end of the straight far too fast, and fought the skidding overseer as best he could, managing a brief grin as he thought of the fleshly, wobbly bottoms on the other side of the cliff, and pressed the car on harder still. At ten to nine he flew past a sign that indicated he'd arrived in the Bay, and breathing a sigh of relief, down shifted the racing gearbox, rumbling on a little slower past the scattering of fisherman's cottages and designer clothes shops. He'd arrived at last.

As he neared the town centre though, the streets became heavily congested with aimlessly wandering, early bird tourists, all of whom seemed to be oblivious to traffic. Desperately he searched the sparse road signs for a car park, as the road ahead narrowed and the brightly clad crowd brushed along his wing mirrors. Finally he managed to squeeze the M3 into a slot on a side street. There didn't seem to be any signs preventing him from doing so, and he quickly gathered together his few belongings, locked up the car and searched frantically for the branch among the throng of bodies and candy floss. On reflection, he really should've had a practice run the day before. But he couldn't afford to waste the petrol.

Roasting hot, dripping with sweat and flustered beyond imagination, something sticky and bright pink clinging to his pinstripe jacket, George eventually burst into Bay Branch's tiny banking hall, glanced around quickly to get his bearings, and dashed over to the welcome desk and a waiting Neanderthal in hair clips.

"*Ohlright Mate?*"

"So, *Butler*, I assume you remember me?" The Evil Ray Varley's words had been carefully loaded with meaning and challenge. His voice as bland and as grey as ever, he rested his skinny forearms on the edge of his desk and made a triangle of his bony fingers. "Surely you recall our first encounter, *hmm?*"

George had always thought that if there was an elephant in the room, it was best to move to another room and leave it alone with its peanuts, but Evil Ray clearly had other ideas. "*Umm*, yes of course, err, sorry again about that Ray, err, *I really didn't mean to…*"

"I'm sure you'll also remember that I prefer it if the staff call me *Mr Varley*, Butler, and I also prefer it if they are here, *on time?*"

"Oh, err, sorry about that Ray, umm, I mean, err, *Mr Varley…*"

The weeks that followed at Bay Branch, were far from his happiest in the Bank. In all three of the branches George had worked in before, he'd always managed to make friends with most of the staff within a few days, even if it had eventually proved too be against their better judgment. It was something that was no doubt spurred on by his hourly offerings to make the tea. But The Evil Ray Varley had long since banned hot drinks from the

Customer facing areas, and staff had to make do with refreshment from the water cooler instead. With his familiar icebreaker confined to the rest room, any attempts George made to bond with his colleagues seemed to wither and die before they had even begun.

Unbeknown to him though, the staff had been poisoned against 'the flash git from the city', as he'd been damningly described by their Branch Manager, long before he'd burst into the banking hall. He wasn't the first exiled trouble maker they'd had to contended with, and he wouldn't be the last.

Evil Ray had earned something of a reputation for managing out troublesome subordinates. During his years at Cottons, he'd also become skilled at remoulding those that the Bank simply wanted to knock back into shape, encouraging them to tow the party line, or else. Like a manipulative, abusive spouse, he'd brainwash the subjects into believing that no one outside of the Bank would ever want them. That there was nothing better waiting for them out there, that they were lucky to have a job at all, and should be grateful, knuckle down and do as they were told. He was very convincing.

Over the years Evil Ray had also cunningly collected together a small staff of subservient, loyal individuals, with their loyalty having been carefully and subliminally programmed into them as soon as they came on board. They were kept in check by the vile Susan, a necessary yet efficient evil that he endured simply to save him getting his own hands dirty.

The five, largely middle-aged staff members were all 'Lifers'. They'd started working for the Bank straight from school and now, like passengers on a decaying train bound on a seemingly relentless, unremarkable journey, they were all waiting for their stop, their pension, and a few lacklustre years of golf and gardening before the lights finally went out for good.

The three cashiers, Doug, Sue and Jason, were all divorcees. Bitter, empty vessels, they kept themselves to themselves, doing just enough to keep Susan from grunting at them, or from Evil Ray giving them a withering stare. Grace, the branches long suffering, solitary CRA, was a despondent sixty-year-old who'd been passed over for voluntary redundancy so many times, she seriously believed she would die at her desk, before she escaped from the Bank. She churned out financial sales in an ambivalent manner, and in a sufficient volume to avoid any stress or detection.

Finally there was Janice, the branches other Customer Advisor, by far the most colourful member of staff. She was a hugely opinionated, pear shaped woman in her mid-fifties, massively animated and a self-appointed expert on everything, especially politics, religion and astronomy. It was only the fact that she kept these opinions and characteristics in check around Ray and Susan, coupled with the endless stream of browbeaten customer referrals she drove into Grace's office, that her presence was tolerated at all. From her vantage point at the Welcome Desk, ears constantly pricked for snippets of information or potential scandal, she'd crowbar herself into customers' conversations as they waited to do their banking, delving into their private affairs, imposing her alleged wisdom and beliefs with all the tact and delicacy of a rusty chainsaw. She was however, the one member of staff who actually talked to George, or rather at him, as during those first few weeks, she'd desperately tried to find out what he'd done wrong, who he voted for, what his religious beliefs were, and what his star sign was.

Matters had reached a spectacular crescendo when the two of them were dispatched to staff The Cove for a morning. The day had gotten off to a particularly bad start when, shortly after arriving at the tiny branch, George discovered he'd left his half of the keys to the safe on his coffee table, twenty-nine and a half miles away. They'd had no choice but to quickly head back to the petrol station cashpoint at the top of the hill, and both withdraw two hundred pound to use as a float, and hope that the businesses paid in early.

Janice went first, quickly dashing back to his car and counting her twenties as though she might be mugged. George meanwhile, made a fuss over finding his wallet. It was getting near pay day. Following his pay cut, he still hadn't sat down to work out his finances yet, and looking at his bank balance wasn't something he especially relished. More importantly, he just didn't know if his account would stomach the transaction. It wouldn't, and as he retreated slowly back to the M3 with the seventy pounds he'd managed to wrestle from the cashpoint, he'd desperately tried to think of an excuse that Janice would believe.

For the rest of the morning, in between interrogating the few customers that wandered into the modest banking hall, she'd been at him. Unyielding and persistent, she'd wanted to know quite why he couldn't withdraw the money, as well as everything else she'd questioned him about previously. Her screeching voice jabbed at him, like endless hot pokers into bare flesh. Eventually, he exploded.

"*Janice*! I'm broke! I got caught chatting up a customer and it was aired on National Television. I don't vote but if I had to, it would be Monster Raving Loony Party. I'm probably a Pagan, and, according to Albert King, I was born under a bad sign!" Thankfully, Janice didn't say anything else, at least for the rest of the morning.

Even worse than Janice's thumbscrews though, were Evil Ray's calculated, malicious moments of 'Punishment Management' and 'Character Assassinations', each blow of which was timed to perfection. In the weeks since he'd arrived at Bay branch, George had struggled to relax even for a second. The threat of the monthly report to HR held with it a shadow that loomed over him, watching his every move, every customer interaction, and every telephone conversation or note he made.

His confidence hadn't been so much been knocked as thrown to the ground and beaten to death by a gang of baseball bat wielding skinheads. Where once he'd relished the moments when a financial sale seemed inevitable, he now dreaded them. Fearing he'd inadvertently do something non-compliant, that would end up on his HR report, and see him queuing for dole money by week's end.

Clearly, Evil Ray knew this all too well, and played on it magnificently. Often appearing out of thin air at George's elbow the second a customer had left the welcome desk, challenging his interaction and examining his paperwork. He'd call his young offender to his office every few hours to sample his work. Although he was perfectly aware that freshly disciplined sellers made for the very worst kind of sales staff, he confronted him about his lack of referrals to Grace too, and why he hadn't offered the last few customers a home insurance quote or credit card.

On the rare occasions that George actually did sell one of the few products that as a Customer Advisor he was allowed too, Evil Ray had dissected and evaluated the sale with all the intensity of a Crime Scene Investigator, the moment he found out. Even calling the customer later that day to interrogate them too, testing their understanding and knowledge of the finer details of the product, desperate to unravel evidence of a mistake, or wrongdoing.

There'd also been the unfortunate matter of making personal telephone calls. After much soul searching, George had decided that he needed to tell his parents a little white lie about his change of location. He'd informed them quite casually over Sunday lunch that he'd been seconded to Bay Branch, to train as a Branch Manager. Foolishly, he'd hoped if he sounded sufficiently nonchalant about the news, he'd avoid the usual 'Butler celebration ritual', something that had existed ever since Michael had come home from Primary school clutching a certificate for finishing the three legged race in first place, even if he had dragged his teammate the final few feet. But it wasn't to be, and his Mum quickly set to work making a huge fruit cake, and planning a special meal for the week ahead.

George felt terrible for lying to them both. But with Michael's unit still off in some far flung corner of the world, doing something secret that, despite Mrs Butler's continued threats towards his Commanding Officer, he still wouldn't clarify (safe in a bunker in the desert, an expertly wielded rolling pin clearly held no fear for him), he had no choice. To burden them now with more bad news would be even more unforgivable than telling them a hugely fictional account of the truth. Or so he kept telling himself.

But once again, he wasn't completely out of the woods, As soon as his Mum had grasped the distance and duration of his daily commute, which as his Dad pointed out, at nearly three hours was longer than some of his son's past relationships, she'd insisted on having the customary 'Three Rings' each day. Just so she'd know he'd arrived safely, at both ends.

Danny had always been very relaxed about staff using the telephone in his branch. But Evil Ray took a different view entirely, and had fined George on his first day for using the phone without asking, taking great pleasure in depositing the reluctantly relinquished fifty pence piece into the charity box.

In order to avoid further reprimands or fines, as well as any parental hysteria, he instead added a quick visit to the bright red phone box, which sat squatly on the quayside, to his morning commute. Dutifully calling home just before nine, counting off the third ring and failing each day to replace the receiver and retrieve his coin, before his Mum cheerfully answered. It was another cost he could well do without.

Sadly, worse still was yet to come. Cotton's NSIB had finally introduced a range of Corporate Uniform. Although in a rare and entirely uncharacteristic move on the Banks part, they did not make it compulsory for existing staff at this stage, only new entrants. George still took immense pride in his collection of business suits, neatly trimmed tailored shirts and interesting collection of knitted silk ties, which he'd collected in much happier, more affluent times. Wearing them to work, even now in his enforced exile, still made his chest swell and lifted his spirits each morning, just enough to get him out the front door.

The permanently grey suited Evil Ray however, clearly didn't approve of his offenders brash pinstripes or physique flattering tailoring. And it had probably been this alone that had made him decide that Corporate Uniform in his branch was mandatory, for all his staff. Not that the others seemed to mind, dull, drab dressers that they were.

Cottons NSIB's idea of Corporate Uniform was simply abysmal. Cheap and nasty, it was fashioned from the sort of thin, synthetic fabrics that would make walking across a carpet, an electrically charged nightmare. Each outfit arrived in a cardboard box, which looked as though it should contain a flat packed bedside table instead, the kind that wouldn't last, and garments were individually wrapped in thin, clear plastic, almost as thick as the fabric itself.

Safe in his apartment, George had very reluctantly tried on his new suit, a grim, grief-stricken look quickly spreading across his already despondent, young face. The shirt material made him clammy, almost immediately, and the shirttails brushed his hairy knees. The suit jacket just about fitted his relatively broad shoulders, but given that the inevitable, pressurized Chinese Tailor probably wasn't given any instruction or budget to do his trade justice, it gaped hugely around his waist. Buttoning it on a windy day was going to be a dangerous business.

The trousers weren't much better, and they'd need taking up by his Mum before his awkward thirty-three and a half inch inside leg could be accommodated. Both the jacket and the trousers made of the very worst sort of polyester money could buy, finished in a faintly unsettling, ribbed pattern. For whose pleasure, it was anybody's guess. One thing was certain, Dean would not have approved.

But at least, during his miserable exile, there had finally been some fantastic news, some cause for real celebration in his life.

"...Whatever you do little bro, don't tell Mum, *promise?*"

"Okay, *I Promise Mike*, I won't, *honest!*"

"I like your M3 by the way. Can I have a blast later?"

"Yeah, of course, no problem Bro. Now, *what were you going to say…?*"

"Okay then. Right, we were on patrol just outside…"

As George had pulled into the little cul-de-sac he knew so well on his usual Sunday mission, a basket of dirty laundry safely secured in the M3's boot, he'd stopped so hard that his antilock brakes nearly had a nervous breakdown. Parked just outside the Butlers' respectable semi, had been Michael's Audi Quattro.

Everything that happened after, but before the brothers had walked into The Bull and Goat for a pre-Sunday Roast pint, had been lost in something of an emotional whirlwind. But it had all been good.

As they'd sat together at the bar, huddled over their beers, the younger of the two became hypnotised by his older sibling once again. Like younger brothers tend too, George had always been secretly in awe of Michael. Especially his sporting achievements, and his way with the ladies, but now the swine had gone and gotten himself a proper 'Action Man' scar down his right cheek as well. It was very impressive, but although it was clearly well healed, it hadn't stopped their Mum fussing over it with great dollops of Germolene. Some things will never change.

Mike had deliberately avoided the subject at home, explaining that being away with the military wasn't like skipping a maths lesson, he couldn't really tell Mum where he'd been hiding all this time. Sensing trouble, Mr Butler senior had soon retreated to check the Quattro's oil level, and after stealing a half-cooked roast potato each, the boys ran off to the pub.

It was quiet, most of the regulars were busy scoffing down their own lunch, and Keithy the barman, always knew when to keep a distance. It went with the job. After the beers were pulled, in a low voice, which had once been reserved for the bedtime horror stories he used to tell his younger brother, Michael told George what little he could about, about what had happened in Iraq.

Although following orders, they were across a line on a map that, officially at least, they shouldn't have been, and so when the snipers opened up, wounding the Commanding Officer with their first few shots, air support was out of the question. As Second in Command, it was left to Michael to rally the squad, tend to the injured man, and find a way out of the kill zone. As shots whizzed past their ears like enraged, heavily armoured bumblebees, they sort cover in a derelict building, and returned fire.

They squad battled for three hours. Each of the seven men suffered an injury of varying severity as the battle raged higher. Mortars began pounding the crumbling remains, ancient bricks and roof timber crashed around them as their ammunition dwindled. Michael was struck in the face by a shard of slate, which had left him with his impressive, three inch scar, and just when it looked as though all that remained was to give the order to fix bayonets, and repel the enemy as best they could, salvation finally arrived.

The American helicopter gunship appeared literally out of the sun. Mini guns blazing, it scattered the enemy, like lambs fleeing from a particularly malevolent sheepdog, deafening the troops on the ground. Following orders wasn't this particular pilot's strong suit, and he'd continued to provide air support, as the injured men, bandaged and patched up as best they could, carried their CO out of harm's way and across the border.

Later, back at the American Forward Operating Base, nursing a row of stitches and an ice cold bottle of Budweiser, Michael was debriefed. When asked how he found the resolve to inspire his men, and hold off what was estimated to be a force of at least eighty rebels, his reply was simple. "Butler optimism Sir. *Bulletproof Butler Optimism*!"

George was awestruck and emotional. This was a world away from playing soldiers in the woods as kids. He'd suddenly felt bitterly ashamed of himself. Ashamed and guilty for even once thinking he had troubles, or that he was having a bad time of it at work. At least nobody shot at him in the banking hall, not even Evil Ray. Not yet, at least.

"...Anyway, like I said little bro, *don't tell Mum!*"

With Michael home safe, the Butler family unit was complete once more, and the Sunday roast dinners even more spectacular. And for a while, things continued to look up for George when, during his fifth week of lonely, poorly attired exile, salvation of sorts wandered into Bay Branch in the form of David Weedon.

He was smart suited, rather than dressed in the new corporate pyjamas, well spoken, and deeply tanned. Somewhere in his late forties, he had greying hair and quizzical, crystal blue eyes. He introduced himself warmly to the new young man at the Welcome Desk, as the local Business Manager, asked Janice how things were in her crypt, before making his way out the back with a sincere promise of returning with tea. George immediately liked him.

Not unlike the rest of Bay Branch, David was also an unashamed 'Lifer', of the Cottons heritage, the difference being, he actually had a rich full life outside of the Bank. Keeping things very much in perspective, he was a perfect example of how you could actually make a work life balance, work.

Throughout his entire career, he'd worked in and around the Bay Area, starting as the tea boy, before climbing the ranks and eventually moving into Business Banking fifteen years ago, hence the suit. Although he'd had his share of misadventure over the years, he was always thought of as a trustworthy, dependant man. It was these qualities that had saved him as a fledgling cashier, when he'd accidental given out five hundred pounds in traveller's cheques to the Captain of a visiting yacht bound for France, rather than fifty. That and the fact that his uncle was the harbour master, and was more than happy to give chase and point out the mistake to the fleeing Captain, on his nephews behalf.

He was married to his wife Gail, a nurse, and had one son, Tim, who was off at University. They owned a modest former fisherman's cottage in the town, just walking distance from the branch where he tended to base himself. On the surface at least, they seemed to be a content average family, meat and potato people, Monday to Friday, nine to five, weekends spent playing golf or tennis, annual holidays to Costa Brava, Vauxhall estate in the drive perhaps. However, if anyone scratched under that surface, they'd soon discover that the Weedon's were all avid surfers. They'd just returned from three weeks on the Australian coast, and they owned a bright blue VW Beetle, with a roof rack and stickers in the windows.

"Now, that was much better George, you might well be getting the hang of it, at last!" David winced as another raging wave crashed into his pupils head, and he went under the water for the third time, eventually coughing and spluttering his way back onto his long board, where he lay flat out again, clutching the edges for dear life.

"*I'm not sure I'm going to survive this Dave!*" They were now a good distance off shore, and picking up some serious waves. Waves that were still sadly lost on the terrified novice. "Can we go in soon, *please?*"

The clouds overhead had thickened, and the sea grown ever more mountainous, but this seemed to just spur on their fellow surfers, all of whom were obviously in the grips of some sort of contagious insanity. The lunatics raced through barrelling tubes of watery death, whopping with delight, before disappearing under the waves in a violent explosion of foam and spray. Others glided weightlessly atop the thundering water, ever quicker, almost as if they were flying low over the surface.

George meanwhile looked on baffled, but somewhat enthralled. As the seawater battered his board, he continued to rise and fall from the crests to the troughs of the waves, with his stomach churning, he often lost sight of his instructor. It was all very unsettling.

"Do you think *I'll* be able to do that one day, Dave?"

"Oh yes, *of course!*" The older man paddled up alongside to offer reassurance and join him in the surging water, "Why don't you go in and dry off, make a fire on the beach perhaps? *I'll be in shortly.*" And with that, David was gone, paddling with all his might across the heaving ocean, further out to sea, at last joining his fellow lunatics in the raging swell. They greeted each other over the din of the crashing ocean in 'Surf Speak'. Words that sounded quite odd coming from David's rather well-spoken mouth. It was 'Gnarly' indeed.

"I'm telling you Arthur, it is addictive - terrifying, *but addictive*! I wasn't sure to start with, but I think I really like it now. And Dave says it empties your mind, puts you right in the middle of nature, and that it's all about the next wave, *Dude!*" George sliced the large Spanish omelette he'd made in half, and heaped a portion onto his neighbour's plate.

"I'm not entirely sure you'd ever be able to completely empty your mind, Sunshine, not that that's a bad thing." The old man sat down shakily at the large table, which filled his apartment, sipped the questionable thin red wine his chef had brought with him, flinched briefly, and reached for his limoncello instead. He carefully examined the meal, trying desperately to remember exactly what it was he'd rehearsed earlier to say his chef. He feared that his memory, along with a growing collection of other vital appendages, wasn't what it once was. "Not that I'm complaining, but isn't an omelette more of a summer dish?"

"Oh, well you know, I thought it might make the rain clouds bugger off if we had this for a change, might make them think it *was* summer!" His defence was weak to say the least.

"We had it yesterday."

"*Really?*"

"Yes, and the day before that…" Arthur paused momentarily to collect his thoughts. How did he practice putting it? What words had he carefully chosen so as not to offend his adopted, and obviously hard up Grandson? "*You know*, with all your dashing about these days, I can always cook for a change, you know, a few evenings a week?"

"Arthur, you can only boil Brussels' Sprouts, *and you hate them*!"

"That is true my Boy, that's true…"

Very reluctantly, George had been economizing of late. It didn't come naturally to him, and after his life in the fast lane, it certainly wasn't something he particularly enjoyed. But unfortunately, after finally sitting down with a calculator and a pile of unopened bank statements, it was clearly a necessity. It was an inescapable fact. He was somewhat financially parched.

To begin with, he addressed his diet. He had no intention of letting his physique wobble again, in any sense of the word, so a relatively healthy, high protein diet was still required. Somehow though, judging by the damning debit card transactions at his local supermarket, he just needed to bring the cost of it down a bit, ideally by at least two thirds.

Free range organic chicken, which had been fed nothing but the best, massaged daily and brought breakfast in bed before eventually being gently and humanely, guided towards the pot, were replaced with tough, stringy birds that had clearly led a miserable life, before the sweet release of the abattoir finally came calling.

Similarly cosseted expensive eggs, large shiny fellows with yolks the colour of a summer sun, were substituted for uneven, emaciated thin shelled offerings, which looked as though they'd been forced through a key hole. It was the same story with bacon and sausages. An old weekend treat that used to make his mouth water at the thought. George had no idea a pig could taste depressed.

Things were bad enough without the weekly, ritual humiliation. Quite why the supermarket insisted on drawing unfair attention to its 'Value

Range' customers, by packing their goods neatly in green and white striped boxes, wrappings and plastic containers, was a mystery. But when they were all heaped together, in a trolley of impoverishment, they just seemed to scream destitution. George had to accept though, that his days of cruising along the isles, absentmindedly flinging products from the 'Premium Range' into his basket were over. From now on, if it wasn't green and white and stripy, he couldn't afford to buy it.

Being the cheapest source of protein at his disposal, eggs soon became a staple ingredient, and very quickly, he adapted his meals accordingly. In particular, he perfected his omelette skills, adding different types of herbs and spices each night, relics from a time when he actually collected them just for fun, to create a Spanish, Chinese or Italian version. Secretly hoping Arthur would think he was just being creative.

To sustain him throughout the day, instead of a lunchbox stacked full of chicken breasts and a handful of fresh pasta or rice; he made huge batches of egg salad instead, going easy on the questionable stripy mayonnaise, and bulking it out with some near solid brown pasta, that no amount of boiling seemed able to soften.

He'd even put his expensive stainless steel blender, a seldom used device that lived a lonely existence behind his pots and pans, to good use tying to perfect homemade protein shakes. It hadn't gone well, and the sickly combination of value eggs whites, and green and white and stripy strawberry milkshake, proved to be less than palatable. Even Fred turned his nose up at a saucer full.

The dramatic decline in the quality of his daily tins of tuna had also not escaped the tiger's attention. The first time his human had heaped the dry, shredded cardboard like mess into his bowl from the stripy tin, Fred sniffed it briefly, gave his human an indignant, unforgiving scowl, and disappeared into the surrounding countryside to murder something fleshy, and far more edible. Difficult times for all concerned.

George had also become inventive with his thrift too. Replacing the expensive fridge light when it blew with a spare sixty-watt lamp bulb that blinded him every time he opened the door, and using up the remnants of the shampoo Summer had left behind to wash the dinner dishes. It left them unusually glossy, and full of body. He unplugged everything that wasn't essential, and dimly illuminated his home each night with mood enhancing tea lights from his vast supply. Relicts both of his days of philandering, and Summer's visit. It resulted in a few knocked shins and stumbles though, especially as the evenings drew in.

Training was another matter. The gym was now an expensive luxury, and had to go. Yet when he'd wandered in the reception of Diamond

Fitness to cancel his membership, something about the way a few of the Gym Bunnies looked down their noses at him made this particular cutback bearable. As he'd handed over his membership card to the orange receptionist with the perfect nails, he felt a small degree of relief as she cut it in two. He pushed open the heavy glass front door with somewhat less effort than he had all those months ago and left for good, without a backward glance.

The challenge now was how to maintain his physique, without a gym to help him do it. But he had an idea. After dropping a few suggestive hints to his Dad, about planning to train at home, he cunningly left a copy of the latest *Argos* catalogue casually lying on the Butler dining room table, neatly folded open on to the weight training pages. The Butler brothers used to do exactly the same thing with Star Wars toys. It had always proved an effective strategy. Anything Kenner could build, Dad could build better.

Sure enough, when George arrived for lunch the next Sunday, he was greeted at the open garage door by a very pleased Mr Butler senior, a full array of dumbbells and bars at his feet, spread expansively over his wife's picnic blanket. There'd be hell to pay. Borrowed weights from the physics lab made up some of the smaller parts of the set, with others having been carefully weighed and machined, before being sandblasted and added to a few threaded bars to assemble a set that would have made even Dean envious. Carefully wrought press up bars, wrapped in rubberised tape for a comfortable, easy grip, and a padded expandable chinning bar to fit in a doorway, completed the set. All he needed now was his Rocky soundtrack and understanding, or at least partially deaf, neighbours. Both of which, fortunately, he had.

Travel was an unavoidable, major expense, yet having seriously tamed his right foot, and learnt how to coast down the hills, George had managed to increase the M3's fuel consumption to something approaching affordable. Although having a performance car like his, and driving it like a Christian, did seem to rather defeat the object of owning it. But as he gently motored to work, he would distract himself on his outbound journey with the superb 'Wake up to Wogan' radio show, and overdose on 80s soft rock on the way home, in preparation for his evening workout.

Slowly, very reluctantly, he began settling into his new routine, grudgingly accepting his frugal, green and white and stripy lifestyle. He often reflected on Michael's story, and his experiences in Iraq, realising time and again how close he'd come to losing him, and how lucky he really was. George decided that it was time to focus his mind on the day's more positive, rewarding aspects, rather than dwelling on negatives.

Now, he relished his drive along the stretch of perfectly straight road which bordered the ocean. A daily prize for having survived the B road perils with his wing mirrors still intact. Always momentarily losing himself with thoughts of Summer, and of their day on the beach, nudist notwithstanding. He treasured his carefully timed lunch breaks, which he spent on the same, sea salt encrusted ancient wooden bench every day, next to the same old retired, silent fisherman. Eating his egg salad in peace, it was a vital, frozen fifty-five minute release from The Evil Ray Varley's prison enclosure.

Each evening, when he'd finally made it back to his apartment, George would dash past his unopened post-box, desperately hoping that the contents weren't spilling out of it yet, open his front door and feed his unimpressed cat. He'd then quickly change into shorts, and begun a homemade workout plan that would last for a gruelling hour, and was followed with a water conserving, 'Navy Shower', which as the seasons changed from Autumn to Winter, left him shivering as he soaped up.

He'd then share an evening omelette with Arthur, more often than not in the old man's apartment these days, with his elderly Granddad making some excuses about having a better table, and served with a bottle of green and white and stripy, eight percent table wine that was unlikely to ever become an acquired taste. Then it was back to his own place in time for the daily call either to, or from, Summer, and a rich, varied conversation that, despite always leaving him with a lingering sense of both disappointment and yearning, was always the highpoint of his day.

Typically the call would last for an hour or so, before ending with them both indulging in the traditional *'no, you hang up first'* game for several more precious minutes. George had no idea how much the calls were costing him. Even if he had opened his post-box and torn apart the phone bill, realising the damage they were doing to his bank account each time the Direct Debit landed, it was the one cost that didn't trouble him. He just needed to talk to her every single day in order to stay sane.

Finally, with a full, if slightly windy belly, and his appetite for Summertime at least suppressed for now, it was then onto his new evening job. From around nine to just past midnight, George would sit at his old, faithful easel, and by candlelight, paint until his eyes became sore from the effort.

"But it's, it's an elephant…?"

"I know, but, *umm*, it's a good elephant, *isn't it?*" Slowly becoming intoxicated by the many joss sticks that burned in unseen corners of the gallery, George tried his very best to keep a pleading, desperate tone from his voice. He failed.

Kayley had taken a fresh look at large canvas that rested on a spare easel, in the middle of her gallery. It was indeed rather good. Very detailed, and the sky was especially noteworthy. But it was mostly of a large, mud splattered elephant, and her gallery was right next to the sea. She hadn't been at all sure it would make for a harmonious relationship. Which was a shame really, she'd rather liked the dishevelled chap. When her Business Banking Manager had suggested that he might have found her a new supplier, she hadn't expected someone like this. She certainly didn't expect him to be another banker.

"It *is* a good elephant, George, a very good elephant. But, well, the thing is, I'm not sure that my Customers would expect to find an elephant in here. You know, in an art gallery, *next to the sea.*" The poor chap. He looked crestfallen. "Have you got anything else I could look at?"

"*Err*, I've got a good one of a tiger at home."

Lately, any glimmer of hope needed to be grasped, like the last morsel of mouldy bread in a Vietnamese prisoner of war camp. And so when David had found out that his new surfing pupil painted, and he'd suggested that he introduced him to a local gallery owner, whose business he banked, the offer was quickly seized with both hands and feet. It was a new skill George had leant since taking up surfing.

Kayley's Place was a small, homely gallery. Nestled on one of the more sort after cobbled streets, the high annual rent was easily met by a steady stream of affluent returning tourist, all of whom had a fondness of her collections of eclectic pottery, quality paintings of the sea, and fine works in pen and ink. Kayley tried to encourage local artist, and scrawled in bright blue letters across her front window, were the words: *If you hear a voice within say 'you cannot paint', then by all means paint, and that voice will be silenced. - Vincent Van Gogh.* It was very inspiring.

George meanwhile, had been reasonably certain that he could paint. He was even more certain that he needed to top up the coffers somehow, and so after surfing practice one Saturday, he'd ventured into the gallery, looking somewhat windswept and hopeful, his favourite A Level piece, wedged firmly under his arm.

"I'm sorry, but I'm not sure I can help you, George. I mean, I really like to promote local artists, but I also need to consider if their work will sell, especially before I give it wall space. Look around you. I mostly sell work that's inspired by the sea, *not African wildlife!*" Kayley looked into his big dark, puppy-dog eyes. If he'd been more confident, more of a cad perhaps, a ladies' man even, she would've definitely suggested sharing drinks as a consolation prize. She had a thing for loveable rouges. "Don't give up the painting though, you're very good."

Sensing a vital opportunity slipping through his trembling fingers, it was time for the once successful CRA to call upon every skill that the Bank's merciless sales courses had ever taught him about objection handling. "But, *err*, but what if, Kayley..." He'd paused. This was the wrong way to start. How did the Trainers tell them do it again? He'd gotten out of practice of late, there was something about using the customer's own words, wasn't there? That was right! "Umm, *what I meant was*, so what *you're* saying Kayley, is you really like my artwork, but the subject's not right. And if I can paint something else, *something of the sea*, you'll put it up and, err, sell it for me?" Danny would've been proud.

Kayley wasn't quite sure what had happened that afternoon. But once the young man with seaweed in his hair had left her gallery, promising to come back the following Monday with a new, more appropriate canvas, she'd had a nagging suspicion that she'd given away a good deal more than she'd intended too. He did have very nice eyes though.

Later that same day, wearing his almost solid, splattered painting shirt, George had sat for three hours staring at a blank canvas. Inspiration had not only deserted him, it had coaxed Talent and Ability along for the ride as well. After years of painting wildlife and pets, how hard could creating a painting of the sea be? Very hard, apparently, and having spent another two hours routing through Arthur's endless piles of books, hoping to find something to get the creative juices flowing, he'd retreated back to his own apartment with nothing but the memory of his stuffy old school library for company.

He'd woken up the following Sunday drained and depressed, feeling slightly guilty that he'd used a Banking Mind Trick to get his foot in the door of Kayley's gallery, only to fail to produce the goods. He'd over promised and under delivered. Something he'd been warned of doing before by Danny, but that had been about selling financial products, not painting.

As he'd sat pecking at his pile of emaciated poached eggs, thinking about his former Manager's good natured debriefs, a thought had fluttered into his head though. He wondered what they'd done with their painting. Was it banished in shame to a cupboard too? Dropping his fork suddenly, George froze. That was it!

As he tore over to Danny and Hannah's that morning, his hair still soaking wet from his brief shower, and still wearing his painting outfit, with no time to waste choosing another, he'd wondered why he hadn't thought of the 'Garson's beach wedding painting' before. After a quick coffee in the presence of the intimidating giant though, he'd dashed back to the apartment, with the painting in the M3's boot as reference, safe in the knowledge that he'd obviously chosen to block out the experience. It was, after all, around the same time as his near death incident on the squash court. He'd probably need a therapist at some point.

From that moment, everything had changed. Inspiration, Ability and Talent were quickly rounded up and pressed into service. The rest of that Sunday had been dedicated to the new canvas, with even the weekly roast dinner having to be put in the fridge for later.

The following Monday lunchtime, with flecks of paint still in his hair, replacing the seaweed, George had strolled as confidently as he'd dared into Kayley's Place. A new painting, simply entitled 'Antigua' replacing the elephant under his arm. She'd loved it. And whilst tossing her long hair seductively over a shoulder, rather taken with his seemingly new found air of confidence, she'd suggested they had drinks after work, to talk about art, naturally. He declined however, respectively of course. His girlfriend would be calling him later from France, and he needed to get back to his easel too.

Since then, he'd begun moonlighting as a freelance artist, specialising in images of the Caribbean. Danny had been very reluctant to lend him their holiday albums again, so instead George collected great armfuls of glossy, tropical holiday brochures from the local travel agent, covering his lounge floor with them as he churned out the canvases. After the first one had sold within a few hours, the race was on to keep Kayley supplied. Whilst Fred relentlessly chased small pebbles around the apartment, he was still somehow managing to find them; his increasingly brightly coloured human tiptoed in between the scattering of catalogues, ignoring the holiday prices, and instead carefully checking his colours, and comparing palm trees and beaches.

To maximize profit, each Saturday afternoon after surfing practice, he enlisted Arthur to help him make his own canvases. Before the night drew in, the two of them cut, nailed and stretched for a few hours, eventually braking out the dwindling remains of the summer limoncello, to celebrate a fresh batch. The old man also diligently quality checked each piece before it was delivered it to the gallery. Working late, the dubious light played havoc with the colour, and a fresh pair of eyes, no matter how old they were, always helped. Even though the appraisal was usually conducted on the old man's doorstep, just before his suited and booted neighbour left for work, he was never anything but balanced and fair. All he wanted was the very best for his adopted Grandson.

George slid back his patio door, despite the cold November air, loosened his awful polyester tie and quickly stood aside as Fred bounded past him, and disappeared into the bedroom. *"Easy there, tiger!* What's got into you?" Pausing, as if expecting a reply, he leant out into the chilly evening air, knowing that his neighbour would have his own door open a fraction too. "Arthur, *I'm back!* I've got something special for tea, I've sold another two paintings - *cool eh*? I'll be there in a bit."

It was Thursday. The weekend loomed eagerly; he didn't have to work this Saturday, and today had been a rare, great day in the Bank. With Evil Ray safely hidden away at a Managers meeting, George had been able to spend ages helping Mrs Whimble. She was another old treasure who'd fallen in love with him. Widowed and totally alone in the world, he'd taken to helping her out with not only her banking, but also anything else that troubled her, each time she'd hobbled into the banking hall. Evil Ray though, having already seen to it that her funds were committed to a five year bond, would often berate him. As there was nothing more to sell her, she was a waste of sales time in his opinion.

But today he did help her, and content and happy, he'd decided to buy some thick, succulent steaks from the local butcher to round off the day in style. Relishing the feeling of being momentarily flush for a change, he'd also indulged in two bottles of rocket fuel strength, Australian Shiraz for good measure. He'd regret it tomorrow, but what the hell.

After changing into his jeans and a treasured chunky, homemade jumper, George bounded out onto his tiny courtyard like an excited puppy, practically chasing the tail he wished he had, and headed for his usual spot by the fence with a bottle and two glasses.

He froze. It could have been for a second, or it could have been for eternity.

His senses suddenly seemed to have deserted him. There was the smashing of glass as, without thinking, he dropped everything and bounded over the fence. Moments later, having used every ounce of skill his Cub Scout first aid badge afforded him, and slowly, like he was wading through a river of congealed mud in shoes of granite, he backed up, unblinking, his heart pounding deep and hard inside his chest.

Somehow, he fumbled his way back over the fence and through his patio door. Reaching for the telephone, delayed by hands that shook uncontrollably, he mechanically dialled the simple three digit number his traumatised instincts led him too. Call over, fighting his way through the thick fog that consumed his mind, he then dialled blindly again. After the third attempt, the telephone started to connect.

"*Bonjour*?"

"*Err*, Summer, *Summertime*?"

"*My Monkey*! You're early darling, is everything okay, have you sold yet *more* paintings? You'll be here in no time at this rate!" The bright, wonderfully sing-song voice washed over him like a blanket of love, carrying with it, just enough warm sunshine to defrost the words that needed to come next.

"Summer, Arthur's gone…"

Chapter 20

Letters, Lakes and Limoncello

A week later.

My Dearest Sunshine,

I'm terribly sorry to burden you with all this fuss, but if you are reading this letter, the chances are good that you have found me in less than perfect health. I do hope that I made it into the fresh air before finally keeling over?

And so, down to business. My life choices have, for one reason or another, left me more or less alone in the world, leaving me no choice but to impress on the kindness of the one true friend I have found on this little island. Someone I would have been proud to call my Grandson. Knowing that you sometimes need a gentle nudge in the right direction when someone is being less than direct, I should point out that this does mean YOU, I'm afraid!

Having sensed for some time now, that vital parts of me were starting to strain at the seams, and sensing that the inevitable was drawing near, I went to see that Nigerian Solicitor chap you mentioned to me when we first met. Charming fellow, extremely limited grasp of the English language, or even our legal system perhaps, but then, we all have our faults, don't we? I've left instruction with him and I would be ever so grateful if you could contact him shortly so that you can deal with my remains, such as they are.

No doubt he'll be in touch with further instruction once he's worked his way through some of the finer points of my will, God help him!

Even now, with my body failing, the thought of the two of you struggling to communicate in that muddled mess of an office of his, brings a warm glow to my heart..!

Finally, you'll soon see that, if you accept the challenge, you have a journey ahead of you. And so, to keep your thoughts occupied on your trip, I've taken the liberty of writing down some thoughts of my own for you to ponder on. To keep you from becoming bored on the road, as it were. You never know, you might find something in there you'll want to hear...

Unable to read anymore for now, and with infinite care, as though tending to an injured butterfly, George folded up the letter he'd already read countless times before, and gently put it back into its envelope for safe keeping, all the while fighting as best he could against yet another crippling wave of weapons grade nausea. Clearly, he'd never mentioned to Arthur his affliction with travel sickness.

The transfer coach's suspension had obviously been fashioned from jelly. As it chugged around yet another never ending bend on its seemingly endless journey to Limone, the small Italian village that the old man, who now lived in a jar safely packed inside George's school rucksack, loved so much, it wallowed horribly, threatening to pitch them off the road at any moment. It had been this way ever since it had left Verona airport, twenty-four minutes ago. And now, of the few passengers that had boarded this out of season, evening trip, one in particular was already somewhat greener than the others. And he still had hours of travel ahead of him.

George swallowed down an extra strength Stugeron tablet with a hearty swig of limoncello for good measure, and rested his sweaty head on the horribly patterned velour seat. He was still struggling to process the events of the past week. Events which had picked him up and swept him away like a raging tsunami, a never ending torrent that held him in a drowning, vice like grip, from which there seemed to be no escape.

From the moment the ambulance crew had taken away the body of his adopted Granddad, his life had changed forever. The younger of the two paramedics, a sweet-looking girl with a schoolgirl ponytail and a scattering of freckles, had given him the envelope, along with a small box that she'd found on Arthurs large dining room table. The box contained the old man's treasured, vintage Omega Seamaster, along with a brief note explaining that if George damaged it in any way; he'd haunt him until the end of time, and the envelope contained the letter that had since become his personal guide. It was his constant companion, and a reminder of his old friend.

He gazed out of the coach window at the passing countryside, at the early snows that sprinkled the mountain tops and the small villages, and at the drooping suspended power lines that seemed to join them together, stretching out over the Italian landscape as far as the eye could see, like an endless line of cooked spaghetti. It would be dark soon, and he desperately hoped that if he kept on drinking the limoncello, a combination of fatigue, alcohol and the side effects of the drugs he'd taken, might temporarily consume him, and he'd drift into a welcome, if inevitably fitful sleep, for the rest of the journey.

His appointment at Mr Obayomi's office had been an experience to remember. George had been quite sure he'd sensed Arthur's presence in that room, doubled over in fits of laughter, as the Nigerian solicitor struggled to explain his responsibilities as sole Executor. As well as intermittently pausing to check his understanding from one of the huge dusty law books that lay strewn about his road accident of an office, he would also periodically rest a huge hand the colour of coal on his clients shoulder for comfort. He meant well though. Bless him.

In the end, after four hours of joint research, both men concluded that at this stage at least, a funeral was probably in order. Anything else could be interpreted and worried about later, once Mr Obayomi had sufficiently recovered from the ordeal, and had located the relevant reference manual.

Although George had felt a degree of responsibility creeping up his hairy legs when he'd first bought his apartment, it had been nothing compared to the sobering effect of the weight that now rested on his shoulders. He'd been left an important task by a trusted, dear friend, and more than anything else, he didn't want to bugger it up.

It soon became apparent that Arthur hadn't given much thought to his death, which was understandable really. Nor did he have any faith in Banks, perhaps even more understandable, preferring instead to collect his pension in cash each week, and distribute it evenly amongst a series of odd shaped jars, labelled accordingly as to their purpose, gas, water, vodka, etc. The remains of his life savings, just over twelve hundred pounds, had been safely stored away in an old shoebox at the back of his battered wardrobe, alongside another overflowing box filled with undeveloped photographic film from his travels.

George hadn't felt at all comfortable sorting through his neighbour's belongings, just one of the many tasks his role as Executor allowed him to do. Although Arthur's home had long since felt like an extension of his own, without the endless banter and constant topping up of glasses, he'd felt like an intruder, picking his way through someone else's life, looking for the cash, for the valuables. And to a degree at least, he was.

But a funeral and cremation needed to be paid for somehow, and there was one more vital thing that had become abundantly clear from his time in Mr Obayomi's office. Providing that it didn't put anyone out, Arthur rather liked the idea of having his remains scattered in Lake Garda, preferably from the shoreline at Limone, but only if it didn't cause too much fuss, of course. George was determined to honour this request, even if it did mean there were now travel costs to consider as well.

He'd collected together the jars of notes and pennies, along with the dusty shoe box, made the necessary calls to the local funeral directors and travel agents, and sat down with a calculator, a large glass of green and white and stripy red wine, and did the math. Money soon proved to be tighter than a fat girl's thong. Even if he walked to the airport and camped in Limone, which considering the early, hard winter, would've probably have meant that he'd freeze to death before he'd even got the lid off the urn, he was nearly a thousand elusive pounds short. That was a lot of paintings to sell.

Without a second thought, he'd packed up his beloved, long saved for electric guitar, flashy new Marshall Amplifier, along with his impressive collection of effects pedals, carefully placed them in the boot of the M3, and drove to the second hand shop he used to turn his nose up at, near Nelson's branch. He could always buy another guitar, one day.

Having been unable to even contemplate working the Friday after Arthur had passed, George had called in sick instead. The grunting Susan, unbelievably the lesser of the two evils, answered the telephone, acknowledging the sad news that there'd been a sudden family bereavement, and that he wouldn't be in today, with a customary, *'Ohlright then Mate.'*

He'd decided for the time being, that he'd keep the news to himself, and not tell his parents. They'd only worry. However, Evil Ray soon scuppered this plan. Immediately after Susan told him why he wasn't coming in, he'd retrieved the young offenders personnel file, looked up his next of kin, and called the Butlers' respectable semi, under the pretence of offering his sympathies. He'd seen this pattern many times before. All of the runts he'd been sent to re-program or manage out eventually crumbled under the pressure. They all inevitably needed a few days off sick to regroup, and Evil Ray always checked out their story. He was just surprised it took George so long to crack. It was almost impressive.

The short call had complicated matters no end. Mrs Butler had panicked and, fearing the worst, frantically called Mr Butler senior home from work. It left George no choice but to explain what had happened to his neighbour, before, as kindly as he could, refusing his parents offers to help with the arrangements. Worst still though, Evil Ray now had fresh ammunition to use against his inmate. It was just as well. He'd been frustratingly compliant of late.

Summer already knew everything. She'd made her highly charged, emotional feelings about leaving France immediately to be with him, and offer her support, abundantly clear on several occasions. But George felt strongly, for reasons he couldn't fully articulate, let alone be expected to defend, that this was something he needed to do on his own. It was between him, his old friend, and possibly Fred, but no one else.

After parting company with his treasured guitar and accessories, and, like an alcoholic sucking the last remnants from a wrapped up bottle of sherry, draining the remaining available funds from his credit card, he finally collected together enough cash to give Arthur the proper send-off he deserved.

In a rare stroke of good luck, George had found that some of the old letters and postcards pinned to the old man's fridge, were from friends he'd met on his travels through Europe, including a couple who lived in Limone. Judging by the terrible pigeon English, which rivalled even Mr Obayomi's, he deduced that they owned some sort of B&B, and that business was still good, despite an unseasonal wet summer.

The postcard was a year old. In spite of still feeling like a trespassing grave robber, George had rummaged through Arthurs drawers until he eventually found a barely touched address book, which contained just a handful of entries, including his neighbours. Each carefully noted in perfect, school teacher handwriting. Over a yet another glass of unpleasant wine, the vintage didn't seem to be improving any with age; he traced the details on the postcard to an entry in the address book, and to a Mr Giuseppe Camisso, and his wife Contessa. There was an address in Limone, and a telephone number. For the first time in days, he felt a small surge of hope.

It had proved to be a difficult conversation, yet one that helped George learn a few new communication skills, which might be useful the next time he talked to his solicitor. Eventually though, after some Italian hysterics on the other end of the line, the Camissos insisted that Mr Arthur's Grandson (this had been a difficult issue to explain, and he eventually just went with it) must stay with them when he came to scatter the ashes. Also, apparently there was to be *senza alcun costo* for *Mr George*. Considering how far he had to stretch his modest budget, he sincerely hoped this meant 'free'.

George returned to Bay branch on Monday, expecting the worst and not being disappointed. Relishing the opportunity to really turn the thumb screws up a few extra notches, Evil Ray had lectured his inmate for a full hour. Dwelling on how he was considering raising further disciplinary action against him, for lying about his reasons for being absent from work, and that he'd left him no choice but to make a full, detailed report to HR. The thin man clearly loved every second of it.

The Evil Ray Varley didn't seem to need to even draw breath during his monotonous speech. The endless thin grey voice was incessant, having the same effect on his victim as a team of nail technicians dragging their collective talons down an oversized black board. When he was eventually allowed to speak again, George had explained that to all intents and purposes, Arthur *was* his Granddad, and that he was all that the old man had in the world. Also, although he wasn't holding his breath here, could he leave early on Thursday for the funeral, and take Friday and Saturday off to travel to Italy, pretty please?

Sensing yet another opportunity to be properly evil, remarkably enough, Evil Ray agreed to the request, although it would need to be taken as holiday, and not as compassionate leave. The deceased was not a relative, regardless of their make-believe relationship. George would also need to catch up on his sales and referral targets before Thursday lunchtime, or he would not be allowed to go. Evil Ray had then immediately set about drafting a challenging, virtually unachievable Action Plan, a great list of stretching sales and referrals objectives. He knew all too well that his victim would toil into the small hours, in order to achieve the targets before the deadline.

Back at the welcome desk, knowing he'd been seized by his short and curlies, not an enviable position to be in, George had reviewed the herculean objectives he'd been set. In just three days, considering he'd already lost half a day being chastised, he needed to book twenty quality appointments, the emphasis being on 'quality', into Grace's diary. He also needed to achieve a further fifteen sales himself, across the limited range of products he was entitled to sell, all of which would be thoroughly checked, to ensure compliance. If there were any mistakes, he wouldn't be going anywhere.

The tourist's and holiday home owners had long since retreated back to the cities, leaving just a scattering of locals to target, most of whom were either elderly or shell fisherman, both of which gave off a curious aroma when you trapped them in an interview room for too long. If he'd been back in the city, he would have had a fair chance of hitting the targets, but here, with a banking hall littered with the likes of Mrs Whimble and Captain Pugwash, his task seemed all but impossible.

Grace tended to stay behind each night for an hour or so, calling Customers, booking them into her own diary, both in an effort to stay busy, as well as to keep her away from her depressing, lonely little bungalow for as long as possible. George had rarely stayed late. With the exception of the time he accidental killed the cashpoint in Nelson's branch, if he was still in a branch after hours, it was usually spent waiting for Billy to get ready for a night on the tiles. They'd been happy days.

Now though, the brief *BBC Watchdog* scandal already a fading memory, Cottons NSIB was back to cunningly promoting the intense Predatory Sales Culture again. Across the country, Managers were being instructed to encourage their staff to stay late, to call Customers and fill the seller's diaries to the brim. Daily faxes were sent to Area Office, numbers downloaded and collated on mass, before the figures were fed up the line in an endless stream of fiction, until they reached the stratospheric heights of Top Management.

As he'd sat hunched at the welcome desk, watching the lights extinguish one by one, save for the ones in Grace's office and the banking hall, the rest of the staff, including Evil Ray, left the branch without a kindly word, or nod of support. Frustrated and humiliated, he'd reviewed the long list of customer prospects, and very reluctantly picked up the telephone. He wasn't doing this for the Bank, or for Evil Ray. He was doing it for Arthur.

One thing became abundantly clear over those few horrible days though. As he'd battled ceaselessly through his lunch breaks, and late into the evenings, ticking off the appointments he'd booked one by one, meticulously checking his own sales before handing them in for marking, it suddenly dawned on him that he wouldn't last six months in this wretched hell hole. And he was quite certain that he didn't belong in the Bank anymore.

George felt as though a big part of his life had become like an unimpressive, disappointing canvas, which he desperately wanted to paint over and begin again. But some of the meatier chunks, some of the pointed lumps of old paint weren't ever going to go away, no matter how much primer he applied. He yearned for a new canvas. Some means of starting over again, of creating a new painting that wouldn't be spoilt by past mistakes. But this was something to worry about later, much later. Right now, he had far more important matters to attend to; this was no time for selfish concerns. It was time for Arthur.

The coach lurched momentarily, as the surly Italian diver wrestled with the belligerent gearbox, jolting his youngest and most off colour passenger from the very fringes of sleep. George straightened up in his seat, glanced out of the window briefly, looking for a lake somewhere out there in the darkness, before leaning forward to see if it would help any with the queasiness. It didn't.

Sitting back and breathing deeply, he reached inside his leather jacket for the old pewter hipflask he'd found lurking in one of Arthur's cupboards, taking another grateful swig of the old man's homebrew. To begin with, he'd been fiercely protective over the last of the summer limoncello. Collecting together and guarding the remains of the precious yellow liquid, as though he expected to be broken into at any moment by some sort of kleptomaniac oenologist, who'd developed an interest in lemon liqueur. On this trip though, it was for drinking, and for eventually for toasting his old friend. Discounting the remnants that sloshed about in the hipflask, he still had a full, chilled thermos safely stowed next to its brewer, carefully wrapped in a change of clothing, snug inside his school rucksack.

George let his mind wander as the distinctive, lemon flavour diluted the sharp bile that had been rising in his throat, threatening to improve the pattern of the seat in front at any moment. He'd chosen to sit as far away from his handful of fellow passengers as possible, yet some memory of where to sit to avoid, or at least minimise travel sickness, told him now that right at the back probably wasn't the best place to be.

Eventually, feeling marginally better, he pulled out Arthur's letter again for another reading. The meaningful sentiments provided a good source of distraction.

... Make love to a beautiful girl in a warm, tropical sea, but be careful of your footing. Try not to collect too many broken hearts. I imagine they'll weigh heavier the older you get. Don't worry if you never find yourself wanting to have children, we're not all meant to share our train sets. Look after your feet and your toes, they're your only means of locomotion and capable of exercising great pain if neglected. If you find the right person to spend your life with, then settle down and enjoy being together without a backward glance, you might not ever find them again, if you send them away...

Thoughts of Summer floated into his head. Did she think he'd sent her away, by refusing her kind offer to come along and help? Hopefully not, she'd seemed to understand how he felt. During one of their many, epic calls last week. He'd been almost able to explain his reason for needing to do this on his own, even managing to use some long words.

He glanced at the large luminous arrow hands of Arthur's old Omega. They still burned brightly in the gloom, despite their age, and although able to survive a three hundred metre dive, George religiously took it off to do the dishes. It would have been just after six at home. His Dad should have fed Fred by now, on his way home from the University, at least that was one meal perhaps, he wouldn't murder and drag into the apartment. He'd left his bedroom window open a fraction, so that the tiger could come and go as he pleased, and given the furry terrorist a stern talking to before he'd left, about not bringing back the remains of any wildlife or livestock. Knowing all too well from blood stained experience, that his words were likely going unheeded.

Or perhaps they weren't? Since that evening he'd found Arthur, spread eagled on his small courtyard, Fred hadn't felt quite himself. Although he'd had seen more than his fair share of death, a great deal of which he'd caused, sniffing the lifeless remains of the gentle old man who used to tickle his ears and feed him custard crèmes, sensing that he was gone from this world, had left him with a gaping hole in his life. In order to fill it, he'd decided to spend more time with his human. It had been a period of adjustment for all concerned.

Lately, George had found that he'd been waking up under a crushing, purring weight, which had then followed him like a shadow throughout his morning routine. Fred even pushed open the bathroom door, sitting precariously on his lap whilst he was on the throne. The tiger met him each evening when he arrived home, something that nearly ended in tragedy and a new bumper the first time, and virtually waved him off with a furry paw every morning. Bless him.

Although disconcerting at first, like having a known serial killer tuck you in each night, the change in behaviour soon became endearing, and exactly what George needed. In dealing with his own grief, Fred had inadvertently become the Tom Cat his human had set out to buy all those months ago. But he still brought home far too many bodies for his liking. Somethings will never change.

To begin with, the journey had been slow. Another coach ahead stopped periodically, to let out passengers out at various hotels along the way, holding up the traffic behind. Once it pulled off the main road though, and he was finally able to finally get past, the enraged driver of the Limone bound vehicle, hugely late for his supper, blasted his horn and thrashed the lumpy diesel engine to within an inch of its life. Desperately trying to coax more speed from the reluctant lump, his efforts caused it to leave great plumes of thick black smoke in its wake, as it was flung it ever faster around the snaking, undulating road.

Unprepared for the change in pace and direction, George inadvertently slid from one end of the long back seat to the other, the cheap velour leaving a minor case of carpet burn through his Levi's. Finally, he managed to grab the armrest at the far end, and fasten his seatbelt. His school rucksack, which was proudly covered in carefully, hand stitched *Star Wars*, Def Leppard and Bon Jovi patches, a collective tapestry of his school years, had slid down the aisle, and now, worryingly enough, rested a few feet away from a suspicious looking passenger.

Fortunately, as the coach raced up yet another hill, it started to slide back towards him and soon, with an outstretched cowboy boot, he was able to hook one of the straps, and pull it back to safety. Immediately, he unzipped the fastenings and checked his precious cargo. Luckily enough nothing, liquid or ash, had spilled.

George had never attended a funeral before, or at least not one he could remember, and this lack of practical experience hampered his ability to organise one. With time limited, and Evil Ray unlikely to allow him to use the branch telephones, arrangements with the Funeral Directors had to be conducted from the public phone box he used each day to call his Mum. The stolen ten minute lunch breaks disappearing in the blink on an eye.

The choice of flowers proved to be difficult, not least due to his extremely limited funds, but reflecting on Arthur's rather wild garden had been inspirational. George explained to the kindly Funeral Director, that his old friend was rather fond of wild flowers, such as daisies, buttercups and bluebells, or anything else that happened to be free and seeded in his few pots for that matter. The Director said that he would speak to his wife, who was rather good at these sorts of things, and told him not to worry. Everything would be alright in the end.

Having miraculously met Evil Ray's impossible targets, and with each sale being very reluctantly deemed compliant, despite a thorough, vindictive evaluation, George arrived for work on Thursday morning dressed for the funeral to save time. He'd borrowed rather an expensive looking black knitted silk tie from Arthur's wardrobe, quite a find amongst the faded chinos and brightly coloured linen shirts he'd favoured, and wore his treasured black pin stripe, along with a matching waistcoat that seldom saw the light of day. Finishing the outfit off with a crisp white cotton shirt that his Mum had washed and pressed by hand especially, it smelt comfortingly fantastic.

Needless to say, turning up out of uniform resulted in yet another trip to Evil Ray's office, and yet another belittling scolding. If he'd had his older brother experiences behind him, he would have reflected that is was just like being back at school again, only thankfully enough, without all the spanking. Perhaps that was next?

Dean had once said that outfits can communicate, and that image can be a powerful tool. And maybe he was right after all, because something gave George confidence that day to stand up to Evil Ray when he started toying with him, questioning whether or not this latest breach of his rules should still entitle him to leave early. Perhaps it was the tie? Whatever it had been, it was enough to see him stand up, and make his chest and shoulders swell.

"I *will* be leaving at lunchtime Mr Varley. *My Granddad needs me*!" It wasn't a request. And it left Evil Ray, alone with his framed corporate pictures, more than just a little shaken by events.

In the end, Arthur's funeral had been a sad, lonely little affair. As he stood by himself in the chapel, and the dreary Minister mumbled a few nondescript, well-practiced words about life and death, George couldn't help but wonder if he'd done the right thing after all. Perhaps he should've invited Summer and his parents along too. Quietly reflecting, listening to the droning speaker with only half an agnostic ear, he realised though that this wasn't to be Arthur's proper send off. This was merely the departure lounge. Once he got his friend to Italy that was when he'd be properly remembered. Sent off in a style of his choosing, not here, not with these cut and paste hollow words that held no meaning for either of them.

Whilst he stood, waiting for it all to be over, he'd at last had what alcoholics like to refer to as 'a moment of clarity'. George had been fretting for days about the actual ash scattering process. What should someone actually do or say when they're flinging mortal remains into a lake? But finally he had it. He'd stand on the shoreline, a heavy crystal shot glass of Arthur's homemade limoncello in his hand, as he'd once lectured him; 'any other type of glass, and you may as well be swigging meths with the tramps'. Then, he'd read his letter aloud and in full, and throw the urn into the lake in order to avoid 'ash back'. He felt certain, Arthur would've approved.

The next day, his frustrated Postie thrust an ominous looking letter into hand, having been unable to get anymore into his post-box. Feeling somewhat embarrassed by the exchange, George headed for the crematorium. Judging by the envelope, the letter was from Mr Obayomi. The hand writing said it all. He couldn't face that now, and stuffed it into his leather jacket pocket instead, next to Arthurs, to be opened later, much later.

After cooling, something he hadn't accounted for, he'd collected the ashes, which were safely entombed in a small wooden urn with a screw lid, and selected from the Funeral Directors budget range. He briefly returned to his apartment, packed a change of clothes, a lunchbox full of egg salad, and the last of the summer limoncello, and had driven to the local short haul airport, as economically as he could manage.

Seriously late and obviously starving now, the coach driver showed no signs whatsoever of letting up, he raced on through the cold November air, triple air horn blasting away at all and sundry, as he sped through the villages and towns towards Limone. George had finally lost his battle against his overwhelming travel sickness, and had vomited uncontrollably into his spare Tightie-whities for a full half an hour. Going commando tomorrow was an inevitable, chilly prospect.

Completely drained in every sense or the word, he sat back in his seat and reached for a stick of chewing gum from his jacket pocket, his hands quivering slightly. The hip flask was also drained of all its limoncello, and he daren't risk opening the thermos in the bucking and weaving coach. He needed to shift focus, to take his mind off things, to regroup his wobbling senses and restore order before he fell out of the coach into Giuseppe Camisso arms when he arrived. He couldn't read the letter anymore. It had already caused one explosive episode.

Letting his mind wander of its own accord, he eventually found himself thinking about his best mate, Barney. Sadly, he'd sensed that they'd slowly drifted away from each over the past year since he'd joined the Bank. Come to think of it now, was he still his Best Mate? Surely friends like them, boys who'd shared adventures like they'd experienced over the years, stayed best mates forever? George made a mental note to call Barney as soon as he got home, to arrange a wild night out in the Pubs where they had cut their teeth as young, painfully unsuccessful, womanisers. Barney would be both physically and biologically unable to decline such an offer. It would be great.

Basking in the warm glow of nostalgia, George let his mind continue to amble about, waiting to see what it would find next in the recesses of his memory to amuse him...

An entirely new mechanical rattle suddenly joined an already overcrowded orchestra of other clattering noises, which the MGB's unwilling, seventy-two mile an hour progress was busy composing. The passengers exchanged worried glances. Barney wound down the reluctant, sticking window, and despite a gale that sent maps and empty crisp packets flying around the cockpit like enraged tropical birds, stuck his head out to inspect the damage, thick red hair billowing wildly.

"Nothing seems to have dropped off yet Mate, and the smoke seems to have died down a bit at last." Looking even more dishevelled than normal, the Navigator sat back down and grinned encouragingly, slowly sealing the window once more. At least this inspection hadn't seen him stand up on the cracked leather seat to look out of the MG's open, full length webesto sunroof, to see if anything had rattled loose. It had been a poor decision at the time, and one that had nearly ended up being an unpleasant ginger stain, on the windscreen of the articulated lorry behind.

The boys had been on the road now for nearly five hours. It was the longest either of them had ever spent in a car before, and unfortunately, despite Mr Butler senior giving the MGB a thorough, comprehensive pre-road trip service, the old girl was starting to show signs of badly needing a tea break. She wasn't the only one.

"*Cup of tea, Barney?*" Gripping the Motolita steering wheel tightly in unseasonal leather driving gloves, George nodded hopefully at his Navigator. The large Thermos flask they'd filled to the brim just before setting off, was now a distant memory, but a memory which required both emptying and topping up. A pit stop was well over due for all those concerned.

"Reckon so Mate, *and maybe a burger two...?*"

George had owned the 1972 classic for just long enough now, to see exactly what his Dad had meant about it needing significant work before it would pass an MOT. And also just long enough to fall deeply in love with the rusty old heap, in spite of all its rather curious smells.

Regardless of any reservations at the time, his Dad had secretly thrived on the restoration project too. It kept him out of the house, and out of harm's way. He'd also hoped that as they toiled together over greasy engine parts, late into the night by the light of a single, naked electric bulb, his youngest son would finally pick up some of the engineering skills he'd already successfully passed on to Michael. He did not.

Naturally, George had a passing interest in what all the oily bits did, but his real interest lay in the bodywork. He desperately wanted to set to work with the filler and spray cans, and transform his pride and joy, making it look pretty and shiny once again. He rather liked shiny things. Alas though, father and son had very different ideas about what bodywork restoration actually entailed. His Dad had strongly suggested he brought home a spot welder from the University, and carefully and methodically patched up the honeycombed shell with neat, perfectly trimmed sections of new steel.

His youngest meanwhile, favoured the much quicker alternative of filler and fibreglass. This was something he could crack on with alone, during the day, without having to wait for the evenings or weekends to be supervised with the potentially lethal welder. He'd also get out on the road much, much sooner.

The boys had finished their A Level exams a few weeks earlier, and now had a long summer holiday ahead of them, with nothing much to do but wait for results that could shape the rest of their lives. Now that they were both eighteen, Barney had been secretly hatching a plan to embark on a wild Club 18-30 holiday. But for now though, he intended to keep this a carefully guarded secret. He knew all too well how George's Mum would react. This topic needed to be snuck up on gently, and handled with infinite care, if his plan had any chance at all of succeeding.

To pass the time, over a few legal beers in their local, the idea of a road trip had been conceived. Barney was keen to check that now they were adults, he could spend a week or so in his best mates company, without wanting to strangle him, and the road trip seemed like a good practice run. At least they would still be in their own country if it all went horribly wrong, as things often tended to where they were concerned.

After four miserable attempts, during which he succeeded in gaining either a minor or major fault in every conceivable section, George finally passed his driving test on his fifth go. The news came as a huge relief to his weary instructor. With the MG's mechanical issues attended to, and the engine purring, if not like a proud lion, then at least like a content, midsized tabby cat, the bodywork, and in particular the gaping hole in the driver side foot well, was all that was holding up his unrestricted mobility.

Mr Butler senior had looked on in despair, as his youngest son slapped great handfuls of pliable filler into the network of holes and crevices. Occasionally losing his arm as yet another section crumbled away under his fingertips, bridging the larger gaps with roughly torn strips of fibre glass, completely failing to heed any of the advice to first kill off the rust.

After weeks of sanding, filling, and then sanding some more, the MG started to look, on the surface at least, almost respectable. One on the rear wings was slightly fatter than its designers had originally intended, and an interesting texture lurked on the bottom of the boot lid, but it was passable enough, and George started spray painting with enthusiastic gusto. His aim and technique were far from expert.

Words could not adequately explain just how stratospherically angry his Dad became when he returned home from work that day, only to find that his son had accidentally splattered his black, shiny vintage motorbikes petrol tank with old English white. He'd been well into the swing of things, and hadn't noticed he'd knocked off the tanks dust sheet in passing.

A week later, gleaming white, having been polished almost back to the bare metal, wire wheels and chrome work shining like the Butler family's best cutlery, the hot August sun threatening to melt all the fibre glass that held it together, the MGB looked spectacular, especially if you squinted a bit.

Thankfully, the decidedly flexible section of floor pan managed to escape the MOT inspector's attention. An old Friend of Mr Butler seniors, and a fellow classic motorcycling enthusiast, he was cunningly distracted from his work, with talk of the challenging Velocette restoration. And after just over an hour of nervously sweating in the corner, the old cars delighted owner was handed a fresh ticket.

Like cardboard scenery for a primary school Christmas play, enthusiastically assembled by year six, the MG's makeover wouldn't last long though. Soon the rust would climb out from under the layers of filler and make its presence felt, ruining the paint work. But for now at least, it would do. The classic car looked the part, which was most important, and it allowed George to get out on the road alone, for the very first time. It was time to start the engine and select a suitable soundtrack.

Mr Butler senior had been surprisingly supportive of the boys plan to embark on a week long road trip. He'd done exactly the same thing, albeit on the back of his motorbike, when he was his son's age, and offered to help plan a suitable route. To his wife though, her youngest was still a schoolboy in short trousers, with scabby knees and wayward hair. Which to a degree at least, he was, and she had her concerns, not least his lack of driving experience, or uncoordinated sense of direction.

George needed to prove himself before the road trip. And for the next few weeks spent all his earnings from the Supermarket on petrol, endlessly filling a tank that seemed to be made from a washing up liquid bottle, and tearing over the surrounding countryside each evening with his startled Dad hanging on for dear life. It was great fun.

As the trip got closer, he became more excited with every passing day. It was going to be great. An opportunity to see new parts of the country, stretch his old cars legs, and to properly get away from home for the first time since he and Barney had been sent packing by a field of Bovine Terrorists. However, aside from being a prelude to a still undisclosed holiday, somewhere hot and sweaty, filled with girls who'd left their morals in their suitcases, his travelling companion had an entirely different outlook on their planned adventure.

Barney's unwavering, unsubstantiated belief that girls would fall willingly into his arms each time he set foot in a new bar, never failed to inspire. He was adamant that in the guise of two hip young men from the South, with no destination in mind, on the road merely in search of the answers, they'd have a stream of northern lasses lining up outside their tent, with their knickers in their handbags. It all sounded rather appealing.

Especially as lately, George was unsure if he and Orang-utan Amy were still an item. They'd had had a sort of argument about the planned road trip, but like everything else about their relationship, it had been a decidedly average exchange of words. If he'd been more experienced in these matters, he'd have probably chalked it up as nothing more than a minor disagreement. Nevertheless, with the boys planning to head out into the great unknown in just a few days' time, he decided that if she made no attempt to contact him before, and with vivid memories of the spectacular Gabriella still burning brightly in his loins, for the purposes of the journey at least, he was a free agent, and would follow the Ginger Womaniser without hesitation. The thought of sharing a tent with him though, was rather worrying.

After narrowly avoiding missing their junction, and being forced against its will to perform a perilous, tyre-squealing, lane-hopping manoeuvre that had nearly caused a pileup, the MG was delighted to be off the motorway and back on a far less stressful A road. And as it rattled on contentedly towards Lake Windermere, it tried to put the whole ordeal behind it.

Mr Butler senior had spent a dusty afternoon in the family loft, looking for the map and pace notes he'd devised, before setting out on his own trip, a half a lifetime ago. It needed some updating of course, new motorways had been built, and some campsites were now busy housing estates, but soon enough the boys had a plan, and route to follow. All they needed to do now was remember to stick to it.

The Lake District was the first of three centres they'd visit. Followed by Scotland, and, finances permitting, finally Wales. On the initial leg of the trip, it was the intention to camp somewhere near Windermere for a night, before heading for the coast over the various mountain passes the next day. They'd then follow the shoreline for as far as possible, come inland and camp for another night, before heading north for Fort William, Scotland. To the boys, it was all very exciting stuff. It was going to be so much better than their last, ill-fated camping expedition.

After misjudging a particularly deceptive bend, the MG's tyres squealed in protest once more, as George wrestled for control, their enormous collection of kit sliding to one side, crashing nosily against the bodywork. There was no doubt that they'd come prepared this time. They'd both been Cub Scouts after all. As well as the usual camping paraphernalia of stoves, tent and sleeping bags, they'd also bought with them a curious collection of clothing. The boys were ready for any occasion, from trekking to sunbathing, and from nightclubbing to shopping. Barney was even prepared to formally meet a visiting dignitary, the green suit being an interesting choice.

Their food stocks, thanks largely to Mrs Butler, would have fed an army for a week. Crammed not only into the family picnic basket, but also a whole fleet of plastic Tupperware boxes, they had enough moist fruit cake between them to sink a battleship. She'd also carefully stitched together a robust coin bag, which she then filled with ten pence pieces, so that her son could make the customary 'Three Rings' each time they arrived somewhere new, and once he'd found a telephone box. Even Barney knew better than to mock this tradition.

Mr Butler senior had been busy organising provisions too. Secretly wishing he was going instead of Barney perhaps, he'd assembled a box of essential tools that might come in useful, should they run into mechanical difficulties, along with a copy of the MGB Haynes manual. The tools were each labelled, and he'd carefully annotated the manual with further notes that his son would hopefully understand, along with detailed hand drawn diagrams, of which tools he would require for which repairs. A partially sighted monkey would've been able to use the kit to rebuild the big end, so hopefully, there was a slim chance that the boys might be able to change a tyre.

"Check the Map again Barney, are you *sure* we're heading in the right direction?" Fortunately, unlike his driver, the Navigator wasn't cursed with crippling travel sickness, and so far at least, they'd managed to stay more or less on course.

"Dude, *trust me*, another half an hour and we'll be in a bar by a lake, surrounded by girls!" Even Barney's freckles looked randy.

"I think we need to find a campsite first, and maybe shower and eat, *I'm bloody knackered*!" It had been a long, long road. And whereas somewhere on the M5, the Navigator had been able to drift off into a cosy, crisps and chocolate biscuit induced afternoon nap, if they'd wanted to stay alive, George had needed to stay awake.

The MGB rumbled its way into the centre of Windermere just after five. It was Friday evening, and whilst the streets weren't exactly crowded, there was a healthy scattering of locals heading either home or to the pub, having happily finished work for the week. A number of easily identifiably, brightly dressed tourists, also steamed up the shop windows and clicked away with their cameras.

Fortunately the tourist information centre stayed open to half past five, and after stopping to ask for directions an embarrassing six times, the boys eventually pulled up outside a wooden building, which resembled a colonial outpost in the mid-west. Whilst George waited vigilantly on the double yellows, Barney ran inside, hoping to be pointed towards a campsite that was within staggering distance of a decent pub, full of desperate girls. Unfortunately, he didn't edit these requests any before asking.

Minutes later he returned, looking crestfallen. He was grasping a solitary piece of paper and not, as they'd expected, a handful of glossy campsite brochures. "Dude, *we've* got a serious problems Mate, *I feel like Baby Jesus!*"

"Barney, what the hell are you talking about?"

"There's no room at the Inn, Mate, or even *Inns* for that matter, not ones that will take us anyway." He hadn't looked this depressed since he'd discovered a girl he'd been making encouraging progress with at a family party, had actually been a distant cousin, and she wouldn't be swayed. "Apparently most of the campsites won't take a couple of male campers!"

"Err, *Barney*, you did explain that, well, you know, we're not, ahem…" George blushed at the thought, and suddenly considered sleeping in the car, alone.

"*Mate*! Of course I did! I actually think that it might have helped if we were! No, they all think we're going cause some sort of trouble, I don't know, get pissed and wake everyone up or something."

"I can't *imagine* what would give them that idea."

"*Me either*! Anyway, the lady gave me the number and address of a place that *might* be okay with us, but I think its miles away…" Barney retrieved the folded map from the foot well, and as always, using his faithful index finger as a guide, traced the village of Lorton, and the Wheatsheaf Inn Camp Site that was scribbled on the scrap of paper. "…*Yep*, here it is, right by that dodgy sounding town we're supposed to be camping near tomorrow!"

"I'm not sure I want to drive there tonight Barney. I mean, Dad said those mountain passes are pretty hard work, *do you want to try them in the dark*?"

"Let me give 'em a call, make sure they'll take us first, yeah?" Without waiting to see if there would be further debate, Barney jumped out of the MG and ran down the road towards a bright red telephone box, clutching the carefully stitched coin bag.

As an afterthought, George opened his driver's door and yelled after him, "*Barney*, call my Mum too, *three rings only*, and see if you can grab me a Cornish pasty!"

"*It's the holy grail of camping*! A pub, with a campsite and shower block, he even said you can get as pissed as you like, and then stagger back when you're ready, I mean *Dude*, you can't ask for more!" The second telephone call he'd made had gone very well indeed, the first, less so. Barney had used up several pounds worth of ten pence pieces, explaining to Mrs Butler, who'd answered the call in a heartbeat, that they were indeed alive and well, had not driven like lunatics at all, promising that they would have a proper dinner, and that he'd make sure her son brushed his teeth properly before going to bed.

With no budget for hotels or B&Bs, there seemed to be little alternative, and after a quick pit stop to empty themselves, and to refill the Thermos at a confused tea house, the boys began their long, perilous trip towards the welcoming campsite, and its adjoining pub.

So far, they'd been blessed with nothing but tranquil, summer weather, and as they left Windermere on the A591, just before six in the evening, the sun continued to shine brightly in a crystal clear blue sky, warming the grinning faces of the two intrepid adventures as they pressed on, the MG's windows firmly wound down, the full length sunroof still wide open. The stereo screwed around to eleven.

The great lake glistened like countless shards of broken glass, as the old car chugged on faithfully, heading first for Waterhead, before following the A593 for a while, eventually turning off onto the narrow single track, which signalled the start of their journey over both the Wrynose and Hardknott passes.

Mr Butler senior had marked this stage on the map as sections that would require extra care and vigilance. And soon enough, as the MG throttled up the first of the steepest roads in England, both boys could see exactly what he'd meant. The landscape was nothing short of spectacular, and the views were endless and unparalleled. But unfortunately the scenery was totally lost on George. He was a fledgling driver at best, and he soon found that trying to pilot an old car with a long bonnet, over unfamiliar, unforgiving terrain, was a daunting, terrifying prospect. Each never-ending hairpin bend, or perilous manoeuvre closer to a sheer drop, just to let an oncoming vehicle pass, reduced him to a quivering, sweaty jelly, trapped within a sticky, cracked leather bucket seat.

To begin with, there'd been another four cars ahead of them. This had made the going somewhat easier, and gave the boys a degree of reassurance each time they rounded yet another corner, to see that none of the lead vehicles had rolled off into a chasm yet. But one by one they chickened out, pulling over nervously to let the car behind take the lead. You couldn't really blame them. The road continued to wind haphazardly, this way and that, and before long, it was the reluctant old MGB's turn to lead the way, much to the reluctance of its crew.

Several times, Barney had to lean out of his window, just to see just how close they were to the edge, as another car passed by, almost knocking off the old chrome wing mirrors. But even worse, sometimes the car would break the crest of a small hill, only for the driver to find the road then swept immediately down and into yet another hairpin bend, on the very edge of a precipice. Blinded by his rising bonnet, George would make his navigator get out, and lead them to safety on foot. With the MG slowly, obediently following on behind.

The going was very, very slow. But as they left the Wrynose pass behind them, they pulled over so that George could mop the sweat from his brow, sip some reassuring tea from the Thermos, and lie down for a moment in the coarse grass to collect his wits again, before tackling Hardknott. It took quite a while, and cost their stores two packets of custard crèmes and a handful of chocolate raisins.

Much later, as they fought their way over the next mountain range, darkness suddenly descended without warning, making progress even more interesting. The other cars had long since given up, performed multiple point turns in the middle of the road, guided by anxious wives and partners, and headed back to Windermere. This left the boys to trudge on into the darkness, all alone.

Before long, it was almost totally pitch black. The MG's vintage headlights battled to cut even the smallest pool of yellowy light on the road ahead. No longer could they see what perils lay in wait along the roadside. Was that gentle slope ahead a flat, harmless area of grass, or a sheer drop into the abyss? It was anybody's guess. And to add insult to potential hurtling death, Barney leant out of the window with a torch from their kit, to help the aging lamps.

George's eyes stung maddeningly from the effort. He didn't dare blink, in case he plunged them into a deep gorge, and his hands were soaked inside the sticky leather driver's gloves. Taking them off was not an option. The road and terrain ahead was as dark of the inside of a walnut, and it seemed that they were totally alone in their quest. Not even a comforting glimmer of light flickered in the blackness.

"*Bloody Hell*! George, *lookout*!" The MG suddenly lurched horribly over onto Barney's side, threatening to launch him from his seat and out of the window into the unknown. There was an ear splitting shriek as aged metal ground horribly against unyielding rock. The car briefly levelled, before slumping over to the driver's side, and skidding to an abrupt, muddy halt. Clearly terrified, the MGB closed its eyes and stalled.

"*You okay Mate*?" George flicked on the map light to take a look at his pale Navigator.

"Oh yeah, *never bloody better*! Come on, let's see what damage you've done."

As expected, they'd left the road. But as the boys examined the area by torchlight, it seemed as though backing it out again, without hitting any of the minefields of rocks, or tearing off the engine sump, should at least be possible.

Reluctant at first, the car was eventually coaxed back into life, and under Barney's supervision, George started carefully reversing out. But before long they stumbled into yet more trouble. The engine's note suddenly changed, becoming massively deeper, almost as though it had suddenly entered puberty. Given its age, it was unlikely though. Something even more enlightening had transformed its tone.

Leaving the engine running, and fearing the worst, they knelt down in the stubby grass beside the car, and peered underneath. The exhaust had cracked cleanly in two. Presumably having been bent to breaking point on one of the rocks that littered the side of the road, the back section now hung from its bracket, like dead man in a noose.

"*Oh, Bugger 'n' Shitting Hell!* The exhaust's buggered!"

"I'm assuming that's some sort of complicated technical engineering term your Dad's taught you then, *is it?*"

Fortunately enough though, the heavily annotated Haynes manual *did* actually contain comprehensive instructions for a temporary road side fix, and one that suited all aspects of their current predicament perfectly.

Starving, in spite of all the crisp packets that littered the foot wells, the boys devoured a tin of Heinz baked beans, which they heated up on their primus stove, grateful for the illumination, and bulked out with a packet of digestive biscuits, whilst they waited for the overworked exhaust to cool. Their reason was twofold.

Carefully following the handwriting and neatly detailed sketches, they cut open the other end of the tin, and sliced it along its length with a pair of tin snips, before prizing it open like a clam shell. George then climbed under the low slung car, as best as his portly belly would allow. Tentatively at first, in case it burnt him, he pushed the fallen half off the exhaust back into its original position, and clamped the modified Heinz tin around the spilt.

Barney then handed him a heavy roll of heat resistant Duct Tape and a few stainless steel cable ties from the tool kit for good measure. He scraped his knuckles a few times, and an inquisitive bug climbed inside his ear, but before long, the tin was firmly held in place, and the exhaust, though not pretty, was at least sealed for now. Covered in mud and oil, and smelling of sweat, baked beans and exhaust fumes, George emerged from under the car a new man. It was a proud moment.

"There, *sorted.* My Dad would be *so* chuffed with that!"

Soon enough the resilient old girl was on her way again, seemingly none the worse for her off-roading experience or roadside surgery. Before long a solitary road sign, a welcome reflective object in a sea of black indicated that, despite Barney's best efforts, they were indeed still heading in the right direction.

But the relentless journey over the mountains, the crash and the subsequent repairs had taken their toll on the driver. With the flush of success at having channelled some of his Dad's engineering skills, now giving way to fatigue, he was strongly in favour of finding somewhere flat and unthreatening to camp for the night. More importantly, he wanted to break out the emergency bottle of Southern Comfort.

A quick scan of the map revelled that they were near Wast Water and Copeland Forest. Foreboding sounding places perhaps, but they at least boasted three campsites, which might, given the hour, be persuaded to let them camp, saving them from roughing it for the night. It was a good plan. Two hours later, they were lost in the woods.

The torch, having been pressed into service as an additional headlamp for several hours, had long since faded and died, its batteries spent. And the MG's dim map light gave more of a cosy glow than anything usefully illuminating. Exhausted, having been on the road for nearly twelve hours, the boys made the decision to pull over, into what they assumed was some sort of gravely car park.

After having another of Mrs Butler's excellent corned beef and mustard baps, they each took a hearty swig of Southern Comfort as a nightcap, and bedded down in the MG. Safely cocooned in their sleeping bags, they soon passed out.

Early the next morning George was awakened from a fitful nightmare, by what he initially assumed was a heavy, unseasonal shower of hailstones. The MG was totally steamed up. Barney, dead to the world as always, seemed to be glued to the passenger side window, snoring peacefully. Suddenly, there was thump of a car door, and the sound of running feet crunching urgently over the gravel. Still dazed and confused by a troubled night's sleep, George rolled about in his sleeping bag, like a reluctant chrysalis, unsure as to whether or not this whole butterfly thing was really worth the effort, and struggled half-heartedly to free his weary arms.

The feet had now reached the MG driver's door, and were joined by a strong pair of hands that rattled the handle violently. So violently, that the whole car rocked from side to side on its wallowing springs. Through the fog of early morning confusion, desperately missing the usual cup of tea that his Mum brought him, George began to suspect that something wasn't quite right with this scene.

Having freed one clammy hand, he started to reach for the window winder. As the MG continued to be brutally rocked on its axles, he paused half way, remembering with dream like disappointment, how his unfortunate habit of pulling the door closed by the winder, had seen it snap off a few days ago in high wind. The need for fresh air was now a lengthy, awkward battle.

Thankfully, the shaking stopped as abruptly as it began. And as Barney snored on undisturbed, the driver rubbed a small circle in the condensation with a corner of his sleeping bag, and peered out to see what had shaken him from his slumber. Parked next to the relatively small MG, the Vauxhall Senator Police Car looked gigantic. But perhaps not quite as gigantic as the imposing police officer that, having retrieved something from his vehicle, was now dashing back towards the classic, brandishing a threatening black truncheon.

Fear, Urgency and Alarm suddenly all awoke at once. Jumping up and down urgently within, they forced George's weary body to act. He grappled with the round stub, all that was left of the severed winder, desperately fighting to lower the window a fraction. Centimetre by agonising centimetre it descended, until chilly morning air at last rushed in through the gap, and he could shout at the uniformed giant. The officer now stood beside the car, raising the truncheon above his head like an axe murderer, presumably preparing to smash in the window.

"Err, *umm*, good morning Officer, *is everything okay?*"

The Policeman froze mid swing, and gazed curiously at the dishevelled teenager, who peered up at him from within the car with pleading eyes. "Oh, *hello*! Is everything alright in there, lad? Only I've had a report about a potential suicide in the area? Is *he* okay? *He looks bloody terrible.*" The Policeman pointed at Barney through the ever widening gap with his truncheon. Panic over, he now looked as though he was holding it for someone else, the potential for violence long since dissipated.

"Oh, umm, *yes, he's fine, Officer,* he always looks like that in the morning." George nudged his Navigator. Having stirred when the icy draft first hit his freckles, he nodded amiably, waving a hand that was still imprisoned within his sleeping bag. It would be a while before all his faculties were available to him.

"*Alright then,* but you can't stay here. be on your way soon boys!" Noting the piles of equipment in the back of the MG, he nodded to himself. "Best find a campsite next time. If you tell them you're *Gay* some of them will let you in…" And with that he was off, showering them in a rooster tail of gravel, kicked up by the Vauxhall's wide rear tyres.

"Err, we're not Gay Officer, he's just my best Mate, *honest*!" But he was long gone, up the road and far away. It was probably for the best.

Having freed one arm, Barney scratched his curly red head, and frowned at his driver. "Morning Officer, *morning officer*! Is that the first thing that came into your head as he's about to stove in your window? *And why didn't you just open the bloody door instead?*"

George looked down at the door handle, back to the remains of the window winder, and then at Barney. "*Oh yeah*, I didn't think of that…"

Barney stretched as best as he could inside his polyester straightjacket, and looked around the cockpit of the MG. Empty cans of coke and discarded crisp packets rattled around his insulated feet. Inadvertently, it seemed he'd been hugging the bottle of Southern Comfort all night, like a treasured teddy bear, and the inside of the car was heavy with the aroma of teenage boys. Reflecting on their road trip so far, how they'd once again survived the elements without even a crossed word, a thought suddenly occurred to him.

"Dude, how do you feel about going to Greece next time?"

Evening had long since given way to night in Italy and Limone sparkled with thousands of lights, each one giving the ancient buildings a warm, yellow ochre glow. They twinkled playfully in the waters of the lake, softening the black, monolithic cliff faces that rose up and encircled the small town. The promenade was lit with a scattering of tall street lamps, twin bulbs hanging down on either side, like empty, burning plant holders. Illuminating the flagstones, the lovingly maintained flowerbeds and tropical ferns, and preventing the passersby from falling blindly into the freezing water.

A few yachts and a collection of other boats bobbed up and down in the gentle swell, protected ever so slightly by a wide, L shaped pontoon that some of the vessels were moored to, ropes slapping half-heartedly against their masts in the chilly breeze, quietly waiting for their turn to get back out onto the lake again. George wandered slowly along the promenade, extremely grateful to be moving under his own steam once more, and even more grateful to have finally gotten off the coach, the horrific journey having finally come to an abrupt, skidding halt in the large car park behind him.

He'd waited around for a while, expecting Mr Camisso to meet him as agreed, but considering they were very late, despite the drivers best efforts to make up time, he must have grown tired of waiting and returned to his B&B. Somewhat anxious, and feeling very alone in the world, George decided it would be best to try and find a telephone box and call before it got too late. According to Arthur's Omega, it was already just past ten o'clock, and as his senses were steadily beginning to recover from the trip, he was suddenly aware that against all odds, he was really quite hungry.

To the left of the promenade there was a scattering of small restaurants. Heavily insulated patrons gesticulated and dined nosily on the outdoor bistro tables, protected from the elements by clear plastic awnings, and large, stainless steel patio heaters. Frozen to the bone, George desperately wanted to rush over to and bear hug one.

Just as he'd plucked up the courage to try out the much loved Italian phrase book, he'd liberated from Arthur's bookcase, in the hope of ordering a large plate of spaghetti bolognaise and a bottle of hearty red, a heavy hand landed on his shoulder and pulled him around to face him, as easily as if he were a rag doll.

"Eh, itsa Mister Georgie, *no?*"

Ten minutes later he got his wish, and was sat in a traditional Italian kitchen, happily tucking into a huge plateful of mouth wateringly delicious, homemade spaghetti bolognaise, and quaffing back goldfish bowl sized glasses of fabulous Bardolino wine, local to the region. Mr and Mrs Camisso, a fabulously warm, generous couple somewhere in their mid to late sixties, were overjoyed to have what they considered an important guest at their table.

They doted on the young Englishman as though he were Royalty. Mrs Camisso heaping on steaming ladles of second and third helpings, showering the dish with a healthy dusting of parmesan cheese, whilst Mr Camisso constantly topped up his glass with the glorious red, always accompanied with a welcome 'Prego', reminding George of Gabriella, and her own, rather explicit kitchen. Clearly, on this adventure, calories and carbohydrate could not be neglected.

Giuseppe Camisso was a squat man with graying, curly hair and an impressive, drooping moustache that obscured his top lip entirely. He was short, with thick, broad shoulders that might have once belonged to a shot putter, and had a vast solid belly, giving him the overall appearance of an old oak barrel with feet. He laughed enthusiastically and genuinely at everything, and slapped his guest heartily on the back at every opportunity. It was beginning to knock the wind out of the younger man.

Contessa Camisso meanwhile, was almost a mirror image or her husband, although thankfully bereft of any moustache. She'd been blessed, or cursed depending on your point of view, with an enormous chest, which had nearly suffocated Arthur's Grandson when she'd first pulled him down towards her, and embraced him in welcome.

The three talked animatedly for a full hour about their dear departed friend. The Camissos' English was far better than their guests Italian, which was largely non-existent, and after Giuseppe had jokingly relieved George of his phrase book, setting it down on the table beside him, they talked endlessly with tears of joy about the great times they'd shared with the old man from England, and of course his beloved, battered house on wheels. Slapping his thighs and banging his great hairy fists on the old wooden table in nostalgic delight, recalling exploits and adventures, Giuseppe constantly slipped back into his native tongue, always saying the same thing. "*Era pazzo in testa, era pazzo in testa!*"

With his fingers slowly walking towards his phrase book to look it up, Giuseppe leaned forward and grabbed George's hand gently, before he had the chance, beaming charmingly into his eyes. "*He was crazy in the head!*"

True to Arthur's letter, he made a mental promise that he'd try and learn the language. After all, Italians did seem to feature heavily in his life from time to time. (*...Try hard to learn a foreign language, it'll help you get by in another country and make you sound much more interesting in your own. Always get the window seat on an aeroplane, it probably won't do you much good if it crashes, but at least the view should be spectacular. Apart from when you visit Italy, only ever drink limoncello you make yourself, there's a recipe pinned to the fridge, and whatever else you do, try to remember to buy un-waxed lemons....*)

After a good deal more Bardolino wine, and checking the contents of the Thermos, tricky things to gage at the best of times, the three of them toasted Arthur's memory with the old man's very own limoncello, and a very weary George was shown to his bedroom.

It was an adorable, quaint little room, with thick windowsills of knotty old pine, stripped floors, elaborate patterned wallpaper from another time, and a single cast iron bed, almost totally consumed with a quilted throw. There was a nightstand and small wardrobe where he could hang his few clothes, and the gold plated lamp, with its gaudy rouge shade and tasselled edging, threw a reddish, warm glow across his temporary home.

He was suddenly aware of just how much he'd had to drink since leaving Verona airport. Although not drunk by any means, he was now, not unlike the Butler's treasured family home, respectably semi-detached. Unfortunately, a combination of shoestring budget, badly timed UK flights, and another gruelling, three hour coach transfer, meant that his time in

Limone was short. He only had a little over thirteen hours left, and he still had important business to attend to.

Naturally, the welcoming Camissos had already invited him to stay for the rest of his natural life, and it had been a difficult offer to decline. But he patiently explained his predicament in loose terms, omitting financial hardships, and promised that he'd return again very soon, hopefully with Summer. This had proved to be a mistake though. The mere mention of a lady friend sparked renewed interest from Mrs Camisso, threatening to detain him for the rest of the night.

George genuinely wanted to return though. Even in the darkness he could understand quite what had drawn Arthur to this place, and why he'd stayed for so long. Coupled with an insatiable yearning to learn much more about the old man, and his adventures around the great Lake, something that he sensed they'd hardly scratched the surface of that evening, not returning one day wasn't even an option anymore. Paying for it though, would be another matter entirely.

Snug and cosy inside his bedroom, with a warm glass of milk and something unbelievably alcoholic that Mr Camisso had given him as a nightcap, the thought of venturing out again into the chilly night air suddenly lost its appeal, and he briefly flirted with the idea scattering the ashes in the morning instead.

Hating himself for his moment of selfish doubt, for even considering changing his carefully conceived plan, he pulled on the thick, homemade knitted jumper he'd discarded in the Camissos' roasting kitchen, wrapped a chunky Christmas scarf tightly around his neck, and with his torso thickened somewhat by the layers, squeezed into his faithful leather jacket. It was just like being tubby all over again. He rather liked it.

The Camissos had given him a huge spare key, hugged him like one of their own, and retreated to bed, with the promise of a massive breakfast and packed lunch to see him on his way. George was still worrying about keeping all this down on his outbound journey, when he carefully stripped everything but Arthur's urn, the remains of the limoncello and one of the old man's carefully wrapped, crystal shot glasses out of his school rucksack, and left the warmth of the Camissos' B&B to venture out into the freezing night air. It was just before midnight.

Rather than head straight to the Lake, he decided to have a little stroll about first. To walk off supper and also to absorb just a bit more of this magical town, before once again boarding that awful coach.

As he ambled alone through the maze of old backstreets, his cowboy boots drew echoes off the tall buildings, as though he were a character in some pre-war spy thriller, his breath leaving wispy clouds that temporarily marked his progress. George marvelled at the foreign architecture, wishing he could spend just one more day here. Perhaps sip a Peroni and an espresso or two at one of the lakeside bars with Giuseppe and Contessa, and talk some more about their crazy mutual friend.

The streets were virtually silent. The few bars and restaurants that were still serving a scattering of locals and die-hard tourists were nearer the centre of town, by a small picturesque harbour. The Camissos' B&B was neatly hidden away, up a zigzagging collection of flagstone streets, just above the promenade from where he'd decided he would launch his friend's ashes.

Completely alone, in a foreign land far from home, sauntering on the very fringes of disorientation, along quietly eerie backstreets that could have conceivably hidden an opportunistic, if not frozen, Italian criminal, George expected to feel frightened. But with Arthur's urn digging into the middle of his back, he followed yet another sign in Italian, he sincerely hoped translated into 'To the Lake', feeling totally unafraid. His mind instead focused entirely on the task ahead. It was an honour, and this was no time for fear.

Despite the awful sense of loss he'd felt since Arthur had passed away, for one reason or other, George still hadn't shed any tears yet. Unlike his Dad, who seemed genetically incapable of crying, he was reminded each time he watched *Born Free* or *Watership Down* that a good old fashioned blub was well within his capabilities. So why hadn't he cried yet?

Twenty minutes later he stood on the edge of the pontoon, having been guided safely by the yellowy street lights. A chilly glass of limoncello in one hand, and the urn, which he'd since tied to a large pebble he'd found in one of the flower boarders, to ensure it sank, grasped firmly in the other. He'd cursed himself for not thinking this through sooner. Of course the urn wouldn't sink without help. It was made of wood!

A suitable pebble was easy enough to find, there were hundreds of them decorating the flower beds and plant pots, but obtaining some sort of string was another matter. After dashing about the promenade for a few minutes, drawing quizzical glances from late night dinners returning to their hotels, he eventually stumbled upon a solitary training shoe. Without giving any thought to the fate of its partner, he quickly relieved it of its laces. He'd lashed the pebble to the urn as best he could, knowing that his Cub Scout Master would've stripped him of his knot tying badge if he ever saw his efforts, his freezing fingers failing on several fumbled attempts to join the two ends together.

Carefully, so as not to spill the dwindling remains of the precious yellow liquid, he knelt and filled the shot glass from the pewter hip flask, shaking it slightly to see if there was enough left for a second round. Thankfully there was, one each then.

Anybody that didn't know the neighbours, or hadn't read the old man's letter, would've perhaps found it a strange mark of respect, as George then pulled off his cowboy boots and woolly socks, and stood barefoot at the water's edge (... *If at all possible, and the weather is with you, try and avoid wearing shoes and socks at all costs...*) Expecting the inevitable tears to roll down his face and turn to icicles at any moment, he sipped the last of Arthur's summer limoncello, the last he'd ever make, and breathed in the chilly air.

He took a moment to allow the alcohol to settle, before reading the letter out loud, pausing occasionally to take another pull from the glass. Eventually, with a contented smile, he read his favourite part, the very end. He folded the precious pieces of paper carefully, put it back into its envelope, and tucked it away into the folds of his leather jacket, with Mr Obayomi's forgotten letter for company.

After topping up his glass for the very last time, George picked up the urn and the pebble clumsily in his other hand, and raised his drink to the heavens. "To you then Arthur, *I'll miss you...*" He drained the limoncello in one swallow, stowed the shot glass in his pocket, braced himself, and threw the urn and its pebble companion into the air, with all his might.

Apart from archery, George had never been good at sports. It was an inescapable, irrefutable fact that he'd long since given up denying. But now that he was at least reasonably strong, and almost fit, it had been his sincere hope that he would be able to muster a decent fling with which to launch his old friend a good distance across the water, before he sank from this world forever. He'd perhaps been a little optimistic.

After nearly dislocating his shoulder, the urn and the pebble spun majestically together in a high arc out over the lake, and to begin with, it seemed as though he'd been reasonably successful. Things started to go wrong however, shortly after release. The pendulum effect of all the spinning put undue strain on his poorly executed knots, and the two objects separated from themselves mid-flight. The pebble, clearly the heavier of the two, immediately shortened its arc and splashed down within seconds, leaving Arthurs' urn sailing on, now free of its burden, for another fifteen feet.

George's heart skipped a beat. He was unable to react for a moment, until a wave of relief washed over him as the urn eventually hit the surface and disappeared below the icy waters. Seconds later, his face turned ashen again, as with an audible plop, it reappeared, bobbing up and down on the gentle waves like a cheerful cotton top. It continued to wobble happily for a moment, until eventually it was caught in a current, and began to drift further away into the darkness. Slowly, it started a new journey of its very own, out into the great beyond.

For a long, long time, the young man on the pontoon stood and did nothing. He watched as the urn got smaller and smaller, until it eventually disappeared into the night. Then, totally involuntarily, his body started to shake. Not from the cold now, he'd long since grown accustomed to the chill, something else entirely was getting a grip on him. Some unseen entity, and apparently it had no intention whatsoever of letting him go.

Before long, it had its way with him, and he was reduced to a collapsed, blubbering mess on the edge of the pontoon, his body trembling uncontrollably, hot tears streaming down his face, warming his cold cheeks.

But these weren't tears of sorrow though. Not entirely at least. The events of the past week had finally caught up with him. Coupled with an unsuccessful attempt to sink a clearly unsinkable urn, he'd reacted in the only way left available, with hysterical, irrepressible laughter. The sort that nearly makes you wet yourself.

Finally, when the last of the shuddering aftershocks had died away, and he eventually stopped exploding each time he thought the seizure had passed, George sat up, wiped his eyes, and dangled his legs over the edge of the pontoon. He looked out across Lake Garda, in the direction that the urn was last seen drifting away into the blackness.

"Well, I suppose *you* thought that was really funny, didn't you Arthur…?"

And somewhere out there, an old man was indeed laughing his socks off. Or rather he would've been, if he ever wore any.

His feet were numb now. Shuffling backwards across the cold, hard surface on his bum, he reached for his boots and his long, woolly socks, quickly pulling them on. The same grateful glee he'd had experienced putting on his shoes after school swimming practice, warming the cockles of his heart. Any comfort was good right now. Taking the long way back to the Camissos' B&B, he strolled unenthusiastically along the promenade, not wanting to leave the Lake side, his cowboy boots tapping his slow progress once more.

It was over. He'd managed to do it. Although far from being the most sophisticated ceremony ever, George felt certain that Arthur would've approved of his Service, especially the bit with the shoe lace and the pebble. So now it was back to England, back to the Bank, and back to the wrath of The Evil Ray Varley. It was a hateful thought. But there was still Mr Obayomi to contend with. He rather enjoyed their interesting exchanges. In some way, he felt as though the old man was there with them in that chaotic office, laughing probably.

George thought about the bulky letter the Postie had forced on him. Perhaps it was ironic that it had travelled all this way next to Arthurs own letter, and that it was here at his farewell? Yet it was still unopened, its contents undigested. Fear of yet more trouble kept its gummed flap sealed. There was something else to consider here though. If George really intended to honour his Granddad by trying to keep to the sentiments of his letter, he wasn't really getting off to a very good start.

What was it he wrote? '...*Don't bury your head in the sand, or even press your face into it for a moment, you should confront your problems and deal with them before they get any worse. And if life hands you lemons, make limoncello (see previous notes for directions)...*' He thought of his bulging mailbox at home. He'd certainly buried more than just his head in the sand when it came to that. His mind was made up. Start as you mean to go on. Arthur would've approved.

Pulling the letter from the warmth of his jacket, George stopped in his tracks, and ran his trembling thumbnail along its seal. If nothing else the pigeon English should cheer him up. Unfolding the letter with shaking hands, he smiled to himself. Mr Obayomi's poorly spelt opening paragraph managing to coax a chuckle. It was attached to a thick wad of papers, a photocopy of something serious and legal by the looks of it. He ignored it for now, reading the long covering letter instead. It would probably be more entraining.

Suddenly he stopped reading. *What was that?*

The wind had picked up, the papers flapped in his grip. That was the problem, he'd been distracted, thinking it would be blown away, he'd read it wrong, perhaps? Pulling the letter taught, like the canvases he and the old man used to stretch in the garden, he read the paragraph again. Mr Obayomi had likely hit the wrong key, copied and pasted something he didn't mean to. Surely that was it? It was a wonder he managed to find his printer at all, let alone the power switch. The silly sod had obviously made a mistake.

George's body didn't seem to agree though. His heart had picked up its pace again, and his adrenaline level, sadly depleted of late, decided that as it was in Italy, it would try a few rounds of triple espressos. Common sense, a seldom used facility, started leaping up and down inside his head too, suggesting that perhaps he should read the attachment as well? It seemed sensible enough.

A nearby bench suddenly looked very inviting. Despite his Mum's warnings of getting piles if he lingered on something cold for too long, he stumbled over to it and sat down heavily, the strengthening wind ruffling his hair. The thick wad of stapled papers was indeed serious and legal. It was a copy of Arthurs will. George flicked through it, not really sure what he was looking for, or even that he wanted to find it.

But finally he did find it. And for once, Mr Obayomi hadn't made a mistake at all. Arthur really had left his adopted Grandson literally everything, from his vast collection of empty limoncello bottles, to his treasured piles of dusty books. His old café racer leather jacket, so old that it was coming back into fashion, his beloved wooden steamer chair, his fourteen foot oak dining room table, the undeveloped box of photographic film from his travels, his impressive stack of Johnny Cash LPs, the huge chopping board he'd bought the last time he was here, and his home. A home that he'd owned outright.

George didn't know what to do, or what to think. He was in shock, proper shock. He felt like a grateful Hobo who'd just been given a warm coat from Oxfam, only to find the winning lottery ticket in the pocket. But he just didn't deserve it, it was too much, he desperately wanted to give it back. Yet he couldn't, the owner had gone, his mind made up. He'd wanted to give the coat to someone who'd appreciate it, make good use of it, now that he was finished wearing it.

The wind whipped through the sheets of paper again, seemingly determined to blow them away. Should he let it go, would that change anything, would it bring back his old friend? He bundled them together, this time stowing them away in his school rucksack for safekeeping, hugging it to his chest after zipping it shut.

What should he do now? What could he do now? He desperately needed to talk to someone about all this. He needed supportive words to help him understand, to help him comprehend exactly what Arthur would've wanted him to do with his legacy, with everything he'd ever owned in the world. It was all far, far too much.

Sadly, the one man who could've answered that question was gone now. All he'd left him as a guide was his letter. *The letter!* George quickly swept the rucksack off his lap and onto the bench. He controlled himself, fought his raging adrenaline. His hands were shaking; he didn't want to tear the precious envelope as he pulled it from his leather jacket. Opening it again, his eyes darted from one line to the next. Something in here would help him, surely?

One sentence was bound to show him which path he should take next. He read line after line, desperate to find one that he'd missed, one that said *'give it to the cats and dogs home'* perhaps. But there wasn't one. No glaringly obvious clue. Frustratingly, there seemed to be nothing to guide him on his way. Welling up, he slumped forward, looking out over the great lake, at the boats that rocked in the waves, still fighting to be free of their restrictive moorings.

The boats! *That was it!*

Quickly holding up the letter, so that he could read it better by the glow of the promenade's lamps, George read his favourite bit again, the very end.

Finally, the flowery pillowcase was pulled from his ruffled head, and the great balls of cotton wool plucked from his cloth ears. At last, he'd found what he was looking for, and typically, it had been there all along, patiently waiting for him to understand.

His young face, once stricken with guilt and with grief, relaxed into a much more familiar, mischievous smile…

"Ah… So that's what you meant, *you old bugger.*"

Bless him.

'…*And finally, remember this, Sunshine. Sometimes in life, you've just got to let go of the wreckage, and find another boat…*'

CPSIA information can be obtained at www.ICGtesting.com
Printed in the USA
LVOW10s1150141215

466503LV00025BA/1365/P